# THE
# *Best*
# AMERICAN
# SHORT STORIES
# 1947

# THE
# *Best*
## AMERICAN
## SHORT STORIES
## 1947

*and The Yearbook of the American Short Story*

*Edited by*
## MARTHA FOLEY

19 47

HOUGHTON MIFFLIN COMPANY · BOSTON

The Riverside Press Cambridge

The Riverside Press

CAMBRIDGE · MASSACHUSETTS

PRINTED IN THE U.S.A.

To
The Editors
of
The 'Little Magazines'
of
America

# ACKNOWLEDGMENT

GRATEFUL ACKNOWLEDGMENT for permission to reprint the stories in this volume is made to the following:

To the Editors of *Accent, The Antioch Review, The Atlantic Monthly, Commentary, Cosmopolitan,* Doubleday and Company, Inc., *Foreground, Good Housekeeping, Harper's Bazaar, Harper's Magazine,* Houghton Mifflin Company, *Mademoiselle, The New Yorker, Partisan Review, Quarterly Review of Literature,* Random House, Inc., *The Sewanee Review, Story, Tomorrow, Town and Country,* and *The Yale Review;* and to Francis L. Broderick, Dorothy Canfield, Truman Capote, Robert Fontaine, Adelaide Gerstley, John B. L. Goodwin, John Mayo Goss, Paul Griffith, Albert J. Guérard, Elizabeth Hardwick, Ruth McCoy Harris, Thomas Heggen, Edward Harris Heth, John Richard Humphreys, Victoria Lincoln, Robert Lowry, May Davies Martenet, Jane Mayhall, J. F. Powers, Samson Raphaelson, Mark Schorer, Allan Seager, Irwin Shaw, Sylvia Shirley, Jean Stafford, Irwin Stark, Wallace Stegner, Niccoló Tucci, John D. Weaver, and Lawrence Williams.

# FOREWORD

*SOME YEARS AGO* the publisher of a short story magazine had the brilliant idea that a natural audience for such a magazine would be those who themselves write short stories. As a result, he compiled a mailing list of the names and addresses of persons who had sent short story manuscripts to magazines, whether accepted or rejected, and of students in adult short story writing courses at colleges and universities. He gathered a list of more than five hundred thousand names!

Unfortunately, the answers to the beautifully worded and printed subscription letter he sent out were almost one hundred per cent identical. 'Thank you for letting me know about your magazine. I am sending you a manuscript. Please deduct the price of your subscription from what you pay me for my short story.'

This is told here because it illuminates the position of the short story in this country. In the foreword to previous volumes of this anthology, I have noted that the short story, ever since the time of Washington Irving and Edgar Allan Poe, has been America's most popular and influential form of literary expression. I also have pointed out that more short stories are written and published here than in any other country in the world. Last year there was a new record in the number of short stories appearing in our magazines and this year has exceeded even that record, both in the number of short stories published and in the number of new authors writing them.

But what I have never stated before and what I believe is true is that such an important medium of expression, a medium which can attract so much interest not only from the reading standpoint but from a subjective standpoint of actually writing them, must reflect any important changes in American moods and life.

Nor is this to judge stories as propaganda. It is a paradox, but the best way to write propaganda is not to write it. To put it another way, the style is the man and what the man believes comes out, willy-nilly, between the lines he writes. I agree wholeheartedly with Arthur Koestler when he says, 'The artist is no leader; his mission is not to solve but to expose, not to preach but to demonstrate. "We make out of our quarrels with others rhetoric, but out of our quarrels with ourselves poetry," said Yeats. The healing, the teaching and preaching the writer must leave to others; but by exposing the truth by special means unavailable to them he creates the emotional urge for healing.'

To what do we find the short story writers of America devoting themselves? First and foremost is a preoccupation with emotional frustration. In other years American writers treated more of frustration from an economic or racial standpoint. But even those stories of the latter type in this collection, notably 'Up the Road a Piece,' by Ruth McCoy Harris, and 'Shock Treatment,' by Irwin Stark, could have been written almost as effectively if the problems in them had hinged on something else than race.

This year the short story writer has been primarily concerned with the 'internal man.' If, in turn, that emotional problem stems out of exterior economic forces, he shows little awareness of it. Sigmund Freud, rather than Adam Smith or Karl Marx, rules his approach. Exceptions are Allan Seager, with his story, 'Game Chickens,' and John Richard Humphreys, who wrote 'Michael Finney and the Little Men.' Both authors have told their stories simply as a matter of interest as narratives without trying deliberately to invoke any emotional participation by the reader.

But whether it be 'The Interior Castle,' by Jean Stafford; 'Day of Gold and Darkness,' by Robert Fontaine; 'Bird Song,' by John Mayo Goss, or 'What We Don't Know Hurts Us,' by Mark Schorer, or any of the majority of stories in this year's anthology, the reader will find writing that, in dealing with emotional problems, crosses the threshold of the psyche.

Therefore, it may be assumed that the American people

today are concerned with a vast searching of souls. Whether this will lead only to a great *weltschmerz* such as troubled for years another emotionally frustrated people, the Germans, or whether it will have more constructive consequences is yet to be seen.

From the standpoint of literary style, *per se*, the stripped, stark school of understatement which prevailed for twenty years, has almost vanished. The tendency is to greater length and more elaboration. As with art and architecture, writing seems to have its cycles of reverting to an extremely simple style, then to add adornment until the rococo, or Victorian, is reached and a new evolution begins.

A number of critics recently have pointed out the influence of Proust on present-day American writing. I think it is too easy a summation. All writing has a literary ancestry, of course. But I myself feel that the same circumstances which led a soul-sick Proust to shut himself up in a cork-lined room to venture out into the streets of Paris only at night are of the same kind influencing American writers. Like Proust's Paris, a gay and lavish America of wide-open frontiers, big Newport and Palm Beach estates, little government restrictions, and easy optimism has gone. Whether Proust's answer, beautiful as is his writing of a lost time, is the only answer American writers will have to decide for themselves.

Apart from that, the influence of any writer of great fame always is over-estimated. At one time, every other new writer appearing on the American scene was accused of imitating Hemingway. First, the critics forgot that Hemingway himself at the beginning had been so accused, one critic going so far as to say that 'Ernest Hemingway is out of Gertrude Stein by Sherwood Anderson' while another critic ran parallel passages from Stein, Anderson, and Hemingway to show the similarity.

I remember a young writer who wrote a story of a fishing trip in the Pyrenees. It appeared in *transition*, the Paris magazine, some time before *The Sun Also Rises* was published. Later it was included in a collection of short stories. Its author immediately was damned as having stolen his story from Hemingway. The truth was both were newspapermen living in Paris, both met the same kinds of people, and both went, as did many others, on fishing trips to the Pyrenees. It is what I mean when I say it is very easy to exaggerate literary influence.

One of the questions most asked me during the past year is what part the American veteran is assuming in the new literature. The answer is, of course, that he is taking a very important part, a part that will be still more important in the next few years. He is only beginning to emerge. The greatest cultural achievement of our country has been to throw open the doors of our colleges and universities to the veterans. It is the first time in history that a returning army has gone to school.

A small minority of the stories here, such as 'Night Watch,' by Thomas Heggen; 'Under the Ginkgo Trees,' by Edward Harris Heth, and 'Return by Faith,' by Francis L. Broderick, touch upon the war. But, among the thousands of veterans now at school, there is a very large number beginning to write. When, to the impact of his war experience, the veteran adds the advantage of a scholastic education at a more mature than usual age, a more appreciative age, the effect upon American writing is bound to be momentous.

Another question often asked is how stories are chosen for re-publication in this volume. It would be convenient if the answer could be reduced to a simple analysis of characterization, style, story content, etc. Once upon a time, professors of literature were quite brash about laying down in textbooks rules for writing. They even drew diagrams. Today it is pretty generally recognized that there are no specific rules for writing. Writing has to come out of the writer's own knowing and feeling. Much depends upon what kind of an individual he is. More depends upon what life has done to him, what his own experience has been. Writing is a matter of many intangibles.

So it is with editing. One could take a flower, for instance, analyze the pigment in its petals, the amount of pollen on its pistil or stamen, the measure of honey concealed within it, the width and length of its stems, but would all those specifications show why it is lovely? In reading the innumerable stories published in our magazines throughout the year, I am in quest of literary adventure. When I feel that I have had an adventure in reading a story, when I think reading it has been a memorable experience, I hope that the readers of this volume also will find it memorable.

The 'little magazines' continue to be most important among all the magazines publishing short stories. It is unfortunate that the average American reader is not aware of their importance. As it is, most readers do not even know of their existence. American writers certainly do. A recent survey showed that eighty per cent of American authors first appeared in the little magazines. The devotion of the editors of these publications to the highest literary standards, often at a great financial sacrifice to themselves and neglect of their own literary careers to further the careers of others, is a publishing phenomenon.

I wish to acknowledge the valuable assistance of Joyce Hartman in preparing this book.

I also wish to recall that this anthology was founded and continued for many years by the late Edward J. O'Brien, the greatest editor of the short story the world has ever known and a remarkable man in his own right, to whom the writers of America long will be indebted.

MARTHA FOLEY

# CONTENTS

# Contents

*(From The Atlantic Monthly)*

# RETURN BY FAITH

## BY FRANCIS L. BRODERICK

*I* WAS sitting on a wooden bench in the poorer residential district of Wilmot. From there I could see the McShanes' house, partially hidden by some oak trees, diagonally across the street. It was already past the hour at which I was to call, but, reluctant to start, I sat wondering what I could say when I was inside their home. Finally, to occupy a few more minutes, I looked again at Mrs. McShane's letter. It said: —

Dear Friend,

I am addressing you as friend for only a good friend of Frank's would take time to write me such a beautiful letter and telling so plainly just what happened to Frank's plane. It meant so much to us for it has been hard to learn any details of his accident. Some general in Washington last April wrote us that Frank's B-24 had been hit by Japanese anti-aircraft guns over one of those small Pacific islands but that other crews had seen some parachutes open and so all hope was not gone. And so we have gone on hoping. Frank's Dad and I have felt terrible ever since we had the bad news. Frank is the oldest of eight — five boys and two girls besides Frank. They are all fine but can't fill Frank's place we were expecting to see him around this time his 21st birthday was Saturday and we sure do miss him he was wonderful at home and the rest of the children all thought there was no one like him they all wait anxiously every day for his return the baby especially she was three yesterday Frank always called her his baby she was born the day after his eighteenth

1

birthday and with him the oldest and mister away it was him that brought her and I home from the hospital where she was born. In all his letters he used to send his love to all the children but special to his Emily; and she runs to his picture every day and asks over and over When Frankie coming home? And so though your letter brought us little hope we were all grateful to hear from you and hope you will be able to visit us like you said. We have a telephone and you could call or write when you can come over or we will go over to see you if you are too busy. Hope you will forgive all the blots I have a terrible pen the only kind that is ever left home with five going to school it is hard to ever get a pen or pencil around here when they are at school. Thanks again for the beautiful letter and I hope I will have the pleasure of meeting you either here or over at yours or any place you say. Hoping and praying that you have a good time on your furlough.

Sincerely,<br>Mrs. Thomas McShane

In my letter I had tried to dissipate all hope of Frank's return. I had tried to be gentle — foolish conceit — in telling Mrs. McShane quite definitely that only one parachute had left the 'Royal Flush' before the explosion and that one man, the tail gunner, had been rescued.

Every detail of that mission was still vivid in my mind because two days before we had lost a whole crew — our first casualties in so many months that no man then flying with our outfit could remember the last. Since the loss had given our boys combat jitters, the group commander had assigned us this lightly defended target; this was to be a 'milk run.' The take-off and flight to the target area were accomplished without mishap. But on arrival at Togo Jima, we found our target blanketed with a high cumulous formation. Frank McShane, who was leading the formation, circled the island several times searching for an opening through which we could drop our bombs. When it finally appeared, we were flying directly into a 100-knot head wind which held us back, so that we were begging for the worst that Jap ground batteries could hurl up at us. Even in this position, it seemed inadvisable to turn off the bombing run, for that would have meant another pass at the island and more target practice for the Jap gunners when we returned to their range of fire. So we stayed on course over the island.

Suddenly a phosphorous shell struck Frank's bomb bay and reserve fuel tank. His plane became an infero. In an attempt to extinguish the blaze he snapped into a steep dive and then chandelled away from the formation so that an explosion would not drag other planes down in his wake. I was watching from the left waist window, my regular observation post, as the fire subsided for a moment and then flared up again into a box of flame, which engulfed the whole ship from the engine nacelles to the vertical stabilizers.

My pilot called back to me, in a voice pitched high with fear, 'Watch for parachutes!' As he spoke, one appeared. The fire paused a moment, then without further warning soared high again. The plane collapsed; its wings, melted off the fuselage by the intense heat, fell limply downward into the clouds; the fuselage itself cracked with a tumult audible above the roar of our engines and even through the high-altitude headgear which we wore. Parachutes appeared and opened, but no one saw any fliers dangling from the twisted shroud lines. My pilot, second in command of the formation, immediately ordered a search of the area and our nine Liberators fanned out in a disorderly pattern over the Pacific. But just one survivor was located and later rescued by a Navy plane.

Intelligence officers back at our base found substantial agreement among the nine surviving crews: many parachutes, but, most probably, only the one survivor. But because they could not positively confirm the deaths of the other men on the crew, Army regulations required that all ten be reported 'missing in action.'

After the six-week delay required by the War Department, I wrote to Frank's mother, for Frank and I had been close friends.

He was a most likable fellow with a ready laugh, and he

found humor even in the tedium of repetitious Army classes. He handled his plane easily, with a sure confidence which his crew shared after one or two flights. With girls he was gawky and bashful. We kidded him about this without mercy, for he was a good-looking chap with black curly hair, blue eyes, and a lean, determined face.

Frank's religious stands used to perplex me. I remember one day how surprised I was to hear him defending with great vigor the Catholic position on birth control. I had never seen him in church and had assumed that he had no interest in things religious. When I asked him about it, he laughed and said: 'Well, I guess I'm what you might call a willing but lazy Catholic. I'm willing, all right, because I accept all the doctrines I learned at school, but when it comes to going to church, I guess I'm just lazy.' Frank had faith, he said, and if good works in the form of churchgoing were required as well, he was prepared to perform them — if the church convened within a hundred yards of his tent. Beyond that distance, he had faith in the Holy Ghost which came perilously close to the sin of presumption.

Once in a while after that, I could drag him off to church. Frank would admit that he was glad he had gone, but he always avoided any commitment toward reform in the future. 'No need for fancy promises,' he would say. 'You won't believe 'em, and I won't keep 'em.' (He was at church the day before his death. I was glad of that.) To this languid faith he added a stoic fatalism not entirely orthodox: he sincerely felt, as so many fliers say they do, that if his 'number came up,' there was little he could do to resist it.

His number had come up.

I still did not know what to say to the McShanes, but I started across the street anyway. Gradually the house, a brown wooden building with a gabled roof, disengaged itself from the trees. Though old, it was in good shape: it had been freshly painted and new shingles dotted the roof like a crazy quilt. Originally built for a single family, it had now been divided, and a partition stretched from the floor of the

front porch to the eaves to assert the independence of each
neighbor from the inquisitiveness of the other. In front,
the lawn had been recently cut and two beds of pansies
drooped over the edges of the gravel pathway to the porch.

As I climbed the steps, the door opened and a woman of
about forty-five came out. 'I'm Mrs. McShane,' she said with
a bit of a brogue. 'We're all so glad you've come; we wanted
to see you so bad.' She was wearing a faded blue sleeveless
housedress and, over it, a red-checked apron which showed
the effects of the day's housecleaning. In contrast to this
drab outfit, she wore bright-colored house slippers beaded
with sea shells — a gift, I recalled, which Frank had sent from
Honolulu when we were there together on rest leave. She
was heavy-set, with the appearance one associates with a
woman who has borne eight children — harried, busy, proud
— and her muscular arms left little doubt that she could
manage her brood with the rod when the occasion demanded.

We stood a moment in the doorway as she took my coat.
Then, as we walked into the parlor, she was saying: 'Lieutenant, I want you to meet my family,' when she stopped
and asked: 'And do they call you "Frank," too?' I said that
they did. 'Well, then, Frank,' she said, pausing over the
name tenderly, 'Frank, this is my family.' First, there was
her sister, Aunt Clara — Mrs. O'Hara — who, Mrs. McShane
warned me, was quite deaf; then the five McShane sons and
one daughter, starting with Harry, who was almost twenty
and expected to be inducted into the Army within a week,
and ending with Kathleen, who was perched restlessly on a
couch between her brother Thomas, Jr., and an elder
brother, William. The other two sons, James and Michael,
sat glumly sharing a chair by the door, curious, but anxious
to go outside and play.

Mrs. McShane sat down on a couch just inside the parlor
and motioned for me to sit beside her. There was an awkward pause for a moment, each of us wanting the other to
start the conversation. Then, while Mrs. McShane murmured that 'Mister was delayed down at the station,' I had
a chance to look around the room.

Across from our couch, a steel engraving of Da Vinci's *Last Supper* covered the wall above the unused fireplace; the frame was chipped in several places. Flanking the fireplace were overstuffed chairs, each with a small table and a lamp beside it. The imitation Persian rug showed signs of wear, a pathway running from the front door to the stairway in the rear. Above the couch where we were sitting, a brightly colored picture of Christ the King was suspended by two gold cords and across the top were the remains of the palms which had been distributed at church on Palm Sunday.

Pictures of the children at various ages were strewn all over the room: on the mantelpiece and tables and on the walls. Over by the window, a picture of Frank which he had had taken in Hawaii was set high on a table, a vase of pansies in front of it. I remembered that picture well: we had joked about Frank's trying to look like a recruiting poster. Mrs. McShane saw me eyeing it. 'Frank sent it back last Christmas,' she said, 'sent it back with a card promisin' to bring the real thing himself this May.' I nodded with embarrassment.

Another clumsy pause, and Mrs. McShane said: 'You didn't leave us much hope, Frank.' I thought that she would go on, but she stopped, urging me with her eyes to talk a little. So I told her again what she already knew from my letter: the same hopeless story. She watched me intently as I spoke, nodding periodically as if I were repeating some familiar piece committed to memory. When I finished, I waited for her comment, and finally, to break the strain of the silence, blurted out: 'I hate to bring this bad news more than I can say, but I really feel that it's better if you can know for sure rather than wait endlessly, hoping for something beyond hope. And much as I hate to say it, this is beyond hope.'

She continued nodding, saying, 'Yes, yes,' absently. Then silence fell over the room except for the restless squirming of Bill and Kathleen. Aunt Clara broke the silence. 'Does he say some hope, Margaret?' she asked in a loud voice. No answer for a moment; then as if waking from a reverie, Mrs. McShane said impatiently: 'He says no hope, Clara.'

'But,' she continued, turning toward me, 'wait till you see

all the papers from some general in Washington and from Frank's squadron commander. They both say there's hope. Here, read them.'

She reached into her apron and drew out a worn envelope addressed to her by the Adjutant General, Washington, D.C. They were the customary documents: the telegram from the Adjutant General which starts: 'The Secretary of War has directed me to inform you . . . '; the follow-up letter in which he confirms that Frank is missing in action; an impersonal letter from Captain Larry Stearns, our squadron commander, with its stereotyped condolences; and an official communication from the Army Personal Effects Bureau stating that Frank's personal belongings would be shipped home as promptly as possible.

The letters from the Adjutant General and from Captain Stearns formed the basis of Mrs. McShane's hopes. That was clear from a glance. In a routine manner, the Adjutant General had explained the meaning of the term 'missing in action': 'This report does not constitute an announcement that subject officer has been lost in action against the enemy. There is no immediate warrant for this conclusion. Subject officer, was, however, separated from his unit after contact with enemy units; his own unit headquarters does not know his immediate whereabouts at this time.' The letter admitted that he might be dead, but it added that he might also be a prisoner of the Japanese, or perhaps hiding from the enemy, though in the Pacific the expanse of ocean limits the chances of survival. The letter warned against despair until Army sources could confirm any of these or many other possibilities.

Captain Stearns's letter aroused even greater hopes, because the McShanes assumed that he was closer to the facts. What they did not realize was that Stearns never knew Frank or his crew, for he had replaced our former commanding officer since Frank's death. His information, drawn from formalized Army reports, was worse than worthless because of the uninformed hope which it raised in an effort to cushion the effect of the news.

While the family watched tensely for a reaction which would confirm its hopes, I read all the letters carefully. When I finished, I realized that they all expected some profound comment, and finding none, I looked through the letters again, stalling for time. What could I say? Something optimistic which would refresh grief-torn hope and cheer them for the first time in three months? An implied hope which, because I was there, would release again their dream of Frank's return? I glanced at Mrs. McShane; her face pleaded. I dropped my eyes and, lacking words, shook my head. The others waited for a comment, but Mrs. McShane understood. I thought that she would cry, but she didn't. Finally, she spoke softly: 'Oh, Frank, we prayed so hard you'd bring us some hope. I know, your letter should have warned us. Even so, we prayed so hard, so hard.'

We were interrupted as the outer door opened and closed. Mrs. McShane rose with a start: 'That'll be Mister,' she said, 'I'll just look at my roast.' And with that she disappeared into the kitchen in the rear, leaving 'Mister' and me to introduce ourselves. Mr. McShane appeared in the living room in a moment, dragging a reluctant three-year-old behind him. This was Emily, 'Frank's baby,' who had been playing next door all afternoon. While she peered at me from under her pink bonnet, Mr. McShane introduced himself. He was wearing the gold-buttoned vest of a railroad conductor and carrying his stiff cap under his arm. He waved me back onto the couch and then sat down across the room in the chair which Kathleen had vacated for him. He was almost bald, but his lean face and blue eyes gave him a striking resemblance to Frank.

'I see you've read all the letters,' he said, nodding toward the envelope from the Adjutant General. 'What news do you bring, Lieutenant?'

I repeated that I was sorry but that I brought no hope at all. He stared at the floor as I spoke, and when I had finished, he was silent for what seemed like eternity. Then he reviewed the whole story. As he finished, he looked over at me and said: 'Of course, we knew really in our hearts after your letter there was little reason for hope, but we hope anyway, especially Mrs. McShane. Somehow we'd feel disloyal to Frank to give up if there's any chance.' His eyes sought the carpet again and he was silent.

Mrs. McShane returned, her face now damp with ill-concealed tears. She greeted her husband with a perfunctory kiss and then, as if to relieve the situation, she made a fuss over Emily and brought her over to the couch. 'Did you say "Howdy-do" to Frank, darling?' she asked her. 'See, I told you Frankie was coming today and here he is.' Emily looked at me and then ran over to Frank's picture and said: 'This Frankie; when this Frankie coming home?' 'This is Frankie, too,' her mother insisted, apparently startled by the grimness of her own jest, 'and he came all the way from Baltimore just to see us. Wasn't that nice?' Emily stared at me again, this time out of the corner of her eye in order to disguise her interest. 'See, darling,' her mother continued, 'this Frankie is in the Army too and flies airplanes.' Finally Emily made up her mind: 'This not my Frankie.' I tried to say that I wished I were her Frankie, but unimpressed, she scampered away to the kitchen, where Aunt Clara was now supervising the roast.

Mrs. McShane settled back on the couch and waited for her husband to ask questions, but when he continued to stare vacantly at the floor, she said thoughtfully: 'You know, Frank, when our Frank went away after his leave at graduation time, little Emily was too young to remember him. All she knows of him is that picture over there and what we'd tell her. I told you Frank said she was his "best girl" — that's what he used to call her, didn't he, Thomas? In all his letters home he'd always ask for her special. We'd read all Frank's letters to her. She was too young to know what he was sayin' most times, but always she listened. Oftentimes we got the feelin' she knew more than we knew.'

Aunt Clara came back into the room, anxious to hear all the conversation and to break in with a word: 'Young man, d'you say you was with Frank when he got shot down?' I

nodded yes. 'And you don't think there's much chance of
him coming back?' I shook my head. She seemed unimpressed. 'Margaret, have you told him about all the hopeful
signs Frank'll be back? Has she, young man?' I shouted that
she had not and that I should like to hear any hopeful news.

Aunt Clara called over to Mrs. McShane: 'Tell him about
it, Margaret. Tell him and see if he don't agree Frank's coming back. He's a good Catholic boy. Tell that by lookin' at
him. He'll understand. Go on and tell him.' With that she
went back to her roast.

Mrs. McShane needed no prodding. 'As I started to say,'
she continued, 'when Frank wrote he'd come home in about
a month, Baby was more excited than any of us. She run
around the block tellin' everyone, "Frankie comin' home
soon." Then evenin's she pesters me all through dinner
askin', "When Frankie comin' home?" Then comes the news
of Frank's accident. We got to tell her that Frank might not
be home for a long time and she cries a lot.

'So we stop talkin' about Frank in front of Emily. I guess
maybe we made too much of a thing out of her bein' Frank's
favorite. Baby seemed to miss all the fuss we'd give her all
the time when we talked about Frank or when his letters
come in. Then about two months ago, the night of the
novena over at church for the boys and girls in service, somethin' funny happens.' She paused, wondering just how to
explain, then continued more slowly. 'I'm tuckin' Emily in
bed and sayin' her prayers with her when she looks up and
says, "Mommy, Frankie comin' home soon." I was so taken,
at first I couldn't say nothin', special after all the bad news
we had. "How do you know?" I asks her. But she just smiles
and don't say nothin'.'

'My wife even tried bribing her with little special favors,'
Mr. McShane broke in, 'something we don't do in this house.'

'I was so anxious,' she explained, 'I tried everythin' to have
her tell me more. But that's all she'd say: "Mommy, Frankie
comin' home soon." Wasn't that the thing, now?'

Mrs. McShane thought it over for a moment, then continued: 'Ever since, she cried only once in a while. It seems

like she knows somethin' the rest of us don't. Sounds funny, but that's the way it seems like; isn't that right, Thomas?' No answer one way or the other.

Bill had been squirming over on his chair. Now slipping off it and coming over to his mother, he nodded toward me and said in a stage whisper: 'Mommy, ask him if Frank will come home a captain maybe, or a major like Jesse O'Hara's uncle.' His father suppressed the suggestion. 'Here now, not now, son. Later maybe.' Mrs. McShane hugged her son and he started back to his seat.

'Mother, perhaps the children should go upstairs for now. They can come down for dinner and talk then,' their father suggested. Mrs. McShane agreed and shooed them out gently: 'Run along upstairs for now, children. You can talk with Frank later at dinner.' The children filed out obediently, all except Harry, who, apparently, was not classified as one of the children.

'It's happened several times since, too,' Mrs. McShane said after the children had disappeared. 'Emily, I mean. About a month ago, on a Sunday, I went over to Mister's mother's house and took Emily along — the children was out and there bein' no one to keep an eye on her. Emily was off playin' in the corner while me and Mother McShane talks. She's quiet a bit, then comes over to me and says it again: "Mommy, Frankie comin' home." Missus was more shocked than me, I guess, 'cause she never heard it before. Both of us tried to find out what Emily means but, like before, that's all she says. And it's happened since then too. Always I try to find out more, but she just smiles or pouts and says the same thing again. Once or twice I think maybe she's tryin' to get a fuss made over her, but she always looks so serious.'

She paused. 'Isn't it possible . . .' I started, but then thought better of it and stopped. 'What, Frank?' Mrs. McShane asked. 'Isn't what possible?' I tried again: 'Don't you think that a baby Emily's age — well, as you say, she likes a fuss to be made over her; all babies do. For her the idea of Frank's return — his letters, for instance — always meant a lot of attention and she learned to associate the two ideas. Then she missed the glory when you all stopped talking about Frank's return. I don't mean glory, exactly; excitement is probably a better word. Now she finds that she receives all kinds of attention by mentioning the magic word: "Frankie."'

I thought to myself that on the night of the novena, probably quite by accident, Emily returned to a subject which her mind had been conditioned to associate with joy and excitement. And it elicited the response which she was unconsciously seeking. She found again the key to her family's heart, and having found it, she used it without understanding its meaning.

I wondered what their reaction to this comment would be, but I could have guessed. They either did not or would not understand.

'I don't know how she can tell,' Mrs. McShane insisted, 'but I feel so strongly she knows somethin'.'

I said nothing further, hoping that she might continue and, in talking, recognize the fantasy in her idea. Instead, she seemed disappointed that I could not share her belief and changed the subject.

'Ever since the word came in from Washington, we've all gone to church every mornin' to pray for Frank. All except Harry,' she added reproachfully. 'He doesn't think God can help us.'

Harry sprang to his own defense: 'God'll do things in His own way anyway, so what's the use of all this jabbering in church?'

Mrs. McShane was apparently accustomed to this irreverence, for she just shook her head sadly and said that she was afraid that Harry was not very religious.

'You know, it's funny,' she continued. 'We moved into this house so we'd be nearer church, and, soon as we done it, we had nothin' but trouble ever since. There's no such thing as an unlucky house. I know that. But just the same, this house has brought nothin' but trouble. We had only just moved in when my sainted mother passed to her reward

— God rest her soul — and not three weeks later comes the telegram about Frank. I declare, if church wasn't just around the block and there bein' no other house available in the parish, I wouldn't stay here five minutes, not five minutes. You'll think that's silly, won't you?' She smiled with some embarrassment. 'Well, I guess I do too. But still, you've got to admit that's too much to be coincidence, don't you think so?'

I agreed there was no such thing as an unlucky house. 'Well, I suppose so,' Mrs. McShane conceded, 'but I want to get away from this place anyway.'

Aunt Clara motioned from the kitchen that the roast was ready. I had reservations on a train scheduled to leave within an hour, so I apologized and said that I should have to leave. Mrs. McShane begged me to stay, but when I explained that I could not, she said that dinner could wait so that no minute of the visit might be lost. She became silent a moment and then abruptly began again, talking very fast as if she had to crowd many things into the few remaining moments.

'It's not like they wrote Frank was killed. All the letters say we mustn't give up hope. You was there, Frank, you saw it happen. That's why we wanted a word of hope from you. When the word first come in, it looked hopeless. But as we thought about it a bit, it didn't seem so bad. Those letters from the general in Washington and from Frank's commander gave us lots of hope. Then these other things start to happen. Baby stops broodin' and seems to know somethin' about Frank. I told you about that. Then later we show all the letters to Father Ronald at the church — do you know him at all? Such a fine and holy man. He told us to pray very hard for Frank so wherever he might be, he'd benefit by our prayers. That was what he *told* us, but I could tell from the look in his eyes he thought Frank would be back. You know,' she added, 'you can tell those things.'

'Oh, Mother, what the hell!' Harry had been sitting in glum silence over by Frank's picture during our talk, but though he had spoken only once, he had indicated his disapproval of his mother's ideas a number of times by stamping out his cigarette impatiently or saying, 'For heaven's sake,' under his breath. I was surprised that he broke into the conversation at all. But now he fairly exploded. 'You know damned well Father Ronald doesn't know any more about Frank than we do. He doesn't know as much. How the hell would he know Frank was coming back?'

'That's no way to talk to your mother,' his father said sharply. 'If you can't speak in a reasonable voice without using blasphemy, get upstairs with the children.'

'I'm sorry, Dad,' Harry responded more quietly, 'but this is all old witch stuff. Father Ronald doesn't know a damned thing about Frank, and it's just superstition to think that he does.'

Mrs. McShane was horrified. 'Harry, you're talkin' against the Church! That's a sin; you know it. Superstition! The saints preserve us, what sort of trouble are you trying to bring down on our house! And in front of company too!'

'All right, all right,' Harry said; then, turning to his father, 'What do you really think, Dad? You don't believe all this hokum of Mother's, do you? Honestly?'

Thomas McShane was unprepared for the question. He stammered and then thought he saw an out. 'I told you, son, that's no way to talk to your mother.'

'All right, Dad,' Harry said with affection in his voice. 'But what do you *really* think?'

'Well,' Mr. McShane said slowly, 'on the face of it, it looks real hopeless. Especially since the Lieutenant here hasn't had anything very hopeful to say. But you can't tell for sure. You read about soldiers every day reported dead and come back. Story about that in tonight's paper. Maybe Mother hopes too much, but if there's any chance, you've gotta hope. Hope, and pray hard. Nothing in this life is certain, son.'

His wife nodded approval and added: 'Harry, how can you give up so easily? So much has happened to bring us hope.'

Harry looked at me and murmured, 'Oh, my God' — to me and to himself — and turned away. In a minute he got up and left the room. I sympathized with him certainly, but it was hardly the moment to take sides.

Thinking back, I realized that our conversation had fallen into a pattern: first, Mrs. McShane had met me on my own ground of facts with the letters from the Adjutant General and from our squadron commander. When I countered those with what I had seen on the mission, we retreated from this plane of reality, where we discussed facts, to the plane of dreams and hopes, where facts were smothered by wishes and where any hope, however nebulous, shielded her from the immediate problem of accepting Frank's death. All her questions during the afternoon sought to evoke some word which would give substance to her dreams. We had now arrived at this peculiarly inverted situation in which she was giving 'information' about Frank rather than receiving it. As long as she continued to talk she held control of the situation, and unconsciously knowing this, she repeated each scrap of ghostly evidence in a variety of forms.

I became used to this technique, but never imagined the final extent to which she would carry it. As I was preparing to leave, she launched one last effort. She had shown my letter to the Mother Superior at Mary Ann's school and when Mother Superior had finished it, Mrs. McShane told me, 'she turned toward me with a gentle smile and said one day when Frank came home, he and his friend, Lieutenant Ryan, would laugh long and hard over the gloom in that letter. "Frank was always intended to be a priest," Mother Superior said. "I know the Lord will surely bring him back to do His work." ' Mrs. McShane paused so that the effect of her statement would not be lost, and concluded, 'I've never had any real doubts since then.'

She was triumphant as she announced this final basis for her hopes, certain that she had at last broken through my best defense. Too amazed for any coherent comment, I murmured: 'I just cannot shake your confidence, can I?'

Mrs. McShane smiled, as if to console me for my failure. 'I think we know how you feel, too, Frank. But faith makes us so sure.'

I marveled at her faith: she denied the reality of my eye-witness account and accepted her hopes as undeniable truth. I saw again the flame over Togo Jima, the consuming heat which melted the wings of the 'Royal Flush' off its fuselage, the 14,000-foot plunge into the Pacific, the rescue planes searching eight hours for ten of the eleven men on the crew. Even in the face of her boundless confidence, I did not need to remind myself that I saw these things happen, that Frank's death was a fact.

But facts had no apparent effect. Only as I left did Mrs. McShane falter a bit and cry. At the door, I knew how totally I had failed to bring her the comfort of definite news, even bad news, for as she hugged me hard, her eyes closed, she said desperately: 'Oh, Frank! Do come back soon!'

I knew that she was not talking to me.

(From The Yale Review)

# SEX EDUCATION

## BY DOROTHY CANFIELD

*I*T was three times — but at intervals of many years — that I heard my Aunt Minnie tell about an experience of her girlhood that had made a never-to-be-forgotten impression on her. The first time she was in her thirties, still young. But she had then been married for ten years, so that to my group of friends, all in the early teens, she seemed quite of another generation.

The day she told us the story, we had been idling on one end of her porch as we made casual plans for a picnic supper in the woods. Darning stockings at the other end, she paid no attention to us until one of the girls said, 'Let's take blankets and sleep out there. It'd be fun.'

'No,' Aunt Minnie broke in sharply, 'you mustn't do that.'

'Oh, for goodness sakes, why not!' said one of the younger girls, rebelliously. 'The boys are always doing it. Why can't we, just once?'

Aunt Minnie laid down her sewing. 'Come here, girls,' she said, 'I want you should hear something that happened to me when I was your age.'

Her voice had a special quality which, perhaps, young people of today would not recognize. But we did. We knew from experience that it was the dark voice grown-ups used when they were going to say something about sex.

Yet at first what she had to say was like any dull family anecdote. She had been ill when she was fifteen; and afterwards she was run down, thin, with no appetite. Her folks

17

thought a change of air would do her good, and sent her from Vermont out to Ohio — or was it Illinois? I don't remember. Anyway, one of those places where the corn grows high. Her mother's Cousin Ella lived there, keeping house for her son-in-law.

The son-in-law was the minister of the village church. His wife had died some years before, leaving him a young widower with two little girls and a baby boy. He had been a normally personable man then, but the next summer, on the Fourth of July when he was trying to set off some fireworks to amuse his children, an imperfectly manufactured rocket had burst in his face. The explosion had left one side of his face badly scarred. Aunt Minnie made us see it, as she still saw it, in horrid detail — the stiffened, scarlet scar-tissue distorting one cheek, the lower lip turned so far out at one corner that the moist red mucous-membrane lining always showed, one lower eyelid hanging loose, and watering.

After the accident, his face had been a long time healing. It was then that his wife's elderly mother had gone to keep house and take care of the children. When he was well enough to be about again, he found his position as pastor of the little church waiting for him. The farmers and village people in his congregation, moved by his misfortune, by his faithful service and by his unblemished character, said they would rather have Mr. Fairchild, even with his scarred face, than any other minister. He was a good preacher, Aunt Minnie told us, 'and the way he prayed was kind of exciting. I'd never known a preacher, not to live in the same house with him, before. And when he was in the pulpit, with everybody looking up at him, I felt the way his children did, kind of proud to think we had just eaten breakfast at the same table. I liked to call him "Cousin Malcolm" before folks. One side of his face was all right, anyhow. You could see from that that he *had* been a good-looking man. In fact, probably one of those ministers that all the women — 'Aunt Minnie paused, drew her lips together, and looked at us uncertainly.

Then she went back to the story as it happened — as it happened that first time I heard her tell it. 'I thought he was a saint. Everybody out there did. That was all *they* knew. Of course, it made a person sick to look at that awful scar — the drooling corner of his mouth was the worst. He tried to keep that side of his face turned away from folks. But you always knew it was there. That was what kept him from marrying again, so Cousin Ella said. I heard her say lots of times that he knew no woman would touch any man who looked the way he did, not with a ten-foot pole.

'Well, the change of air did do me good. I got my appetite back, and ate a lot and played outdoors a lot with my cousins. They were younger than I (I had my sixteenth birthday there) but I still liked to play games. I got taller and laid on some weight. Cousin Ella used to say I grew as fast as the corn did. Their house stood at the edge of the village. Beyond it was one of those big cornfields they have out West. At the time when I first got there, the stalks were only up to a person's knee. You could see over their tops. But it grew like lightning, and before long, it was the way thick woods are here, way over your head, the stalks growing so close together it was dark under them.

'Cousin Ella told us youngsters that it was lots worse for getting lost in than woods, because there weren't any landmarks in it. One spot in a cornfield looked just like any other. "You children keep out of it," she used to tell us almost every day, "*especially you girls*. It's no place for a decent girl. You could easy get so far from the house nobody could hear you if you hollered. There are plenty of men in this town that wouldn't like anything better than — " she never said what.

'In spite of what she said, my little cousins and I had figured out that if we went across one corner of the field, it would be a short-cut to the village, and sometimes, without letting on to Cousin Ella, we'd go that way. After the corn got really tall, the farmer stopped cultivating, and we soon beat down a path in the loose dirt. The minute you were inside the field it was dark. You felt as if you were miles

from anywhere. It sort of scared you. But in no time the
path turned and brought you out on the far end of Main
Street. Your breath was coming fast, maybe, but that was
what made you like to do it.

'One day I missed the turn. Maybe I didn't keep my mind
on it. Maybe it had rained and blurred the tramped-down
look of the path. I don't know what. All of a sudden, I knew
I was lost. And the minute I knew that, I began to run, just
as hard as I could run. I couldn't help it, any more than
you can help snatching your hand off a hot stove. I didn't
know what I was scared of, I didn't even know I *was* running,
till my heart was pounding so hard I had to stop.

'The minute I stood still, I could hear Cousin Ella saying,
"There are plenty of men in this town that wouldn't like
anything better than — " I didn't know, not really, what she
meant. But I knew she meant something horrible. I opened
my mouth to scream. But I put both hands over my mouth
to keep the scream in. If I made any noise, one of those men
would hear me. I thought I heard one just behind me, and
whirled around. And then I thought another one had tiptoed up behind me, the other way, and I spun around so
fast I almost fell over. I stuffed my hands hard up against
my mouth. And then — I couldn't help it — I ran again —
but my legs were shaking so I soon had to stop. There I
stood, scared to move for fear of rustling the corn and letting
the men know where I was. My hair had come down, all
over my face. I kept pushing it back and looking around,
quick, to make sure one of the men hadn't found out where
I was. Then I thought I saw a man coming toward me, and
I ran away from him — and fell down, and burst some of
the buttons off my dress, and was sick to my stomach — and
thought I heard a man close to me and got up and staggered
around, knocking into the corn because I couldn't even see
where I was going.

'And then, off to one side, I saw Cousin Malcolm. Not a
man — The minister. He was standing still, one hand up
to his face, thinking. He hadn't heard me.

'I was so *terrible* glad to see him, instead of one of those men, I ran as fast as I could and just flung myself on him, to make myself feel how safe I was.' . . .

Aunt Minnie had become strangely agitated. Her hands were shaking, her face was crimson. She frightened us. We could not look away from her. As we waited for her to go on, I felt little spasms twitch at the muscles inside my body — 'And what do you think that *saint,* that holy minister of the Gospel, did to an innocent child who clung to him for safety? The most terrible look came into his eyes — you girls are too young to know what he looked like. But once you're married, you'll find out. He grabbed hold of me — that dreadful face of his was *right on mine* — and began clawing the clothes off my back.'

She stopped for a moment, panting. We were too frightened to speak. She went on: 'He had torn my dress right down to the waist before I — then I *did* scream — all I could — and pulled away from him so hard I almost fell down, and ran and all of a sudden I came out of the corn, right in the backyard of the Fairchild house. The children were staring at the corn, and Cousin Ella ran out of the kitchen door. They had heard me screaming. Cousin Ella shrieked out, "What is it? What happened? Did a man scare you?" And I said, "Yes, yes, yes, a man — I ran — !' And then I fainted away. I must have. The next thing I knew I was on the sofa in the living-room and Cousin Ella was slapping my face with a wet towel.'

She had to wet her lips with her tongue before she could go on. Her face was gray now. 'There! that's the kind of thing girls' folks ought to tell them about — so they'll know what men are like.'

She finished her story as if she were dismissing us. We wanted to go away, but we were too horrified to stir. Finally, one of the youngest girls asked in a low trembling voice, 'Aunt Minnie, did you tell on him?'

'No, I was ashamed to,' she said briefly. 'They sent me home the next day, anyhow. Nobody ever said a word to me about it. And I never did either. Till now.' . . .

By what gets printed in some of the modern child-psy-

chology books, you would think that girls to whom such a
story had been told would never develop normally. Yet, as
far as I can remember what happened to the girls in that
group, we all grew up about like anybody. Most of us
married, some happily, some not so well. We kept house.
We learned — more or less — how to live with our husbands;
we had children and struggled to bring them up right — we
went forward into life just as if we had never been warned
not to.

Perhaps, young as we were that day, we had already had
enough experience of life so that we were not quite blank
paper for Aunt Minnie's frightening story. Whether we
thought of it then or not, we couldn't have failed to see that
at this very time Aunt Minnie had been married for ten
years or more, comfortably and well married, too. Against
what she tried by that story to brand into our minds, stood
the cheerful homelife in that house, the good-natured, kind,
hard-working husband, and the children — the three rough-
and-tumble, nice little boys, so adored by their parents, and
the sweet girl baby who died, of whom they could never
speak without tears. It was such actual contact with adult
life that probably kept generation after generation of girls
from being scared by tales like Aunt Minnie's into a neurotic
horror of living. . . .

Of course, since Aunt Minnie was so much older than we,
her boys grew up to be adolescents and young men while
our children were still little enough so that our worries over
them were nothing more serious than whooping cough and
trying to get them to make their own beds. Two of our
aunt's three boys followed, without losing their footing, the
narrow path which leads across adolescence into normal
adult life. But the middle one, Jake, repeatedly fell off into
the morass. 'Girl trouble,' as the succinct family phrase put
it. He was one of those boys who have 'charm,' whatever we
mean by that, and he was always being snatched at by girls
who would be 'all wrong' for him to marry. And once, at
nineteen, he ran away from home, whether with one of these
girls or not we never heard, for through all her ups and

downs with this son, Aunt Minnie tried fiercely to protect him from scandal that might cloud his later life.

Her husband had to stay on his job to earn the family living. She was the one who went to find Jake. When it was gossiped around that Jake was in 'bad company' his mother drew some money from the family savings-bank account, and silent, white-cheeked, took the train to the city where rumor said he had gone.

Some weeks later he came back with her. With no girl. She had cleared him of that entanglement. As of others, which followed, later. Her troubles seemed over when, at a 'suitable' age, he fell in love with a 'suitable' girl, married her and took her to live in our shire town, sixteen miles away, where he had a good position. Jake was always bright enough.

Sometimes, idly, people speculated as to what Aunt Minnie had seen that time she went after her runaway son, wondering where her search for him had taken her — very queer places for Aunt Minnie to be in, we imagined. And how could such an ignorant home-keeping woman ever have known what to say to an errant wilful boy to set him straight?

Well, of course, we reflected, watching her later struggles with Jake's erratic ways, she certainly could not have remained ignorant, after seeing over and over what she probably had; after talking with Jake about the things which, a good many times, must have come up with desperate openness between them.

She kept her own counsel. We never knew anything definite about the facts of those experiences of hers. But one day she told a group of us — all then married women — something which gave us a notion about what she had learned from them. . . .

We were hastily making a layette for a not especially welcome baby in a poor family. In those days, our town had no such thing as a district-nursing service. Aunt Minnie, a vigorous woman of fifty-five, had come in to help. As we sewed, we talked, of course; and because our daughters were near or in their teens, we were comparing notes about the bewildering responsibility of bringing up girls.

After a while, Aunt Minnie remarked: 'Well, I hope you teach your girls some *sense*. From what I read, I know you're great on telling them "the facts," facts we never heard of when we were girls. Like as not, some facts I don't know, now. But knowing the facts isn't going to do them any more good than *not* knowing the facts ever did, unless they have some sense taught them, too.'

'What do you mean, Aunt Minnie?' one of us asked her uncertainly.

She reflected, threading a needle: 'Well, I don't know but what the best way to tell you what I mean, is to tell you about something that happened to me, forty years ago. I've never said anything about it before. But I've thought about it a good deal. Maybe —'

She had hardly begun when I recognized the story — her visit to her Cousin Ella's mid-western home, the widower with his scarred face and saintly reputation and, very vividly, her getting lost in the great cornfield. I knew every word she was going to say — to the very end, I thought.

But no, I did not. Not at all.

She broke off, suddenly, to exclaim with impatience: 'Wasn't I the big ninny? But not so big a ninny as that old cousin of mine. I could wring her neck for getting me in such a state. Only she didn't know any better, herself. That was the way they brought young people up in those days, scaring them out of their wits about the awfulness of getting lost, but not telling them a thing about how *not* to get lost. Or how to act, if they did.

'If I had had the sense I was born with, I'd have known that running my legs off in a zigzag was the worst thing I could do. I couldn't have been more than a few feet from the path when I noticed I wasn't on it. My tracks in the loose ploughed dirt must have been perfectly plain. If I'd h' stood still, and collected my wits, I could have looked down to see which way my footsteps went and just walked back over them to the path and gone on about my business.

'Now I ask you, if I'd been told how to do that, wouldn't it have been a lot better protection for me — if protection was what my cousin thought she wanted to give me — than to scare me so at the idea of being lost that I turned deef-dumb-and-blind when I thought I was?

'And anyhow that patch of corn wasn't as big as she let on. And she knew it wasn't. It was no more than a big field in a farming country. I was a well-grown girl of sixteen, as tall as I am now. If I couldn't have found the path, I could have just walked along one line of cornstalks — *straight* — and I'd have come out somewhere in ten minutes. Fifteen at the most. Maybe not just where I wanted to go. But all right, safe, where decent folks were living.'

She paused, as if she had finished. But at the inquiring blankness in our faces, she went on: 'Well now, why isn't teaching girls — and boys, too, for the Lord's sake don't forget they need it as much as the girls — about this man-and-woman business, something like that? If you give them the idea — no matter whether it's *as* you tell them the facts, or as you *don't* tell them the facts, that it is such a terribly scary thing that if they take a step into it, something's likely to happen to them so awful that you're ashamed to tell them what — well, they'll lose their heads and run around like crazy things, first time they take one step away from the path.

'For they'll be trying out the paths, all right. You can't keep them from it. And a good thing, too. How else are they going to find out what it's like. Boys' and girls' going together is a path across one corner of growing up. And when they go together, they're likely to get off the path some. Seems to me, it's up to their folks to bring them up so, when they do, they don't start screaming and running in circles, but stand still, right where they are, and get their breath and figure out how to get back.

'And, anyhow, you don't tell 'em the truth about sex' (I was astonished to hear her use the actual word, tabu to women of her generation) 'if they get the idea from you that it's all there is to living. It's not. If you don't get to where you want to go in it, well, there's a lot of landscape all around it a person can have a good time in.

'D'you know, I believe one thing that gives girls and boys

the wrong idea is the way folks *look!* My old cousin's face, I can see her now, it was as red as a rooster's comb when she was telling me about men in that cornfield. I believe now she kind of *liked* to talk about it.'

(Oh, Aunt Minnie — and yours! I thought.)

Someone asked, 'But how *did* you get out, Aunt Minnie?' She shook her head, laid down her sewing. 'More foolishness. That minister my mother's cousin was keeping house for — her son-in-law — I caught sight of him, down along one of the aisles of cornstalks, looking down at the ground, thinking, the way he often did. And I was so glad to see him I rushed right up to him, and flung my arms around his neck and hugged him. He hadn't heard me coming. He gave a great start, put one arm around me and turned his face full towards me — I suppose for just a second he had forgotten how awful one side of it was. His expression, his eyes — well, you're all married women, you know how he looked, the way any able-bodied man thirty-six-or-seven, who'd been married and begotten children, would look — for a minute, anyhow, if a full-blooded girl of sixteen, who ought to have known better, flung herself at him without any warning, her hair tumbling down, her dress half-unbuttoned, and hugged him with all her might.

'I was what they called innocent in those days. That is, I knew just as little about what men are like as my folks could manage I should. But I was old enough to know all right what that look meant. And it gave me a start. But, of course, the real thing of it was that dreadful scar of his, so close to my face — that wet corner of his mouth, his eye drawn down with the red inside of the lower eyelid showing —

'It turned me so sick, I pulled away with all my might, so fast that I ripped one sleeve nearly loose, and let out a screech like a wildcat. And ran. Did I run! And in a minute, I was through the corn and had come out in the backyard of the house. I hadn't been more than a few feet from it, probably, any of the time. And then I fainted away. Girls were always fainting away; it was the way our corset-strings were pulled tight, I suppose, and then — oh, a lot of fuss.'

'But, anyhow,' she finished, picking up her work and going on, setting neat, firm stitches with steady hands, 'there's one thing, I never told anybody it was Cousin Malcolm I had met in the cornfield. I told my old cousin that "a man had scared me." And nobody said anything more about it to me, not ever. That was the way they did in those days. They thought if they didn't let on about something, maybe it wouldn't have happened. I was sent back to Vermont right away, and Cousin Malcolm went on being minister of the church.

'I've always been,' said Aunt Minnie moderately, 'kind of proud that I didn't go and ruin a man's life for just one second's slip-up. If you could have called it that. For it *would* have ruined him. You know how hard as stone people are about other folks' let-downs. If I'd have told, not one person in that town would have had any charity. Not one would have tried to understand. One slip, *once,* and they'd have pushed him down in the mud. If I had told, I'd have felt pretty bad about it, later — when I came to have more sense. But I declare, I can't see how I came to have the decency, dumb as I was then, to know that it wouldn't be fair.' . . .

It was not long after this talk that Aunt Minnie's elderly husband died, mourned by her, by all of us. She lived alone then. It was peaceful October weather for her, in which she kept a firm roundness of face and figure, as quiet-living countrywomen often do, on into her late sixties.

But then Jake, the boy who had girl trouble, had wife trouble. We heard he had taken to running after a young girl, or was it that she was running after him? It was something serious. For his nice wife left him and came back with the children to live with her mother in our town. Poor Aunt Minnie used to go to see her for long talks which made them both cry. And she went to keep house for Jake, for months at a time.

She grew old, during those years. When finally she (or something) managed to get the marriage mended so that Jake's wife relented and went back to live with him, there was no trace left of her pleasant brisk freshness. She was stooped and slow-footed and shrunken. We, her kinspeople, although we would have given our lives for any one of our own children, wondered whether Jake was worth what it had cost his mother to — well, steady him, or reform him. Or perhaps just understand him. Whatever it took.

She came of a long-lived family and was able to go on keeping house for herself well into her eighties. Of course, we and the other neighbors stepped in often to make sure she was all right. Mostly, during those brief calls, the talk turned on nothing more vital than her geraniums. But one mid-winter afternoon, sitting with her in front of her cozy stove, I chanced to speak in rather hasty blame of someone who had, I thought, acted badly. To my surprise this brought from her the story about the cornfield which she had evidently quite forgotten telling me, twice before.

This time she told it almost dreamily, swaying to and fro in her rocking-chair, her eyes fixed on the long slope of snow outside her window. When she came to the encounter with the minister she said, looking away from the distance and back into my eyes: 'I know now that I had been, all along, kind of *interested* in him, the way any girl as old as I was would be in any youngish man living in the same house with her. And a minister, too. They have to have the gift of gab so much more than most men, women get to thinking they are more alive than men who can't talk so well. I *thought* the reason I threw my arms around him was because I had been so scared. And I certainly had been scared, by my own cousin's horrible talk about the cornfield being full of men waiting to grab girls. But that wasn't all the reason I flung myself at Malcolm Fairchild and hugged him. I know that now. Why in the world shouldn't I have been taught *some* notion of it then? 'Twould do girls good to know that they are just like everybody else — human nature *and* sex, all mixed up together. I didn't have to hug him. I wouldn't have, if he'd been dirty or fat and old, or chewed tobacco.'

I stirred in my chair, ready to say, 'But it's not so simple as all that to tell girls —' and she hastily answered my unspoken protest. 'I know, I know, most of it can't be put into words. There just aren't any words to say something that's so both-ways-at-once all the time as this man-and-woman business. But look here, you know as well as I do that there are lots more ways than in words to teach young folks what you want 'em to know.'

The old woman stopped her swaying rocker to peer far back into the past with honest eyes. 'What was in my mind back there in the cornfield — partly, anyhow — was what had been there all the time I was living in the same house with Cousin Malcolm — that he had long straight legs, and broad shoulders, and lots of curly brown hair, and was nice and flat in front, and that one side of his face was good-looking. But most of all, that he and I were really alone, for the first time, without anybody to see us.

'I suppose, if it hadn't been for that dreadful scar, he'd have drawn me up, tight, and — most any man would — kissed me. I know how I must have looked, all red and hot and my hair down and my dress open. And, used as he was to big cornfields, he probably never dreamed that the reason I looked that way was because I was scared to be by myself in one. He may have thought — you know what he may have thought.

'Well — if his face had been like anybody's, when he looked at me the way he did, the way a man does look at a woman he wants to have, it would have scared me — some. I'd have cried, maybe. And probably he'd have kissed me again. You know how such things go. I might have come out of the cornfield halfway engaged to marry him. Why not? I was old enough, as people thought then. That would have been Nature. That was probably what he thought of, in that first instant.

'But what did I do? I had one look at his poor horrible face, and started back as though I'd stepped on a snake. And screamed and ran.

'What do you suppose *he* felt, left there in the corn? He must have been sure that I would tell everybody he had attacked me. He probably thought that when he came out and went back to the village he'd already be in disgrace and put out of the pulpit.

'But the worst must have been to find out, so rough, so plain from the way I acted — as if somebody had hit him with an ax — the way he would look to any woman he might try to get close to.

'That must have been — ' she drew a long breath — 'well, pretty hard on him.'

After a silence, she murmured pityingly, 'Poor man!'

*(From Harper's Bazaar)*

# THE HEADLESS HAWK

## BY TRUMAN CAPOTE

*They are of those that rebel against the light; they know not the ways thereof, nor abide in the paths thereof. In the dark they dig through houses, which they had marked for themselves in the daytime: they know not the light. For the morning is to them as the shadow of death: if one know them, they are in the terrors of the shadow of death.*
—Job 24: 13, 16, 17

*V*INCENT switched off the lights in the gallery. Outside, after locking the door, he smoothed the brim of an elegant panama, and started toward Third Avenue, his umbrella-cane tap-tap-tapping along the pavement. A promise of rain had darkened the day since dawn, and a sky of bloated clouds blurred the five o'clock sun; it was hot, though, humid as tropical mist, and voices, sounding along the gray July street, sounding muffled and strange, carried a fretful undertone. Vincent felt as though he moved below the sea. Busses, cruising crosstown through Fifty-seventh Street, seemed like green-bellied fish, and faces loomed and rocked like wave-riding masks. He studied each passerby, hunting one, and presently he saw her, a girl in a green raincoat. She was standing on the downtown corner of Fifty-seventh and Third, just standing there smoking a cigarette, and giving somehow the impression she hummed a tune. The raincoat was transparent. She wore dark slacks, no socks, a pair of huarachas, a man's white shirt. Her hair

31

was fawn-colored, and cut like a boy's. When she noticed Vincent crossing toward her she dropped the cigarette, and hurried down the block to the doorway of an antique store.

Vincent slowed his step. He pulled out a handkerchief, and dabbed his forehead: if only he could get away, go up to the Cape, lie in the sun. He bought an afternoon paper, and fumbled his change. It rolled in the gutter, dropped silently out of sight down a sewer grating. 'Ain't but a nickel, bub,' said the newsdealer, for Vincent, though actually unaware of his loss, looked heartbroken. And it was like that often now, never quite in contact, never sure whether a step would take him backward or forward, up or down. Very casually, with the handle of the umbrella hooked over an arm, and his eyes concentrated on the paper's headline — but what did the damn thing say? — he continued downtown. A swarthy woman carrying a shopping bag jostled him, glared, muttered in coarsely vehement Italian. The ragged cut of her voice seemed to come through layers of wool. As he approached the antique store where the girl in the green raincoat waited, he walked slower still, counting one, two, three, four, five, six . . . at six he halted before the window.

The window was like a corner of an attic; a lifetime's discardings rose in a pyramid of no particular worth: vacant picture frames, a lavender wig, Gothic shaving mugs, beaded lamps. There was an oriental mask suspended on a ceiling cord, and wind from an electric fan whirring inside the shop revolved it slowly round and round. Vincent, by degrees, lifted his gaze, and looked at the girl directly. She was hovering in the doorway so that he saw her greenness distorted wavy through doubled glass; the elevated pounded overhead and the window trembled. Her image spread like a reflection on silverware, then gradually hardened again: she was watching him.

He hung an Old Gold between his lips, rummaged for a match, and, finding none, sighed. The girl stepped from the doorway. She held out a cheap little lighter; as the flame pulsed up, her eyes, pale, shallow cat-green, fixed him with alarming intensity. Her eyes had an astonished, a shocked

look, as though, having at one time witnessed a terrible incident, they'd locked wide open. Carefree bangs fringed her
forehead; this boy haircut emphasized the childish and rather
poetic quality of her narrow, hollow-cheeked face. It was the
kind of face one sometimes sees in paintings of medieval
youths.

Letting the smoke pour out his nose, Vincent, knowing
it was useless to ask, wondered, as always, what she was living
on, and where. He flipped away the cigarette, for he had not
wanted it to begin with, and then, pivoting, crossed rapidly
under the El; as he approached the curb he heard a crash of
brakes, and suddenly, as if cotton plugs had been blasted
from his ears, city noises crowded in. A cab-driver hollered:
'Fa crissake sistuh get the lead outa yuh pants!' but the girl
did not even bother turning her head; trance-eyed, undis-
turbed as a sleepwalker, and staring straight at Vincent, who
watched dumbly, she moved across the street. A colored boy
wearing a jazzy purple suit took her elbow: 'You sick, Miss?'
he said, guiding her forward, and she did not answer. 'You
look mighty funny, Miss. If you sick I . . . ' then, following
the direction of her eyes, he released his hold: there was
something here which made him all still inside. 'Uh —
yeah,' he muttered, backing off with a grinning display of
tartar-coated teeth.

So Vincent began walking in earnest, and his umbrella
tapped code-like block after block. His shirt was soaked
through with itchy sweat, and the noises, now so harsh,
banged in his head: a trick car horn hooting 'My Country,
'Tis of Thee,' electric spray of sparks crackling bluely off
thundering rails, whiskey laughter hiccuping through gaunt
doors of beer-stale bars where orchid juke machines manufactured U.S.A. music — 'I got spurs that jingle jangle
jingle . . . ' Occasionally he caught a glimpse of her, once
mirrored in the window of Paul's Seafood Palace where
scarlet lobsters basked on a beach of flaked ice. She followed
close with her hands shoved into the pockets of her raincoat.
The brassy lights of a movie marquee blinked, and he remembered how she loved movies: murder films, spy chillers,

wild west shows. He turned into a sidestreet leading toward the East River; it was quiet here, hushed like Sunday: a sailor-stroller munching an Eskimo pie, energetic twins skipping rope, an old velvet lady with gardenia-white hair lifting aside lace curtains and peering listlessly into rain-dark space — a city landscape in July. And behind him the soft insistent slap of sandals. Traffic lights on Second Avenue turned red; at the corner a bearded midget, Ruby the Popcorn Man, wailed, 'Hot buttered popcorn, big bag, yah?' Vincent shook his head, and the midget looked very put out, then: 'Yuh see?' he jeered, pushing a shovel inside the candle-lit cage where bursting kernels bounced like crazy moths, 'Yuh see, de girlie knows popkern's nourishin'.' She bought a dime's worth, and it was in a green sack matching her raincoat, matching her eyes.

This is my neighborhood, my street, the house with the gateway is where I live. To remind himself of this was necessary inasmuch as he'd substituted for a sense of reality a knowledge of time, and place. He glanced gratefully at sour-faced, faded ladies, at the pipe-puffing males squatting on the surrounding steps of brownstone stoops. Nine pale little girls shrieked round a corner flower cart begging daisies to pin in their hair, but the peddler said 'Shoo!' and, fleeing like beads of a broken bracelet, they circled in the street, the wild ones leaping with laughter, and the shy ones, silent and isolated, lifting summer-wilted faces skyward: the rain, would it never come?

Vincent, who lived in a basement apartment, descended several steps, and took out his keycase; then, pausing behind the hallway door, he looked back through a peephole in the paneling. The girl was waiting on the sidewalk above; she leaned against a brownstone banister, and her arms fell limp — and popcorn spilled snowlike round her feet. A grimy little boy crept slyly up to pick among it like a squirrel.

For Vincent it was a holiday. No one had come by the gallery all morning, which, considering the arctic weather, was not unusual. He sat at his desk devouring tangerines, and enjoying immensely a Thurber story in an old *New Yorker*. Laughing loudly, he did not hear the girl enter, see her cross the dark carpet, notice her at all in fact until the telephone rang. 'Garland Gallery, hello.' She was odd, most certainly, that indecent haircut, those depthless eyes — 'Oh, Paul. *Comme çi comme ça,* and you?' — and dressed like a freak: no coat, just a lumberjack's shirt, navy blue slacks and — was it a joke? — pink ankle socks, a pair of huarachas. 'The ballet? Who's dancin? Oh her!' Under an arm she carried a flat parcel wrapped in sheets of funny-paper — 'Look, Paul, what say I call back? There's someone here . . . ' and, anchoring the receiver, assuming a commercial smile, he stood up: 'Yes?'

Her lips, crusty with chap, trembled with unrealized words as though she had possibly a defect of speech, and her eyes rolled in their sockets like loose marbles. It was the kind of disturbed shyness one associates with children. 'I've a picture,' she said. 'You buy pictures?'

At this, Vincent's smile became fixed: 'We exhibit.'

'I painted it myself,' she said, and her voice, hoarse and slurred, was Southern. 'My picture — I painted it. A lady told me there were places around here that bought pictures.'

Vincent said, 'Yes, of course . . . but the truth is —— ' and he made a helpless gesture —— 'the truth is I've no authority whatever. Mr. Garland — this is his gallery, you know — is out of town.' Standing there on the expanse of fine carpet, her body sagging sideways with the weight of her package, she looked like a sad rag doll. 'Maybe,' he began, 'maybe Henry Kleeman, up the street at Sixty-five . . . ' but she was not listening.

'I did it myself,' she insisted softly. 'Tuesdays and Thursdays were our painting days, and a whole year I worked. The others, they kept messing it up, and Mr. Destronelli . . . ' Suddenly, as though aware of an indiscretion, she stopped and bit her lip. Her eyes narrowed: 'He's not a friend of yours?'

'Who?' said Vincent, confused.

'Mr. Destronelli.'

He shook his head, and wondered why it was that eccentricity always excited in him such curious admiration. It was the feeling he'd had as a child toward carnival freaks. And it was true that about those whom he'd loved there was always a little something wrong, broken. Strange, though, that this quality, having stimulated an attraction, should, in his case, regularly end it by destroying it. 'Of course I haven't any authority,' he repeated, sweeping tangerine hulls into a wastebasket, 'but if you like I suppose I could look at your work.'

A pause; then, kneeling on the floor, she commenced stripping off the funny-paper wrapping. It originally had been, Vincent noticed, part of the New Orleans *Times-Picayune*. 'From the South, aren't you?' he said. She did not look up, but he saw her shoulders stiffen. 'No,' she said. Smiling, he considered a moment, decided it would be tactless to challenge so transparent a lie. Or could she have misunderstood? And all at once he felt an intense longing to touch her head, finger the boyish hair. He shoved his hands in his pockets, and glanced at the window. It was spangled with February frost, and some passerby had scratched on the glass an obscenity. 'There,' she said.

A headless figure in a monklike robe reclined complacently on top a tacky vaudeville trunk; in one hand she held a fuming blue candle, in the other a miniature gold cage, and her severed head lay bleeding at her feet: it was the girl's, this head, but here her hair was long, very long, and a snowball kitten with crystal spitfire eyes playfully pawed, as it would a spool of yarn, the sprawling ends. The wings of a hawk, headless, scarlet-breasted, copper-clawed, curtained the background like a nightfall sky. It was a crude painting, the hard pure colors molded with male brutality, and, while there was no technical merit evident, it had that power often seen in something deeply felt, though primitively conveyed. Vincent reacted as he did when occasionally a phrase of music surprised a note of inward recognition, or a cluster of words in a poem revealed to him a secret concerning himself: he felt a powerful chill of pleasure run down his spine.

'Mr. Garland is in Florida,' he said cautiously, 'but I think he should see it; you couldn't leave it for, say, a week?'

'I had a ring and I sold it,' she said, and he had the feeling she was talking in a trance. 'It was a nice ring, a wedding ring — not mine — with writing on it. I had an overcoat, too.' She twisted one of her shirt buttons, pulled till it popped off and rolled on the carpet like a pearl eye. 'I don't want much — fifty dollars; is that unfair?'

'Too much,' said Vincent, more curtly than he intended. Now he wanted her painting, not for the gallery, but for himself. There are certain works of art which excite more interest in their creators than in what they have created, usually because in this kind of work one is able to identify something which has until that instant seemed a private inexpressible perception, and you wonder: who is this that knows me, and how? 'I'll give thirty.'

For a moment she gaped at him stupidly, and then, sucking her breath, held out her hand, palm up. This directness, too innocent to be offensive, caught him off guard. Somewhat embarrassed, he said, 'I'm most awfully afraid I'll have to mail a check. Could you —— ' the telephone interrupted, and as he went to answer she followed, her hand outstretched, a frantic look pinching her face. 'Oh Paul, may I call back? Oh, I see. Well, hold on a sec.' Cupping the mouthpiece against his shoulder, he pushed a pad and pencil across the desk: 'Here, write your name and address.'

But she shook her head, the dazed, anxious expression deepening.

'Check,' said Vincent, 'I have to mail a check. Please, your name and address.' He grinned encouragingly when at last she began to write.

'Sorry, Paul . . . whose party? Why the little bitch, she didn't invite . . . hey!' he called, for the girl was moving toward the door. 'Please, hey!' Cold air chilled the gallery, and the door slammed with a glassy rattle. Hellohellohello. Vincent did not answer; he stood puzzling over the curious information she'd left printed on his pad: D. J. — Y.W.C.A. Hellohellohello.

It hung above his mantel, the painting, and on those nights when he could not sleep he would pour a glass of whiskey and talk to the headless hawk, tell it the stuff of his life: he was, he said, a poet who had never written poetry, a painter who had never painted, a lover who had never loved (absolutely) — someone, in short, without direction, and quite headless. Oh it wasn't that he hadn't tried — good beginnings, always, bad endings, always. Vincent, white, male, age 36, college graduate: a man in the sea fifty miles from shore; a victim, born to be murdered, either by himself or another; an actor unemployed. It was there, all of it, in the painting, everything disconnected and cockeyed, and who was she that she should know so much? Inquiries, those he'd made, had led nowhere; not another dealer knew of her, and to search for a D. J. living in, presumably, a Y.W.C.A. seemed absurd. Then, too, he'd quite expected she would reappear, but February passed, and March. One evening, crossing the square which fronts the Plaza, he had a queer thing happen. The archaic hansom-drivers who line that location were lighting their carriage lamps, for it was dusk, and lamplight traced through moving leaves. A hansom pulled from the curb and rolled past in the twilight. There was a single occupant, and this passenger, whose face he could not see, was a girl with chopped fawn-colored hair. So he settled on a bench, and whiled away time talking with a soldier, and a fairy colored boy who quoted poetry, and a man out airing a dachshund: night characters with whom he waited — but the carriage, with the one for whom he waited, never came back. Again he saw her (or supposed he did) descending subway stairs, and this time lost her in the tiled tunnels of painted arrows and Spearmint machines. It was as if her face were imposed upon his mind: he could no more dispossess it than could, for example, a dead man rid his legendary eyes of the last image seen. Around the middle of April he went up to Connecticut to spend a week-end with his married sister; keyed-up, caustic, he wasn't, as she complained, at all like himself: 'What is it, Vinny, darling — if you need money . . .' 'Oh, shut up!' he said. 'Must be love,' teased his brother-in-law. 'Come on, Vinny, 'fess up; what's she like?' And all this so annoyed him he caught the next train home. From a booth in Grand Central he called to apologize, but a sick nervousness hummed inside him, and he hung up while the operator was still trying to make a connection. He wanted a drink. At the Commodore Bar he spent an hour or so downing four daiquiris — it was Saturday, it was nine, there was nothing to do unless he did it alone, he was feeling sad for himself. Now in the park behind the Public Library sweethearts moved whisperingly under trees, and drinking-fountain water bubbled softly like their voices, but for all the white April evening meant to him, Vincent, drunk a little and wandering, might as well have been old, like the old bench-sitters rasping phlegm.

Now in the country, spring is a time of small happenings happening quietly, hyacinth shoots thrusting in a garden, willows burning with a sudden frosty fire of green, lengthening afternoons of long flowing dusk, and midnight rain opening lilac; but in the city there is the fanfare of organ-grinders, and odors, undiluted by winter wind, clog the air; windows long closed go up, and conversation, drifting beyond a room, collides with the jangle of a peddler's bell. It is the crazy season of toy balloons and roller-skates, of courtyard baritones and men of freakish enterprise, like the one who jumped up now like a jack-in-the-box. He was old, he had a telescope and a sign: 25¢ See The Moon! See The Stars! 25¢ No stars could penetrate a city's glare, but Vincent saw the moon, a round, shadowed whiteness, and then a blaze of electric bulbs: Four Roses, Bing Cro — he was moving through caramel-scented staleness, swimming through oceans of cheese-pale faces, neon, and darkness. Above the blasting of a jukebox, bulletfire boomed, a cardboard duck fell plop, and somebody screeched: 'Yay Iggy!' It was a Broadway funhouse, a penny arcade, and jammed from wall to wall with Saturday splurgers. He watched a penny movie (*What The Bootblack Saw*), and had his fortune told by a wax witch leering behind glass: 'Yours is an affectionate nature' . . . but he read no further, for up near the jukebox there was an attractive commotion. A crowd of kids, clapping in time to jazz music, had formed a circle around two dancers. These dancers were both colored, both girls. They swayed together slow and easy like lovers, rocked and stamped and rolled serious savage eyes, their muscles rhythmically attuned to the ripple of a clarinet, the rising harangue of a drum. Vincent's gaze traveled round the audience, and when he saw her a bright shiver went through him, for something of the dance's violence was reflected in her face. Standing there beside a tall ugly boy, it was as if she were the sleeper and the Negroes a dream. Trumpet-drum-piano, bawling on behind a black girl's froggy voice, wailed toward a rocking finale. The clapping ended, the dancers parted. She was alone now; though Vincent's instinct was to leave before she noticed, he advanced, and, as one would gently waken a sleeper, lightly touched her shoulder. 'Hello,' he said, his voice too loud. Turning, she stared at him, and her eyes were clear-blank. First terror, then puzzlement replaced the dead lost look. She took a step backward, and, just as the jukebox commenced hollering again, he seized her wrist: 'You remember me,' he prompted, 'the gallery? Your painting?' She blinked, let the lids sink sleepily over those eyes, and he could feel the slow relaxing of tension in her arm. She was thinner than he recalled, prettier, too, and her hair, grown out somewhat, hung in casual disorder. A little silver Christmas ribbon dangled sadly from a stray lock. He started to say, 'Can I buy you a drink?' but she leaned against him, her head resting on his chest like a child's, and he said: 'Will you come home with me?' She lifted her face; the answer, when it came, was a breath, a whisper: 'Please,' she said.

Vincent stripped off his clothes, arranged them neatly in the closet, and admired his nakedness before a mirrored door. He was not so handsome as he supposed, but handsome all the same. For his moderate height he was excellently proportioned; his hair was dark yellow, and his delicate, rather snub-nosed face had a fine, ruddy coloring. The rumble of running water broke the quiet: she was in the bathroom preparing to bathe. He dressed in loose-fitting flannel pajamas, lit a cigarette, said, 'Everything all right?' The water went off, a long silence, then: 'Yes, thank you.' On the way home in a cab he'd made an attempt at conversation, but she had said nothing, not even when they entered the apartment — and this last offended him, for, taking rather female pride in his quarters, he'd expected a complimentary remark. It was one enormously high-ceilinged room, a bath and kitchenette, a backyard garden. In the furnishings he'd combined modern with antique and produced a distinguished result. Decorating the walls were a trio of Toulouse-Lautrec prints, a framed circus poster, D. J.'s painting, photographs of Rilke, Nijinsky and Duse. A candelabra of lean blue candles burned on a desk; the room, washed in their delirious light, wavered. French doors led into the yard. He never used it much, for it was a place impossible to keep clean. There were a few dead tulip stalks dark in the moonshine, a puny heaven tree, and an old weather-worn chair left by the last tenant. He paced back and forth over the cold flagstones, hoping that in the cool air the drugged drunk sensation he felt would wear off. Nearby a piano was being badly mauled, and in a window above there was a child's face. He was thumbing a blade of grass when her shadow fell long across the yard. She was in the doorway. 'You mustn't come out,' he said, moving toward her. 'It's turned a little cold.'

There was about her now an appealing softness; she seemed somehow less angular, less out of tune with the average, and Vincent, offering a glass of sherry, was delighted at the delicacy with which she touched it to her lips. She was wearing his terry cloth robe; it was by yards too large. Her feet were bare, and she tucked them up beside her on the couch. 'It's like Glass Hill, the candlelight,' she said, and smiled. 'My Granny lived at Glass Hill. We had lovely times, sometimes; do you know what she used to say? She used to say, "Candles are magic wands; light one and the world is a story book."'

'What a dreary old lady she must've been,' said Vincent, quite drunk. 'We should probably have hated each other.'

'Granny would've loved you,' she said. 'She loved any kind of man, every man she ever met, even Mr. Destronelli.'

'Destronelli?' It was a name he'd heard before.

Her eyes slid slyly sideways, and this look seemed to say: There must be no subterfuge between us, we who understand each other have no need of it. 'Oh, you know,' she said with a conviction that, under more commonplace circumstances, would have been surprising. It was, however, as if he'd abandoned temporarily the faculty of surprise. 'Everybody knows him.'

He curved an arm around her, and brought her nearer. 'Not me, I don't,' he said, kissing her mouth, neck; she was not responsive especially, but he said — and his voice had gone adolescently shaky — 'Never met Mr. Whoozits.' He slipped a hand inside her robe, loosening it away from her shoulders. Above one breast she had a birthmark small and star-shaped. He glanced at the mirrored door where uncertain light rippled their reflections, made them pale and incomplete. She was smiling. 'Mr. Whoozits,' he said, 'what does he look like?' The suggestion of a smile faded, a small monkeylike frown flickered on her face. She looked above the mantel at her painting, and he realized that this was the first notice she'd shown it; she appeared to study in the picture a particular object, but whether hawk or head he could not say. 'Well,' she said quietly, pressing closer to him, 'he looks like you, like me, like most anybody.'

It was raining; in the wet noon light two nubs of candle still burned, and at an open window gray curtains tossed forlornly. Vincent extricated his arm; it was numb from the weight of her body. Careful not to make a noise, he eased out of bed, blew out the candles, tiptoed into the bathroom, and doused his face with cold water. On the way to the kitchenette he flexed his arms, feeling, as he hadn't for a long time, an intensely male pleasure in his strength, a healthy wholeness of person. He made and put on a tray orange juice, raisin-bread toast, a pot of tea; then, so inexpertly that everything on the tray rattled, he brought the breakfast in and placed it on a table beside the bed.

She had not moved; her ruffled hair spread fanwise across the pillow, and one hand rested in the hollow where his head had lain. He leaned over and kissed her lips, and her eyelids, blue with sleep, trembled. 'Yes, yes, I'm awake,' she murmured, and rain, lifting in the wind, sprayed against the window like surf. He somehow knew that with her there would be none of the usual artifice: no avoidance of eyes, no shame-faced, accusing pause. She raised herself on her elbow; she looked at him, Vincent thought, as if he were her husband, and handing her the orange juice, he smiled his gratitude.

'What is today?'

'Sunday,' he told her, bundling under the quilt, and setting the tray across his legs.

'But there are no church bells,' she said. 'And it's raining.'

Vincent divided a piece of toast. 'You don't mind that, do you? Rain — such a peaceful sound.' He poured tea. 'Sugar? Cream?'

She disregarded this, and said, 'Today is Sunday what? What month, I mean?'

'Where have you been living, in the subway?' he said, grinning. And it puzzled him to think she was serious. 'Oh, April . . . April something-or-other.'

'April,' she repeated. 'Have I been here long?'

'Only since last night.'

'Oh.'

Vincent stirred his tea, the spoon tinkling in the cup like a bell. Toast crumbs spilled among the sheets, and he thought of the *Tribune* and the *Times* waiting outside the door, but they, this morning, held no charms; it was best lying here beside her in the warm bed sipping tea, listening to the rain. Odd, when you stopped to consider, certainly very odd. She did not know his name, nor he hers. And so he said, 'I still owe you thirty dollars, do you realize that? Your own fault, of course . . . leaving such a damn fool address. And D. J., what is that supposed to mean?'

'I don't think I'd better tell you my name,' she said. 'I could make up one easy enough: Dorothy Jordan, Delilah

Johnson; see? There are all kinds of names I could make up, and if it wasn't for him I'd tell you right.'

Vincent lowered the tray to the floor. He rolled over on his side, and, facing her, his heartbeat quickened. 'Who's him?' Though her expression was calm, anger muddied her voice when she said. 'If you don't know him, then tell me, why am I here?'

Silence, and outside the rain seemed suddenly suspended. A ship's horn moaned in the river. Holding her close, he combed his fingers through her hair, and, wanting so much to be believed, said, 'Because I love you.'

She closed her eyes. 'What became of them?'

'Who?'

'The others you've said that to.'

It commenced again, the rain spattering grayly at the window, falling on hushed Sunday streets; listening, Vincent remembered. He remembered his cousin Lucille, poor, beautiful, stupid Lucille who sat all day embroidering silk flowers on scraps of linen. And Allen T. Baker — there was the winter they'd spent in Havana, the house they'd lived in, crumbling rooms of rose-colored rock; poor Allen, he'd thought it was to be forever. Gordon, too. Gordon, with the kinky yellow hair, and a head full of old Elizabethan ballads. Was it true he'd shot himself? And Connie Silver, the deaf girl, the one who had wanted to be an actress — what had become of her? Or Helen, Louise, Laura? 'There was just one,' he said, and to his own ears this had a truthful ring. 'Only one, and she's dead.'

Tenderly, as if in sympathy, she touched his cheek. 'I suppose he killed her,' she said, her eyes so close he could see the outline of his face imprisoned in their greenness. 'He killed Miss Hall, you know. The dearest woman in the world, Miss Hall, and so pretty your breath went away. I had piano lessons with her, and when she played the piano, when she said hello and when she said good-by — it was like my heart would stop.' Her voice had taken on an impersonal tone, as though she were talking of matters belonging to another age, and in which she was not concerned directly. 'It was the end of summer when she married him — September, I think. She went to Atlanta, and they were married there, and she never came back. It was just that sudden.' She snapped her fingers. 'Just like that. I saw a picture of him in the paper. Sometimes I think if she'd known how much I loved her — why are there some you can't ever tell? — I think maybe she wouldn't have married; maybe it would've all been different, like I wanted it.' She turned her face into the pillow, and if she cried there was no sound.

On May twentieth she was eighteen; it seemed incredible — Vincent had thought her many years older. He wanted to introduce her at a surprise party, but had finally to admit that this was an unsuitable plan. First off, though the subject was always there on the tip of his tongue, not once had he ever mentioned D. J. to any of his friends; secondly, he could visualize discouragingly well the entertainment provided them at meeting a girl about whom, while they openly shared an apartment, he knew nothing, not even her name. Still the birthday called for some kind of treat. Dinner and the theatre were hopeless. She hadn't, through no fault of his, a dress of any sort. He'd given her forty odd dollars to buy clothes, and here is what she spent it on: a leather windbreaker, a set of military brushes, a raincoat, a cigarette lighter. Also, her suitcase, which she'd brought to the apartment, had contained nothing but hotel soap, a pair of scissors she used for pruning her hair, two Bibles, and an appalling color-tinted photograph. The photograph showed a simpering middle-aged woman with dumpy features. There was an inscription: Best Wishes and Good Luck from Martha Lovejoy Hall.

Because she could not cook they had their meals out; his salary and the limitations of her wardrobe confined them mostly to the Automat — her favorite: the macaroni was so delicious! — or one of the bar-grills along Third. And so the birthday dinner was eaten in an Automat. She'd scrubbed her face until the skin shone red, trimmed and shampooed her hair, and with the messy skill of a six-year-old playing grown-up, varnished her nails. She wore the leather wind-breaker, and on it pinned a sheaf of violets he'd given her; it must have looked amusing, for two rowdy girls sharing their table giggled frantically. Vincent said if they didn't shut up . . .

'Oh yeah, who you think you are?'

'Superman. Jerk thinks he's superman.'

It was too much, and Vincent lost his temper. He shoved back from the table, upsetting a ketchup jar. 'Let's get the hell out of here,' he said, but D. J., who had paid the fracas no attention whatever, went right on spooning blackberry cobbler; furious as he was, he waited quietly until she finished, for he respected her remoteness, and yet wondered in what period of time she lived. It was futile, he'd discovered, to question her past, still she seemed only now and then aware of the present, and it was likely the future didn't mean much to her. Her mind was like a mirror reflecting blue space in a barren room.

'What would you like now?' he said, as they came into the street. 'We could ride in a cab through the park.'

She wiped off with her jacket-cuff flecks of blackberry staining the corners of her mouth, and said, 'I want to go to a picture show.'

The movies. Again. In the last month he'd seen so many films, snatches of Hollywood dialogue rumbled in his dreams. One Saturday at her insistence they'd bought tickets to three different theatres, cheap places where smells of latrine disinfectant poisoned the air. And each morning before leaving for work he left on the mantel fifty cents — rain or shine, she went to a picture show. But Vincent was sensitive enough to see why: there had been in his own life a certain time of limbo when he'd gone to movies every day, often sitting through several repeats of the same film; it was in its way like religion, for there, watching the shifting patterns of black and white, he knew a release of conscience similar to the kind a man must find confessing to his father.

'Handcuffs,' she said, referring to an incident in *The Thirty-Nine Steps*, which they'd seen at the Beverly in a program of Hitchcock revivals. 'That blond woman and the man handcuffed together — well, it made me think of something else.' She stepped into a pair of his pajamas, pinned the corsage of violets to the edge of her pillow, and folded up on the bed. 'People getting caught like that, locked together.'

Vincent yawned. 'Uh huh,' he said, and turned off the lights. 'Again, happy birthday, darling, it *was* a happy birthday?'

She said, 'Once I was in this place, and there were two girls dancing; they were so free — there was just them and nobody else, and it was beautiful like a sunset.' She was silent a long while; then, her slow Southern voice dragging over the words: 'It was mighty nice of you to bring me violets.'

'Glad —— like them,' he answered sleepily.

'It's a shame they have to die.'

'Yes, well, good night.'

'Good night.'

Closeup. Oh, but John it isn't for my sake after all we've the children to consider a divorce would ruin their lives! Fadeout. The screen trembles; rattle of drums, flourish of trumpets: R.K.O. PRESENTS —

Here is a hall without exit, a tunnel without end. Overhead, chandeliers sparkle, and wind-bent candles float on currents of air. Before him is an old man rocking in a rocking chair, an old man with yellow-dyed hair, powdered cheeks, kewpie-doll lips: Vincent recognizes Vincent. Go away, screams Vincent, the young and handsome, but Vincent, the old and horrid, creeps forward on all fours, and climbs spiderlike onto his back. Threats, pleas, blows, nothing will dislodge him. And so he races with his shadow, his rider jogging up and down. A serpent of lightning blazes, and all at once the tunnel seethes with men wearing white ties and tails, women costumed in brocaded gowns. He is humiliated; how gauche they must think him appearing at so elegant a gathering carrying on his back, like Sinbad, a sordid old man. The guests stand about in petrified pairs, and there is no conversation. He notices then that many are also saddled with malevolent semblances of themselves, outward embodiments of inner decay. Just beside him a lizard-like man rides an albino-eyed Negro. A man is coming toward him, the host; short, florid, bald, he steps lightly, precisely in glacé shoes; one arm, held stiffly crooked, supports a massive headless hawk whose talons, latched to the wrist, draw blood. The hawk's wings unfurl as its master struts by. On a pedestal there is perched an old-time phonograph. Winding the handle, the host supplies a record: a tiny worn-out waltz vibrates the morning-glory horn. He lifts a hand, and in a soprano voice announces: 'Attention! The dancing will commence.' The host with his hawk weaves in and out as round and round they dip, they turn. The walls widen, the ceiling grows tall. A girl glides into Vincent's arms, and a cracked, cruel imitation of his voice says: 'Lucille, how divine; that exquisite scent, is it violet?' This is cousin Lucille, and then, as they circle the room, her face changes. Now he waltzes with another: 'Why Connie, Connie Silver! How marvelous to see you,' shrieks the voice, for Connie is quite deaf. Suddenly a gentleman with a bullet-bashed head cuts in: 'Gordon, forgive me, I never meant — ' but they are gone, Gordon and Connie, dancing together. Again, a new partner. It is D. J., and she too has a figure barnacled to her back, an enchanting auburn-haired child; like an emblem of innocence the child cuddles to her chest a snowball kitten. 'I am heavier than I look,' says the child, and the terrible voice retorts, 'But I am heaviest of all.' The instant their hands meet he begins to feel the weight upon him diminish; the old Vincent is fading. His feet lift off the floor, he floats upward from her embrace. The victrola grinds away loud as ever, but he is rising high, and the white receding faces gleam below like mushrooms on a dark meadow.

The host releases his hawk, sends it soaring. Vincent thinks, no matter, it is a blind thing, and the wicked are safe among the blind. But the hawk wheels above him, swoops down, claws foremost; at last he knows there is to be no freedom.

And the blackness of the room filled his eyes. One arm lolled over the bed's edge, his pillow had fallen to the floor. Instinctively he reached out asking mother-comfort of the girl beside him. Sheets smooth and cold; emptiness, and the tawdry fragrance of drying violets. He snapped up straight: 'You, where are you?'

The French doors were open. An ashy trace of moon swayed on the threshold, for it was not yet light, and in the kitchen the refrigerator purred like a giant cat. A stack of paper rustled on the desk. Vincent called again, softly this time, as if he wished himself unheard. Rising, he stumbled forward on dizzy legs, and looked into the yard. She was there, leaning, half-kneeling against the heaven tree. 'What?' and she whirled around. He could not see her well, only a dark substantial shape. She came closer. A finger pressed her lips.

'What is it?' he whispered.

She rose on tiptoe, and her breath tingled in his ear. 'I warn you, go inside.'

'Stop this foolishness,' he said in a normal voice. 'Out here barefooted, you'll catch — ' but she clamped a hand over his mouth.

'I saw him,' she whispered. 'He's here.'

Vincent knocked her hand away. It was hard not to slap her. 'Him! Him! Him! What's the matter with you? Are you' — he tried too late to prevent the word — 'crazy?' There, the acknowledgment of something he'd known, but had not allowed his conscious mind to crystallize. And he thought: Why should this make a difference? A man cannot be held to account for those he loves. Untrue. Feeble-witted Lucille weaving mosaics on silk, embroidering his name on scarves; Connie in her hushed deaf world listening for his footstep, a sound she would surely hear; Allen T. Baker thumbing his photograph, still needing love, but old now and lost — all betrayed. And he'd betrayed himself with talents unexploited, voyages never taken, promises unfulfilled. There had seemed nothing left him until — oh, why in his lovers must he always find the broken image of himself? Now as he looked at her in the aging dawn his heart was cold with the death of love.

She moved away, and under the tree. 'Leave me here,' she said, her eyes scanning tenement windows. 'Only a moment.'

Vincent waited, waited. On all sides windows looked down like the doors of dreams, and overhead, four flights up, a family's laundry whipped a washline. The setting moon was like the early moon of dusk, a vaporish cartwheel, and the sky, draining of dark, was washed with gray. Sunrise wind shook the leaves of the heaven tree, and in the paling light the yard assumed a pattern, objects a position, and from the roofs came the throaty morning rumble of pigeons. A light went on. Another.

And at last she lowered her head; whatever she was looking for, she had not found it. Or, he wondered as she turned to him with tilted lips, had she?

'Well, you're home kinda early, aren't you, Mr. Waters?' It was Mrs. Brennan, the super's bowlegged wife. 'And, well, Mr. Waters — lovely weather, ain't it? — you and me got sumpin' to talk about.'

'Mrs. Brennan' — how hard it was to breathe, to speak; the words grated his hurting throat, sounded loud as thunderclaps — 'I'm rather ill, so if you don't mind — ' and he tried to brush past her.

'Say, that's a pity. Ptomaine, must be ptomaine. Yessir, I tell you a person can't be too careful; it's them Jews, you know. They run all them delicatessens. Uh uh, none of that Jew food for me.' She stepped before the gate, blocking his path, and pointed an admonishing finger: 'Trouble with you, Mr. Waters, is you don't lead no kinda *normal* life.'

A knot of pain was set like a malignant jewel in the core of his head; each aching motion made jeweled pinpoints of color flare out. The super's wife babbled on, but there were blank moments when, fortunately, he could not hear at all. It was like a radio — the volume turned low, then full blast. 'Now I know she's a decent Christian lady, Mr. Waters, or else what would a gentleman like you be doing with —— hm.

Still the fact is, Mr. Cooper don't tell lies, and he's a real calm man, besides. Been gas meter man for this district I don't know how long.' A truck rolled down the street spraying water, and her voice, submerged below its roar, came up again like a shark. 'Mr. Cooper had every reason to believe she meant to kill him — well, you can imagine, her standin' there with them scissors, and shoutin'. She called him an Eyetalian name. Now all you got to do is look at Mr. Cooper to know he ain't no Eyetalian. Well, you can see, Mr. Waters, such carryings-on are bound to give the house a bad — '

Brittle sunshine plundering the depths of his eyes made tears, and the super's wife, wagging her finger, seemed to break into separate pieces: a nose, a chin, a red, red eye. 'Mr. Destronelli,' he said. 'Excuse me, Mrs. Brennan, I mean excuse me.' She thinks I'm drunk, and I'm sick, and can't she see I'm sick? 'My guest is leaving. She's leaving today, and she won't be back.'

'Well, now, you don't say,' said Mrs. Brennan, clucking her tongue. 'Looks like she needs a rest, poor little thing. So pale, sorta. Course I don't want no more to do with them Eyetalians than the next one, but imagine thinking Mr. Cooper was an Eyetalian. Why, he's white as you or me.' She tapped his shoulder solicitously. 'Sorry you feel so sick, Mr. Waters; ptomaine, I tell you. A person can't be too care — '

The hall smelled of cooking and incinerator ashes. There was a stairway which he never used, his apartment being on the first floor, straight ahead. A match snapped fire, and Vincent, groping his way, saw a small boy — he was not more than three or four — squatting under the stairwell; he was playing with a big box of kitchen matches, and Vincent's presence appeared not to interest him. He simply struck another match. Vincent could not make his mind work well enough to phrase a reprimand, and as he waited there, tongue-tied, a door, his door, opened.

Hide. For if she saw him she would know something was wrong, suspect something. And if she spoke, if their eyes met, then he would never be able to go through with it. So he pressed into a dark corner behind the little boy, and the little boy said, 'Whatcha doin', Mister?' She was coming — he heard the slap of her sandals, the green whisper of her raincoat. 'Whatcha doin', Mister?' Quickly, his heart banging in his chest, Vincent stooped and, squeezing the child against him, pressed his hand over its mouth so it could not make a sound. He did not see her pass; it was later, after the front door clicked, that he realized she was gone. The little boy sank back on the floor. 'Whatcha doin', Mister?'

Four aspirin, one right after the other, and he came back into the room; the bed had not been tidied for a week, a spilt ashtray messed the floor, odds and ends of clothing decorated improbable places, lampshades and such. But tomorrow, if he felt better, there would be a general cleaning; perhaps he'd have the walls repainted, maybe fix up the yard. To-morrow he could begin thinking about his friends again, accept invitations, entertain. And yet this prospect, tasted in advance, was without flavor: all he'd known before seemed to him now sterile and spurious. Footsteps in the hall; could she return this soon, the movie over, the afternoon gone? Fever can make time pass so queerly, and for an instant he felt as though his bones were floating loose inside him. Clop-clop, a child's sloppy shoefall, the footsteps passed up the stairs, and Vincent moved, floated toward the mirrored closet. He longed to hurry, knowing he must, but the air seemed thick with gummy fluid. He brought her suitcase from the closet, and put it on the bed, a sad cheap suitcase with rusty locks and a warped hide. He eyed it with guilt: where would she go? how would she live? When he'd broken with Connie, Gordon, all the others, there had been about it at least a certain dignity. Really, though — and he'd thought it out — there was no other way. So he gathered her belongings. Miss Martha Lovejoy Hall peeked out from under the leather windbreaker, her music-teacher's face smiling an oblique re-proach. Vincent turned her over, face down, and tucked in the frame an envelope containing twenty dollars. That would buy a ticket back to Glass Hill, or wherever it was she

came from. Now he tried to close the case, and, too weak
with fever, collapsed on the bed. Quick yellow wings glided
through the window. A butterfly. He'd never seen a butterfly in this city, and it was like a floating mysterious flower,
like a sign of some sort, and he watched with a kind of horror
as it waltzed in the air. Outside somewhere the razzledazzle
of a beggar's grind-organ started up; it sounded like a
broken-down pianola, and it played *La Marseillaise*. The
butterfly lighted on her painting, crept across crystal eyes,
and flattened its wings like a ribbon bow over the loose head.
He fished about in the suitcase until he found the scissors.
He first purposed to slash the butterfly's wings, but it spiraled
to the ceiling and hung there like a star. The scissors stabbed
the hawk's heart, ate through canvas like a ravening steel
mouth, scraps of picture flaking the floor like cuttings of
stiff hair. He went on his knees, pushed the pieces into a
pile, and slammed the lid shut. He was crying. And through
the tears the butterfly magnified on the ceiling huge as a bird,
and there were more: a flock of lilting, winking yellow,
whispering lonesomely, like surf sucking a shore. The wind
from their wings blew the room into space. He heaved forward, the suitcase banging his leg, and threw open the door.
A match flared. The little boy said: 'Whatcha doin', Mister?'
And Vincent, setting the suitcase in the hall, grinned sheepishly. He closed the door like a thief, bolted the safety lock
and, pulling up a chair, tilted it under the knob. In the still
room there was only the subtlety of shifting sunlight and a
crawling butterfly; it drifted downward like a tricky scrap
of crayon paper, and landed on a candlestick: *Sometimes he
is not a man at all* — she'd told him that, huddling here on
the bed, talking swiftly in the minutes before dawn — *sometimes he is something very different: a hawk, a child, a butterfly*. And then she'd said: *At the place where they took me
there were hundreds of old ladies, and young men, and one
of the young men said he was a pirate, and one of the old
ladies — she was near ninety — used to make me feel her
stomach: 'Feel,' she'd say, 'feel how strong he kicks?' This
old lady took painting class, too, and her paintings looked*

*like crazy quilts. And naturally he was in this place, Mr.*
*Destronelli. Only he called himself Gum. Doctor Gum.*
*Oh he didn't fool me, even though he wore a gray wig, and*
*made himself up to look real old and kind. I knew. And*
*then one day I left, ran clear away, and hid under a lilac*
*bush, and a man came along in a little red car, and he had a*
*little mouse-haired moustache, and little cruel eyes. But it*
*was him. And when I told him who he was he made me get*
*out of his car. And then another man, that was in Phila-*
*delphia, picked me up in a café and took me in an alley. He*
*talked Italian, and had tattoo pictures all over. But it was*
*him. And the next man, he was the one who painted his toe-*
*nails, sat down beside me in a movie because he thought I*
*was a boy, and when he found out I wasn't he didn't get*
*mad but let me live in his room, and cooked pretty things for*
*me to eat. But he wore a silver locket, and one day I looked*
*inside and there was a picture of Miss Hall. So I knew it was*
*him, so I had this feeling she was dead, so I knew he was*
*going to murder me. And he will. He will.* Dusk, and
nightfall, and the fibres of sound called silence wove a shiny
blue mask. Waking, he peered through eyeslits, heard the
frenzied pulsebeat of his watch, the scratch of a key in a lock.
Somewhere in this hour of dusk a murderer separates himself from shadow and with a rope follows the flash of silk legs
up doomed stairs. And here the dreamer staring through his
mask dreams of deceit. Without investigating he knows the
suitcase is missing, that she has come, that she has gone; why,
then, does he feel so little the pleasure of safety, and only
cheated, and small — small as the night when he searched
the moon through an old man's telescope?

Like fragments of an old letter, scattered popcorn lay
trampled flat, and she, leaning back in a watchman's attitude,
followed her gaze to hunt among it, as if deciphering here
and there a word, an answer. Her eyes shifted discreetly to
the man mounting the steps, Vincent. There was about him
the freshness of a shower, shave, cologne, but dreary blue
circled his eyes, and the crisp seersucker into which he'd

changed had been made for a heavier man: a long month of pneumonia, and wakeful burning nights had lightened his weight a dozen pounds, and more. Each morning, evening, meeting her here at his gate, or near the gallery, or outside the restaurant where he lunched, a nameless disorder took hold, a paralysis of time and identity. The wordless pantomime of her pursuit contracted his heart, and there were coma-like days when she seemed not one, but all, a multiple person, and her shadow in the street every shadow, following and followed. And once they'd been alone together in an automatic elevator, and he'd screamed: 'I am not him! Only me, only me!' But she smiled as she'd smiled telling of the man with painted toenails, because, after all, she knew.

It was suppertime, and, not knowing where to eat, he paused under a street lamp that, blooming abruptly, fanned complex light over stone; while he waited there came a clap of thunder, and all along the street every face but two, his and the girl's, tilted upward. A blast of river breeze tossed the children's laughter as they, linking arms, pranced like carousel ponies, and carried the mama's voice who, leaning from a window, howled: rain, Rachel, rain — gonna rain gonna rain! And the gladiola, ivy-filled flower cart jerked crazily as the peddler, one eye slanted skyward, raced for shelter. A potted geranium fell off, and the little girls gathered the blooms and tucked them behind their ears. The blending spatter of running feet and raindrops tinkled on the xylophone sidewalks — the slamming of doors, the lowering of windows, then nothing but silence, and rain. Presently, with slow scraping steps, she came below the lamp to stand beside him, and it was as if the sky were a thunder-cracked mirror, for the rain fell between them like a curtain of splintered glass.

*(From The Yale Review)*

# DAY OF GOLD AND DARKNESS

## BY ROBERT FONTAINE

*S*AM nearly always drank beer. Today he ordered brandy, at the Eighth Street Grille. He was not quite sure whether it was the warm, spring goldness of the day or what, but he ordered brandy.

'Stuff's worth a fortune these days,' the bartender said. 'Coneyyack's scarce, believe me.'

Sam sniffed the brandy and grinned.

'You know,' he said wistfully, 'sometimes I don't love my wife. I mean sometimes I *think* I don't.'

He looked up at the moose head on the wall. The bartender aimlessly whisked several flies from the bar. Sam finished the brandy.

'How *is* the little woman?' the bartender asked perfunctorily.

Sam grinned. 'She's not so little any more.'

'They get that way,' the bartender agreed, philosophically, wiping invisible dust from the bar. 'Especially in back,' he added as if a mental image had appeared in his mind.

He filled Sam's empty glass. Sam drained it thoughtfully but much more briskly than before. Then he blinked his eyes as if, inside him, something bright stirred, like the quick gleam of golden fish in deep waters.

A little sheepishly he took out a picture from his jacket pocket. It was bent and creased. He showed it to the bartender.

'That's a horse I bet on once,' he said.

'Nice legs,' the bartender observed.

'I won a lot of money on that horse,' Sam said, almost belligerently. 'That was the first and only race that horse ever won. Just the one time I bet on him. I read the dope sheets after. I used to keep track of him.'

'Sure, you were grateful. Naturally. A horse does something for you —.'

'It's funny that he should win just when I needed him. Never after. Just once.' Sam thought about it. Then he put the picture back.

'Lots of things don't even happen once,' the bartender said. He put the red rubber stopper back in the brandy bottle and put it away.

Sam ran his hands over his eyes.

'Sick?' the bartender asked.

'No,' Sam said. 'You just made me think of something that happened a long time ago. I mean something that *didn't* happen a long time ago.'

The sharp corners of the barroom were rounding a little for Sam, and the crude pictures seemed brighter. He started to leave, a soft smile on his face.

'Hey!' the bartender called. 'You don't want to be running that cigar store for nothing. You're forgetting all your groceries.'

He pointed to a pile of parcels that contained carrots, cabbage, lettuce, garlic salt, paper napkins, and six bottles of beer.

'I'll be back,' Sam said. 'Plenty of time before dinner.'

He went on to Eighth Street a little unsteadily. The golden afternoon sun was lighting up a new world Sam hadn't seen in some time. The people were looking brighter, and the spring blue of the sky was like the eyes she would have had.

For it was that remembrance of her that made the shimmering light around everything — the people; the newsstand; the gift shoppe; the man playing the violin in the street; the horse pulling a cart of fresh vegetables.

It was a dream that had come into his mind when he was

eighteen or nineteen and had slowly been receding into his subconsciousness. Once in a while after he had first been married, it would shine for a moment, and he would smile to himself, like a man not quite asleep yet.

Now, for a long time, he had not thought of it at all. But, today, with the late sun and the brandy editing the street, he walked along, towards Fifth Avenue, in sweet, sad confusion, startled now and then by the colors of things in windows and the sound of people's scraps of words and their high laughter.

The dream came up, soon, just as he neared the Avenue.

He remembered now exactly what it had been. For years in the dusty, hot streets of his home town, he had thought of it. He had thought of it sometimes suddenly, while playing baseball in a vacant lot; at the movies; in church; at school, and often just before going to sleep.

It was a dream of having just one perfect evening with a girl. Taking her to dinner and then driving in a car away some place where there would be a small white farmhouse with a red barn.

They would not talk much about it, and the old farmer who rented rooms would understand, because the sky would be a Vermont turquoise green, and apple blossoms would be around, and there would be the low, wistful moo of a patient cow.

You could smell the earth and the grass; and you could taste things at the farmer's table — late at night, before you went to bed. Freshly baked pie and creamy milk and cold chicken.

Afterwards you would walk out and look at the stars, and there would not be anything to say because the stars and the pie and apple blossoms and the moo of the cow and your both being there would have said it all. Or almost all. Not quite.

She would be just that special way. Young and slim and white, with a red mouth and blue-green eyes and a head that went back when she laughed, with white, glittering teeth, small and even, deepening the red softness of her mouth.

The night then would fold its arms around them in soft blackness, and they would be, gently, lovers. And after the love and the frightened, slightly puzzled, happy little smiles, a deep and undreaming sleep.

In the morning early: clean rain beating on the roof and making the world new and fresh and clean. Giving it, and you and her a new start, a new belief, a charge and a challenge. All somehow inextricably woven into the night that had been and the rain that was washing the world clean.

There was no more to it, after that. You would never see her again nor she you.

He turned up the Avenue, his breath coming a little fast, his face flushed, small beads of perspiration on his brow. The sun was turning from golden to a copper-red-gold.

Well, never had the dream come true, of course. He had married Rose, and there had been Atlantic City, and then a little cigar shop and the days chasing each other around in tender circles.

Once or twice it had been remembered, but not often in the quiet peace with Rose.

Only today (when the dream seemed like yesterday's dream, or the day before yesterday's, and still to come true — not at all one of the things that never even happen but one of the things that just happen once) — only today and at this moment —

He felt for a second a little dizzy.

He stopped, blinked his eyes to get the golden fringe off them, and then, quite suddenly, and as he had thought he would fifteen years or more ago, he saw her.

She went past him quickly and softly as a summer wind-cloud. But it was she! How could he mistake the faint revelation of lace; the long swiftness of the legs; the small firmness of the breasts; the blue-greenness of the eyes; the scarlet promise of the mouth.

He turned to follow her, triumphant.

She was walking speedily, and he hurried after, not wanting to lose her in the crowd. She would know, of course. She had been dreaming, too.

He hurried on, feeling a little faint and frightened and wonderful.

Forgotten were Rose and the groceries and dinner and the bartender and everything. The thing that doesn't even happen once could happen now. Could happen as soon as he caught up to her.

She seemed away ahead of him now, and he began to run. Breathing heavily and almost in panic, he rushed by startled strollers, coming home from work or shopping or the movies.

Then, when he came up close to her, almost where he could have spoken and she would have recognized and understood, he paused — to hold the moment fluttering sweet —

Abruptly she turned into a small shop, and he felt a choking.

He stood puzzled and then started into the shop. A square mirror in front of him, and others on the side and in the shadow, threw back his face at him, as if in pity and scorn.

That checked him like a lasso around his neck, pulled back taut.

It was an oldish face they handed him. A face that had red splotches and dark circles and tired lines. Above the face they cruelly gave him, there was a wrinkled lostness and the thinning hair.

He turned away from the mirrors and out onto the street. A cloud had hidden the sun, which was not any longer golden, and he felt a chill.

This was not the girl. Or if it were the girl, he was not the boy. He felt alone and lost.

He turned back down Eighth Street and started to run. He ran all the way to the Eighth Street Grille. Ran in and grabbed his parcels.

'You look like you seen a ghost,' the bartender said. 'Hey, the Dodgers lost again. What a dope, that Durocher!'

Sam ran out past him, parcels opening and paper flapping. It was almost dark. It was later than he had thought.

He rushed through street after street till he came to his own, leaving a trail of carrots, lettuce, and leaves of cabbage behind.

The door was unlocked, and he almost fell into the house. He stumbled up the stairs and fell, faint, at the landing.

The noise attracted Rose. She came flying out, solid, kind, and worried.

'Sam, what's the matter, Sam? You ran? You shouldn't run, Sam. Your heart isn't so good. Suppose you stopped to hear the end of the game. What difference? Don't run. You'll be sick.'

'I'm all right,' he said, getting up. 'I lost some carrots and lettuce.'

'That's all right. You better lay down.'

'I'm all right now. It was just the sun, and I had a couple of drinks.'

'You shouldn't drink before sundown. Not before sundown.'

Rose took the groceries, and Sam lay down on the couch. He felt peaceful now, and not afraid.

Rose sat beside him, dabbing his forehead with a cool wet towel.

'Nellie called,' Rose said gently. 'She wants us to go up the Hudson River on the Day Line next Sunday — the leaves are just coming out and all.'

Sam didn't open his eyes.

'That'll be nice,' he said softly, 'with the leaves just coming out, especially.'

# THE MAN IN THE MIRROR

## BY ADELAIDE GERSTLEY

*H*E woke to the air-conditioned comfort of his apartment at the Attorneys' Club. In summer the enervating heat was shut out; in winter the temperature was held to an exact seventy degrees. Everything he wanted in life was here inside the sheltering walls of the club: food cooked to please his finicking appetite, obsequious servants who knew his little idiosyncrasies, physical fitness in the athletic department where he exercised daily for ten minutes and swam three times the length of the tank.

Through habit he woke promptly at seven although there was no reason for him to rise early. It was still dark, but outside the ventilator on his window sill he could see the sooty and forlorn city snow clinging.

Unblinkingly wide awake, he sat up and the mirror over the pickled pine bureau showed him a neat, spare man who could have been any age. He had been fair and ruddy when he was young; now he was graying, but his skin was pink as befits one who has regular massage and regular elimination. His blue-striped pajamas, tailored by Sulka of finest sea-island cotton, were neat and unmussed, for he seldom tossed in his sleep. Even the shock of yesterday's news had not disturbed him overmuch. The important thing was that no one knew that Molly had been his mistress. He would have to make certain new arrangements now; but at his age there was no hurry.

Bathed and gargled, he drew the silken cord of his robe

around his narrow hips as the waiter entered on the stroke of half past seven and set down the unvarying breakfast tray. While the man stood by as was his custom, Charlie lifted silvered covers to be sure the orange juice was properly iced, the glass of hot water with lemon steaming, the two pieces of toast dry and crisp, the coffeepot hot to his touch. Yes, all was well; the man would get his quarter this morning.

But he did not glide out in his usual self-effacing manner. Charlie looked up with the hot water halfway to his lips to see that the waiter, who had always been a blank face with an uplifted arm bearing food, had turned into a man with working lips and pitying eyes.

'What is it?' Charlie spoke sharply, for he was afraid he knew what the waiter was going to say and he felt it an impudence.

'We all feel so bad, sir, about Mrs. Smith.' He looked as if he were going to cry. 'In the midst of life we are in death, sir, I always say.'

'Yes. Yes.' Charlie broke off a piece of toast with a dismissive snap. 'I'm sure everyone in the club will miss her.' He unfolded the newspaper and pretended to scan the headlines as the waiter sidled out.

*Oh, Molly! I never thought you'd be the one to leave me while I still needed you. You never told me you had a bad heart. And now you'll never know that I had you down in my will for a nice little income. You wouldn't have had to work any more and Joan could have had her teeth straightened by a good orthodontist.* The newsprint blurred, for he had been very fond of Molly — almost too fond, he sometimes thought.

It was five years now since he had first realized that the round and frolicsome girls of his youth had all swelled into fat ladies or shriveled into skinny wenches. Five years had passed since he had first taken the compact, smiling little housekeeper out to dance and to dine on lobster after many tentative and cautious lunches at obscure taverns and many small attentions: candy, flowers, a Christmas doll for her five-year-old Joan.

'How about a whole evening just for us?' he had asked that first time. And with a subdued twinkle in her blue eyes, she had answered, 'I could have Joan sleep in the linen room for one night in case I'm out very late.' He squeezed her hand and she looked demurely aside.

He wasn't looking for wild and exhausting romance. He had seen too many of his contemporaries ruin their health trying to assuage the passions of some youngster to whom love-making was still a novelty. No, thank you; let them boast of their palpitating virgins and worry each month. He preferred a good-natured, settled little woman like Molly with the additional excellence of being safely divorced and forbidden by her church to marry again. With her there would be no jealous husband or father to beat him up or shake him down and there would be no tearful pleas for marriage. She was just about perfect for him.

'I love lobster.' She probed into a claw and looked up with smiling, promising, merry eyes. A fluff of transparent white between the lapels of her dark suit hinted of firm pinkness underneath. A little blue hat matched her eyes and showed her wavy brown hair with its occasional thread of gray. Her only ornament was a small twist of gold-colored metal on one shoulder. He'd get her something better. Maybe even real gold.

Of course he had chosen a place that his married friends would not ordinarily visit; but she was so pleasant and quiet in appearance that he wouldn't have felt embarrassed even if someone he knew had come in.

In the taxi going back to the club, his arm around her cuddlesome shoulder, he was freshly sure he had found a very good thing in Molly. But he'd have to make arrangements to get the child permanently out of the way. She couldn't sleep in the linen room too often. People would talk.

He got off on his own floor. The convenience of it! Her room was just above his suite and he had only to walk one flight up the indoor fire escape.

Without anything having been said, he knew her door would be ajar. But he hadn't realized how sweetly her hair would ripple over her shoulders or how tenderly she would smile at him when he closed the door with a little click. Closed the door on lonesomeness.

'I came up to kiss you good night. Did you have a good time?'

'Such a good time, Ducky-dumpling!'

Soft arms reaching up to circle his neck . . . pet names . . . 'And shall Mommy stroke her baby boy's poor tired head?'

Love — smiling, happy, grateful, undemanding love. Five years.

But it was over now. He put it out of his life with a little click like the closing of another door.

He supposed Joan — unattractive child — must have been called home from her boarding school and he would have to go to see her. He would be kind, of course, but he must tread carefully. She had no claim on him — no claim at all. Let her father take care of her if he were still alive and if he had ever existed, that anonymous Smith.

He pursed his lips over the rack of ties, then selected a gray one with the smallest pattern of dark blue. Let no one think he was in mourning; still, when someone you know has passed away, a certain somberness of attire is fitting. Yes, the mirror told him he was suitably dressed.

He tested the door knob from the outside to make certain the lock had caught, then, habit-bound, he turned toward the fire escape. Molly waiting upstairs, her door ajar a faint-lit crack. Molly of the soft round face and the soft, prematurely gray curls laughing, 'It's a short leap up, Ducky-dumpling, but it's a long hike back.'

Today the room was dim and every chair was filled. An elevator boy shining with buttons, the steward in his cutaway, two maids in maroon with crisp white aprons, the chef immaculate in his tall nodding cap. As if pulled by an invisible cord, they all rose when he entered and lowered blank faces. Molly had been one of them; they knew, damn them, every one of them knew; or else why did they all scuttle off at once without a backward glance, leaving him uncomfortably alone with the forlorn figure of the child huddled on the day bed.

He tried to pull her tight-pressed hands away from her face, but she shook her head wildly and made a strangled sound.

'Now Joan, you must be a brave little girl.' Her light braids were dark with dampness where they strained away from her high shiny forehead and, conquering repugnance, he tried to pat her head.

Quick as a frantic trout she flung herself away from his touch.

'Joan!' There was the least little quiver of impatience in his voice. 'I can't talk to you unless you take your hands off your face and look at me.'

'You don't really want to talk to me.' But abruptly she lowered her hands and sat up, smoothing her crumpled dress. 'You hardly ever came here before when I was home.'

He was prepared for the piteous, teary little face, but he flinched before the beseeching regard of those swollen gummy eyes. As if he hadn't done enough for her while her mother was alive! He was hurt — yes, really he was hurt. And what she said wasn't true. More than once on a long dull Sunday, he had driven Joan to the gates of her school in the suburbs. Molly beside him, soft lips curving with happiness because he was being kind to her little girl, Joan bouncing from one window to the other in the back seat, her week-end things in a paper bundle until he had bought her a little suitcase at the drugstore where they stopped for sodas.

She had looked longingly at the tan canvas carryall with leather binding and a lock. But he thought the little shrimp pink box printed with dolls and kittens was cuter. It cost sixty-nine cents.

'There now, you're a real young lady with grown-up luggage.'

'Say thank you to Uncle Charlie, Ducky.' Why did Molly call everyone 'Ducky'?

The suitcase was at Joan's feet on the day bed now, battered, with the gray cardboard curling up from one broken corner. They both looked at it.

'I came to see you lots of times.' It was ridiculous to be on the defensive with a ten-year-old child — as if he owed her some duty of affection. Hadn't he helped Molly keep her in that school, and hadn't it cost a lot of money? But it was that or having her underfoot all the time. 'And didn't I buy you presents every birthday and Christmas?'

The child swung her knobby legs to the edge of the bed and sat up straight. A glimmer of interest flicked in her drowned eyes. 'You gave me my stationery.' She drew a small square box out of the pink suitcase and opened it with lingering fingers. Notepaper, a gay circus with giraffe and elephant and clown capering down the margin and across the top, 'Joan' printed in loops of varicolored flowers. 'I wish — '

'What do you wish?'

But her eyes filled with tears again and she shook her head violently. 'She said I should never ask you for anything.'

'You want some more paper; is that it?'

Timidly she nodded and again covered her face with her hands. In spite of himself he was touched. She was really Molly's child, impractical, easily pleased by some trifle that appealed to her foolish heart.

He touched her shoulder and rose. 'You'll get some more paper and maybe something else too. Maybe a surprise. And I'll be up to see you again.'

When Molly's sister came from Topeka, they'd have a talk. Of course he had no responsibility; but still, sometimes at the club when an old employee died, the members got together a purse for the dependents. He'd see what could be done — in an impersonal way, of course.

'Now, Joan, don't let me leave you crying.' But she was prone on the bed and didn't look up. Hesitating helplessly at the door, he saw one of her hands go out to touch the garish stationery box.

He reached his office on the stroke of half past nine, cheeks glowing from the nippy air.

'Good morning, Miss Macklin.' He hung his Oxford top-coat on the curved wooden hanger, brushing a fleck of dust from the black velvet collar.

'Good morning, Mr. Porter.' The stoop-shouldered secretary looked up from her machine. 'Your mail is on the desk and there's a telegram. I opened it, but I didn't think it necessary to call you at the club.' She lowered her spectacled eyes and her fingers began their industrious rattle, but not before he was aware that she had been gazing at him with more than usual interest.

So she knew too! This was what happened when you allowed your affections to become involved with a person not of your own station. First the servants at the club, now the faithful Macklin; all mousing, prying at his privacy, trying to thrust their unwanted sympathy at him. It was most presumptuous of them.

His inner office was a refuge with rows of heavy lawbooks, pages still stiff between their sober covers, and his mother's picture framed in silver on his desk. He took a piece of chamois that he kept in the top drawer and rubbed it over the frame, a little devotion that he always performed personally. Then he sat back and lit the first cigarette of the five he permitted himself each day.

He riffled through the mail, laying the telegram to one side. The recommendation of stock analysts, advertisements for men's wear, annual reports of corporations. And, as always, requests for donations — did people think that because he gave an annual subscription to the United Charities he was made of money? But once get the reputation of being a sucker, and they had you forever.

The telephone buzzed discreetly. Miss Macklin's voice. 'Will you speak to Mr. Jenkins?'

Jenkins was chairman of the house committee at the Attorneys' Club and a great kidder. He probably wanted permission to take some visitors to see his suite. It was quite a show place.

'Charlie? Hope I'm not interrupting you in an important conference.'

Charlie said, 'Not at all,' and waited. The men often chaffed him about his nonexistent law cases; but they were probably jealous of a fellow lawyer who could retire and devote himself to looking after his investments.

'I looked for you this morning at the club, but I guess I missed you. Suppose you're pretty blue today.'

Charlie felt his heart begin to beat louder. Servants were one thing; they waited on you, knew your habits, your personal routine; and they didn't matter so much. But when your friends encroached on your privacy, it began to be uncomfortable.

'I don't know what you mean.' Immediately he knew he had said the wrong thing. If people knew, there was no use trying to pretend they didn't.

'Come off it, Charlie. If you didn't feel blue about Mrs. Smith, you wouldn't be human. You can't fool all of the people all of the time, you know.'

'All right.' Charlie could hear his own voice getting high and squeaky. 'I feel blue. I feel terrible. So what do you want? I'm not in conference, but as it happens I'm pretty busy.' He poked at the pile of trivial mail, eyed the still unread telegram.

'Well, you know Molly was at the club for over seven years, so we're getting up the usual collection for Joan. Poor little kid; I just went up to see her and she looks like a drowned rabbit. Can we count on you?'

He breathed more easily. Just routine with a little kidding thrown in. And he was relieved that he hadn't been the only one to visit the child. Not much expense; little gossip. His comfortable life inviolate. 'Sure. Sure, Whatever the rest of you do, I'll match.'

There was silence at the other end of the line and he thought the connection was broken. Then, 'I thought you'd want to — ' Then, 'It's your money.' Another silence. Then, 'I suppose if you want to do something more on the side, it's your affair.'

'I don't always do all my charities publicly,' said Charlie. Pointedly, he thought. It was an old topic of argument between him and the other men. They were always after him for donations to boys' clubs and leagues for this and that, and he had acquired quite a technique for putting them off.

'Yes. That's what you tell us. Well. Be seeing you.'

Charlie rattled the receiver. He hadn't had a chance to say good-by. But this time the connection was really broken.

Immediately came another buzz and Miss Macklin's voice. 'Will you see Mrs. Zaus now, Mr. Porter?'

'Who's Mrs. Zaus?' he asked irritably. Zaus? He had no client by that name.

He heard a small gasp. 'The telegram, Mr. Porter. I thought you were expecting her.'

The woman pounced into his office almost before he had time to put the telephone down. She was a meager woman of indeterminate age and she settled herself into the comfortable chair at the foot of the desk with something at once bold and nervous in her demeanor. Above her sallow face her hair was aggressively, unnaturally black. She loosened her largely plaided thick coat to show a ruffled black chiffon dress.

'So you're Charlie.' She watched him intently as she fumbled in a lumpy handbag and extracted a stiff, new, black-bordered handkerchief. 'I guess you'd never take me for Molly's sister.'

Helpless resentment boiled beneath Charlie's smooth face and he felt red creeping up his neck. How could Molly let him be implicated with her impossible family? First the whining child, now the ill-bred sister. And by what right did this woman approach him?

'I'm sorry you had to come on such a sad errand, Mrs. Zaus,' he said politely. 'But I think the gentleman for you to see is Mr. Jenkins at the club.' There! That would get back at Jenkins and his hints!

'That's just where I thought you could help me.' She touched the handkerchief to the corner of a dry and beady eye. 'You see, it was quite an expense making the trip to Chicago and paying for Molly's funeral and all. And there's Joan to take care of, too. Molly always said you — '

He rose abruptly. Blood hammered in his temples and his collar felt tight.

'What is it you want?' A little voice deep inside him cried, 'Caution! Caution!' but this woman revolted him so that he must get rid of her at any cost.

'Why, Charlie!' She crouched back in her chair; then tittered inanely. 'I guess I can call you Charlie; I've heard so much about you. And you call me Eva. I don't want anything special. Only it was so expensive coming up here; it didn't seem worth while to make that long trip just for Molly's funeral, God rest her soul.' She raised the handkerchief again. 'I thought you people at the club made Molly so comfortable; I thought maybe I'd stay awhile as long as I made the trip anyway. Let Joan finish her year at school. She's dead set on it. And I thought maybe you'd say a word for me to that Mr. Jenkins. See, if I had Molly's job, I could stay. Of course, I'd need a little help for Joan; but I guess that wouldn't bother a rich, kind, gentleman like you.' Her smile fawned on him. 'And you wouldn't need to worry. I wouldn't talk out of turn.'

'I'll see,' he said hollowly. 'You'll have to give me time to think.' Think? Thought was impossible. What could he do?

She simpered and was gone. He sank back, wiping his wet forehead.

One phrase beat at him. 'Maybe I'd stay awhile.' Why, that meant — ruination! His peace, his comfort, his routine; everything he had built up during all the years since the death of his mother. It was bad enough for Molly to die and leave him again bereft — for in some ways she had been like a second mother to him — but in dying she had bequeathed him a legacy of trouble the like of which he had never known in all his orderly life. The servants laughing at him behind his back. The men at the club — it would be just like Jenkins to give this impossible woman a job if only to see him squirm. And little Joan! Reaching for him with skinny hands, grabbing for his heart because she knew that in him there was some tie to her mother. It was not to be borne.

'Miss Macklin!' He didn't stop to use the telephone; he strode to the door and flung it open. 'Get me a drawing room to Palm Beach. Tonight.'

He began to throw papers indiscriminately into his brief case. Miss Macklin's voice came through the open door. 'There's nothing tonight but an upper berth but you can have a drawing room tomorrow. Will tomorrow do?'

'Yes. Yes.' Tomorrow would have to do, for an upper berth was, of course, unthinkable. At best he hated to subject himself to the discomforts of traveling and strange hotels; but he was ready to face even those to get out of this mess!

His rooms at the club had never looked so covetable, half an hour later, when he stood vacillating among his gaping suitcases. Which things would he need on this undesired trip? How could he possibly get ready in one day? At random he opened the shallow drawers in his built-in closet where dozens of shirts lay side by side inviting his twice-daily selection. Which ones? And underwear — would he use the summer weight or the winter? Sometimes the weather changed even in those warm climates and it was dangerous not to be adequately dressed. On the other hand, he hated to be hot and perspiry. He wished Molly were here to help him. No, no; Molly was the cause of all this!

He piled garments on every chair and table. He would have to work fast. As he fussed from end to end of his apartment, he noticed a square of envelope sticking under his door. It hadn't been there when he came in. He turned it over in his fingers and saw the crude, penciled drawing of a stamp in the corner. So. Joan was trying to get around him again. Her horrible aunt had probably put her up to it.

Clowns and elephants with 'Joan' in bright flowery letters. Paper incongruously gay for a little girl who had just lost her mother.

'*Dear Uncle Charlie,*' he read. '*You are giving me more writing paper so I thought I would write you a letter on this one. Please do not let Aunt Eva take me away I would rather*

*stay here where you are. And Mother. Please let me stay
with you. I will be quite and good. And not bother. Love
from Joan.'*

And beneath the signature, a row of 'X's.'

The harassed middle-aged man, the only neat object in his
crumpled domain, stood still for a long moment. An unac-
customed moisture prickled at his eyelids. He blew his nose.
He *had* promised to come to see Joan again. Poor little kid!
He'd have to let her down easy.

As he emerged from the fire escape on the floor above, he
heard the sound of sobbing. He stopped at the half-open
door, caution reasserting itself. After all, why should he display his private affairs to servants? That awful aunt — !

'He promised to come back.' Joan's voice, choked and
reedy, reached him.

Then a shrill tone. 'He'll come back. Don't you worry.
He'll come back if I have to go out and get him myself.' In
imagination he could see Eva, sly and bold, with the ghost
of a smirk on her narrow lips.

'I want Uncle Charlie.' A blubbering moan made Charlie
shudder.

'Now you be quiet. Isn't Auntie here? Don't you want
me?'

'No. I want Uncle Charlie. Uncle Charlie. Uncle Char —
lie!' The child's voice rose in thin hysterical wails. Why,
everyone in the club would hear! Inch by careful inch, he
eased the door closed and, trembling, hurried down the fire
escape again.

His hands shook so fast that he could hardly dial his telephone. 'Miss Macklin. My plans are changed. I find I must
leave tonight. Yes, the upper berth. Yes, even the upper
berth.'

Charlie, surrounded by his heaped-up luggage, swayed
with the sickish motion of the train and drew his overcoat
more tightly around him. Foul, oily smoke from the engine
seeped clingingly through the cracks in the vestibule. He

shivered, partly with cold and partly with disgust. But even the drafty vestibule was better than the stifling car he had just left. The air conditioning wasn't working, and the porter refused — simply refused — to do anything about it. Said it wasn't his work. Charlie thought with longing of the employees at the Attorneys' Club, so respectful, so obliging.

He couldn't go into the club car because he had to wait to see the conductor. There was a little trouble about his berth.

Quite a good deal of trouble, in fact.

When the redcap had struggled in with Charlie's bags, bent under the load, and Charlie stepped to section six, an elderly lady surrounded by wraps and bundles had the forward-riding seat. The other seat, which was the unhappy portion of anyone unfortunate enough to occupy an upper berth, was also filled. Filled to overflowing. Charlie eyed with aversion a husky individual with an honorable-discharge button on his very new green tweed suit who publicly embraced a small birdlike wench with bleached hair.

While the redcap put two of the larger suitcases down and mopped his brow, Charlie waved his Pullman reservation authoritatively. 'I believe you're in my space.'

'No we ain't, Buddy.' The male disengaged his hand and fumbled in his inside pocket. 'See?' He held out his slip. 'We got upper six. And we're staying right here. See?'

Two in an upper berth. Limbs. Sweat. Disgusting. Aloud, he said, 'We'll hear what the conductor says when he comes through. This is *my* space.'

The giant roared, 'O.K. We'll see.' And added derisively, 'Keep your shirt on, Momma's boy.'

Someone tittered and Charlie was aware of interested heads beginning to crane in his direction; so he hastily waved his baggage to the vestibule and followed it. The engine howled mournfully and Charlie echoed it inwardly with all his heart.

He showed his tickets and told his story, holding his fat wallet conspicuously, when the conductor came through the car he had just left.

'You understand I'd prefer a compartment or even a

lower.' His fingers delicately searched among the bills. Should he offer the man a five, or would a couple of dollars be enough? After all, it *was* his berth. He hated to waste money, but his comfort was at stake.

'Not a chance.' The conductor relaxed against the door. 'This train is packed as tight as a sausage.'

'Then if you'll tell those people to get out — '

'You wouldn't want to do that.' The man screwed his face into a ponderous wink. 'It seems they were just married today and as soon as the porter made the berth up, they — '

'Yes. I see.' Wearily Charlie put his wallet back. 'I suppose I'll have to sit in the club car.' A dreary prospect, but at least a comfortable chair.

The conductor removed his cap and scratched his head. 'Well sir, I'm sorry, but they take the club car off in fifteen minutes. They put another one on in the morning, but that isn't going to do you any good, is it?' He laughed awkwardly. 'Well, there's always the men's room. You wouldn't want me to interfere with the newlyweds, now would you?'

The men's room reeked with cigar smoke and perspiration. Charlie dropped his Oxford overcoat on the cracked leather bench. The black velvet collar, soot-flecked, looked up at him reproachfully.

He didn't care. He lowered his tired haunches to the bench. The endless night stretched ahead of him, so he picked up a crumpled newspaper.

The venomous little headline shocked him more than reports of starvation abroad and unemployment at home. 'TOURIST-JAMMED FLORIDA FRIES IN 98° HEAT.' His comfortable, spacious, air-conditioned apartment! And — suddenly his eyes widened in staring horror as he realized the worst — he had no hotel reservation!

A man across the room was looking at him. Such an unkempt man with thin, florid cheeks, dirt-streaked, and wildly working lips. But after a moment he recognized that he was alone and that there was no other man. It was only himself in the mirror.

*(From Story)*

# THE COCOON

## BY JOHN B. L. GOODWIN

*W*HEREAS downstairs his father had a room the walls of which were studded with trophies of his aggressive quests: heads of ibex, chamois, eland, keitloa, peccary, and ounce, upstairs Denny had pinned upon his playroom walls the fragile bodies of Swallowtails, Nymphs, Fritillaries, Meadow Browns and Anglewings.

Although his father had maneuvered expeditions, experienced privation, waded through jungles, climbed upon crags for his specimens, Denny had blithely gathered his within the fields and gardens close to home. It was likely that his father's day as a collector was over; Denny's had just begun.

Denny was eleven and his father forty-six and the house in which they lived was a hundred or more years old though no one could be exact about it. Mr. Peatybog, the postmaster in the shriveled village, said as how he could recall when the circular window on the second-story landing hadn't been there and Mrs. Bliss said she knew that at one time what was now the kitchen had been a taproom because her father had told her about it. The heart of the house, as Denny's father put it, was very old but people had altered it and added on and covered up. Denny's father had added the room where his heads were hung, but Denny's playroom must have been the original attic because where the rafters of its high, abrupt ceiling were visible the nails in them were square-headed and

76

here and there the timbers were still held together with wooden pegs.

But the playroom, where Denny also slept, appeared to the casual glance anything but old. The floor was carpeted in blue, the curtains were yellow and the bedspread blue and white. The wallpaper, which his mother had chosen for him before she left, was yellow willow trees on a pale blue ground and to an alien eye the butterflies pinned on the walls seemed part of the design. It had been a long time since Denny's father had been up in the room and although he knew that his son's collection of Lepidoptera, as he called them, was pinned upon the walls he did not know and therefore could not reprimand his son for the damage they had done the pretty wallpaper. Under each specimen a putty-colored blot was spreading over the blue paper. It was the oil exuding from the drying bodies of the dead insects.

In one corner of the room was a chintz-covered chest in which lay the remains of Denny's earlier loves; battered trains and sections of track, an old transformer, batteries covered with cavernlike crystals of zinc salts, trucks, and wind-mills no longer recognizable as much more than haphazard, wooden arrangements of fitted blocks and sticks, books crumpled and torn with Denny's name or current dream scrawled aggressively in crayon across the print and pictures, a gyroscope, a rubber ball, its cracked paint making a mosaic of antique red and gold around its sphere, and somewhere at the bottom weighed down with tin and lead and wood more than any corpse with earth and grass, lay a bear, a monkey, and a boy doll with a scar across one cheek where Denny had kicked it with a skate. In another corner the symbols of his present were proudly displayed. The butterfly net leaned against the wall, and close to the floor on a wooden box turned upside down stood Denny's cyanide bottle, tweezers, and pins, the last shining as dangerously bright as minute surgical instruments in their packet of black paper.

After almost a year of collecting butterflies, Denny had found that a certain equivocal quality could be added to his pursuit if he were to collect not only the butterflies but also the earlier stages of their mutations. By cramming milk bottles, shoe boxes, and whatever other receptacle the house might offer with caterpillars and pupae he was, in the cases of those that survived, able to participate in a sort of alchemy. Intently he would squat on his haunches and gaze into the receptacles, studying the laborious transformations, the caterpillar shedding skin, the exudation that is used to hitch its shroudlike chrysalid to twigs or undersides of leaves, and then the final unpredictable attainment of the imago. It was like opening a surprise package, for as yet Denny had not learned to tell what color, size, or shape worm would turn into a Dog's Head Sulphur, Mourning Cloak, or Tiger Swallowtail.

As late summer approached, Denny insisted that the servant girl refrain from opening the windows wide in order to air out his room. The sudden change in temperature, he said, would disturb the caterpillars and pupae. Even though the girl reported to his father that Denny's room smelled unhealthily from all the bugs and things, the man did no more than mention it to Denny in an offhand manner. Denny grunted to show that he had heard and did no more about it, and as his father was writing a book on his jungles and crags and beasts, he had really very little concern about what went on upstairs.

So it was that an acrid smell of decaying vegetable matter resolving itself into insect flesh pervaded Denny's bright attic room and the oily blotches on the walls beneath his specimens spread ever so slightly, discoloring the paper more and more.

In a book, 'Butterflies You Ought to Know Better,' which an aunt had sent him for Christmas, Denny read that a suitable 'castle' for a caterpillar could be made by placing a lamp chimney, closed at the top, upon a flowerpot filled with earth. He prepared this enclosure, purchasing the lamp chimney from the village store with his own money. It was such an elegant contrivance and yet so magical that he decided to save it for an especially unusual specimen. It was not until a late afternoon in October that Denny found one worthy of the 'castle.'

He was exploring a copse between two fields. Because of the stoniness of its ground it had never been cultivated and lay like a sword between the fertility of the fields on either side. Denny had never trespassed on it before and dared to now only because of his growing self-confidence in his power over nature. A month ago he would have shied away from the area entirely, even taking the precaution to circumvent the two fields enclosing it. But he felt a little now the way he thought God must feel when, abject within its glass and cardboard world, the life he watched took form, changed, and ceased. Protected from unpleasant touch or any unpredictable action, Denny watched the metamorphosis from worm to chrysalid to miraculously vibrant petal. It lay within his power to sever abruptly the magical chain of their evolution at any point he chose. In a little way he *was* a little like God. It was this conceit that now gave him the courage to climb over the stones of the old wall and enter the half acre of dense woodland.

The autumn sun, already low, ogled the brittle landscape like some improbable jack-o'-lantern hanging in the west. What birds were still in that country spoke in the rasping tone of the herd; the more melifluous and prosperous had already gone south. Although the leaves on the trees displayed the incautious yellows of senility and ochres of decay, the underbrush such as cat briar and wild grape were mostly green. Armed with his forceps and his omnipotence, Denny explored each living leaf and twig.

Brambles tore his stockings and scratched his knees but, except for vulgar tent caterpillars in the wild cherry trees, Denny's efforts went unrewarded. It was dusk when, searching among the speculatively shaped leaves of a sassafras, Denny found a specimen beyond his most arrogant expectations. At first sight, due in part to the twilight, it looked more like some shriveled dragon than a caterpillar. Between it and the twig a filament stretched and this, added to the fact that when Denny touched it gingerly he could feel its puffy flesh contract the way caterpillars do, convinced him that it was no freak of nature or if it was it was a caterpillar freak and therefore nothing to fear. Tearing it cautiously with his tweezers from the twig, he put the monster in the Diamond Match box he always carried with him and, running breathlessly, blind to briar and brambles, Denny headed home.

It was suppertime when he got there and his father was already at the table, his left hand turning the pages of a book while with his right hand he ladled soup into his mouth. Denny had clattered up the stairs before his father was aware of his presence.

'You're late, son,' he said in the moment between two printed sentences and two spoonfuls of soup.

'I know, Father,' Denny replied without stopping, 'but I got something.'

Another sentence and another spoonful.

'How many times have I told you to be explicit? *Something* can be anything from a captive balloon to a case of mumps.'

From the second landing Denny called down, 'It's just *something*. I don't know what it is.'

His father mumbled, and by the time he had finished a paragraph and scooped up the last nugget of meat out of his soup and had addressed his son with the words, 'Whatever it is it will wait until you have your supper,' Denny was peering at it through the glass of the lamp chimney.

Even in the bright electric glare it was reptilian. It was large for a caterpillar, between four and five inches long Denny guessed, and was a muddy purple color, its underside a yellowish black. At either extremity it bore a series of three horny protuberances of a vermilion shade; they were curved sharply inward and stiff little hairs grew from them. From its mouth there protruded a set of small grasping claws like those of a crustacean. Its skin was wrinkled like that of a tortoise and the abdominal segments were sharply defined. The feet lacked the usual suctionlike apparatuses caterpillars have but were scaly and shaped like tiny claws.

It was indeed worthy of its 'castle.' It was not to be found in any of the illustrated books Denny had. He would guard it and keep it a secret and finally, when he presented its metamorphosis into a winged thing to the world, his father's renown as the captor of extraordinary beasts would pale beside his own. The only thing he could guess at, and that because of its size, was that it was the lava of a moth rather than that of a butterfly.

He was still peering at it when the servant girl brought up a tray. 'Here,' she said, 'if you're such a busy little gentleman that you can't spare time for supper like an ordinary boy. If I had my way you'd go hungry.' She set the tray down on a table. 'Pugh!' she added. 'The smell in this room is something awful. What have you got there now?' And she was about to peer over Denny's shoulder.

'Get out!' he shrieked, turning on her. 'Get out!'

'I'm not so sure I will if you speak like that.'

He arose and in his fury pushed her hulk out the door, slamming it and locking it after her.

She started to say something on the other side, but what it was Denny never knew or cared, for his own voice screaming, 'And stay out!' sent the young girl scurrying down the stairs to his father.

It was typical of the man that he merely commiserated with the girl, agreed with her on the urgency of some sort of discipline for his son, and then, settling back to his pipe and his manuscript, dismissed the matter from his mind.

The following day Denny told the girl that henceforth she was not to enter his room, neither to make the bed nor to clean.

'We shall see about that,' she said, 'though it would be a pleasure such as I never hoped for this side of heaven were I never to enter that horrid smelling room again.'

Again his father was approached and this time he reluctantly called his son to him.

'Ethel tells me something about you not wanting her to go into your room,' he said, peering over his glasses.

'I'd rather she didn't, Father,' Denny replied, humble as

pie. 'You see, she doesn't understand about caterpillars and cocoons and things and she messes everything up.'

'But who will see to the making of your bed and dusting and such?'

'I will,' asserted Denny. 'There's no reason why if I don't want anyone to go into my room I shouldn't have to make up for it somehow, like making my own bed and clearing up.'

'Spoken like a soldier, son,' the father said. 'I know the way you feel and if you're willing to pay the price in responsibility I see no reason why you shouldn't have your wish. But,' and he pointed a paper knife of walrus tusk at the boy, 'if it isn't kept neat and tidy we'll have to rescind the privilege; remember that.'

His father, grateful that the interview had not been as tedious as he had anticipated, told his son he could go. From then on Denny always kept the key to his room in his pocket.

Because caterpillars cease to eat prior to their chrysalis stage and Denny's caterpillar refused to eat whatever assortment of leaves he tried to tempt it with, Denny knew that it had definitely been preparing its cocoon when he had plucked it from the sassafras branch. It was very restless, almost convulsive now, and within the lamp chimney it humped itself aimlessly from twig to twig, its scaly little claws searching for something to settle upon. After a day of such meanderings the caterpillar settled upon a particular crotch of the twig and commenced to spin its cocoon. By the end of twenty-four hours the silken alembic was complete.

Though there was now nothing for Denny to observe, he still squatted for hours on end staring at the cocoon that hung like some parasitic growth from the sassafras twig. His concentration upon the shape was so great as he sat hunched over it, that his eyes seemed to tear the silken shroud apart and to be intimately exploring the secret that was taking place within.

Now Denny spent less and less of the days out in the open searching for the more common types of chrysalid with which he was acquainted. Such were for him as garnets would be to a connoisseur of emeralds. His lean, tanned face became puffy and the palms of his hands were pale and moist.

The winter months dragged on and Denny was as listlessly impatient as what was inside the cocoon. His room was cold and airless, for a constant low temperature must be kept if the cocoon was to lie dormant until spring. His bed was seldom made and the floor was thick with dust and mud. Once a week the girl left the broom and dustpan along with the clean sheets outside his door, but Denny took only the sheets into his room where they would collect into a stack on the floor for weeks at a time. His father took no notice of his condition other than to write a postscript to what was otherwise a legal and splenetic letter to his wife that their son looked peaked and upon receiving an apprehensive reply he casually asked Denny if he was feeling all right. The boy's affirmative though noncommital answer seemed to satisfy him and, dropping a card to his wife to the effect that their son professed to be in sound health, he considered himself released from any further responsibility.

When April was about gone Denny moved his treasure close to the window where the sun would induce the dormant thing within it into life. In a few days Denny was sure that it was struggling for release, for the cocoon seemed to dance up and down idiotically upon its thread. All that night he kept vigil, his red and swollen eyes focused on the cocoon as upon some hypnotic object. His father ate breakfast alone and by nine o'clock showed enough concern to send the servant girl up to see if everything was all right. She hurried back to report that his son was at least still alive enough to be rude to her. The father mumbled something in reply about the boy's mother having shirked her responsibilities. The girl said that if it pleased him, she would like to give notice. She was very willing to enumerate the reasons why, but the man dismissed her casually with the request that she stay until she found someone to take her place.

At ten Denny was positive that the cocoon was about to break; by ten-thirty there was no longer any doubt in his mind. Somewhat before eleven the eclosion took place.

There was a convulsive movement inside and the cocoon opened at the top with the faint rustle of silk. The feathery antennae and the two forelegs issued forth, the legs clutching the cocoon in order to hoist the body through the narrow aperture. The furry and distended abdomen, upon which were hinged the crumpled wings, was drawn out with effort. Immediately the creature commenced awkwardly to climb the twig from which the cocoon was suspended. Denny watched the procedure in a trance. Having gained the tip of the branch and unable to proceed farther, the insect rested, its wings hanging moist and heavy from its bloated body. The abdomen with each pulsation shrank visibly and gradually, very gradually, the antennae unfurled and the wings expanded with the juices pumped into them from the body.

Within an hour the metamorphosis of many months was complete. The beast, its wings still slightly damp though fully spread, fluttered gently before the eyes of the boy. Though escaped from its cocoon, it lay imprisoned still behind the glass.

Denny's pallor was suddenly flushed. He grasped the lamp chimney as if he would hold the insect to him. This was his miracle, his alone. He watched with a possessive awe as the creature flexed its wings, although it was still too weak to attempt flight. Surely this specimen before him was unique. The wings were easily ten inches across and their color was so subtly gradated that it was impossible to say where black turned to purple and purple to green and green back into black. The only definite delineations were a crab-like simulacrum centered on each hind wing and upon each fore wing, the imitation of an open mouth with teeth bared. Both the crabs and the mouths were chalked in white and vermilion.

By noon Denny was hungry, yet so overcome with nervous exhaustion that he almost decided to forego the midday meal. Aware, however, than an absence from two meals running would surely precipitate an intrusion by his father with the servant girl as proxy, he reluctantly left his room and went downstairs to face his father over luncheon.

Despite his compliance, the father was immediately aware of the transformation in his son.

'Spring seems to have put new life into the lad,' he said, turning over the page of a book. 'You're like your mother in that respect and in that respect only, thank God. She never did do well in cold weather.'

It was the first time he had mentioned the mother to the son since he had been forced to explain her departure obliquely some five years before. The boy was shocked. But as the opportunity had arisen, he hastily decided to follow up the mention of his mother. It was unseemly that he should disclose any sentiment, so he hesitated and calculated before putting his question. 'Why doesn't she write or send me presents?' he asked.

His father's pause made him almost unbearably aware of the man's chagrin in having opened the subject. He didn't look up at the boy as he answered. 'Because legally she is not allowed to.'

The remainder of the meal was passed in silent and mutual embarrassment.

Denny returned to his room as soon as he could respectfully quit the table, and while unlocking the door for an awful moment the possibility that the moth might have escaped, might never really have been there, scorched Denny's mind. But it was there, almost as he had left it, only now it had changed its position; the spread of its wings being nearly horizontal and in this position Denny realized that the lamp chimney was too narrow to allow it free movement.

There was no receptacle in the room any larger and in Denny's mind there paraded the various jars, the vases, and other vessels in the house that had from time to time in the past served as enclosures for his specimens. None of them was large enough. Without sufficient room, the moth as soon as it attempted flight would in no time at all damage its wings. In a kind of frenzy Denny racked his brains for the memory of some container that would satisfy his need. Like a ferret his thoughts suddenly pounced on what had eluded them. In his father's room a huge crystal tobacco jar with a lid of repoussé silver stood on an ebony taboret beneath the smirking head of a tiger.

There was no time to lose; for within five hours after emerging from the cocoon a moth will try its wings in flight. Breathlessly Denny bounded down the stairs and for a moment only hesitated before he knocked upon his father's door.

'Yes?' his father asked querulously, and Denny turned the knob and walked in.

'Father —' he began, but he had not as yet caught his breath.

'Speak up, boy, and stop shaking. Why, even confronted by a rogue elephant I never shook so.'

'I want to b-b-borrow something,' the boy managed to stammer.

'Be more explicit! Be more explicit! What do you want? A ticket to Fall River? A hundred-dollar bill? A dose of ipecac? The last would seem the most logical to judge from your looks.'

Hating his father as he had never hated him before, the boy spoke up. 'I want to borrow your tobacco jar.'

'Which one?' the father parried. 'The elephant foot the President gave me? The Benares brass? The Dutch pottery one? The music box?'

The boy could bear this bantering no longer. 'I want that one.' And he pointed directly where it stood half full of tobacco.

'What for?' his father asked.

The boy's bravura was suddenly extinguished.

'Speak up. If you make an extraordinary request you must be ready to back it up with a motive.'

'I want it for a specimen.'

'What's wrong with all the containers you have already appropriated from kitchen, pantry, and parlor?'

Denny would not say they were not big enough. It might arouse sufficient interest within his father so that he would insist on seeing for himself what this monster was. Denny had a vision of his father grabbing the moth and hastening to impale it upon the study wall, adding it to his other conquests.

'They won't do,' Denny said.

'Why won't they do?'

'They just won't.'

'Be explicit!' his father thundered at him.

'I want to put some stuff in it that won't fit in the others.'

'You will stand where you are without moving until you can tell me what you mean by "stuff." ' His father laid down his glasses and settled back in his chair to underscore the fact that he was prepared to wait all day if need be.

'Chrysalids and dirt and sticks and food for them,' the boy mumbled.

The man stared at Denny as if he were an animal he had at bay.

'You intend to put *that* filth into *that* jar?'

Denny made no answer. His father continued.

'Are you by any chance aware that that jar was a gift from the Maharana of Udaipur? Have you any faintest conception of its intrinsic value aside from the sentimental one? And can you see from where you stand that, beside any other objections I might have, the jar is being employed for what it was intended for? And if for one moment you think I am going to remove my best tobacco from my best jar so that you can use it for a worm bowl you are, my lad, very much mistaken.'

The man waited for the effect of his speech and then added, 'Go and ask Ethel for a crock.'

It was useless for Denny to attempt to explain that he wouldn't be able to see through a crock. Without a word he turned and walked out of the room, leaving the door open behind him.

His father called him back, but he paid no mind. As he reached the second landing Denny heard the door slam downstairs.

A half hour had been wasted and, as he had been sure it would, the moth, having gained control over itself, was in the first struggles of flight.

There was only one thing to do. Denny went to the corner where he kept his equipment. Returning, he lifted the lid from the lamp chimney and reaching inside with his forceps he clenched the moth with a certain brutality, though he took pains to avoid injury to its wings. Lifting it out, the beauty of so few hours, Denny once again felt his omnipotence. Without hesitation he plunged the moth into the cyanide jar and screwed down the lid.

The wings beat frantically with the effort that should have carried the moth on its first flight through the spring air. Breathless, Denny watched for fear the wings would be injured. The dusty abdomen throbbed faster and faster, the antennae twitched from side to side; with a spasm the abdomen formed a curve to meet the thorax. The eyes, still bearing the unenlightened glaze of birth, turned suddenly into the unknowing glaze of death. But in the moment that they turned Denny thought he saw his distorted image gleaming on their black, china surfaces as if in that instant the moth had stored his image in its memory.

Denny unscrewed the cap, plucked out the moth and, piercing its body with a pin from the black paper packet, he pinned the moth to the wall at the foot of his bed. He gave it a place of honor, centering it upon a yellow willow tree. From his bed he would see it first thing in the morning and last thing at night.

A few days and nights passed, and Denny, though still on edge, felt somewhat as a hero must returning from a labor. The untimely death of the moth had perhaps been fortuitous, because now in its death the creature was irrevocably his.

The meadows were already filled with cabbage butterflies, and Denny would go out with his net and catch them, but they were too common to preserve and so, having captured them, he would reach his hand into the net and squash them, wiping the mess in his palm off on the grass.

It was less than a week after the death of the moth when Denny was awakened in the night by a persistent beating on his windowpane. He jumped from bed, switched on the light, and peered outside. With the light on he could see nothing, and whatever it had been was gone. Realizing that though the light made anything outside invisible to him it would also act as a lure to whatever had tried to come in, he went back to bed leaving the light on and the window open. He tried to stay awake but soon fell back into sleep.

In the morning he looked about the room, but there was no sign of anything having entered. It must have been a June bug or possibly a lunar moth though it had sounded too heavy for one, thought Denny. He went over to look at the moth on the wall, a morning ritual with him. Although he could not be sure, the dust of one wing seemed to be smudged and the oily stain from the body had soaked into the wallpaper considerably since the day before. He put his face close to the insect to inspect it more fully. Instinctively he drew back; the odor was unbearable.

The following night Denny left his window wide open and shortly before midnight he was awakened by a beating of wings upon his face. Terrified and not fully conscious, he hit out with his open hands. He touched something and it wasn't pleasant. It was yielding and at the same time viscid. And something scratched against the palm of his hand like a tiny spur or horn.

Leaping from bed, Denny switched on the light. There was nothing in the room. It must have been a bat and the distasteful thought made him shudder. Whatever it had been, it left a stench behind not unlike the stench of the spot on the wall. Denny slammed the window shut and went back to bed and tried to sleep.

In the morning his red-rimmed eyes inspecting the moth plainly saw that not only were the wings smudged but that the simulacra of crabs and mouths upon the wings seemed to have grown more definite. The oily spot had spread still farther and the smell was stronger.

That night Denny slept with his window closed, but in his dreams he was beset by horned and squashy things that pounded his flesh with their fragile wings, and awakening in fright he heard the same sound as he had heard the previous night; something beating against the windowpane. All night it beat against the closed window and Denny lay rigid and sleepless in his bed and the smell within the room grew into something almost tangible.

At dawn Denny arose and forced himself to look at the moth. He held his nose as he did so and with horror he saw the stain on the paper and the crabs and the mouths which now not only seemed more definite but also considerably enlarged.

For the first time in months Denny left his room and did not return to it until it was his bedtime. Even that hour he contrived to postpone a little by asking his father to read to him. It was the lesser of two evils.

The stench in the room was such that although Denny dared not leave the window open he was forced to leave the door from the landing into his room ajar. What was left of the light in the hall below, after it had wormed its way up and around the stairs, crawled exhaustedly into the room. For some perverse reason it shone most brightly upon the wall where the moth was transfixed. From his bed Denny could not take his eyes off it. Though they made no progress, the two crabs on the hind wings appeared to be attempting to climb up into the two mouths on the fore wings. The mouths seemed to be very open and ready for them.

That night no sooner had the beating of wings upon the window awakened Denny than it abruptly ceased. The light downstairs was out and the room was now in darkness. Curling himself up into a ball and pulling the sheet over his head, Denny at length went off to sleep.

Sometime shortly afterward something came through the door and half crawled and half fluttered to the bed. Denny awoke with a scream, but it was too muffled for either his father or Ethel to hear because what caused him to scream had wormed its way beneath the sheet and was resting like a sticky pulp upon Denny's mouth.

Floundering like a drowning person, the boy threw back the covers and managed to dislodge whatever had been upon his mouth. When he dared to, he reached out and turned on the light. There was nothing in the room, but upon his sheets there were smudges of glistening dust almost black, almost purple, almost green, but not quite any of them.

Denny went down to breakfast without looking at the moth.

'No wonder you look ghastly,' his father said to him, 'if the smell in this house is half of what it must be in your room, it's a wonder you're not suffocated. What are you running up there? A Potters' Field for Lepidoptera? I'll give you until noon to get them out.'

All day Denny left the window of his room wide open. It was the first of May and the sun was bright. As a sop to his father he brought down a box of duplicate specimens. He showed them to his father before disposing of them.

'Pugh!' said his father. 'Dump them far away from the house.'

That night Denny went to bed with both the door and window locked tight in spite of the smell. The moon was bright and shone all night unimpaired upon the wall. Denny could not keep his eyes off the moth.

By now both crabs and mouths were nearly as large as the wings themselves and the crabs were moving, Denny could swear. They appeared in relief, perhaps through some trick of chiaroscuro induced by the moonlight upon the dusty white and red markings. The claws seemed upon the verge of attacking the mouths, or were the so terribly white teeth of the mouths waiting to clamp down upon the crabs? Denny shuddered and closed his eyes.

Sleep came eventually, only to be broken in upon by the beating of wings against the windowpane. And no sooner had that ceased and Denny become less rigid than the thing was at the door beating urgently as though it must be let in. The only relief from the tap-tapping was an occasional, more solid thud against the panel of the door. It was, Denny guessed, caused by the soft and fleshy body of the thing.

If he survived the night Denny vowed he would destroy the thing upon the wall or, better than losing it entirely, he would give it to his father and he in turn would present it to some museum in Denny's name. Denny for a moment was able to forget the persistent rapping which had now returned to the window, for in his mind he saw a glass case with the moth in it and a little card below upon which was printed

*Unique Specimen Lepidoptera. Gift of Mr. Denny Longwood, Aged 12.*

All through the night, first at the window, then at the door, the beating of the wings continued, relieved only by the occasional plop of the soft, heavy body.

Though having dozed for only an hour or two, with the bright light of day Denny felt his decision of the night before indefensible. The moth smelled; that was undeniable. The matter of the crab and mouthlike markings seeming to expand and become more intense in their color could probably be explained by somebody who knew about such things. As for the beating against the window and the door, it was probably as he had at first surmised, a bat or, if need be, two bats. The moth on the wall was dead, was his. He had hatched it and he knew the limitations of a moth dead or alive. He looked at it. The stain had spread so that now its diameter was as great as the spread of the wings. It was no longer exactly a stain, either. It looked as if a spoonful of dirty cereal had adhered to the wall; it was just about the color of mush. It will stop in time like the others; just as soon as the abdomen dries up, thought Denny.

At breakfast his father remarked that the smell as yet hadn't left the house, that it was in fact stronger if anything. Denny admitted it might take a day or two more before it was completely gone.

Before the meal was over his father told Denny that he was looking so badly that he had better see Dr. Phipps.

'How much do you weigh?' he asked.

Denny didn't know.

'You look,' his father said, 'all dried up like one of those pupae you had upstairs.'

The moon shone bright again that night. In spite of his

logic of the morning Denny felt sure that the movement of the white and vermilion crabs up to the white teeth and vermilion lips was more than just hallucination. And the beating of wings started at the window again. Then at the door. Then back to the window. And, in a way, worse than that was the plop now and then of the body against the barrier. Though he tried to rise and look out when it was at the window, his limbs would not obey him. Hopelessly his eyes turned to the wall again. The crablike spots clicked their tiny claws together each time the wings struck against the windowpane. And each time the plump, squashy body went plop the teeth snapped together between the thin-lipped mouths.

All at once the stench within the room became nauseating. There was nothing for Denny to do but make for the door while whatever it was still pounded at the window. As much as he feared and hated him, his father's cynical disbelief was to be preferred to this terror.

Denny refrained from switching on the light for fear that it would reveal his movements to the thing outside. Halfway across the room and shivering, he involuntarily turned his head and for a moment his feverish eyes saw what was outside before it disappeared.

Denny rushed for the door and unlocked it, but as he twisted the knob something beat against the other side of the door, pushing it open before Denny could shut the door against it.

When luncheon was over Ethel was sent upstairs to see what had happened. She was so hysterical when she came down that Denny's father went up to see for himself.

Denny lay in his pajamas on the floor just inside the door. The skin of his lonely and somewhat arrogant face was marred by the marks of something pincerlike and from his nose, eyes, ears, and mouth a network of viscid filaments stretched across his face and to the floor as though something had tried to bind his head up in them. His father had some trouble in lifting him up because the threads adhered so stubbornly to the nap of the blue carpet.

The body was feather light in the father's arms. The thought that the boy had certainly been underweight passed inanely through his father's mind.

As he carried his son out his eyes fell upon a spot on the wall at the foot of the bed. The pattern of a willow tree was completely obliterated by a creeping growth that looked like fungus. Still carrying his son, the man crossed over to it. A pin protruded from its center and it was from this spot, Mr. Longwood could tell, that the terrible smell came.

(From *The Atlantic Monthly*)

# BIRD SONG

## BY JOHN MAYO GOSS

*M*IKE, the Hospital attendant, whisked the collar of the oversize, canvas lumber-jacket up around Beresford's ears and grinned. 'That coat looks good on you, fella,' he said. 'A little big, but it's cold out and those sleeves will keep your fingers warm.' He held up a cap of black cloth, round as a casserole, with visor and ear-tabs provided with strings to tie beneath the chin. 'Here's just the hat to go with it.' Beresford tried to strike a comic attitude as Mike pulled the thing hard down on his head, but it was no use. He could not, he knew, be funnier-looking than he was.

'Who's coming for you, Georgie? Your wife? Oh, oh — the little French babe, hey? Well, you be careful, Georgie — don't forget to come back.'

Mike was young but his manner was fatherly; his arm lay across Beresford's shoulder as they walked away from the clothes room, down the long corridor, past the small, neat kitchen and dining room. 'Now you go up front and listen to the radio, George.' (Hop along, my boy, Papa's busy.)

The common room crossed the corridor at its top like a T. The big hall with its high, grilled windows and solid furniture served as meeting place, reading and writing room, library, and game room for the ward. Well patronized on weekdays, on a Sunday morning such as this, when no doctors came and there were no treatments, insulin shots, or occupational classes, it was a case of standing room only. There

95

was a restlessness here, like flotsam in flowing water; a sitter here, another there, would be pulled to his feet and away. Even as Beresford stood alert in the doorway, a chair in the row against the wall, almost next to him, was vacated and he slid into it, pulling out of his uncomfortable coat.

As many patients as could find places were seated about two center tables, reading magazines and the morning papers. At the end of one, 'Aunt Nellie' Nelson and 'One-Eye' Connor, dignified in overalls, were playing checkers. At the opposite end a slap-bang card game was in progress.

Swinging around these groups of furniture and humanity, a number of tireless individuals were finding release for their energy in marching single file, counterclockwise, in a rhythm unbroken except when one would flop triumphantly into a vacant chair or another would hesitate in his stride to twirl a knob of the radio. This last diversion, imparting endless variety to the programs and volume, gave a kaleidoscopic accompaniment of sound to the pervading activity.

Beresford glanced at the electric wall-clock. A quarter of ten — his wife should have been here an hour ago. A sweep of uncertainty left him clenching and unclenching his hands on the rough canvas of the coat in his lap. He took out a cigarette and cast around for someone already smoking, for matches in the pocket are considered a hazard for patients in state hospitals.

On the far side of the room, an attendant, loud-mouthed Bill Pfluger, spread himself throughout one of the big chairs and George could get a light from him — probably. But to be beholden to Pfluger even for a match was distasteful. Just now Pfluger was expanding his body and soul before those of the mentally deficient who sat about him. With Olympian authority, his great face red with the exertion, he proclaimed his opinions.

'Why, that punk'd have no more chance against Louis — ' George heard distinctly across the wide room, above the exhortations of a fleeting sermon just caught from the air by an indefatigable marcher. Pfluger waved a cigar in the face of the nearest of his audience. 'You don't know nothin', you poor goddam — ' 'Nothing is beyond our strength if we hold — ' intoned the air-borne sermon.

Three chairs away Graber had a cigarette going. Graber was a husky man with whom George often had confidential conversations, but he was unpredictable. Sometimes he had to be tied in his bed — only yesterday he had assailed the outer door of the ward with a frenzy that would have shattered the glass if it had not been made to withstand such emergencies. Now Graber offered a light without a word, looking intently only at the tips of the cigarettes as they met.

Urie, a mute with a shaved head, was sitting in Beresford's chair when he turned back, but it was not usurpation — merely the guarding of his friend George's seat against seizure. Urie got up at once, and when Beresford thanked him he writhed like a patted dog.

George breathed his cigarette long and deeply. The waiting and the flickering radio were wearing down his earlier exultation. He was getting nervous; his stomach was vacant and fluttery. Oh, Lord, what could be holding Denise?

Around and around the walkers went. Young Peters (he wet the bed at night) paused at the radio, jerky as a squirrel, and took his twirl. The instrument came in on short wave: 'Calling all cars, calling all cars. Watch for — ' Police, eh? It reminded Beresford of a refrain from a play a long time ago — *Liliom*, wasn't it? — 'Look out, here come the damn police, the damn police, the damn — '

George sat stiffly, his face dead-pan. Infrequently a thumb or finger twitched in almost imperceptible gesture. He wasn't going to get jittery today, he was telling himself, whatever happened. Not on this day of days, the day he had thought might never come, this day of proving himself, of rebirth. Nothing must shake him. This was the day of good-bye to that drawn-faced Beresford who had crept around crying to himself, 'They've got to let me out of here. I'm all right now — they've got to let me out.'

A twitter of birds — canaries, a cageful of canaries — sang

through the room. 'Gluck's Cake, Light as a Feather.' Canaries in a broadcast — too damn farfetched. A line of verse leaped into Beresford's mind, bright and fixed as a neon sign: 'Bird-song at morning, and star-shine at night, bird-song at morning — '

The marchers moved in quicker cadence. Pfluger's voice rose more positive and profane. The room swung in inexorable movement. Someone laughed shrilly.

Beresford finished his cigarette in one long drag and forced himself to relax. How about your achievement of ten days ago? (That's a good thing to think about.) When you sat beside the doctor before his wretched 'class' and, when your turn came, finally answered his questions, quickly and naturally as anyone should: —

'What day is it?'

'Wednesday, the thirteenth of November, 1940, Doctor.'

'How old are you? When is your birthday?'

'Three weeks ago I was forty-six, Doctor.'

(I'm living, Doctor. I am of my own generation. I am not a child nor an old man, not unborn or dead, just miraculously George Beresford, groped back out of oblivion to consciousness, to sanity.)

'Good! Very good indeed, Beresford. Nicely oriented. I am proud of you. One of my best patients.'

And then a little later, 'A day with your wife now? Well, I don't know, Beresford. Her influence on you has not been soothing. You recall after some of her visits — '

'Yes, Doctor, but I was worried about her then — desperate. I'm all right now, and she has a job and a room.'

So it had been arranged. Denise had been telephoned to come for him; he was to spend the day with her. (Don't look at the clock, Beresford — don't look. So, you see, only twenty-seven minutes since the last time. She'll be here. She will not fail you after all these months.)

No, he thought, she won't fail me. I failed her but she won't fail me. Whatever happened, ever, we were in it together. Nothing was too bad for us to share. Where I went, you went, drink for drink, always. I couldn't leave you in

France, could I? Are you sorry now? Ah, no, you liked it on the farm; those were five good years — or four and three-quarters. 'Oh, but this is *merveilleux*,' you said. Remember? 'I love it here. See, I can milk the cows and in the garden I am content.'

We came close to it there, *ma chère*. And we knew it. 'Let's drink to it,' we said. 'Let's drink in the long winter evenings before the fire. Let's drink in the mornings and in the afternoons. Let's drink to be happier. Let's drink to keep it as it is. You and I against the world, Denise.'

Fog, wisps of fog, seeping into the old house, haze impalpable but ponderable, fog over the garden, over the elms, mist clinging to my face. Flashes of lightning through the fog, shattering, shuddering glimpses of terror. Where are you, Denise? Hold me, for the love of God, hold me fast!

Beresford drew a hand across his eyes, as a diver does coming to the surface, and sat back again in his chair. Those last days — how were they for you, Denise? And after? This town is not Paris, ah, no. This town is hard and ugly when you have no money, no friends.

But today, at last, you can tell me. A job and a room! Carefully Beresford drew a small, folded paper from his pocket. 'Lavinia St.' I don't know it, he thought, but no matter. All we need is a safe and quiet corner, all by ourselves, away from these smirking guards and goggling inmates. You don't come to see me very often any more but I don't blame you for that. Those short, urgent, dumb moments were agony for us both.

Have you a fireplace in your room? Of course not. But pictures, maybe. I'll bet *Sainte Thérèse* is looking down from the wall. And the little water-color that hung in the hall at the farm — did you bring that in? You liked it so. Is there a tree outside your window?

Mike came to the door and beckoned to Beresford. On the instant, as George jumped to his feet, young Lolly, one of the walkers, fell like a board in front of Graber. Lolly was six feet tall, had a girlish face and a constant giggle, and fell down here and there. Graber stayed impassive though the

falling body brushed his legs. Pfluger parted himself from
his chair and his educational endeavors, picked up Lolly's
limp figure, and departed with it towards the limbo of the
dormitory. Pfluger maintained his cigar in his mouth, and
one of Lolly's shoes scraped across the floor.

Clutching his coat and cap, almost stepping on Pfluger's
heels in his eagerness, Beresford followed the guard's wide
back, straining with its burden, out into the corridor.
Denise, at last, he was certain.

Standing beside Mike's desk was a taxi driver gazing in
fascination at the scarecrow figure of Lolly draped in
Pfluger's arms. Mike looked up from a note he was reading
and Beresford shivered in premonition.

'Your little Frenchy can't make it, George. Ain't that
tough?' It was an exaggerated sympathy. 'But the dame she
lives with says come on down. She sent a cab for you.' Mike
fingered the note and examined Beresford speculatively. 'I
guess that's all right. Wanna go?'

Beresford hugged his lumber-jacket tighter. 'Yes,' he said.
'Yes, I — would like to go.'

The driver took his turn at speculative examination. You
could feel his wariness: riding one of these birds around
might not be so hot. Things went on in this place. But he
followed unprotesting as Mike led the way down the corridor
and unlocked the door to the stairway.

'There y'are, George. Give her my love — and don't forget
to come back.'

Beresford grinned and waved casually as people do on the
outside. He fixed the loops over the buttons on his coat as
he and the taxi driver descended the metal stairs, and tilted
his cap a little to one side.

'Wanna ride in front, bud?' the driver asked.

Probably scared I'll bean him from the back seat, but
maybe he's just being friendly, George thought, and climbed
in as quickly as he could.

'How long you been in there, bud?'

Beresford had to concentrate on the question. They had
passed out of the stone gates of the Hospital grounds and

were on the edge of town, a section of factories and freight yards which he had never known well, but which seemed now familiar in every detail. He did not want to talk.

'Not very long,' he replied.

Even the smoke hanging low and white over the locomotives, solid and white in the cold air against the gray sky, he had seen before, exactly as it was now. He read the names on the factories and warehouses, still there, steady and normal, names that he knew. They stopped for a streetcar, and a girl got on, a pretty girl with brown hair and rosy cheeks. She wore a brown hat and a brown coat with a fur collar.

They drove fast down the almost deserted, Sunday morning street. They would reach the middle of town in a few blocks.

'Isn't Lavinia Street on the south side?' he asked politely.

'North side — near north. It's Bertha's place we're heading for.' Launched into conversation, the driver continued, 'Ain'cha never been there? Say, is that little Frenchy your wife?'

Beresford was startled out of his thoughts. 'Why, yes,' he replied loudly. 'My wife is French.'

'Them Frenchies is sure full of hell. She's a good kid, though. I've drove her lotsa times. I do a lot of work for that gang at Bert's. They always ask for Eddie.'

What was the fool saying? But almost immediately, before George could ask for an explanation, the cab had turned and pulled up at the side of a dingy frame building, a store building from the look of it. There were filling stations on the other three corners of the intersection.

'Here y'are, bud. No, it's all paid for. Any time you want a cab, just ask for Eddie.' The driver leaned out as the taxi pulled away and called, 'Don't forget to go back home, bud.'

Beresford stood on the sidewalk, only the tips of his fingers showing from his coat sleeves, and wished to God he had stayed in the cab. He walked slowly to the corner. 'Lavinia St.' the marker said.

It's the wrong number then, he told himself. That smart

taxi driver. He fumbled for the address slip through his
buttoned jacket. '92 Lavinia St.' This won't be 92.

The raw wind helped George back down the side street
to the spot where he had been deposited. At the far end
of the building was a door. Upon it were nailed two metal
figures, a nine and a two. His upward glance found four
shaded windows on the upper floor. 'Oh, my Lord, it can't
be a — *bordel*.' Say it fast, Beresford. Say it in French and
you won't be sick.

Yet it did not have the right look about it, somehow, for
that. Too honestly bare. Without giving himself time to
think, he punched at the bell with a numb finger.

A strong female voice responded so quickly that it seemed
the button must have been in direct electrical contact with
it. 'Come in. Come on up,' the voice commanded.

The stairway, narrow and unlighted, mounted steeply.
Whatever light there might have been was blocked by the
wide figure of a woman on the top step.

'Say, ain't this our George?' the figure shouted. 'Come
right on up. I seen you get outta Eddie's cab. I got your
little Frenchy tucked away waiting for you. She ain't feeling
so hot this morning.' Beresford had groped his way to the
upper floor and was greeted with a dig in the ribs. '*You*
know, George, Saturday night.'

Beresford grinned, desperately friendly. 'May I — see her?'
he asked.

'You sure can, George. That door right there. Say, I'm
Bertha. I run this place. It ain't much, but there's no funny
business — men only, except Denise. I sure think the world
and all of that little girl. You go right in, George. Nobody'll
disturb you.'

Of course it's all right here, it's only a rooming house,
Beresford thought. It's just me — the old head still goes
rocketing. But I wasn't afraid, he thought. I came up.

Denise was propped up in bed; her head turned to look
at him as he entered. His first glance saw only that her eye
and cheekbone were discolored by a faded bruise. She was
trying to smile, half welcoming, half pleading. He crossed

the little room in two strides and kissed her on the mouth, quickly. Her breath was strong of overnight whiskey.

'I wanted to go for you,' she whispered in French.

Beresford nodded. He understood perfectly. He had done the same thing often enough himself. There was no question of forgiveness.

He sat on the edge of the bed, turning his cap in his hands. He should be talking to Denise, hugging her. Go on and talk, he goaded himself. Where are all those things you had to talk about?

Heavy footsteps tramped past the closed door.

The room was small and mean — bedbug mean. Except for a cheap dresser, there was no furniture but the dirty white iron bed, which sagged under even his light weight. Hanging beneath a shelf were Denise's dresses. With a lump in his throat George recognized most of them.

Denise was looking at him, smiling still, but frowning a little too, looking at him a little uncertainly. Her hair was dark on the pillow, her eyes dark and questioning.

He found her hand and gripped it hard. She was a little thinner, he thought, her highish Breton cheekbones a little more noticeable than he remembered. He bent and kissed her again, longer this time, lifting her shoulders to hold her close. Ah, this was better. This was Denise, brave and gallant, doing the best she could.

'Soon you can be out, *mon homme*?' she whispered. 'Soon we can go back to the farm?'

Back to the farm? Back to the old furniture, the silver, the pictures on the walls? Go fishing in the creek again with Denise, work in the garden with her, play with the dogs? What about that letter from the bank? There was no money. What was it that he had to do about that? He must see about everything, so many things. Not now — some day. He couldn't think about them now.

A bang on the door shook the light wall and a man shouted, 'How you comin', Frenchy?'

'*Va-t'en*, go to 'ell, *sale cochon*,' Denise called back. Even as he gripped his knees in panic, Beresford cursed himself for a weakling. Wasn't that Pfluger's voice? Could it be? Had he followed him? Did they put a tail on you when you went out? Then George heard Bertha, good-natured, 'On your way, you big bum,' and the man's answering chuckle. It wasn't Pfluger; Pfluger was at the asylum. He was working himself up over nothing again.

Denise was talking. She was telling him, vivaciously now, that *Berthe* was *formidable.* 'She makes the men here march straight as soldiers,' she said, and showed George with stiff hands how straight the men must march. 'But a good heart. She guards me well. She sees that I eat much. *Vraiment,* it is not so bad here, *mon Georges.*'

As he looked at her his heart constricted in pity, in remorse, in a love greater than he had known for her. No word of reproach from her, though it was as if he had led her by the hand and left her in this — this joint. Left her to fight for her life with no help from him. And she tries to cheer me up. He must get her out of here.

'Denise — '

With the clang of a hammer on sheet metal, Bertha's voice came from just outside. 'Hey, get up and get some clothes on, dearie,' she ordered and opened the door. 'I'm cooking you and George a nice dinner. Do you like fried chicken, George? Bet you ain't had none for a while. Say, how they been treating you anyhow?' She blanketed Beresford in heartiness. 'Hey, look at the poor guy sweat. Take off that hot coat, George. Make yourself at home.' She helped him unbutton it and threw it over the scrolled and battered foot of the bed.

Turning, Beresford saw, propped against the mirror of the dresser, a small, unframed photograph, a picture of himself, taken, he well remembered, in Belfort just before they had moved up into the Argonne.

'Golly,' he thought, peering closely, 'was I as young as that?' The boy in the photograph gazed back with arrogant confidence, fresh as his gold bars and Sam Browne belt, in a proud pose of 'Look who won the war.' Then what was that spectacle staring back at Beresford from the mirror? The old tweed coat was familiar, but that curious, intent face, the eyebrows raised in half-circles, the eyes stretched until the whites showed, that face which looked as if an invisible hand were clawing all the features downward, whose face was that? Mirrors were not numerous at the Hospital. There was only one small one in the ever populous washroom, and George had not had a good look at himself for a long time. Through a knothole, he thought. He squinted and lifted the corners of his mouth. That's better.

A squashed package of cigarettes lay on the dresser. He took one and turned around, still squinting. Denise was watching him intently — and Bertha, too, standing there with fists on her hips.

'No matches, hey, George?' Bertha seemed to know everything. 'Put this box in your pocket and light one whenever you goddam please. You're on your own today. I'd give you a snort — the babe here could use one — but I don't know, they're plenty ornery out there, I guess. How about a bottla beer?' She was gone with the last word.

Denise squirmed from the covers and sat on the edge of the bed, her shoulders back, stretching, her breasts tight against the jacket of an old pair of his pajamas, the sky-blue pair. 'What a girl!' said Beresford (Forget that specter staring at your back from the mirror). 'You are still wearing my clothes.'

'But naturally. Like that, *mon Georges à moi* is with me every night.' She's talking to me as if I were a child, thought Beresford. 'You want a *coup, Georges?*' She pulled a black pint bottle from beneath the pillow. 'I saved a little. Maybe it help you.'

Beresford could only shake his head. Nothing's changed — nothing at all, except himself. In how many places, on how many mornings, one or the other brought out the rest of a bottle, proudly, loyally. How could he tell her that the sight of the bottle appalled him now, that he was scared to take a drink, scared of the Hospital, inside and out, scared of himself, of everything?

How had Bertha been so quick — back already with two

glasses, accurately foamed, in her hands? She gave one to Beresford. It did look good — Hell, what's a glass of beer! — and he took a long swallow. The sharp beer taste cut through the mentholated hospital taste in his mouth, into his nose, through his head, throughout his body, jolting his senses. He put the glass of beer on the dresser.

'Come on over and take a look at my apartment,' Bertha said, 'while the kid here gets dressed. I got it fixed nice.'

Beresford had followed too many guards and nurses to hesitate at authority's voice. That was the way you showed them you were all right, he had learned — by not thinking, by doing what you were told. But his shoulders sagged as he followed Bertha.

On the threshold of a room across the hall he stopped, trembling like a wary animal. In the window opposite, across a welter of shiny furniture and garish decoration, there hung a pair of caged canaries. Canaries — he did not mind canaries. He had never thought about canaries. But this cage — this cage —

Bertha caught his fixed expression. 'You like canaries?' she asked. 'Denise is nuts about 'em. I got some more in here.'

To be sure, in the next room, where there were two windows, two cages hung, a pair of yellow birds in each. All were silent and motionless until, swinging her wide hips through a narrow channel between bed, tables, and chairs, Bertha put her mouth close to a cage and made small, sipping sounds. A gentle murmur came in reply; then, altogether, all three cages were alive with song, rising, falling, interweaving, clear notes and half notes, shimmering madly through the room.

Beresford wanted to turn and run. *Now* he knew what that cage had meant. His mind, feverish with strain, sparked and flashed. This was connected with the Hospital; this was where they broadcast that canary stuff from — 'Gluck's Cake.' It was a beastly scheme they were trying out on him. They were showing him he could not get away even for a day.

They knew what he was doing all the time — they would always know.

A slow, resistless movement commenced, around and around him, he at its center, a helpless atom in a cosmic carousel, its music a chatter of bird song. His upper lip glistened with sweat, his hands were clenched. Bertha glanced at him and raised an eyebrow.

'Hey, you wanna go back to Denise, George? I — I gotta fix dinner.' He followed her submissively, scarcely conscious of moving. The canaries subsided to nervous tweets, then all were still.

Denise was standing in her doorway, laughing and talking with a big fellow in a leather coat, breeches, and puttees. She had on a dressing gown, black with red flowers, one that Beresford had never seen before, and she had made up her face and fixed her hair.

'This is my 'osban',' she said as Beresford came up. 'He been seek, you know. *Georges, mon coco,* this is my good fran', Meestaire Bob Scott, *un grand detectif.* He good sona-beech.' She laughed and rolled her eyes at the big man.

'We been teaching your wife English, Beresford.' The detective grinned down at George and extended a hand. 'Heard about you,' he said. 'Been taking a little rest cure up on the hill.' He patted Denise on the shoulder. 'A great little Frenchy you got here.'

A detective! 'The damn police, the damn police — ' They were after him all right, slipping up on every side, spying him out, waiting to grab him. He squeezed past into Denise's room; he would be safer in Denise's room. He sat on her bed, elbows on his knees, head in his hands, and stared at the floor.

Denise came and sat beside him — Bob Scott had disappeared. She said softly, in French, 'He is truly good fran', *mon Georges. Bon type.* You would like him. He found a job for me making sandwiches in a tavern.'

Beresford could only nod. He was thinking, thinking; he must fit the detective into his place. The canaries were taken care of, but the detective — was there something awful about the detective? Was this something worse than he had thought down there on the sidewalk?

It was very hard to think. The giant circle slowly revolving was sweeping everything up. Denise and the detective, Bertha and Pfluger, the song of canaries in cages, the taxi driver, the four shaded windows and the narrow stairs, all were absorbed in the deliberate, swinging wheel. They came and went, approaching and receding, now large, now small, now sharply defined, now dissolving, nebulous, into the background.

Denise had taken his hand and was holding it against her breast, stroking the hand. 'You feel bad?' she was whispering. 'Don't worry, *mon Georges*. It is all right.'

His trembling quieted. He drew a long, shaky breath as a drunken man will do when fighting for control — and Bertha's voice bugled to come and get it. Oh, God, for a few minutes peacefully with Denise!

But not now. She was waiting for him at the door; she led him back to the kitchen. The kitchen was a cubicle, no more; its walls bulged with the stress of holding a refrigerator, a table, three chairs, and Bertha.

'Now fill 'er up, George,' Bertha urged as they sat down. 'You ain't et good for a long time. More'n that — here, let me — ' The muscles of her bare forearm rolled as she gripped the iron skillet and his plate was heaped.

Bertha's off-color blonde bangs, wet with perspiration, were stuck against her brow. The air was turgid with the fumes of hot grease.

She talked on undiscouraged. This was a decent rooming house, she was assuring Beresford. No women — she run it strict. A clattering and bumping in the hall broke the monologue as two men passed the open door, one supporting the other, almost dragging him.

'Listen, you lousy bums!' Bertha shouted, harsh with authority. 'You get into your room and if I hear a peep out'n either of you I'll throw you out on your cans.'

'Nice guys,' she commented good-humoredly to George, 'but they get a little high week-ends.'

Across from George, Denise was looking at her food, her hands in her lap. Beresford managed a swallow of mashed potato as he looked at her, but his first piece of chicken wadded against the roof of his mouth. His thoughts distilled into misery absolute. As clearly as if it were a great painting before his eyes he saw, it seemed, all the wrongness of his life with Denise.

You were going to give her a chance, he thought. You were the noble guy who was going to pull her up to sit beside you before all the world. She is sitting beside you now, Beresford — that's Denise looking at her food, her hands in her lap — and that's a tear that's running down her cheek. And here *you* are, Beresford —

'Ain'cha hungry, George?' Bertha's voice was like a blow. 'You gotta come and see us often now.'

A bell rang. Beresford jumped. Bertha went to answer the telephone in the hall. 'Who? Yes, he's here. Yeah sure, I'll get him there. No, I won't let him out. Hell, no, he won't be late.'

Beresford sat stiff. The Hospital, calling about him! The swing circled again, faster, dizzying. Outside, a siren wailed its lost-soul way along the street. 'The damn police —' They were surrounding the house; they had come to take him back.

Bertha switched on a small radio on top of the refrigerator as she rolled back to the table. She was complaining about having to wet-nurse a lot of goddam drunks and get them back to work.

But Beresford was not listening. A little tearing sound of static had come from the radio, then 'Tune in again next Sunday at the same hour. The following announcement is transcribed.'

Beresford waited, holding his breath. It couldn't be — A clear, ineffably musical whistle, a broken run, a rivulet of melody, 'Gluck's Cake, Light as a Feather,' then the burst of bird song.

'Listen.' Bertha grinned and pointed toward the door. From her own apartment her own feathered pets were responding, not to be outdone, singing for greatly more than they were worth. The sound beat upon Beresford's face; he felt their wings drumming on his eyes and cheeks. He was submerged in their song.

'Ain't that sweet?' asked Bertha.

Never had the swing been so swift, never so crushing. This was the end. He could stand no more. He jerked to his feet, jostling the table. He held to the table corner.

A small voice was trying to tell him, 'You are George Beresford, you are George Beresford. You were born — ' No use, small voice, you are too far away.

But another voice came and it was clearer — it was very clear. 'Get back to the Hospital, Beresford,' the clear voice said. 'Get back to the Hospital.'

Denise and Bertha had risen too. 'I must go,' George forced himself to speak. 'I must get back. I'm all right. It's just nerves — nerves. I'll have to go.'

Bertha shook her head. 'And he ain't et nothin', poor guy. It's a lousy deal. He ain't got no luck. But if you think you oughta go, George, I'll call Eddie.'

Denise led Beresford back to her room, picked up his coat and held it for him. She seemed to know he must hurry, but for a moment she held him by the hands, turning them slowly, gripping them hard. She smiled at him — his Denise — her eyes steadfast on his own.

'It is better than you think, *mon Georges*,' she said. 'It is almost. Next time — '

But he was numb, his throat dry wood. He could only kiss her clumsily, dutifully, as if she were a distant relative.

At the head of the stairs he turned, tried to grin, half saluted. Denise, in her doorway, smiled back — or did she? Her mouth curving upward, slackened, seemed to melt; her face disintegrated. Both her hands went slowly to her cheeks and she vanished into her room.

Bertha went down the stairs before him, her hips working like rubbery loaves as she hurried. 'Get him there as quick as you can,' she told the cab driver and crumpled money into his hand.

The Hospital — already? It had taken so much longer going in. But this was George's building all right. He climbed the stairs, the clean, cold, iron stairs, up to his ward on the top floor. Never before had he climbed those stairs alone. Now, as he returned, for the first time he had a feeling of freedom. He felt superior and privileged, as if he were a senior in college again, and he trod with a firmer step. He took off his cap. His jacket seemed to fit better now and he unbuttoned it and let it swing.

Mike answered the buzzer. 'Why, *Mister* Beresford! Back so soon?'

Ignoring him, Beresford dropped his coat and cap in the clothes room and walked up the corridor. The ward was still. Two groups of visitors were in the dining room, bags of fruit and cookies on the tables before them. The red-checked tablecloths and curtains lifted the scene to a warm domesticity.

Turning right before he came to the common room, Beresford entered one of the dormitories. *His* dormitory. The beds in two rows were lined up exactly, each with its meticulously draped green cotton cover. Some of the windows were open and the white curtains waved contentedly.

From a cardboard box beside a bed — *his* bed — he took a candy bar and commenced eating it slowly. He was hungry and he let the chocolate dissolve on his tongue and crunched the almonds with relish. From a window he watched groups of visitors coming and going from the cars wedged along the curb. The sun had come out and it was a fine, sparkling, late fall day, perfect football weather.

He balled the paper covering of the candy bar, dropped it into a wastebasket, and walked into the common room. It was as peaceful as a religious library. Its only occupant was Graber, smoking a cigar and flipping the pages of a magazine, obviously bored, but also, Beresford was glad to perceive, obviously in a good humor. George took the seat next to him and pulled out a package of cigarettes.

'Take one of these,' said Graber and proffered a cigar. 'I got five bucks from my brother yesterday and sent down to the commissary for some of their best. Pretty fair. Where you been all day?'

'Thanks, Grabe. I've been down in the city visiting my wife.' Beresford hoped the remark sounded casual.

Graber looked at him sharply. 'Have you? Swell! Your first time out, isn't it?' His eyes narrowed. 'Did they tell you to get back so early? It's only two o'clock.'

'No — but it didn't work out so well.'

'That's too damn bad. Feel all right?' Graber was acute.

'Well, no — that is, I feel fine now, but when I was down there — I got the jitters — had to get out.' He paused. 'I hope to God it's not always going to be like that.'

'Hell, no, George. There's nothing the matter with you any more. Look, fella, you've been in here quite a while. Lock the sanest guy in the world up in this place for a few months and he would start getting ideas — ideas about the outside, I mean. Everything's wrong here, but everything's right on the outside — get me?'

Beresford nodded. ' "I dreamt that I dwelt in marble halls," ' he said beneath his breath.

'What? Anyway, a guy sits here and forgets how screwy things were in the world. God, look at this sheet.' Graber extended the magazine he had been reading to arm's length and slapped it violently to the floor. 'Things aren't perfect out there, Beresford, by a hell of a sight — whatever you've been hoping. What was the matter? Wasn't your cute little wife glad to see you? Or was she living on the wrong side of the tracks?'

Graber drew hard on his cigar in scorn. 'I've seen plenty of guys get knocked off balance again the first time they stuck their heads out.' Philosophic calm reigned again. 'All you have to do, George, is take your time — you'll be O.K. Take me now — seven years —' Graber fell silent.

They sat for a moment smoking their cigars. Beresford crossed one leg over the other. It was good to sit here next to Graber — what a sound, understanding fellow he was.

The sunlight slanted in a close angle through the west windows, lying in rectangular blocks of brightness on the dark floor next to the wall, animating the whole end of the room like footlights before a stage. From their cigars, thin fillets of smoke ascended, steady in the stillness, as blue and clear, as pale yet as vivid, as the outside sky.

Beresford smiled — two businessmen they might have been, two men of affairs anywhere, idling an hour in their club lounge in the hush of a Sunday afternoon.

*(From Tomorrow)*

# THE HORSE LIKE SEPTEMBER

## BY PAUL GRIFFITH

*W*HEN SUMMER RIPENED, the ranchers in St. Johns drove their cattle to the highest pastures on the mountains, hoping the herds would finish the dry end of summer there and, when September brought rain again to the lower land, come down fattened and ready for the long trek to market. Careful watch was kept. Boys were sent to ride fence and to report the condition of the mountain grass and the average weight of the new calves. August had almost passed, with the grass still green and water plentiful, and the ranchers began to calculate the summer's profit. Then came the wild horses.

Where they had come from no one knew. In fact, many had assumed that wild horses now lived only in the tales of old men, along with Geronimo and the dead towns to the south. A few who were not so old could remember seeing them, great proud horses with deep scars beneath their manes, but no one claimed to have seen one now for a quarter of a century.

They had come two weeks ago, sweeping up from the dry lands and plundering the mountains' fresh meadows, breaking fences, trampling precious grass, muddying the precious streams. But the horses had not been seen.

Although extra boys were sent to ride fence, they had found only a track in the dust of a trail, a bright strand of hair caught on a barb, the broken fences and the torn grass. In spite of this, the young ranchers met together in the café

114

to plan what they should do to protect their property. They laid their plans and waited.

Then, one afternoon, Humpy's oldest boy rode into town and told how he had found the carcass of a small lion, its head stove in, its body trampled to pieces. Only wild horses could have killed a lion in such a way. And he had seen their trail. It went up into the first mountain. So it was decided in the café that the younger men would go out the next morning and do what had been planned. Boys and old men would stay home, for it would be a hard ride, and dangerous, with the rifles. Nat would go with Jim and Ralph and Humpy — so called for the knot of hard flesh he bore on his shoulder.

That evening, Nat and his wife, Emily, talked of the wild horses. It was then that Emily first spoke of the sorrel. She had always wanted one, she said, ever since she was a child. 'It would make everything we have perfect,' she said, looking at their house which stood alone on the highest and finest land below the mountains. Emily was proud of the house she kept so clean and surrounded with blue lupine. She was proud of Nat, and she was proud that they had made a success of their ranch. She was proud in the way a woman is proud of her children, wanting the best of everything for them, as she leaned on Nat's arm that evening. She was thinking of the sorrel. It would make everything perfect, and she knew that her desire had created desire in Nat. She knew he would bring one home, if possible, for her.

In the morning she woke first. She wakened Nat and kissed him, and then they both rose and hurried to get ready for the hunt. When breakfast was over, Emily quickly made sandwiches and laid them neatly in the righthand pocket of the saddlebag. Fastening the flaps, she flung the saddlebag over her shoulder and stepped into the yard, hurrying down to the corral where Nat was saddling Antelope. He was ready, wearing his chaps, his rifle clean in its leather case; and when she had tied the saddlebag behind the cantle, he mounted Antelope and then leaned down to kiss her goodbye. He said he would bring back a sorrel if he could.

Emily smiled at him excitedly. 'Oh, yes, Nat,' she said,

'I hope there is a sorrel. I do love the color so, all red and yellow. It's like September. I hope there is one, Nat. I've always wanted a horse like that.'

'I'll try,' he said. 'It would be fine.' He looked down at her, lovingly, and kissed her. Then he rode down the lane, allowing his look to lie for a moment on his green and rich land.

He met Jim, Ralph and Humpy at the turn. Riding southward, they talked with excitement. Gradually, Humpy urged his horse ahead, half-trotting. The horses responded to the riders' anticipation and rattled their bits, jogging and holding their ears high, listening to the voices and the tantalizing jingle of spurs under their bellies.

The plan had been that they divide in pairs, one climbing the mountain from the plain that separated Nat's ranch from the mountains, the other circling the mountain and climbing from the south by way of the mining camp, and thus maneuvering the wild horses between them, driving them to the top of the mountain where there was smooth grass and space in which to shoot cleanly. It was obvious, however, that those who rode directly from the plain would meet the horses first, for the northern side of the mountain was rich in streams and fresh grass. And so, silently, each man had made up his mind to go by the north. The plan was altered without a word, by common recognition of each one's desire to take a wild horse for himself, or his wife.

Crossing the plain, climbing the trail that arched over the foothills, the four men grew silent. At the first, lowest pasture on the mountain all was well. The men surveyed the strong fences without expression. There was no trace of the wild horses. Even below, on the trail where the small lion had been killed, there were only the tracks of coyotes who had stolen the bones. But the men said nothing to each other, riding steadily, peering steadily about them.

Humpy rode ahead, urging his horse ahead with his spurs. Bent over, he kept his hand upon the rifle slung from the saddle and stared into the brush and at the climbing trail. Then Ralph suddenly pointed at him riding so far ahead.

Jim snickered. They all knew how excitement made Humpy sullen. Without smiling, Ralph leaned from the saddle and picked a pebble from the trail and hurled it into the trees along the trail.

At the moment when the pebble struck a tree, Humpy half-stood in his stirrups, drew his rifle and pointed the barrel into the quivering brush. Then he heard Ralph's laugh, and without looking back he pushed the rifle back into its case and urged his startled horse back into the trail. Bent beneath the weight of the hard flesh on his shoulder, his nerves strained to the glitter of each leaf along the trail.

Then the others began to argue how best to take a wild horse. Each knew the bullet should enter the neck halfway between the jaw and the shoulders, in the very center of the neck's curve, piercing the strong flesh and inflicting shock and first fear on the animal, but cleaving through cleanly, leaving veins and nerves unharmed, as through a bull's-eye. It was their grandfather's proudest tale, and though they each knew exactly how it should be done, they argued to ease anticipation.

As they entered the second mountain pasture, Humpy kicked his horse's side, spurring him far ahead on the trail. The others did not talk. They sat straight in their saddles, peering ahead, listening to the sound of Humpy's horse climbing. He was above them now. Although the trail grew continually steeper, they did not pause to let the horses rest. As rocks clattered against their hooves, the horses rolled their eyes with nervousness, puffing, their flanks black with sweat. Then came Humpy's cry: 'Here they are! The horses!' Shrill and far away, the words were meaningful only by the excitement heard in them. And they came with the sound of Humpy's spur striking his horse's belly and the clatter of hooves against the hard trail.

Nat, Ralph and Jim rushed up the trail after him. As they entered a green pasture, neat and square as a park set in the rough mountain timber, they saw Humpy disappearing into the trees, following the trail as it led higher to the mountain's peak. He was galloping, his gun held to his shoulder, his horse miraculously guided without reins, which dangled between its knees. Then they saw Humpy's horse take fright at the reins and swerve, turning into the trees. The rifle was wrenched from Humpy's grip and fell among the trees as a bullet cut into the leaves. Humpy fell, and his horse rushed on in its fright, ripping the saddle on the sharp limbs of the forest, and then stopped and peered back at what had happened. Humpy was not hurt. Before the three men could ride to him, he was on his feet, face white, pointing up the trail with both hands. 'I saw 'em,' he said. 'Right up there. I saw 'em.'

Nat spoke to him irritably: 'All right, Hump, get back on your horse. We'll get them.' Humpy went to his horse, mounted and sat there with his seat of ripped padding blowing around him. The others rode ahead of him. They waited for the sweat to dry on his face and the blood within him to quiet, for his horse to stop its rattling breathing, before they spoke of what he had seen. Finally, he spoke. 'There were three of them,' he said. All of them turned to him: 'Only three?' He nodded, and they became silent again, each one seeming to ride more steadily, with more determination. Finally Nat asked him the important question: 'What kind?'

'Big. Big ones.'

'No, I mean what kind.'

'Two bays. Maybe one was black. I don't know. And a red.'

Nat stiffened. Emily's sorrel was there, and he could be certain now that the hunt was real, that his desire had an object beyond his imagination and Emily's pride. He felt certain that the sorrel would make everything perfect, as she had said, that the horse would be the one last thing needed to make their green ranch a success. Thinking, he grew impatient and concentrated his attention on the horses' fatigue, muttering as they paused on the trail to rest and catch their wind.

When it became apparent that Humpy's horse would break

its throat and lungs for the strain of climbing so steadily under the prodding of Humpy's spurs, Humpy silently pulled off the trail and dismounted, allowing the others to go on without a word. Walking a higher ridge a moment later, Nat looked down on him lolling and smoking and pulling at the grass, and waved. Humpy saw the motion, but turned his head aside. 'Damn him,' Nat said, feeling the irritability grow in him, weighing down his spurs with the fatigue of carrying excitement too long. But neither Jim nor Ralph spoke. They were watching the trail. Jim was leading, and just as Nat expressed his feelings he leaned excitedly from his saddle and plucked something from the sharp branch of a dead tree. He held it up triumphantly, a swatch of hair, bright red and gold. 'We're right,' he shouted. 'Come on.'

Thereafter, no one spoke. Nat stared at the swatch dropped on the trail and pushed his weight into the motion of Antelope's climbing. The brief stops angered him, but as they approached the highest meadow on the smooth peak of the mountain, he felt less strained. His eyes, like Jim's and Ralph's, sharpened, but at the last pause before they reached the meadow he sat calmly as Antelope drew in the air, waiting until the horses were easy and ready again to employ their full strength. Nat thought of the meadow, the greenest on the mountain, water flowing there in a long pool, protected from the wind by large boulders. Certainly the horses would be there, enjoying the grass saved for the herds in case of a late summer's drought.

Then, circling a clump of piñon trees, they reached the meadow. Its strong fence was broken, the wire glistening on the ground, the poles broken and marked with hooves. The horses were there, standing before the boulders with their ears erect. Humpy had been wrong. There were four, two bays, a black and a red.

For a moment both men and horses were still. Nat stared at the sorrel. Taller than any horse he had seen, the red was exactly what Emily wanted, the coat sleek and short, burnished with sweat and sun, the legs tapered, the feet hard and sure. The mane and tail were yellow and long enough to blow about the red body. Nat relaxed, as if the desire within him had momentarily been satisfied by sight.

Then with his finger he released the safety-catch of his rifle, and Jim and Ralph imitated his motion, all three men drawing their guns to their shoulders and peering down the sights to the horses before the great boulders. The horses were standing with taut muscles and quick ears. Suddenly and quietly, they rushed behind the rocks.

The three men followed. As their own horses jumped forward, they snapped their safeties and returned the rifles to their cases. They saw the four horses crossing the southern side of the pasture, running free with the long gait of the unsaddled horse. The men galloped after them. Nat spurred Antelope gently and touched his neck with encouraging fingers. Hooves were almost silent in the thick grass. If the men could reach the place where the trail led down from the mountain there would be ample time to draw steady aim and fire into the rushing necks.

Nat was leading. Antelope moved under him swiftly, hooves cutting the grass and stepping lightly on both stones and gullies; but unthinking in his desire, Nat urged him on faster and faster. Behind him he could hear Jim's and Ralph's horses snorting. Then he reached the edge of the pasture and entered trees again, plunging down the dark steep trail. Before him the wild horses slowed, hind legs bent and sliding on the rocky trail, going in single file with the sorrel leading. They were too far below, there were too many branches, their flight was too fast for Nat to shoot. He kept Antelope to their speed. Occasionally the horses disappeared, and he would spur Antelope down the steepness, watching the forest below him move.

The south side of the mountain was steep, but shorter and curving in to the foothills. Halfway down the trail was the only pasture. It had poor grass, and it was seldom used, for there the trail split, one fork dropping to the miners' camp, the other easing suddenly northward into the dunelike foothills that rose from the plain bordering Nat's ranch. Nat did not think of this consciously. During the hunt his mind worked secretly, informing his muscles of directions and intents of which he was unaware. Antelope responded to the measure of his weight in the saddle, to the meaning of the spur. Now, unconsciously, Nat had made his plan. In the pasture he would cut the sorrel from the other horses and turn him into the northern trail, pushing him to the empty plain where for a mile or more there was nothing to hinder his shooting cleanly.

Suddenly Antelope gained on the four horses. The bay that followed the others, a mare, kicked her legs into the leaves and turned back the whites of her eyes. The pasture was ahead. Across the parched grass Nat saw the horses running, the red first. His lean red body flamed in the sun, yellow mane and yellow tail seemingly caught up from the pale dried grass in the pasture. Behind him ran the black and the bays. They were crossing the pasture, moving toward the southern trail. Nat urged Antelope to fullest speed, and they circled past the mare showing her white eyes, past the black, almost to the sorrel running through the white grass. Trees rose up close before them, fencing the pasture with dark limbs. Still the bays and the black followed the sorrel to the southern trail. With a shout Nat leaned forward in the saddle. Antelope replied, leaped close before the black, moved to the left of the sorrel and suddenly turned him back to the north. Nat pursued him across the pasture, pushing him alone into the northern trail. The black and the bays stopped, looked about, saw Jim and Ralph close behind, then hurried down the southern trail. On the northern trail, Nat was chasing the sorrel alone, running easily in the shadow of the trees, mane and tail seemingly the only motion around the red body.

Antelope kept the pace, stumbling close behind the red. But for the leaves and sliding earth, there was a chance of cleaving the red neck with a bullet. But Nat waited, without even fingering the rifle. Soon they came to the foothills, where the horses eased their legs to a smooth trail, the sorrel losing his color in the red dust they raised. They were almost silent, except where marsh grass rattled in the gullies and mud splashed and cactus shattered beneath hooves. Down to the plain, down past the few cottonwoods, they came to the emptiness of the barren land between the mountains and Nat's ranch. Nat knew this land, and he recognized its advantage. Hemmed in by the mountain and the high wire fence he had built on the border of his ranch, he could guide the sorrel, take his time to shoot, crease the neck neatly and lead the groggy horse back to be tamed for Emily to ride. He pressed his knee into Antelope's shoulder.

The sorrel ran straight across the plain, never deviating from the trail. Antelope followed to the right of the trail, so that Nat watched the sorrel from the side. Slowly he drew his gun, lest its glint cause the horse to swerve, and raised it to his shoulder. Having wrapped the reins loosely about the horn, Nat allowed Antelope to have his head, trusting him to follow as he had been taught, not too close to scare the sorrel into swerving, close enough to keep him running and without a moment to feign a change of direction. Yet the sorrel increased his speed, and Nat laid the rifle across his lap, touching Antelope's belly with his spur. They did not gain. Antelope was breathless, the wind sounding in his throat, his maned whitened with foam, red and white flicking from his mouth. But the high fence was ahead, and just this side of the fence the small stream that separated Nat's ranch from the plain, the stream which rose there at the edge of the plain and gave Nat's land its green richness. The trail which the sorrel followed led to the fence, to the gate strung with wire.

Nearing the fence, the sorrel slowed, Antelope imitating his pace close behind him. Nat raised the rifle and held it ready to his eye, waiting to see which way the sorrel would swerve, ready to cleave the neck with the bullet as soon as it turned in either direction. The sorrel stopped, muscles quivering, eyes turning up and down the fence. Antelope stopped. Nat was ready, waiting for the sorrel to turn. And then the sorrel jumped, neither to the right nor to the left, but directly ahead, so that his neck was never exposed, so that there was no way of shooting cleanly. Hind feet pushed against the edge of the small stream, he leaped toward the green grass beyond the fence, red arc over the wire. Then, with a cry as shrill as a woman's, the sorrel dropped his forefeet on the grass. His belly, and then his hindlegs, dropped on the wire.

Nat and Antelope stood still with surprise. They watched the sorrel twist into the wire, his belly bright with the barbs caught there, his legs crimson with blood. He struggled for a moment, and Nat saw the wire push into his flesh, the blood come forth. Then Nat slid out of the saddle, waded the shallow stream and stood looking down at the sorrel. The great horse lay still, its only motion the flow of blood, the twinkle of the barbs. Nat raised the rifle and drove a bullet into the red head. The yellow mane tossed. And then there was only the motion of the blood, pumping still with heavy throbs.

He led Antelope back to the ranch and let Emily, who was waiting in the corral, unsaddle and feed him. Nat walked to the house. He sat in the dark kitchen and drank a cup of hot coffee. Emily came to him and put her hand on his shoulder, looking into his face.

'Did you see him at all, Nat?'

'Yes, I saw him.'

'Sorrel?'

'Yes. Red, yellow, big.' He sat staring into the empty cup.

'Like I always wanted, Nat?'

'Yes, Em, like you wanted.' He got up and went to the window, carrying the cup with him. Emily waited for a moment and then questioned him, watching him sharply.

'What happened?'

'He got away.'

'Got away free?'

Nat turned toward her: 'Not away free. He jumped the fence and got caught. I had to shoot him.'

'Oh. Wasn't there any way?'

'I tell you it was impossible. He didn't turn his neck once. He didn't give me a chance.'

'Impossible?'

'Yes, Em. Impossible.'

'Nat, you're tired.'

'I tell you it was impossible.'

'Nothing's impossible. I don't care about the horse, but nothing's impossible.'

'Well, I care about the horse.'

'Oh, don't go on so, Nat. Don't let it get you down. We've got too much to be upset about a thing like that. I don't care about the horse, really.'

'All right,' Nat was almost shouting at her from the window, 'forget it. But don't forget there are a lot of things beside this ranch of ours, a lot of things we never heard of, a lot of things I bet we couldn't have if we wanted them. I'm not sure we're right thinking we've got too much. I wouldn't be surprised if we really didn't have much at all.'

Emily stared at him for a moment. Then she tightened her mouth and set about preparing supper. Nat stood silently by the window. And they ate without speaking, Nat rising when he had finished and going to the bedroom to lie down on the bed. Washing the dishes, Emily didn't understand what had happened. She could not think what Nat's failure to capture the horse had meant to him. Wearily she looked out at their ranch, almost invisible in the darkness beyond the windows. And then she suddenly smiled, half-yawning, to herself. It was ridiculous. She herself had started Nat's discontent by wanting the horse.

*(From Story)*

# TURISTA

## BY ALBERT J. GUÉRARD

*T*HEY sat side by side against the wall of Sanborn's cocktail lounge, drinking quietly and watching the boy and girl, honeymooners, at the table across the room. It was eight o'clock, and there was no one else in the room. If it hadn't been for the Mexican waiter lounging against the door to the kitchen they might have been back in the States. The boy and girl were Americans, very tanned and in their self-consciousness looking about nineteen.

It was a nice clean bar, Irene thought, and they had been there almost an hour. It was the last day of their trip to Mexico, and they looked at the boy and girl because they were afraid to look at each other.

But she couldn't help sometimes looking into the mirror above the boy and girl, and seeing Frank's hard, white face beside her own — white and angry even though he hadn't shaved for two days, and the black stubble ran from his ears to his chin in a thickening line. She couldn't help looking up every time he took some of the ice with his Scotch and cracked it between his teeth. Every time she heard the crunching sound of the ice she wanted to scream. But there wasn't much she could do about that. She sipped her daiquiri and tried to get the picture, the sharp focused image, out of her mind.

'You're being unreasonable,' he said. And again she enjoyed the pleading, the almost helplessness in his voice.

She didn't answer.

125

'Please, dear. I don't want to have to make a scene.'

She laughed, feeling a little drunk. For a moment she turned to him, seeing the new, the different face. 'That's good! That's really good. You don't want to have to make a scene! I should think they were your specialty by now.'

He looked down into his glass. 'I haven't needed you very often. Why do you have to pick tonight of all nights to get your back up?'

She looked at the boy and girl across the room. They were whispering.

'I've told you a dozen times, Frank. I'm simply not going on to Laredo tonight. I've been getting things for other people all over Mexico. I want to go around for myself tomorrow — get some things for myself.'

He grunted, and beckoned to the waiter. 'Haven't you got gypped enough already? All that Shalimar that turned out to be colored water. And those phony antiques. *Camero* — one more Scotch and soda. Not plain water. Soda.' He gesticulated in explanation. *'Agua de Tehucan.'*

'That's not soda water,' she said, watching the waiter go away with the glass. 'It's mineral water.'

'Well, he'll see I don't want plain water anyhow. I don't intend to get typhoid the last day with their filthy water. And listen, Irene, you can get all that stuff — bracelets and so forth — in San Antonio. At least you'd know what you're getting.'

The phrase stuck in her mind. *At least you'd know what you're getting.* She looked at the little blonde girl across the room, and she wanted to say, *And what are you getting?*

'Well, Frank,' she said quietly. 'It was you that wanted to get to Monterey so you could go to Sanborn's for dinner. And have an air-conditioned room for tonight. And here we are.'

'Oh, God!'

'They'll hear you,' she said. 'You'll corrupt the young.'

He fumbled with a package of cigarettes, almost tore it open.

'All right,' he said. 'Lay it on. I suppose I deserve it.

Only can't you please give me hell when we get to Laredo?
It's only two hours.'

'I'm not giving you hell. I just want to stay and buy myself
a couple of bracelets in the morning.'

The waiter returned before Frank could say anything else.
He was carrying a tray with two glasses, one filled and the
other empty, and a bottle of mineral water. Before they
could stop him, he had poured the bottle of mineral water
into the empty glass.

'Damn! I knew it! I knew this would happen.' He handed
the glass of mineral water back to the waiter. 'I don't want
that. I wanted Scotch and soda. *Soda!*'

The waiter looked baffled. He held the glass in his hand.
'*Agua de Tehucan,*' he explained.

'*Quiero* Scotch and soda,' Frank insisted. '*Scotch con
Agua de Tehucan. Mixado.*'

The waiter looked at her for help.

'It's all right,' she said. 'I'll drink it.'

'But damn it, Irene, it isn't all right. I can't drink their
water.'

'All right,' she said. 'I think it's got soda anyway.' She
tasted the drink. 'It's Scotch and soda.' She smiled at the
waiter. '*Buen. Gracias.*'

The waiter walked away shaking his head.

'I don't see why we've got to just sit back and take it,'
Frank said. 'I don't see why we've got to pay for a bottle of
mineral water we don't want.'

'You can afford it.'

'That's not the point. It's the principle of the thing.'

'Ah,' she said. 'Principle! Isn't that the word you
used . . .'

'Just because we're tourists, we don't have to take anything.'

She laughed and took another drink. 'Tourists. *Turista!*
I'd almost forgotten the little red sticker on the car.' She
turned in time to see him wince when she mentioned the car.
Anyway, he was feeling it. '*Turista!* Purpose of visit: *Recreo.*
And what have we recreated? Or are we the ones who were
supposed to be recreated?'

'Stop it, Irene!' His voice lashed at her. Then he ran his hands through his hair, and she noticed that the gray hairs seemed thinner than the others. Well, he looked his forty-five now. When he spoke again, it was almost as though he had got down on his knees, there was such a change in his tone. 'I'm sorry, darling. But when we're in trouble. When we're really in trouble . . .'

'*You* were driving. Remember that, dear!'

'All right. All right.'

'Don't forget that, Frank.'

'But if only you hadn't insisted on our driving down. We'd have been so much more comfortable in the train, anyway. And we'd have saved on rubber.'

'Oh,' she said. 'So that's where I come in. So that's my part of it.'

He was so angry that he could hardly get the glass to his mouth. But he was trying not to show it. 'I'm not blaming you for anything,' he said. 'I've just got to get out of here. And now you get your back up and want to stay over because of a damned bracelet.'

'It isn't just a bracelet,' she said quietly.

'Well, what is it? I'll get you anything you want in San Antonio. What is it you want?'

She looked across at the boy and girl and said, 'It isn't anything you can buy me in San Antonio. Or anywhere else.'

'Don't be dramatic,' he said. 'Two daiquiris and you go soft.'

'I'm not much older than she. Maybe five years older.'

'Older than who?'

'That girl over there.'

'So what?' Frank said. 'You're a damn sight better looking. But listen, Irene, where's all this getting us?'

'Getting us?' She stood up quickly, feeling that she couldn't stand talking any more. She had to be outside, in the dark. And where was it getting her? In the end she'd give in, as she always did. They'd go on to Laredo tonight. 'I'll go out and look for a bracelet now. If I find one tonight I guess we can go.'

He stood up and signaled to the waiter.

'No,' she said, and even as she said it she realized it was the first time in their three years she'd ever told him what to do. 'You stay here. I'm going out by myself.'

'But it's late, dear. You shouldn't go out alone.'

'Well,' and she looked straight into his gray eyes. 'Well, I'm going to.'

Outside it had turned cold. And she stood for a moment in the doorway, wondering — from three years' habit — whether she shouldn't go back for her coat. That's what Frank would want her to do. He had protected her so carefully during their two weeks in Mexico: from heat and cold, from the germs of the market places she had foolishly wanted to visit, from bad food and bad water and bad hotels. They had left the bullfight at the first sign of a cloud; they had scrupulously avoided Acapulco, with its blazing, dangerous sun. Nothing must happen to her, she reflected bitterly. She was his possession, his young and pretty wife.

She started up the street toward the Cathedral Plaza, without her coat, a little surprised not to find herself surrounded by the troop of boy guides and peddlers who had followed them from the car. Then she began to pick them out of the darkness: the slim shadows congregated in the doorways watching her — unmoving, hostile, and suspicious. They stood in twos and threes, and stopped their whispering as she passed, until in the street's darkness it seemed the sharp clicking of her heels had blotted out all the city sounds: the wheezy music from the Plaza bandstand and the rumble of traffic as well as the chattering boys. The little innocents, she thought. They were afraid of her, of *her* even though she was now alone. She walked a little faster in her embarrassment, thinking of how Frank had turned angrily upon them, that troop of squirming laughing boys, and shouted that single word. She wanted to gather them up in her arms, all of them; ask their forgiveness, bring back those soft cries, those brown, friendly smiles.

At the corner across from the Gran Ancira — the hotel

they had driven so madly to reach — an old legless man sat against the wall holding a basket of flowers where his legs should have been. She opened her pocketbook and fished for a peso, wondering whether to pin the gardenia on her dress or tuck it in her hair. Perhaps when the boys saw her buy a flower . . . she looked hungrily at the clusters of gardenias, knowing she wouldn't dare buy any, because of the germs — like all those dangerous wonderful pulpy fruits she had not been allowed to taste: the lush bright yellow mangoes and papayas, the tiny platanito bananas, the guavas and red Ciruela plums. And how she had wanted to press those roadside clusters of flowers to her face that morning, when everything was bright and fresh after the early rain; before the accident. She threw the peso into the basket, and when she saw the old man's wrinkled blind face turn up to her, in the half-darkness, she remembered what Frank had said about their indifference to death. If they held on like this . . .

And as she walked she thought of the ritual of death, the formulas of courted dangers. Was it indifference to death, or rather the very opposite, fear of death in the blood, which had evolved the elaborate sacrifice of the bullfight? The bull, so full of energy and pulsing life, brought face to face with unknown enemies, with a final unknown lover who would kill him at last; or even the twisting, dainty matador permitting the great animal to graze him closer and still closer with every dodge and turn. She had understood little, but at least she had seen with how much ceremony and form they honored the coming of death.

Far above a bell began to ring out the hour. Nine o'clock! She came to herself with a start, thinking of Frank sitting at the bar back at Sanborn's, desperately afraid. Poor Frank! Now that they were driving more slowly it would be midnight before they reached the border, even if they left right away. And every minute more added to the chance of arrest, of someone's checking up on the few cars that had gone through that day and understanding enough to phone to the customs at Laredo. And to be perfectly honest, wasn't that what she really wanted? Wasn't that the only thing that could drive away the ever-returning image, keep it out of the way, blot the hard fixed picture from her mind?

She sat down on one of the benches near the bandstand and watched the conductor wave to the players. What she had to know was whether she might not, if she had been in Frank's place, have done the same thing. It had all happened so suddenly, and could she hold him responsible for a mere reflex action, for a wrong choice where there was no time for choice at all? The sharp, unexpected turn in the road, the violent side sweep of the car as the brakes shrieked; and the sudden bewildering immobility of the green lush jungle, with only the gentlest aftersway of the car to tell them that there had ever been any motion there. Where coolness had rushed by and through them with the swiftly changing forest there had been suddenly no air at all: only an absolute and blanketing heat that left them staring and exhausted, seemingly not breathing at all. Then, behind their turned and straining backs, the sound that had set them in motion again, that had driven Frank to smash the car back in gear and shoot ahead: detection! out of the incredible silence, the regular *pit-pit, pat-pat, pit-pit, pat-pat* of a galloping horse. And moments later, a half mile down the road, the horse itself and its startled rider reining in to watch them speed by. Once they had passed the horse and rider, of course, there was no question of turning back — not for Frank at least. She saw again, as though they were back in the car now, the white ridge of his knuckles as he held the steering wheel until she thought it would crack under his hands. He had driven ahead for sixty miles without once relaxing, without lifting his eyes from the road, or saying a single word.

But that was ten hours ago. And now, she thought, he's sitting back there in the cocktail lounge. And he's not so sure, now.

The boy and the girl were still sitting across the room, so Frank and Irene had to whisper. Irene was glad it was that way. She watched Frank's face in the mirror as she talked, and it had turned soft. There was nothing left of that hard, controlled angry poise, and seeing his disordered features and the thin hair matted and tangled where he had run his hands through it, she understood how she once could have loved him. But that was three years ago. She took a quick sip from her glass and went on, 'It might as well be now as later,' she said. 'It had to happen sometime.'

'Why? We've got on all right. As well as people do.'

'You don't need me. You never did.'

'It was because of you I was hurrying,' he insisted. 'I wanted you to have a comfortable air-conditioned room to-night. I guess I was wrong. But there's thousands killed every year. Millions, if you take the whole world.'

'It's not just that,' she said. 'But you didn't stop. Or you went right on.'

'I saw he was dead. There was nothing I could do about it.'

'He might not have been,' she said. 'And his family. You could have done something.'

He shrugged his shoulders and took a long drink. 'They don't stay with their families. You know that. He was at least fourteen.'

'You don't know,' she said.

'I'll bet they don't. You see too many of them hanging around by themselves. Shiftless. What kind of a future would a boy like that have?'

'Yes,' she said. 'And Mexicans are indifferent to death, aren't they?'

'All right, Irene, go ahead and lay it on. I just know if we'd stopped there's no telling what might have happened to us. The book says that's a very primitive region. Until the highway went through there wasn't any connection with the rest of Mexico. Savages.'

She found herself smiling — though inside she was thinking of what he had said, that the boy might never have seen an automobile until he was seven or eight.

'Then you could have reported it at Valles. You could still report it here.'

He turned to her and took one of her hands. His own were sweating. 'But he's dead, Irene! He's dead now. It's over. It's something that's happened and I'm sorry as hell for it. But that's no reason to let it wreck our lives.'

'It didn't take today to do it,' she said, looking directly at him. 'But this is as good a time as any.'

'But I want you.' He looked at her with bloodshot eyes. 'I love you, darling. I need you.'

She turned away from him; and the boy and girl seemed much farther from them now. The girl was looking at her watch, and Irene thought: *Oh God — don't let them go!*

'I'm sorry, Frank. But I think it's better this way.'

He looked down at the table, and she could see that his lips were trembling. 'Irene?'

'Yes.'

'I don't know just how to say this, but . . . well, I guess I haven't needed you very much. But something like what happened today sort of takes it out of you. I don't know what's wrong with me.'

She said nothing.

'Please come with me, Irene. You've just got to go. I can't go by myself. I'm afraid.'

'There's nothing I could do.'

'It's just I'm afraid to face them at the customs. By myself, that is. When we get to Laredo you can go home by train.'

'I'm not going home.'

'Or anywhere you like. I'll do anything you say if you'll just stick with me for another three hours. It's only a hundred and fifty miles.'

She looked up to see if he was telling the truth. 'You mean after Laredo . . . there won't be any more?'

'There won't be any more, if that's the way you want it.'

She looked again at the boy and girl across the room, and now the small cocktail lounge seemed enormous, they were so far away. She looked back at Frank's face, trying to find the fear there. And there seemed no further need to whisper.

'All right,' she said. 'I'll go with you. But only as far as Laredo.'

He bent over quickly and kissed her hand. His lips were very dry. 'I'm going to the men's room,' he said. 'I'll be back in a minute. Then let's go.'

She leaned far back against the wall and watched the boy and girl.

But it was fantastic, the clarity of the image after so many hours. She had only to shut her eyes, and there it was: the road scooped white and perfect out of the vast green tangle of dripping trees for a hundred yards, then sharply curving out of sight. A few miles south there was still the gray, gauzy curtain of rain, but above the road the sun blazed down as though nothing had happened. Even the silence of the forest, compact of a thousand tiny sounds — birds chattering and water dripping and insects whirring or rustling — was part of the utter unbelievable placidity of the scene into which, from a speed of seventy miles an hour, they had so abruptly descended. The white and brown figure lying on the road fifty or so yards back was almost irrelevant, merely a white flat strip of cloth beneath a brown face, leaving a miniscule red stain on the road. Then again, as regular as her pulse, the *pit-pat, pat-pat* of a horse galloping on the pavement toward them.

She opened her eyes again, and saw her drink on the glass-topped table in front of her, here at Sanborn's in Monterey — and across the small cocktail lounge the boy and girl surreptitiously sticking their tongues out at each other, very tense and embarrassed, and very much in love. The girl sat stiffly, her hands folded on her lap except when she took a drink. Then for a moment Irene could see the flash of the girl's new rings. Had there ever been a time, even three years ago, when she too had felt just married, and been self-conscious about her rings?

But it was strange how so small an object, the white, flat body with its brown face and its tiny red stain, could imprint forever that placid scene — the green, dripping forest, the hot, intolerant sun, the myriad tiny sounds that added up to a single crushing silence. Even after her third drink, there was no shading of the riotous green, no softening blur of detail. The only change was the momentary coming of other images she thought she had forgotten: particularly the sight on their way down of as many as a hundred buzzards congregated on the side of the road and waiting in the trees, remarkably still and unafraid as a lean brown dog paddled through them toward the bushes where their dead quarry lay. And the old woman climbing toward them up the pyramid at Teotihuacán, wrinkled, with her basket of masks and jade. There were others and these. But always, perhaps every thirty seconds and whenever she closed her eyes, the dead unmoving body, the green forest, and the white perfect road. The three daiquiris really hadn't done any good at all.

Across the room the boy and girl were talking louder now, and she listened to them discuss whether they would go to Saltillo tomorrow, or on toward Mexico City. And she tried to imagine them arriving in one after another of the little towns she had seen along the Pan-American Highway, irresponsible and without plans, not knowing where they would stay. She imagined them in an old battered Ford, dusty and laughing, trying first the tourist courts and then the cheaper hotels, driving slowly and curiously along the main street with half a dozen Mexican boys on the running board to shout advice. There had been none of that for them. The American Express had arranged everything. But these two! The boy's open collar and dirty saddle shoes, the girl's bobby socks and beer jacket, told her what kind of a time they would have.

Well, she had had her trip too. And if she hadn't left Frank when he was strong, she couldn't leave him now. It would almost be cheating herself to leave him when now for the first time since their marriage he had asked her for something. Those other times on the trip, there had been nothing she could do: when he had raged up and down the Avenida Francisco Madero because the American Express office was closed from one-thirty to four or when, in Taxco, they had been given a room without a view. She had merely stood aside, embarrassed, superfluous. But tonight, for the first time, he was not angry but afraid. He might even be sick. He had been gone for more than ten minutes.

But the boy, sitting across the room, in his white ducks! Wasn't it just the inescapable whiteness of the Mexican boy lying on the hot pavement, under the startling noonday sun? The dark brown face and the white, white trousers. If they had even picked him up and thrown him into the wild overgrowth of the roadside, where only the buzzards and the lean wary dog could find him! As it was, he would still be lying on the flat highway, even though so many hours had passed. She could not visualize him anywhere else. They may have picked him up, of course, put him in some kind of room, prepared him for burial even. But she had to see that stretch of road for herself. Until she did, he would lie there in his white trousers, a fixed, permanent image, an imperishable white stain.

Poor Frank, she thought. He too would see it like that, always. Poor Frank, with his firm granite face now sagging and uncomposed, sick with fear. She signaled to the waiter to bring another drink.

She heard the door to the kitchen open and looked up, expecting to see the waiter with her drink. But it was Frank, holding out his hands to her. It was no wonder that he had been away so long. She had time, in the moments before she made up her mind, to notice everything. He had combed his hair to hide the thin strands of gray: it was now sleekly black and immaculately in place. The blue handkerchief which matched his silk tie perked jauntily from his breast pocket. Even his shirt, which had rumpled from the heat of the day, was smooth and his shoes glistened in the electric glare. He might have been leaving for a board meeting, she thought, so well did his tailored smile fit in with everything else. He stood above her, smiling down; confident, strong, and tall. 'Are you ready, dear?'

She could say nothing. She motioned to the seat beside her; he frowned slightly and sat down.

'Hadn't we better leave, Irene? It's getting on ten o'clock.'

'I ordered a drink,' she said. 'It'll be here in a minute.'

He took out a cigarette and lit it carefully. For a few seconds he held the lit match and watched it burn toward his fingers. The flame scarcely wavered at all. Then, with a single, accurate flick of his index finger, he put it out.

'Do you think you ought to? You've had three already.'

She looked toward the door to the kitchen. 'Everything will be all right now, won't it?' Could this ironic tone, once so deliberate and difficult, have become natural to her now?

'Of course!'

'I'm glad,' she said at once. 'You needn't wait for me. I'll pay for my drink.'

'Don't be silly. Of course I'll wait.'

'You don't understand. I'm not going with you.'

She heard the table legs scratch on the tile floor. But she turned to see him still sitting there, smiling again, indulgent. She had to look at him, take it that hardest way.

'I mean it,' she said. 'You don't need me. You're all right now.'

His smile was still infinitely patient. 'You ought to grow up, Irene. You're just wasting time.'

'I know. That's what I'm good for.'

'All right,' he said. 'But let's go, dear.' There was the slightest menace in his voice, and she remembered the boys scattering into the darkness after he had shouted at them.

'But don't you see, Frank? I'm not afraid of you. I'm not afraid of you any more.'

'What a thing to say! Why should you be afraid of me? Listen, Irene — I've been very patient.'

'Yes,' she said. 'All things considered, very. But I'm the one that's being patient now.'

'It's nearly ten o'clock. You said you'd go as far as Laredo with me. You said.'

'I know I said it. But I've changed my mind. I'm not going.'

She was sorry she had to slap him. It wasn't any way to end things, and the waiter — who had just come through the kitchen door with her drink — stood in a corner of the room, embarrassed. Even the boy and girl were leaving, though they had pretended not to see. She stared at her drink on the little table and told herself that at least it hadn't been anger. She had slapped him deliberately and accurately, because it was the only way to make him go.

The boy and the girl paid for their drinks and went out without looking back. Then she saw the waiter coming toward her, not smiling at all, and she reached for her drink.

'I am sorry, Madame. I must close the lounge.'

'Yes,' she said. 'Just a minute.'

'It is nearly ten o'clock.' The waiter turned away.

'Please,' she said. 'I am very sorry.'

'It is all right. It is not yet ten.'

'No. I mean I'm sorry that this happened. I did not want to make a scene.' She spoke very slowly, so he would understand.

'It is nothing, Madame.'

'But it is embarrassing for you. It is not good for the reputation of the lounge. But I would like you to understand that this was necessary.'

'Yes,' he said. 'There is no need. Madame does not need to explain.'

'Thank you. He won't be coming back.'

The waiter studied his fingernails.

'We all have our quarrels. *Esta la vida!* I am sure the Señor . . .'

'No,' she said. 'He is going back to America. To Laredo.' She handed him a ten-peso bill. 'Please keep it. And I hope you understand. I am very sorry.'

Then she was walking, a little stiffly, feeling the drinks for the first time. *I suppose he'll be waiting for me,* she thought, *I suppose he'll be out in the car.* But when she got out to the street, the car was gone.

And there again were the darker shadows of the little boys. A car drove by noisily — an old Ford coupé — and she knew it was the American boy and girl. 'Goot-by!' several of the little boys called as they passed. She stood in the doorway to

Sanborn's, wondering which way she should go, and she could still hear the chug-chug of the old Ford, far down the street. Then, to her surprise, she heard herself say aloud, 'I want to buy a bracelet.'

For perhaps a minute none of the shadows moved. Then, as though he had come from nowhere, a very small Mexican boy with what looked like a large bag of marbles was standing in front of her. He said nothing, and he looked very frightened. He might have been six.

She knelt down on the pavement so the boy's face was level with her own, and she tried to smile. But she felt the tears coming, and it was hard to hold on. She pointed to the bag in the boy's hand.

'What have you got in that bag?' she asked. The boy moved a little nearer. But he was still afraid. 'Please,' he said, looking at the wall behind her. 'You want rings?'

'Yes,' she said. She held out her hands to him, and saw her own rings twinkle faintly in the light from the doorway. 'Yes, I want to buy your rings. All of them.'

He stared at her.

'Look!' she said, and she pulled off first her large engagement ring and then her thin platinum wedding ring. 'Look,' and she put her rings in her pocketbook. 'I need some new rings.'

'*Non entien*,' the little boy said.

She looked at the circle of faces to see if anyone understood, but the boys only stared back at her. Then she smiled, and very gently took the little bag out of the boy's hand. Something in this moment seemed so familiar to her that she held the bag in her hand without opening it, puzzled. Then she remembered how, ten or twelve years before, she alone of all the girls in the school had dared to play marbles with the boys.

She looked around at the semicircle of boys, and several of them had begun to smile. She opened the little bag and emptied it onto the sidewalk. There were two ivory crucifixes, a little round mirror, a brooch in the figure of a bird, and three jade rings. She picked them up and examined them one by one.

'You want rings?' the boy said. *'Cincuenta centavos.'*

'Oh yes!' she said. 'I do want them. I'll buy them all.'

She reached into her pocketbook and took out two ten-peso bills, and handed them to the little boy.

'For them all!' she said, and began to put the rings and crucifixes into her pocketbook. It was only then that all the boys began chattering at once. She took the largest ring and slipped it on her third finger.

*'Gracias!'* she said. *'Muchas gracias!'*

The next thing she knew she was standing up, and it was as though not ten but a hundred boys were tugging at her arms, trying to sell her things. *They think I'm crazy,* she thought. *But let them think it.* Wherever she moved she touched a bag of trinkets or a basket, and now the tears were really coming fast. And when she felt a bouquet of gardenias thrust into her hand she could hold back no longer. She took the flowers and crushed them against her mouth, felt the fine, thin leaves bruising against her lips and on her tongue; pressed them closer and closer until she could smell them everywhere, and the deep living smell was running through her, through her heart. 'Oh yes!' she heard herself crying. 'Oh yes! Everything! I want everything now!'

*(From The Sewanee Review)*

# THE GOLDEN STALLION

## BY ELIZABETH HARDWICK

*MARTHA FISKE* met the young soldier at a party. There were several other soldiers present, but he was the only one she noticed. He was about six feet tall and had the gracefully heavy body of an athlete. His face was large and handsome with prominent, well-shaped features, but his mouth and eyes were curiously small. Perhaps it was the remarkable alertness of those small eyes that made him look like a wicked little urchin. A narrow, white scar was just barely visible on his cheek. At first she couldn't identify the special quality that drew her to him. And then he smiled and she knew. His smile was tender and childlike and made him appear momentarily helpless. This smile — it was hardly more than a downward twisting of his mouth — had the effect of an apology, as if he meant to say that though he might be good looking and confident there was an inviolable delicacy in him. The young soldier quickly became the center of attention. Perhaps this was natural since he was sitting in the middle of the room, but she didn't think it such an accident as that. To her he assumed authority because he was a specimen of manhood far removed from the husbands who were telling stories heard many times before and exhibiting the limitations of their interests. He was also unlike his fellow soldiers. They were rawboned, commonplace boys who seemed extremely uncomfortable and kept saying, 'Thank you, Ma'm,' at every turn. The handsome soldier ingeniously disowned any possible connection with

141

the other boys and never acknowledged, by a reference to the army, their common identity. In thus cutting himself off from his comrades, he also repudiated the generosity of the hospitable civilians. He seemed to accept his presence at the party as a natural tribute to his personality, rather than his soldier status.

She watched him all through the evening and noted that he did not get drunk and that his moods alternated between boredom of a tolerant, not unpleasant, sort and amusement which was, she felt, a bit patronizing. He said nothing about himself, at least not where he was from, what he had been or hoped to be. It is true he was asked, but he simply did not bother to answer. And yet, for all his lack of interest, she noticed he became distressed when the conversation lagged and it was always he who started it again. At such times he would look down at his glass, cough, as if to get attention, and then say, 'Are the autumns in Kentucky always cool?' She observed he was not the least interested in the question. He looked away, in the manner of a faithful servant who had performed an expected duty and could now retire, when the men started to give comparative figures on cold and hot spells and to mention frozen pipes or prolonged summer droughts. He would then be silent and withdrawn until the next break in the conversation provided the opportunity to pay some-one a casual compliment. The compliments, also, were pre-sented as an obligation to some mysterious source.

Only once did Martha Fiske speak directly to the soldier, because she was both shy and aloof and did not talk much except with those seated next to her. When she was with more than one person she hardly spoke above a whisper and, though she was exceedingly civil and much given to sympa-thetic inquiries about the health and happiness of her friends, she knew her conversation lacked animation because of her reticence about her own affairs. From the first, the soldier's talent for asking the question most likely to appeal to the listeners had interested her. She put it down as an instinctive affability not unlike her own automatic courtesy. The soldier abruptly left his chair and went to the window. He stood there for some time in silence, as if he were absorbed in the view. Immediately she saw the paradox of his body that was similar to the strength and weakness of his face. Though he was strong, his movements were slow and deliberate. It was not that he appeared physically weak, but that he seemed to be burdened with an inner fatigue that was at once elegant and rather absurd. The guests were visibly startled when he suddenly said, 'I've been lots of places and a new town is like a new person to me. There are certain hidden qualities that give a place its meaning. Just like a person.' He paused and everyone stared at him. What other young man would have the daring to speak as he did? He spoke as an actor, more or less formally, without joking, mumbling or qualifying. 'There is always some symbol, if you have the sort of mind that likes those things. I mean something that will recall the town. Even *here* there must be a distinctive thing.' He hadn't a definite accent, but one would have guessed from the general nature of his behavior that he came from a large city. It occurred to Martha Fiske — she felt herself a bit more understanding of odd young men than the others — that he might be thoroughly artificial. She didn't object. On the contrary, it gave his personality a gloss she admired.

The men seemed particularly embarrassed by his question and for a moment no one attempted an answer. Then she, from the comparative isolation of the corner in which she was sitting, said, 'There is a golden stallion weather vane on top of the courthouse.'

The soldier stretched and yawned before he actually turned to look at her. 'I beg your pardon?' he said, though she felt certain he had understood her. He moved away from the window and again took the chair in the middle of the room. Martha Fiske knew he was looking at her and she allowed herself the briefest glance at his face. At first she saw only that stubbornly maintained composure which distinguished him, but, as she continued to stare at him, she noticed that his lips trembled slightly.

'A golden stallion,' he said, after forcing her to repeat. And then he laughed and turned his head around the room so that he brought everyone into his amusement. 'Perhaps that's it.' His laughter was nothing more than a few staccato grunts and there was not a trace of mirth in it. Again she looked up at him in her guarded way. Their eyes met and an odd feeling came over her. She believed he had tried to give her some personal attention he had denied the others.

He seemed distracted and annoyed when someone said, 'Martha knows everything of that sort. She knows all about antiques and the names of historical places. If it's a symbol you want, she can give it to you.'

'I wasn't thinking of historical symbols,' he replied, 'but something a bit less traditional. However, the golden stallion will do very well.' He put his hand over his eyes and sighed very deeply. He was taller and stronger than anyone else in the room, and yet when he sighed there was a general flash of self-conscious laughter meant to reprimand him for the pose he had assumed. He made no response to the laughter and it vanished.

She found, later, that she was not clear about the rest of the evening. The conversation with the soldier had changed her from an observer to a participant in the party and this, because of her spontaneous interest in him, put her under a strain. The only thing she was certain of was that something had been established on this night. His head inclined in her direction when he spoke and when he was silent his eyes were fastened upon her face. In her usual way, she left just as the evening reached its peak. Though there was no particular reason for her departure, she, too, had her eccentricities and being the first to leave a party was a convention of her behavior. She was aware there was something planned in the act beyond the mere fatigue of social life. It was, she supposed, one of the tiny, harmless ways in which she sought to distinguish herself and had, no doubt, been inherited from her father who had said that in order not to be a mediocrity one had either to arrive places late or to leave them early. Also she had developed a certain technique for getting away with the least confusion. She merely slipped behind the circle of chairs, disappeared into the bedroom and then, al-

most on tiptoe and with her head down, came back to wave
a vague and apologetic good night to her friends. Her way
was so shy that people instinctively let her get away without
the usual chatter. She was at the door before the hostess had
time to reach her. To her surprise the soldier was standing
beside her in the half-darkness of the hall.

'Good night,' she said.

She watched him for a moment. He was standing very
close to her. And there it was — that way he had of pleading
with her without saying a word. Already she was thinking
of their exceedingly good possibilities for friendship. He
continued to look at her and she felt obliged to give him
some evidence of her feeling. She said, 'I live very close to
the college where you are stationed. Right across the street,
in fact.'

'I know,' he said, quite softly. 'I know.'

His hand had fallen on her sleeve and she, from timidity,
drew away. Still he said nothing, though there was the suggestion of impatience in his silence. 'Will you come over
sometime? Will you?' she said.

He smiled and nodded.

She started down the steps and was almost to the street
when she heard him, as if he were laughing, call to her,
'What is your name?'

'Martha Fiske,' she answered.

'Mrs.?' he asked.

She stopped and turned around. However, there was no
need for her to answer, because the door of the house had
closed and she could no longer see the soldier.

Martha Fiske did not sleep well that night. She was disturbed by her thoughts of the soldier. It was not that she
feared she had been too eager in her invitation. (She had
long ago realized that a quiet, timid life gave one all sorts
of privileges.) It did not matter that she might have been
overheard and, since she was a married woman living alone,
reproved for entertaining male visitors. Actually she was
blessed with an extraordinary independence. She had always

lived in her own way and the fact that this way was undramatic was merely the accident of her nature. Had she had emotions of another sort, those, too, would have been expressed without fear. In thinking of the soldier she concluded that she liked him because he was similar to the other young men who had come, too late, into her life and who were the only people she had ever truly cared for. Indeed he was not, as the others had been, somewhat girlish, but he shared with them an indefinable singularity. She was almost thirty — it occurred to her the soldier might be older than she, but for some perverse reason she liked to think him younger — and had not discovered until a few years ago that there were men with whom she could have both security and excitement. Her youth had been as normal as possible for a shy, almost taciturn girl. Her mother had once told her she was not hearty enough for most men's taste and she readily admitted her difficulty in overcoming that period of semi-formality that precluded even the most superficial intimacy. Yet, she had had many friends and there had always been men who were, in an unspecified way, her suitors. As a rule these men were themselves fainthearted and unequal to the rigors of romance, but they seemed to find her a pleasant and acceptable companion. And, as she had expected, she had married one of the men for whom she felt neither friendship nor love, but only a high degree of tolerance. She had married a doctor, Robert Fiske, because he had asked her to do so. They had lived together one month before he was called away to the army. He had been gone more than a year now.

The mainstay of her existence was her flair for decorations and her limited knowledge of period architecture, furniture and the like. Though this was largely a hobby, she sometimes accepted money for the selection of frames and drapes or the evaluation of an old piece of furniture some circumspect buyer had discovered on the back porch of a Negro shack. Her interest deepened and she had decided, several years before, to take classes in art appreciation at the College. For the most part this was an unhappy decision. Her life became miserable the moment she stepped into the classroom. She hadn't the slightest notion what was going on, couldn't understand a thing the teacher said or spell more than one out of a dozen names under discussion. She knew hardly a fact about art history except that certain buildings in the town were part of something called the Greek Revival and that Henry Clay's garden had been laid out by L'Enfant. Her pretensions were slight, but this daily reminder of her ignorance threatened to destroy the little confidence she had and so, after a few months, she discontinued the classes and fell back upon her familiarity with corner cupboards, antique glassware, and portraits by the Kentuckian, Jouett. However, her excursion into study bore some fruit in that she made a number of new friends. She was a strikingly handsome woman, tall, with long, almost black, hair which she wore in a severe and rather out-of-date fashion. Her clothes were ordered from New York and were too odd to please the bachelor doctors, lawyers, and tobacco buyers with whom she associated, but they found immediate approval among several of the young male students. Perhaps her face was something like a monkey's, as one of the boys had said, but at the same time there was real distinction in her fine eyebrows and prominent cheek bones. She learned from these young men that she had *style* and, though she maintained her extensive reserve, her heart was deeply touched by their enthusiasm and friendship. It was not long before the young men started to come to her house and even her mother, with whom she had lived until the latter's death, found them interesting and lively. For two or three years Martha Fiske had experienced a sweetness of male companionship that was the most satisfactory thing in her life. The house was frequently noisy with the sounds of records by Beatrice Lillie and Marlene Dietrich and obscurely bawdy songs by night club performers whose names she could not remember. She heard of great stage performances, of public characters who drank or took dope and had fabulous love affairs with other public characters. The boys knew an astonishing number of details about the lives of famous people. She heard a lot about Dorothy Parker, though she could not, to her great distress, remember any of the anecdotes. She was happy to experience the lives of the famous, but that alone would not have given her satisfaction. She liked best to hear the intimate difficulties of her new friends and to brood over their accounts of family dissension. She learned their secret spirit, hurt pride and petulant iconoclasm. Never had she come so close to another person and never had she been so serenely impersonal. Her life was enriched, also, by the boys' ambitions to take singing, dancing or acting lessons and, in those days, her acquaintanceship seemed to be a catalogue of great people to come. But one by one the boys had disappeared, usually with one of her checks in his pocket, either to New York or to the army. She was driven back to her old life and to the friends who seemed now unusually lethargic. Again she felt odd and timid and said yes when Robert Fiske asked her to marry him. Often she thought she would have consented to the proposal of any respectable man, because she believed women should marry and also because she felt her chances for making other friends like the young boys were over.

When her husband went away, she didn't miss him much. Their one month together had been uncomfortable, because he was more or less inhibited by her silence which he took as evidence of an artistic temperament. She was aware her manner made her husband less communicative than he might otherwise have been, but she didn't know how to bring him into her life. Sometimes she dreamed she would get to know him as intimately as she had known the young boys. She hoped he might tell her his fears, angers and ambitions, his memories of childhood. When a certain amount of time had passed without his indicating a need to unburden himself, she decided he was happy and had nothing to say. This conclusion made her, on the contrary, very melancholy because it deprived her of the opportunity to exercise her talent for sympathy. Writing letters to her husband had been, from the first, an almost intolerable burden. She never knew if she had put in enough *dears* or if her desire for his return seemed sincere. When she had, as all decorum demanded, to write 'I love you' her fingers began to quiver. The months passed and she found it impossible to think of him as any-thing except a man who was away and to whom she had to write.

On the morning after the party she felt unusually alert and happy. Though she almost always slept well, she super-stitiously considered the restless night a good omen. She sat at her window and watched the soldiers drilling on the grounds across from her house. The rows of brown uniforms had never before seemed particularly romantic; but, today, with the bright sun covering the field and the flags flying on the building, she found herself thinking of the old-fashioned comic operetta encampments and the rough gaiety of movies about the Foreign Legion. (There was no rôle in these ready-made day dreams she could play, for there was nothing of the ragamuffin, gypsy coquette in her. In all her dreams she remained the same: a dignified, Southern woman who was the sympathetic observer of life's exciting frivolities.) She did not think very much about the soldier, except to regret not having set a definite date for their meeting. How-ever, her way was naturally slow and untroubled and she could let things happen as they would. As usual she went out in the afternoon to attend to shopping and business. When she returned there was a note in her mail box saying the soldier would visit her at eight in the evening. It was signed with the initials, T. J., and she realized she had for-gotten his name. For some minutes she studied his hand-writing. The script was exceedingly large and irregular, like that of a child.

The soldier didn't arrive at eight. The night outside was clear and cool. She was pleased the wind had risen, because it gave her an excuse to make a fire in the grate and that was the domestic duty she most loved. She waited for him, but without impatience. Her mind was beautifully empty and tranquil when she was alone. She gave herself so completely to her solitary dreaming that she was startled when the bell finally rang. It was well past nine o'clock. She did not hurry to answer; instead she stopped and observed, as if the first time, the rather commonplace austerity of her living room. Though she was not often critical of herself or of others, she did in brief moments of tension, such as the arrival of the soldier, experience the wildest and most agonizing sense of personal inferiority. Tonight this fleeting sensation of inadequacy gave her a capricious desire to destroy all the things she had so painstakingly collected. Suddenly she was skeptical of the value of her tables, frames and bird prints. They became the undeniable emblems of her provincialism. The aspect of the soldier she remembered most vividly was his way of making things *small*. Now that she was to see him she felt herself diminished. The town in which she lived shrank and all her possibilities were worthless.

When she opened the door, her first impression was that the man standing before her was a stranger. Of course, she knew the next moment it was the young soldier, but she was unprepared for the change in him. What could it be? A kind of general shabbiness, she decided. When he saw her look at him his expression changed and he managed to recover some of his former self-possession.

'Am I late?' he said, hesitantly.

'Yes, you are,' she answered. She pointed to the living room and he walked past her.

She did not immediately ask him to sit down and he, in some confusion, said, 'I'm sorry. I didn't realize it was so late.' He shrugged his shoulders in a vague gesture of repentance. She was rather annoyed that he should think her angry about the time, because she wasn't at all responsive to the conventions of social behavior. Her curtness came out of her surprise that the soldier had so many personalities. He had only to change his posture to be another human being. One moment he was impressive and the next he was guarded, feeble, second rate. He seemed a little less in every way than she had thought him. The fine color of the personality she had seen the night before had faded. What she saw meant to her that he was, after all, *nobody,* really nothing exceptional. She was glad and it gave her the courage to be open with him. Very quickly she organized her new impressions of his appearance. His hair grew low on his forehead; his face, at times extremely handsome, could also be merely ordinary. At the door he had reminded her of nothing so much as an appealing little beggar who, with cap in hand and eyes downcast, made the most of the pathos and contempt he aroused.

'I have no memory for names,' she said, ignoring his apology. 'Perhaps I didn't hear yours clearly last night.'

'My name is Tony,' he said. 'Tony Jones. It suits me, doesn't it?'

'I don't know,' she said seriously. When he said nothing, she asked him to sit down.

There was, certainly, an initial measure of awkwardness in their meeting. She, however, saw it as only a surface coolness and was surprised that she felt little real discomfort with Tony Jones. Perhaps they could not talk freely, and yet their very lack of crisp, nervous brightness seemed to her a miracle. They had the melancholy ease of friends. The soldier took off his coat and lighted a cigarette. She watched, without any embarrassment at all, this real entrance into her life which was symbolized by his coat on her sofa and the leisurely way he was settling himself for the evening. A wave of excitement came over her when she realized how deeply the image of the soldier had impressed her. It did not matter that the image was as yet blurred. What she had responded to was the man himself, that part of his nature which was naked and unalterable and which she felt mysteriously destined to discover. She knew by instinct theirs was one of those haphazard meetings that must mean something to both, either for evil or for good. The mere fact that she had been very deeply touched by him, without even being sure she liked him, was enough to draw them into some common history, however short.

When they were comfortably seated before the fire, Tony Jones, with the polite incaution that had stamped all their brief conversations, said, 'I like you. I suppose you noticed it.'

'If you do, I'm glad you told me,' she said. No matter what he said, his eyes were always cold. They seemed to belong to another face.

'We don't need to begin in the usual way, then,' he went on. 'I don't see any reason why we shouldn't accept each other from the start.' When she did not comment he added, 'As friends only. You needn't fear anything else.'

The neatness of his speech oppressed her slightly. The flat clarity of his conversation succeeded only in making his character, that which she was extremely anxious to comprehend, more and more obscure. She remembered now something told her at the party: the soldier had been *nowhere,* in the military sense. He was a recent recruit and had, therefore, probably suffered none of the currently possible disasters.

'Do you mind the army very much?' she asked. He lifted his shoulders to indicate it meant nothing one way or another. She had not supposed it would. His absorptions, whatever they were, went far back into his life and could not be displaced by public history. This she also accepted with relief, because she was unskilled in the specific anxieties that war might produce in intricate personalities; and, further, it was additional proof that he was nothing beyond himself, nothing he hadn't always been.

He looked carefully around the room and she thought his eyes stayed for an unnecessarily long time upon a collection of old fans visible through the glass doors of her cupboard. At last he said, 'Well, your house is very nice. If it is necessary to be away from really exciting places, then certainly it isn't too much to ask for a little comfort and ease.'

She didn't know whether or not he meant to compliment her house and, thereby, to show a similarity of taste. Since she had decided he was only a compelling nonentity, it didn't matter much that he seemed to turn her more important preoccupations into casual whimsicalities.

'What exciting places are you missing?' she asked. She took a cigarette from the box on the table and he came to her with a light. His savage little eyes met hers over the flame.

'Lots of places,' he said. He was smiling brightly and turning his head to show the good line of his profile. 'I was silly at the party, wasn't I?' he asked, looking at her attentively. 'I often put on acts. It doesn't do to let everyone get close to you. With people I like, I'm different.' The soldier had very short teeth that were somehow too square and regular. He smoked one cigarette after another and there was always a cloud of smoke around him. For the first time he noticed the portrait of Martha Fiske on the side wall. It had been done when she was in her teens by an itinerant painter who had flourished sketches of the Morgan and Vanderbilt families before the eyes of every prospective customer in the county and had, thereby, got many commissions. The portrait was elegantly sober. The planes in her face had been rejected for a perfectly smooth, oval-shaped countenance and an exquisitely proportioned gloominess of expression that had delighted her mother. Martha Fiske recalled the painter's stories of the great banquets his wealthy patrons had given in appreciation of his work. He was a liar, she thought now. Something in Tony Jones's manner, his way of appraising, made her skeptical. When the soldier had finished with the picture, he went to the desk and took down a volume which her father, at some expense, had had printed. It was titled, *Stories of Our Family*. He flipped through the pages and stopped over photographs of Martha Fiske in the arms of a Negro nurse, her parents in their wedding clothes, and a reproduction of a French menu around which an anecdote, very dear to her father, was told.

He put the book away and sat down again. 'What do you think of me?' she asked.

'Nobody is as typical as you would seem to be,' he said. He was looking at her now with the same unabashed calculation in which he had examined her belongings. When she put her hand, self-consciously, on her forehead, he said, 'What are you afraid of? Don't hide.'

'I'm not hiding,' she said.

She saw now his cautious, despairing smile. 'You want to suffer, don't you?' he said, almost tenderly. He didn't wait for her reply. 'Well, you can't because that's my rôle.'

'Why should you suffer?' she said. Actually she had not been prepared for the obliqueness of his conversation. The young boys to whom she had become attached had been far simpler than this and she had understood them on their own terms.

'I just do,' he said. His voice rose in dramatic enthusiasm and she listened to him, not as if he were telling the truth, but as if he were repeating speeches he had learned for particular occasions. 'There are so many things. Things you don't know about me now and won't know later. You may think I'm well-adjusted and all that, but I'm not. God, if you could only imagine what life is for some people. You think you worry and suffer and conceal, don't you?' He had moved closer to her and she wanted to draw away until she noticed he was totally preoccupied with the contemplation of his marvelously diversified self. 'You don't wake up not wanting to live, do you?' he insisted.

'No, I suppose I don't,' she said.

He nodded impatiently. 'You will never know, I hope, what it is to feel that your whole life has been a mistake that can never be rectified. Have you had such an experience?'

She was, for all practical purposes, incapable of thought about general attitudes. If he had spoken to her of a particular, even a dreadful, event, she might have been able to make it a part of herself and to give him her peculiarly somber compassion; but here in this room which was, to her, a warm, golden rectangle of security she found it impossible to think of his diffuse sorrows. Instead she was listening to the familiar sounds of her life: the crackling of the coals as they broke apart and the fearful screams of a cat who had roamed into her yard.

'You didn't answer me,' Tony Jones said. 'You aren't always uneasy like I am, are you?'

'I can't say. I'm not sure I know what you mean,' she said at last. She had not been looking at him and when she did turn his way she was puzzled to see how calm he was, how boyishly relaxed by his own thoughts.

'What mistakes have you made?' she said. He smiled in an impudent way she didn't like. 'Tell me,' she said, rather imperiously.

He looked down at the carpet and, with those unmotivated variations in mood she had noticed before, seemed to withdraw from her. 'Not so fast, Mrs. Fiske. Not so fast,' he said.

'I'm sorry,' she said.

'Sorry?' The word seemed to please him, for he brushed his hand lightly over hers.

They fell into a lengthy silence which pleased her by providing the opportunity for further impressions of him. His hands, she saw, were short and tough and his fingers had the efficient strength of a workman's. And yet these same fingers could tremble furiously in evidence that his physical strength was often assaulted and nullified by his delicate nervous system. Though he made no effort to talk, she believed silence tormented him. He could be as motionless as an icon and yet betray a need that the world around him be active. After a time he took a sheaf of papers out of his pocket. There were letters, cards, snapshots, an address book and the usual loose scraps of paper. He turned each item over slowly, at times scowling and again smiling in what seemed to be the memory of the contents. Here, evidently, were the numerous odds and ends of his private life. Here were the remnants of the wandering he had done and the places to which he might return. He stacked the papers neatly and put them back in his pocket. 'Have you a telephone, Mrs. Fiske?' he asked.

'My name is Martha,' she said, not looking at him.

'Have you a telephone?' he repeated. She pointed to the hall and he got up without a word of explanation. His voice was loud enough when he requested the number, but during his conversation nothing was audible to her except his occasional effort to laugh. She did not wish to overhear him; in fact, a kind of numbness had come over her. She went to the bedroom to get the fringed, pink shawl she sometimes wore in the house and when she returned he was waiting for her.

'You are very nice,' he said brightly. 'If only all of us had the sense to confine ourselves to nice people. And you are very good looking, even if you don't show yourself off enough. You must consider yourself a beautiful, desirable woman. It will make you more confident.' He threw himself into this speech with the zeal of a hopeful salesman.

Who are you and how and where were you given form? she longed to ask. She was fiercely eager to invade the grave in which he had willfully buried himself and to disinter what she believed was a pathetically anguished heart. She wondered why she felt obliged to check herself. Why? Because she believed he would lie to her if she asked him for the kind of information she cherished. Instead she was cold to him and said reproachfully, 'Do you consider yourself a handsome man?'

'I guess so,' he answered quickly. 'But to make you feel better I'll admit I'm not always certain.' There was a mirror over the mantel and he, as if to annoy her, got up to look at his reflection. When he turned around again, he gave her his short-lipped, abbreviated smile and said, 'What do you think I'll look like when I'm older? I often worry about it. Thank God, my hair is thick!'

To her surprise, she saw that he was not altogether jesting. He waited for her response. 'You will always be handsome,' she said. She did not care what he was, apparently, vain, mendacious and counterfeit. These matters were outside her interest; she sought something in him not above the traits he had revealed, but below them. She sought the open wound which gave off the poisons.

Again he drew the packet of letters and papers out of his pocket. Perhaps he was not interested in them, she thought, and only wished to make himself seem important. 'Do you write so much?' she said, hesitantly.

'God no! I never write. People write to me. Lots of people.'

'Does that make you proud?' she asked. A trace of anger had defiled her usually indifferent manner.

'Not at all,' he said, dryly. 'It's just a fact. People like me and I can't believe that's wrong. You are probably afraid people won't love you, but I happen to be afraid they will care too much. I have a fear of being loved, yet I can't disregard affection. Whenever I have it I hold on to it, because I'm not sure it will come again.'

'I thought you didn't want it,' she said.

'I want it in general. It's only in particular instances that it begins to suffocate me.'

She took in his words one by one, as if there were no connection between them. Her mind was powerfully obstinate and she could sit there with an orderly and discreet smile on her lips even though she could not assimilate these fragments of his soul. As she listened to him, she thought that if he had any judgment at all it was only an animal shrewdness acquired for protection. She knew herself to be uninformed and at times she was aware of the large amount of indolence that constituted the very core of her nature; but she was without fear and, therefore, was quick to recognize it in others.

Tony Jones was now speaking very softly. By an act of will he seemed to be able to throw himself into a gentle hypnosis and to linger there in a submissive dream. 'Do you know what I want more than anything in the world?' he said. 'I want to love someone. That's all I ask . . . to fall in love.'

'To fall in love? That shouldn't be difficult.' She spoke in an unemphatic whisper for she, too, had fallen under a spell, the wonderful hallucination their meeting had been from the first moment.

Her answer seemed to distract him. 'Perhaps it is easy for you, but that lack is the greatest terror of my life. It won't happen to me. Can't happen, ever.' His voice broke at the end of the sentence. And then he did a very strange thing. His eyes filled with tears and he began quite suddenly to sob. She had never before heard a cry like it. It was a dry, fretful whimper such as a child might make in a disturbed sleep.

'Tony . . .' she said helplessly. She could not bring herself to touch him. She could only repeat his name over and over, 'Tony Jones. . . . Tony Jones. . . .' He buried his face in his hands and, after a moment, the sobs disappeared. He did not look at her and remained so still she could hardly hear his breathing.

'What do you want to tell me?' she asked, unable to bear the terrible quiet that followed his crying. During their silences he seemed to be alone in the world; he was that orphan she had adopted the first time she saw him smile.

Finally he said, 'Would you believe I cry often? It may not seem like me, but I've always done it. Naturally, I would never reveal this to anyone except you.'

She thought of the warm purity of his dark skin and the strong line of his jaw. She kept looking at him and he seemed to find solace in her presence, because he began to talk about himself. In a way that was at once halting and eager, he told her that he was the son of a Detroit factory worker, a tired, simple-minded man. His life had been lived in the shadow of The Company for which his father, brothers, aunts, uncles and neighbors worked. He spoke cautiously of his mother and said that she had given herself to God with the same ferocity in which the others offered themselves up to the factory. Her days and nights were a furious tirade against dancing, picture shows and card playing. She was delicate, thin and angry from too much feeling, and he remembered best her light brown hair that fell to her waist — she didn't believe in cutting it — and the pale softness of her skin. When asked he admitted that he never wrote to her, even though he always wanted to do so. It seemed that his real break with his home dated from his meeting with a red-haired German jeweler who had extensive connections in a more cultivated and fastidious society. He hated this man passionately and could not think of him without anger. Tony Jones left home to live in Chicago, New York and St. Louis where, as he said vaguely, he had friends.

Where were those parents? Martha Fiske wondered. In

some little, grey box of a house upon which the sun shone all day long without relief? And where was the red-haired man with the rings and silver bracelets, the man who stood behind the glass counters and brushed the dust from the velvet mats? She, by comparison with Tony Jones, had experienced nothing. Her greatest awareness — it had persisted until her middle twenties — had been of her parents rather than herself. She had been only the daughter of a man and woman whose character freed her from the obligation to develop personality. If she told anecdotes about her youth, they concerned something her parents did or said, or their parents before them. Tony Jones's childhood seemed utterly incomprehensible to her.

At last he had consumed the random crumbs of his life. (That was the way it worked for him. He gave out nothing; instead he let her watch him devour himself.) He said, sheepishly, 'You like furniture, don't you? Everyone should have interests and that is your choice.'

'Yes, I suppose it is,' she said. If she had dared she would have told him that she had no real interests and that this fact gave their association its grave urgency. She was, and believed him to be, a person with a few needs and many habits, but without that which could be called a mind.

When the time came for him to leave they were both rather stiff. He put on his coat and she followed him to the door. Somewhat sadly they looked at each other. His weary movements, the slight way his shoulders dropped, gave his appearance an old-fashioned solemnity. How strange and dark his face is, she thought — dark like her own hair and brows. We might have come from any country, she said to herself. The little scar on his cheek seemed to twitch as a patch of light from the living room fell on his face.

He grasped her hand tightly before he left. The moon was still high and she watched him make his slow way across the street. She stood at the door until she began to shiver from the cold and until Tony Jones had disappeared into the black fields that surrounded his quarters.

During the weeks that followed, the routine of Martha Fiske's life was somewhat altered. The days had become tiresomely long and she found it difficult to occupy herself with household duties. Her yard was covered with fallen leaves and she made no move to sweep them away or to hire someone to do it for her. In some ways her house was brighter than ever and she was more and more conscious of her appearance. (Her clothes had now become rather bizarre. She ordered several lemon yellow dresses and wore them with long strands of jet beads draped around her neck and jeweled combs in her hair. She had red, Japanese style shoes, studded with shining yellow and green nails.) She was negligent, however, of that which presupposed a settled life and about which she had to make plans. She did only those things necessary for the pleasure and comfort of a particular day. With the soldier she drifted along in a remarkably uneventful fashion that was much to her liking. Their conversation was repetitious; their meetings lacked atmosphere and drama. He asked nothing of her and did not even try to discover the old and hidden motives of her behavior. She mentioned, on an occasion, one of the young boys and he became so scornful she could not continue. 'Oh, God,' he said. 'You don't need to tell me anything more. They turn up everywhere . . . always the same.' She and the soldier were locked in the present, because they shared no past and mentioned no future. Yet, sometimes when she was alone in the house, she knew that something was happening. It was neither an event nor a feeling, but a kind of corrosion they both had to undergo. Slowly and painlessly, they were wearing down into slightly different shapes.

Not long after her meeting with Tony Jones she gave the first of a long series of parties. The guests were usually bold young people she didn't like at all. The girls had halos of crimped, blonde hair and their faces were covered with a heavy powder mask that made them look like mummies. They laughed all the time, but not as she had thought young people laughed. Instead every sound they made carried the habitual innuendo of a burlesque barker. The boys were sometimes soldiers and most often bleached-skin young men who worked all day and drank all night. She sat there among them and was always rather conscious of her brilliant dresses, her smooth dark hair and the angularity of her face. Being absolutely lifeless when confronted with this violently meaningless activity, she began to think of herself as not a person at all, but the stationary object on a stage set, the powerful, inanimate image around which all action revolved.

The more informal of these parties grew out of the soldier's insatiable lust for company. For a stranger, he knew a surprising number of people and he no sooner came into her house than he began to telephone everyone in his address book. Though he considered these acquaintances unusually dull, he evidently felt no need to explain or to justify his desire for their company. After a time even these numerous, if haphazard, gatherings failed to satisfy him and he could find excitement only in more ambitious parties to which he would invite a different sort of person, this time trim salesgirls and stenographers, young men who sold insurance policies or worked in banks, and again a few soldiers from the barracks. He seemed to have met some of his friends in bars and they had, in turn, introduced him to others. At the parties he was very restless and kept stirring the fire and lighting cigarettes for everyone, but he did not talk unless he had to in order to keep the conversation going. She began to suspect he deliberately censored himself out of some notion that the less he said the more impression he made. In this he was not altogether mistaken, because his detachment did perplex his friends and his gentleness could be rather frightening. She came to understand the parties and to see that he was frantically trying to reproduce the apartment life of unattached, young city people. She even knew now the sudden pallors and tremblings that attacked him came out of his recurrent fears that he wasn't living at all.

The moments that followed the departure of the guests made the evenings worth the trouble. Then Martha Fiske had the most of Tony Jones. He faced each day as a crisis and at the end, having come through, he always experienced

a relaxation that softened and warmed him. He became talkative and was even gay in his condemnation of those who had
just left. These ordinary people became either pathetic or
strikingly comical by his precise, talented mimicry. He
sighed and yawned and talked, as she went about emptying
the ashtrays and gathering up the glasses. When she was
alone with him she felt as if she were thrown back into a
remembered childhood existence of great purity. Her adult
life, up until their meeting, seemed merely a kind of loiter-
ing in a half-human state.

He said to her one evening, 'You see how meaningless life
is? I told you I only wanted someone I could love, but where
is that to be found?' In the end he always came face to face
with his private gloom: the inability to love.

'Maybe you are too hard on people,' she said.

'I'm not hard on them,' he said. 'I'm more interested than
you are and that makes me critical.'

She was standing by the window, absent-mindedly fingering the folds in the curtains. 'I'm not interested in people,
but I'm interested in you,' she said. 'You might as well tell
me everything. I don't even know how you've lived.'

'Money?' he said. She hadn't meant that exactly, but she
nodded. 'You won't hate me if I tell you? Well, suppose you
do. I can't be anything except myself.' He took a deep
breath. 'I don't need to worry about money. I think I've
said before that people like me. It's true and it pays.'

'What sort of people?'

'Oh, women . . . and men. Don't give me any lectures,
please. I've been nice to them. I'm never cruel or selfish.
If I had money I'd give it to anyone, but I don't have it.
Everyone prefers the giving.'

She smiled at him and he, foolishly, took it as a reproach.
(When would he learn that she pitied him as she would a
mutilated animal and therefore did not scold, but nursed
and indulged?) 'Why are you smiling?' he demanded.

'It means nothing,' she said. He came to her and put his
hand on her shoulder, again demanding. 'I meant nothing,'
she repeated.

How could she mean anything when she was thinking at
this moment of the powerful contentment they shared?
Didn't he sometimes take a nap while she sat beside him and
gazed sweetly at his relaxed, dreaming face and his fine dark
hair? No doubt there were a thousand places in which he
might be tense with the clash of personalities; here they
knew the beauty of an undemanding affection.

'Why do you like me? Why do you come to see me?' she
asked.

He laughed, possibly to indicate to her that his answer
would not be serious. 'It's always my policy to tell the truth.
Or maybe I should say to tell the truth when I can get by
with it. I see you because you are near my quarters and I
like company. Of course, if I weren't fond of you, you
wouldn't be a good companion. You have helped me.'

'Have I?'

'Yes, you have. And I have helped you by knowing what
you want out of life.'

'What do I want?' she said.

'You want to look after me, or someone like me. I need
looking after.' There was nothing in his voice. It was flat
and dead.

'Are you weak?' she asked.

'Oh, very,' he said.

She thought, later, a great deal about their conversation
and though she remembered the words she hadn't any definite frame to fit them into. The weeks went by and she was
more or less happy. Sometimes his visits were separated by
several days. Once he was gone for an entire week end and
he later told her he had been in Cincinnati. He gave her a
detailed account of a house party and spoke quite contemp-
tuously of the people at whose house it had been given.
Something in his manner, a nervousness and loss of confidence, made her think the week end hadn't gone particularly
well. This grieved her deeply and it may have been from
that moment she started to love him fiercely. She tried to
imagine people for whom Tony Jones would be an ordinary
man, one to be treated without special favor, and she ended

by despising those who could thus reduce him. Once she had admitted her love, a mysterious and lawless power burst forth in her. It was stronger than his humiliations and moods, stronger than his indifference. It came upon her so quickly and with such force it almost wiped him out of her thoughts, since it was her love, and not Tony Jones himself, that startled and invigorated her.

He was deeply absorbed in the details of his personality and these were gradually revealed to her. Oddly enough, he believed himself to be in poor health. He spoke of diseases, approaching blindness and the like. She took these revelations lightly, partly out of her knowledge of his temptation to exaggerate and partly from her belief she could work miracles if any of these dread expectations came true. At times he seemed to her ridiculous and worthless, but she was patient because she had always accepted him as a sort of underworld hero. Nothing he could do touched her feelings. Had she not known these evils from the first? She waited one evening for him to come, waited until midnight and he had not appeared. When the clock struck twelve, she started to put out the lights, but was actually powerless to do so. During the past months she had, like the soldier, developed that tenacious self-assurance of a desperado. If she left her light on, he could not pass her house without stopping. This was an act of extortion, done for itself alone, and without regard for the value of seeing him.

It was almost dawn when she heard a rap on her door. He looked stern and unpleasant as he entered the house and it was not until he had removed his coat that she noticed he was bleeding. The blood was thick on his chin and a few dark drops stained his collar.

'What is it?' she said. He evidently had forgot the wound, because his face was deeply set in that strangely peasant-like haughtiness that always astonished her with its fierceness.

'I shouldn't have come here, but I saw the light,' he said severely. 'You are a fool. It's very late.' His inflamed eyes were almost hidden in the dark cave of his eyelids. 'Why are you up at this hour?'

'You let me know you, wanted me to know you,' she said softly. He seemed confused when she smiled at him. His anger did not alarm her. Here he was, that choleric, tyrannical waif who might at this moment have broken out of an institution and come to her for refuge. They were indeed conspirators. 'You let me know you,' she repeated.

'My God! My God!' he said impatiently. Again she saw the little clump of blood on his chin. 'What happened?' she said.

He brushed his hand over the wound. 'Just a fight. It's nothing.'

She led him to the chair and got a pan of water and a towel from the kitchen. 'I have to touch your face,' she said. 'It will be the first time.'

'You needn't do it, you know. I don't ask you to.' She trembled a bit as she approached him, because his body seemed as rigid as if he were in a cataleptic state. He did not move at all when she unbuttoned his collar.

Very gently she worked the towel over his face and neck. His skin was still cold from the wind. 'Don't you want to tell me what happened?' she said.

'I was downtown,' he said. 'I got into a fight with two men.'

'They hurt you,' she said, her voice almost vanishing over these terrible words. 'They hurt you.'

'Yes, they did.' He opened his eyes widely now and stared at her curiously. She tried to imagine where this had taken place, the beginning and end of it. Nothing came to her except a vision of Tony Jones wandering in and out of dark streets. She could not conceive of this secretive, forbidding figure in conflict with the ordinary hoodlums of the town.

'I'm sorry,' she said.

'Don't be sorry,' he said quickly. 'I wanted them to.' He continued to stare at her until she wondered what outrages of feeling he was attempting to hide. Her fingers touched his forehead and brushed against his hair.

'Wanted them to hurt you?' she asked.

'Yes.'

'Why?' She drew away from him. His face was now clean and she saw that there was only a slight scratch on his chin.

'I like it,' he said. His voice seemed hollow and tired now and she too felt suddenly weary. She heard an old truck rattling up the street. It was now passing her dreary, cold house and she had a longing to see the face of the driver, to see how some other human being might look in this hour or so before daylight.

'I will take care of you,' she said at last. She said it simply, as she might have said that she would take the ashes out of the grate in the morning or pick up the magazine that had fallen to the floor.

'You will have lots of wounds to nurse if you take care of me,' he said insistently.

At this moment he looked rather lonely and she too felt cut off from all familiarities. He was old and wise in ways unknown to her. 'Will there be more?' she asked.

'There will be when I feel like it.' His head was thrown back against the chair and her limp arm touched his shoulder. 'You might even make a few wounds of your own if you love me. Do you think you could love me that much?'

'I might do anything almost, if I could learn what you mean.' She pulled his head down on her chest. Her hands were long and rather bony. She had always thought them ugly, but now as they smoothed his hair they seemed to have a peculiar beauty all their own. 'If I knew . . .' she repeated. Though her voice was soft and calm, she was overpowered by a kind of inner frenzy. She could not even make the effort to understand what he had told her because of the wild beating of her heart. 'My love! My love!' she said over and over to herself.

The time came for the departure of the soldiers. It was rumored that the entire camp was to be disbanded. Martha Fiske accepted the fact, though she did not connect it with Tony Jones. It was not easy to imagine him subject to orders not of his own making. She gave little thought to his leaving, largely because her mind was occupied with other matters. Her mother's death, seven months ago, began to worry her. Whenever she remembered the old lady she fell into a torpor that often lasted for hours. At times she thought of her father and then, again, of her husband. She had written her husband that she didn't love him and he had not answered. In this instance she felt neither pity nor anxiety. He was fit for something better than the life they had had together and she believed he would easily discover a new one. More than anything else she brooded over her own hardness. In the strictest terms, she had done nothing that couldn't have been known by all; yet she fretted, not because of guilt but because she was no longer innocent. Considering her hardness, or rather the inflexibility of her will, she often pitied Tony Jones. Her determination operated only with regard to the soldier and she was able to see it for what it was: a perilous heresy that must be accepted without reservation if she were ever to have peace again. In other respects, she was still timid and indefinite, still a soft-spoken, prudent woman. She often wondered how she had managed to outbalance him and she found no explanation except in her love.

Finally the night of their last meeting arrived. Even this event did not fully enter her consciousness. She approached it as if it were an obligatory ritual which had for her no personal content. Tony Jones came to her house in the evening. The night was dark and cold and for some hours there had been intermittent rainstorms. 'We have always met at night,' she said to him.

'Have we?' His hands were busy folding and unfolding his cap. She saw that he was not going to take off his coat, that he had come only to say goodbye and to leave her forever. 'Well, it's been nice,' he said uneasily. 'It hasn't been quite like anything else.' He turned to look at her living room. As he did so, he tried rather unsuccessfully to smile. 'Well . . .' he said again. Beads of perspiration stood out on his lip and his voice was unsteady.

She had left the front door open and was watching the night outside. 'We have never been in the sun together,' she said. It had been a long time since she had actually had conversations with him; instead her whole mind was absorbed in her own delirious monologue.

Her coat was hanging in the hall and she put it on. 'At least we shall have been in the rain together,' she said.

He stepped back from her. 'It's cold and damp. I hate this weather,' he said without a pretense of good humor.

She smiled at him as she tied a scarf over her hair. 'Where will you be sent from here?' she asked. Together they went through the door and out into the rain. The sky was low and dark and the streets were slippery. She put her arm through his. His damp coat brushed against her cheek as they walked.

'It's better that you don't know where I'm going,' he said. 'I think this sort of thing demands that I disappear. I always used to do that as a civilian and I can, in a sense, do it again.'

'Disappear? Why should you want to do such a thing?' She tried to see his face, but it was almost hidden by his coat collar. Is it possible, she asked herself, that he doesn't know what has taken place between us? Does he think he can leave the town as he came into it?

'I hate the rain,' he repeated desperately. 'I must go back. We're leaving early in the morning.' He was begging now. She had grown accustomed to his sorry, trapped little whine, to his bent head and angry breathing. But even when he was most childish there was a cunning energy in him. At times she thought his real strength lay in his hesitations, his anxiety and lack of will. They protected him.

'Where are you being sent?' she repeated. She felt him slow his pace to prepare an answer. (He could hardly take a breath now that she didn't anticipate.)

'Pray for me,' he said with exaggerated lightness. 'I could use a little of your courage. I'm not young enough to get by so easily now.' He looked at her and his eyes widened with astonishment. She knew he was frightened by her calm, persistent questioning, her tearless face, and he seemed at that moment to realize that this was not the end, but the beginning with her.

She had no interest at all in his ridiculous verbal games. What little there was to be said must come out now. 'You didn't answer my question,' she said impatiently.

He began then to abuse her and to try, as his last means of escape, to hurt her. 'So there's a golden stallion weather vane on the courthouse,' he said crossly. 'Yes, I think that suits you.'

'What do you mean?' she said.

'There will be another. . . . There are lots of golden stallions.'

'I don't think so,' she said.

They walked on past the houses until she turned into the park that surrounded the public library. The caretaker's cottage was almost hidden by the darkness, but she could hear the rain beating on the roof and pouring out of the gutters. They stepped now on soggy ground and made their way through the trees that led up to the library. One tiny corridor light glowed in the square stone building. When they came to the porch she said, 'It will be dry here.' They climbed the steps to the shelter and stood there for a long time looking at the circular darkness of the park out of which a few scanty tree branches pointed up to the sky. He was behind her, breathing heavily, waiting. . . .

'Tell me where you are going!' she said in a sudden fury. Her voice was sharp and clear.

'You are married. Remember that,' he said. He was wearing his soldier's cap, that article of clothing he most despised because it seemed to reduce him to the common herd. The cap had slipped down to his eyebrows.

'I'm not. You know I'm not. The marriage never touched me.' She spoke with a flat finality that sent him into a violent, but hopeless, anger.

'It's these damned small towns,' he groaned. Before her view his face seemed to vanish. In the dim light he had no features at all — only those vigilant, untamed little eyes. 'They aren't good for me, these places! People are too serious. You don't know when to stop.'

'Perhaps that's it,' she said calmly. The town clock struck

eleven. She counted the strokes wearily, for she had suddenly lost her energy. The quiet that followed the striking of the hour depressed her. Here there was nothing of his past or of hers. They might have been two tramps wrestling with some ugly destiny on the steps of a public building. She had heard of the vagrants who prowled about the park. There were none here now. Only she and Tony Jones were out in the night.

'Tony . . . I have money,' she said softly, offering it to him openly as compensation for his losses. For a long time she had known that he, in asking her to understand him, had suffered a kind of accident that had left him powerless. 'I have more than people realize. Wherever you go there will be a nice place for you and when the war is over we can live as you like. Any city will do for me.' She put her body in front of him and forced him to look at her. He bit his lip deeply and with a clenched fist brushed the rain from his face. For a moment she had thought he might strike her.

'I don't care,' he said. His voice was so low and broken it was almost a growl. 'Damn you and this place! Damn you!'

He drew back from her and started for the steps. Suddenly he was running away, through the park, back to his barracks. She watched him from the porch. At the edge of the park he passed through the street light, into the darkness and then back to the light, like a rabbit startled by an automobile. He stopped now, his back toward her. The rain was pelting down on him. She hardly breathed as she waited for him to move again. It seemed hours before he turned around and looked in the direction of the shelter. He will wait, she thought. He is mine. She walked forward to meet him in the darkness.

*(From The Antioch Review)*

# UP THE ROAD A PIECE

## BY RUTH McCOY HARRIS

*S*OMETHING WAS AILING GRAMPA. Sis could tell it plain as day, but she did not let on. If she let on, Grampa might sit down again. They had to go on, had to get there before dark.

'Where we goan, I reckon they just now gitten up,' Sis said, lifting her eyes to the round red sun just showing over the trees. 'Reckon they is got on they fine clothes, sitten down in they fine chairs.'

'I smells meat fryen,' Grampa said. 'I smells coffee.' He sniffed the air like a bird dog.

'Sho' do smell good, don't it, Grampa? Smell like more.'

'Sho' do. Ummp-mmmm!'

'They at a fine table. They got bacon and aigs for breakfast.'

'Aigs!'

'Bacon and aigs. Ever' mornen. Two aigs!'

'Now, Sis,' Grampa grinned. 'You know good and well ain't no niggahs eat no two aigs ever' day.'

'Two aigs. Gits in they fine cars and rides around. Has chicken ever' day. And grapes!' Her eyes opened wide at her own extravagance. 'Yes, sir. Chicken and dumplen.'

'Ummp-ummmmph!'

The dust felt soft as kitten fur under Sis's skinny black feet, and the September sun was warm upon her skinny black face, early in the morning as it was. She looked at Grampa and thought how old he was, older than anybody.

171

She thought how it was that Grampa seemed older, every step he took, putting his feet carefully one in front of the other, like sticks of stove wood. Older and younger at the same time. Sis seemed to herself older than Grampa, responsible for him, after the day and night upon the road.

'I'm thirteen,' she said aloud. She liked to say it; thirteen was much older than twelve. 'I'm goen on fourteen. How old is you, Grampa?'

'I old,' Grampa said. 'I older than anybody. I so old, they's no tellen.' He slowed his steps, almost stopped. 'I tired, Sis. Old and tired. I got to take me a little rest.'

Sis started praying again. 'Lord Jesus, help Grampa,' she prayed inside herself. 'Something ailen him. Sweet Jesus, help him; he ain't got much farther to go. Help Grampa to git there. We *got* to git there.'

She saw a blue jay like a flash of sky, lighting on the limb of a wild plum tree, scolding and fussing at them as they trudged along.

'Lookayondah that old jaybird, Grampa!' Sis said aloud, without stopping her inward prayer. 'Sweet good Jesus, help him to keep putten one foot in front the other. You *knows* we near 'bout there,' she could not help adding impatiently. 'You *knows* us got to git there.' She looked slyly at Grampa. 'Look at him. Here how he do.' Sis imitated the jaybird's noisy scolding, putting her head on one side and making her eyes sharp and mean.

'Here how he go. He go like this. . . . Here how the sweet mocking bird go. He say . . .' and Sis whistled some of the mocking bird's many songs.

'That last ain't no mocking bird. That last a crow.'

'This here a mocking bird mocking a crow.' Sis laughed, seeing Grampa laugh. They laughed together, free and careless, and each looking at the other would laugh still more. When Grampa laughed, his black face was wiped clean and new. It was like being back at home, safe and happy with Lady.

When they had left, they had simply shut the door behind them. The house was still back there, away back down the

road, Sis thought with surprise. If they were back in the
little one-room shack, it would be as if they had never left,
except that Lady was not there.

After the funeral everything had been too quiet. Sis could
not bear to be in the house alone. And Grampa would not
come in, even with the dark coming on. Sis tiptoed past the
narrow white bed without looking, past the scrubbed pine
table where the layer cake and the bottled drinks had been
spread. The bare boards creaked and Sis felt death and
darkness in the room, felt a hand reaching out toward the
back of her neck.

'Grampa!' Sis screamed, and ran out the back door to
crouch beside Grampa in his old chair. He held his Bible in
his hand, and his old pipe. Sis could see dimly the scars the
gallberry broom had left in the baked earth.

'I here, Sis,' Grampa said patiently. 'I setten here.'

Nothing could induce either of them to go inside, where
the sweet rambling roses smelled of the grave and the odor-
less zinnias stood prim in bottles and jars.

'Niggah buryen make me lonesome,' Grampa said im-
personally, as if the funeral had not been Lady's, his own
granddaughter and this child's mother. 'Niggah make too
much noise and laughs. Then it so quiet and lonesome.'

'Sister? Oh, Sister! Where you all?' The voice, rich and
brown and warm, poured through the house and washed
away the breath of death. 'I declare. Out here in the dark!
You all catch malarium. Come on in out the black.' Mis'
Mott, big and brown, lighted the kerosene lamp. It made a
shadow behind the bed. They never expected to go to sleep,
but they lay down, the old man on his sagging couch, the
child on her pallet, soothed by Mis' Mott's cheerful manag-
ing. The black at the window was graying, the lamplight
fading when they awoke.

Grampa did not argue when Sis told him. He turned to
stare, groping for his old shoes, but he did not argue.

'Lady say us got to go anyhow? Just us?'

'She say go ahead.'

'Sudie, too?'

A curtain dropped over the brightness of Sis's eyes. 'Not this time, Grampa. Not now.' Not ever. Sudie would never go.

Sis could hear Lady saying it. 'Sudie ain't worth a chew tobacco. Sudie a no-count niggah. Ever how Sudie do, you do the different. Don't you never let me catch you take after Sudie.'

Sudie and her four little blue-eyed children, with their hair too soft and brown and their skin too light. Sudie could never go, but she did not care. She did not feel the thing that Sis felt, the thing driving her on. Lady had talked to Sudie the way she talked later to Sis, but Sudie always laughed and put on her high-heeled shoes and the thick red lipstick and ran out of the house. And now she lived alone, with the four children, her belly big and heavy again. She was always singing and laughing, laughing at Lady and Sis.

They each took their most valuable possessions, tied in a little bundle. Sis took her red dress and her shoes that were almost new and the little red pocketbook Lady had given her long ago. It was full of pennies, with three nickels like prizes among them. Grampa had his Bible that he could not read.

They passed Mr. Jeff Webb's big white house, sitting back from the road, where Lady had worked. They passed other painted houses behind their dusty evergreen bushes, passed the cotton gin and the planer mill, the courthouse and the stores. After more houses and the filling station came the other edge of town, with its shacks like Lady's, straight up and down boards weathered gray, with cracks between and a chimney made of sticks and mud.

No one was stirring at Sudie's house or at Mis' Mott's. At Aunt Lucy Carter's they had hot corn pone and bacon drippings for breakfast, but ask as she would, Aunt Lucy could get nothing out of them.

'Just a little trip,' was all Sis would say. 'Just up the road a piece.'

'I bet you all going to Hattiesburg,' Aunt Lucy said, scandalized, for Lady was not good cold in the ground, but Sis would not say. They left Aunt Lucy standing by the chinaberry tree in her yard. The road stretched like an inviting finger. Sis could hardly stand it, her feet wanted so much to run and skip, but she walked along slowly, the way Grampa had to walk.

'I got to go in the bushes,' Grampa said, stopping. Sis crept behind a bush, too, and then waited for Grampa. But when he came back, he sat down. 'Got to sit a little,' he said. 'Old Grampa tired.'

They sat down in the shade, for the autumn sun was already merciless. Grampa had drops of perspiration on his forehead, below his kinky white hair. Grampa was a great big tall man, but he was so stooped nobody knew how tall he had once been.

'Time to go now, Grampa?' Sis kept asking, but Grampa would only shake his head drowsily.

It was Mr. Jeff's car that stopped.

'Howdy, Sis. What you waiting here for?'

Sis nodded toward Grampa. 'We goan to Hattiesburg. Grampa's tired.'

Mr. Jeff laughed. 'He got tired mighty quick. You all ain't good started. Get in. I'm going to Hattiesburg.'

They got into the back seat of the splendid car and sat on the splendid upholstery. Some folks would spread an old quilt first, but Mr. Jeff would let them get right in. Even if he was the sheriff, Sis was not afraid of him. She sat marvelling at the miles flowing behind them. It was like riding in the golden chariot.

'Where's Lady?' Mr. Jeff asked them, after a while. 'Lady never showed up to help Mrs. Webb during court last week.'

They could only stare at each other. How could it be that he did not know of the heavy earth and the flowers piled above Lady?

'Mamma daid,' Sis's lips trembled to say the words.

'Dead! Well, I'll declare!' Then, 'Lady was a good worker. I've heard Mrs. Webb say many's the time, she wouldn't have anybody help her but Lady.' It was his tribute, his flowers for the grave, and it brought the tears to Sis's eyes.

At the edge of town, Mr. Jeff parked the car and Sis almost

fell out for staring at the piles of vegetables in a store window.

'Look out, girl,' Mr. Jeff said sharply. 'You'll break your neck.' He locked the car. 'I'll be going back about sundown,' he said.

They did not tell him they would not be going back with him. He would never give it another thought, if he did not find them waiting.

Sis held Grampa's arm, partly to steady him, but mostly to comfort herself. There were people everywhere, soldiers talking Yankee talk and ladies in fine clothes and colored folks like themselves. Grampa, bewildered, bumped into a lady.

'Look out, Uncle,' she said good-naturedly, 'You're in town now.'

Luckily they made no turns. The street led straight through the town and became an open highway again. Sis was empty and thirsty, but she had no idea where to get anything.

'I thirsty,' Grampa said. It was the beginning of a refrain. Every time Sis felt joyful and light, thinking of the wonders ahead, Grampa would say it again. Say it or sit down by the road, fanning himself with his old hat. Once he went to sleep, and Sis, her eyes darting about the scrub oak and pine saplings, saw a grapevine. It had no grapes, but she saw another and another, and finally climbed a tree, her dress falling away from her bare body, and came down with a handful of the sharp little grapes.

'Ummp, ummph! Foxgrapes,' Grampa said, wadding them, stems and all, into his mouth. 'They not ripe. I remembers when I was a slave boy, eating foxgrapes in the fall after the frost.'

He had never been a slave, Sis knew, and his remembering was mixed up with the stories he had heard. He thought he had come across the water in the dark hold of a ship, and described whippings and travellings and battles, even his own birth. No one believed him, but they listened.

They saw a white cottage ahead. Sis told Grampa they

would ask for a drink of water. But then the dog started barking, just inside the picket fence, a big fierce yellow dog. Grampa stopped in the middle of the road.

'Go on and bark,' he said to the dog. 'I know you. You know better to bite old Grampa, you old barken dog, you.' But he went no nearer.

'Prince. You, Prince! Shut up!' The voice was shrill and cross.

'Come on, Grampa,' Sis urged. 'Le's don't mess with that old dog.'

Grampa would not budge. A tired bedraggled white woman came out of the screen door. 'Prince!' she screamed. Then she saw them. 'What you all standing there for?' she called to them. 'Why don't you go on; standing there fretting my dog?'

But she held the dog by the neck and told them where the pump was. 'Hurry up, now, and don't put your mouth on the spout. There's a tin cup.'

Grampa was so slow Sis could not wait. She pumped hard until the water splashed out fast and cold; then she bent over and put her mouth to the cold wet spout. They heard the woman calling.

'Come on, Grampa,' Sis begged. 'She might let that old dog loose.'

'I ain't scared of no old dog,' Grampa said, as he filled the cup again. But when the woman came muttering around the corner of the house, dragging the dog by his neck, Grampa moved with dignity toward the gate.

The sun still burned them when it was halfway down the western sky. Sis could not understand it. She had been watching for the place, expecting it at every turn of the road. Surely it would be at the top of that hill; surely it was down in that low swampy valley. But the road ran on and on, white in the blinding sunlight.

'Boy,' Sis said to a Negro child they met, 'Boy, where the Piney Wood School?' She called him 'Boy' to sound important, to show him she was a person going somewhere on business.

The boy tugged at his faded overalls. 'Huh?'

'Where Jackson? Jackson up thisaway?'

He nodded. 'I been there. On the bus. It ain't far. Rat on up the road a piece.'

Grampa walked slower and slower. He hardly lifted his feet, and his shuffling made a scraping sound on the pavement that scared Sis. She tried to push him with her thoughts, with her own urgency, and forgot to entertain him with chatter.

The sun sank lower, behind the trees, and left the woods black and threatening. Night was coming, not far away; night full of danger, full of things with teeth and claws, and soft cold brushing things out of graves.

'Come on, Grampa,' Sis begged. 'We got to hurry.'

'I old, Sis,' he apologized. 'I too old. Us better go back.'

'Back?' She tried not to scream at him. 'We can't go back. It's right up yondah.' She peered ahead. 'Look like I see it up yondah,' she murmured slyly. 'I sees it rat up yondah, look like.'

'You don't see nothing up yondah,' the old man told her. 'I got to rest some more.'

'You sit down, I goan walk rat on off and leave you. Goan walk rat on.'

Grampa smiled. But he glanced up at the sky and saw that the sun was gone. He did not sit down.

They were surprised when the rattly old car stopped. Two stylish young Negro girls sat on the front seat and their father, wearing overalls, was in the back.

'We thought you all old Mr. Plum and Sarah May,' said the girl driving, racing the engine, getting ready to drive on.

'Oh, Miss,' Sis could not hide her desperation. 'Oh, lady!' She could not let them leave her and Grampa among the wildcats and han'ts. 'Us . . . we . . . we wants to git up towards Jackson.'

She wiped away the tears of relief when they were safely in the car. Nothing could discourage her, once out of the threat of darkness, not the sullenness of the girls when they heard the man asking her and Grampa to spend the night, not the hostility of the black woman waiting at a board shack like their own, not the way they invited her and Grampa into the kitchen so reluctantly, ashamed of the food. Sis and Grampa slept on a pallet before the gaping fireplace. Sis was surprised to hear the girls giggling behind her back, before she had stretched out good. She saw them putting on their fine dresses and their bracelets at sunup, leaning over the cracked mirror to put on lipstick until their mouths shone thick and red, like bloody gashes.

'Where you all going, Jackson?' the black woman, already knowing, asked them as they got into the car.

'To the Piney Wood school,' Sis said. 'To get educated.'

'Piney Woods!' They were impressed. 'I got a girl friend went there. Runs a typewriter and ever'thing.'

'We goan buy us a car.' It was the younger girl, not to be outdone. 'Cost us eight hundred dollar. A fine car, near'bout new.'

'Eight hundred dollar!' It was almost the first time Grampa had spoken, drowsing away in the car as it bumped over the ruts back to the highway.

'Yeah. Eight hundred dollar.' She let each silver dollar clank impressively. 'We makes good money at the plant.'

'You could buy a farm! House too.' Grampa stared at her.

'We got a farm. Farm enough to do us.' Her bitter voice told them the hours she had bent chopping the cotton and picking it, the weary miles of furrow she had travelled over the meager and begrudging land. 'We don't want no more farm.'

They waved goodbye at the highway, stood watching the car go back the way they had come.

How different, to be travelling in the brightening morning, with stomach comfortably full. How happy the journey, how light her heart. Sis could have run, yelping like a puppy. It was only that Grampa walked the same as before, dragging his feet.

But nothing could hold down the joy inside Sis and she sang in her sweet thin voice. How could she doubt, in the early new day, that they would get to the school? She kept watching. She expected to see it just ahead, at the top of the next hill, showing beyond the next turning. She would see it, all of a sudden, right there in front of them.

But the road ran on and on. After each turning there would be only more and more highway, stretching endlessly. When they passed through a little town, Sis, remembering, stopped in a store and bought a box of crackers and a bottle of pickles. She saw the redheaded boy grinning as she counted the pennies out of her pocketbook. Sis stuck out her lower lip sullenly and switched the tail of her skirt as she walked out into the sunlight again.

With the crackers and the pickles she felt fortified for anything, and Grampa, too, was encouraged.

On they walked, forever and ever, up hill and down, sometimes through woods of pine and oak, sometimes past fields of cotton just bursting its bolls, showing a little white. The corn was parched and yellow; dust softened the green of tree and bush.

Sis was not tired, even when the angry sun stood high above, burning her head through her hair. But she was watching Grampa. He must not stop. She would never let him stop again until they got there. She opened the bundle and handed some crackers to Grampa.

She watched the way he ate the crackers, writhing his lips about them, waiting for them to be soft enough to swallow. He did not look at Sis, and he did not strain his eyes ahead looking for the place. The way Grampa looked, it did not matter much to him, one way or the other.

Sis could not understand the ebbing of her courage, the fear, round and heavy in the pit of her stomach, every time she looked at Grampa. Something was ailing him. He looked ashy, as Lady had done before she died. They could only go on, but Sis was afraid.

It was then that the blue jay alighted on the plum tree. Sis felt the weight lifted from her when Grampa laughed at her imitation of the jay bird. But his feet still dragged. They were quiet, Sis and Grampa, but inside she began the praying again. She felt ashamed of herself, finally.

'Grampa, you looks tired. You want to rest?'

'I'm all right, child.'

Sis was proud of him. The day before, he had been complaining all the way. Now of course it was past the complaining time. Sis saw how he favored one foot a little.

'Your feets hurt you, Grampa?' She wished he were back in his old chair by the back door, and she beside him. What had made her start on a trip so far, to a place so unknown? What good was school to Grampa, older than time itself? She could not think what had driven her to do it.

'My feets all right, child,' Grampa said. 'I got a little stitch in my side is all. Nothing much.'

'Mamma said to come. She said not to go off and leave you, you so old.'

'Um-humm.'

'Said I goan learn to read and write at the school. Said I got to.'

'Ummm-ummmph!' Grampa had heard this many times. 'A niggah that can read and write, he can do anything, git anywhere.' Grampa did not know this for a fact; he was quoting Lady.

Sis could feel the heaviness in the pit of her stomach; sometimes it rose and stuck in her throat. She kept glancing at the sun, hardly started on its downward course. She wished Grampa would complain and fuss; his patience scared her. Maybe the school would be at the next turning. It had to be up there at the next turning of the road.

When Grampa fell down, he did not fall all at once. He leaned forward a little, as if he were listening. He cocked his head to one side, listening, and then his knees buckled under him, and he slid to the ground noiselessly and easily as if he had been practicing all his life. He gave a little grunt, 'Ummmfff!' of anger or surprise, and lay still.

Sis watched him. She could not believe what her eyes saw. She stood and looked at him lying still in the road before she screamed.

'Grampa! Grampa!' Her childish screams came out of a mouth that hung open, and the salty tears ran into it. She shook him wildly, taking his arms and tugging and pulling, trying to get him to his feet again. She had known all the time that once he was down he would never get up. He lay at the side of the highway. An automobile whizzed by so close it almost ran over Grampa's foot.

'Git up, Grampa!' she kept begging. 'Oh, git up. Oh, git up. Oh, Grampa, git up!'

She managed to pull him a little farther to the side of the road after another car had whizzed by his feet. A car might run right over Grampa, lying in the road, run over him before the driver saw him.

Although she was frenzied, she could not truly believe for a long time that Grampa was dead. It was simply that he was so hard to get started, once he stopped. She needed Grampa to be walking beside her. With him lying still, she was scared, lost.

Finally she began to know that Grampa was dead. He was gone, like Lady. That changed everything. She stopped her wailing and her moaning. Grampa was dead and it was her fault. She had killed him.

At the same time, it was not she, Sis, who had killed Grampa. He had died during the journey, but the journey itself had not been a thing they could take or not. Lady had said they must go; Sis knew they had to go; Grampa had not argued against it at all. The trip had to be made; there was something driving her, stronger than any of them. She could not leave Grampa all by himself in the shack and he had died on the trip.

But she was still terrified. With Grampa not there, she was alone, a child in a far-off land, not knowing where she was going, not daring to turn back. She could not stay. She had to get on up the road.

Sis saw a buzzard in the tip of an old dead tree. Buzzards always knew about death. Even before it happened, they knew.

Sis looked down at Grampa. She moved his bundle nearer his hands; his Bible was in it. She glanced up at the sky again to see where the sun stood and without another look at the old man she walked steadily up the road.

Sis knew what she was doing. She knew the horror of not being properly buried, the greatest concern of Grampa's life. She knew about the burial insurance back home, knew he had expected to be buried where Lady was, among his friends, with God watching.

But she walked on. What else could she do? There was no going back, no bringing Grampa back to life; no physical possibility of looking after his body from which his soul had already gone.

It was completely beyond her power and so out of her hands. Sweet Jesus God would have to take care of Grampa's body.

Sis did not feel like skipping and jumping any more. The sun was dropping in the west; hunger was gnawing at her stomach. Her thoughts seemed light and far away, dancing up above the top of her head.

It might be right ahead. At the school, they would know what to do about Grampa. They would know everything at the school. But of course the school was thousands of miles away; she would keep walking until she, too, fell down like Grampa and never got up again. She kept thinking of herself and Lady and Grampa, standing in the kitchen, eating the good hot cornbread and the hot turnip greens. Cold buttermilk. Side meat fried, and molasses.

She passed a filling station where two or three cars were parked. Some white boys, nearly grown, stood drinking from enormous bottles. She could taste the cold orange flavor as she watched out of the corner of her eye. It would be sweet and a little acid going down her throat. Cold and sweet and wet. She heard them laughing and talking as she hurried past, a thin little Negro girl with knobby knees.

The dusk came on with surprising suddenness. The sun had appeared to stand quite high in the west, above the treetops. Then all at once it dropped behind the tallest trees. There were long shadows. From the woods the dark was creeping toward the road. Sis gave a little cry of despair and tried to quicken her steps. Night coming and she not there. She would never be there. She shivered. Jesus God had seen how she had done Grampa. Jesus was mad with her.

'Keep rat on walking,' the voice said. 'It ain't far. Just up the road.' It was Lady's voice and Sis felt the warm tears come to her eyes.

'Grampa,' she said to Lady. 'Grampa.'

'I knows. You couldn't help it.'

'He ain't buried.'

'You can't help it,' Lady insisted. 'You just a little girl. Us niggahs, we got to do the best we can. Jesus looking after Grampa. You just keep on. You goan git there.'

'You said to come.'

'You got to. You goan learn a heap at school.'

'Reading and writing,' Sis said, wiping her eyes.

'Ever'thing. Goan learn ever'thing. Be big and rich. Goan ride in a fine car and have plenty firewood. Plenty quilts. All you wants to eat. Apples and oranges. Meat ever' day. Goan have money to give to them what ain't got nothing to eat. Goan be a schoolteacher and teach the chillun what ain't got nobody to teach them. You got to git there.'

'Mama,' Sis cried, wiping her eyes again. 'Mama, you stay with me.'

She did not know whether Lady was really there. She knew about ha'nts, but they were cold and creepy, not warm and comforting like Lady.

The car ground to a stop. Sis turned in surprise. She had not heard it approaching.

'Git in, girl,' somebody ordered.

'Aw, Pete, for the love of God,' another voice said. 'She ain't nothing but a young'un.'

'Git in, girl,' the first voice said.

They were the boys she had passed at the filling station. Sis was puzzled. She was so relieved to hear human voices that she could not understand the little throb of fear in her.

'Git in, git in,' Pete said. 'You want to ride or not?'

Sis giggled. 'I sho' does. I tired.'

She got into the back seat, beside one of the boys. 'Aw, for the love of God, Pete,' the boy not driving kept saying. 'You all make me sick.'

'Shut up, Ralph,' Pete jeered good-naturedly. 'Where'd we put that liquor, Ed? You remember?'

'Sure.' Ed spoke from his place beside Sis. 'Keep on going. I'll tell you.'

Sis shrank back into her corner when the boy reached toward her. She sat rigid as a pole as she felt his hand on her.

'She ain't got nothing on,' Ed stated. 'Not a damn thing but a dress.' Pete laughed raucously, but Ralph kept saying, 'Aw, for the love of God. This makes me sick at the stomach.'

'Listen to the Christer. Sixteen years old and he acts like he was born yesterday. Where is that liquor, Ed?'

'Hey, stop. Wait a minute. Wait, I think we put it right back there.'

Pete stopped, put the car into reverse. Sis pushed hard into her corner. The boys were all staring into the darkness.

'Naw, this ain't it,' Ed said. 'It must be a little farther on.'

'Aw, nuts,' Pete muttered. 'How come we put it there anyhow?' They drove on slowly, still peering into the blackness.

'Wait a minute,' Ralph said quickly. 'Here it is. This is the place.'

'You sure? I can't see a wink.'

When the car stopped the three boys got out. 'You stay right there, girl,' Pete called back, 'if you don't want your brains beat out.'

Sis heard them crashing about. She was too paralyzed to move. Much as she feared the boys, she was still more afraid of the dark woods.

A voice spoke softly into her ear, making her jump.

'Beat it, girl,' Ralph said. 'Here, this way. I got the door open. Go down the road a little ways and hide until we're gone.' Sis stood up, felt beside her for the little bundle.

'Ain't you got no sense?' he hissed. 'Don't never get in no more cars with white boys if you don't want . . .' and he ended up with a mouth full of obscenity. 'Beat it.'

Sis stumbled out of the car and ran through the darkness, crashing blindly into bushes. She stumbled over a log and fell and crouched where she had fallen, like a rabbit crazed by hounds.

'Hey, Ralph,' said Pete's voice very near. 'I don't see no big oak tree. Where in hell is that liquor?'

'Maybe it ain't the place,' Ralph admitted.

'Oh, the hell you say. Come on.' She heard more crashing, then, 'Hey, she's gone!'

'What?'

'That little blackbird is gone.'

'Well, let her go. Let's get going. I got 'bout enough of this.'

When the car had gone, its lights dipping into a hollow and disappearing, Sis got up again and ran along the side of the road. She was past crying, past any feeling except numbness and a creeping at the back of her neck, where a hand was reaching out toward her. She wanted Lady to come back, but there was nobody, nothing.

She heard and trembled at all the little night noises, the insects and the murmur of the leaves in the dark. She heard the far-off bay of a dog, the lonesome whistle of a distant train. She could not stop, but how could she go on? She was breathing in gasps, and in her side a pain caught her and did not let go. When she saw the lights of a car like a probing finger, she stepped off the road into the woods. It was the boys again; she could hear their voices as the car moved slow and threatening, making long shadows about her. Then, the car gone, she was back at the road again, far more afraid of the black woods than of any people.

Time had no beginning or end. There was only the pain under the bottom of her foot, where a blister had burst, and the ache in her side and the ache in her throat. Black woods and black despair. But she kept on walking. If she stopped a minute the hands would grab her. Even when she saw distant car lights again she stepped only a few feet off the road.

Sis never knew when she sank down. She had either fainted or gone to sleep on her feet. One moment she was walking, fearing the distant car lights; the next she opened her eyes and saw the paling of the eastern sky, the first wash of pink. She felt herself trembling, shivering, for the night had been cool with a touch of fall in the air, and the ground where she lay was wet with dew.

The road was right beside her, stretching away into the distance. Where it rose from the low swampy place, she could see the sun shining on the cement, whitening it with daylight and hope.

'It ain't far now. It just up this old road,' Sis said aloud. She stood up carefully, keeping her weight off her blisters. She ached all over, but she picked up her little bundle and walked on, her heart as light as spongecake to see the daylight again.

'Just rat at the top of that hill and there it will be. Spelled out in great big words, like Mama taught me from the letter. A great big old building, maybe, all shining like diamonds. Great big letters so I can read it.' Sis could read only three words, 'Piney Woods School,' because those were all Lady knew to teach her.

It was not at the top of the hill. For the first time, Sis wondered whether possibly she had passed it. The sun had come up and the whole sky was brightening. The trees became green instead of gray. Sis heard a squirrel chattering and turned her head to look.

She stared. She could not believe her eyes. It was an iron arch, with the words spelled out in big iron letters, 'Piney Woods School.'

Sis could read them plain as day, just as Lady had taught her. To think they were there. She knew, reading the words, that she had actually never in this world expected to see them.

Her mouth stretched into a wide grin. She said the words aloud, stepped inside the arch, turned and looked back to see that she was truly inside, gave a skip. Saw nothing but a little dirt road through the trees, but she never doubted what was ahead.

Well inside the fence, Sis slipped off into the woods grown friendly in the daytime.

When she was hidden, she lifted her old dress over her head and stood skinny and naked. Proud Sis took her red dress out of the bundle and slipped it over her head. She put on the shoes, a size too small, arrogantly ignoring the pain of the blister. She reached back to button her wrinkled dress, then, wadding the old dress carelessly, stuck it deep into a red haw bush.

Proudly Sis took her little pocketbook in her hand, and gingerly walked to the dirt road again. Proudly she marched, stepping firmly upon the burning blister, pinched in her shoes. Her face was radiant and impudent with joy. Her face was ashy with dust, her legs scratched and rusty.

'Piney Wood!' she cried, her face transfigured, her sorrow past and forgot. She saw a cluster of unpretentious brick buildings ahead of her and stood still for a moment, seeing palaces. She began to skip awkwardly, on toward the buildings.

*(From The Atlantic Monthly)*

# NIGHT WATCH

## BY THOMAS HEGGEN

*T*HIS ship lying at anchor in the glassy little bay is a Navy cargo ship. You can tell it as a cargo ship by the five hatches, by the house amidships, by the booms that bristle from the masts like so many mechanical arms. You know it as a Navy ship by the color (dark, dull blue), by the large numbers painted on the bow, and incontrovertibly by the thin ribbon of the commission pennant flying from the mainmast.

The U.S.S. *Reluctant* operates in the rear areas of the Pacific. Most of the time it stays on its regular run: from Tedium to Boredom and back; about five days each way. It makes an occasional trip to Monotony, and once it made a run all the way to Ennui, a distance of 3000 nautical miles from Tedium. It performs its dreary and thankless job, and performs it well, if not inspiredly. How many enemy planes has it shot down? None. How many fired upon? None. How many subs sent to the bottom by her guns? None. How many fired upon? Well, there was once. This periscope; the outlook sighted it way off on the port beam, and the Captain got very excited. 'Commence firing!'

The five-inch and the two port three-inch guns fired for perhaps five minutes, but they didn't really do very well; the best shell was five hundred yards off the target and there were many that weren't even in sight. 'We'll ram!' the Captain shouted. 'Hard left!' The ship bore down on the periscope; it seemed dead in the water. At one thousand yards it was positively identified as the protruding branch of a small floating tree. The branch had a big bend in it and didn't even look much like a periscope.

You say that the men aboard her are not heroes? Well, perhaps; but I should urge moderation and the judgment deferred. I am perfectly willing to see 'heroism' retired from the conversation, for it is always an embarrassing word, and suspiciously ubiquitous. But I am not so sure that it is inapplicable here. I think I should insist, for instance, upon its extension to Lieutenant Roberts.

Lieutenant Roberts is a young man of sensitivity, perceptiveness, and idealism; attributes which are worthless and even inimical to such a community as this. He wants to be in the war; like filings to a magnet, he is powerfully drawn to the war and to the general desolation of the time; but he is held off, frustrated, defeated by the rather magnificently non-conductive character of his station. He is the high-strung instrument assuming the low-strung role; the violin playing bass. To convert like this, from a higher to a lower tempo, requires the invention of a sort of self-imposed, self-maintained reduction gear, and Roberts supplied this. He geared himself to the tempo of the ship and made the adjustment with — I do not believe the words are misplaced — gallantry, courage, and fortitude. I would call him a kind of hero.

All the officers, with the exception of the Doctor and Mr. Ronad, the supply officer, had at one time or another submitted letters to the Bureau requesting a change of duty. This was their privilege, and presumably the Bureau gave just consideration to such letters. These officers, however, turned in their requests perfunctorily and without hope; for all of them were absolutely certain that there existed at the Bureau a yeoman, probably a Wave, whose sole duty consisted in dropping all such correspondence, unopened, into a roaring incinerator.

As incontestable proof of this theory they cited the fact that in fifteen months the only officer transferred from the ship had been an ensign named Moulton, who had been aboard only six months and who had never submitted a letter. Naturally, there was some ill-will toward Moulton, who it was felt was undeserving of such good fortune; but for the most part the officers accepted the stroke philosophically and even, their theory confirmed, with a certain satisfaction.

While the officers may or may not have been right in guessing the disposition of their requests, there can be no doubt at all that they correctly gauged the futility of them. As a matter of policy — a policy, clearly, of pure spite, since he had many times expressed his desire to be rid of the whole passel of officers — the Captain always forwarded these letters with the endorsement: 'Not recommending approval.' That way they were licked from the start.

While all the other officers were content to submit their one letter, make their one gesture and let it go at that, Lieutenant Roberts did not give up so easily. One month to the day after he had written his first request he appeared in the yeomen's office and had the letter retyped verbatim and presented again to the Captain. The Captain muttered, then sputtered, then roared; but he had no choice other than to forward it, with, of course, the same negative endorsement. Every month after that — without fail, it was exactly a month — the procedure was repeated: Lieutenant Roberts would submit the same letter and the Captain with the same curses would apply the same endorsement.

It might seem that this was a foolish and futile business and in the main Roberts would agree, but not entirely. As he explained to his friend Pulver, he felt that it had a certain nuisance value. He reasoned that, if anyone at the Bureau did indeed read these letters, sooner or later that person was going to get so goddamned angry with him that he would be transferred to the Naval equivalent of Siberia — which, by comparison with his present station, he did not consider at all undesirable. And he knew for an agreeable fact that, every time the yeoman appeared bearing his letter, the Captain's digestion was effectively ruined for at least one meal.

Regularly on the fourteenth of every month Roberts would appear in the ship's office and turn in his letter to the grinning yeoman. One month, on the fourteenth, he did not appear and the next morning, while he was sleeping in after the midwatch, there came a knock on his stateroom door. It was about ten o'clock; Roberts had just awakened and was lying in his bunk, arms crossed beneath his head, debating whether to get up and go down to the wardroom for a cup of coffee. So he was willing to be disturbed.

'Come in,' he called.

Steuben, the satyr-faced little yeoman, entered. He had a letter in his hand and he was grinning. 'Good morning, Mr. Roberts,' he said.

Roberts said, 'Good morning, Mr. Steuben,' and smiled at the formality.

'Mr. Roberts?'

'Yes?'

'You know what day it is?'

Roberts rubbed his head with his knuckles. 'Tuesday, isn't it?'

'Mr. Roberts,' Steuben said significantly, 'it's the fifteenth!' Steuben grinned in satisfaction. 'I can't let you slip up, you know.'

'No, hell no,' said Roberts. 'I'm glad you didn't. We've got to keep those letters rolling in.'

Steuben nodded at the sheet in his hand. 'Same one?'

Roberts nodded. 'Same one.' Then, as the yeoman started for the door, he sat up. 'No, wait a minute. Can I see that?' As Steuben handed him the letter he said: 'By God, maybe we ought to change it a little. Maybe it would change our luck.'

He read the familiar letter to himself and then he read aloud the third and concluding paragraph, dwelling questioningly on each word: 'It is therefore requested that I be ordered to duty aboard a combatant ship, preferably a destroyer or cruiser.' He flicked the letter with his hand. 'What do you think, shall we change that?'

Steuben considered soberly. 'Yeah, let's change it,' he said.

'All right,' said Roberts. 'Give the correspondence a little variety and improve the grammar at the same time. How's to make this read, "It is requested comma therefore comma"? Think that will do it?' He passed the letter back.

'Yeah, hell yes,' Steuben said. 'That's a lot better. Gives it more punch, you know. I'll fix it right up, Mr. Roberts.' He grinned again and put his hand on the doorknob.

Roberts reached down for the cigarettes on the desk and lit one. 'You know, Steuben,' he said, 'by God, maybe that's all it needed. Maybe the Captain will like it better now.'

'He will, Mr. Roberts. I bet he will.'

'Yep,' said Roberts. 'I think he'll appreciate that.' After Steuben went out he sat for a moment on the edge of the bunk, smoking. He looked at his watch: ten thirty. He stretched and rubbed his head. He might as well get up and go have some coffee. He remembered that Keith had a new copy of *Life* with a girl in a zebra-striped bathing suit on the cover. He would go down and read that while he drank his coffee.

As he slipped a leg into his khaki trousers he thought again: 'It is requested comma therefore comma.' Yes, by God, that did it, that fixed it up. A split participle — no wonder his orders hadn't come! No doubt the Bureau had a policy concerning split participles. Putting on his shoes, he could see clearly the fate of all his previous letters; the Wave yeoman opens the envelope, reads the letter, gasps as she comes to the defective part, and in a shocked voice says to Commander Doark: 'Commander, here's a letter from an officer who's split a participle.' And the Commander, looking up coldly from his desk, says: 'Well, you know what to do with it, Carrigan.' And without a word Carrigan drops it into the blazing incinerator.

Yep, by God, that was all it needed. Roberts felt almost good as he started down to get the copy of *Life* with the girl in the zebra-striped bathing suit on the cover.

It seemed to Lieutenant Roberts that he had just fallen

asleep when the flashlight shone in his face, awakening him for the watch. He had been dreaming, and in his dream his dead mother was there; it was summer at his home and he was going out to play tennis. His mother was sitting on the porch drinking a Coca-Cola and as he went out she said: 'On your way back pick up some pastry for supper.' And he got into the car and started off and at the corner he smashed right into another car; and when the driver of the other car got out and came toward him he saw that it was Captain Morton.

The flashlight shone questioningly in his face and he was fully awake by the time the messenger called: 'Mr. Roberts. Mr. Roberts. It's eleven thirty, sir. You have the watch.'

Roberts put a hand to his eyes and rubbed them. 'Okay,' he said. 'Thank you.' The messenger went out, stumbling in the darkened stateroom against the chair. Carefully, he pulled the door to behind him; he knew that Mr. Roberts would get up; you only had to call Mr. Roberts once. Roberts lay on his back not moving a muscle, numbly, tiredness an actual ache in his legs, considering the fact that sleep was over and now for four hours — another four of the hours without end that wheeled past ceaselessly like ducks in a shooting gallery — he must get up and stand in the darkness.

Here we go again, he thought; and as he lay there he felt the old, incipient despair that for two hours he had eluded returning again. To stop it he stopped his mind; he had learned well how to do that. He lay there and all he was doing was breathing and listening. In the hot, pitch-dark little room there were four distinct sounds. There was the noisy breathing of Langston in the bunk above him — a long, wheezing inspiration, then a pause, then a wet, angry snort. There was the hissing drone of the blower in the overhead and the whirring of the fan that wearily pushed the heavy air over to the bunks.

Over on the desk the cheap alarm clock ticked evenly, tirelessly, stridently. Roberts raised his head and looked at the luminous dial: eleven thirty-five. He lay still a moment longer; then he stretched and sat up. In the darkness he reached to the deck and put on his stockings and shoes and still without turning on a light he found the rest of his clothes and put them on. As he went out he closed the door quietly, although he could have slammed it fifteen times without awakening Langston.

He went down to the wardroom, where one overhead light burned dimly. It was deserted; a few old and much-thumbed magazines were strewn about the tables. There was no one in the pantry either; not even the steward's mate with the watch. Incuriously, Roberts looked through the refrigerator for something to eat and, finding nothing, poured himself a cup of coffee from the Silex and sat down at a table. He picked up a six-month-old copy of *Time* and looked at the book section to see if he had read it. He had; he threw it aside. He drank the black coffee in deep swallows and felt better; it smothered some of the weariness, his legs felt better, he could stand the watch now. He stretched again, shook his head like a swimmer with water in his ear, put on his cap, and walked slowly up the two ladders to the charthouse. There he initialed the Captain's night-order book — always the same: 'Call me at any time if in doubt' — and looked at the chart. The closest land was four hundred miles. He went out into the wheelhouse.

Usually, before he took the officer-of-the-deck watch, Roberts would stand at night in the rear of the wheelhouse and let his eyes adjust to the darkness. Tonight, though, as soon as he stepped into the wheelhouse, he could see. A bright moonlight was streaming through the portholes and almost right away he could make out every object in the room and every person. He asked the helmsman: 'Where's Mr. Carney?' and the helmsman told him: 'Out on the port wing.' Roberts went out on the wing and found Carney leaning on the pelorus.

Like all watch-standers about to be relieved, Carney was jovial. 'Welcome,' he said. 'And good morning.'

Roberts smiled wryly. 'Good morning, goddamn it,' he said. He waited quietly for Carney to give him the dope.

'Well,' Carney began, 'we're steaming along in this here

ocean at ten knots, seventy-two r.p.m., and the base course is two five eight and that's what we're steering. No zigzag, no nothing; everything's peaceful.'

'I trust Stupid's gone to bed,' said Roberts.

'Stupid's gone to bed.'

'Okay,' said Roberts. 'Anything else?'

'Nope, nothing else. No course changes.'

'Okay,' Roberts said. 'I've got it.'

'Okay.' Carney made a gestured salute. He stood around a moment, trying not to appear too anxious to go below. 'Hell of a bright night,' he said.

'It really is.'

Carney shifted his cap back on his head and yawned. 'Okay,' he said vaguely, and slouched off into the charthouse to write his log and turn in.

Roberts had the watch. For maybe the thousandth time in two and a half years Roberts had the watch. He walked back out on the wing, leaned against the windshield, and looked out at the sea and the night; and for the first time he noticed what an incredible night it was. The moon — what an enormous moon! It had risen yellow and round and fat, and now that it was higher it had shrunk a little, but still it was round and full, and no longer yellow but molten, incandescent silver. The light it spread was daylight with the harshness filtered out, unbelievably pure and even and dimensionless. On the bridge you could have read a newspaper: it was that bright.

The moon now was on the port quarter and all the way to the horizon it parted the water in a wide, white glistening path that hurt the eyes; and back where the horizon should be there was really none at all; there was only this pale blue, shimmering haze where sky and water merged without a discernible break. And the sea was even more remarkable: Roberts had never seen the sea quite like this. There wasn't a ripple anywhere; there was only the faintest hint of a ground swell, an occasional bulge of water. The surface, glazed as it was with moonlight, looked heavy, coated, enameled: it was that perfect.

The ship slid through the water with an oily hiss, and the bow cut the fabric like a casual knife. At the stern, the wake was a wide, frothing rent, but further back it was healing and not so wide, and far, far back the fabric was whole and perfect again.

Lord, thought Roberts, this sea is a phony, a mirage, an illusion. There couldn't be a sea like this. It's a lie, a myth, a legend. It isn't real.

And a not at all faint rebutting voice answered him: Don't you wish it weren't?

Yeah, said Roberts, I do for a fact: I wish it weren't.

And then he added: But this ship can't be real. There couldn't possibly be a ship like this.

The voice concurred: You're right there. There couldn't be.

But there is, Roberts said.

But there is, the voice agreed.

'Like a damn millpond,' said a voice at his side; a more audible and more physical voice. Roberts looked up at Dolan, the second-class quartermaster.

'The smoothest I ever saw it,' Roberts said.

'It really is.' Dolan looked about, almost squinting in the shiny moonlight. 'What a hell of a night to be out in this place!'

'I was thinking the same thing.'

Dolan, his eyes still scanning the water, shook his head defeatedly. 'Man, that beats me.' He was young, only twenty-one or so, but he was a smart one; savvy; shrewd. He had been aboard not quite a year, and in that time he had established himself as one of the most formidable crapshooters on the ship; the company was fast. From his first day aboard, he had stood his watches with Mr. Roberts, and a nice feeling had grown up between the two.

When the two stood a watch there wasn't any nicely shaded officer and enlisted man relationship; there wasn't even any awareness of difference. They just stood and talked together: two men with the background of the United States, the bond of this ship, a mutual dislike of the Captain; stood and gossiped and speculated and told stories and reminisced; things two men together are apt to do anywhere. Their watches were really one continued conversation which they could resume at any time without consciousness of a break.

'Crap game tonight?' Roberts asked.

'Yeah,' Dolan said. 'I played till about eleven, then I quit.'

'How'd you make out?'

'Lousy. That's why I quit. I went in with a hundred and I dropped that and then I borrowed fifty from Vanessi and I came back a little but then I dropped that too. So I figured it was time to get out of there.'

'Who won all the money?'

'Vanessi. Dowdy and him. That guy Vanessi was up about eight hundred bucks when I got out. He was hotter than a firecracker.'

Dolan was quiet a moment, then he said suddenly: 'By the way, did you hear about Dowdy? Him and the old man?'

'No. What did he do?'

Dolan laughed delightedly, an obviously choice morsel to give. 'That guy, you know what he did? Tonight? The old man called him up, something about the boats, and when they got through, the old man started crying the blues to Dowdy about the officers on here; what a miserable bunch of officers there was, and what a miserable outfit the Navy is, and how he wished he was back in the merchant service and could get hold of some of the officers back there. And then he says to Dowdy: "I know the officers on here hate my guts. That's all right; I don't care about that. Now tell me what the crew thinks of me." And Dowdy looks at him and says, "You really want to know, Captain?" And then he says: "Okay, you asked me and I'm telling you, Captain. They think you're an ass." '

'Well I'll be damned!' Roberts said. He clapped the pelorus. 'Say, that's fine! He really said that?'

'Absolutely! He said, "Captain, they think you're an ass." And he said the old man turned blue in the face, he was so mad; and at first he couldn't even talk, he was that mad.

Then he told Dowdy to get the hell out of his cabin!'

'Say, that's fine,' Roberts said admiringly. 'Dowdy should get decorated for that — the Navy Cross at least. I'm going to see to it that Dowdy gets recommended for the Navy Cross.'

The two worked on the Dowdy incident until its possibilities were exhausted; then they moved on to other matters. Dolan did most of the talking: he was a garrulous young man with impressively complete information on all strata of shipboard life, which he passed on faithfully to Mr. Roberts. Roberts, in turn, supplied opinion when asked, advice when asked, and a certain amount of information on officers' doings, which were somewhat inaccessible to Dolan's probing. Like all good gossip sessions, theirs was a reciprocal affair, and like a good session it served its purpose; it passed a weary hour.

Dolan looked at his watch. 'Jeez, a quarter of two,' he said. 'Okay if I go down for some coffee?' Roberts said it was, although it always took Dolan half an hour to get a cup of coffee.

'Shall I bring you some?' Dolan said, starting down the ladder. Roberts shook his head.

Alone on the wing again, he took his glasses and studied the horizon. There was nothing there; there was nothing at all in the night but this ship, the point of reference in infinity, and this sea that planed away in all directions to the curving line of its visible limits. A little wind had come up, and on the sea there was a little swell; the ship rolled in it ever so gently and slowly. Roberts watched as the foremast wheeled in a stately arc against the stars of the Southern Cross, a pointer tracing on the blackboard of the sky. A quarter of two: well, that was good; that was better than he expected. That's where it paid to have someone to talk to, someone like Dolan; the time went down so much more easily.

A quarter of two. Two hours down, two to go. It was when you were alone like this, nothing to do, no one to talk with, that the time went hard. It was a hundred times better to run in convoy and be busy as hell; a station to keep, the zigzag plan to run, ships to watch out for. It was when you were alone like this, no ships and no Dolan to engage the front of your mind, that it got bad. You started thinking then, and that was always bad. Never think: that was one of the two great lessons Roberts had learned. The other was, once started, how to stop thinking. When his mind started to work in the all too frequent pattern — subjectively, wishfully, unrealistically or too realistically, and, in the end, despairingly — there was only one thing to do and that was to stop it; to wipe his mind blank and clean as a slate washed with a sponge, and to keep it that way.

He had learned to do that, and he considered the knowledge a priceless boon. He could stand for hours as he did now, his mind shuttered like a lens; and the tiny corner of it that would never quite close completely engrossed with such an external as the mast pirouetting among the stars, or the phosphorus that flared in the bow wave. And sooner or later the watches always ended — he had learned that too — they always ended.

There were footsteps on the ladder and Dolan was back. He busied himself for a moment in the wheelhouse, getting the two o'clock readings; then he came out. He was eating an apple and he handed one to the officer.

'Clocks go back an hour tomorrow night,' Dolan said between bites. 'Not on our watch though.'

'Midnight?' Roberts said.

'I guess so. Jeez they'd better. I think we've caught all the long watches so far. And then when we go the other way and the clocks go ahead we miss all of those.'

Dolan worked on his apple down to the core and then threw it over the side. 'What time does Frisco keep?' he asked suddenly.

'Frisco?' Roberts said. 'I think plus seven. Why?'

'Plus seven,' Dolan mused, 'plus seven. We're in minus eleven now. That's six hours difference.' He ticked off on his fingers. 'Man, do you know what time it is in Frisco right now? It's eight o'clock!'

'That's right,' said Roberts. 'Eight o'clock yesterday.'

'Sonofabitch!' Dolan was impressed. 'Think of that, Mr. Roberts. Eight o'clock. Just the time to be starting out in Frisco!'

Roberts didn't say anything and the quartermaster went on: 'Man, how I'd like to be down on Turck Street right now. Just going into the old Yardarm. Things would just be starting to pop down there! Were you ever in the Yardarm, Mr. Roberts?'

Roberts smiled. 'Once.'

'I knew it!' Dolan chuckled. 'I knew it! I might have known you'd get down there. It's all right, ain't it, the old Yardarm?'

'A little strenuous,' Roberts smiled.

'More beasts down there than you can shake a stick at!' Dolan was getting enthusiastic in his recollection. 'You know what, Mr. Roberts? The last time I was there, that was a year ago, man, I found a fine little beast down there. Cutest little doll you ever saw, blonde, a beautiful figure, really a beautiful girl. I was pretty stupid drunk but I saw her and I started dancing with her and, boy, I sobered up in a hurry. I said, "Let's go some place else, baby," and she said, "Let's go," and we went out the door and I said, "Where we going?" and she just says, "Come with me." And she led me and we got in her car and she drove me out to her apartment 'way out by U. C. Hospital. She had an apartment all to herself and this fine car and, man, I was shacked up with her for a month. Her old man owned three bars and she was always getting me liquor and I was driving all over town in that Plymouth convertible and all the time shacked up with that fine beast. That was all right!' He shook his head wonderingly.

Dolan was all wound up now. He went on and on, recalling other conquests in San Francisco. Roberts listened for a while but gradually his mind wandered. He nodded his head at the right places, and smiled at the right places, but he was no longer listening. Against his will, knowing he shouldn't be doing it, he was thinking of San Francisco; he was back there himself now, reconstructing his own version of the town. He was thinking of eight o'clock, the hour when the evening came to life; drawing upon his intensely maintained recollections of two and a half years ago. He was thinking of the signs lighting up along Geary Street, and the lineup waiting for taxis in front of the St. Francis, and the cable cars climbing Nob Hill, and the dusk settling on Nob Hill, filling up from the bay and from the city below.

Eight o'clock in the nice bars — the St. Francis and the Cirque room at the Fairmount and the Top of the Mark and the Zebra room at the Huntington — the air bright and murmurous with the laughter and the clink of glasses and the foolish, confidential talk and over it all, soft and unheard and really astonishingly sad, the deep, slow rhythms of American dance music. And the girls, the fine, straight clean-limbed American girls in their tailored suits, sitting, leaning forward, each talking with her escort, one hand extended on the table and just touching his sleeve. Or dancing tall and proud to the music that promised them bright and lovely and imperishable things.

And at the bar all the young officers, the bright-eyed, expectant young officers, watching the girls, looking for something — they didn't know what — something that called at night with the dusk and the neon lights and swore to them that tonight, this very night, in this town, this bar, something of desperate loveliness was going to happen if only they found the right girl, found the right bar, drank enough liquor, smoked enough cigarettes, heard enough talk, laughed enough. But they must hurry, they must hurry; the bars were closing, the trains were leaving, the ships were sailing, youth itself was running out. What was it they were seeking? It wasn't just a girl, although a girl was necessary. A girl wasn't the total; she was just a factor. It was more than that, Roberts thought; what was it?

And the angry, critical refuting voice arose inside him and answered: Why you goddamn knucklehead! Who're you trying to kid? The bars are so goddamn noisy you can't yell from one table to the next. The women are a bunch of beasts with dirty bare legs and stringy hair. The boys are out for just one thing. Who're you trying to kid, anyway? . . .

Dolan was asking him something. He wanted to know: 'Any chance of this scow ever getting back to the States?'

Roberts said mildly, 'You know better than that.'

'Yeah,' Dolan said, 'I guess so. But the engineers keep saying we've got to get in a yard pretty soon.'

'And they've been saying that for two and a half years. There's nothing wrong with these engines that can't be taken care of right out here.'

Dolan shook his head sadly. 'Yeah, this bucket will be running around here till the war's over.' He added determinedly: 'But this kid is sure as hell going to get back before then. As soon as I get eighteen months in, if they don't send me back then, whiz over the hill I go!'

Roberts turned and smiled. 'What are you going to do, swim?'

'If necessary!' Dolan said emphatically. 'If necessary! Do you know there are thousands of bastards lying around the States who've never been to sea? Yeomen and storekeepers and all that crap. Thousands of them!'

'That doesn't help us any.'

'No, but it should,' Dolan said. 'How long have you been out of the States, Mr. Roberts?'

'How long? Two and a half years. Thirty-three months exactly.'

'Kee-ri-st!' Dolan said, impressed. 'That's a long time! How come?'

Roberts pinched his ear thoughtfully. 'I have a theory that all my records have blown out the window at the Bureau.'

'But thirty-three months! That's a *long* time!'

Yes, Roberts thought, it probably was a long time. He wasn't sure just how long, but it must have been quite long. He thought of his little sister for a greater comprehension of thirty-three months than the calendar provided. Thirty-three months had been long enough for his little sister, four

years younger, to meet a man, fall in love with him, marry
him, and bear a child for him. It was long enough for his
sister, who had been slim and blonde and pretty, to become,
according to the evidence of the camera, no longer slim, no
longer pretty, and more than thirty-three months older. It
had been long enough, he wondered, for how many couples
to fall in love and marry and have children? If all the
couples who met and married in that period were to march
four abreast past a given point, how long would the procession take? A hell of a long time, he decided; probably another two and a half years. . . .

'I know one thing,' Dolan was saying, 'when I do get back
I'm sure as hell going to get married. Little girl in Lakeland,
Florida. Cute as hell. Did I ever show you her picture?'

Roberts shook his head and Dolan said: 'I got it right
here.' He pulled a wallet out of his dungaree pants and in
the ample moonlight they stood and examined the likeness
of a round-eyed, gentle-looking girl with bobbed blonde
hair. 'Very pretty girl,' Roberts said.

'I'm going to marry that gal,' Dolan said, 'and then when
I get out I'm going to settle down right there in Lakeland
and raise ferns. Make a million dollars growing ferns.'

'Ferns?'

'Hell, yeah. There's a lot of money in them. People just
don't realize. You can make a lot of money growing ferns
if you get a little good ground.'

'I didn't know,' Roberts said politely.

'Yeah, hell yes,' Dolan said. 'What are you going to do
when you get out?'

Roberts picked up a pair of glasses and raised them to his
eyes. 'I haven't the faintest idea. Run a chain of whore-
houses, maybe. Grow ferns. Sell apples. Shine shoes.'

'What were you doing before you came in?'

Roberts looked through the glasses a moment without
answering; then he put them down. 'I was going to school,'
he said. 'Medical school. I'd just finished my first year.'

'Medical school? How come they got you in this outfit?'

'I came in. It was my own idea.'

'Yeah, but how come? The draft couldn't get you in medical school, could it?'

'No.'

'And you still joined this outfit?' Dolan insisted. 'When you didn't have to?'

Roberts smiled crookedly. 'That was right after Pearl Harbor. For some reason I felt that I had to get in the war.' He shrugged as though to dismiss the subject. 'I don't understand it myself now.'

But Dolan was not to be put aside. 'Jeez,' he said. 'I shouldn't think you would. If I had a chance like that to stay out I sure as hell wouldn't be here now!'

'Jeez,' he said again; and after a moment: 'How many times a day do you kick yourself, Mr. Roberts?'

'Several hundred,' Roberts said quietly. 'An average of several hundred.'

'Are you going back to medical school when you get out?'

Roberts shook his head and squinted up at the foremast. 'Too old,' he said. 'I was twenty-three when I came in, I'm twenty-six now, I'll be twenty-eight when I get out. That's too old. I'd have to take a year of refresher work, then three more years of med school, then two years interning. That would make me thirty-four before I even started practicing. That's too much.'

The quartermaster was quiet a moment. 'Jeez,' he said after a moment, softly. 'Why in the *hell* did you want to get in the war?'

Roberts' answer wasn't really an answer at all. 'I didn't know then that there were such things as auxiliaries,' he mused. 'I just took for granted that I'd get on a can or a wagon or a carrier right in the middle of it. Instead I end up on a tanker in the Atlantic and this thing out here.'

'Jeez,' Dolan said again. He shook his head doubtfully and looked at his wrist. 'Three o'clock,' he announced, 'five after.' He went into the wheelhouse to get the readings. He came back and leaned on the pelorus and the two stood together and looked out at the sea. A minute passed, and then another, and then, like an army in rout, the watch collapsed, fell apart, was finished. One minute it was three o'clock, and the next it was four. One minute Dolan was telling a story about the girl friend of Dowdy's who got her picture in *True Detective* for shooting her husband, and the next it was three thirty and time to call the reliefs. And from three thirty, the clock jumped to a quarter of four and Dolan was making an informal salute and spieling all in one breath and almost in one word, 'I've been relieved sir Garrity has the watch,' and then there was Pauley standing beside him, rubbing his eyes and yawning.

'A hell of a time to get a man up,' Pauley mumbled.

And the watch was over, swallowed, put down. 'It is that,' Roberts agreed. 'It is that.'

Pauley scowled around the horizon. 'What's the dope?'

'Two five eight. Seventy-two turns. No course changes. No zigzag. Stupid has a call in for six.'

Pauley nodded. 'I saw that. Okay,' he said. 'I got it.'

'Okay,' said Roberts. He turned to go.

'Say,' called Pauley, 'have you got *God's Little Acre?*'

'No, I don't have it. Keith had it the last time I saw it.'

'He's too young to be reading that,' Pauley pronounced soberly.

'That's very true.' Roberts went on into the charthouse to write his log. When he had finished he sat for a moment slumped on the stool at the chart table, rubbing his eyes. He considered for a moment going down to the wardroom for something to eat, then he remembered there was nothing there. He got up slowly and went down the ladder to his room.

Nothing had changed: it could have been seconds that he had been gone. Langston was still breathing with the same rhythm and the same intensity. With the same whine the fan was pushing the same air across the room. The clock ticked on and on. Roberts undressed in the dark and got into bed. He lay on his back, his arms cradled beneath his head, his eyes open and staring into the darkness. Helplessly, before he could stop himself, he thought again of San Francisco. Now, as he saw it, it was midnight there and the bars were letting out; the couples walked arm in arm down the streets and the women laughed, and all of them were rich with the knowledge of some incomparable party to follow. A boy and a lovely, slender girl with shining black hair came out of the Mark and stepped into a taxicab, and as the taxi pulled away the girl lay back in the seat and turned to the boy with a slow, happy, secret smile. And down the steep face of California Street, past the careless, oblivious couples, a young man walked alone, back to the ship, the camp, the empty hotel room; another night spent of the dwindling supply, and nothing bought. What was he looking for? What was he missing? What had he lost?

And then the sudden, angry voice clamored: Will you knock it off? Will you for Pete's sake knock it off?

Abruptly as turning out a light Roberts stopped thinking, shut off his mind, composed himself for sleep. Mechanically, through the tiny corner left open, he calculated the day ahead: four hours of sleep now, the four to eight watch in the afternoon, and then all night in — no watch until eight the next morning. A whole night in — that was something to look forward to.

*(From Town and Country)*

# UNDER THE GINKGO TREES

## BY EDWARD HARRIS HETH

*T*HE SIX men sitting under the ginkgo tree were listening to a short-wave rebroadcast of the Jack Benny show. The reception was not even fair; only fragments of voices here and there were understandable, like occasional waves on a rough sea leaping tongue-like into a boat. Much of the time there was only a grinding noise. But even though they could not understand, it made the men feel less far away. The voice of Rochester, though they could not understand his jokes or what made the audience laugh, made the men more comfortable because they recognized the voice; they thought of people at home listening to the same broadcast. A quiet obbligato of laughter came from the men each time their people at home laughed at Rochester and they felt for a moment a small part of the world they once had known.

The six men looked up as Gill joined them, but did not speak. He had just been moved up from base by plane and outrigger canoe and by the path cut through the jungle. He squatted down beside them, reminded by the broadcast of Sunday nights in New York. He raised the mosquito net from his face over his helmet to wipe the thick hot dampness from his jaw.

He could tell by looking at the men that they were tired, hopelessly tired, not alone from fighting or forcing supplies forward but simply from being there, from being away from home. They were exhausted by their suspension from life.

The hot stars overhead did not help them any. They were a link, like Rochester's voice, that made their isolation more complete: they only added to the distance from home because the men had seen these same stars in Ohio or Oregon. Even the heat was foreign.

A plane droned above them. By its sound they all recognized it as a Zero, but they were too tired, too lonely, even to glance up to see if the plane had spotted them and would summon others to bomb them. But they switched off the short-wave, calmly, as they might turn off a tap or close a door.

Gill glanced up at the sky and grinned at the men. 'My name's Gill,' he said. 'I just came up from base. Replacement.'

'Gill?' one of the men asked. 'Do you have relatives in Cambridge, Mass.? I knew some Gills there when I went to school. I'm Kavanaugh.'

'Gill's the first name,' Gill said. 'Gill Champion.'

'Oh, Gilbert,' Kavanaugh said. 'Bob Nissen, meet Gilbert Champion.'

'No,' Gill laughed. 'It's just Gill, not Gilbert. Two *l*'s.'

'How long ago were you in Cambridge?' a man asked. 'I'm Ben Sweet. Kavanaugh and I both went to school there. Funny thing, meeting out here.'

'I'm not from Cambridge. I didn't say I was,' Gill said.

It was like meeting friends over a drink in a bar. The men looked curiously and politely at Gill, lean, tall, at his dark matted hair as he pushed back his helmet, at the grin on his full lips. He was surprised at the courtesy of the tired, isolated men in the jungle until he learned that all six had gone to Eastern colleges. They had formed a colony among themselves, the way the baseball or movie fans formed colonies. And even in the hot jungle they kept a fraternity-like bond in which the youngest, named Lenicheck, was like a neophyte, running errands or lighting cigarettes for the older men though they were all of the same rank.

In the village the natives began singing. It was a strangely beautiful sound, Gill thought, watching it fall like a cool breeze against the tired faces of the men, relaxing their muscles, the stiff jaws, and aching eyes. It was not barbaric but gentle and lonely sounding. A pair of the enormous cockroaches moved over the short-wave set. Kavanaugh shot his cigarette at the cockroaches and they slid like two black dead balls down the side of the case. Lenicheck had been looking steadily at the case — Gill saw his eyes in the dark light like two holes of terror. Going to sit beside him, Gill felt the quick eagerness with which the boy made room for him under the ginkgo tree.

For the loneliness was plain in Lenicheck, even though he had his five friends from the Eastern colleges. It was not so much of missing people as of being lost where he was. His hair was short and reddish, his body slight. He was far too thin. He looked more tired than any of the others. More than with any of the other men, the youth was being burned slowly out of him, though he was the youngest of the lot.

Lenicheck looked up nervously as Captain Barker came through the dark. Barker tipped his heavy head backward to wipe the heat from his throat with his handkerchief, as he approached the men. He was shy and heavy-set, still under thirty, and well liked by the men he commanded.

'You men aren't playing that radio, are you?' he asked. He glanced down at the set. 'There's some Jap planes around. Oh, it's turned off,' he said, slightly embarrassed and wiping the soiled handkerchief around his red neck. 'That's good.' He nodded, looking at the men, whom he knew would be back in action within twelve hours. 'I've got a detail for someone.' He dropped his handkerchief, stooped to retrieve it, shaking it carefully, always afraid of the ticks and roaches on the jungle floor that could snatch at the piece of cloth quicker than a man's hand. 'One of the native guides will go along, but he won't go alone.'

The men, tired, suffocating, looked in silence at the Captain.

'Well, we can't trust a native alone,' the Captain explained like someone accused. 'Sometimes they just never come back.'

'What is it?' Kavanaugh asked.

'Well, the men up ahead at the hill need something. They need something badly. It's about a three-hour trek one way, but a native will go along to show the way. It's safest to make the trek at night.'

'What do they need?' Kavanaugh asked.

'Well, they need something. It's toilet paper,' the Captain said, smiling shyly while he dabbed at his throat. 'Supplies must have got mixed up. A hell of a thing to leave out.'

The men did not laugh, feeling a sudden and sober comradeship for the men up ahead because they needed something.

'I'll go,' Gill said.

'I'll go,' Lenicheck said.

'Well, that's right, you're the youngest, Lenicheck,' Captain Barker said, and dropped the handkerchief again. 'But you've had a tough day yourself, Champion.'

'Just traveling,' Gill said. 'Not fighting.'

'If you don't mind going,' the Captain said, nodding reflectively.

'Well, then you two had better catch an hour's sleep and start out. Report to me when you're ready.'

He picked up the handkerchief, shook it, and went back into the darkness again.

Once the Captain was gone, the men began to joke with Gill and Lenicheck about their mission and its nobility and the pleasure of walking a jungle trail by night. But they did not joke brutally. It was only a way of giving courage, to young Lenicheck especially, and to cover their own relief because they were not going, not through cowardice, but because they were exhausted and hot and tomorrow would be fighting again.

Lenicheck and Gill went to the huts to get some sleep. They lay down on adjoining mattresses but then did not sleep at once, Gill learning what the boy's loneliness was. Lenicheck lay on his back, his hands under his head, and might have been lying on a hillside, looking at the moon. He could not sleep.

'Cambridge is outside Boston, isn't it?' Lenicheck asked. 'That's where Yale is, isn't it?'

'No. Harvard,' Gill said. 'Yale's at New Haven.'

'Oh, sure, that's where Nissen went. Then you're a Harvard man. That's pretty good.'

'No, they got that mixed up about me and Cambridge,' Gill said, laughing. 'I've never been in Cambridge.'

'You didn't go to college?'

'Yes. Wisconsin.'

'Well, that's not a bad school, is it?' Lenicheck said, and sounded patronizing, so that Gill smiled in the blackness of the hut. 'I'm from Dartmouth. Wonderful winter sports.'

'I've been there visiting,' Gill said, 'yes, it's wonderful.'

'You've been there?'

'Yes, I have.'

For a moment Lenicheck was silent, bringing one hand out from under his head to touch it briefly over his eyes. 'I never have,' Lenicheck said.

This was Lenicheck's loneliness. Gill did not answer. It was a strong and bitter loneliness, to make Lenicheck pretend he had been to college like his five friends, and after knowing Gill only an hour to tell him this. It was an angry loneliness because Lenicheck had never been to college at all but had to quit high school to go to work. But with his five friends he could almost feel he had gone to one of the wonderful colleges, Harvard or Princeton or Dartmouth. It was not the education, because he had educated himself well; but it was the life, the excitement. Lenicheck, in the fantastic jungle, thought of fantastic proms and clubs and stadiums.

'I said I never went,' he repeated.

'I know. That's all right,' Gill said. 'I'm sorry you had to miss it.'

'Is your home in Wisconsin?' Lenicheck asked.

'It was. It's where I was born. But for the past five years it was New York.'

'New York City?' Lenicheck quietly asked.

'Yes.'

Then Gill could sense Lenicheck's thin body stretching

taut on the mattress across from him, as though he heard
of New York City with a tight, painful ecstasy. 'I'm from
Idaho. Boise. I never went further east.'

'You will,' Gill laughed.

'Oh, I will!' Lenicheck said, and Gill could hear the boy's
body racked with pain. He spat the words out; there was
blood in his mouth from their hurt. 'I suppose you knew
lots of girls there?'

'Quite a few.'

'What kind?' and the words writhed, as his body writhed
with hunger and longing and fear.

'One sang in a nightclub.'

'You did not,' Lenicheck said, and laughed faintly, the
laugh torn from his lips, believing, disbelieving, worship-
ping, envious, his arms and legs beginning to tremble with
his loneliness for life, for girls and nightclubs and music
and drunken gay endings, his head dropping asleep over a
shining white-clothed table among the half-empty glasses
and compacts and frail handkerchiefs left behind by the
girls. 'You did not,' he repeated, icy cold in the hot jungle,
and all the blood leaving him in sudden fright that Gill
might agree with him. He might say it was all a lie, like
Dartmouth — that he did not know a girl who sang in a club,
or had never even been in New York.

Gill heard that the boy was crying. He did not speak but
in the darkness reached out his hand to lay it on Lenicheck's
head to comfort him and let him know he was there. He remained silent, so the boy need not know that he knew there
were tears running down his burnt, thin face. He only lay
there thinking of the wonder of the boy beside him, sweating
in the jungle and crying and dreaming about New York and
afraid he would never get there.

Gill kept his eyes on Lenicheck's back moving ahead of
him. Under the thin cotton shirt he could see the muscles
tighten as occasionally he shifted the load he carried from
one shoulder to the other. The sticky vines grabbed at the
load Gill carried, as he had watched the native carry it, on

top his head. When it could pierce the jungle, the rising sun brushed in almost friendly fashion across Lenicheck's back. He kept moving determinedly on under the trees ahead of Gill, as though he had no notion of what had happened.

Gill blinked, trying to steady his eyes. The growing light played tricks with him. Repeatedly, through the crinkled foliage of the ginkgo trees, he thought he could catch the glossy flesh of the native carrier. It was several hours since the native had deserted them, yet his eyes kept glimpsing him behind the tree trunks, as though he had not left at all, and were following along behind them, and would finally reappear to show them the way back to the trail. He did not mention it to Lenicheck. He knew the guide would not return. They could only keep on pushing their way through the vines, hoping to come upon a clearing, or an encampment, or upon the men on the hill whom they should have reached many hours ago.

There was no sign that they were near the hill country. No slight undulation began on the jungle floor to show they were nearing the low hills. It remained flat, with a warm smell of decay sifting up from the dead tremendous leaves. The heat was beginning again like something that had lain there all night, waiting for the light to lift it up again. It rose vaporously, pressing small drops of moisture from the falls of the orchids that hung leechlike against the trees.

Lenicheck halted. He shifted his load from one shoulder to the other. His streaked face grinned. 'This is the God-damnedest place.'

Gill laughed. Then he looked around him. Alone, only himself and Lenicheck, he saw the jungle for the first time. They were helpless inside it. He did not see it now from the safety of an Army encampment or an outrigger canoe, being paddled along the dipping, salmon-colored coast by friendly natives.

Yet he saw the wonder in it, and its impervious beauty as it existed only for its own necessity and pleasure, without need of man. It knew nothing except the rain and sun that nurtured it. It was a chaos of survival, the ropelike vines reaching out to strangle the trees while the trees grew stout to burst the vines apart. Gill ran his hand under his chin, feeling again the wet heat that rushed up from the floor; and glanced at Lenicheck.

Lenicheck saw nothing of the jungle. Before beginning once more to move forward through the trees, over what no longer bore any trace of being a trail, he turned his eyes to Gill. There was something distant in them, searching, having no cognizance of where he was, lost in the jungle. But also there was no fear in them. Rather, a confidence, as though some distant world made it possible for him to continue his trek through the jungle that always grew denser and more web-like with its ropes of vines.

Gill was thinking about the guide who had deserted them, after they had been on their way only an hour; for no reason he had suddenly dropped the load from his head and bolted among the trees, a black shadow vanishing swiftly among blacker shadows. Lenicheck spoke again.

'I like to hear you talk,' Lenicheck said.

For the first hour after the native had bolted, Gill had kept up a flow of talk; to ward off their helplessness, to conceal from Lenicheck that the trail was growing always more elusive, until all at once Gill had known that they had lost it, stumbling forward in the darkness. He had talked about his trip up by plane and canoe. He asked questions about the five men who were Lenicheck's friends. He asked about the fighting up near the hill.

Now Lenicheck even whistled a few notes of a tune. The rising light seemed to give him strength. He had not once asked whether Gill knew where they were going, or how soon they might reach the hill. 'Lots of men don't know how to talk,' Lenicheck said over his shoulder. 'They just give out a lot of words. But I get something out of you.'

Gill hesitated, drawing the net from his helmet over his face as the waking jungle drew the insects up from the matted floor. 'What do you want to talk about?'

'Tell me more about New York City.' Lenicheck did not turn around, but Gill saw his back go more erect. It stiffened, a rod of pain. 'About the girl you knew there. The singer.'

Around noon they had dropped their loads. They were no longer looking for the hill, or intent on their detail, but simply on finding their way back to something they knew. They had only taken one ration along, and eaten that several hours ago, still confident that they would have found their way long before this.

But a strange thing had come over Lenicheck. He had listened earlier, trekking through the hot morning, to Gill talk about New York City, the theatres and nightclubs, streets and shops, and how anything could be bought in New York City and anything one wanted could be done. He listened with a rigidity in his burnt, thin body as Gill told about the singer, a girl named Susan Bright. How tall was she? Lenicheck needed to know; what color hair; her eyes; what kind of voice; and whether she drank and danced. And how old, Lenicheck needed to know; was she too old for someone like himself, who was twenty-one, and did Gill think he could ever date a girl like that in New York City?

A hunger was plain in every movement he made. They walked more freely now, since they had discarded their loads, no longer even remembering the ridiculous nature of their mission. But Lenicheck walked with a much heavier weight. He held himself taut, like someone being whipped. His footsteps wove slightly. His reddish hair looked hotter and wilder than the noon sun racing down through the trees.

Gill saw the desperation that was coming over Lenicheck. They had not yet said to each other that they were lost, that their traipsing through the jungle was aimless and endless. Gill's eyes felt a rim of pain along their lower lids, from searching through the trees for some familiar sight. Flies slid and hummed and darted against their faces. The parched air was painful to breathe. Lenicheck's back was a rag of sweat. But it was not from fright or the baking sun. It was the strange thing that had come over Lenicheck. As they wound the jungle more and more weblike around themselves, a driving haste made him walk still faster, as if he kept pulling himself toward some distant day.

He talked much, and a little incoherently, of the distant day. Repeatedly Gill tried to draw him back to things he knew. He tried to make him talk of Boise, Idaho, where he had been born. But Lenicheck only tipped his head to one side, listening to something else, not to what Gill was saying. And after a moment of listening, asked in almost a whisper, 'That singer, that Susan Bright — is she your girl? I mean, do you go with her steady?'

Gill wanted to make Lenicheck sit down to rest; but knew that his rapid pace was as necessary as his flow of blood. 'No.' And after a moment he added, looking up idly through the trees. 'There's a couple of girls I like much better.' For he suddenly knew something else and, knowing it, could not tell Lenicheck that the singer was really his girl.

Lenicheck brushed fiercely at the flies that hummed at his face. 'I'm going to New York City. After this business. When it's over, I mean,' he said, making it sound that he was saying nothing, and was not waiting painfully for what Gill would answer.

Gill's voice was steady. It held only the silence and monotony of the jungle. 'When you get to New York, I could get you a date with Susan. I'll fix you up.'

'You could not,' Lenicheck said, as he had said it the night before. He laughed with the sound sneering in his throat. 'You'd never do that. You couldn't. Unless she's a four-eyes or got club feet. I'll bet she isn't even a singer.' Lenicheck laughed. 'You could not,' he said again, the words scarcely forced from his lips.

'I've got her picture with me,' Gill said.

'You have not. I'll bet she's a beaut. Like Vera Vague.'

Gill took out the snapshot and, without lessening pace, handed it forward to Lenicheck. Lenicheck did not look for a moment, seeming not even interested, and when he looked took only one glance, dropping his hand again to his side.

'Do you like her?' Gill asked.

He could hardly hear the answer; the buzzing of the insects was louder. 'She's all right.'

'I could get you a date easy enough — '

'She's all right,' Lenicheck repeated.

He sounded as if he had seen much better. But the blood was pounding in him and on the back of his shirt Gill could see the sweat pour freely.

'Keep the snap if you want,' Gill said.

'What for?'

Gill laughed, a hollow sound in the jungle. 'Get acquainted with her. Get to know her. The first day you get to New York, I'll fix up a date.'

'You will not.'

'Sure I will,' Gill laughed. 'I'm giving her to you. She's not exactly my type. I've got other girls I like. I'm giving you a girl for keeps.'

Lenicheck said nothing and as though it were only a piece of paper stuffed the snapshot inside his shirt.

The heat rose damp and rank from all sides of the jungle. They rested against a tree trunk. There was not a sound in the jungle until all things took on a sound of their own. They could hear the leaves growing and even the thick shadows of evening, coming early, slid in with a leaping sound. Gill looked at his watch and saw nine minutes to six and after a dozen years looked again and saw it was eight minutes to six.

Lenicheck did not look frightened or worried. The orchid he had picked an hour ago and stuck in the buttonhole of his shirt already hung limp with thirst like their own. They took a drink from their canteens, just wetting their mouths, because they did not know how long the water would have to last. Lenicheck took out the flower and briefly stuck its stem into the neck of his canteen then grinned at Gill.

'How much do these things cost in New York City?'

'Orchids?'

Lenicheck nodded.

'About five bucks,' Gill said.

'For just one?' Lenicheck laughed. But he enjoyed it. He envied the opulence of paying five dollars for just one flower, in some distant and wonderful city to which he would go someday, when here in the jungle they could be picked by the armful.

Gill saw him looking into the distance. But his lips were moving quietly like a mute's. His eyes pierced through the thick vines, their ropes alive with ticks and parasites, and he saw much further; and from his slowly moving lips Gill could tell he was repeating the names he had told him earlier in the day, the names of the clubs he was going to visit someday, Ruban Bleu, the Stork, Coq Rouge.

'Where do they wear them?' Lenicheck asked suddenly.

Gill was tired. He was not tired so much from his own exhaustion as from trying to conceal Lenicheck's own exhaustion from him. For a moment he did not even want to answer. They should not have halted to rest, he was thinking, because now as they leaned against the sharp bark of the ginkgo trees everything seemed aimless. There was no purpose in forcing themselves up again, because there was no place to go — any direction he might pursue was blind, hopeless, fruitless. He had closed his eyes for only a second, forcing himself to answer Lenicheck, and was turning to him when he saw how Lenicheck was laughing.

He was holding the orchid against his chest. 'Here? On the breast?' he was asking. His laugh came in a short hiccough. He looked sheepish, a little frightened. The fingers holding the flower were quivering. They might have touched warm, round flesh, pinning on the orchid. All his wiry body was alive with life and the things he still would do; his eyes gleamed with the things they still would see.

Gill tried to shake the exhaustion from him. Whatever he tried to say then seemed heavy, the words lost and meaningless like the shadows sliding under the moist leaves. 'They wear them a lot in the hair,' Gill said. 'Pinned on one side, over the ear. Or flat on top the head.'

Lenicheck stuck the flower behind one ear. The pale color took on a washed-out look against his fiery stubble of hair.

The shadows were coming quickly, piling over the trees and vines, but with them came a thin rush of cool air. It was easier to breathe.

Lenicheck with the ridiculous flower behind his ear leaned back against the tree. But he was grinning. At the same time something else made his grin empty. He was worried about something. He was somehow getting up nerve. Despite the rush of cool air, he was sweating more than before. The rivulets ran down his thin cheeks, shining faintly in the little light left to them. His whole body seemed to be working at something. The nerves and muscles were so tight they might have torn open the flesh. In his thin growth of reddish beard was a second beard of sweat.

Then Gill saw what was happening. The vacuous grin hung on Lenicheck's lips — Lenicheck himself seemed absent. He had got himself to New York City. He had a date with the singer. He was sitting at a white-clothed table, his head swaying from too much to drink, his ears deafened with the music, and his eyes dimmed from the crowds and glasses and the dancers. And he had pinned the orchid in her hair.

Only once did Lenicheck come back. For a moment, as the night kept growing, he put his arms around one of the hanging trunks of the vines. It looked like having them around something real. His eyes closed. Then he dropped his arms, opening his eyes. 'We're lost, aren't we?' he asked.

Gill nodded. Lenicheck also nodded, almost thoughtfully, and leaned back against the tree. The shadows leapt around them like frightened birds.

(From Cosmopolitan)

# MICHAEL FINNEY AND
# THE LITTLE MEN

# BY JOHN RICHARD HUMPHREYS

*I*N ANY ONE of the many Banbury tavern bars talk
doesn't have to run very dry before someone brings up
the name of Mike Finney. In Banbury, of late, Mike
Finney's name and a glass of beer have assumed a peculiar
association, because it's over a beer glass that the question
most often arises: 'What the Sam Hill ever got into Finney,
anyway?'

The only man in town with a possible answer is Claude
Conroy, a Banbury old-timer and head man at the Conroy
fish hatchery. Conroy has a clear memory of the night the
change took place in Finney because that was the night in
the middle of which Finney dragged him out of bed and
hustled him out to Neg Deering's place, talking all the while
like a drunken maniac.

To hear Conroy tell it, Neg and Finney must have had
a binge out there at Elm Island Lake big enough to last
Finney the rest of his life. And certainly no one has seen
Neg Deering since. Anyway, something momentous happened to Finney that night. Since then he's been close-
mouthed about the whole affair, but everyone knows he slips
out to Deering's cottage at Elm Island Lake every chance he
gets and spends hours in the pump house jabbing a fish pole
down the water pit under the pump. . . .

Finney's memorable night began with a telephone call
from Neg about seven o'clock in the evening. A half hour

221

later he had left the house, telling his wife he wouldn't be back till morning, and driven away muttering to himself.

Dusk was thickening the woods and fields by the time Finney reached the lake. He turned into the narrow lake road and drove down between the tall trees fencing the tire tracks and passed the first of the winter-boarded cottages. Leaves were just beginning to turn from green to brilliant frost-stung colors.

Neg's hillside cottage faced the lake, isolated on the tree-dense shore. Neg had a light on in the front room. Finney stopped the car in front of the closed garage doors. As he got out and shut the car door, he heard Neg coming down the driveway from the front of the house.

Neg had on a suede jacket that flapped as he walked and his face was white in the dusk. 'Did you bring it?'

'Yeh, I brought it,' Finney said. 'It's in the back.'

Neg nodded, 'Swell, swell. Let's get it inside.'

Finney opened the back of the car. 'You gone nuts up here or something?' He leaned inside, wrapped his arms around the bulky object and pulled it out.

Neg said, 'Look, Finney, leave it with me will you, just a couple of days. How about it?'

Finney shook his head and stood looking at Neg. 'Can't do it, Neg. Like I told you, I can't do it.'

'Well, let's get it inside,' Neg said and Finney started toward the door of the pump house. 'No! This way,' Neg said. 'Here, let me take it.'

'Why not put it in the pump house? What do you want to lug it all the way around front for?'

Neg started on down the drive. 'I keep the pump house locked.' Finney shook his head and followed. Neg kept saying, 'You'll never know how much I appreciate this, Finney. This is a big favor. You'll never know.'

'All I want to know,' Finney said, following him up on the porch, 'is what you want it for. What have you got out there in the lake?'

Neg stood by while Finney opened the door. 'Can't tell

you now,' he said. 'Tell you later. Can't tell you all at once. You wouldn't believe me. You'd either say I was a liar or tell me I'd gone nuts.'

Neg set the helmet down in a corner of the living room. It was a homemade diving helmet, a cut-down boiler with a compressed-air tank and a window for the diver's face. Neg stood up rubbing his hands. 'That's swell. That's swell.'

Finney thought Neg looked a little wild around the eyes, and he sat down in an armchair, watching Neg's face.

'You'll see,' Neg said. 'In the morning: As soon as it's light. Then you'll see.'

'I'll see what?'

'You'll see. You'll see,' Neg said. 'How about a drink?'

'I think you owe me one,' Finney said, 'after that wild trip out here.'

'Yeah, a drink. We'll have a drink. Come on out in the kitchen.'

Neg stopped in the kitchen doorway and looked across the room at the water pail. 'Oh, wait,' he said. 'I'm out of water. Unless you want it straight. I've got whisky. Better get water anyway. Do you mind taking the car to another cottage up the road a ways?'

Finney looked at the back door, the door to the pump house. 'Pump's broken,' Neg said quickly. 'I've got to get it fixed.'

'Let me take a look,' Finney said. He felt Neg reach for his arm as he passed, but Neg missed and Finney crossed the floor hearing Neg behind him. He took hold of the knob. The door was locked.

'Neg,' Finney said, 'there's something screwy as hell going on out here. What's up?'

Neg looked back at him a minute, and there was definitely a wild look in his eyes. Then he turned away and walked over to the pail. 'For God's sake, Finney, will you trust me? Will you trust me till morning?'

'It's not a question of trusting you, Neg. I want to know what's going on. I don't like the looks of things. What's up?'

'Look,' Neg said, 'go get the water for me, will you? I'll

tell you just where to go. There's a pump you can get at about a half mile from here.'

'You want me to get it?' Finney said, his eyebrows rising, his finger pointing at his chest. 'You want me . . .'

It was at this point that the pounding inside the kitchen cupboard began. Neg heard it first, and the look in his eyes got wilder and wilder. 'Okay,' Neg said. 'We'll get it together. Let's go.'

'What's that?' Finney said, looking at the cupboad where the doors were tightly closed and padlocked.

It was a hollow distant pounding, not the sound of struck wood, but the sound of remote drums, and the sound of something else that was like the movement of water.

'That?' Neg said. 'Oh, that. That's rats or something. You ought to see some of the rats around here.'

'You keep them locked in there?' Finney said.

Neg waved his hand toward the cupboard in embarrassment. 'No, I — oh, I got reels and stuff in there. I'll show you where to get the water.' He started for the doorway.

Finney followed. 'Neg,' Finney said, 'I want to hear right now what's going on around here. I want to hear it right now or I'm packing my helmet back in the car and heading for town.'

They went down the porch steps together, Neg carrying the pail, and went around to the car, crossing the moonlit ground. . . .

Finney was a good Christian and a fine family man. He ran the Banbury hardware store, and his wife and daughter helped him. He read the Grand Rapids Herald every morning of the week, including Sunday; and on Sunday he bought the Journal-American for the additional funnies and the magazine section. He liked to read about ghosts but, never having seen one in his life, he was pretty sure they didn't exist. Still he liked to read about them and about the strange 'supernatural' things that happened to other people.

Finney had walked down a hundred dark staircases, up a hundred back alleys and had never run across anything more disturbing than a prowling alley cat. He scoffed at spiritualist meetings, fortunetellers, palm readers, gypsy curses and all that junk. And once (although he would have rather confessed beating his own mother than reveal this secret) he had stood up in a dark room and challenged all ghosts in general. No ghost had appeared and it had settled his mind on the matter of their existence.

So far as Finney was concerned life was a straight logical routine. You got up in the morning, shaved, had breakfast and went down in the store for the day's work. Every day was the logical same. That was one reason Finney looked forward to his hunting and fishing trips every year. And he'd built a diving helmet to catch a little of the feeling of mystery there might be in life.

To Finney it was inconceivable that the murders, robberies, divorces and other lurid stories he read about in the papers could ever happen to him. But on this momentous evening his curiosity had been just strong enough to make him go out to his garage and get out his diving helmet and drive to Neg's place. Neg had made it sound pretty urgent, but he hadn't explained what it was all about.

Finney had known Neg most of his life. Neg wasn't a dumb guy or the kind that filled his head up with a lot of crazy ideas. They'd grown up in Banbury and had gone to the same school, even played on the same football team. After high school Neg got a job on the Grand Rapids Herald and finally moved from home into the city; but he spent a lot of time in the cottage his folks had on Elm Island Lake. Finney came out to the lake enough so they kept running into each other, enough at least so Neg knew he had a diving helmet. But they'd never been very close friends.

So when Neg began to tell him about the treasure hidden at the bottom of the water-filled pit under the boards of the pump house, Finney laughed in his face.

They were driving down the narrow road between the trees, turning around and around with the road, sweeping the blackness with their headlights. Finney kept his grip on the wheel and threw his head back and laughed.

'No, I'm not kidding,' Neg said. 'That's why I keep it locked. I don't want anyone to get in there.'

'You telling me,' Finney said, 'there's water enough under that pump for you to use a diving helmet?'

'Yes. That's what I'm telling you. I'm telling you there is. I told you you wouldn't believe me.'

'This where we get the water?' Finney slowed down the car.

'That's it. Pull up there by the side. Look, Finney, we'll get this gold together. We'll share and share alike.'

Finney laughed. Then he remembered the pounding behind the padlocked kitchen cupboard: faraway and liquid-like. And he stopped laughing.

The pump squeaked in the dark shed under the flashlight in Finney's hand, and the water roared into the pail. Neg stood on the boards and pumped the handle up and down. The boards were like the ones in Neg's pump house. You could pull them up.

When the pail was filled they went out to the car and drove back to the cottage. It was a warm night and the crickets were singing away under the leaves of the woods.

When they got back Neg fixed the drinks. He brought the whisky out and they mixed it with water. They sat around in the living room awhile and talked about the old days. Neg built a fire in the fireplace and turned out all the lights.

Once Finney asked Neg to let him look at the pump house but Neg said no, to wait. 'The first thing in the morning,' Neg said, 'I'll show you the first thing.'

And then Finney figured out what the look was Neg had around his eyes. It was the look of a man who has made up his mind to do something, and he's scared stiff. And he doesn't want me around when he does it, Finney thought; he wants me out of the way.

So when they went upstairs and went to bed in separate rooms, Finney didn't go to sleep. He lay awake and listened.

About two hours passed before he heard what he wanted. It was the sound of a door opening, the door to Neg's room.

Finney listened, heard Neg's slippers in the hall and then on the stairs.

Finney threw back the blankets and got up. He went to the door of his room and waited, giving Neg time enough to get downstairs and get at whatever he was about. Then he softly opened the door and felt along the dark walls to the stairs. He went down the steps, feeling along the banister until he came to the bottom. The light was on in the kitchen.

He stepped barefooted and quietly across the floor until he could see through the kitchen door. He saw Neg first. Neg was sitting on the kitchen table. And then he saw what Neg was looking at because the cupboard doors were unlocked and open.

It was a large, glass jar, at least three feet high, and inside was a little man with his hands and face pressed against the glass looking back at Neg. The jar was filled to the top with water.

'Neg! My God, Neg! What is it?'

The creature in the glass pushed away from the side, and the water swirled.

Neg got up from the table and turned to Finney with the eyes of a sleepwalker. 'What are you doing here?'

Finney quickly crossed the kitchen to the cupboard. 'Neg. What is that thing?'

The little man whipped his feet and his face returned to the glass. Little gills opened and closed on his neck, just below the ears. His mouth blew a stream of bubbles, and Finney saw the teeth were fanged.

'Get away,' Neg said. 'Get away from it!'

Finney stepped back.

Neg took his arm, his fingers cutting in through the cloth. 'Do you see it? Do you believe it? There it is, look.'

Neg pointed at the jar, his finger a few inches from the glass. The little man moved back and then rushed furiously forward at the pointing finger, legs thrashing the water, hands pounding against the glass.

'It hates me,' Neg said, 'Lord, how it hates me!'

The little man's teeth were opening and snapping shut in rage and fury.

'What is it?' Finney said hoarsely.

Neg stepped quickly to the open cupboard doors and closed them. Then he carefully took the lock and snapped it shut. Finney could still hear the creature pounding and banging against the side of the glass.

Neg was neither a good Christian nor a good family man. His only family were his parents who still lived in Banbury. So far as his Christian standing was concerned, it didn't go far. It was reliably reported the only church services he ever attended were Baptist evening meetings when liquor caught him in a sentimental mood.

At the Grand Rapids Herald he was considered a good but undependable reporter so far as his working hours went. Or if you wanted to look at it another way you could always depend on Neg to disappear once or twice a year on a prolonged drinking jag. Once he'd disappeared for two years and come back with wild tales about life in the Florida swamps. That was Neg. But anybody who'd believe a word he said about his crazy adventures was a plain fool.

Neg, unlike Finney, was inclined to listen to anything a fortuneteller or a gypsy had to say. In fact, he never faced a fortuneteller without a tight feeling in his stomach that now at last something black and dire would be revealed.

Neg, in his forties, was still young enough in mind to consider that he had been born for a signal fate, for a certain fateful day on which an act of his would, forever after, affect the entire world for better or worse. He felt that the passing of his days was not so much a matter of routine as a marking of time.

Neg's fateful day began early on the first morning of his week's vacation at Elm Island Lake. It began in a manner so completely illogical that, had it happened to Finney, it would have shocked him into total disbelief. Finney would have blamed it on liquor, an upset stomach, anything rather than have to accept the incident as factual.

Neg, early that first morning, had left a fishing pole propped against the pump and gone off in search of wood.

As he told the incredulous Finney later, after Finney had seen the little man with his own eyes, 'You know how you'll do,' he said. 'Sometimes you'll leave the worm on the hook. That's the way it happened. I'd been out on the lake the night before, fishing for bullheads, and the next morning there was still a worm on the hook. I didn't even notice if there was a worm on or not. I just leaned the pole up against the pump and went off looking for wood. Well, listen Finney, that hook with the worm on it dropped down between the two sections of the boards under the pump; it fell down between those two sections and dangled in the water. With the worm still on it, see?

'Well, so help me, when I got back with the wood and piled it up I turned around because something sort of caught my eye near the pump. It was the pole. It had fallen down and was hopping around on the boards. It stunned me. I'm telling you, it knocked the wind out of me, that pole hopping around on the boards like there was a fish on the other end of the line. It took me a couple of minutes just to get over to the pump and pick up the pole. That's all I did at first. Just picked up the pole and held it. I couldn't think of anything else to do, and it *did* feel like a fish on the other end of the line. All I could think of was what the hell is a fish doing down in the water under the pump?

'So I pulled those sections of the board back and yanked up on the line. At first I thought it was a fish because it came out fast. It was just a blur on the end of the line. I tossed it over my head, and it hit against the wall of the pump house. When I turned around to look, there it was standing up, jerking at the hook in its mouth. A man, honest to goodness, a tiny full-formed man standing there. He was staring at me and jerking on the hook and screaming; yes, screaming; and then I saw him tear back to the pump pit. He ran across the ground just like you or I would, and jumped into the water. And right then the pole in my hands started jerking again. All I could think of doing was cutting the line loose. I got out a jackknife and cut quick.

'Then I ran over to the pump pit and looked down at the water. The water was still whirling around a little and there was blood on the surface. I'm telling you the truth Finney, that's how it happened. You saw one of them. I've got one there in the kitchen.'

'Let me see that pump house,' Finney said slowly. They were sitting in the front room, and Neg had his head in his hands staring at the floor. 'Let me take a look at it, Neg.'

Neg stood up slowly. 'I don't even like to go out there. I'm scared of the place, but I guess it will be all right at night. They seem to stay down in their hole when it's night. Did you see the teeth those things have?'

'Yeah, I saw them,' Finney said.

Neg shook his head in a bewildered way. 'That's why I keep the one in the cupboard locked up. I've been afraid one of these days he'd get out and go looking for me. They can breathe air, Finney, just like you or me.'

'Let me take a look at the pump,' Finney said.

'I have to lock the door to keep them in there. Whole mobs of them come out and run around that shed all day. I've sat here for two days now and listened to them. Honest, they hold meetings and yell and swear and keep daring me to come in there. So help me Finney, I can't believe it myself but they speak English, just like you or me. Listen, Finney, I've often wondered if with those teeth of theirs they could chew through the door. I mean it. What do you think?'

'I don't know,' Finney said slowly. 'I can't quite believe the whole thing yet.'

Neg was feeling in his pocket. He brought his hand out and held a ring of keys. 'I'll show you,' Neg said. 'Bring the flashlight.'

They went out to the kitchen, and Neg put the key in the lock. The lock slid back, and Neg put his hand on the knob and turned it. He pushed the door open wide and Finney stood behind him, looking into the pump house. The light from the kitchen dimly filled the shed, highlighting the long slim pump and the wood piled along the far wall. Moonlight came in through the only window and made a yellow, crossed square on the ground by the pump. The shed was empty. Neg placed his hand against Finney's chest so he would wait. They stood in the doorway looking and listening. 'Okay,' Neg whispered. He motioned for Finney to follow and went quietly down the three steps to the dirt floor. Then he and Finney tiptoed to the edge of the pump pit where the board sections had been pulled away, leaving the black square of the hole around the bottom of the pump. The pump disappeared down into the darkness.

Neg turned his head to Finney and put his finger against his lips. They waited a moment, and then Neg reached over and took the flashlight from Finney's hands. He held the head toward the pit and flicked the beam on.

There was a startled movement of water in the pit, as though a fish near the surface had flipped its tail. They stood looking down at the glittering, rippling surface of the water. 'Caught them,' Neg whispered. 'Did you see that?'

They got on their knees at the edge of the pit and looked down in the water, holding the light steady. They waited a minute or two, and then Finney distinctly saw something swimming to the surface. He saw the tiny face come looming up in the light, and then the body twisted and it was gone. 'See them?' Neg said. 'That was one. It's full of them. They live down there.'

'Where did they come from?'

'I don't know,' Neg said.

'How deep is it?'

'I don't know. That first day, you know ... I tried to find out then. I had a long cane pole here in the shed. I shoved that down in the water and I couldn't hit bottom, but you know what happened? While I had that pole in the water something down there grabbed it. I almost fell in the pit. It almost pulled me in. I let go of the pole, and it went right down out of sight.'

'You mean it didn't come back up?' Finney said.

Neg shook his head. 'No sir. It stayed down there.'

'How could it?'

'It did. Right out of sight.'

'Hold it a minute,' Finney said. 'How deep down does this pump go, I wonder.'

'A hundred feet, I think. I think that's it.'

'Then it couldn't be more than a hundred feet deep.'

Neg nodded. 'That's why I want to go down there. See now? Finney, this is a great discovery. Those are men. That's a race of people, a lost race of humans. Did you ever read about Atlantis?'

Finney nodded.

'It's like that Finney. My God, think of it. Think of what we've discovered. They're going to have to revise Darwin. They're going to have to rewrite the history of man. There's a whole country down there, and it must have air because they've got noses and mouths and ears. Finney, maybe we could go down there past the water, take off the helmet and walk around.'

'That one in the kitchen,' Finney said. 'How did you catch him?'

'A net,' Neg said. 'With a net.'

The flashlight beam moved around the dark corners of the pit and over the surface of the water. No more of the little men appeared. 'I'll show you something else,' Neg said. 'Come on.'

They got up and went back in the kitchen. Neg locked the pump house and led Finney into the front room and over to a big wooden chest near the stairs. 'I'll show you something,' Neg said.

Finney watched him open the top of the chest and then stepped over to look in. 'What is it?'

'Look.' Neg held it up in his hands.

'Chain mail, isn't it?' Finney said. He shook it in the room light and dropped it back.

'They'll never bite through that. I'll wear that when I

go down.' Neg slapped a thick coiled rope with the back of his hand. 'I'm going to lower myself down with this. I'm scared, but I've got to go because it's my discovery. Mine. I'm ready to try it right now.'

'Now?'

'Sure. Why wait for morning? I'll take the flashlight with me. It works under water.'

'Look,' Finney said excitedly, 'I've got an idea.'

'Yeah?'

'I'll go get Conroy. He'll know all about this. I want him to see this.'

'Who?' Neg said. 'Conroy? The guy that runs the fish hatchery?'

'Sure.'

'What'll he know? All he knows is bass.'

'No, Conroy would have to know about every kind of fish. Maybe this is just a rare fish. Let me get him . . .'

Conroy said, 'Finney, this is the most idiotic bosh I've ever heard in my life.'

The speedometer figures on the lighted dashboard registered like numerals on an idiotic roulette wheel.

Finney leaned forward over the wheel, sighting ahead with the car lights. 'Bosh? Wait till you see what I've seen with my own eyes.'

White desultory road signs appeared and passed like gowned figures, like Finney's challenged ghosts, to stand as soldierlike honor guards along the way.

Conroy settled down in his overcoat, muttering and glaring through the windshield, thinking of the way Finney had burst into his house and hauled him out of bed. Hauled him out of bed in the middle of the night, Finney had, and stood him on his feet yelling about little men running around in Neg's pump house. Conroy shook his head, settled down further and muttered, 'Little men,' sniffing at the reek of whisky in the car. Hauled him out of bed, he had, to drag him out to Neg's so he could watch them go diving for little men in Neg's pump pit. Conroy jabbed his hands down in the pockets of his overcoat and thought of Finney's bare feet on the pedals of the car.

He'd stood in Conroy's bedroom in his bare feet with a raincoat over his pajamas shouting that Conroy had to go with him, he didn't care what time of night it was. And Conroy, who had never seen Finney drunk in his life before, got dressed and went, more because he was worried about Finney's going completely off his nut than anything else.

Conroy had said carefully, 'What's in the well pit, you say?'

'Little men. Little men, I'm telling you.' Then he'd stopped a minute as though his reason was returning, and he'd looked steadily across the bedroom at Conroy. Then he'd said, 'Conroy, I want to know one thing before we go any further. I want just one thing verified. It's something Neg told me just before I left. Do we humans have the remnants of what used to be gills in our bodies? Do we?'

'Why yes, Finney. I guess that's true enough. Now why don't you sit down a minute and rest yourself?'

Then Finney had started in again, raving about a little man in Neg's cupboard, so Conroy had finished dressing and gone with Finney. But now that they were in Finney's car he was starting to get sore. The nearer they came to Neg's cottage the madder he got.

Gigantic trees sailed by with ghostly arms whitened under the car lights. 'Why me?' Conroy said, twisting around in the seat. 'What the hell you want me for?'

'Maybe it's a fish,' Finney said. 'If it's a fish you can tell, can't you?'

'But why now?' Conroy said, 'Why in the middle of the night? Couldn't you wait till morning? It doesn't make sense, I don't care how excited you are or what's happened. Why me in the middle of the night? And another thing I don't get: this chain armor business. That's the most idiotic thing I've ever heard. Where would he get it? He's only been out there a few days.'

'I tell you he's got it. He's got it out there. I've seen it with my own eyes.'

Conroy sat bundled in his coat in the corner of the car, staring out ahead, his eyes watery and stiff with sleep, as though this were still a part of his sleep, an aggravating dream. 'I don't care, Finney. This isn't like you. The whole thing isn't like you. Since when have you been chummy enough with Neg to take your diving helmet clear out there and stay all night without knowing what he wanted it for? Since when? And this thing he had in the jar . . . why wouldn't he show it to you right off the bat? I don't get it, Finney. I'm just telling you, Finney, this sure as hell better not be a joke. It better not.'

'You wait. You wait,' Finney said.

They drove over the country roads, through the night, grinding the tires into the gravel roadbed until they came to the lake road that went down to Neg's cottage.

Finney pulled the car in beside the house and stopped in front of the garage. Then he and Conroy got out and went around to the front porch. Finney began shouting as they went up the steps, 'Hey, Neg. Neg . . . I've got Conroy.'

They went in the front door, into the living room, and then Finney stopped and froze like a statue in front of the open chest by the stairs. 'Gone,' he said. 'It's gone,' he shouted.

'What's gone?' Conroy said, his hands deep in the pockets of his coat, staring in an angry, perplexed way at Finney.

Finney pointed into the chest. 'The armor's gone. It's gone, and the rope's gone.' He yelled, 'Neg. Hey, Neg.' He took a quick look around the room and let out another yell. 'My helmet!'

Finney ran to the kitchen, and Conroy followed suspiciously.

'Look,' Finney yelled and pointed. 'Look.' The cupboard doors were open and the glass jar that had been on the inside shelf had fallen to the floor and broken. Water was soaking darkly into the floor around the table. 'The shed,' Finney said. 'He's gone down already. Damn him. Damn him.'

Finney flicked on his flashlight, aiming the beam through

the open doorway into the pump house. Conroy frowned and followed him slowly. He stood in the doorway at the top of the steps and watched Finney at the pump.

The shed was dark and quiet, lighted by window moonlight and the light of the kitchen doorway. Conroy's legs made two dark shadows down the pump-house steps. He said, relaxed and easy, 'Go on, Finney.'

Finney held his light on the pump and on the rope tied to the top of the pump that ran down into the dark water. 'See, look there,' he said. 'Look. He's down.'

Conroy took his hands out of his pockets and came down the steps as Finney grabbed the rope and pulled up. The end of the rope flipped out of the water with a tiny splash and Finney stared at the frayed end with open mouth. 'My God,' he said slowly, 'it's been cut. They've cut it. My God, he's down there with them now.'

'He's what?' Conroy said.

'The rope. The rope,' Finney shouted, waving it in his hands. He shoved the flashlight into Conroy's hand. 'Hold this. Hold it on that hole.'

Conroy pointed the beam into the open pit around the pump and looked down a moment at the surface of the water, and then up at Finney running frantically around the pump house.

Finney came running back with a cane pole in his hands.

'So they cut it did they? Now what are you doing?' Conroy said.

'He's down there,' Finney yelled. 'I don't know if we can reach him . . . We've got to.' He dropped on his knees by the side of the pit and jabbed the pole down into the water. The pole slicked through three feet of water and jarred to a halt. Finney raised and jabbed the pole against the bottom three or four times before he stopped and stared at the roiling muddy surface of the water.

'It's caved in,' Finney said as though he were speaking about the sky. 'They've caved it in so he can't get back.'

The moonlight came in through the shed window and fell across Finney's back where he knelt by the pump pit.

'Sure they did,' Conroy said. 'They caved it in. And you wouldn't kid me, would you, Finney?'

Claude Conroy may be the only one in Banbury other than Finney who has any idea what happened that night, but Conroy says it was liquor and Finney isn't talking. Finney is waiting. He knows as sure as God made little apples that one of these days Neg Deering will come digging his way back. And when he does this world is going to open its ears to one of the strangest stories it's ever heard. They can call him as crazy as they want to, but Finney's just waiting.

*(From The New Yorker)*

# DOWN IN THE REEDS
# BY THE RIVER

## BY VICTORIA LINCOLN

*W*HY are we never prepared, why do all the books and all the wisdom of our friends avail us nothing in the final event? How many deathbed scenes we have read, how many stories of young love, of marital infidelity, of cherished ambition fulfilled or defeated. There is nothing that can happen to us that has not happened again and again, that we have not read over a thousand times, closely, carefully, accurately recorded; before we are fully launched on life, the story of the human heart has been opened for us again and again with all the patience and skill of the human mind. But the event, when it comes, is never anything like the description; it is strange, infinitely strange and new, and we stand helpless before it and realize that the words of another convey nothing, nothing.

And still we cannot believe that personal life is, in its essence, incommunicable. We, too, having lived the moment, are impelled to convey it, to speak the words so honest in intent, so false in the final effect. Now, after so many years, I want to tell you about Mr. deRocca, although it is a queer story — not a story at all, really, only an incident in the life of a young girl — simply to show that it was not what you would have expected. It was not like the books or the whispered, ugly confidence that you remember from your school days; it was quite, quite different. I want to tell you, although I know from the outset that I shall fail, as we all fail.

But now that I come up to it, I hesitate. It should have
been evil, frightening, all wrong; of course it should. It
should have been the repellent accident that can queer an
emotional development for years to come. And still, when
it was happening, it was not like that at all.

I was fourteen, a wiry, red-headed, unimaginative little
tomboy, fond of sand-lot baseball. My parents were dead,
killed in an accident a year before, and I lived with an aunt
and uncle in Braeburn Heights, a suburb of a small city in
Kansas. Bereft, rudely transplanted from the life I had
known — a happy-go-lucky life in the brown hills of California — I was lonely beyond words. I had grown up in the
careless warmth of love, and for my Aunt Elsa's genuine, if
worried, kindness I could feel nothing but ingratitude. The
house was strange, the neighboring children were strange,
with their neat, pretty bedrooms, their queer talk of dates,
and formals, and going steady. I felt dry and hard and empty
inside myself, day after day. I used to take my bicycle and
ride out into the country, but the country was strange, too,
and ugly to my eyes, all flat and dull.

And then, one day, I found White Creek Row. It was the
town's Hooverville, a row of shanties between the creek and
the railroad, little huts like the playhouse that I had built
back in the hills with the children of our Mexican gardener
— a tragic, shocking, sordid shantytown, as I see it now. But
to my enchanted eyes it was romantic and delightful and,
more than that, comprehensible, as my aunt's house in
Braeburn Heights was not.

It was in White Creek Row that, unknown to Aunt Elsa,
I made my first real friends in Kansas. The squatters in the
row were shy of me at first, as I was shy of the people in
Braeburn Heights. My decent clothes, my bicycle, made me
alien, an object for suspicion and resentment. And still,
somehow or other, I managed to scrape an acquaintance
with Posy Moreno, an acquaintance that grew into love.

She was a gentle creature with a mop of soft black curls
piled high on her head and a womanliness, at sixteen, that
made me feel, for the first time, glad that I, too, was growing

near to womanhood. She lived in the last shanty in the row with her little brother Manuel, and next door was Mrs. Grimes, her self-appointed duenna. She was very proud of Mrs. Grimes' watchfulness.

'Me, I'm never chasing with the feller,' she used to say, 'but if I was to chase with the feller, Mrs. Grimes she's knock me down, you bet. She's not let anybody get fresh with Posy Moreno.'

'I wouldn't want anyone bossing me like that,' I said once. And Posy, lifting her head in the pride of her womanhood, replied, 'You not need. You just a kid.' But as we became better acquainted she treated me less and less like a kid.

Through our long afternoons on the creek bank, listening to her conversation, I would sit spellbound, infinitely flattered that she considered me a girl and not a child, feeling within myself a new softening, a shy preening, a tremulousness delicious and unfamiliar.

Besides Posy and Manuel, the only other child on the row was Chuck Hansen, who was twelve. I liked him, too, and I used to let him ride my bicycle while Posy and I talked. I could never hear enough about life in the row, and the people who lived in it. They had everything, I used to tell myself, everything that anybody could want, for I was too young to understand the need for security, for dignity. They had everything, and they had got it all free — even a church.

Mrs. Grimes had wanted the church, and Mr. deRocca, who had been a carpenter in Italy, had built it for her, although he was a freethinker and had accompanied every hammer blow, so Posy told me, with a lot of bad talk about religion being made up by rich people to keep poor people quiet.

How I wished I might have been there to see him, sitting on the roof, pounding down the shingles that were made from flattened tin cans, with his delicate, hard little old hands, and shouting all the time, 'Opium of the people. You getta pie in a sky when you die!' The church even had a piano, with a good many keys that still sounded, nice and loud, if not true, and Mrs. Grimes played gospel hymns on it by ear.

Mr. deRocca would not go to the prayer meetings. He lived in the best shanty in the row, and in his front yard was a beautiful American flag laid out in bits of broken brick and slate and white stones. I admired it intensely and used to stop before his house, the better to enjoy it, but Posy would shy off and draw me away, throwing up her head with a sort of wild-pony elegance. 'Better we're not hanging around here,' she would say. 'Mr. deRocca, he's liking the girl.'

I did not understand. Would anyone so old want a wife as young as Posy, I wondered. It must be that, I decided, when Posy told me that Mrs. Grimes had not let Mr. deRocca help with the building of Posy's shack. I supposed they thought it would not be fair to encourage him. But I saw no reason why the caution should also apply to me. I was charmed by the little I had managed to see of Mr. deRocca. He seemed to be a very clever, very nice old man.

And now I come to my story, and it is hard to tell. It is hard to tell because I should have been so different. Perhaps there were undertones that I have forgotten. That is likely, for the memory has a curiously clear and classic air, quite unlike life as I have since found it — the nymph and the old satyr frozen in attitudes of timeless innocence under the box elders by the creek bank, the sacred grove where liquid Peneus was flowing and all dark Tempe lay. And still, still, I remember it like that. If there was fear, if there was guilt, they came later.

One afternoon, Chuck Hansen met me on the cinder track, looking wistful. 'I don't guess you'll want to stay today, Connie,' he said. 'Mrs. Grimes and Posy, they went uptown.' He rubbed the handle bars of my bicycle with his hands, hard, as if he were fondling a horse. 'Guess you won't have much to stick around for,' he said humbly.

How nice he was, I thought, never teasing.

'Well, listen, Chuck,' I said. 'I'm tired, a little. I'll go down and walk around a while and sit on the creek bank.'

His grin made me feel warm and pleasant. I began to saunter along the front of the row. Mr. deRocca was sitting on a packing case by his door, eating an onion. His face, lifted to the sky, wore the blank, peaceful expression of one enjoying the quiet of a village street after a procession has passed, the look of remembering in quietness.

I came along very slowly, watching Mr. deRocca from the corners of my eyes. He wore a plaid flannel shirt, ragged and, of course, unironed, but fairly clean, and the neck was unbuttoned. I noticed how the flesh under his chin was firm and didn't hang down in wattles, and the cords in his neck didn't stick out. He looked harder and nicer than other old men.

How old was he, really? About fifty, I should guess now, looking back; maybe a little less. But if I had known it then, it would not have changed my picture of him at all. Fifty to eighty in those days were all of a piece in my mind. Mr. deRocca was an old man. And he was nice. As I came very close, I realized with a sudden throb of excitement that he had been watching me all along, just as I had been watching him. Watching me and waiting for the moment to speak, just as I had been, with him. I turned, pretending to have seen him for the first time. I smiled at him. The white teeth gleamed in the thin, brown face; the elegant, small, brown paw that held the onion described a vast semicircle of greeting. 'Hi, kid,' he said. 'Looka for da Posy? She's a not home.'

I did not answer. I had realized, quite abruptly, that it was the sight of him sitting down there below me, fully as much as Chuck's longing hands rubbing the handle bars, that made up my mind for me up there on the embankment, and I turned shy, hoping that he would not guess it.

'I always like to look at that flag, Mr. deRocca,' I said.

'Come on in a yard,' he said. 'Looka good. It's a pretty, hey?'

We stood together, eyeing the charming sight in a sort of shared pride. He pulled out another packing case from the corner of the house and waved me to it with the flattering charm of a courtier.

'Please to sit,' he said. 'Scusa.' He went in the house for a second and returned, extending his hand with the same grave courtesy. 'You like-a onion?'

I looked at it dubiously. Father had disliked salads, saying firmly that hay was for God-damned Frenchmen, and Aunt Elsa's were of the pineapple, cream cheese, and mayonnaise school. Raw onions were new to me, and alarming. But it was so lovely, being treated like a lady, that I could not disappoint him.

I took it and bit into it gingerly. The sharp, pungent, biting juice ran over my tongue, the firm, fleshy layers crunched between my teeth in a stinging, breathtaking ecstasy of delicious pain.

'Oh!' I cried in sincere delight. 'It's good!' Then, with the snobbery of the young guest who does not wish his host to think him ignorant of the wines he is offered, I added, 'It's one of the best onions I ever ate.'

'Sure,' he said proudly. 'Sure, you bet it's a good, it's a fine. I grow.'

I regarded him happily, rejoicing in his kingly acceptance of the compliment, so unlike the mincing, genteel self-depreciation which, of all the mannered compulsions of the Heights, I found most unfamiliar and most dismal.

I went on with my compliments, sincerely, but also eager for the continuing pleasure of his openness. 'You have a wonderful house,' I said. 'The church is wonderful, too. You're a fine carpenter.'

His eyes glowed and he swayed his head from side to side, like someone keeping time to music. 'You bet I'm a good,' he replied. 'I'm a learn in a Old Country, worka slow, take-a pain, think for the job, for looka pretty, not think for hurry up, getta money. I'm a good like nobody's business.'

'I should think you'd get lots of jobs,' I said, 'and be rich.'

He shrugged. 'Bad a time,' he said. 'Everywhere bad a time. Smart a man everywhere hungry, no work. Someday come a good time.' He finished the onion and wiped his thin lips on the backs of his neat little fingers. 'Someday, different time, all be good, not graba, graba, be man and man together, not dog and dog. First a big fight, maybe, then all be good.'

I remembered something we had studied in social science.
I leaned forward, trying to look intelligent and grownup.
'You mean a revolution?' I said. 'Are you a Communist, Mr.
deRocca?'

'Pah!' he replied. 'Not!' He spat to one side, to emphasize
his attitude. Then, with a flashing, all-embracing smile: 'Lots
good in de Comunista, lots smart. I read, I like, good. Only
alla time boss, boss. Boss so bad like we got here, now. I'm
a no like all a time boss. I am Anarchista, me.'

'What's that?' I asked.

'Everyone's treat everyone else right. No push around, no
boss. People no gotta lot of stuff, graba, graba. No law, no
boss, everyone a same. Treata them right, they treata you
right. All good.'

It sounded lovely.

'What do you call that? Anarchista? I guess I'm Anarchista, too,' I said.

He threw both arms wide, embracing me in the universal
fellowship. 'That's a fine. You smart a kid.'

Master and disciple, we sat happily together in the blissful
country of utopian anarchy, regarding the flag of America
spread out at our feet with absent, gently admiring eyes.
Gradually, the conversation took a personal turn.

'You name a Constansia?'

'Constance.'

'Pretty name,' he said. 'Pretty name for pretty girl. Nice
when a pretty girl have a pretty name.'

No one had told me I was pretty since my mother died.
I was grateful to him, but unbelieving. 'I have awful red
hair,' I said.

'Pretty,' he said. 'Pretty hair, pretty eye, pretty shape.
How old?'

'Going on fifteen.'

He smiled, as if I could not possibly have been a nicer age,
as if it were a peculiar grace and wisdom in me to be going
on fifteen.

'Last year, da little kid,' he said. 'Next year, da woman,
look at da fella, think for da fella. Now she not know
what she think — that right?'

I was deeply struck with the truth of his words. It was what I had been feeling in my inarticulate way all the time I was sitting with Posy on the creek bank, admiring her womanly young beauty, listening to her sternly virtuous, so very sex-conscious conversation, hoping that she did not still think of me as just a little kid.

I looked earnestly at Mr. deRocca sitting on his packing case, as if I could discover in the glowing, friendly eyes the source of his remarkable understanding. He was old, but I thought suddenly that he was handsome, as handsome as my father had been. His features were so sharp and delicate, his body so fine-boned, the shoulders so narrow, compared with the Mexicans with whom I unconsciously classed him. A fleeting wonder passed through my mind if all Italians were like him, so little and handsome and wise.

He held out his hand toward me, palm up and slightly cupped, almost as if he were coaxing a tame bird with seed. 'That right?' he said again, quite soft.

I was surprised at my voice when I answered. It was unfamiliar — low and a little unsteady. 'That's right,' I said.

He stood up, smiling more than ever. 'Come on down a creek bank,' he said. 'I show you where I gotta good catfish net. Other guy wait to fish, watch, work. Me, I sit and they come.'

Thinking back, remembering, I wonder for the first time if he spoke in any conscious analogy. I do not believe that he did.

I followed Mr. deRocca trustfully down the creek bank, under the box-elder trees. At the water's edge, he turned and looked at me, and I saw the changed look in his eyes. It was as if the door had opened and I were looking upon a landscape that was both strange and familiar. I glanced around me, and I saw that the box elders grew thick where we stood, that we were in a place that was private, sheltered from the eyes of the world. Suddenly, I understood everything that Posy had said. I knew what she meant when she said, 'He's liking the girl.'

'Show me the net,' I said nervously.

His eyes smiled at me, reassuring, his voice quieted me. 'Pretty soon,' he said. 'Right down here.' But he made no move toward going on. Instead, he put out a lean, brown paw and touched my head. 'Pretty,' he said. 'Pretty hair.'

His hand slipped down my back and around my waist, the fingers firm and hard against me, warm through my cotton dress. And again he paused, his eyes still smiling with that same gentle reassurance.

He was old at the game, I see now, and grown wise in method, wise and patient. If he had hurried, if he had let me see his eagerness, I should have been terribly frightened, I should have run away crying. I should have run away full of fear and hate, and the fear and hate would have lived in me a long time.

But he stood, smiling at me, until I was used to his arm, his hand, feeling it not as a sexual advance but as warm, human affection in my body that was aching for human affection, for the demonstrative love on which I had thrived through a warm, loving childhood. He was quiet until I felt my fear dissolve in gratitude for the kindness of his arm, his firm, affectionate hand.

It was easy, then, for him to turn me against him, to hold me firm and close, stroking my hair, firm and close against him, waiting till his accustomed, patient hands should tell him that I was ready for more.

I knew that I must be doing something bad, and still I could not feel that it was bad yet, not yet. And his slowness made me confident that I was free to decide if it was really bad, that he would let me go quickly the minute I thought it had begun to be bad. It still did not seem bad when he kissed me, or when his kissing changed and made me feel all soft and strange inside, or when his hands began to describe all the differences that the year had made in my body, and to tell me silently that they were beauties, richness, a bounty of which to be proud.

Once he made a little motion to draw me down in the thick grass, and I had the sense to be frightened, but he felt it at once and waited, and I waited, too, sure that I would know when I should run away, growing softer and stranger by the moment, forgetting everything outside me. I was wholly lost when I heard Posy's shrill voice calling my name, and heard her pushing through the branches down the creek bank.

Mr. deRocca let me go and dropped to his knees at the water's edge. 'Like a this,' he said. 'I'm a tie right here, da fish swim right in. Some net, hey?'

He looked over his shoulder and saw Posy. She was white and out of breath. 'Connie!' she cried. 'I don't know where you are. I'm scaring.' She snatched at my hand, too relieved, too wrought up, to look at my revealing face. 'Come along outa here,' she said. Then, remembering her manners, 'Hello, Mr. deRocca.'

She yanked me back to the row. 'You crazy,' she scolded me. 'What you think, you go down there with deRocca? I'm telling you he's liking the girl.'

'You said I was just a kid. That's what you said,' I repeated.

'I know,' she said. 'Well, I'm crazy. Just as soon Chuck he tell me you down here, I'm knowing I'm crazy. You no kid, not for looks. No more. Was a little while ago, now no more. Mother of God, I'm scaring.' She paused, momentarily suspicious. 'What you going down in there with deRocca for?'

'He said he was going to show me his catfish net.'

'Ha, I bet! You poor kid, you got no sense. What he say? He talk dirty?'

No,' I replied with perfect truth. 'He talked just as nice as you and Mrs. Grimes.'

'Thanks God,' said Posy, over and over again. 'Thanks God.'

In the unpleasant shock of nearly being caught out, all the new feeling that I had learned — the lovely, soft, flowing, flowering openness — was driven back in me, and the present moment closed above it so completely that the afternoon might have been lived years before, or not at all, by anything

I felt in myself. Instead, I was troubled by an unwilling anger against Posy, as if she were making a disproportionate fuss.

Something of this she must have felt, or perhaps she now decided that my unwary innocence had been scolded long enough, for she took my hand, smiling again, as if, for her, too, the incident had suddenly dropped away out of sight.

'Come now,' she said. 'Is early yet, you don't got to going home, come now down to the house. We don't say nothing from this to Mrs. Grimes.'

'No, Posy, no, I've got to get home,' I said.

All the way home, I pedalled hard, as if I were very late — so hard that there was no room in me for anything else. Even before I saw the letters lying on the hall rug, where they had fallen from the mail slit in the door, I could tell from the silence that the house was empty. I stood in the sun that poured in at the open doorway, absorbing gratefully the quality of an empty house. I had not realized at all, as I forced myself home, faster and faster, how I would need, once I had got there, to be alone. I shut my eyes and sighed heavily, feeling the silence, the aloneness all through me like a merciful, unexpected blessing.

What had happened that afternoon, what had really happened? It wasn't only that I had let Mr. deRocca kiss me and touch me like that. It was something that had happened in me. There was something in me — and in the world, too — that I had never known was there before, something powerful and lovely, something powerful and new.

I stood there alone in the quiet house, in the sunshine, with my eyes closed. 'I wish,' I thought slowly, 'that Posy hadn't come. I wish . . .'

Suddenly, I knew that I had begun to be bad right there in Mr. deRocca's front yard, before we had ever gone down to the creek. I knew that I had been bad all along, terribly bad. Fear and guilt rose in me like a storm, shaking my body until my teeth chattered and I had to sit on the bottom step of the stairs and lean against the wall to hold myself still.

'If Posy knew,' I thought, 'if she knew about me, if she knew what I did, I'd die. I should die, I'd die.'

Aunt Elsa found me like that when she came in a few minutes later. 'Why, Connie!' she cried. 'What is it, dear? You're sick.'

'I got a chill,' I said. 'Just right now.'

'Let me hang up my coat, dear,' she said, 'and I'll get you right into bed. Why, you poor baby!'

I let her help me up the stairs. I clung to her motherly warmth all the way, hungry for it, like a child that has been lost and found again. 'Oh, Aunt Elsa,' I cried. 'I'm so glad you're home.' And her gentle voice soothed me again and again. 'There, dear, there. You're going to be all right. There, poor little girl. Aunt Elsa'll put you to bed. Yes, she will. Of course she will.'

In the complex agony of the moment, I was broken wide open. She's real, too, I thought in slow wonder; Aunt Elsa is real, too. She was my mother's sister.

I caught at her light, smooth dress, hiding my face in it. She smelled nice, clean and fresh with a light perfume. I let my head fall against her shoulder, and it was soft and firm, comforting, comforting.

'Oh, Aunt Elsa,' I cried, wondering because it was true, because it had not been true before, at all, and now it was wholly true. 'Aunt Elsa, I love you.'

That is the story, and that is all. When I woke in the morning, the ecstasy and the shame alike were gone. I had shut my mind upon them, as I had learned earlier to shut it upon grief and loss.

Oddly enough — for the defense mechanism seldom works that way — I still liked Mr. deRocca. Apparently, his attempted seduction had been quite impersonal, for, as I used to pass his yard, walking up the row to Posy's house in the warm, dusty August afternoons, he would always wave his little paw at me and say, 'Hi ya, kid,' amiably, but with no attempt to detain me.

For my own part, I always felt a tingling as I passed him;

not enough to be unpleasant — just a sort of shy, quickening self-consciousness. It made me avoid his face as I replied, 'Hello, Mr. deRocca.' My voice, as I spoke, was always a trifle breathless. I told myself that it was funny how I hardly remembered that afternoon by the creek at all. But as I passed his house, I always stood up straight and moved slowly, and tried to look grownup.

*(From Mademoiselle)*

# LITTLE BASEBALL WORLD

## BY ROBERT LOWRY

*H*ELEN turned it on very low so that nobody else in the house would know she was listening (she'd sworn before them all never to listen again, because they had kidded her about it), and then as soon as she'd heard the score she turned it off and sat staring at the back yard.

The score was five to two in favor of the Cubs and it was only the last half of the third inning with the Reds at bat — who was batting? Lombardi? Lombardi was a good hitter, you couldn't tell what they were going to do now . . . of course the Reds would lose, they always lost, they did so many completely stupid things just when they got you all excited about how good they were that you wanted to throw the radio out of the window. Who was batting anyhow? She turned on the radio again, very softly, and listened, leaning forward in her rocker.

'Lombardi on second, Harry Craft at bat with one ball and two strikes —' Lombardi on second! She leaned forward to listen.

'All right,' said the announcer, 'Bill Lee is ready —' and the black-eyed buxom girl rocked back and forth in the rocker before the radio. She was ready too, it was evident, she was waiting for whatever was sure to come. She just had no faith at all in the Reds any more, they lost yesterday and they'd lose today, they weren't going to be leading the League for much longer. . . . Like what happened yesterday, they were winning until the first of the ninth, then that

Johnny Vander Meer let the bases get full by walking so many, and Hartnett came in to pinch-hit and made a home run, and that was the end of your old ball game. That was the way they always did — got you all worked up then betrayed you.

'. . . hits a long fly ball into right field — and he's *out!*'

'Oh my God,' Helen said, and snapped the radio off.

She went to the kitchen, got herself a glass of water, then came back into the dining-room. She sat stiffly in her rocker, staring out at the back yard. She wouldn't turn it on for ten minutes, then she'd see what happened. Not that she expected anything good to happen.

But all the radios up and down Hutton Street were blaring forth the game, and before three minutes were up she couldn't resist, she switched it on.

' — and the Reds are out in front again! Now let me turn you over to Dick Bray who has a few words to say about the Breakfast of Champions . . .'

She'd missed the best part — the score and everything. There was that Dick Bray talking away in his tenor voice about Wheaties, the Breakfast of Champions — he wouldn't tell it.

'Shut up about your Wheaties and tell us the score,' she said out loud. 'We know all about your Wheaties, just shut up and tell us something we want to know.'

But no, he just wouldn't. Finally Red Barber came on to announce the first half of the fourth, and she found out the Reds were leading six to five.

Well, that was better than nothing — she rocked away in her rocker. They'd lose it anyhow, though. They always did something good then went ahead and lost it anyhow. They didn't care how hard you rooted.

She'd certainly done her part — been here by her radio since the opening game in spring, shouting at the announcer, getting angry when the Reds fumbled, furious when the Giants or Cards or Phillies made a run. Anyhow the Reds were leading the League, even if they wouldn't win the pennant. It was the last of July, everybody else on that street was sure they were going to be champions and play in the World Series, but she laughed at that, you never could depend on them just when you thought they were so good. That was when they always lost.

'Well, the Reds are out in front now with that one-run margin,' Red Barber said, 'but we still have six-long-innings to go and — '

'Six long innings is true,' Helen said right back. 'And don't kid yourself that plenty can't happen between now and then.'

She sure did know, this was her second year listening and they sure made plenty of mistakes. Of course she *wanted* them to win — tuned in even on Sunday when the club officials wouldn't let the game be broadcast in detail because it hurt attendance. She read the papers in front of the radio then and waited for the pause in the recorded music when Red Barber gave the runs, hits and errors.

Seven days out of the week she was here, but she didn't care. People could just leave her alone to sit here, they could mind their own business. Her mother never told her to go out and get a job or anything, but she knew that was what they were all thinking and she didn't care. Her brother Tom would make some remark to her, and she'd tell him off. Just let me alone, just go away and never speak to me.

She didn't care if she *never* went out of the house again. She almost never did either, except to go downtown to the library. She hated clothes, she hated getting all dressed up. She felt so conspicuous on the streetcar. Wearing those silly gloves.

They didn't understand, nobody else had anything wrong with them. They didn't have to wear silly gloves when they went out. Tom thought he was smart and could do anything he wanted, go anywhere he wanted. He was a boy seventeen, a year younger than she was — she'd wanted a sister anyhow.

Well, yesterday she'd told off her mother all right. Her mother had said, 'Why don't you ever go out any more? Why don't you and some of your girl friends go to the movies?' She'd told her mother then. 'Because of my hand, that's why.

Because I'm crippled,' she'd said right out. Her mother had begun crying and Helen hadn't even felt sorry. 'Now you know, so just stop crying. I'm not ever going anywhere again, so just don't bother me. I'm not ever going to go out and get all dressed up and wear those silly gloves again.'

They could all just leave her alone, she was happy. She was glad she was all through with high school — glad she had no friends — glad she didn't have anything to do but listen to the baseball game — glad she was crippled. If anybody didn't like it they could just not look at her, that was all. She knew she was ugly and they could just all stay away.

Baseball was more interesting anyhow. She'd never seen a game but that didn't matter, she didn't want to. She knew all the players, she read the papers and listened to all the sports broadcasts and she liked the players better than any people she knew. Paul Derringer was the best of them — he was tall and slender and always going out to the night clubs so sometimes he couldn't play the next day. She liked little Eddie Joost too — he was like a grade-school boy, never failing to do something crazy like fumbling the ball when it was an easy play. Ernie Lombardi supported a lot of his relatives out in California and she felt he played awfully serious — not like Frank McCormick who was good-looking and so sure of himself.

Her mother asked once how could she know what a ball game looked like if she'd never seen one, and she'd got mad and told her mother she didn't *want* to know. But she knew all right — she could picture Harry Craft 'shifting his chaw of tobacco from the left side of his mouth to the right and stepping up to the plate' or Whitey Moore 'pounding his fist in the palm of his glove and glancing over at first.' Red Barber was a really good announcer, he could say funny things about the players and make it all humorous. Of course he made a lot of mistakes too, sometimes got so excited he forgot what he was saying, and you had to wait till he calmed down to find out if it was a hit or an out.

Well, here we go into the first of the ninth, she thought. Cubs at bat. The Reds better watch out with their old one-run lead — they always were leading up to the last inning just to throw the game away by making errors. Who was batting anyhow?

'Quit talking about last inning and tell us who's batting,' she said to Red Barber, and he answered by saying: 'Whambo! It's a *hard* bouncing ball down to Joost at third — and Joost *fumbles!* He makes the throw to first — but too late! — and Wilson is tucked away there safely with —— '

'Did you do those dishes?'

She turned scarlet and whirled around on her mother standing in the doorway. 'Let me alone!' Helen shouted. 'Can't you see I'm listening?'

'If you don't do them I'll do them,' her mother said. 'They've been around here all afternoon and I'm sick of seeing them.'

Her face was toward her mother but her plump body was bent eagerly toward the radio.

'Just tell me,' her mother began again, but Helen really turned on her then: 'Now you made me miss who was next at bat! Don't bother me! I'll do them! Just let me alone!'

It was a long fly ball — Craft would never catch it — going back, back, the sun in his eyes — oh, he caught it! She looked around then, and her mother was gone.

The rest of the inning was nothing, a ground ball and a strike-out so the Reds won and they were lucky they did. She turned the radio off and rocked away. She had to admit that she *wanted* them to win even if she didn't really believe in them — days they won she felt so good.

Her brother came into the room from outside. 'What'd they do today, lose?'

She felt her hand clench. 'Well, they almost did but they didn't,' she said. 'It was a crazy game — the Cubs got five runs in the third inning, then the Reds got three more runs and it was six to five. So the Cubs couldn't do anything till the first of the ninth and Wilson got on first — that crazy Eddie Joost had a ground ball and he fumbled it. The next batter up hit a long fly and I thought Craft would never catch it — he had to go all the way back to the stands. So they won all right — but I bet they're still shaking in their boots!'

'That's all right,' Tom said, 'just so they won. It won't be long till they have the pennant clinched, if they just keep winning.'

'Well, they better do better than they're doing if they're going to beat out St. Louis,' Helen said. 'All the fumbles they've been making. Wait'll the series next week when they meet the Cards. Johnny Mize made two home runs yesterday.'

'That don't mean anything,' Tom said. 'How about Lombardi yesterday? He made a home run and a double.'

'Yes, he has to hit a home run or not get anything, he's so slow! Red Barber said that double yesterday would have been a triple if Bill Werber or Craft had hit it. The other team makes fumbles and everything and they still get old Lombardi out.'

'How about Goodman?' Tom asked. 'He made a triple yesterday.'

'Goodman!' she shouted. 'Don't talk to me about Goodman! Today when he came up to the plate in the first the crowd was clapping and everything because of that triple and all he did was stand there while Bill Lee whizzed three of them over and he went back to sit down. The crowd was so stunned it didn't know what to say. All Red Barber said was, "Well, that's the way it goes" — Red Barber says such dumb things sometimes.'

She was feeling all warmed up, the way she always did whenever she talked about baseball. Her brother was the only one in the family who really knew anything about it. He'd played on the Turkey Bottoms Blues when he'd been in grade school, so she always liked to hear what he had to say. Sometimes she would even flatter him by asking his opinion on something.

'I feel like going sometime,' Tom said. 'I haven't seen them play all this season.'

'It costs too much,' Helen said. 'It costs a dollar and ten cents just for regular seats.'

She felt him looking at her intently, but she wouldn't look back at him. She never did know what he was thinking. 'Let's get tickets and go to the World Series if the Reds win,' he said.

Helen's hand clenched up tight and the color all drained out of her face. She couldn't answer, maybe he was making fun of her because she just sat here all day, she looked at one of the Gruber fox terriers smelling at something in the back yard.

'I think Cokie Myers' father can get me tickets, he works at the park,' Tom said. 'Should we go if I can get them?'

'You can't get them,' she said loudly. 'So just don't bother me!'

'I can get them.'

'Just don't bother me!' she said. 'You can't get them so just don't even talk to me about it!'

'I tell you I can get them!' he said, getting mad too. 'Will you go if I get them?'

She jumped up from the chair, her face white, her hair all mussed. 'Just leave me alone!' she shouted at him. 'Just quit making fun of me and leave me alone!' And she went out into the kitchen and turned on the hot water for the dishes.

At supper table that night she got so mad, her mother and her brother were so optimistic about the Reds and they didn't know anything about it. When they said some of the things they did, she just couldn't help but shout at them. They always thought the Reds were going to win.

'They're not going to win tomorrow,' she shouted. 'They always lose on Friday. Joe Aston in the sports page yesterday analyzed how many times they lost on Friday, and it turned out to be eight or ten times.'

'That doesn't mean anything,' Tom said, breaking a piece of white bread and mopping up gravy with it. 'They're in a winning streak now and they're going to keep on going. I bet you they win tomorrow.'

She just got furious, she waved her hand and could hardly speak he made her so mad. 'Why? Why?' she demanded, leaning forward, her black eyes jumping out of her head, her hair flying all over. 'How can you say they're going to win tomorrow?'

'Because of Derringer, that's why.'

'Yeah, yeah, Derringer!' Helen stopped eating altogether and sat back in her chair. 'Look what he did in his last game — got knocked out of the box in the second inning by the Boston Bees! Derringer! Don't talk to me about Derringer!'

'Well, Derringer *is* good,' her mother put in innocently. 'He's a good pitcher,' she added.

Helen turned on her mother with a fixed expression of horror, her left hand clenched in close to her and her right thrown out as if to defend herself. 'Good pitcher! Yes! Good pitcher! He pitches good when he wants to, but that's only about twice a month! I know him!'

For five minutes there was silence while her mother and brother ate, but she could hardly eat anything, they made her so mad. Then she turned on Tom suddenly when he was just about to put a forkful of peas into his mouth and said: 'You should have heard the booing the crowd gave Joost today when he dropped that bunt! Boy!'

She liked to sit in the dark like this — the kitchen light was on but it didn't shine on her rocker by the radio at all. The *Round the Town* program had been a disappointment — Dick Bray and Red Barber hadn't had time to do anything but give their opinions on the Reds' pennant chances, and she already knew what their opinions were, they were so optimistic.

There was just dance music now and she didn't feel like dialing around. She was tired, she'd been so keyed up all day. She was glad her mother was upstairs lying down and her brother was out to Ray's Place. Sometimes she just didn't want to be with anybody at all, she just wanted to be alone. She only felt natural when she was alone, and they didn't like her anyhow. She didn't care, they could just leave her alone if they didn't like her.

Well, her father would be down soon — she heard her

mother up now, waking him. 'Come on, William, get up —
it's ten o'clock.'

She went out to the kitchen and poured herself a glass
of milk. She began to feel better, thinking about the day's
game — wait till her father heard what almost happened in
the ninth inning!

'Hello, Helen,' he said — he was still sleep-dazed, she
hardly felt he saw her out of his eyes. It was funny, when he
got up in the evening he seemed about a foot smaller than
when he came home from work in the morning. He was
dressed in his blue work shirt buttoned at the collar and his
brown whipcord pants. He was a small man with a potbelly
and arms too thin and long for his body. She always felt
strange with him, maybe because he looked so different — his
face was altogether different from hers, he had a strong nose
with a little bend in it and small gray eyes under gray eyebrows. A kind of bony face. She looked like her mother —
round like her mother, with large dark eyes and full lips.

'Old Bucky Walters thought he was so good today!' she
said as he went to the icebox and brought out a large plate
of sliced tomatoes and cucumbers and a bottle of beer. 'He
had to go and let the Cubs get three hits in the first inning,
and everybody thought the Reds were sunk.'

He poured salt and pepper over the salad and opened the
beer. 'Yeah?' he said, sitting at the table.

'Then they got two more runs in the second, and we got
two runs. That made it five to two. You should have heard
the crowd booing the umpire when he called Frey out at
third in the fourth inning! That was when Werber singled
and it looked like we were going to get some runs. The umpire was the only guy who believed old Frey was out. Roger
Baker said it was the worst booing he'd heard in years.'

He drank the beer and wiped the foam off his mouth. He
was always so quiet when he was sleepy — he only really
talked a lot when he came home tanked up from Ray's Place
in the afternoon.

'Well, who won?' he asked finally.

'Oh, we won,' Helen said, hating to tell him the end of

the game first. 'But it's a wonder. Roger Baker almost threw a fit when Joost fumbled in the ninth inning and the Cubs had Wilson on first. We were only leading by one run — six to five. But then Goodman did something good for a change — he made a one-handed catch all the way back to the stands with the sun in his eyes and, boy, the crowd really cheered then, I thought the radio was coming apart. Then there was a ground ball and a strike-out and that was all. Oh I forgot to tell you, they put in Gene Thompson to pitch in the eighth inning.'

'Gene Thompson?' he said. 'I didn't know he was playing with the Reds any more.'

'Sure he is. They always talk about trading him but they never do. He did pretty good too, except for that last inning. If Goodman hadn't been awake for a change Thompson would just have another loss on his record.'

She followed him out in the hall, where he put on his blue work coat. 'Tomorrow the Giants come to town, then we'll see! Carl Hubbell is supposed to pitch — and after what he did to the Reds last time they better be lying awake tonight thinking about it.'

She followed him back into the kitchen — he stuffed lots of kitchen matches into his pockets for his stogies. She watched him, trying to think of something else to say, as he took out his gold pocket watch and noted the time. She always felt desperate when he was leaving in the evening, she hadn't told him half of what happened.

'Ten forty,' he said. 'Got to get down there.'

She followed him to the front door. 'Everybody's so sure they're going to win the pennant,' she said, 'but I'm not so sure. If they can take two games out of three from the Giants they'll be all right.'

'Oh, they'll win,' he said. 'Good night.'

She watched him through the window, lighting a stogie on the front porch, and then she turned and went upstairs. She didn't feel tired now, she felt all excited again. But she thought she might as well go to bed anyhow, there was nothing else to do.

She went right on through August with them, never missing a game, and she never gave them the benefit of the doubt but they kept winning anyhow, she didn't know how because they did so many things wrong. She still wouldn't believe they were going to be champions even when they were within two games of clinching it. They'll do something, she kept thinking, they always do. And besides Johnny Vander Meer has a sore arm and can't pitch.

But then they took a game from Philadelphia and they were only one game away from the pennant and she was so nervous the next day because they didn't play, they were on their way back to Cincinnati to meet St. Louis, and that was the hardest team of them all — St. Louis had all the batters, Johnny Mize, Enos Slaughter, all of them.

She didn't talk back to Red Barber very much during that St. Louis game, she just sat there, her heart high in her chest, both her hands clenched, listening to every play.

It was the last half of the ninth and Frey was on second, the score was still nothing to nothing and she wasn't making a sound. Jimmy Ripple was coming up to the plate and Red Barber gave a long description of everything he did — dusted his hands with dirt, picked up the bat, stepped over to the plate. She was leaning forward, her head almost touching the radio, her teeth tight together, when suddenly the scream of the crowd hit her full in the face —

'It's a smashing line drive into left field and Frey is rounding third —'

He was scoring, he was scoring! She couldn't sit down, she jumped up and walked around the room, her mouth open, her eyes blazing, her hand clutched in tight against her breast.

' — and the Cincinnati Reds are now —'

All of Hutton Street was screaming, Mrs. Must next door was screaming to her husband Allen who was out in the back yard: 'Allen, Allen, they did it —'

She stood very still in the middle of the room, no longer hearing the radio, her body full and free, all her doubts gone. Should I go up and wake him? she thought, but instead she ran out on the front porch where her mother and Tom were sitting in the swing.

'They —' she said, but they already knew, they were both standing up shouting something at Mr. Keager across the street and here came Mrs. Gruber over from next door.

'What's the matter?' Mrs. Gruber asked.

'The Reds just won the pennant,' Tom said.

'My God, I thought war was declared or something.'

Helen's mother was beaming, 'Tom's going to get tickets and take you,' she said.

'What?' Helen asked, looking from Tom to her mother.

'Tom's getting tickets from Mr. Myers to one of the World Series games and he's going to take you.'

She felt like crying — she hated them, they were always making fun of her. 'You leave me alone,' she said, the tears popping into her eyes. She began to scream: 'All of you just leave me alone, I'm happy the way I am so just leave me alone!' She ran off the porch around to the back yard.

'I don't care!' she said. 'I'm not going!'

Tom had the tickets in his hand. 'You want me to tear them up?' he asked. 'Just say tear them up and I'll do it right now.'

She didn't know what to say — she knew why he'd gone and got them, just because she didn't want him to. He was always making fun of her, she listened to the game all the time and he thought she was silly. That's why he'd got the tickets, just to show her up.

'You can go by yourself!' she shouted and ran out on the front porch. She just wanted to get away, she hated them.

But they were at her day and night, they acted as if they couldn't understand why she wouldn't go. As if she wanted to get all dressed up and wear those silly gloves!

Her mother kept pounding away at her till she thought she'd go crazy. 'It would be so nice for the two of you to go out together once in a while,' her mother said, and that almost made her burst a blood vessel.

'Nice!' she said. 'Nice! Do you think I want to go out

with *him?* He doesn't like me and I know it! He can just go out by himself whenever he wants to.'

'Why don't you go with Tom?' her father said one evening while he was eating his snack. 'He got those tickets and now you won't go with him.'

Somehow she never really got angry with her father, he didn't talk at her like her mother did. But now she felt so emotional she couldn't answer him, and she left the room. They were all the same — none of them understood. None of them would leave her be. They all had to keep picking on her.

The day before the game she found her mother pressing her blue dress.

'You can do all that you want,' Helen said, 'but I'm not going!'

Her mother didn't answer her — just went on pressing. And Helen sat down and watched her mother working, wishing she'd argue. 'Tom doesn't want to take me anyhow — he just did it because you made him.' But still her mother didn't answer and Helen got up and left the kitchen.

The sun wasn't even up — she looked at the alarm clock beside her bed. Five twenty. And then she remembered, this was the day! Today we'll see, she thought. Today we'll know whether they're any good or not. Derringer was going to pitch — she wished it were Bucky Walters. Derringer was more brilliant sometimes, but Bucky could really be depended on more.

She wondered if Tom would try to make her go — well, she wasn't going, he could put that in his pipe and smoke it. All of them could try to make her go but she wouldn't.

She couldn't stay in bed, she was too excited, she'd never been so excited about anything in her life before. She got up and dressed and went downstairs. There were some peaches in the icebox so she ate them and drank a glass of milk. Then she went out on the front porch and Hutton Street looked so strange, the air smelled good and the street was quiet, deserted. Just Mr. Timpkins' car parked down the street and none of the kids who were always around. Wait a minute — here came Mr. Kobble up the street. She dashed back into the house, she didn't want him to see her.

At eleven she was sitting on the front porch reading the *Ladies' Home Journal* but not really getting anything out of the story because she was so excited, when Tom came out. She wouldn't look up at him but he came over to her anyhow.

'You better get dressed,' he said.

She still didn't look at him, there was a strange feeling in her chest. She surprised herself when she jumped up. 'All right then, I will.' And she went into the house and up the stairs.

When she was all dressed she stared at herself in the mirror. I don't look so fat when I'm fixed up, she thought. She wore her blue dress with the little white collar, and on her head was the hat she'd got last spring — a white hat that sat back from her face and had a black bow on it. She hadn't been out for three months, she'd almost forgotten how neat and clean it felt to be all dressed up with her girdle on and everything.

'You can wear your new gloves,' her mother said when she arrived down in the kitchen. And she didn't get mad, she just took the gloves from her mother and started working the left one on. She had a hard time, the hand always persisted in clenching up hard whenever she wanted to do anything with it, but finally she got it and then worked the right one on by using the edge of the kitchen table. Tom and her mother did not watch her. Tom was looking out of the back door and her mother was washing a skillet at the sink.

She wished her mother wouldn't come out on the porch with them, but she didn't say anything. She felt so strange all dressed up, she just knew that people were staring out of their windows at her as she came down off the porch steps behind Tom — for a moment she almost decided to dash back into the house but then they were on their way, going past Mrs. Must's. Tom turned once at the top of the street and waved to his mother, but she didn't want to even look at that house, besides it was silly.

They climbed the footbridge over the railroad tracks and then they were standing side by side at the car stop on Eastern Avenue. She couldn't resist glancing at Tom as they stood there — he did look handsome in his brown suit and his tie. She got car tickets out of her handbag. 'Here, drop these,' she said, as the trolley came swaying toward them from the end of the line. And then they were on the car, bumping against each other as they sat on the straw seat.

Part of a swarm, she moved forward toward the high wall that was the ball park, Tom somewhere behind her, but she didn't look around. She felt that life had caught her and was dragging her along toward something she must know . . . something so inevitable she could not escape now even if she struggled. She was carried in through a doorway cut in the green wall, Tom was handing the tickets, then they were free again, going up the ramp into the grandstand. And suddenly she thought: is this the day I've been waiting for two years? The struggle she had put up against coming certainly did seem ridiculous now that she was here — nobody noticed her, they all just rushed along, nobody stopped and laughed at her and stared at her gloved hands.

They were following an usher down to their seats and she was so busy watching her step she didn't get a good look at the field till she sat down — and then she looked, and she could not believe it. It was little! It was a dozen times smaller than she'd expected — she looked at the center field wall over which Lombardi had hit so many home runs and it did not seem any distance at all. She looked at the diamond itself — the distance between the bases was so short. And she had not known about the signs out there surrounding the outfield — signs advertising insurance, loans, suits of clothes, ham. They made everything so commercial.

Tom bought two bottles of Coke. 'Did they really charge you fifteen cents each for these?' she asked. Everywhere were men in white suits selling things to the crowd — popcorn, Cracker Jacks, score cards, souvenir pins. Red Barber had never mentioned all of this.

But the players didn't have anything to do with it, she thought. These were just a lot of people trying to make money off the game, they didn't really care about baseball. . . . Well, it wouldn't be long now, the groundkeepers were smoothing out the infield. She watched them, trying to feel the excitement she always had at home just before the game, but she couldn't — two men on her left were discussing Florida and in front of her a Spanish-looking fellow was pressing kisses on the cheek of a little blonde. Wasn't anybody interested in the game?

'Where's the broadcasting booth?' she asked Tom.

'It's up above us, you can't see it,' he said. 'But look down there, there's Dick Bray interviewing people.'

'*Fans in the Stands*,' she said — but Dick Bray was lost in a knot of people, she couldn't see him.

Then the band was playing — *The Star-Spangled Banner* — and everyone was standing. Why did she always feel so silly standing — feeling everyone would look at her? 'There's the Reds!' Tom said, nudging her.

She started, she strained toward them, even bending forward a little. They came stringing out on the field from their dugout, tiny loping men, each one like the other way down there — and she didn't know them!

She didn't know a single one of them. Had she been foolish enough to think they would be bigger than life, that she could actually see and know each one? They were all alike in their white suits with the big numbers on the back — just miniature men, who seemed to have nothing to do with her or the rest of the crowd. And here came Derringer out to the mound — but it was not really Derringer at all, Derringer was taller than Gary Cooper, Derringer was nonchalant, masterful, and this was just a tiny man in a white suit.

The game was starting — Derringer threw to Wilson. But she couldn't see the ball. She realized, as the first inning progressed and Detroit had men on base, that the game itself was just like the park — it was all in miniature, it wasn't like the game she'd imagined at all. They were just a lot of little men down there standing around, and she didn't know any of them. Even when the ball was hit nobody seemed to do very much — one man out in the field ran around a little and then there was someone on first or second, Derringer had the ball again and was throwing to the plate.

Detroit was making runs but she didn't care — she didn't know any of those men, she didn't care what they did. The crowd was screaming because Detroit was scoring again but she felt disgusted — she felt unclean. It isn't mine at all, she thought, it belongs to everybody and it isn't anything.

It was the second inning but she wasn't even watching any longer, she wasn't even trying to identify the players . . . she could not even look at them, she studied the ads on her score card. Her stomach was swimming in her, she felt she would drown if she had to stay the whole game, her head was bursting. Just to get out of here, to run away from here she didn't care where. . . . 'Tom,' she said, but he didn't hear her, he was shouting something down at the players.

She stood up and someone behind her pushed her shoulder and said, 'Sit down!' but she kept on going, stumbling over people, rushing to the aisle.

When she got to the exit Tom was beside her. 'You going?' he asked. She didn't answer, she walked on. 'You can't leave now — '

She saw the sign, LADIES REST ROOM, and she rushed toward it, not even looking around at him. Nobody inside at all, that was good. She slumped down in an armchair, it was over. The crowd was screaming out there but she didn't care — she didn't care whether the Reds won or lost.

And suddenly she saw herself as she had been — in that sloppy house dress, sitting by the radio for two years. It was a dream, she thought, it wasn't real. I made it all up myself. There is no such person as Paul Derringer, Bucky Walters and Lonnie Frey and Bill Werber — they are all just people I made up. No one has ever seen them but me.

I have just told lies, that's all, she thought. I lied to myself every day of the week. It's all really a silly game, with nothing important happening in it, but I made it the most important thing in the world. I acted as if they were playing just for me, and here they were playing for everybody. They would not know me if they saw me, and I did not know them. Really it was just a silly dream.

Thinking this she began to feel better. She'd been sick, that was it. And after you'd been sick for two years you wanted to wash yourself clean and never be sick again.

These silly gloves, she said to herself, working off the left-hand one, these silly gloves that I've been wearing all my life. She had to use her mouth to pull off the other. Then she pushed up her sleeves and began. She washed her crippled hand last and most thoroughly.

Finished, she dried with a paper towel. So it was all over. It wasn't real and I don't want it. Now I will just have to change, that's all. I will have to be someone different.

She picked up her handbag and started to reach for the gloves, then turned quickly and hurried to the door.

*(From Quarterly Review of Literature)*

# FATHER DELACROIX

# BY MAY DAVIES MARTENET

*F*ATHER DELACROIX was always speakin' about 'man' but I can't recollect ever hearin' him talk about *men.* And women — well it was like he was a deaf man who knew there was such a thing as sound but noise was somethin' he would never have to take account of. That's how it seemed about Father Delacroix and women. I think people kept rememberin' that and just couldn't believe themselves when it all came out about Alma Stuart. And of course she was no woman exactly, just sixteen with bows in her long hair and nobody takin' notice of how she really looked if you looked at her good. Now if she was colored instead of a white girl we'd none of us ever have thought of her as only a child. She was slow-laughing and her body put you in mind of fine fruit under the baby-like clothes her father put on her from his store.

I come near workin' there, in the store, instead of the church. First thing when I came here to Raleigh I heard Mr. Stuart was hiring a man to scrub up and carry bundles and I went to see him and he said I could have the job. But before we got through talkin' he found out I went to Hampton for that year and he said he didn't want any educated nigger. I was walkin' out of his office but he followed me with his face as smooth as if he'd just handed me a size of hog chittlins. He pushed a dollar towards me. He said he couldn't have me because sooner or later a half-educated colored man was bound to come out with notions that would turn off his customers. That made hirin' me a luxury he couldn't afford, he said, even though he liked me. I took that dollar. I hadn't eaten anything that day and I bought some food but that night I sent fifty cents to Dr. Armstrong for Hampton.

Mr. Stuart was still talkin' when we come out of his office and Mr. Sanders Grimsley was standin' there on the stair-landing. I didn't know who Mr. Grimsley was then but he had heard all we said. I thought he never even saw me but when I was halfway downstairs he said, 'Wait boy.' I turned around and he said, 'You'll find my mare at the hitching-post. You can look after her 'til I come down.'

When he came down he asked my name and wrote on a card and told me to take it to Father Delacroix at the Rectory.

'Aubert Delacroix is your man, Charlie,' he said. 'He is from New Orleans but I understand he has frequented Mrs. Howe's drawing-room in Boston. There will be no question of your turning off the customers with him, I think. Though I daresay the Stuarts and the Duprés may not be as satisfied as they have been.'

I was settin' the stirrup over his black shiny boot and it jerked out of my hand and there was dust up my nose before I could say anything. Mr. Grimsley sat smart as a knifeblade on his mare goin' down the street.

That's how I got to be the Sexton at St. Mary's.

Father Delacroix was just new-come to Raleigh then. He was sent to be under Father Farrell. The old priest wasn't kep' to his bed yet like he was later but he was already sick. Father Delacroix really did everything from the start. Work! I never saw a man who could do so little sleepin' and eatin' and no restin' atall. And every day I'd look to see if some-thin' wouldn't show in his pink-colored face. But it never did. And it wasn't just because he was so young and strong. If it'd been that it'd been all right. But sometimes I'd think I'd leave because I couldn't stand it. Did he have a young face? He didn't have any age face and I knew he was a twenty-eight year old man.

In those days Alma Stuart was drivin' a pony-cart to church. Then next year she went off to that Seminary in Fayetteville. She would never stay there. Every month or so she'd be at home on some excuse and then Mr. Stuart would be carryin' out one thing and another from the store to please her. He would have parties invitin' all the people to 'cheer up my Baby' who had got 'too run-down' with all her studyin'. Some of the ladies and gentlemen would say what else could you expect with a man so foolish about his motherless child and some would say, 'Fiddlesticks! She damn well ought to be made to stay down yonder!'

I used to earn right much extra by helpin' out for the parties. Like Mr. Grimsley said, some of the church members and Mr. Stuart didn't seem pleased about my bein' Sexton, but Mr. Stuart always let me serve for extra help and paid good too. He was a rich man and owned half the land around the town and everybody always came to the parties. Maybe Father Delacroix wouldn't've gone of his own taste but he liked to be friendly and anyway Mr. Stuart gave more than anybody to the church.

At first I expected Mr. Grimsley must be an important member of St. Mary's parish but he went to the Presbyterian church once a month and everybody said that was only to satisfy his sister, and he never came near Father Delacroix. I didn't see him for a long time after I went to St. Mary's. I found out Father Delacroix's father and Mr. Grimsley was Majors together at Vicksburg twenty-five years before. One day I carried a message down to the Courthouse and I saw Mr. Grimsley and it looked like to me he had just won a case. I didn't know then he could have been a judge but wouldn't. I spoke to him and said I thanked him for givin' me my chance.

He said, 'You individually, Charlie, have no chance. I gathered you had fully realized that and it interested me very much.'

'Mr. Grimsley, Sir,' I said, 'I meant I think one of the reasons I got the chance over at the Catholic church is because Father Delacroix's Father was your friend.'

Mr. Grimsley looked at me and if he had said anything it would have been 'You impudent black damn fool!'

What he did say presently was 'I doubt if Aubert Delacroix conceived any sentiment about my acquaintance with his father. You know as well as I do he hired you for some real humanitarian reason.'

But Mr. Grimsley never called the Catholics 'Romans' behind their backs like most of the Presbyterians does at some time or another and I think maybe nobody knew how he really felt. Except Father Delacroix. Once he went to see Mr. Grimsley and he came back and I heard him say, 'There's nothing so difficult as a just man who has a prejudice.' But his tones and his face wasn't nothing compared with Mr. Grimsley's that time later in the courtroom. I mean when Mr. Grimsley would look across at Father Delacroix up there on the stand sayin' nothin' to the other lawyer and nothin' and nothin' and then when he was made to, just sayin' those same little sentences over again.

When Alma Stuart came home from the Seminary for the last time she made tracks over here to the church. In three weeks she sure enough had a path showin' in the grass across the lot that was between Mr. Stuart's back garden and the Rectory. She and little Katy Dupré was in charge of the flowers and altar linen. In a month there was a new organist an' it was Alma Stuart.

I used to hear her practicin' and she could get along right nicely, tum tum *tee* tum, like clock chimes. So it almos' smacked me down that Sunday when I come back durin' service and heard what she was doin' with that organ. Hangin' on to the low notes and tremblin' and smashin' at the right-hand chords. It was July by now and Father Delacroix hadn't never seen her yet.

Hones' before God that's what I mean. I reg'n she talked to him every day. But she was like one of his ideas, that's all. Like me. I used to think maybe I was his favorite idea. I had to be helped and deserved education. He even started me on some Latin words.

But that hymn she was playin'. It pulled me over to where

I could see through the window back of the choir. There they was, damp at the necks of their robes, strugglin' to match up with the music, holdin' on to words and then rushin' 'em out and so busy they couldn't listen. I called it a hymn. Well, some of the ladies in the pews began to fan themselves and the men whose faces was turned up had a waitin' look. I don't know if anybody knew what they was hearin' and I cant remember what I thought. I jus' remember listenin'. Until I saw the little mirror she had set up on the organ rack.

In this mirror in one corner I could see the back of Father Delacroix and then there was her eyes lookin' pale, almos' gold-colored. Watchin. Her chin was cut off but there was deep places at the corners of her mouth. By this time the big notes was droppin' out like blood and other ones was slidin' around the air like the incense they sometimes had. She really couldn't play music but that's how it was. And her eyes never winked.

Seems like he'd've had to feel it. This wasn't the kind of starin' that's two holes in your back. This would touch you all over like it was some kind of actual stuff. But he just knelt down as safe and bright as one of them ornaments with a glass dome over it.

After church she was the last one out an' she went walkin' close along side him to the Rectory askin' did he like the flowers, did it suit him how she played. 'Miss Alma,' he said real kindly, 'Maybe you should practice to steady your tempo a bit.' And then he stood a while politely. Green light came down out of the branches over them and was on her face. He smiled and nodded at that face, goin' towards his door, and she held absolutely still and just in that minute anybody would have felt sorry for her.

It was durin' the next week Father Farrell took to his bed for good. This made Father Delacroix have to do more than ever which was a kind of short-lastin' mercy because it gave him an excuse to stay away. And he needed that. Because it was only the next Saturday morning when the thing happened that changed everything.

She'd been comin' every day all week to practice and wait around to get near him. Just like she always did. Only now she was different. She was quarrellin' an' pickin' an' harryin' him into contradictin' himself over every little thing. Then she would have a smile over her face so her eyes was drawn in slits an' if words could really be claws he'd a' been welted from head to foot.

Most all the Guild ladies was down directin' things that Saturday. They brought flowers and talked and went away again by eleven o'clock. All except her. I was gettin' down the big cross that had to be cleaned and she was standin' on my work-box reachin' up her arms for it when he walked in the church. He got almost up to us and then right in the middle of takin' a step he stood still. He stayed there and looked at her and he saw her. When I was young I used to wonder how it was with Adam when he first woke up after the Lord breathed into him, and now I saw Father Delacroix's face and I knew all about it. It takes it out of you to see things born just like it does when you see them die and maybe that's why I cant remember how his face really looked. The best I can do is remember the feeling of seein' it, though I'm always tryin' to get back to how he looked right then.

Soon as I could I said, 'Miss Alma.' I even bumped the cross a little. 'Here, Miss Alma,' I said. But it was too late. She had seen his look too. And there was part of it I knew she could understand.

'Now Charlie,' she said. She spoke real slow and she was smilin'. She arched and swayed a little standin' there and she sort of sighed and stretched out her arms before she took the cross. 'Do be careful,' she said.

She handed it to Father Delacroix and waited 'til he had put it up very gentle by the wall. Then she said, 'Please, Father,' and kind of teetered at the edge of the box. He held out his hand and she took hold, curlin' her fingers under his wrist, and I saw the dark red color that came even over the back of his neck.

I guess he was fifteen pounds thinner before they finally

got him over to one of the parties Mr. Stuart was so crazy about. He came in late and when I saw him I knew what a long time he must've been walkin' up and down in his room. It had got so he worried Father Farrell whose rooms was right under his and sometimes Father Farrell would knock on the wall with his cane to stop him. One afternoon I heard the old man's voice call out, 'My Son, try to rest.'

Father Delacroix stuck his head out of his own window and he called back down sayin', 'Forgive me, Father.'

The old priest said, 'Never mind, Son, but you must not let this extra burden of work overstrain you or you will fail our people and our God.'

It was queer how Mr. Stuart never took it in. I can see how everybody else missed it with her ribbons and dresses and her still makin' curtsies to the oldest ladies and Father Delacroix keepin' himself so scarce. But at first I really puzzled over her father.

Now this night when Father Delacroix came to the party I clean upset a tray when I saw Mr. Stuart go out on the porch. I'd seen them go out there and I knew anybody could see as good as day in that full moon. But in a minute Mr. Stuart was back leadin' her towards the piano and clappin' his hands all in a happy flourish. Father Delacroix came an' sat down just inside the door, but Mr. Stuart didn't even glance at him. Nobody did. Little Katy Dupré was playin' the chords for the song an' she was standin' under the chandelier foldin' her hands and breathin' in with her lashes down against her cheek. All the time she was singin' Mr. Stuart was watchin' her and lookin' like one of those joyful pink men on a valentine.

Father Delacroix gave up tryin' to keep his eyes away from her. He just sat there with his face kind of broken-apart lookin'. That oughtn't to surprised me because how would you expect the face of anybody to look who had gone through boy-age of his body and through bein' young and come to the tearin' strengths of a man all in the time of one swelling of the moon?

It was almost right at the beginning in court when the

Solicitor (that was young Hunt Taylor) when he said, 'Your
Honour, the witness Charles Tucker knows something he is
not telling.'

Old Judge Pearsall said, 'He is your witness, Sir. You can
question him.'

'Charlie,' Mr. Taylor said, 'I want to know *why* you
wouldn't mow the lawns on that afternoon of August the
third.'

Hunt Taylor was a smart young man. Father Farrell
couldn't come to court but Mr. Taylor had found out about
that afternoon how Father Farrell was urgin' me to cut the
grass. It was the day after the party, a hot day with no color
in it. About four o'clock I saw her slip in the side vestibule
where the stairs leads up to Father Delacroix's rooms. You
cant go anywhere else from that vestibule. So then I took
my trowel and sat down in the border under Father Farrell's
window. I poked and clipped at things some but I could
hardly bring myself to moving. I had to wait and listen.
But this wasn't for any reason, because I knew it was the
time now, and nobody could do anything. Still I had to sit
there.

Father Farrell couldn't have seen her go in and everything
was quiet overhead. And yet presently the old man called
out to me. 'What is it?' he said. 'What is it Charlie? Why
don't you go mow the grass? What are you doing? You're
supposed to cut the grass.'

He raised up in bed 'til he could look over the sill. His
thin hair was out in tufts like there was a wind blowing in his
room. But not a breath was moving the heat anywhere.

He kind of cried out. 'Why are we waiting? I mean you,'
he said. 'Go away and do your work.'

I soothed him down and he lay back quiet a while. Soon
his old hands was scratchin' over the sheets and he said 'I
wish the storm would come. Nobody can breathe properly
if the air is like this.'

I never saw her comin' down 'til she had got over in the
open lot. It was almost twilight when I looked up and saw
her dress glimmerin' in the long burnt-out grass before she
was hid by trees.

That same night the Doctor's buggy drove up to the Stuart's. The Doctor didn't stay long and before midnight they came to get Father Delacroix. They say he must never have left his room all that time. When they came in one lamp was burnin' and he was lyin' on the cot with his hands crossed behind his head and he just looked at them real quiet. Then they told him they were takin' him for rape and he just got up without sayin' anything and went down to the jail with them.

There wasn't nothing in the paper about it until the trial came up. But you'd of thought it was written in the sky. Mr. Stuart was partly the cause of that. Because even in the street sometimes you could hear him shoutin' at her. He wouldn't go down to the store and he began to get drunk in the nights. One time he hollered out he would kill her.

You ought to seen the faces of the Presbyterians when they would drive past St. Mary's on their way to church Sundays.

And you ought to seen them when Mr. Grimsley came out and said he was goin' to take the case for Father Delacroix.

At the trial she sat between Mr. Stuart and his sister from Georgia. But she acted like she never saw them before. Except when she gave her testimony. Then she would look at her father and when he would get paler her voice would get stronger.

Father Delacroix sat with his hands against his temples and his fingers cupped out over his eyes. That first time she got on the stand he looked up at her with his lips apart a little and even as far back in his head as his eyes had gone now they showed light for a minute. But after she had talked a while he put his hands back up over his eyes and he never looked at her again. I mean never.

On the stand he was like I said. Sayin' nothin'. It was more like he couldn't hear them than as if he was stubborn. And even young Hunt Taylor who ought to been satisfied began shoutin' and pacin'.

When they began the second half of the trial I was called as witness again.

Mr. Grimsley hadn't no sooner begun than he said, 'It has been repeatedly stated that no outcry or sound of struggle was heard. I submit that the charges are false because we are concerned not with rape but with seduction.'

Right quick the solicitor asked if Mr. Grimsley wanted it on the record that he claimed that the defendant, while wearin' the robes of priesthood, had seduced a young girl of seventeen?

'I do not,' Mr. Grimsley said. 'I made no such claim.' He looked around for a minute before he said 'In fact that is not at all what I meant to suggest.'

Then there wasn't any sound anywhere 'til Hunt Taylor said, 'Why — you — !' and a kind of a roar came over the courtroom, rolling above his words about 'defaming' and 'vile insinuation' and 'this tragic child.' Mr. Stuart jumped up and the noises in his throat got lost with benches creakin' everywhere and this sound that was washin' back from the walls over everybody shiftin' in their places. Then Judge Pearsall was bangin' with his little mallet. I looked at Father Delacroix but I might as well have looked for some sign from a stone at the bottom of a pool.

There was somethin' to see in her face, though. Have you ever looked at a cat and it seemed like to you it was laughin' at you? I mean without movin' its face somehow it gave you the idea it was laughin'? Well, she put out her hand on her father's coatsleeve and that's the way her face was.

After that when court was out for lunch I went up to see Mr. Grimsley in his office. He used to be right at the head of the stairs in the old Eden Building then. I'd only just got there when I noticed all of a sudden everything was dead quiet in the Square outside. I looked out the window and there was little knots of people standin' around and I just barely saw Mr. Stuart steppin' under the portico to come in. I thought he had somethin' under his arm. Downstairs the men who was in the hall stopped talkin'. Mr. Grimsley's door was open and we could hear the feet shufflin', movin' back, and then plunk — plunk — plunk real steady while Mr. Stuart was comin' up the steps.

Right light and quick Mr. Grimsley stepped over and pushed his door to. He didn't lock it. I don't think he even quite closed it all the way. 'Edward!' he said when Mr. Stuart got right outside the door. 'Go away Edward, because you know there is no sense of honour in your coming to horse-whip me.'

Mr. Grimsley kind of leaned on his wrist on the doorknob and crossed his ankles the way you might see a gentleman do at a party listenin' with his head back. He said, 'In the beginning you could have sent Alma quietly away to France to the Convent where you will send her in the end. This need never have been. Why did you do this? Did you think no man would defend him?'

I was tryin' to think how Mr. Stuart must look so still on the other side of that door. Then Mr. Grimsley said, 'I know the answer is "no" Edward, because you are not a coward. If you had been much concerned with Aubert Delacroix you would have dealt with him yourself. But do you know what makes you avenge yourself against your daughter? Because that is what you are doing. That is all you are doing.'

After a minute somethin' hit on the door and dropped. Then we heard Mr. Stuart's feet very slow on the stairs goin' down.

Mr. Grimsley walked over and sat at his desk and I went outside and picked up the horsewhip and brought it to him.

That afternoon there was more people than ever turned away from the courtroom. It was winter now but they had to open all the windows with everybody packed in there like they was. Father Delacroix was on the stand. I felt as tired as Mr. Grimsley looked when he said, 'Your witness, Mr. Solicitor.'

Hunt Taylor stood up. 'Aubert Delacroix,' he said, 'you have not attempted to dispute the Prosecutrix' account of your brutal actions on that afternoon. *Why?*'

Father Delacroix didn't speak or move at all.

'Because her account is accurate. Isn't it?' Hunt Taylor's voice was so loud and he shouted *'Isn't it?'* again.

After a long time Father Delacroix said, 'I dont think so.'

Hunt Taylor rocked back on his heels. 'You don't *think* so!' he said and he looked all around at everybody. 'You had best be definite,' he said, 'Your behavior was definite enough.'

You could see Hunt Taylor's teeth under his mustache. But Father Delacroix just sat there.

Hunt Taylor said, 'Is the Prosecutrix' account of this crime accurate or is it not?' When he got no answer he said, 'If the Court pleases will you instruct the witness to answer the question?'

So Judge Pearsall told Father Delacroix to answer and the solicitor asked again if it was like she said it was.

'I don't know,' Father Delacroix said.

This time Hunt Taylor didn't need to do nothin'. But he had to right himself from backin' on his heels again and the way that room was then it sounded like gunshots when his feet hit the floor.

After while he gave a big showy sigh. 'Well,' he said, 'perhaps you can tell me your version of this thing, how you *think* it was, how it *seemed* to you.'

'Objection!' Mr. Grimsley called out, and the Judge said, 'Objection sustained.'

But the thing was Father Delacroix had answered this time. He had said, 'It seemed all right —' and yet there wasn't one smirk in that courtroom, ' — just simple and clear at last,' Father Delacroix said.

Mr. Grimsley got leave to question him again. 'Listen to me my boy,' he said, 'and please do as I ask. Tell me what happened when Alma Stuart came into your room.'

But he said just what he always said before. Those same sentences which was the most that he would say all together durin' the whole trial.

'I looked up and saw her,' he said. 'Her arms were raised and together. I opened my arms, she walked into them, and I put them around her.'

I didn't go to court that last day when Hunt Taylor and Mr. Grimsley had their turns to talk to the jury. I stayed in the church and that night when I thought it was time I went downtown and they told me about it.

They told me Father Delacroix was acquitted.

Everybody was sayin' over and over again how Mr. Grimsley had saved Father Delacroix's life. They said it until I had to go away and walk out on the Durham road.

Because I know with a black man as long as he's breathin' and in his skin he's alive, but with some white men that's not so. I'd been lookin' at Father Delacroix after he was down off the stand that last time and someway it'd come to me that he was dead. As dead as if his head was brought in on a platter.

*(From Quarterly Review of Literature)*

# THE DARKNESS

# BY JANE MAYHALL

*A*LTHOUGH he was fifteen years old, when he heard that his mother was going to die, he believed it instantly. It was Lillian, his sister and elder, who argued with the doctor, croaking and coughing up tears, her eyes bulging until she looked like a frog. The boy merely stood as if in contemplation, then walked to the sink to get a drink of water. As he gulped the tasteless liquid, he looked through the bluish end of the glass and watched his sister's face, the flat head and lean teapot nose. Meanwhile, the doctor was standing helplessly by, with a melancholy expression like a whipped dog, and occasionally whining his sympathy at them.

Abstractedly, the boy set down the glass and moved through the swinging kitchen door into the dining room. He saw that the blinds of all the windows had been drawn down to a neat two inches below the window sills. A wry grin stung his mouth. The funeral would go off in good order too. With banks of flowers and tangled ferns, Lillian must have it all planned in her head by now. It needed only that late comer, death. John made a faint hissing sound between his teeth and stopped to look at himself in the dull gloom of the parlor mirror. He saw his image framed familiarly in that watery depth, with the intimate knowledge of furniture behind him, furniture warm and overstuffed like domesticated animals. He turned and faced the dark room. Then without pausing, he walked lightly to the stairs and went up.

His mother was awake. She lay with the pink bedspread coming to her elbows. The sun was bright and gay in the room, reflecting on the dresser and its ten-cent store perfume bottles, sending up rays of light like colored quartz. Here the blinds reached to the ceiling and the window was flung open, a breeze glittering the voile curtains. John leaned against the door, his breath diminishing in him like a sigh of relief.

When his mother looked up, he smiled. How pretty she looked! Her skin was pale as a child's, smoothed by its thinness. The dark eyes, rich with fever, regarded him questioningly. She had been ill for seven months and it was always her unspoken question to him — why am I ill? It was because he looked thoughtful that she asked him this. She never asked anyone else. John blinked his eyes and walked forward against the swimming radiance of the room.

'Those idiots!' he laughed, perching on the edge of the bed, 'Those idiots! They're gossiping about your health again.' He chuckled easily and picked up a magazine.

Her body tensed like a wire. He saw its livid line, acute beneath the spread.

'What?' she asked in a low voice, 'What are they saying?'

'Oh, Lillian talks of potato soup, while Doc Creighton insists on tapioca. I say,' he glanced up boyishly, 'let you decide for yourself.'

Out of the corner of his eye, he saw her relaxing. Casually he shuffled the pages of the magazine between his fingers. He would have to play for time while Lillian got hold of herself, if she ever would. Ah, the sheer tactlessness of her distress. As long as he remembered, nothing had ever mattered to her but a relentless self-expression. When peddlers came by with shoestrings or pencils to sell, it was always Lillian who invited them in, not to buy anything, but to tell them about herself. When he came home from school, he would see her in her housedress, a dust cap knotted on her low forehead, leaning forward in the old horsehair divan —

she would be talking greedily to a broom salesman who would be standing uncomfortably in the middle of the room, or with his back against the staircase, ready to leave when he could. But she chattered on, recalling in detail how many trips she made to the grocery, the movie she had seen last week, the amount of money her father had left when he died a postal clerk. While John and his mother kept silent, a bond of reserve between them.

'Where is Lillian, now?' said his mother.

'Still in the kitchen, I guess,' he murmured over the magazine. But his heart wrenched and he saw again his sister's face suspended over the checked apron, her features monstrous and magnified with grief, her neck red as if she had been bending over a hot stove. Suddenly, with abrupt candor, he stared into his mother's eyes.

'Lillian thinks,' he said, 'that sickness in the family is a three ring circus and she's the ringmaster.'

His mother laughed softly. 'Poor Lillian,' she said. 'She's high-strung, John. Not like you.'

The boy flushed with undisguised pleasure. His mother had not complimented him often, and hardly ever contrasting the brother and sister. But since her illness, small personal praises escaped her lips, she looked at him tenderly. John and his mother had become closer. It seemed that life hurried around them while they went more slowly, slowly — . The boy put his head against the bedpost and felt joy like a sedative go through his veins. The quiet room. The sun was like a weight, pressing him down. He could die here.

'I wonder,' he asked, 'do you mind so much light in the room?'

'No,' his mother answered. 'I wish that the walls were glass. It makes me feel — ' the blank word rose quietly, ' — alive.'

John stretched his legs and went to the window, picking up the dark-hued medicine bottles from the sill, smelling them. The world of sickness was a strange one, but he was growing used to it. It had, he thought, its laws, its truths, its falsities. Once he had read that in war a man can degenerate until he is nothing more than a wound under a bandage. But contrarily, a man could also be a thin spider's thread of hope, perilously suspended between suffering and nothing at all. Was she suffering? He stole a glance at her. The disease worked in curious ways. Sometimes she exclaimed that she felt so well, why, she might walk out into the backyard. He saw her moving through the shining dark hedges, the moist earth clinging to her old shoes. Other times, those other times, the pain seemed enough to change the whole world, it was like an ocean which rolled up, filling the air, absorbing the elements. And anyone who passed or knew of her suffering, anyone was pulled like a frail swimmer into the currents, dragged by the undertow. And then his body rode her suffering like the shocks of a wave, going, going into the vast regions of insensibility.

But insensibility never came. She was superbly conscious. And his own forbearance from comments, his restraint from applauding her courage — this told her that he understood. How well he understood, thought the boy. The two of them together, it was a welding of powers. He picked up a small camphor bottle and noting that it was empty, tossed it into the wastebasket.

The boy started back across the room to his mother, but another sound invaded his consciousness. It was his sister's step on the stair, the unmistakable and heavy high-heeled tread, slow with pompous dignity.

With a wretched feeling of excitement, John whirled and walked to the door.

'Hey, Lillian,' he said good-humoredly, out into the hall. 'Is that you?' He turned around, winking at his mother. 'Well, for Chrissakes, can't I have a minute with her, without *you* butting in?'

Listening intently, he heard his sister make some uncertain utterance and then go slowly back down the stairs. He extended the palms of his hands in a gesture of mock annoyance. They shone with the dry sparkle of perspiration. He was trembling. He felt himself bending, there was no ballast in his thoughts. For an instant, he might have jabbered out anything. He might have said — .

The word was cancer. He had spoken it calmly at first. But the trouble came afterwards. For once said, there it took root and began to grow over the thoughts, a lichen riven to rock. The maleficent name should be cut away, blotted out. But he knew it had taken tissue in the mind of his sister. As soon as the doctor had told them, he saw it blossom in Lillian's face, its secret like a poisonous plant, ready to be devoured by anyone. And how she would like to feed that venom to her mother — and in turn to sup the gall of the older woman's despair. Ah! he knew Lillian. Nothing would so much placate her insatiable appetite. For that hunger which drove her to ask reassurance from strangers, broom salesmen, vegetable vendors — what an exquisite morsel this was!

His mother said, 'You should be nicer to Lillian. She's a good girl.'

He smiled. 'The salt of the earth,' he said.

His mother lifted her hands, the wrists like pale fish swimming in air. 'Have you ever,' she exclaimed breathlessly, 'ever seen such weather!'

John felt a windy onrush of relief. Following her glance, he looked out, adjusting his eyes to the effortless blue of the sky. And he said gently, 'No, never.'

Sitting down in a rocking chair, with his eyes still focused on the sky, he crossed his knees and put his head back. The chair went softly, 'Creak-creak,' and he stopped. Turning he saw that his mother had closed her lids and was resting easily. Whether she slept or not, he did not know. Her eyes were closed, darkness encased in darkness. There was no sound in the room. But there was. It slipped like a snake into his consciousness. For awhile he could not tell what it was. Then it turned quietly and became articulate. It was their breathing. How one keeps on breathing. It was a slack winnowy sound like grasses being parted at their roots, the tops scarcely rustling. He listened as one laved into slumber. He felt the passing of time.

Two weeks later, on the first of June, Lillian came and

stood by the door. Her huge shallow face was warped, anxious. She was twisting her apron in her hands.

'I — ' she began witlessly, 'I told Brother Lampton to come over.'

'What?' his mother could hardly speak. 'You told the preacher to come?'

'Yes,' an arrogant piety puckering her lips. 'Thought it would be a *comfort* to you.'

'Ah,' exclaimed the boy, rashly crossing the room.

The dying woman looked from one to the other, and flexed her tired fingers. 'Well,' she rested her eyes on the ceiling. 'Let him come. Perhaps — ' a sly smile passed her face, 'we'll comfort him!'

Lillian waited in the doorway, clasping her hands together, looking as if she were about to sneeze. Then she said petulantly, 'I only did it for your own good. Nothing I do in this house seems to — '

'Lillian,' his mother reached out her thin arms and he could almost see the clear unveiled bone. 'Lillian, you have been an angel. You have!' she repeated and sank back exhausted.

Lillian came further into the room, her mouth moving as if from thirst. 'How do you feel?' she asked presently.

'I — ' his mother's voice was falling away, he could hardly hear it. 'I would like — some potato soup, I think.' The last word was a whisper. The two of them bent to hear, then Lillian glanced up and looked triumphantly at her brother.

'I'll make some,' said the daughter.

And she went downstairs.

With a quick movement, John sat down beside his mother. When Lillian came between them, he felt without strength. The boy regarded her wordlessly. A fear crossed his breast. Suppose she were to die now, while he was afraid and without strength to support her. But suddenly her eyelids fluttered and she looked up.

'You're tired,' she said faintly. 'Why don't you take a nap, John?'

'No,' he said. 'I'm not sleepy.'

It was true. He was never weary these days. His heart beat tirelessly like a lover's. Why should he be tired? His pulse raced with passion. What idleness there was ahead of them! He could foresee only endless days, time sunk in the restless ennui of waiting. Summer was coming. It warmed the earth with a portentous fever. The boy looked out of the window and saw the gnarled plum tree in the back yard. It was blooming again, as if magically, the white siftings of blossom spraying fountain-wise from the black trunk and through the green. Oh, how restful it was. The grape arbor throwing its shadows over the moist brick wall, it ran the length of the yard to the alley gate. How slowly the leaves were loosened from the hard clumps of bud. The future was imminent and yet came so easily. He foresaw the ripened bunches of fruit. In autumn they would drop to the grass, purple like blood. He foresaw the lopped-off calendar of days. And yet it was not death he foresaw. Rather, he felt that everything was becoming more animate, alive to them. So much that it was terrifying. As he sat quietly in the rocking chair, sometimes it seemed that the thin timber of the floor and the cheap rose-twined paper that covered the walls — all the surfaces of the room appeared to glow with a terrible brilliance. And he often imagined that he and his mother were two insects in a globe of light and could not be reached except by crushing the world into darkness. . . .

Brother Lampton came at three o'clock. He was a large preacher with hairy ears and quivering nostrils. He stood by the bed, his long-necked head lowered to a docile interest. But he could not keep back the great neighing pulpit voice. It whinnied over his bony teeth and struck the air forcibly.

'How are you!' his lips parted in a thunderous smile.

John's mother, shy of her sickness, held out her hand to the preacher.

'I am fine,' she said.

His thick ungual palm slipped over the covers and rested for a moment on her fingers. '*That's* fine!' he struck the bed with his closed fist. 'That's fine!' Wetting his long upper lip with the lower, he reflected solemnly for a moment, then

threw back his head and laughed. 'Good, good!' he emphasized heartily. Panting from the exertion of that cordiality,
he lumbered to his feet and exclaimed, 'We're praying for
you, never fear!'

John watched his mother's face. She had changed in the
last weeks, the features were sharp, illuminated almost to
transparency. The sunlight danced like water-motes over
her face, the fine silver brown hair flowed like rough shallows
covering the pillow. How beautiful she was. Even with the
change. As he watched her, John knew that he loved the
change, he would follow it with his eyes. Were he blind, he
would still perceive it —

She said almost inaudibly to the preacher, 'Thank you.'

The boy knotted his hands, then relaxed the knuckles. 'It
is getting,' he announced inappropriately, 'late, isn't it?'

He heard Lillian, in the corner, move with disturbed
politeness. Her starched apron rattled like paper.

'Well,' exclaimed the boy recklessly, 'it is, isn't it?'

Lillian's powdered face made an adult grimace and
frowned at her brother. John noticed that under the curling-
iron curls, a limp red ribbon stuck out its little forked
tongue. The preacher's visit was a social occasion which she
would not give up easily.

'Oh,' said the preacher, 'I had no idea of the time — ' he
squinted bewildered at the boy, his big eyelids folding over
the corners of his eyes.

'Why,' Lillian's voice was trembling, 'You only just came.'

'I know, I know.' The large man lifted his black cloaked
arm like a command. Underneath the coat, the boy saw a
pair of candy-striped suspenders. Then he dropped his hand
in a rapid gesture of supplication and said, 'The works of
the Lord are exceedingly strange.' His hoarse breath was
calmed to a minor commotion. His head was lowered and
on his neck the unclipped mane rose stiffly erect. He was
praying.

'But in life or in death,' the word *death* was delicately
accented, 'Thou, oh Lord, art with us.' His great hawking
whisper was gathering momentum. 'For as the rain cometh

down and the snow from heaven, and returneth not thither, but watereth the earth, and maketh it bring forth and bud, that it may give seed to the sower and bread to the eater: so shall my word be that goeth forth out of my mouth: It shall not return unto me void. But it shall accomplish that which I please, and it shall prosper in the thing whereto I sent it. Ahem!' With a large engulfing cough, the preacher covered his mouth with a handkerchief and blinked twice around the room. When he removed the handkerchief, he was smiling. His fleshy tongue, stuck between his uncovered teeth, was at once both tough and servile. Was it he, John thought dreamily, was it he who had licked the boots of heaven — ?

That night, his mother woke up and said aloud in the darkness, 'I'm not afraid.'

John came over from the window and lit the lamp.

'Why should you be?' he said.

'I had a funny dream.' She looked up at him. 'I dreamed that I was two hundred years old, with ivy growing round my face. If I had been as young as you,' she smiled, 'I would have been afraid. But I wasn't afraid.'

John listened intently. The morphine always gave her such dreams. But he understood them. He could soften their sharp isolation into reality. That was the reason she told him. The dreams were a secret from others.

'I dreamed,' she went on as the boy waited. 'I dreamed that I had met all the people who have died. And it was not strange at all. Aunt Mamie, you remember her?' His mother's voice rose like a child's. 'Aunt Mamie could never take a bath without getting heat prickles.' The woman smiled deeply into the lamplight. 'She was there. And everyone was so quiet, John. I thought — ' her voice sank, level with the darkness. 'I thought, it must be snow falling. And it was, everywhere. But nobody was cold. What do you think of that?' She looked into her son's eyes, as if she had spoken rationally. He almost believed that she had. His own identity he felt fading into her world. With a long drowning gaze, like a swimmer in long strokes against the tide, he followed her.

He said quietly, 'I'll leave the light on.'

The next evening, Lillian asked John to go to the store for her. She was in the kitchen talking to the doctor. The doctor had been there all day. He stood over the white enamel breakfast table, looking down absently, cradling a hypodermic syringe in his hand. He held it as carelessly as a pencil, John thought. While Lillian talked without interruption.

'How long can this go on,' she chattered. 'The house needs cleaning. I'm a wreck. Oh God — '

John listened indifferently. He walked out of the back door and around the house, noting as he passed that the hollyhocks had not yet bloomed. Crowded against the whitewashed fence, their stiff buds curled like serpents' heads. He crossed the yard and crushed one in his palm. The odor was acrid with a faintly ashen tang.

Without thinking he walked a block up the street and went into the grocery. Its vegetable coolness struck him like dusk and he shivered.

'A quart of milk,' he said and observed the storekeeper's hands. In front of the white apron, they seemed whiter, clean and large as an undertaker's. The boy picked up the cold package of milk from the counter. He walked out of the store.

As he came to his house, he looked without interest at its box front, like the other houses on the street, its narrow porch suspended between two windows; the porch, somehow, resembled a shelf. There was a heavy twilight which cast a greenish aura over the houses. But then, without warning, in the gray green air, John suddenly saw his sister. She was walking off the shelf, coming rapidly toward him. How strange she looked! Her skirt flew behind her like the tail of a swan. Without concern, he watched its calm glide coming toward him.

'What?' he asked and with snobbish serenity turned his head away from her.

'Oh,' her hooked fingers sought his own. 'Brother, brother, she is going fast. The doctor says it's a coma.'

'Don't be silly.' The boy jerked away. 'She'll never go into a coma.'

They walked clumsily into the house, the screen door squeaking behind them. The boy turned quietly to his sister, his voice thick with anger. 'You're a liar,' he said. 'A liar and a show-off. That's what you are!' he flung out, going to the kitchen.

But she followed after, her nose sloping toward him like a pointed finger. 'I tell you,' she said. 'It's true. I'm not lying! She's *unconscious!*'

With a snarl, the boy pushed her aside and rushed through the house, up the stairs.

The doctor was standing beside the pink bedspread, a peculiar expression on his face. Or it had no expression, the doctor's face was impassive and sweet, seeming to have ripened like a stone. When the man saw John, he moved humbly aside. The boy advanced ponderously and stood a moment as if waiting. Then he knew. It dawned on him with amazing simplicity. She was, he thought, after all, dead. Her eyes were closed.

But something strained at his throat, an objection, a rebuke. Like rocks breaking inside him, it seemed to scatter all his love. Her eyes, darkness against darkness. The boy looked at her unbelievingly, angrily. How unfriendly her closed face was! The boy bent over.

'Mother,' he exclaimed, fury overcoming him like an agony. 'Mother!'

So this was how it had ended! He, who would have followed her anywhere — he, who would have listened to anything she might have said — he, who had endured and was silent. How he could have praised her, how he could have propounded her worth! Did she know how loyal he was? Did she know that he had forsaken the world to follow her? Now he realized it. In her mute face, he saw the traitorous truth. *She* had forsaken him. The boy sucked his breath, trembling with wrath. Her motionless brow, receding into the shadows, the face cold and empty as a wax flower. Ah, he cried, what did she care for him now?

*(From Accent)*

# PRINCE OF DARKNESS

## BY J. F. POWERS

### I. MORNING

*I* SHOULD'VE KNOWN you'd be eating breakfast, Father. But I was at your Mass and I said to myself that must be Father Burner. Then I stayed a few minutes after Mass to make my thanksgiving.'

'Fine,' Father Burner said. 'Breakfast?'

'Had it, Father, thanking you all the same. It's the regret of my life that I can't be a daily communicant. Doctor forbids it. "Fast every day and see how long you last," he tells me. But I do make it to Mass.'

'Fine. You say you live in Father Desmond's parish?'

'Yes, Father. And sometimes I think Father Desmond does too much. All the societies to look after. Plus the Scouts and the Legion. Of course Father Kells being so elderly and all . . .'

'We're all busy these days.'

'It's the poor parish priest's day that's never done, I always say, Father, not meaning to slight the ladies, God love 'em.'

Father Burner's sausage fingers, spelling his impatience over and over, worked up sweat in the folds of the napkin which he kept in view to provoke an early departure. 'About this matter you say Father Desmond thought I might be interested in — '

'The Plan, Father.' Mr. Tracy lifted his seersucker trousers

293

by the creases, crossed his shining two-tone shoes and rolled warmly forward. 'Father . . . '

Father Burner met his look briefly. He was wary of the fatherers. A backslider he could handle, it was the old story, but a red hot believer, especially a talkative one, could be a devilish nuisance. This kind might be driven away only by prayer and fasting, and he was not adept at either.

'I guess security's one thing we're all after.'

Father Burner grunted. Mr. Tracy was too familiar to suit him. He liked his parishioners to be retiring, dumb or frightened. There were too many references made to the priest's hard lot. Not so many poor souls as all that passed away in the wee hours, nor was there so much bad weather to brave. Mr. Tracy's heart bled for priests. That in itself was a suspicious thing in a layman. It all led up to the Plan.

'Here's the Plan, Father . . . ' Father Burner watched his eye peel down to naked intimacy. Then, half listening, he gazed about the room. He hated it too. A fabulous brown rummage of encyclopedias, world globes, maps, photographs, holy pictures, mirrors, crucifixes, tropical fish and too much furniture. The room reproduced the world in exact scale, all wonders and horrors seemingly, less land than water. From the faded precipices of the walls photographs viewed each other for the most part genially across time. Three popes, successively thinner, raised hands to bless their departed painters. The world globes simpered in the shadows, heavy-headed idiot boys, listening. A bird in a blacked-out cage scratched among its offal. An anomalous buddha peeked beyond his dusty umbilicus at the trampled figures in the rug. The fish swam on, the mirrors and encyclopedias turned in upon themselves, the earless boys heard everything and understood nothing. Father Burner put his big black shoe on a moth and sent dust flecks crowding up a shaft of sunlight to the distant ceiling.

'Say you pay in $22.50 every month, can be paid semi-annually or as you please, policy matures in twenty years and pays you $35.67 a month for twenty years or as long as you live. That's the deal for you, Father. It beats the deal Father

Desmond's got, although he's got a darned good one, and I hope he keeps it up. But we've gone ahead in the last few years, Father. Utilities are sounder, bonds are more secure and this new legislation protects you one hundred per cent.'

'You say Ed — Father Desmond — has the Plan?'

'Oh, indeed, Father.' Mr. Tracy had to laugh. 'I hope you don't think I'm trying to high-pressure you, Father. It's not just a piece of business with me, the Plan.'

'No?'

'No. You see, it's more or less a pet project of mine. Hardly make a cent on it. Looking out after the fathers, you might say, so they'll maybe look out after me — spiritually. I call it heavenly life insurance.'

Slightly repelled, Father Burner nodded.

'Not a few priests that I've sold the Plan to remember me at the altar daily. I guess prayer's one thing we can all use. Anyway it's why I take a hand in putting boys through seminary.'

With that Mr. Tracy shed his shappy anonymity and drew executive markings for Father Burner. He became the one and only Thomas Nash Tracy — T. N. T. It was impossible to read the papers and not know a few things about T. N. T. He was in small loans and insurance. His company's advertising smothered the town and country; everybody knew the slogan T. N. T. spells Security. He figured in any financial drive undertaken by the diocese, was caught by photographers in orphanages and sat at the heavy end of the table at communion breakfasts. Hundreds of nuns, thanks to his thoughtfulness, ate capon on Christmas Day and a few priests of the right sort received baskets of scotch. He was a B. C. L., a Big Catholic Layman, and now Father Burner could see why. Father Burner's countenance softened at this intelligence and T. N. T. proceeded with more assurance.

'And don't call it charity, Father. Insurance, as I said, is a better name for it. I have a little money, Father, which makes it possible.' He tuned his voice down to a whisper. 'You might say I'm moderately wealthy.' He looked sharply at Father Burner, not sure of his man. 'But I'm told there isn't any crime in that.'

'I believe you need not fear for your soul on that account.'

'Glad to hear it from you, a priest, Father. Oft times it's thrown up to me.' He came to terms with reality, smiling. 'I wasn't always so well off myself, so I can understand the temptation to knock the other fellow.'

'Fine.'

'But that's still not to say that water's not wet or that names don't hurt sometimes, whatever the bard said to the contrary.'

'What bard?'

' "Sticks and stones — " '

'Oh.'

'If this were a matter of Faith and Morals, Father, I'd be the one to sit back and let you do the talking. But it's a case of common sense, Father, and I think I can safely say if you listen to me you'll not lose by it in the long run.'

'It could be.'

'May I ask you a personal question, Father?'

Father Burner searched T. N. T.'s face. 'Go ahead, Mr. Tracy.'

'Do you bank, Father?'

'*Bank?* Oh, bank — no. Why?'

'Let's admit it, Father,' T. N. T. coaxed, frankly amused. 'Priests as a class are an improvident lot — our records show it — and you're no exception. But that, I think, explains the glory of the Church down through the ages.'

'The Church is divine,' Father Burner corrected. 'And the concept of poverty isn't exactly foreign to Christianity or even to the priesthood.'

'Exactly,' T. N. T. agreed, pinked. 'But think of the future, Father.'

Nowadays when Father Burner thought of the future it required a firm act of imagination. As a seminarian twenty years ago, it had all been plain: ordination, roughly ten years as a curate somewhere (he was not the kind to be sent to Rome for further study), a church of his own to follow, the fruitful years, then retirement, pastor emeritus, with assistants doing the spade work, leaving the fine touches to him, still a hearty old man very much alive. It was not an uncommon hope and in fact all around him it had materialized for his friends. But for him it was only a bad memory growing worse. He was the desperate assistant now, the angry functionary aging in the outer office. One day he would wake up and find himself old, as the morning finds itself covered with snow. The future had assumed the forgotten character of a dream, so that he could not be sure that he had ever truly had one.

T. N. T. talked on and Father Burner felt a mist generating on his forehead. He tore his damp hands apart and put the napkin aside. Yes, yes, it was true a priest received miserably little, but then that was the whole idea. He did not comment, dreading T. N. T.'s foaming compassion, to be spat upon with charity. Yes, as a matter of fact, it would be easier to face old age with something more to draw upon than what the ecclesiastical authorities deemed sufficient and would provide. Also, as T. N. T. pointed out, one never knew when he might come down with an expensive illness. T. N. T., despite himself, had something . . . The Plan, in itself, was not bad. He must not reject the olive branch because it came by buzzard. But still Father Burner was a little bothered by the idea of a priest feathering his nest. Why? In other problems he was never the one to take the ascetic interpretation.

'You must be between thirty-five and forty, Father.'

'I'll never see forty again.'

'I'd never believe it from anyone else. You sure don't look it, Father.'

'Maybe not. But I feel it.'

'Worries, Father. And one big one is the future, Father. You'll get to be fifty, sixty, seventy — and what have you got? — not a penny saved. You look around and say to yourself — where did it go?'

T. N. T. had the trained voice of the good and faithful servant, supple from many such dealings. And still from time to time a faint draught of contempt seemed to pass through it which had something to do with his eyes. Here,

Father Burner thought, was the latest thing in simony, unnecessary, inspired from without, participated in spiritlessly by the priest who must yet suffer the brunt of the blame and ultimately do the penance. Father Burner felt mysteriously purchasable. He was involved in an exchange of confidences which impoverished him mortally. In T. N. T. he sensed free will in its senility or the infinite capacity for equating evil with good — or with nothing, the same thing, only easier. Here was one more word in the history of the worm's progress, another wave on the dry flood that kept rising, the constant aggrandizement of decay. In the end it must touch the world and everything at the heart. Father Burner felt weak from a nameless loss.

'I think I can do us both a service, Father.'

'I don't say you can't.' Father Burner rose quickly. 'I'll have to think about it, Mr. Tracy.'

'To be sure, Father.' He produced a glossy circular. 'Just let me leave this literature with you.'

Father Burner, leading him to the door, prevented further talk by reading the circular. It was printed in a churchy type, all purple and gold, a dummy leaf from a medieval hymnal, and entitled, 'A Silver Lining in the Sky.' It was evidently meant for clergymen only, though not necessarily priests, as Father Burner could instantly see from its general tone.

'Very interesting,' he said.

'My business phone is right on the back, Father. But if you'd rather call me at my home some night —'

'No thanks, Mr. Tracy.'

'Allow me to repeat, Father, this isn't just business with me.'

'I understand.' He opened the door too soon for T. N. T. 'Glad to have met you.'

'Glad to have met you, Father.'

Father Burner went back to the table. The coffee needed warming up and the butter had vanished into the toast. 'Mary,' he called. Then he heard them come gabbing into the rectory, Quinlan and his friend Keefe, also newly ordained.

They were hardly inside the dining room before he was explaining how he came to be eating breakfast so late — so late, see? — not *still*.

'You protest too much, Father,' Quinlan said. 'The Angelic Doctor himself weighed three hundred pounds and I'll wager he didn't get it all from prayer and fasting.'

'A pituitary condition,' Keefe interjected, faltering. 'Don't you think?'

'Yah, yah, Father, you'll wager' — Father Burner, eyes malignant, leaned on his knife, the blade bowing out bright and buttery beneath his fist — 'and I'll wager you'll be the first saint to reach heaven with a flannel mouth!' Rising from the table, he shook Keefe's hand, which was damp from his pocket, and experienced a surge of strength, the fat man's contempt and envy for the thin man. He thought he might break Keefe's hand off at the wrist without drawing a drop of blood.

Quinlan stood aside, six inches or more below them, gazing up, as at two impossibly heroic figures in a hotel mural. Reading the caption under them, he mused, 'Father Burner meets Father Keefe.'

'I've heard about you, Father,' Keefe said, plying him with a warmth beyond his means.

'Bound to be the case in a diocese as overstocked with magpies as this one.' Father Burner threw a fresh napkin at a plate. 'But be seated, Father Keefe.' Keefe, yes, he had seen him before, a nobody in a crowd, some affair . . . the K. C. barbecue, the Youth Center? No, probably not, not Keefe, who was obviously not the type, too crabbed and introversive for Catholic Action. 'I suppose,' he said, 'you've heard the latest definition of Catholic Action — the interference of the laity with the inactivity of the hierarchy.'

'Very good,' Keefe said uneasily.

Quinlan yanked off his collar and churned his neck up and down to get circulation. 'Dean in the house? No? Good.' He pitched the collar at one of the candles on the buffet for a ringer. 'That turkey we met coming out the front door — think I've seen his face somewhere.'

'Thomas Nash Tracy,' Keefe said. 'I thought you knew.'

'The prominent lay priest and usurer?'

Keefe coughed. 'They say he's done a lot of good.'

Quinlan spoke to Father Burner: 'Did you take out a policy, Father?'

'One of the sixth-graders threw a rock through his windshield,' Father Burner said. 'He was very nice about it.'

'Muldoon or Ciesniewski?'

'A new kid. Public school transfer.' Father Burner patted the napkin to his chin. 'Not that I see anything wrong with insurance.'

Quinlan laughed. 'Let Walter tell you what happened to him a few days ago. Go ahead, Walter,' he said to Keefe.

'Oh, that.' Keefe fidgeted and seemingly against his better judgment began. 'I had a little accident — was it Wednesday it rained so? I had the misfortune to skid into a fellow parked on Fairmount. Dented his fender.' Keefe stopped and then, as though impelled by the memory of it, went on. 'The fellow came raging out of his car at me. I thought there'd be serious trouble. Then he must have seen I was a priest, the way he calmed down, I mean. I had a funny feeling it wasn't because he was a Catholic or anything like that. As a matter of fact he wore a Masonic button.' Keefe sighed. 'I guess he saw I was a priest and . . . ergo knew I'd have insurance.'

'Take nothing for your journey, neither staff, nor scrip,' Quinlan said, 'words taken from today's gospel.'

Father Burner spoke in a level tone: 'Not that I *still* see anything wrong with insurance. It's awfully easy,' he continued, hating himself for talking such drivel, 'to make too much of little things.' With Quinlan around he played the conservative; among the real righthanders he was the enfant terrible. He operated on the principle of discord at any cost. He did not know why. It was a habit. Perhaps it had something to do with being overweight.

Arranging the Dean's chair, which had arms, for himself, Quinlan sank into it, giving Keefe the Irish whisper. 'Grace, Father.'

Keefe addressed the usual words to God concerning the gifts they were about to receive. During the prayer Father Burner stopped chewing and did not reach for anything. He noted once more that Quinlan crossed himself sloppily enough to be a bishop.

Keefe nervously cleared the entire length of his throat. 'It's a beautiful church you have here at Saint Patrick's, Father.' A lukewarm light appeared in his eyes, flickered, sputtered out, leaving them blank and blue. His endless fingers felt for his receding chin in the onslaught of silence.

'*I* have?' Father Burner turned his spoon abasingly to his bosom. '*Me?*' He jabbed at the grapefruit before him, his second, demolishing its perfect rose window. 'I don't know why it is the Irish without exception are always laying personal claim to church property. The Dean is forever saying *my* church, *my* school, *my* furnace . . .'

'I'm sorry, Father,' Keefe said, flushing. 'And I'll confess I did think he virtually built Saint Patrick's.'

'Out of the slime of the earth, I know. A common error.' With sudden, unabated displeasure Father Burner recalled how the Dean, one of the last of the old brick and mortar pastors, had built the church, school, sisters' house and rectory, and had named the whole thing through the lavish pretense of a popular contest. Opposed bitterly by Polish, German and Italian minorities, he had effected a compromise between their bad taste (Saint Stanislaus, Saint Boniface, Saint Anthony) and his own better judgment in the choice of Saint Patrick's.

Quinlan, snorting, blurted: 'Well, he did build it, didn't he?'

Father Burner smiled at them from the other world. 'Only, if you please, in a manner of speaking.'

'True,' Keefe murmured humbly.

'Nuts,' Quinlan said. 'It's hard for me to see God in a few buildings paid for by the funds of the faithful and put up by a mick contractor. A burning bush, yes.'

Father Burner, lips parched to speak an unsummonable cruelty, settled for a smouldering aside to the kitchen. 'Mary, more eggs here.'

A stuffed moose of a woman with a tabbycat face charged in on swollen feet. She stood wavering in shoes sliced fiercely for corns. With the back of her hand she wiped some cream from the fuzz ringing her baby-pink mouth. Her hair poked through a broken net like stunted antlers. Father Burner pointed to the empty platter.

'Eggs,' he said.

'Eggs!' she cried, tumbling her eyes like great blue dice among them. She seized up the platter and carried it whirling with grease into the kitchen.

Father Burner put aside the grapefruit. He smiled and spoke calmly. 'I'll have to let the Dean know, Father, how much you like *his* plant.'

'Do, Father. A beautiful church . . . "a poem in stone" — was it Ruskin?'

'Ruskin? *Stones of Venice,*' Father Burner grumbled. '*Sesame and Lilies,* I know . . . but I never cared for his *style.*' He passed the knife lovingly over the pancakes on his plate and watched the butter bubble at the pores. 'So much sweetness, so much light, I'm afraid, made Jack a dull boy.'

Quinlan slapped all his pockets. 'Pencil and paper, quick!'

'And yet . . . ' Keefe cocked his long head, brow fretted, and complained to his upturned hands. 'Don't understand how he stayed outside the Church.' He glanced up hopefully. 'I wonder if Chesterton gives us a clue.'

Father Burner, deaf to such precious speculation, said: 'In the 19th century Francis Thompson was the only limey worth his salt. It's true.' He quartered the pancakes. 'Of course, Newman.'

'Hopkins has some good things.'

'Good — yes, if you like jabberwocky and jebbies! I don't care for either.' He dispatched a look of indictment at Quinlan.

'What a pity,' Quinlan murmured, 'Oliver Wendell couldn't be at table this morning.'

'No, Father, you can have your Hopkins, you and Father Quinlan here. Include me out, as Sam Goldwyn says. Poetry, I'll take my poetry the way I take my liquor, neat.'

Mary brought in the platter oozing with bacon and eggs.
'Good for you, Mary,' Quinlan said. 'I'll pray for you.'

'Thank you, Father,' Mary said.

Quinlan dipped the platter with a trace of obeisance to Father Burner.

'No thanks.'

Quinlan scooped up the coffeepot in a fearsome rush and held it high at Father Burner, his arm so atremble the lid rattled dangerously. 'Sure and will you be about having a sup of coffee now, Father?'

'Not now. And do you mind not playing the wild Irish wit so early in the day, Father?'

'That I don't. *But a relentless fate pursuing good Father Quinlan, he was thrown in among hardened clerics where but for the grace of God that saintly priest, so little understood, so much maligned . . .* ' Quinlan poured two cups and passed one to Keefe. 'For yourself, Father.'

Father Burner nudged the toast to Keefe. 'Father Quinlan, that saintly priest, models his life after the Rover Boys, particularly Sam, the fun-loving one.'

Quinlan dealt himself a mighty mea culpa.

Father Burner grimaced, the flesh rising in sweet concentric tiers around his mouth, and said in a tone both entrusting and ennobling Keefe with his confidence: 'The syrup, if you please, Father.' Keefe passed the silver pitcher which was running at the mouth. Father Burner reimmersed the doughy remains on his plate until the butter began to float around the edges as in a moat. He felt them both watching the butter. Regretting that he had not foreseen this attraction, he cast about in his mind for something to divert them and found the morning sun coming in too strongly. He got up and pulled down the shade. He returned to his place and settled himself in such a way that a new chapter was indicated. 'Don't believe I know where you're located, Father.'

'Saint Jerome's,' Keefe said. 'Monsignor Fiedler's.'

'One of those P. N. places, eh? Is the Boss sorry he ever started it? I know some of them are.'

Keefe's lips popped apart. 'I don't quite understand.'

Quinlan prompted: 'P. N. — Perpetual Novena.'

'Oh, I never heard him say.'

'You wouldn't, of course. But I know a lot of them that are.' Father Burner stuck a morsel on his fork and swirled it against the tide of syrup. 'It's a real problem all right. I was all out for a P. N. here during the depression. Thought it might help. The Dean was against it.'

'I can tell you this,' Keefe said. 'Attendance was down from what it used to be until the casualties began to come in. Now it's going up.'

'I was just going to say the war ought to take the place of the depression.' Father Burner fell silent. 'Terrible thing, war. Hard to know what to do about it. I tried to sell the Dean the idea of a victory altar. You've seen them. Vigil lights — '

'At a dollar a throw,' Quinlan said.

'Vigil lights in the form of a V, names of the men in the service and all that. But even that, I guess — Well, like I said, I tried . . . '

'Yes, it is hard,' Keefe said.

'God, the Home and the Flag,' Quinlan said. 'The poets don't make the wars.'

Father Burner ignored that. 'Lately, though, I can't say how I feel about P. N.'s. Admit I'm not so strong for them as I was once. Ought to be some way of terminating them, you know, but then they wouldn't be perpetual, would they?'

'No, they wouldn't,' Keefe said.

'Of course the term itself, perpetual novena, is preposterous, a solecism. Possibly dispensation lies in that direction, I'm not theologian enough to say. Fortunately it's not a problem we have to decide.' He laid his knife and fork across the plate. 'Many are the consolations of the lowly curate. No decisions, no money worries.'

'We still have to count the sugar,' Quinlan said. 'And put up the card tables.'

'Reminds me,' Father Burner said earnestly. 'Father Desmond at Assumption was telling me they've got a new machine does all that.'

'Puts up card tables?' Quinlan inquired.

'Counts the collection, wraps the silver,' Father Burner explained, 'so it's all ready for the bank. Mean to mention it to the Dean, if I can catch him right.'

'I'm afraid, Father, he knows about it already.'

Father Burner regarded Quinlan sceptically. 'Does? I suppose he's against it.'

'I heard him tell the salesman that's what he had his assistants for.'

'Assistant, Father, not assistants. You count the collection, not me. I was only thinking of you.'

'I was only quoting him, Father. *Sic*. Sorry.'

'Not at all. I haven't forgotten the days I had to do it. It's a job has to be done and nothing to be ashamed of. Wouldn't you say, Father Keefe?'

'I daresay that's true.'

Quinlan, with Father Burner still molesting him with his eyes, poured out a glass of water and drank it all. 'I still think we would do with a lot less calculating. I notice the only time we get rid of the parish paper is when the new lists are published — the official standings. Of course it's a lousy sheet anyway.'

Father Burner, as editor of the paper, replied: 'Yes, yes, Father. We all know how easy it is to be wrathful or fastidious about these things — or whatever the hell it is you are. And we all know there *are* abuses. But contributing to the support of the Church is still one of her commandments.'

'Peace, Pere,' Quinlan said.

'Figures don't lie.'

'Somebody was telling me just last night that figures do lie. He looked a lot like you.'

Father Burner found his cigarettes and shuffled a couple half out of the pack. He eyed Quinlan and the cigarettes as though it were as simple to discipline the one as to smoke the others. 'For some reason, Father, you're damned fond of those particular figures.'

Keefe stirred. 'Which particular figures, Fathers?'

'It's the figures put out by the Cardinal of Toledo on how

many made their Easter duty last year.' Father Burner offered Keefe a cigarette. 'I discussed the whole thing with Father Quinlan last night. It's his latest thesis. Have a cigarette?'

'No, thanks,' Keefe said.

'So you don't smoke?' Father Burner looked from Keefe to Quinlan, blacklisting them together. He held the cigarette hesitantly at his lips. 'It's all right, isn't it?' He laughed and touched off the match with his thumbnail.

'His Eminence,' Quinlan said, 'reports only fifteen per cent of the women and five per cent of the men made their Easter duty last year.'

'So that's only three times as many women as men,' Father Burner said with buried gaiety. 'Certainly to be expected in any Latin country.'

'But fifteen per cent, Father! And five per cent! Just think of it!' Keefe glanced up at the ceiling and at the souvenir plates on the moulding, as though to see inscribed along with scenes from the Columbian Exposition the day and hour the end of the world would begin. He finally stared deep into the goldfish tank in the window.

Father Burner ploughed up the silence, talking with a mouthful of smoke. 'All right, all right, I'll say what I said in the first place. There's something wrong with the figures. A country as overwhelmingly Catholic as Spain!' He sniffed, pursed his lips, and said: 'Pooh!'

'Yes,' Keefe said, still balking. 'But it *is* disturbing, Father Burner.'

'Sure it's disturbing, Father Keefe. *Lots* of things *are.*'

A big faded goldfish paused to stare through the glass at them and then with a single lob of its tail slipped into a dark green corner.

Quinlan said, 'Father Burner belongs to the school that's always seeing a great renascence of faith in the offing. The hour before dawn and all that. Tell it to Rotary on Tuesday, Father.'

Father Burner countered with a frosty pink smile. 'What would I ever do without you, Father? If you're trying to say

I'm a dreadful optimist, you're right and I don't mind at all.
I am — and proud of it!'

Ascending to his feet, he went to the right side of the
buffet, took down the card index to parishioners and returned with it to his place. He pushed his dishes aside and
began to sort out the deadheads to be called on personally by
him or Quinlan. The Dean, like all pastors, he reflected, left
the dirty work to the assistants. 'Why doesn't he pull them,'
he snapped, tearing up a card, 'when they kick off! Can't
very well forward them to the next world. Say, how many
Gradys live at 909 South Vine? Here's Anna, Catherine,
Clement, Gerald, Harvey, James A., James F. — which James
is the one they call "Bum"?'

'James F.,' Quinlan said. 'Can't you tell from the take?
The other James works.'

'John, Margaret, Matthew — that's ten, no eleven. Here's
Dennis out of place. Patrick, Rita and William — fourteen
of them, no birth control there, and they all give. Except
Bum. Nice account otherwise. Can't we find Bum a job?
What's it with him, drink?'

Now he came to Maple Street. These cards were the remains of little Father Vicci's work among the magdalens.
Ann Mason, Estelle Rogers, May Miller, Billie Starr. The
names had the generic ring. Great givers when they gave —
Christmas, $25.00; Easter, $20.00; Propagation of the Faith,
$10.00; Catholic University, $10.00 — but not much since
Father Vicci was exiled to the sticks. He put Maple Street
aside for a thorough sifting.

The doorbell rang. Father Burner leaned around in his
chair. 'Mary.' The doorbell rang again. Father Burner
bellowed. 'Mary!'

Quinlan pushed his chair away from the table. 'I'll get it.'

Father Burner blocked him. 'Oh, I'll get it! Hell of a bell!
Why does he have a bell like that!' Father Burner opened
the door to a middle-aged woman whose name he had forgotten or never known. 'Good morning,' he said. 'Will you
step in?'

She stayed where she was and said, 'Father, it's about the

servicemen's flag in church. My son Stanley — you know him — '

Father Burner, who did not know him, half nodded. 'Yes, how is Stanley?' He gazed over her shoulder at the lawn, at the dandelions turning into poppies before his eyes.

'You know he was drafted last October, Father, and I been watching that flag you got in church ever since and it's still the same, five hundred thirty-six stars. I thought you said you put a star up for all them that's gone in the service, Father.'

Now the poppies were dandelions again. He could afford to be firm with her. 'We can't spend all our time putting up stars. Sometimes we fall behind. Besides, a lot of the boys are being discharged.'

'You mean there's just as many going in as coming out, so you don't have to change the flag?'

'Something like that.'

'I see.' He was sorry for her. They had run out of stars. He had tried to get the Dean to order some more, had even offered . . . and the Dean had said they could use up the gold ones first. When Father Burner had objected, telling him what it would mean, he had suggested that Father Burner apply for the curatorship of the armory.

'The Pastor will be glad to explain how it works the next time you see him.'

'Well, Father, if that's the way it is . . . ' She was fading down the steps. 'I just thought I'd ask.'

'That's right. There's no harm in asking. How's Stanley?'

'Fine, and thank you, Father, for your trouble.'

'No trouble.'

When he came back to the table they were talking about the junior clergymen's examinations which they would take for the first time next week. Father Burner interrupted: 'The Dean conducts the history end of it, you know.'

'I say!' Keefe said. 'Any idea what we can expect?'

'You have nothing to fear. Nothing.'

'Really?'

'Really. Last year, I remember, there were five questions

and the last four depended on the first. So it was really only one question — if you knew it. I imagine you would've.' He paused, making Keefe ask for it.

'Perhaps you can recall the question, Father?'

'Perfectly, Father. "What event in the American history of the Church took place in 1541?"' Father Burner, slumping in his chair, smirked at Keefe pondering for likely martyrs and church legislation. He imagined him skipping among the tomes and statuary of his mind, winnowing dates and little known facts like mad, only at last to emerge dusty and downcast. Father Burner sat up with a jerk and assaulted the table with the flat of his hand. 'Time's up. Answer: "De Soto sailed up the Mississippi."'

Quinlan snorted. Keefe sat very still, incredulous, silent, utterly unable to digest the answer, finally croaking, 'How odd.' Father Burner saw in him the boy whose marks in school had always been a consolation to his parents.

'So you don't have to worry, Father. No sense in preparing for it. Take in a couple of movies instead. And cheer up! The Dean's been examining the junior clergy for twenty-five years and nobody ever passed history yet. You wouldn't want to be the first one.'

Father Burner said grace and made the sign of the cross with slow distinction. 'And, Father,' he said, standing, extending his hand to Keefe, who also rose, 'I'm glad to have met you.' He withdrew his hand before Keefe was through with it and stood against the table knocking toast crumbs onto his plate. 'Ever play any golf? No? Well, come and see us for conversation then. You don't have anything against talking, do you?'

'Well, of course, Father, I . . .'

Father Burner gave Keefe's arm a rousing clutch. 'Do that!'

'I will, Father. It's been a pleasure.'

'Speaking of pleasure,' Father Burner said, tossing Quinlan a stack of cards, 'I've picked out a few lost sheep for you to see on Maple Street, Father.'

## II. NOON

He hung his best black trousers on a hanger in the closet and took down another pair, also black. He tossed them out behind him and they fell patched at the cuffs and baggy across his unmade bed. His old suede jacket, following, slid dumpily to the floor. He stood gaping in his clerical vest and undershorts, knees knocking and pimply, thinking . . . what else? His aviator's helmet. He felt all the hooks blindly in the darkness. It was not there. 'Oh, hell!' he groaned, sinking to his knees. He pawed among the old shoes and boxes and wrapping paper and string that he was always going to need. Under his golf bag he found it. So Mary had cleaned yesterday.

There was also a golf ball unknown to him, a Royal Bomber, with one small hickey in it. Father Desmond, he remembered, had received a box of Royal Bombers from a thoughtful parishioner. He stuck the helmet on his balding head to get it out of the way and took the putter from the bag. He dropped the ball at the door of the closet. Taking his own eccentric stance — a perversion of what the pro recommended and a dozen books on the subject — he putted the ball across the room at a dirty collar lying against the bookcase. A thready place in the carpet caused the ball to jump the collar and to loose a pamphlet from the top of the bookcase. He restored the pamphlet — Pius XI on 'Atheistic Communism' — and poked the ball back to the door of the closet. Then, allowing for the carpet, he drove the ball straight, *click,* through the collar, *clop.* Still had his old putting eye. And his irons had always been steady if not exactly crashing. It was his woods, the tee shots, that ruined his game. He'd give a lot to be able to hit his woods properly, not to dub his drives, if only on the first tee — where there was always a crowd (mixed).

At one time or another he had played every hole at the country club in par or less. Put all those pars and birdies together, adding in the only two eagles he'd ever had, and you had the winning round in the state open, write-ups and action shots in the papers — photo shows Rev. Ernest 'Boomer' Burner, par-shattering padre, blasting out of a trap. He needed only practice perhaps and at his earliest opportunity he would entice some of the eighth-grade boys over into the park to shag balls. He sank one more for good measure, winning a buck from Ed Desmond who would have bet against it, and put the club away.

Crossing the room for his trousers he noticed himself in the mirror with the helmet on and got a mild surprise. He scratched a little hair down from underneath the helmet to offset the egg effect. He searched his eyes in the mirror for a sign of ill health. He walked away from the mirror, as though done with it, only to wheel sharply so as to see himself as others saw him, front and profile, not wanting to catch his eye, just to see himself . . .

Out of the top drawer of the dresser he drew a clean white silk handkerchief and wiped the shine from his nose. He chased his eyes over into the corner of the mirror and saw nothing. Then, succumbing to his original intention, he knotted the handkerchief at the crown of the helmet and completed the transformation of time and place and person by humming, vibrato, 'Jeannine, I dream of lilac time,' remembering the old movie. He saw himself over his shoulder in the mirror, a sad war ace. It reminded him that his name was not Burner, but Boerner, an impediment removed at the outset of the first world war by his father. In a way he resented the old man for it. They had laughed at the seminary; the war, except as theory, hardly entered there. In perverse homage to the old Boerner, to which he now affixed a proud 'von,' he dropped the fair-minded American look he had and faced the mirror sneering, scar-cheeked and black of heart, the flying Junker who might have been. 'Himmelkreuzdonnerwetter! When you hear the word "culture," ' he snarled, hearing it in German, 'reach for your revolver!'

Reluctantly he pulled on his black trousers, falling across the bed to do so, as though felled, legs heaving up like howitzers.

He lay still for a moment, panting, and then let the inner-

spring mattress bounce him to his feet, a fighter coming off
the ropes. He stood looking out the window, buckling his
belt, and then down at the buckle, chins kneading softly with
the effort, and was pleased to see that he was holding his own
on the belt, still a good half inch away from last winter's
highwater mark.

At the sound of high heels approaching on the front walk
below, he turned firmly away from the window and considered for the first time since he posted it on the wall the
prayer for priests sent him by a candle concern. 'Remember,
O most compassionate God, that they are but weak and frail
human beings. Stir up in them the grace of their vocation
which is in them by the imposition of the Bishops' hands.
Keep them close to Thee, lest the enemy prevail against
them, so that they may never do anything in the slightest
degree unworthy of their sublime . . .' His eyes raced through
the prayer and out the window . . .

He was suddenly inspired to write another letter to the
Archbishop. He sat down at his desk, slipped a piece of paper
into his portable, dated it with the saint's day it was, and
wrote, 'Your Excellency: Thinking my letter of some months
ago may have gone amiss, or perhaps due to the press of
business —' He ripped the paper from the portable and
typed the same thing on a fresh sheet until he came to 'business,' using instead 'affairs of the Church.' He went on to
signify — it was considered all right to 'signify,' but to re-
signify? — that he was still of the humble opinion that he
needed a change of location and had decided, since he believed himself ready for a parish of his own, a rural one
might be best, all things considered (by which he meant
easier to get). He, unlike some priests of urban upbringing
and experience, would have no objection to the country. He
begged to be graced with an early reply. That line, for all
its seeming docility, was full of dynamite and ought to break
the episcopal silence into which the first letter had dissolved.
This was a much stronger job. He thought it better for two
reasons: the Archbishop was supposed to like outspoken
people, or, that being only more propaganda talked up by

the sycophants, then it ought to bring a reply which would reveal once and for all his prospects. Long overdue for the routine promotion, he had a just cause. He addressed the letter and placed it in his coat. He went to the bathroom. When he came back he put on the coat, picked up the suede jacket and helmet, looked around for something he might have forgot, a book of chances, a box of Sunday envelopes to be delivered, some copy for the printer, but there was nothing. He lit a cigarette at the door and not caring to throw the match on the floor or look for the ashtray, which was out of sight again, he dropped it in the empty holy water font.

Downstairs he paused at the telephone in the hall, scribbled 'Airport' on the message pad, thought of crossing it out or tearing off the page, but since it was dated he let it stand and added 'Visiting the sick,' signing his initials, *E. B.*

He went through the wicker basket for mail. A card from the Book-of-the-Month Club. So it was going to be another war book selection this month. Well, they knew what they could do with it. He wished the Club would wake up and select some dandies, as they had in the past. He thought of *Studs Lonigan* — there was a book, the best thing since the Bible.

An oblique curve in the road: perfect, wheels parallel with the center line. So many drivers took a curve like that way over on the other fellow's side. Father Burner touched the lighter on the dashboard to his cigarette and plunged his hams deeper into the cushions. A cloud of smoke whirled about the little Saint Christopher garroted from the ceiling. Father Burner tugged viciously at both knees, loosening the binding black cloth, easing the seat. Now that he was in open country he wanted to enjoy the scenery — God's majesty. How about a sermon that would liken the things in the landscape to the people in a church? All different, all the same handiwork of God. Moral: it is right and meet for rocks to be rocks, trees to be trees, pigs to be pigs, but — and here the small gesture that says so much — what did that mean that men, created in the image and likeness of God, should be? And what — He thrust the sermon out of mind, tired of it. He relaxed, as before an open fireplace, the weight of dogma off his shoulders. Then he grabbed at his knees again, cursing. Did the tailor skimp on the cloth because of the ecclesiastical discount?

A billboard inquired — 'Pimples?' Yes, he had a few, but he blamed them on the climate, the humidity. Awfully hard for a priest to transfer out of a diocese. He remembered the plan he had never gone through with. Would it work after all? Would another doctor recommend a change? Why? He would only want to know why, like the last bastard. Just a slight case of obesity, Reverend. Knew he was a non-Catholic when he said Reverend. Couldn't trust a Catholic one. Some of them were thicker than thieves with the clergy. Wouldn't want to be known as a malingerer, along with everything else.

Another billboard — 'Need Cash? See T. N. T.'

Rain. He knew it. No flying for him today. One more day between him and a pilot's license. Thirteen hours yet and it might have been twelve. Raining so, and with no flying, the world seemed to him . . . a valley of tears. He would drive on past the airport for a hamburger. If he had known, he would have brought along one of the eighth-grade boys. They were always bragging among themselves about how many he had bought them, keeping score. One of them, the Cannon kid, had got too serious from the hamburgers. When he said he was 'contemplating the priesthood' Father Burner, wanting to spare him the terrible thing a false vocation could be, had told him to take up aviation instead. He could not forget the boy's reply: *But couldn't I be a priest like you, Father?*

On the other hand, he was glad to be out driving alone. Never had got the bang out of playing with the kids a priest in this country was supposed to. The failure of the Tom Playfair tradition. He hated most sports. Ed Desmond was a sight at a ball game. Running up and down base lines, giving the umpires hell, busting all the buttons off his cassock. Assumption rectory smelled like a locker room from all the equipment. Poor Ed.

The rain drummed on the engine hood. The windshield wiper sliced back and forth, reminding him a little of a guillotine. Yes, if he had to, he would die for the Faith.

From here to the hamburger place it was asphalt and slicker than concrete. Careful. Slick. Asphalt. Remembered . . . Quinlan coming into his room one afternoon last winter when it was snowing, the idiot, prating:

> *Here were decent godless people:*
> *Their only monument the asphalt road*
> *And a thousand lost golf balls . . .*

That was Quinlan for you, always spouting against the status quo without having anything better to offer. Told him that. Told him golfers, funny as it might seem to some people, have souls and who's to save them? John Bosco worked wonders in taverns, which was not to say Father Burner thought he was a saint, but rather only that he was not too proud to meet souls halfway wherever it might be, in the confessional or on the fairways. Saint Ernest Burner, Help of Golfers, Pray for Us! (Quinlan's come back.) Quinlan gave him a pain. Keefe, now that he knew what he was like, ditto. Non-smokers. Jansenists. First fervor is false fervor. They would cool. He would not judge them, however.

He slowed down and executed a sweeping turn into the parking lot reserved for patrons of the hamburger. He honked his horn his way, three shorts and a long — victory. She would see his car or know his honk and bring out two hamburgers, medium well, onions, pickle, relish, tomato, catsup, his way.

She came out now, carrying an umbrella, holding it ostensibly more over the hamburgers than herself. He took the tray from her. She waited dumbly, her eyes at a level with his collar.

'What's to drink?'

'We got pop, milk, coffee . . . ' Here she faltered, as he knew she would, washing her hands of what recurrent revelation, rather than experience, told her was to follow.

'A nice cold bottle of beer.' Delivered of the fatal words,

Father Burner bit into the smoking hamburger. The woman turned sorrowfully away. He put her down again for native Protestant stock.

When she returned, sheltering the bottle under the umbrella, Father Burner had to smile at her not letting pious scruples interfere with business, another fruit of the so-called Reformation. Watch that smile, he warned himself, or she'll take it for carnal. He received the bottle from her hands. For all his familiarity with the type, he was uneasy. Her lowered eyes informed him of his guilt.

*Was* he immoderate? Who on earth could say? *In dubiis libertas,* not? He recalled his first church supper at Saint Patrick's, a mother bringing her child to the Dean's table. She's going to be confirmed next month, Monsignor. Indeed? Then tell me, young lady, what are the seven capital sins? Pride, Covetousness . . . Lust, Anger. Uh. The child's mother, one of those Irish females built like a robin, worried to death, lips silently forming the other sins for her daughter. Go ahead, dear. Envy. Proceed, child. Yes, Monsignor. Uh . . . Sloth. To be sure. That's six. One more. And . . . uh. Fear of the Lord, perhaps? Meekness? Hey, Monsignor, ain't them the Divine Counsels! The Dean, smiling, looking at Father Burner's plate, covered with chicken bones, at his stomach, fighting his vest, and for a second into the child's eyes, slipping her the seventh sin. *Gluttony,* Monsignor! The Dean gave her a coin for her trouble. She stood awkwardly in front of Father Burner, lingering, twisting her gaze from his plate to his stomach, to his eyes, finally quacking, Oh Fawther!

Now he began to brood upon his failure as a priest. There was no sense in applying the consolations of an anchorite to himself. He wanted to know one thing: when would he get a pastorate? When would he make the great metamorphosis from assistant to pastor, from mouse to rat, as the saying went? He was forty-three, four times transferred, seventeen years an ordained priest, a curate yet and only. He was the only one of his class still without a parish. The only one . . .

and in his pocket, three days unopened, was another letter from his mother, kept waiting all these years, who was to have been his housekeeper. He could not bear to warm up her expectations again.

Be a chaplain? That would take him away from it all and there was the possibility of meeting a remote and glorious death carrying the Holy Eucharist to a dying soldier. It would take something like that to make him come out even, but then that too, he knew in a corner of his heart, would be only exterior justification for him, a last bid for public approbation, a short cut to nothing. And the chaplain's job, it was whispered, could be an ordeal both ignominious and tragic. It would be just his luck to draw an assignment in a rehabilitation center, racking pool balls and repairing ping pong bats for the boys — the apostolic game-room attendant and toastmaster. Sure, Sarge, I'll lay you even money the Sox make it three straight in Philly and spot you a run a game to boot. You win, I lose a carton of Chesters — I win, you go to Mass every day for a week! Hard-headed holiness . . .

There was the painful matter of the appointment to Saint Patrick's. The Dean, an irremovable pastor, and the Archbishop had argued over funds and the cemetery association. And the Archbishop, losing though he won, took his revenge, it was rumored, by appointing Father Burner as the Dean's assistant. It was their second encounter. In the first days of his succession, the Archbishop heard that the Dean always said a green Mass on Saint Patrick's Day, thus setting the rubrics at nought. Furious, he summoned the Dean into his presence, but stymied by the total strangeness of him and his great age, he had talked of something else. The Dean took a different view of his narrow escape, which is what the chancery office gossips called it, and now every year, on repeating the error, he would say to the uneasy nuns, 'Sure and nobody ever crashed the gates of hell for the wearing of the green.' (Otherwise it was not often he did something to delight the hearts of the professional Irish.)

In the Dean's presence Father Burner often had the sensation of confusion, a feeling that someone besides them stood

listening in the room. To free himself he would say things he
neither meant nor believed. The Dean would take the other
side and then . . . there they were again. The Dean's position
in these bouts was roughly that of the old saints famous for
their faculty of smelling sins and Father Burner played the
role of the one smelled. It was no contest. If the Archbishop
could find no words for the Dean there was nothing he might
do. He might continue to peck away at a few stray foibles
behind the Dean's back. He might point out how familiar
the Dean was with the Protestant clergy about town. He did.
It suited his occasional orthodoxy (reserved mostly to con-
found his critics and others much worse, like Quinlan, whom
he suspected of having him under observation for humorous
purposes) to disapprove of all such questionable ties, as
though the Dean were entertaining heresy or at least felt
kindly toward this new 'interfaith' nonsense so dear to the
reformed Jews and freshwater sects. It was very small game,
however. And the merest brush with the Dean might bring
any one of a hundred embarrassing occasions back to life,
and it was easy for him to burn all over again.

When he got his dark room rigged up in the rectory the
Dean had come snooping around and inquired without staying for an answer if the making of tin-types demanded that
a man shun the light to the extent Father Burner appeared
to. Now and again, hearkening back to this episode, the
Dean referred to him as the Prince of Darkness. It did not
end there. The title caught on all over the diocese. It was
not the only one he had.

In reviewing a new historical work for a national Catholic
magazine, he had attempted to get back at two Jesuits he
knew in town, calling attention to certain tendencies — he
meant nothing so gross as 'order pride' — which, if not necessarily characteristic of any religious congregation within the
Church, were still too often to be seen in any long view of
history (which the book at hand did not pretend to take),
and whereas the secular clergy, *per se,* had much to answer
for, was it not true, though certainly not through any superior virtue, nor even as a consequence of their secularity —

indeed he would be a fool to dream that such orders as those
founded, for instance, by Saint Benedict, Saint Francis and
Saint Dominic (Saint Ignatius was not instanced) were without their places in the heart of the Church, even today, when
perhaps . . .

Anyway 'secular' turned up once as 'circular' in the review.
The local Jesuits, writing in to the magazine as a group of
innocent bystanders, made many subtle plays upon the unfortunate 'circular' and its possible application to the person
of the reviewer (their absolute unfamiliarity with the reviewer, they explained, enabled them to indulge in such
conceivably dangerous whimsy). But the direction of his
utterances, they thought, seemed clear, and they regretted
more than they could say that the editors of an otherwise
distinguished journal had found space for them, especially in
wartime, or perhaps they did not rightly comprehend the
course — was it something new? — set upon by the editors and
if so . . .

So Father Burner was also known as 'the circular priest'
and he had not reviewed anything since for that magazine.

The mark of the true priest was heavy on the Dean. The
mark was on Quinlan, it was on Keefe. It was on every priest
he could think of, including a few on the bum and his good
friend and bad companion Father Desmond. But it was not
on him, not properly. They, the others, were stained with it
beyond all disguise or disfigurement — indelibly, as indeed
Holy Orders by its sacramental nature must stain, for keeps
in this world and the one to come. 'Thou art a priest forever.' With him, however, it was something else and less, a
mask or badge which he could and did remove at will, a temporal part to be played, almost only a doctor's or lawyer's.
They, the others, would be lost in any persecution. The
mark would doom them. But he, if that *dies irae* ever came
— and it was every plump seminarian's apple-checked dream
— could pass as the most harmless and useful of humans, a
mailman, a bus rider, a husband. But would he? No. They
would see. I, he would say, appearing unsought before the
judging rabble, am a priest, of the order of Melchisedech.
Take me. I am ready. *Deo gratias.*

Father Burner got out the money to pay and honked his horn. The woman, coming for the bottle and tray, took his money without acknowledging the tip. She stood aside, the bottle held gingerly between offended fingers, final illustration of her lambishness, and watched him drive away. Father Burner, applying a cloven foot to the pedal, gave it the gas. He sensed the woman hoping in her simple heart to see him wreck the car and meet instant death in an unpostponed act of God.

Under the steadying influence of his stomach thrust against the wheel, the car proceeded while he searched himself for a cigarette. He passed a hitch-hiker, saw him fade out of view in the mirror overhead, gesticulate wetly in the distance. Was the son of a gun thumbing his nose? Anti-clericalism. But pray that your flight be not in the winter . . . No, wrong text: he would not run away.

The road skirted a tourist village. He wondered who stayed in those places and seemed to remember a story in one of the religion scandal sheets . . . ILLICIT LOVE in steaming red type.

A billboard cried out, 'Get in the scrap and — get in the scrap!' Some of this advertising, he thought, was pretty slick. Put out probably by big New York and Chicago agencies with crack men on their staffs, fellows who had studied at *Time*. How would it be to write advertising? He knew a few things about lay-out and type faces from editing the parish paper. He had read somewhere about the best men of our time being in advertising, the air corps of business. There was room for better taste in the Catholic magazines, for someone with a name in the secular field to step in and drive out the money-changers with their trusses, corn cures, nontangle rosary beads and crosses that glow in the dark. It was a thought.

Coming into the city limits, he glanced at his watch, but neglected to notice the time. The new gold strap got his eye. The watch itself, a priceless pyx, held the hour (time is money) sacred, like a host. He had chosen it for an ordination gift rather than the usual chalice. It took the kind of courage he had to go against the grain there.

'I'm a dirty stinker!' Father Desmond flung his arms out hard against the mattress. His fists opened on the sheet, hungry for the spikes, meek and ready. 'I'm a dirty stinker, Ernest!'

Father Burner, seated deep in a red leather chair at the sick man's bedside, crossed his legs forcefully. 'Now don't take on so, Father.'

'Don't call me "Father"!' Father Desmond's eyes fluttered open momentarily, but closed again on the reality of it all. 'I don't deserve it. I'm a disgrace to the priesthood! I am not worthy! Lord, Lord, I am not worthy!'

A nurse entered and stuck a thermometer in Father Desmond's mouth.

Father Burner smiled at the nurse. He lit a cigarette and wondered if she understood. The chart probably bore the diagnosis 'pneumonia,' but if she had been a nurse very long she would know all about that. She released Father Desmond's wrist and recorded his pulse on her pad. She took the thermometer and left the room.

Father Desmond surged up in bed and flopped, turning with a wrench of the covers, on his stomach. He lay gasping like a fish out of water. Father Burner could smell it on his breath yet.

'Do you want to go to confession?'

'No! I'm not ready for it. I want to remember this time!'

'Oh, all right.' It was funny, if a little tiresome, the way the Irish could exaggerate a situation. They all had access to the same two or three emotions. They all played the same battered barrel organ handed down through generations. Dying, fighting, talking, drinking, praying . . . wakes, wars, politics, pubs, church. The fates were decimated and hamstrung among them. They loved monotony.

Father Desmond, doing the poor soul uttering his last words in italics, said: 'We make too good a thing out of confession, Ernest! Ever think of that, Ernest!' He wagged a nicotined finger. Some of his self-contempt seemed to overshoot its mark and include Father Burner.

Father Burner honked his lips — plutt! 'Hire a hall, Ed.'

Father Desmond clawed a rosary out from under his pillow. Father Burner left.

He put the car in the garage. On the way to his room he passed voices in the Dean's office.

'Father Burner!' the Dean called through the door.

Father Burner stayed in the hallway, only peeping in, indicating numerous commitments elsewhere. Quinlan and Keefe were with the Dean.

'Apparently, Father, you failed to kill yourself.' Then, for Keefe, the Dean said: 'Father Burner fulfils the dream of the American hierarchy and the principle of historical localization. He's been up in his flying machine all morning.'

'I didn't go up.' Sullenness came and went in his voice. 'It rained.' He shuffled one foot, about to leave, when the Dean's left eyebrow wriggled up, warning, holding him.

'I don't believe you've had the pleasure.' The Dean gave Keefe to Father Burner. 'Father Keefe, sir, went through school with Father Quinlan — from the grades through the priesthood.' The Dean described an arc with his breviary, dripping with ribbons, to show the passing years. Father Burner nodded.

'Well?' The Dean frowned at Father Burner. 'Has the cat got your tongue, sir? Why don't you be about greeting Father O'Keefe — or Keefe is it?'

'Keefe,' Keefe said.

Father Burner, caught in the old amber of his inadequacy, stepped over and shook Keefe's hand once.

Quinlan stood by and let the drama play itself out.

Keefe, smiling a curious mixture more anxiety than amusement, said: 'It's a pleasure, Father.'

'Same here,' Father Burner said.

'Well, good day, sirs!' The Dean cracked open his breviary and began to read, lips twitching.

Father Burner waited for them in the hall. Before he could explain that he thought too much of the Dean not to humor him and that besides the old fool was out of his head, the Dean proclaimed after them: 'The Chancery phoned,

Father Burner. You will hear confessions there tonight. I suppose one of those Cathedral jokers lost his faculties.'

Yes, Father Burner knew, it was common procedure all right for the Archbishop to confer promotions by private interview, but every time a priest got called to the Cathedral it did not mean simply that. Many received sermons and it was most likely now someone was needed to hear confessions. And still Father Burner, feeling his pocket, was glad he had not remembered to mail the letter. He would not bother to speak to Quinlan and Keefe now.

## III. NIGHT

'And for your penance say five Our Fathers and five Hail Marys and pray for my intention. And now make a good act of contrition. *Misereatur tui omnipatens Deus dimissis peccatis tuis . . .*' Father Burner swept out into the current of the prayer, stroking strongly in Latin, while the penitent, a miserable boy coming into puberty, paddled as fast as he could along the shore in English.

Finishing first, Father Burner waited for the boy to conclude. When, breathless, he did, Father Burner anointed the air and shot a whisper, 'God bless you,' kicking the window shut with the heel of his hand, ejecting the boy, an ear of corn hucked clean, into the world again. There was nobody on the other side of the confessional, so Father Burner turned on the signal light. A spider drowsy in his web, drugged with heat and sins, he sat waiting for the next one to be hurled into his presence by guilt ruddy ripe, as with the boy, or, as with the old ladies who come early and try to stay late, by the spiritual famine of their lives or simply the desire to tell secrets in the dark.

He held his wrist in such a way as to see the sweat gleaming in the hairs. He looked at his watch. He had been at it since seven and now it was after nine. If there were no more kneeling in his section of the Cathedral at 9:30 he could close up and have a cigarette. He was too weary to read his Office, though he had the Little Hours, Vespers and Compline still to go. It was the last minutes in the confessional that got him — the insensible end of the excursion that begins with so many sinewy sensations and good intentions to look sharp at the landscape. In the last minutes how many priests, would-be surgeons of the soul, ended as blacksmiths, hammering out absolution anyway?

A few of the Cathedral familiars still drifted around the floor. They were day and night in the shadows praying. Meeting one of them, Father Burner always wanted to get away. They were collectors of priests' blessings in a day when most priests felt ashamed to raise their hands to God outside the ceremonies. Their respect for a priest was fanatic, that of the unworldly, the martyrs, for an emissary of heaven. They were so desperately disposed to death that the manner of dying was their greatest concern. But Father Burner had an idea there were more dull pretenders than saints among them. They inspired no unearthly feelings in him, as true sanctity was supposed to, and he felt it was all right not to like them. They spoke of God, the Blessed Virgin, of miracles, cures and visitations, as of people and items in the news, which was annoying. The Cathedral, because of its location, described by brokers as exclusive, was not so much frequented by these wretches as it would have been if more convenient to the slums. But nevertheless a few came there, like the diarrheic pigeons, also a scandal to the neighborhood, and would not go away. Father Burner, from his glancing contact with them, had concluded that body odor is the real odor of sanctity.

Through the grating now Father Burner saw the young Vicar General stop a little distance up the aisle and speak to a couple of people who were possible prospects for Father Burner. 'Anyone desiring to go to confession should do so at once. In a few minutes the priests will be gone from the confessionals.' He crossed to the other side of the Cathedral.

Father Burner did not like to compare his career with the Vicar General's. The Archbishop had taken the Vicar General, a younger man than Father Burner by at least fifteen years, direct from the seminary. After a period of trial as Chancellor, he was raised to his present eminence — for reasons much pondered by the clergy and more difficult to discern than those obviously accounted for by intelligence, appearance and, post facto, the loyalty consequent upon his selection over many older and possibly abler men. It was a medieval act of preference, a slap in the face to the monsignori, a rebuke to the principle of advancement by years applied elsewhere. The Vicar General had the quality of inscrutability in an ideal measure. He did not seem at all given to gossip or conspiracy or even to that owlish secrecy peculiar to secretaries and so exasperating to others. He had possibly no enemies and certainly no intimates. In time he would be a bishop unless, as was breathed wherever the Cloth gathered over food and drink, he really was 'troubled with sanctity,' which might lead to anything else, the cloister or insanity.

The Vicar General appeared at the door of Father Burner's compartment. 'The Archbishop will see you, Father, before you leave tonight.' He went up the aisle, genuflected before the main altar, opened as a gate one of the host of brass angels surrounding the sanctuary, and entered the sacristies.

Before he would let hope have its way with him, Father Burner sought to recast the expression on the Vicar General's face. He could recall nothing significant. Very probably there had been nothing to see. Then, with a rush, he permitted himself to think this was his lucky day. Already he was formulating the way he would let the news out, providing he decided not to keep it a secret for a time. He might do that. It would be delicious to go about his business until the very last minute, to savour the old aggravations and feel none of the sting, to receive the old quips and smiles with good grace and know them to be toothless. The news, once out, would fly through the diocese. Hear about Burner at Saint Pat's, Tom? Finally landed himself a parish. Yeah, I just had it from McKenna. So I guess the A. B. wasn't so sore at the Round One after all. Well, he's just ornery enough to make a go of it.

Father Burner, earlier in the evening, had smoked a cigarette with one of the younger priests attached to the Cathedral (a classmate of Quinlan's but not half the prig), stalling, hoping someone would come and say the Archbishop wanted to see him. When nothing happened except the usual small talk and introductions to a couple of missionaries stopping over, he had given up hope easily. He had seen the basis for his expectations as folly once more. It did not bother him after the fact was certain. He was amenable to any kind of finality. He had a light heart for a . . . an American of German descent. And his hopes rose higher each time and with less cause. He was a ball that bounced up only. He had kept faith. And now — his just reward.

A little surprised he had not thought of her first, he admitted his mother into the new order of things. He wanted to open the letter from her, still in his coat, and late as it was send her a wire, which would do her more good than a night's sleep. He thought of himself back in her kitchen, home from the sem for the holidays, a bruiser in a tight black suit, his feet heavy on the oven door. She was fussing at the stove and he was promising her a porcelain one as big as a house after he got his parish. But he let her know, kidding on the square, that he would be running things at the rectory. It would not be the old story of the priest taking orders from his housekeeper, even if she was his mother (seminarians, from winter evenings of shooting the bull, knew only too well the pitfalls of parish life), or as with Ed Desmond a few years ago when his father was still living with him, the old man losing his marbles one by one, butting in when people came for advice and instructions, finally coming to believe he was the one to say Mass in his son's absence, no need to get a strange priest in, and sneaking into the box to hear confessions the day before they took him away.

He would be gentle with his mother, however, even if she talked too much, as he recalled she did the last time he saw her. She was well-preserved and strong for her age and ought to be able to keep the house up. Once involved in the social life of the parish she could be a valuable agent in coping with any lay opposition, which was too often the case when a new priest took over.

He resolved to show no nervousness before the Archbishop. A trifle surprised, yes — the Archbishop must have his due — but not overly affected by good fortune. If questioned, he would display a lot of easy confidence not unaccompanied by a touch of humility, a phrase or two like 'God willing,' or 'with the help of Almighty God and your prayers, Your Excellency.' He would also not forget to look the part, reliable, casual, cool, an iceberg, only the tip of his true worth showing.

At precisely 9:30 Father Burner picked up his breviary and backed out of the stall. But then there was the scuff of a foot and the tap of one of the confessional doors closing and then, to tell him the last penitent was a woman, the scent of apple blossoms. He turned off the light, saying 'Damn!' to himself, and sat down again inside. He threw back the partition and led off, 'Yes?' He placed his hand alongside his head and listened, looking down into the deeper darkness of his cassock sleeve.

'I . . .'

'Yes?' At the heart of the apple blossoms another scent bloomed: gin and vermouth.

'Bless me, Father, I . . . have sinned.'

Father Burner knew this kind. They would always wait until the last moment. How they managed to get themselves into church at all, and then into the confessional, was a mystery. Sometimes liquor thawed them out. This one was evidently young, nubile. He had a feeling it was going to be adultery. He guessed it was — and up to him to get her underway.

'How long since your last confession?'

'I don't know . . .'

'Have you been away from the Church?'

'Yes.'

'Are you married?'

'Yes.'

'To a Catholic?'

'No.'

'Protestant?'

'No.'

'Jew?'

'No.'

'Atheist?'

'No — nothing.'

'Were you married by a priest?'

'Yes.'

'How long ago was that?'

'Four years.'

'Any children?'

'No.'

'Practice birth control?'

'Yes, sometimes.'

'Don't you know it's a crime against nature and the Church forbids it?'

'Yes.'

'Don't you know that France fell because of birth control?'

'No.'

'Well, it did.  Was it your husband's fault?'

'You mean — the birth control?'

'Yes.'

'Not wholly.'

'And you've been away from the Church ever since your marriage?'

'Yes.'

'Now you see why the Church is against mixed marriages. All right, go on.  What else?'

'I don't know . . .'

'Is that what you came to confess?'

'No.  Yes.  I'm sorry, I'm afraid that's all.'

'Do you have a problem?'

'I think that's all, Father.'

'Remember, it is your obligation, and not mine, to examine your conscience.  The task of instructing persons with regard to these delicate matters — I refer to the connubial relationship — is not an easy one.  Nevertheless, since there is a grave obligation imposed by God, it cannot be shirked. If you have a problem —'

'I don't have a *problem*.'

'Remember, God never commands what is impossible and so if you make use of the sacraments regularly you have every reason to be confident that you will be able to overcome this evil successfully, with His help. I hope this is all clear to you.'

'All clear.'

'Then if you are heartily sorry for your sins for your penance say the rosary daily for one week and remember it is the law of the Church that you attend Mass on Sundays and holy days and receive the sacraments at least once a year. It's better to receive them often. Ask your pastor about birth control if it's still not clear to you. Or read a Catholic book on the subject. And now make a good act of contrition . . .'

Father Burner climbed the three flights of narrow stairs. He waited a moment in silence, catching his breath. He knocked on the door and was suddenly afraid its density prevented him from being heard and that he might be found standing there like a fool or a spy. But to knock again, if heard the first time, would seem importunate.

'Come in, Father.'

At the other end of the long study the Archbishop sat behind an ebony desk. Father Burner waited before him as though expecting not to be asked to sit down. The only light in the room, a lamp on the desk, was so set that it kept the Archbishop's face in the dark, fell with a gentle sparkle upon his pectoral cross and was absorbed all around by the fabric of the piped cloth he wore. Father Burner's eyes came to rest upon the Archbishop's freckled hand, ringed, square and healthy.

'Be seated, Father.'

'Thank you, Your Excellency.'

'Oh, sit in this chair, Father.' There were two chairs. Father Burner changed to the soft one. He had a suspicion that in choosing the other one he had fallen into a silly trap, that it was a game the Archbishop played with his visitors: the innocent ones, seeing no issue, would take the soft chair, because handier; the guilty would go a step out of their way to take the hard one. 'I called Saint Patrick's this morning, Father, but you were . . . out.'

'I was visiting Father Desmond, Your Excellency.'

'Father Desmond . . . '

'He's in the hospital.'

'I know. Friend of his, are you, Father?'

'No, Your Excellency. Well' — Father Burner waited for the cock to crow the third time — 'yes, I *know* the man.' At once he regretted the scriptual complexion of the words and wondered if it were possible for the Archbishop not to be thinking of the earlier betrayal.

'It was good of you to visit Father Desmond, especially since you are not close to him. I hope he is better, Father.'

'He is, Your Excellency.'

The Archbishop got up and went across the room to a cabinet. 'Will you have a little glass of wine, Father?'

'No. No, thanks, Your Excellency.' Immediately he realized it could be another trap and, if so, he was caught again.

'Then I'll have a drop . . . *solus*.' The Archbishop poured a glass and brought it back to the desk. 'A little wine for the stomach's sake, Father.'

Father Burner, not sure what he was expected to say to that, nodded gravely and said, 'Yes, Your Excellency.' He had seen that the Archbishop wore carpet slippers and that they had holes in both toes.

'But perhaps you've read Saint Bernard, Father, and recall where he says we priests remember well enough the apostolic counsel to use wine, but overlook the adjective "little." '

'I must confess I haven't read Saint Bernard lately, Your Excellency.' Father Burner believed this was somehow in his favor. 'Since seminary, in fact.'

'Not all priests, Father, have need of him. A hard saint . . . for hardened sinners. What is your estimate of Saint Paul?'

Father Burner felt familiar ground under his feet at last. There were the Pauline and Petrine factions — a futile business, he thought — but he knew where the Archbishop stood and exclaimed: 'One of the greatest — '

'Really! So many young men today consider him . . . a bore. It's always the deep-breathing ones, I notice. They say he cuts it too fine.'

'I've never thought so, Your Excellency.'

'Indeed? Well, it's a question I like to ask my priests. Perhaps you knew that.'

'No, I didn't, Your Excellency.'

'So much the better then . . . but I see you appraising the melodeon, Father. Are you musical?'

'Not at all, Your Excellency. Violin lessons as a child.' Father Burner laughed quickly, as though it were nothing.

'But you didn't go on with them?'

'No, Your Excellency.' He did not mean it to sound as sad as it came out.

'What a pity.'

'No great loss, Your Excellency.'

'You are too . . . modest, Father. But perhaps the violin was not your instrument.'

'I guess it wasn't, Your Excellency.' Father Burner laughed out too loud.

'And you have the choir at Saint Patrick's, Father?'

'Not this year, Your Excellency. Father Quinlan has it.'

'Now I recall . . . '

'Yes.' So far as he was concerned, and there were plenty of others who thought so too, Quinlan had played hell with the choir, canning all the women, some of them members for fifteen and twenty years, a couple even longer and practically living for it, and none of them as bad as Quinlan said. The liturgical stuff that Quinlan tried to pull off was all right in monasteries, where they had the time to train for it, but in a parish it sounded stodgy to ears used to the radio and split up the activity along sexual lines, which was really old hat in the modern world. The Dean liked it though. He called it 'honest' and eulogized the men from the pulpit — not a sign that he heard how they brayed and whinnied and just gave out or failed to start — and each time it happened ladies in the congregation were sick and upset for days afterward, for he inevitably ended by attacking women, pants, cocktails, communism, cigarettes and running around half naked. The women looked at the men in the choir, all pretty in surplices, and said to themselves they knew plenty about some of them and what they had done to some women.

'He's tried a little Gregorian, hasn't he — Father Quinlan?'

'Yes, Your Excellency,' Father Burner said. 'He has.'

'Would you say it's been a success — or perhaps I should ask you first if you care for Gregorian, Father.'

'Oh, yes, Your Excellency. Very much.'

'Many, I know, don't . . . I've been told our chant sounds like a wild bull in a red barn of consumptives coughing into a bottle, but I will have it in the Cathedral, Father. Other places, I am aware, have done well with . . . light opera.'

Father Burner frowned.

'We are told the people prefer and understand it. But at the risk of seeming reactionary, a fate my office prevents me from escaping in any event, I say we spend more time listening to the voice of the people than is good for either it or us. We have been too generous with our ears, Father. We have handed over our tongues also. When they are restored to us I wonder if we shall not find our ears more itching than before and our tongues more tied than ever.'

Father Burner nodded in the affirmative.

'We are now entering the whale's tail, Father. We must go back the way we came in.' The Archbishop lifted the lid of the humidor on the desk. 'Will you smoke, Father?'

'No, thanks, Your Excellency.'

The Archbishop let the lid drop. 'Today there are few saints, fewer sinners and everybody is already saved. We are all heroes in search of an underdog. As for villains, the classic kind with no illusions about themselves, they are . . . extinct. The very devil, for instance, where the devil is the devil today, Father?'

Father Burner, as the Archbishop continued to look at him, bit his lips for the answer, secretly injured that he should be expected to know, bewildered even as the children he toyed with in catechism.

The Archbishop smiled, but Father Burner was not sure

at what, whether at him or what had been said. 'Did you see, Father, where our brother Bishop Buckles said Hitler remains the one power on earth against the Church?'

Yes, Father Burner remembered seeing it in the paper; it was the sort of thing that kept Quinlan talking for days. 'I did, Your Excellency.'

'Alas, poor Buckles! He's a better croquet player than that.' The Archbishop's hands unclasped suddenly and fell upon his memo pad. He tore off about a week and seemed to feel better for it. His hands, with no hint of violence about them now, came together again. 'We look hard to the right and left, Father. It is rather to the center, I think, we should look, to ourselves, the devil in us.'

Father Burner knew the cue for humility when he heard it. 'Yes, Your Excellency.'

With his chubby fingers the Archbishop made a steeple that was more like a dome. His eyes were reading the memo. 'For instance, Father, I sometimes appear at banquets — when they can't line up a good foreign correspondent — banquets at which the poor are never present and at which I am unfailingly confronted by someone exceedingly well off who is moved to inform me that "religion" is a great consolation to him. Opium, rather, I always think, perhaps wrongfully and borrowing a word from one of our late competitors, which is most imprudent of me, a bishop.'

The Archbishop opened a drawer and drew out a sheet of paper and an envelope. 'Yes, the rich have souls,' he said softly, answering an imaginary objection which happened to be Father Burner's. 'But if they had Christ they would not be themselves, that is to say, rich.'

'Very true, Your Excellency,' Father Burner said.

The Archbishop faced sideways to use an old typewriter. 'And likewise, lest we forget, we would not be ourselves, that is to say — what? For we square the circle beautifully in almost every country on earth. We bring neither peace nor a sword. The rich give us money. We give them consolation and make of the eye of the needle a gate. Together we try to reduce the Church, the Bride of Christ, to a streetwalker.'

The Archbishop rattled the paper, Father Burner's future, into place and rolled it crookedly into the typewriter. 'Unfortunately for us, it doesn't end there. The penance will not be shared so equitably. Your Christian name, Father, is — ?'

'Ernest, Your Excellency.'

The Archbishop typed several words and stopped, looking over at Father Burner. 'I can't call to mind a single Saint Ernest, Father. Can you help me?'

'There were two, I believe, Your Excellency, but Butler leaves them out of his *Lives*.'

'They would be German saints, Father?'

'Yes, Your Excellency. There was one an abbot and the other an archbishop.'

'If Butler had been Irish, as the name has come to indicate, I'd say that's an Irishman for you, Father. He does not forget to include a power of Irish saints.' The Archbishop was Irish himself. Father Burner begged to differ with him, believing here was a wrong deliberately set up for him to right. 'I am not Irish myself, Your Excellency, but some of my best friends are.'

'Tut, tut, Father. Such tolerance will be the death of you.' The Archbishop, typing a few words, removed the paper, signed it and placed it in the envelope. He got up and took down a book from the shelves. He flipped it open, glanced through several pages and returned it to its place. 'No Ernests in Baring-Gould either. Well, Father, it looks as if you have a clear field.'

The Archbishop came from behind the desk and Father Burner, knowing the interview was over, rose. The Archbishop handed him the envelope. Father Burner stuffed it hastily in his pocket and knelt, the really important thing, to kiss the Archbishop's ring and receive his blessing. They walked together toward the door.

'Do you care for pictures, Father?'

'Oh, yes, Your Excellency.'

The Archbishop, touching him lightly on the arm, stopped before a reproduction of Raphael's Sistine Madonna. 'There is a good peasant woman, Father, and a nice fat baby.' Father Burner nodded his appreciation. 'She could be Our Blessed Mother, Father, though I doubt it. There is no question about the baby. He is not Christ.' The Archbishop moved to another picture. 'Rembrandt had the right idea, Father. See the gentleman pushing Christ up on the cross? That is Rembrandt, a self portrait.' Father Burner thought of some of the stories about the Archbishop, that he slept on a cot, stood in line with people sometimes to go to confession, that he fasted on alternate days the year round. Father Burner was thankful for such men as the Archbishop. 'But here is Christ, Father.' This time it was a glassy-eyed Christ whose head lay against the rough wood of the cross he was carrying. 'That is Christ, Father. The Greek painted Our Saviour.'

The Archbishop opened the door for Father Burner, saying, 'And, Father, you will please not open the envelope until after your Mass tomorrow.'

Father Burner went swiftly down the stairs. Before he got into his car he looked up at the Cathedral. He could scarcely see the cross glowing on the dome. It seemed as far away as the stars. The cross needed a brighter light or the dome ought to be painted gold and lit up like the state capital, so people would see it. He drove a couple of blocks down the street, pulled up to the curb, opened the envelope, which had not been sealed, and read: 'You will report on August 8 to the Reverend Michael Furlong, to begin your duties on that day as his assistant. I trust that in your new appointment you will find not peace but a sword.'

(From Good Housekeeping)

# THE GREATEST IDEA IN THE WORLD

## BY SAMSON RAPHAELSON

*S*HIRLEY DOCKSTEDER and Thelma Bassler, both stenos, congenial yet with different interests, so there was always something to talk about, were loafing in the little back yard of their little apartment on this Sunday afternoon in May. It was an old-fashioned, brownstone house, and there was a tree in the yard and there were some terrace chairs, and if you looked carefully, at an angle, between the hotel and the brownstone house next door, you could catch a glimpse of Central Park. Shirley was drying her dark, pretty hair in the sun, rubbing it occasionally with a towel, which she would drop to the flagstones on top of the news section, which naturally you don't read but comes in handy to keep a towel from getting dirty. Then you concentrate on the magazine section, the movie section, the funnies, and always, at the end, conscientiously, the help-wanted ads, to see the jobs you might be applying for if you weren't lucky enough to be secretary to Mr. Grimsted of the Universal Advertising Agency at $40 a week minus withholding tax and social security, netting exactly $34.50. She was in slacks and a blouse and slippers, and her legs were bare where she had rolled up her slacks to get the sun. Wearing dark glasses and stretched out on the slatted wooden terrace chair, Shirley Docksteder, twenty-two, was the equal of any debutante in self-respect, appearance, and the luxurious knowledge that her dresser drawers contained an adequate supply of nylon stockings.

336

In the open doorway of the little apartment, seated on the worn marble step, Thelma, in a $2.98 striped blouse, $7.49 jodhpurs, and $1.77 bedroom slippers over her bobby-soxed feet, was vigorously saddle-soaping her $6.59 genuine imitation English leather jodhpur boots. Thelma was a few years older than Shirley, not quite so pretty, figure somehow not precisely so fetching, and yet devoid of jealousy — who could ask for anything more?

'Yesterday a man came into the store with a beautiful English saddle.' Thelma squeezed the excess water out of the sponge and loaded the sponge extravagantly with the thick yellow soap. 'It cost two hundred dollars new. My boss gave him twenty-five for it, and it's on sale for forty.'

Shirley dropped the magazine section and picked up the movie section.

'All day, whenever I could get away from my desk, I sneaked over to look at that saddle. It's so beautiful.' Thelma sighed, then vigorously rubbed the soap into the under edge of the boot, where the perspiration gets into the seams and rots the leather and the thread unless you keep it nice and soft. The sunlight, getting out from behind the house next door, fell into her lap. 'Isn't this a nice day? And if I *had* the saddle, have I got a horse?' Thelma set the boot in the shade, so it wouldn't dry too rapidly, and picked up the other boot.

Shirley let the newspaper drop to her lap, stared up into the prettiest sight in the world — leaves of a tree against the sky. 'What's a good name for a tire?' Shirley asked while Thelma dipped the sponge again into the little bowl of water. 'Did you ever in your life think of entering a prize contest? Alvin says *somebody's* got to win, and why shouldn't it be Alvin? I wouldn't be surprised if he does. And then — well, I guess he'll want me to marry him right away. What name would make people desire a rubber tire? Let's see. Tires are mostly named after people.' She contemplated the potentials for magic, then sadly: 'The president's name of Alvin's company is Mr. Schnellenbacher.'

Thelma was busily mopping off the extravagant surplus of saddle soap. She paused, boot in hand. 'Sometimes I wonder, am I crazy, every Sunday sitting in the subway all the way up to Van Cortlandt to ride horseback. Why don't I walk a block and ride in Central Park? Just to save a vulgar dollar and a half. What am I saving it for — my grandchildren, for heaven's sake?'

Shirley picked up the towel, rubbed her wet hair thoughtfully. 'I think I like Alvin Smiley. I'm engaged to him and — yes, I do like him. Someday — probably after we're married — I'll fall in love with him. That's the best way. Two years ago, when I was a kid, I used to dream of meeting a fellow and going mad over him — a fellow who looked exactly like a movie star. I couldn't make up my mind whether he should look like Jimmy Stewart or Clark Gable, on account of I couldn't make up my mind which I loved most. I still can't.' The sun was wandering off her left leg, and she readjusted her body, trying to postpone to the last possible second the moment when she'd have to drop the newspapers from her lap, get up, change the position of the chair, get back into the chair, roll up her sleeves and adjust the neck of her blouse to a V generous for violet rays but modest for the eyes of a chance male, reroll her slacks to the previous line above her knees, pick up the newspaper, find the page she was looking at, and remember what had been going on in her mind before she moved, which might have had very little to do with what she had been reading.

Thelma now had the right boot on her foot and was briskly rubbing it with a soft rag — not any old soft rag, but a special one with blue binding, which was on sale in the store where she worked, designed especially for this ritual, and priced at fifteen cents.

Shirley picked up the newspaper again. 'It says here that Jimmy Stewart is in town. Tonight he makes a personal appearance. I wonder if Alvin and I should go. The contrast between Alvin and Jimmy might — well, you know — What I'm hoping is, I'm hoping that when I see him in person, I'll be disappointed. Somehow, you always expect them to be

eight feet tall or something, and when they're only five feet
ten or something, well, it kind of relieves you.'

Thelma took the bedroom slipper off her left foot, rested
her arms on her knees meditatively. 'One thing about Van
Cortlandt, you do meet a nice class of fellows — fellows with
futures.'

'I know. They're all an assistant to somebody.'

'Yeah — assistant office manager, assistant to the president.'

'Alvin says it's a new type — you work up from the top.
In Bloomington, Indiana, when he met me, he said: "You
watch. One year after I'm back from overseas, you'll be the
wife of an assistant sales manager." At the time, I thought
that was a depressing remark. Well, here I am.' She lay there
lazily, amiably thinking it out: 'You know, I think all the
ecstasy is somewhere else — I mean not here and now — I
mean, well, it's in the past — or someday it'll happen — or
you read about it. Probably it's all overestimated. Yeah,
that's probably it. That's the way I sum it up.'

Both girls were silent in the easy and bearable May sun,
both contemplating the little back-yard tree.

'One of those fellows,' Thelma ruminated, 'the nicest of
them all — he's not exactly handsome, but a type you could
take seriously — I don't know what got into me, Shirley. I
told him I had a horse of my own on Long Island. It happened three weeks ago, and honestly I've been so ashamed
that I canter past every time.' She briskly began the ritual
of the rag on the left boot, then paused, sweetly relaxed and
unhappy. 'Tell the truth, I didn't say a horse. I said horses.
And oh, my, I think I made a remark about a groom. I never
told such a fib in my life before — not on horseback.'

Shirley said dreamily, 'I met Alvin on foot.'

She picked up the funnies, and Thelma returned with
vigor to the mystical satisfaction of softening and polishing
leather. Clay Randolph, the Negro janitor, who was leaving
on his vacation, brought his new assistant through the basement door to point out severely where he had failed to sweep
the flagstones clean. And while the younger Negro toiled

with a broom delicately, so that the dust would not disturb the tenants, Clay discovered a loose screen in a window and drawing a screwdriver from his jeans, went to work.

'Be out o' yo' way in a minute, ladies. Go to church dis mo'nin', Miss Docksteder?'

'No, I had to wash my hair.'

'I always say God is everywhere,' Thelma remarked, 'in the trees, in the home, and on the bridle path.'

'God is only one place, Miss Bassler — de Baptist Church. When I was in de Ardennes Bulge, drivin' a truck through dat shellfire, I say: "Merciful God, no Baptist Church in dis country! Ain't *my* fault. You know dat! Forgive me my sins an' save my life!" An' He did. I ain't missed a single Sunday in de Third Baptist Church since I come back.

Thelma squeezed out the sponge for the last time. The younger Negro maneuvered the dust into his dustpan.

Shirley picked up her towel and gave her hair a final rubbing. 'I'm a Presbyterian myself — that is, I was when I was a kid. I used to love being in church. But when I grew older, I got acquainted with the people who sat in the other pews and — oh, I don't know, either they didn't belong in the church or God didn't belong there. And I still don't know what to think. So I feel guilty when I don't go, and when I do go, I — I feel guiltier.'

Thelma clicked the top shut on the tin saddle-soap box. 'You're just not religious, that's all. The world's full of different types.'

'You an atheist,' said Clay, working with leisurely swiftness. 'Can't be two ways 'bout de Lawd.'

Shirley looked genuinely worried as she angled her body another fraction of an inch to the sun. 'Clay, do you think I'll be damned?'

'Yes, ma'am. You is kindhearted, but dat don' count.'

And now, through the open door of the apartment came Alvin Smiley like a breeze, like a March breeze into the mild May stillness, twenty-five years and six feet of energy, resourcefulness, optimism, and bright remarks. Do you know your front door was open? Aren't you glad it's me instead of some other burglar?' he remarked brightly as Shirley greeted him with a warm smile. 'Stay where you are, darling,' he cried. 'Don't get up!' He bent over and gave her a kiss and for a flickering moment lost his assurance and asked humbly, 'How are you, sweet?'

Responding to his humbleness, Shirley took his hand, held it close to her cheek. 'Waiting for you, dearest.'

Shirley's love in the bag for the moment, Alvin turned boundingly to Thelma, making an expression of mock regret. 'Gee, Thelma, can you ever forgive me? I forgot to bring you a bale of hay!'

Thelma rose with dignity. Rag, soap box, bowl, and sponge in her hands, she went into the apartment, pausing only for a parting shot. 'I overlook that remark, considering the source.' She then winked at Shirley, and Shirley smiled back at her as if to say, 'These men — we can't live with them, but we can't live without them!'

As the door closed behind Thelma, Alvin concentrated on the janitor. 'Clay! You are about to earn thirty-seven cents.' He tossed a coin to the colored man. 'That's half a dollar. Go to the nearest drugstore, get me a special-delivery stamp, and squander the change.' With that off his mind, he turned to Shirley. 'Now, darling — ' He brought a letter carefully out of his pocket. 'I have here a little gem which I have written on the subject of tires.'

'Excuse me, Mr. Smiley,' said the hesitant and unhappy Clay. 'But I'se leavin' on my vacation dis afternoon, and de train goes at — '

Alvin's friendly hand on Clay's shoulder stopped him. 'Pack faster — take a later train — be an executive.' Clay still hesitated. Alvin's quick eye caught the other Negro, who was trying to melt unobtrusively into the basement. 'Who's that?'

'Dat's my new helper. He ain't supposed to wukk on Sundays, but I jes — '

Alvin snatched the half-dollar from Clay's hand, reached the helper in two strides, and dropped the coin into the helper's shirt pocket. 'Son, you know what I want — you know where to get it. Start your career with a bang.'

The two colored men — both war veterans, Clay with decorations for fearlessness and lightninglike thinking in more than one perilous moment — were unable to cope with this situation and found themselves sidling out of the yard simply because Alvin was addressing Shirley with the blithe assumption that he and she were alone.

'Now, Miss Docksteder,' said Alvin, as Shirley, with wonder and dismay, watched the two Negroes disappear, 'is your mind nice and fresh?' He drew a crisp, folded, typed letter from the envelope. 'Listen to this!' He paused, entranced by the phrases in his letter. 'Doggone, but it's a honey!' The sensuous ripple and glint of newly washed hair competed for his attention; he took Shirley by the hand, drew her out of the chair and over to a bench under the tree, sat them both down, and encircled her with his free arm, being careful all the while not to rumple or smudge the precious letter. 'How —' he kissed the tip of her nose — 'can I think of anything but you when I'm near you? And when I'm away from you — well, when I got the idea in this letter, what do you think I was sitting and dreaming about?'

'Tires?'

'Don't be like that. I was dreaming about you.'

Shirley, her faint effort at the sardonic easily spent, tucked her arm into his and cuddled closer. '*Were* you?' Funny about Alvin. He was very — well, sure of himself, and yet he needed confirmation all the time.

Alvin, easily confirmed, returned to the letter. 'Now listen,' he began, then paused to explain. 'And remember, at the same time, that the president of our company owns two hotels and a whole real-estate development in Atlantic City. But don't let that influence you! After all, this name must stand on its own feet. It's the public that's buying these tires. Ready?' Slowly, savoring each syllable: ' "Atlantic City Tires." ' He regarded her solemnly. 'Is it the greatest idea in the world, or just okay?'

Shirley, taken aback, said, 'Well — it's a little sudden.'

'You're unimpressed!' said Alvin.

Shirley reached hastily for his coat sleeve, soothed it. 'Give me a few minutes. It's — it's like — like seeing a new painting — or hearing a symphony for the first time. I'm sure it's wonderful.'

'What do you get out of working for an advertising agency if you can't see the possibilities in an idea like this?'

Shirley sparred for time. 'The thought came to you while you were — uh — dreaming of me?'

Alvin brightened. 'Yeah! I was loafing in my bedroom, the Sunday sun in the open windows, and I began contemplating the future — you and me — married — the honeymoon. What's the next thought?'

'Niagara Falls.'

'Darling!'

Shirley added two and two. 'Oh! You want our honeymoon in Atlantic City!'

'And you don't like Atlantic City.'

'Oh, *no*. That is, I hadn't thought about it. When I was in high school, I sort of used to imagine Niagara Falls — it's not very original, but you know how kids are.' She cuddled closer to him, made her voice sound enthusiastic. 'Anyway, I'm sure Atlantic City will be heavenly.'

Alvin laid the letter aside carefully on the adjacent table and, grateful for such devotion, really embraced her. 'We couldn't go anywhere else now, could we?'

'I wouldn't want to!' She relaxed in his arms.

'I hope that boy doesn't get lost,' Alvin remarked suddenly.

'He'll be back soon,' she reassured him, drew him back into the comfort of the bench, into the certainty of marriage, a home, a future. 'Now let's concentrate on Atlantic City. I see what you mean! Darling, it *is* a great idea. The power of the ocean — that's what you're after, isn't it?'

'Right!' Alvin was happy. He picked up the letter, read from it: ' "Tires that surge across the open road like the bounding sea — everlasting like the tides." '

'And they're as restful,' said Shirley, inspired, too, 'as the beach on a weekday afternoon!'

'You've almost got it.' Alvin nodded with sober approval. He read: ' "They give you a ride as balmy as the seaside on a summer night." Get the point? The *ride* ties it in — *that's* what's balmy.'

Shirley sighed with genuine admiration. 'It's awfully good. You know, I really think it's perfectly wonderful.'

'No kiddin'!' Alvin was deeply touched. He sprawled happily beside her. 'If I win the prize, what do you say we get married?'

Shirley grew a little pale. 'You mean — right away?'

'The same week! You know darn' well they couldn't afford to have a prize winner being *assistant* sales manager. I'll become sales manager — that guy isn't half as good as me right now, and he knows it — and they'll double my salary. How about it, lambie pie?'

Shirley made a deep decision. 'All right,' she said very quietly.

'You mean it?' asked Alvin, who to his own surprise was astonished.

'Yes.' With sudden intense feeling: 'Yes, I do mean it. Let's get married, prize or no prize!' She turned her face up to him and held him tightly as he kissed her. 'Oh, darling, darling,' she said, clinging to him, 'when'll you know about the prize?'

'Wednesday noon at the employes' luncheon.'

'That's three days from now. We can get married Thursday!'

'But suppose I don't — That's ridiculous. Of course I'll win.'

'Of course! But even if you don't — oh, Alvin, I guess I'm being selfish, but I want a home. I know I'll never be president of the Grimsted Agency, and I know I'll never find a *lovelier* husband than you.'

It was a pretty picture, indeed, this handsome couple, this fine, dynamic young man and this lovely, gentle girl on a Sunday in May.

The fine, dynamic young man gradually began to chuckle. 'You're very cute. I sit here looking at you — the high-school girl from Bloomington who thought me commonplace, who only kissed me once. And why? Because I was going overseas.'

'Don't tease me.'

'Running around with a lot of insignificant college kids, sophomores and freshmen, when I was a senior and the best doggone business manager the Athletic Association ever had. Materialistic — that's what you called me! And now — You really are growing up, aren't you?' He nodded with wonder and respect.

Shirley took one of his strong hands in hers, held it tightly, desperately. 'That must be it. I want — yes, at last I know what I want. Somebody to believe in, to live for, to plan for — to love. The typewriter and the office and, oh, someday being advertising manager of a department store — it's all like a — a dress I might have seen in a window, and then I tried it on and it wasn't for me. Here I am, Alvin — I — maybe it's the springtime, I don't know what it is — but won't you please dream a big dream and let me help you make it come true? Give me something I can put my heart into, will you, dear? It's the only talent I have, my heart.'

'Gee,' said Alvin with even greater wonder, 'when I think of all the mismated couples in the world!' He thought of all the mismated couples in the world for a few moments, and then he gently drew her fingers down on his hand so he could look at his wrist watch. He became anxious. 'I wish that guy'd get back with the stamp. The entries must be posted by midnight, lambie, and if I don't get this into a mailbox right away, Lord knows if there'll be another collection before — '

Shirley covered up his wrist watch, drew him loungingly beside her, rested her head on the back of the bench, pursuing her dream, her marriage, her home, her future. 'Let's live in the country.'

'Right!' Alvin succumbed happily to her mood. 'In a

good, select suburb, with a Tudor house three minutes from the station.'

'Someplace near a brook, where our son can play barefoot.'

'We'll have big shots for dinner three times a week. Let the kid meet men of distinction and power.'

'And when he grows up,' said Shirley, listening only to herself, 'let's give him the finest education. Let him be great.'

'You bet. The right diploma hands you plenty of prestige — you get in with a big corporation. The little guy hasn't a chance any more. It's the era of salaries, but what majestic ones.'

'I don't care whether he makes money or not. I want him to be —'

'Listen, sugarplum, you care whether I make money, don't you?'

'Yes, dear, but —'

'You want a six-burner electric range in that kitchen, don't you, and an electric dishwasher? And a bathroom all tile from floor to ceiling? Well, don't you think his wife'll want the same, only better? And where is he going to meet that glorious little girl?'

'On a bus. On a Fifth Avenue bus, please!'

Alvin played with her glimmering curls. He not only was practically positive that he had his heart's desire, but he was tasting a new, unexpected pleasure: She had a mind, and he was its master, too. 'That's not the way it's done, sweetness. I'm a Cleveland boy myself, but I've learned a thing or two. If you go to Yale, you meet the girls from Vassar. If you go to Harvard, you meet the Radcliffe and Wellesley girls. And on a Fifth Avenue bus who do you meet? The conductor. Get me, angel face?'

Shirley turned suddenly and regarded him so steadily that he was shaken.

His competent mind raced swiftly back over what he had said. Had he been out of step? Had he said one single thing that wasn't right, sure, incontrovertible? 'What are you thinking?'

Shirley's shining, honest eyes reassured him. 'Nothing —

only that I intend to be a good wife,' she said, and the way she said it, it was clear to Alvin that he had not only her heart and mind but her soul as well, which really perked him up. She went on, deeply earnest, withholding nothing. 'I'm going to learn how to — oh, if there's anything I hate it's a half-hearted marriage! I — don't laugh at me, dear — but I think people should be heroic. I mean women. I think they should give — everything. I mean, no matter who you're married to, whether he's a burglar or a — a wonderful fellow like you, his ideas should be — if he's a Republican, she should be a Republican, even if she comes from a Democratic family, which I don't — you know very well my father is a Republican. Oh, Alvin, I'm going to make myself over. I have a lot of kid ideas to get rid of. If I miss, just tell me what they are, and I'll — Oh, you're so definite. You know what you want. You see things so clearly, like — like — ' She paused, stumbling on the peak of resolve and consecration — and was suddenly, tenderly amused because Alvin, who could be a god for only just so long, was again looking at his wrist watch, worried about the time, a young man anxious about a thousand dollars. 'Like,' she finished gaily, 'like if you need a special-delivery stamp, you're going to go and get it with your own two bare hands — and darling, I'm for you!' She was on her feet, pulling him up, pushing him gently toward the door.

'You don't mind?' Alvin was a little doubtful, a little guilty, as she led him through the apartment, past the half-open door to the bedroom, where Thelma was studying herself before a mirror.

'Of course not, dear.' She opened the front door.

'Don't think I don't appreciate every word you said. It was — I'll remember it all my life — it was like being in church. It was more beautiful than the wedding ceremony in the prayer book. It was — '

'Hurry, dear. Your prize is my prize, isn't it?'

'That's right!' Alvin brightened up. He gave her a quick kiss, hastened through the ancient and beautiful and slightly dilapidated wrought-iron gate, paused, saluted her. 'Remember — Atlantic City!'

'Atlantic City!' Shirley returned his salute, stood watching him as he half-walked, half-ran toward Columbus Avenue.

She went back into the apartment, her mind suddenly a blank, and slowly but surely moved to the yard, to the long, low chair where she had been sitting in such sweet idleness half an hour ago. She moved the chair into the sun, stretched out on it again, rolled up her slacks scrupulously, picked up the newspaper. Unseeingly, she began to read. 'The tragic lack of a dynamic spiritual principle, an activating tradition, in American life — ' It was the wrong section. She dropped it, found the movie page, straightened it out on her lap, tried to read, to drift, to harmonize with the back yard, with May, with the Sunday afternoon, with half an hour ago.

Thelma appeared in the doorway. 'Like the ensemble?'

Shirley turned, inspected her friend carefully. Thelma wore a chic and modest little brown sports hat, informally suitable for equestrianism, and a trim, heather-colored, ready-made riding coat. In her hand she carried a crop, a little shyly, as one not to the crop born.

'Stunning,' Shirley said.

Thelma concealed her pleasure at this verdict with a little businesslike frown. 'I wonder should I wear the riding coat or just a light sweater and look like all the other stenos on horseback.'

'Oh, wear the coat. You're the type, and why not accent yourself boldly?'

These were just the words Thelma needed. They had the authority of a dictum from Paris. 'Yeah, I think so, too.' She turned, started to go. 'Well, see you later.'

'Thelma — '

'Yes?'

'Where would you rather go for a honeymoon — Niagara Falls or — or Atlantic City?'

'Niagara Falls, of course.'

'Thanks. Have a good time.'

'Oh, I will.'

Thelma was gone. Shirley settled back, picked up the movie page, read again that Jimmy Stewart was making a personal appearance today, dropped the movie page. She felt guilty about Jimmy Stewart and about what she had asked Thelma. Firmly and forever she gave up Jimmy Stewart — and Niagara Falls. Rummaging among the cultural plenitudes of the newspaper, she found the classified section and turned to the help-wanted ads, to see the jobs she might be applying for if she weren't lucky enough to have such a good job — and to be engaged to Alvin Smiley.

*(From Harper's Bazaar)*

# WHAT WE DON'T KNOW HURTS US

# BY MARK SCHORER

*T*HE MID-AFTERNOON winter sun burned through the high California haze. Charles Dudley, working with a mattock in a thicket of overgrowth, felt as steamy and as moldy as the black adobe earth in which his feet kept slipping. Rain had fallen for five days with no glimmer of sunshine, and now it seemed as if the earth, with fetid animation, like heavy breath, were giving all that moisture back to the air. The soil, or the broom which he was struggling to uproot, had a disgusting, acrid odor, as if he were tussling with some obscene animal instead of with a lot of neglected vegetation, and suddenly an overload of irritations — the smell, the stinging sweat in his eyes, his itching skin, his blistering palms — made him throw the mattock down and come diving out of the thicket into the clearing he had already achieved.

'Is it hard?'

He looked up and saw Josephine, his wife, sitting on the railing of the balcony onto which the French doors of their bedroom opened. She was holding a dust mop, and a tea towel was wrapped around her head, and her face seemed pallid and without character, as it always did to Charles when she neglected to wear lipstick.

He snorted instead of replying, and wiped his muddy hands on the seat of his stiff new levis. Then he walked over to the short flight of steps that led up to the balcony from the garden, and lit a cigarette.

'It looks as though the ground levels out up there where you're working,' Josephine said.

'Yes, it does. Somebody once had a terrace up there. It's full of overgrown geraniums that are more like snakes, and a lot of damned rose vines.'

'You've got the pepper tree almost free. It's going to be very nice, isn't it?'

He looked up at the pepper tree, with its delicate, drooping branches and the long gray tendrils that hung down from the branches to the ground. He had chopped out the broom as far up the incline as the tree, and now he could see that a big branch of the eucalyptus at the very edge of the property had forced the top of the pepper tree to grow out almost horizontally from the main portion of its trunk. 'Look at the damned thing!' he said.

'It's charming, like a Japanese print.'

'I'm going to hate this house long before it's livable,' he said.

'Oh, Charles!'

'I didn't want to buy a house. I never wanted to own any house. I certainly never wanted to own a miserable, half-ruined imitation of a Swiss chalet built on an incline that was meant for goats.' Vehemently he flipped his cigarette up into the pile of brush he had accumulated.

Josephine stood up and shook out the dust mop. 'Let's not go into all that again. There was no choice. It's no pleasure for me, either, living the way we are, nor is it for the children.' She paused, and then she added a cold supplement. 'I sometimes think that your disinclination to own anything is a form of irresponsibility.' She turned swiftly and went into the house.

He stood staring after her, frowning a little, for it seemed momentarily that with studied intent she had cracked the bland habit of her amiability. But in a minute she reappeared in the doorway and said matter-of-factly, 'I heard on the radio that Boston has had eighteen inches of snow.' Then she went back inside.

'Are you trying to make me homesick?' he asked of no one

as he started back up the incline, and he remembered the frozen river, snow blowing over the Esplanade, and city lights faint in a blizzard.

He began again to chop at the roots of the broom. All right, he told himself, so he was being unpleasant. He did not like the idea of being pinned down by a mortgage to a place his firm had picked for him. He did not even like the idea of being pinned down by a mortgage. To own something was, to that extent, to be owned, and he did not like the feeling. His idea of a good way to live was in a duplex apartment owned by someone else, in Charles River Square, or, better than that but always less likely, in a duplex apartment owned by someone else, on the East River. He connected happiness with a certain luxury, and, probably, sexuality with elegance and freedom. These were not noble associations, he was aware, and he knew that it was foolish to let impossibilities, as they faded, become forms of minor torture. This knowledge made him chop more angrily than ever at the broom.

It was vegetation with which Charles felt that he had a peculiar intimacy, perhaps the only thing in California which, in the several weeks they had lived there, he had really come to know. And he loathed it with a violence which he recognized as quite undue, and which, now, made him feel childish and curiously guilty. Yet he could not laugh away his loathing. The stuff was ubiquitous, and sprang up anywhere at all the minute the ground was neglected. If it grew up in a patch, it began a foolish competition with itself, and the thin, naked stalks shot ten and twelve and fourteen feet into the air, all stretching up to the sun for the sake of a plume of paltry foliage at the top. Then the foliage tangled together in a thatch, and when you had managed to chop out the shallow roots of the tree, you still had to extricate its trivial but tenacious branches from those of all its neighbors to get it out of the clump. Once it was out, the wood was good for nothing, but dried up into a kind of bamboo stalk so insubstantial that it did not make even decent kindling. As a tree it was a total fraud, and in spite of the nuisance of its numbers, and of its feminine air of lofty self-importance, it was, with its shallow roots in this loose soil, very vulnerable to attack. Charles beat away at it in an angry frenzy, as if he were overwhelming, after a long struggle, some bitter foe.

He did not hear his son come up the incline behind him, and the boy stood quietly watching until his father turned to toss a stalk up on the pile in the clearing. Then the boy said, 'Hi.' He said it tentatively, almost shyly, as though his father's responses were unpredictable.

'Hi, Gordon.'

'What're you doing?'

'Can't you see? How was school?'

'It stinks,' he answered doggedly, his dark eyes half-averted and sorrowful.

Charles felt a twinge of pain for him. 'Cheer up. Give it time. You'll get to like it after a while.'

'I'll never like it,' Gordon said stubbornly.

Charles took up his mattock again. 'Sure you will,' he said as he began to swing it.

'Nobody likes me.'

Charles let the mattock come to rest and, turning once more to the boy, he spoke with an impatient excess of patience. 'You say that every day. I've told you it isn't true. You're a new boy in the school, and you came in the middle of the term, and there's never yet been a new boy who entered a school late and made friends right away. You're nearly nine, and you can understand that. Anyway, I'm tired of explaining it to you.'

'When can I get a paper route?'

Charles laughed without humor. 'My God, boy! Give us a chance to get settled.'

'I need money.'

'You get an allowance.'

'I need more money,' the boy insisted. 'I want a paper route. How do kids get them?'

'You can work for me. You can get in there with a hedge shears and cut out all those vines.'

The boy looked at his father despairingly and shook his head. 'No, I need a lot of money.'

'You can earn a lot of money working for me,' Charles said, swinging his mattock.

'I need a dollar,' Gordon said faintly.

His father did not hear him, and he did not turn from his work again until presently he heard his daughter calling him shrilly from the foot of the hill on which the house stood.

'What is it?' he called back. She was climbing the path, and he saw that she had a white envelope in her hand.

Then Gordon broke into rapid, desperate speech. 'I need a dollar. I'll pay it back out of my allowance. Remember yesterday I told you about that dollar I found? I have to pay it back.'

Charles stared at him. 'What dollar?'

Gordon glanced wildly over his shoulder. His sister, holding the menacing white envelope in one hand and her workman's tin lunchbox in the other, was halfway up the hill, coming along the side of the house. Pleadingly, Gordon looked back at his father. 'The dollar. Remember? I told you I found it. You wanted to know what I did with it.'

'What dollar?'

He sighed. 'You didn't listen! You never listen!'

Charles patted his shoulder. 'Now take it easy. Don't get excited. Tell me again. I don't think you told me anything about a dollar yesterday.'

'The dollar I found. You asked me what I did with it, and I told you I gave it to Crow, and you said I should have brought it home to you.'

'That Crow! I thought you were joking.'

Penelope, the six-year-old, was behind him now, and Gordon's shoulders sagged in despair. 'I wasn't joking,' he said almost wearily as Penelope handed his father the letter. 'You never really listen.'

Charles read the precise handwriting on the envelope. 'Mr. or Mrs. Dudley,' it said, and in the lower left-hand corner, 'Courtesy of Penelope.' He opened the envelope and read the message:

Dear Mr. and Mrs. Dudley —

Gordon became involved in some difficulty about a dollar today, and I wish you would help me. The dollar was lunch money belonging to a girl who says she left it deep in her coat pocket, in the cloak room, yesterday. When I brought it up with Gordon, he immediately said that he did not steal it. He says that he found it on the floor, and he also says that he told his father about it yesterday and that his father said he should have brought it home to him, and now he is fixed in his confusions. He gave it to an older boy named Will Crow, who spent it, and I have told Gordon that he will have to return a dollar to the girl tomorrow. Gordon is a very worthwhile little personality, but I do not think he has been entirely happy here at the Crestview School, and therefore, if you can help me straighten this out to his own best interest, I will be ever so grateful.

Sincerely yours,<br>
Gertrude Grandjent,<br>
Principal.

Charles groaned in exasperation. 'My God, why did you have to drag me into it? What will that woman think?'

Gordon's lips were trembling. 'You remember? I did tell you, didn't I?'

'Yes, I remember now. I remember very clearly that you told me you found it on the way to school, and when I asked you what you did with it, and you said you gave it to Crow, naturally I said you should have brought it home. *Listen,* Gordon —' The very simplicity of the boy's strategy infuriated Charles, and it was with an effort that he controlled his temper. He said, 'Penny, you go in now and tell your mother you're home.'

Penny was staring at her brother. 'What did Gordon do?'

'Run along, Penny, as I told you.'

She went down the incline reluctantly, staring back over her shoulder, and when she had gone into the house, Charles turned to Gordon again and said, 'Sit down.'

They sat down side by side on the damp slope. Gordon said, 'Will you lend me a dollar and keep my allowance until it's made up? I have to take it back tomorrow.'

'We'll talk about that later.' Charles tapped the letter with his muddy hand. 'Why did you tell me you found it in the street?'

Gordon looked away but answered promptly. 'I knew if I told you I found it in school, you'd have said I should have taken it to the office.'

'So you lied to me instead. That was better?'

Gordon did not answer.

'Answer me.'

'Yes.'

'Yes, what?'

'I lied.'

That was that. Charles started over. 'Why did you tell Miss Grandjent that you did not steal it when she hadn't even said that you had?'

'I knew that's what she thought.'

'How did you know?'

'I just knew.'

Charles hesitated. When he spoke again, his voice was warmer, friendly, almost confidential. 'What's the little girl's name, Gordon?'

'She's not little. She's in high fourth.'

'What's her name?'

'I don't know. Joan, I guess.'

'What color is her coat?'

Gordon glanced at his father sharply. 'I don't know. I never noticed it.'

Charles bit his lip in exasperation and stood up. 'Let's go inside.' He led the way in.

Josephine was standing on a chair in the middle of the living room. She was dusting the hideous chandelier of dark metal and colored glass which hung from the center of the ceiling. It was only one of many distasteful features in the house which the Dudleys hoped to rid it of, but it was hard to find men to do all the necessary work, and none would promise to do it quickly. An electrician had torn away a good deal of plaster and lathing, and a carpenter had ripped out some bookshelves and ugly mantels and taken down most a wall between the dining room and a useless hallway, but neither had returned, and painters, plasterers, paper hangers had not yet come at all. The Dudleys had decided to leave most of their belongings in storage until the work was done, and to bring nothing out of storage that they cared about. The result was that the house was almost fantastically disordered and bleak and squalid, and while Josephine managed to keep an even temper under these conditions, Charles, who found them very trying, did not.

He stood in the doorway of the living room now and said to her, 'Why do you bother?'

'The light was so dim,' she said, and then, seeing his expression, asked quickly, 'What's wrong?'

'Another problem.' He came heavily into the living room and gave her the letter. She read it standing on the chair, her face expressionless. Then she stepped down and went out into the hall where Gordon was lurking and said, 'Come in, dear.'

There was one old sofa in the room, and Josephine sat down there with Gordon. Charles sat facing them on the single straight chair. Josephine took Gordon's hands and said, 'Now tell me everything, Gordon, just the way it happened.'

The boy's face was composed in a kind of stolid determination, but when he raised his moody eyes from the bare floor to his father, his chin began to tremble, his eyelids fluttered, and suddenly the dogged expression broke in despair, his body sagged, his head fell back against the sofa, and he burst into harsh sobs. Josephine put her arm around his shoulders and held him close while he cried, and she shook her head sharply at Charles as he jumped up impatiently. He sat down again. Finally Gordon stopped crying, almost as abruptly as he had begun.

'How did it happen, Gordon?' his mother asked.

He straightened up and stared at the floor again. 'Nothing happened. I just came in the cloak room and saw it on the floor. I took it and put it in my pocket, and at recess I gave it to Crow.'

'Didn't anyone see you pick it up?'

'There wasn't anyone else there.'

'In the cloak room? Before school? Why not?'

'I was late.'

'Late? But why? You left here in plenty of time.'

'I stopped on the way and played with a cat.'

Josephine frowned. 'So there was no one else there at all to see you?' she asked meaningfully.

'No.'

Josephine glanced at Charles. He drew his lips apart and, with a heavy satiric edge, said, 'Well, Gordon, that's too bad! If there'd been someone else there, you could prove that you hadn't — '

Josephine broke in. 'Tell me just where the dollar was, Gordon,' she said softly, and her voice had no relation to the look in her eyes as she glared at Charles.

'On the floor.'

'But exactly where? Was it near the little girl's coat?'

'She isn't little.'

'Was it near her coat?'

'I don't know which coat is hers.'

'Was it near any coat?'

'It was on the floor, near all of them. They hang on a rack, and it was on the floor near them.'

Josephine paused, and Gordon wriggled his shoulders out from under her arm and slumped in the corner of the sofa, away from her. 'When can I get out of here?' he asked.

'When you start answering our questions,' his father said sharply. 'You insist that you didn't steal it?'

Gordon raised his lids slowly, as if they were very heavy, and stared out at his father from under his brows. 'I found it on the floor.'

Josephine spoke brightly. 'Very well. We have settled that. But Gordon, surely you don't think that because you found it on the floor, it belonged to you? Don't you see that it was just as much stealing it as if you had really taken it from the pocket of the person it belonged to?'

'Not as much,' Gordon said.

'But it wasn't *yours!* You knew that.'

The boy nodded.

'Well, then —'

'Someone else would have found it!'

'But would someone else have kept it?'

'I didn't keep it.'

Charles leaped up from his chair. 'That's the point! Why in God's name did you give it to that Crow rat?'

'He's my friend,' Gordon said with simple defiance, and then he slid off the sofa and lay on the floor.

'Your friend! A fine friend!' Charles shouted in disgust, standing over him. 'Get up!'

Gordon did not make any effort to move, and Josephine grasped Charles's arm. 'Let me,' she said quietly. 'Sit down.'

'Nonsense!' he cried angrily at her, and pulled his arm free of her touch. 'I'll take over now.' He seized the boy by the shoulders and pulled him up on the sofa. The jerk which he gave his body made the boy's head bob back and forward like a doll's, and he slumped against the sofa back almost as if he had been injured, dull eyes staring out of his pale face. 'Now listen to me, Gordon. I don't know if you took that money out of someone's pocket or not, but it looks, from the way you're behaving, as if you did. Anyway, you took it. It didn't belong to you, you knew that, and yet you took it. Do you see that there is no difference between the floor and the pocket as long as you kept it?'

'I didn't keep it,' Gordon repeated, but almost listlessly.

'Oh, my God!' Charles ran his hand through his hair, and the rumpled hair gave him a sudden wild look. 'Listen,' he said as quietly as he could, 'we are all having a very hard time here. We are trying to live in a house that isn't fit to live in. I am trying to get used to a new office. Your mother —'

Josephine said, 'Don't bother about me.'

'I will bother! We are all having a tough time, and Gordon can't think of anything better to do than to get into this mess at school. Of all the friends you could pick, you pick that nasty Crow brat, who is too old for you by three years and is a snide little —'

'Charles!'

Gordon lay back on the sofa. He looked ill and defeated.

'Will you admit that you stole that dollar? That taking it from the floor was just as much stealing it as if you had taken it from the pocket?'

'Yes,' he answered faintly.

'Speak up!'

'Yes, I *do!*' Gordon cried, and turned his face away.

Then the room was very still. Josephine stood stiffly beside the couch, her eyes fixed on Charles with dismay. Charles sagged a little, as if he, too, were defeated. And Gordon might have been asleep or dreaming, so remote had he suddenly become. Then they all heard a sly noise at the door, and Charles and Josephine swung toward it. Penelope stood there, embarrassed to have been caught. She giggled and said, 'Why did Gordon steal money?'

'Go away,' Charles said.

'Go to your room, dear,' Josephine said, 'or go outside.'

'But why did Gordon steal money?'

Charles walked to the girl, gave her a little push, and closed the door on her face. Then he came back to the sofa. He sat down next to Gordon, and when he spoke, his voice was nearly lifeless. 'You want to earn that dollar. All right, you can, Gordon. First go to your room and write your five sentences. Do them quickly for a change, and then go out into that patch of broom with the hedge shears and cut down all the vines you can find in it. You have an hour left before it gets dark.'

Gordon's eyes dreamed over his father's face, and then he slowly got up and left the room. His parents watched him go, and when he had closed the door softly behind him, Charles broke out. 'What is it, what stubbornness, that makes that boy so impenetrable? Did he steal that money or not? I haven't the slightest idea. All I could do was force him to admit that there was no difference between the two things.'

Josephine was looking at him with studied appraisal.

'Well?' he challenged her.

'You forced his admission. Did that gain anything? And what did it lose? How much did it hurt him? Is it of very great importance whether he stole it or not?'

'I don't know what's more important.'

'No, I really think you don't.'

'Well?'

'What's more important is why he took it, and what he did with it, and why he did that. What's more important is that he's a miserable little boy, and that you haven't made the slightest effort to understand *that*. All you've done is played the heavy parent, shown him that you don't trust him or believe him, and left him with a nice new layer of solidified guilt, and what is he supposed to do with *that?*'

'Let's skip the psychology for a change,' Charles said. 'There is an old-fashioned principle of honesty and dishonesty.'

'There's a more old-fashioned one of simple perception!' Josephine's face was red with anger. She stood in the middle of the bare room and looked rapidly around her, as if she felt a sudden desperate need, a hunger, for objects. But there was only the sofa, the chair, and Charles. Her eyes came back to him.

'Have you thought of his difficulties at all? Just the simple matter of his writing, for example? He came from a school where the children printed, and he printed as well as anyone. He comes here where the children do cursive writing, and of course he's made to feel like a fool, and he has to practice at home to learn it when other boys are playing. Or have you once helped him with that? Have you even suggested a sentence he might write? No. All you've done is to give him the extremely comforting bit of information that new boys, especially if they enter school late, have a hard time making friends! The one friend he has made you deride. No, don't interrupt. I know he's a horrid boy. I don't want Gordon playing with him either. But you haven't the sense to see that what has brought them together is that they are both pariahs. I think Gordon's giving that dollar to that dreadful boy is one of the most touching things I've ever heard of!'

'If what you've told me about Crow is true,' Charles said quietly, 'I won't have Gordon playing with him, and that's that.'

'Because Crow taught him some nasty words and told him some nasty, mistaken things about sex! You're perfectly right. But you can't just stand there and say no to him! If you were half a father, you would have told him yourself. *You* should be his friend! You're the one who should be giving him a decent attitude toward those things. You *are* his father, after all.'

'Oh, listen — He's not even nine!'

'All right. But he's getting it, isn't he? And all wrong?' And then, without warning, she sat down heavily on the single chair and began to sob, her reddened face lifted, her mouth twisted in sorrow, tears streaming down over her cheeks. 'All *wrong!*' she wailed.

Charles went to her quickly and, half standing, half kneeling beside the chair, awkwardly put his arms around her. 'Josephine, listen —'

'Oh, I know!' she sobbed. 'We all get in your way. We're all a nuisance that you're saddled with! We all just *bother* you! I know! It just isn't your idea of the way to live. You really hate it, don't you?'

His arms tightened. 'Darling,' he said, 'don't be a damned fool. Listen, I love you, I love the kids. Why, little Penny, I —'

'Oh, yes. Penny, sure! She's tractable! She doesn't raise any problems. That's different!'

'You're crazy. Gordon, too. You. Maybe I'm not much good with him, but that doesn't mean . . . And listen . . . I'll try. I'll go out there now.'

She dug in her pocket for a piece of Kleenex. She blew her nose and wiped her eyes. She pulled the tea towel off her head and shook out her hair. Then she blew her nose again. 'I'm all right now,' she said, getting up. She picked up the dust cloth which she had flung over the back of the chair, and she said, 'It's probably just this awful house, the way we have to camp. I'm going to get cleaned up and dress, and

I'm going to find a table cloth, and we'll have dinner at a table tonight, instead of sitting on the floor with plates in our laps.'

He said, 'Good girl! I'll go and fix it up with Gordon.'

Charles went into Gordon's room. It was empty. He glanced at the table where Gordon worked and saw that there was a sheet of writing there. Then he looked out of the window and saw the boy on his hands and knees in among the remaining broom. He crossed the hall to the bedroom where Josephine was dressing. 'I may not be very subtle with him, but I seem to get results,' he said. She merely glanced up at him, and as he went out on the balcony, down the steps, and up the slippery incline, he felt no satisfaction whatever in his remark.

'How's it going?' he asked the boy.

Gordon glanced over his shoulder. 'All right,' he said, and turned at once to his job. The hedge shears made a busy, innocent sound.

Charles found his mattock where he had dropped it, and began to chop at the edge of the overgrowth again. Immediately his nostrils filled with the poisonous smell he had noticed before, his hands began to chafe, and even though the heat of the sun had gone in the late afternoon, sweat broke out with a prickling sensation all over his face and body. Once more he was tense with irritation, and he said, 'That awful smell! What is it?'

'I don't know,' Gordon replied without looking up.

'Like something decaying.'

The boy did not answer, and Charles chopped angrily away at a root. When it came free, he shook the earth off and tossed the slim tree down the slope. 'This crazy, piddling stuff!' he shouted, and then reminded himself that it was only a kind of exaggerated weed, a thing that grew everywhere, so futile that it could not even send down a decent root and was hardly designed as a personal affront to him. Or was it? He laughed and started to chop at the next root, but stopped at once. 'I'm quitting for today,' he said. 'Come on, let's go in.'

Gordon said, 'No, I'll work a while. I want to earn the money.'

'Oh, let it go. We'll fix that up.'

Gordon stared at him. 'I want to earn it,' he said, and went on clipping at the rose vines.

'All right,' Charles said, 'but come in soon. You'll have to wash up thoroughly to get that muck off.'

He went back into the house by way of the bedroom, but Josephine was no longer there. He went into Gordon's room, but she was not there, either. On the table lay the white sheet of ruled paper covered with the boy's writing, his five sentences in their hasty, uncertain, and very large cursive characters. Charles picked it up. The first sentence was, 'I am going to cut vins.' The second was, 'I am going to ern mony.' The third was, 'The sun is shining.' The fourth was, 'When it rains here it rains hard.' The last, which seemed to have been written with greater care, with a kind of precision and flourish which his writing had never shown before, was, 'You hate me and I hate you.'

Charles took a sharp breath and held it, then sagged. After a moment he walked to the window and put his forehead against the cool glass. He stared out into the desolate garden, at the bare earth and the darkening tangle, and tried to think. When he heard Josephine moving on high heels somewhere in the rugless house, he began to fold the sheet of paper, and he folded it again and again, until it was a small hard square. This he stuffed deep into his pocket.

He came into the hall and saw Josephine standing in the center of the barren living room. She looked tall in an old but still handsome black housecoat, a straight, severe garment which hung from the tightly belted waist in heavy folds, and was without ornament or color anywhere. Her hair was pulled tautly away from her face, and her face was smooth and white, and her mouth was painted dark red.

She was detached from the room, from the house, and utterly from him — remote and beautiful, cold in resolution. Never in the ten years he had known her had she appeared so wonderfully in possession of herself. And, helplessly, Charles turned away.

He went into the boy's room again, and looked out to see
the boy. But twilight had obscured the garden now, shadows
hung about it like veils, and Charles could hardly see into
the trees. Then he thought that he saw Gordon's shape,
hunched on the ground among the slim trunks, and he went
out quickly to find him. Perhaps, even now, after everything, it was the boy who, somehow, could help.

*(From Foreground)*

# GAME CHICKENS

## BY ALLAN SEAGER

*WHEN* I finished high school in Memphis, Tennessee, it was in the middle of the year. The graduation exercises were held about the first of February and the next day I went out to look for a job. I intended to work for a year and a half, save all my money and go to Yale or, if I could not get in, I was going to ship out to Hamburg, Germany, on a cattle boat. I cannot remember now why Hamburg seemed to be more important than Gravesend, Cherbourg, or Stockholm. I believed Yale to be a difficult college to enter so that I felt an alternate choice was necessary and I may have heard that a great many cattle boats went to Germany.

I particularly wanted a job in the office of one of the big cotton factors on Front Street facing the levee, a cobbled ramp that sloped down to the River. If you worked for a cotton factor, you wore very good clothes which meant at that time four button, no-padding-in-the-shoulder jackets and narrow trousers with sharp creases and during working hours the suit would be covered with wisps of cotton lint. Inevitably you went to all the debutante parties and many of your colleagues were young Englishmen from Liverpool, and this semed to be a strange romantic fact. I tried all the offices on Front Street but I didn't get a job. We were Yankees and I had no connections. I didn't get a job anywhere else either.

After looking for a week or so I began to get discouraged.

I felt that I was no good. Although I had taken the platitudes of the principal address at graduation with a grain of salt, I had unconsciously accepted more of their message than I realized. I took to spending more and more of my afternoon swimming at the YMCA to bolster up my self-esteem. I was local champion at fifty and one hundred yards. It was a small sixty-foot tank in a room with a low ceiling. When I took the water my kick made a loud booming noise that made everybody stop and watch and had even drawn fat business men out of the barber shop and off the rubbing tables. I swam a good deal and I thought I was getting myself in shape for the outdoor racing season which began in June.

It was there that I met George L'Hommedieu. The first time he told me his name, he called it 'Lommadoo' and he spelled it out immediately with a certain pride and then said it was a nuisance as a name. I saw him come out of the showers one afternoon. He was about twenty-four or five with a good enough build but I knew he could not swim because he walked gingerly over the wet tiles as if they were hot and he tried the water with his toe before he climbed down the ladder at the shallow end. That first day he stood timidly around up to his waist patting the water. Occasionally he screwed up his face and lay down on his side in it, straightening up immediately to cough and spit and wipe his eyes. He seemed to want to swim but he knew nothing about it. As I swam by him he seemed to admire the display, so I volunteered to teach him and in a week he could swim the length of the pool. His arms looked stiff and brittle as he did it and he always swallowed quite a lot of water when he tried to breathe but anyone could tell it was a crawl stroke he was attempting and not a nasty feminine side stroke. At the pool we became quite good friends.

He told me he was a graduate of the University of Illinois and this was a recommendation to me because any college man was not only a Bachelor of Humane Letters, or something, he also knew about liquor and women. When I saw him in his clothes, I thought at first he worked for a cotton factor; he was dressed with the same elegance. I asked him but he said, no, he worked for the Illinois Board & Filler Company. It seemed to be a dull name and I did not inquire further. Although he was a Yankee like me and alone in Memphis, he got around a good deal. He mentioned the names of two or three debutantes and I was sure he led an exciting life. I was a little proud that I had taught him to swim. He became a proxy through whom I could imagine the conquest of the wild beautiful Mississippi girls who were drawn up to Memphis from the river towns of the Delta to 'come out' every winter. Some were girls from towns with the same names as theirs: I remember Elizabeth Banks of Banks, Miss. I thought she looked like Corinne Griffith and I hoped she was kind to George and saved him some 'no-cuts' at the dances. Actually, I can see now, he was a lonely young man who probably spent most of his evenings at the boarding house reading magazines on the bed in his room.

He got me the job I had been looking for and while working on it, I walked out of a room three minutes before a murder, maybe five minutes, anyhow, it was as close as I have ever been. We were sitting on the edge of the pool one afternoon and he asked me if I wanted a job. I told him I did and he said I could have his. He was quitting to work for a glass company up North and his home office had told him to find someone to replace him. The job was nothing, he said, very simple, very easy. I told him I was two months past my seventeenth birthday and I had never had any business experience.

'That's all right. Don't worry. There's nothing to this job. Meet me here tomorrow and I'll take you out to look the place over,' he said.

The Memphis branch of the Illinois Board & Filler Company was at the extreme north edge of town. Beyond it lay river bottoms and gum-tree woods. When I first saw the place, I was troubled and frightened. It seemed tremendous, and George had explained on the way out that my title would be Manager. I doubted whether I could manage all this. Something would be sure to come up that I wouldn't know how to handle. There were several long dingy grey two-story buildings made out of corrugated iron. They were laid out almost in the shape of a U. Between the ends of the U was a small corrugated iron building painted a dull red. This was the office. It sat on a small patch of gritty neat grass and there was a drooping tree. We got out of George's Ford and went in.

It was an old office. The walls were made of pine boards painted a mustard color and bulging here and there. Against one wall stood an old-fashioned high standing desk. There was also a battered oak flat-top desk with a swivel chair, a rickety adding machine, a huge black safe with a rustic scene on the door and a rusty little baseburner stove. Two rush-bottomed chairs with wire between the rungs stood in corners.

George knelt at once in front of the safe and spun the knob around the dial forward and back. I could hear the tumblers clank faintly.

'This is a hell of a safe,' George said as he swung the door open. He brought out a bottle of gin from the top shelf and stood to one side to let me look in. 'We keep coal in there. Coal, gin, and the stamps. They're the only valuables. No money comes through this office.' In the main coffer of the safe was about a bushel of soft coal.

'What's the combination?' I asked. I thought it sounded businesslike.

'There isn't any. Just give it a whirl,' he said.

I asked him what the Illinois Board & Filler Company made.

'Oh,' he said as if he thought he had already told me. 'Egg-case fillers. We sell fillers and flats and knocked-down cases.'

This meant as little to me then as it does to you. George went into an adjoining room, where the files and typewriter were, I learned later, and brought out, folded up and dusty, one of these cardboard crisscross things they put eggs in. Unfolded it was a large square network of three dozen little squares. A case of eggs holds thirty dozen, hence there would be ten of these networks — fillers, in fact — five on each side. The wooden egg-case made of 3/16″ gum or 7/32″ cottonwood was sold in a bundle, the sides, the ends and the top and bottom all bound together, and the dealer had to make a box out of it himself.

George passed me the gin bottle and said, 'Good luck.' I thought he meant good luck with the gin but afterward I was ashamed to realize he was toasting my fortunes on the job. I did the genteel thing. I took as small a drink as I dared, coughed only once and by blinking rapidly kept the tears from running down my face. Italians made the Memphis gin, a standard product that smelled like *Hearts & Flowers* perfume. I was glad it was not their 'brandy,' a liquid made of corn whiskey, peach flavoring and red pepper. George took several swallows with great ease while I watched admiringly.

He told me he had been authorized by the home office in Illinois to pay me $110 a month. This seemed to me a large salary but he explained apologetically that it really was small because there was so little to do most of the time, nothing but sit there all day long and hope that freight agents from the railroads would stop in and talk. The reason they were freight agents was because they were affable fellows who could tell a good story and he kept the gin in the safe for their entertainment. I could come to work the next day and he would stay with me two weeks to show me the ropes. Then he was going North.

Pat as he said this, the screen door opened and a thin little wizened man came in.

'Cathey, this is Mr. Seager. He's taking my place,' George said.

Cathey rolled a twig from one side of his mouth to the other and said in a high voice, 'Uh-huh.'

He would have been about five feet, eight inches long if you had laid him out flat on a table and measured him but he was only about five feet tall as he stood there because he was all humped over into his pants pockets. He wore a large fuzzy grey fedora hat covered with grease spots and wisps of cobweb. His shirt was blue and dirty and he had on a pair of black trousers that shone down the thighs from the oily dirt that was ground into them. He was about thirty-five years old and he had a long sagging face. As he stood there, the face did not change; he did not glance up from the floor; he looked like a man alone on a street corner.

'Cathey's the foreman. He knows about everything. If you want to know anything, ask him,' George explained.

It seemed to me that I ought to acknowledge the introduction in some way. At seventeen manners are not consideration for other people; they are a display you make to prove you have them. I stepped briskly forward with my hand stuck out and said, 'How are you, Mr. Cathey?'

He rolled his light eyes up at me and down again. He pulled a hand slowly out of his pocket and held it three inches in front of his thigh. I could take it if I wanted to. I took it, limp, thin, and moist, and squeezed it once and let it go. He put it back in his pocket. George went on talking to me about the job. Cathey stood looking at the floor, occasionally moving the twig from one corner of his mouth to the other by hand, then spitting, and after a few minutes, he turned around and walked out of the office.

'Doesn't he ever talk?' I asked George.

'Who, Cathey? Sure he talks. He knows all about this place. He could run it all by himself. He can read and write.'

After George had gone and I had settled into the work, I found there was really very little to do just as he had said. The factory 'ran' four months a year. The rest of the time we shipped orders out of stock and I kept banker's hours. I used to take a Poplar Avenue street car, pick up the morning mail, and board a Thomas Street car for the factory. The Thomas Street cars were the oldest in Memphis. They ran very slowly, rocking backward and forward, and it was nearly nine-thirty when I reached the office which was at the end of the line. It would take me about an hour to answer a letter or two (in longhand) and write up the orders and bills of lading. Cathey came in, sometimes silently, sometimes saying ' 'morning,' pick up the orders and bills and walk out. He and one colored man made up the orders and before noon I would see our old ratty Ford truck taking the cases and fillers down to the depot to be shipped. At twelve-thirty I took the street car back downtown, had a malted milk and a sandwich, picked up the afternoon mail and was trundled sedately back again. There was another hour's work and I was finished for the day. I had to stay there, though, because somebody might call up on the phone. During the off season there were only three people in this huge clump of buildings, Cathey, J. T., the Negro, and myself.

At first I spent some time exploring the place. The factory had made cottonseed oil during the War but none had been made there since. The windows were thick with a gummy dust, almost opaque, and inside the light was dim. Long festoons of old ragged cobwebs hung everywhere with lint and chips of wood caught in the loops. The floor was damp and against the wall in heaps of dust and corners, some kind of pale weed sprouted. There were structures I took to be vats, blistered and rusty, and wherever there was machinery the lines of its curves, spokes and joints were broken by the thick coating of grease someone had put on them to preserve them. In some of the rooms there were metal bins full of moldy cottonseed hulls and it was from these that the whole factory took its rank and rubbery odor. Rats lived on the hulls.

The rats were monstrous and Cathey's terrier would never go inside the factory. They had lived there battening on the greasy hulls so long unmolested that they were full of confidence and they usually moved at a slow trot shaking all over with their fat. They did not seem to see, hear, or smell very much. You could walk up within a yard of one, then at some point he would become aware of you and slash like lightning at your shoe or ankle. I did this just once and then I let them alone.

Once after a tour of these gloomy buildings I was coming out of a doorway into the sunlight when I saw a chicken yard in front of me. I had never noticed it before. Chickens were just chickens to me and I was about to pass by when I saw they were not ordinary chickens.

I walked over to the wire fence and looked down at them. I had never actually seen any before but I knew from pictures in the *National Geographic* that these were game chickens.

'Them are game birds,' I heard Cathey's high voice say, and, turning, I found him at my elbow.

'What do you do with them?' I asked.

There was an accent of soft scorn in his voice. 'Fight 'em.'

I was young and ignorant especially with people and half consciously but helplessly I blurted out the obvious. 'It's against the law, isn't it?'

It was as if he were overlooking a breach of etiquette. 'I fight 'em Sunday mornings over there in the bottoms with the niggers.'

'With gaffs?'

He spat over the fence and a young cockerel jumped and fluttered. He swung his pale eyes at me deliberately and said, 'Uh-huh.' Maybe he thought by looking at my face he could tell just what kind of a damned fool I was. He knew he was going to have to work with me, damned fool or not, and he hunched his shoulders and leaned over with his forearms crossed on a thin little fencepost and resumed politely but without any polite inflections. 'We git over there about ten o'clock Sunday morning and we fight two, three mains for ten dollar side bets.' He spat again. 'Make money.'

The cocks stood up high off the ground. They had long serpentine necks that gleamed in the sun. Some were a beautiful greenish black, others a reddish bronze, others a kind of dirty speckled grey. Everything had been bred off them but muscle. They stepped around stiff and alert, stopped, scratched, and stopped, the neat reptilian heads turning slowly, blinking, one claw lifted, and then ran quickly on.

'They's good blood in those birds. *Im*ported. Those grey ones are Irish Greys. You know Paul Dickson down at Rosedale?'

'No. Who's he?' I said.

'Got a big place down there. He keeps a big string of game chickens. I got 'em from him.'

I would have liked to ask him more about cockfighting but I didn't want him to think I was any stupider that he did already. I said, 'Well, I better be getting back to the office,' and just as I said it before I had turned away from him, I saw him smile, a slow hoist of his sagging cheeks that let out his orange broken teeth. He knew I had no work to do and I had been stupid again.

As spring came and the weather got warm, I tried to find things to do. I practised typing about an hour a day sitting on a tall three-legged stool. I was anxious to get ahead (of whom I didn't stop to think) and I considered buying a book on poultry so that I might learn the business from the egg up. I tried conscientiously to envision the industry as a whole: the farmer, the wholesaler, the salesman, the manufacturer, and the Home Offices but I was always stopped by a sort of sneaking thought that egg-case fillers were not very important. I know now that this was not a sneaking thought. It was a conviction that I was unwilling to recognize then and it made me inefficient in the little work there was. I made mistakes steadily.

I had to keep a simple set of books on expenditures and payrolls. I knew they were simple but within two weeks of my start, I was 3c out and I never did find that three cents. Once a month I took an inventory of the stock on hand and one warm April day with a light breeze and the toad-frogs chirping and clunking in the bottoms beyond the factory, I walked right past a whole warehouse full of fillers and I showed a 1500-case loss on my inventory. Three days later I had a special delivery letter from the President of the company. It began conventionally enough, 'Dear Mr. Seager,' and opposite the salutation above the body of the letter was typed, '*In re*: Monthly Inventory.' It continued.

'*Yours of even date received and contents noted. Would say in reply* (and here the style blew up) *just what the hell are you doing down there, Allan?*' Then he explained, more formally, my mistake.

The worst came a few weeks later although I did not hear about it for a long time. A letter came in cancelling an order.

The letter-paper was charred brown around the edges and on it the customer said his whole establishment had burned up. I thought for half an hour about the shock and distress of having your business burn up and then I sat down on my stool to compose a consoling reply. I wanted it to be warm, humane, and sympathetic for I felt that this would help the prestige of the I. B. & F. CO. I began, 'I am terribly sorry to hear about your fire. Fire is so relentless and uncaring . . . .' There was a lot more of this and it was not until six months later that Uncle Joe Thomson, the salesman, a shrewd old man with an Elk's tooth, brown vici kid shoes and a wad of *Peachy Plug* always sleeping in his cheek, came in off the territory and said there was a fellow over in Marked Tree, Arkansas, that thought I was crazy.

When the weather got hot in May, my attempts to improve grew more sporadic and they withered completely in the summer when the little iron office building used to take enough heat so it jumped up and down. Nobody came to visit the place then, not even the freight agents, and I sat stripped to the waist with my feet on the desk, reading *The Faerie Queene* and *The Adventures of Gargantua and Pantagruel*. The sweat used to run off my hands and forearms to my elbows and drop off to the floor. There was always a puddle under my elbows. I got through both books during the hot weather. I had picked them because they were good and thick and would last me a long time. I did not want to be lugging books back and forth on the street car from the library.

Cathey spent a lot of his time sitting next to the cold boilers in the factory; some of it with the game chickens and a little of it talking to me in the office. He never stayed long because it was too hot and after he saw the puddles under my chair he would urge me to come sit by the boilers with him but I thought that was the same as sitting down cellar and I had heard it would give you rheumatism. I got my name in the paper whenever I took part in a swimming race during the summer, and I think this made Cathey look more kindly on me. Anyhow, he became affable and, for him, talkative.

He had been a soldier in France during the War. I wanted to hear about his experiences. It went this way:

'Yeah, I shot a German.'

'How?'

'Just shot him, that's all.' And then he would stare at me again with his faint blue eyes.

Or he would answer, 'Sure, I been to Paris.'

'What was it like?'

'Well, it's bigger than Meffis, more spread out.'

'Was it a beautiful place?'

'It was all right.'

The only thing touching his War experience that he seemed willing to discuss at length was the crudity of the French. They were a barbarous, uncivilized people. He had been sent to a rest camp near some village behind the lines and he had been shocked by the privies. They were not like anything he had ever seen and they were much worse. 'They ain't human, goddamn it. They got these damn little old houses and they ain't nothing in 'em but a couple of handles and. . . . ' He had been glad to leave France and get back to civilization.

Unlike many American soldiers, he had scorned the French women because you couldn't understand a damn word they said even when they were talking English. Yet he was a hot lover. He told me about affairs he had contrived in Mississippi with waitresses, farm girls, and married women. (He was married himself.) He was proud of the married women but I could never imagine how this ugly scrawny little man could attract any woman because I believed you had to be handsome, vigorous, and rich for the job. I got one inkling, though. He was going on one day about a brakeman's wife in some river town. He said in a matter-of-fact tone he had gone with her fifteen times in one night. Ordinarily I never questioned anything he said or made any comment on it but this was the kind of statistic that had been hashed over pretty thoroughly my senior year in high school and I said, 'The hell you did.'

As if I had pressed a button he began to shake all over and

stride up and down the room, swearing in a high voice almost falsetto with rage. I just sat and shook my head.

At last he jerked off his fuzzy hat and threw it on the floor and kicked it.

'I *did*. I swear I did. I did it. Yes, sir,' he shouted. It is the only time I ever saw him with his hat off. His forehead was a shiny greasy white and he was bald with wild uncombed strands of hair fluffed up from the sides of his head. He was uglier than ever yet his passion gave him a kind of dignity, at least you could take him seriously as a human being. He looked at me waiting for me to acknowledge him. He was not exactly angry, not at me anyhow. My doubts seemed to have tainted the memory of the night with the brakeman's wife and he was waiting for me to make it right again and the anger was the shock that his past could be tampered with.

At last I said, 'OK.'

He picked up his hat without any embarrassment and went out and began to handle his game chickens.

Along about October the factory began to 'run.' I had very little to do with it. One morning I saw smoke coming out of one of the smaller chimneys. I went out to the shop and found all the machines running, each operated by a colored woman. That afternoon Cathey led them all into the office to sign the payroll sheet.

'They git fourteen dollars a week,' he said. He turned to the first one. 'What's your name?' he bawled.

'Willie Sue Mawson,' she said and tittered. Then the whole line tittered.

'Kin you write it?'

'Naw, suh,' she said.

'Write down Willie Sue Mawson,' he said to me. I wrote it down.

'Make your mark,' he said and jerked her forward by the arm. She took the pencil and made a shaky cross after her name. There were about twenty women in all. Three or four could write their names and one printed it out in block letters. When they all had signed, they began to file out of the office. Cathey stood beside the door jocosely patting the young ones on the behind, and they cooed and giggled.

My easy days were over. I came to work at eight o'clock in the morning because there was a much larger mail every day, more bookkeeping, a constantly shifting inventory, and I had to dicker with the railroads for empty freight cars. If I got to the office a little early I would see the colored women drifting past my windows toward the shop. Few of them wore stockings although the mornings then were getting sharp. Most of them had broken men's shoes on their feet and occasionally one of them would wear a man's staved-in hat. They walked beautifully, languidly, cackling and giggling in high shrill voices. I never did anything but just barely notice them and I never could tell them apart.

One morning I had to go out in the factory to get Cathey to check a shipment of strawboard with me. He was in the machine room overseeing the work of the women. I told him what I wanted and we went out to the siding and opened the freight car that had just been switched in. It was full of big rolls of yellow strawboard about four feet high. It didn't take us more than five minutes to count them. We shut the car again and Cathey returned to the machine room. I added up my figures and started back to the office. I was always in a hurry those days and it was shorter to go through the old factory past the huge gloomy power wheels and the bins of cottonseed hulls.

I came out of the building and was crossing the road to the office when I noticed Cathey coming toward me. He was walking slowly all humped over looking at the ground as he usually did. He was too busy himself to come to the office unless he wanted something so I waited.

He took a twig out of his mouth and spat. He looked up at me and gave his weak yellow grin. 'One of them nigger wenches just killed another one out in the shop,' he said.

'Killed her?' I suppose I said. 'How?'

'Cut her.' He sliced the air beside his throat with his forefinger.

I had already started walking toward the machine shop

very fast and Cathey had to hustle to keep up with me. He resented it and took it out in the high complaining tone of his voice, 'We wasn't gone five minutes. God-damn 'em.'

I didn't say anything. I guess it was because I had to see the body first.

Cathey said, 'Ain't no need to hurry thisaway. She'll keep.'

She lay on the floor beside a machine. There was a long bloody gash in her neck and a big pool of blood on the floor. Already the floating lint from the strawboard was settling on its surface. Her eyes were open and her hands lay open by her sides as if she expected to receive something. I don't think I had ever seen her before in my life.

There was no one near her. The other women stood in a group about ten feet away staring down at the body. Cathey had shut off the machines and the place was very still. I could hear a loud passionate whisper somewhere at the back of the group, 'I tole her. Didn't I tell her, Loreen? I swear I tole her a hundid times.' It was evidently the voice of the woman who had done the cutting.

Suddenly Cathey shouted, 'Now, god-damn it, all y'all git back to work. And git her out of here.' He threw the power switch and the wheels began to turn and the belts started flapping. The women drifted back to their machines.

I said loudly to Cathey, 'What were they fighting about?'

He nodded his head toward the door and started for it. I followed him. The day had turned out warm and bright with a haze in front of the red gum trees across the bottoms. We walked slowly up the bumpy cinder roadway toward the office.

'What were they fighting about?'

'Hahda I know? They're always fightin about somethin.'

'We ought to send for the sheriff, don't you think?'

He stopped dead and looked at me. 'Sheriff?'

'To pick up the woman with the razor. It's murder.'

He began to quiver, walking back and forth across the road cutting and slicing with his empty hands. 'God-damn it, don't call no sheriff. They got enough to do. Come way out here?' he shouted. It was hard for him to say what he meant he was so angry. 'God-damn it to hell, they're just niggers. The law don't want iny part of a nigger killin.'

I said nothing. I was balked by the intensity of his anger and by the stink of the cottonseed hulls and the dull red of the gum trees. It was a strange country. They had their own ways of doing things here and maybe I had better not monkey with them.

'I been to ever nigger shanty in North Meffis to git this women. I gotta git one more now. I don't wanta git two more. You call the sheriff and he taken her to jail and I got to start out again, askin, askin. . . . ' He stopped, and putting a hand on a post, he jumped lightly over his chicken fence and caught one of his cocks. He began kissing it. He took its bill between his lips, cooing and clucking as he would to a child, and stroking its long black shining neck.

He turned to me with the bird in his arms, smiling. 'You have to get 'em used to this. When they git hurt in a fight, you spit in their mouths. It'll put 'em right back on their feet sometimes. Why, I seen it when . . . . ' He went on telling about cockfights and how game birds should be handled. I stood there and I must have been listening to him because I didn't hear the car go by or if I did I thought it was our truck.

I saw the car when it came back, though. I don't know how they sent word for someone to bring it. No one had used the phone. Maybe some one of the women had run down the railroad tracks back of the factory. It was an old Model-T touring car with the top down. One of the wilted fenders flopped loosely up and down and the colored boy driving it kept slamming the front door that wouldn't shut and steering with one hand. Three women sat in the back seat. The one on the far side was old. I could see grey hair sticking out under her red head-rag. The near one was about sixteen. Her hair stuck out in stiff pigtails and I could see the neat pattern of parts on her skull like a map. The one in the middle wore a man's dirty felt hat and her throat was bound up with a piece of calico. Just as they passed me, the front wheels went over a small culvert and the head jerked to one side with a dreadful limpness. As the hind wheels struck the tile, it jerked back to the other side. I saw the old woman trying to straighten it up again and at last she put her hand up on the back of the seat and held the head erect so that it would not show when they passed down the street.

I did not think Cathey had noticed the car. He was still talking to his game cock but when the car turned out our front gate into Thomas Street, he looked up and said slyly, cheerfully, 'They'll be some sure enough big doings now. They always have a brass band at them funerals.'

(From The New Yorker)

# ACT OF FAITH

## BY IRWIN SHAW

*PRESENT* it to him in a pitiful light,' Olson was saying as they picked their way through the almost frozen mud toward the orderly-room tent. 'Three combat-scarred veterans, who fought their way from Omaha Beach to . . . What was the name of the town we fought our way to?'

'Königstein,' Seeger said.

'Königstein.' Olson lifted his right foot heavily out of a puddle and stared admiringly at the three pounds of mud clinging to his overshoe. 'The backbone of the Army. The noncommissioned officer. We deserve better of our country. Mention our decorations, in passing.'

'What decorations should I mention?' Seeger asked. 'The Marksman's Medal?'

'Never quite made it,' Olson said. 'I had a cross-eyed scorer at the butts. Mention the Bronze Star, the Silver Star, the Croix de Guerre with palms, the Unit Citation, the Congressional Medal of Honor.'

'I'll mention them all.' Seeger grinned. 'You don't think the C.O.'ll notice that we haven't won most of them, do you?'

'Gad, sir,' Olsen said with dignity, 'do you think that one Southern military gentleman will dare doubt the word of another Southern military gentleman in the hour of victory?'

'I come from Ohio,' Seeger said.

'Welch comes from Kansas,' Olson said, coolly staring down a second lieutenant who was passing. The lieutenant made a nervous little jerk with his hand, as though he expected a salute, then kept it rigid, as a slight, superior smile of scorn twisted at the corner of Olson's mouth. The lieutenant dropped his eyes and splashed on through the mud. 'You've heard of Kansas,' Olson said. 'Magnolia-scented Kansas.'

'Of course,' said Seeger. 'I'm no fool.'

'Do your duty by your men, Sergeant.' Olson stopped to wipe the cold rain off his face and lectured him. 'Highest-ranking noncom present took the initiative and saved his comrades, at great personal risk, above and beyond the call of you-know-what, in the best traditions of the American Army.'

'I will throw myself in the breach,' Seeger said.

'Welch and I can't ask more,' said Olson.

They walked heavily through the mud on the streets between the rows of tents. The camp stretched drearily over the Reims plain, with the rain beating on the sagging tents. The division had been there over three weeks, waiting to be shipped home, and all the meagre diversions of the neighborhood had been sampled and exhausted, and there was an air of watchful suspicion and impatience with the military life hanging over the camp now, and there was even reputed to be a staff sergeant in C Company who was laying odds they would not get back to America before July 4th.

'I'm redeployable,' Olson sang. 'It's so enjoyable.' It was a jingle he had composed, to no recognizable melody, in the early days after the victory in Europe, when he had added up his points and found they came to only sixty-three, but he persisted in singing it. He was a short, round boy who had been flunked out of air cadets' school and transferred to the infantry but whose spirits had not been damaged in the process. He had a high, childish voice and a pretty, baby face. He was very good-natured, and had a girl waiting for him at the University of California, where he intended to finish his course at government expense when he got out of the Army, and he was just the type who is killed off early and predictably and sadly in moving pictures about the war, but he had gone through four campaigns and six major battles without a scratch.

Seeger was a large, lanky boy, with a big nose, who had
been wounded at St.-Lô but had come back to his outfit in
the Siegfried Line quite unchanged. He was cheerful and
dependable and he knew his business. He had broken in five
or six second lieutenants, who had later been killed or
wounded, and the C.O. had tried to get him commissioned in
the field, but the war had ended while the paperwork was
being fumbled over at headquarters.

They reached the door of the orderly tent and stopped.
'Be brave, Sergeant,' Olson said. 'Welch and I are depending
on you.'

'O.K.,' Seeger said, and went in.

The tent had the dank, Army-canvas smell that had been
so much a part of Seeger's life in the past three years. The
company clerk was reading an October, 1945, issue of the
Buffalo *Courier-Express*, which had just reached him, and
Captain Taney, the company C.O., was seated at a sawbuck
table which he used as a desk, writing a letter to his wife, his
lips pursed with effort. He was a small, fussy man, with
sandy hair that was falling out. While the fighting had been
going on, he had been lean and tense and his small voice had
been cold and full of authority. But now he had relaxed,
and a little pot belly was creeping up under his belt and he
kept the top button of his trousers open when he could do
it without too public loss of dignity. During the war Seeger
had thought of him as a natural soldier — tireless, fanatic
about detail, aggressive, severely anxious to kill Germans.
But in the last few months, Seeger had seen him relapsing
gradually and pleasantly into the small-town hardware merchant he had been before the war, sedentary and a little shy,
and, as he had once told Seeger, worried, here in the bleak
champagne fields of France, about his daughter, who had
just turned twelve and had a tendency to go after the boys
and had been caught by her mother kissing a fifteen-year-old
neighbor in the hammock after school.

'Hello, Seeger,' he said, returning the salute with a mild,
offhand gesture. 'What's on your mind?'

'Am I disturbing you, sir?'

'Oh, no. Just writing a letter to my wife. You married, Seeger?' He peered at the tall boy standing before him.

'No, sir.'

'It's very difficult.' Taney sighed, pushing dissatisfiedly at the letter before him. 'My wife complains I don't tell her I love her often enough. Been married fifteen years. You'd think she'd know by now.' He smiled at Seeger. 'I thought you were going to Paris,' he said. 'I signed the passes yesterday.'

'That's what I came to see you about, sir.'

'I suppose something's wrong with the passes.' Taney spoke resignedly, like a man who has never quite got the hang of Army regulations and has had requisitions, furloughs, and requests for courts-martial returned for correction in a baffling flood.

'No, sir,' Seeger said. 'The passes're fine. They start tomorrow. Well, it's just — ' He looked around at the company clerk, who was on the sports page.

'This confidential?' Taney asked.

'If you don't mind, sir.'

'Johnny,' Taney said to the clerk, 'go stand in the rain someplace.'

'Yes, sir,' the clerk said, and slowly got up and walked out.

Taney looked shrewdly at Seeger and spoke in a secret whisper. 'You pick up anything?' he asked.

Seeger grinned. 'No, sir, haven't had my hands on a girl since Strasbourg.'

'Ah, that's good.' Taney leaned back, relieved, happy that he didn't have to cope with the disapproval of the Medical Corps.

'It's — well,' said Seeger, embarrassed, 'it's hard to say — but it's money.'

Taney shook his head sadly. 'I know.'

'We haven't been paid for three months, sir, and — '

'Damn it!' Taney stood up and shouted furiously. 'I would like to take every bloody, chair-warming old lady in the Finance Department and wring their necks.'

The clerk stuck his head into the tent. 'Anything wrong? You call for me, sir?'

'No!' Taney shouted. 'Get out of here!'

The clerk ducked out.

Taney sat down again. 'I suppose,' he said, in a more normal voice, 'they have their problems. Outfits being broken up, being moved all over the place. But it's rugged.'

'It wouldn't be so bad,' Seeger said, 'but we're going to Paris tomorrow. Olson, Welch, and myself. And you need money in Paris.'

'Don't I know it?' Taney wagged his head. 'Do you know what I paid for a bottle of champagne on the Place Pigalle in September?' He paused significantly. 'I won't tell you. You wouldn't have any respect for me the rest of your life.'

Seeger laughed. 'Hanging is too good for the guy who thought up the rate of exchange,' he said.

'I don't care if I never see another franc as long as I live.' Taney waved his letter in the air, although it had been dry for a long time.

There was silence in the tent, and Seeger swallowed a little embarrassedly. 'Sir,' he said, 'the truth is, I've come to borrow some money for Welch, Olson, and myself. We'll pay it back out of the first pay we get, and that can't be too long from now. If you don't want to give it to us, just tell me and I'll understand and get the hell out of here. We don't like to ask, but you might just as well be dead as be in Paris broke.'

Taney stopped waving his letter and put it down thoughtfully. He peered at it, wrinkling his brow, looking like an aged bookkeeper in the single, gloomy light that hung in the middle of the tent.

'Just say the word, Captain,' Seeger said, 'and I'll blow.'

'Stay where you are, son,' said Taney. He dug in his shirt pocket and took out a worn, sweat-stained wallet. He looked at it for a moment. 'Alligator,' he said, with automatic, absent pride. 'My wife sent it to me when we were in England. Pounds don't fit in it. However . . .' He opened it and took out all the contents. There was a small pile of francs on the table in front of him when he finished. He counted them. 'Four hundred francs,' he said. 'Eight bucks.'

'Excuse me,' Seeger said humbly. 'I shouldn't have asked.'

'Delighted,' Taney said vigorously. 'Absolutely delighted.' He started dividing the francs into two piles. 'Truth is, Seeger, most of my money goes home in allotments. And the truth is, I lost eleven hundred francs in a poker game three nights ago, and I ought to be ashamed of myself. Here.' He shoved one pile toward Seeger. 'Two hundred francs.'

Seeger looked down at the frayed, meretricious paper, which always seemed to him like stage money anyway. 'No, sir,' he said. 'I can't take it.'

'Take it,' Taney said. 'That's a direct order.'

Seeger slowly picked up the money, not looking at Taney. 'Sometime, sir,' he said, 'after we get out, you have to come over to my house, and you and my father and my brother and I'll go on a real drunk.'

'I regard that,' Taney said gravely, 'as a solemn commitment.'

They smiled at each other, and Seeger started out.

'Have a drink for me,' said Taney, 'at the Café de la Paix. A small drink.' He was sitting down to tell his wife he loved her when Seeger went out of the tent.

Olson fell into step with Seeger and they walked silently through the mud between the tents.

'Well, *mon vieux?*' Olson said finally.

'Two hundred francs,' said Seeger.

Olson groaned. 'Two hundred francs! We won't be able to pinch a whore's behind on the Boulevard des Capucines for two hundred francs. That miserable, penny-loving Yankee!'

'He only had four hundred,' Seeger said.

'I revise my opinion,' said Olson.

They walked disconsolately and heavily back toward their tent.

Olson spoke only once before they got there. 'These raincoats,' he said, patting his. 'Most ingenious invention of the war. Highest saturation point of any modern fabric. Collect more water per square inch, and hold it, than any material known to man. All hail the quartermaster!'

Welch was waiting at the entrance of their tent. He was standing there peering excitedly and shortsightedly out at the rain through his glasses, looking angry and tough, like a big-city hack driver, individual and incorruptible even in the ten-million colored uniform. Every time Seeger came upon Welch unexpectedly, he couldn't help smiling at the belligerent stance, the harsh stare through the steel-rimmed G.I. glasses, which had nothing at all to do with the way Welch really was. 'It's a family inheritance,' Welch had once explained. 'My whole family stands as though we were getting ready to rap a drunk with a beer glass. Even my old lady.' Welch had six brothers, all devout, according to Welch, and Seeger from time to time idly pictured them standing in a row, on Sunday mornings in church, seemingly on the verge of general violence, amid the hushed Latin and the Sabbath millinery.

'How much?' Welch asked loudly.

'Don't make us laugh,' Olson said, pushing past him into the tent.

'What do you think I could get from the French for my combat jacket?' Seeger said. He went into the tent and lay down on his cot.

Welch followed them in and stood between the two of them. 'Boys,' he said, 'on a man's errand.'

'I can just see us now,' Olson murmured, lying on his cot with his hands clasped behind his head, 'painting Montmartre red. Please bring on the naked dancing girls. Four bucks' worth.'

'I am not worried,' Welch announced.

'Get out of here.' Olson turned over on his stomach.

'I know where we can put our hands on sixty-five bucks.' Welch looked triumphantly first at Olson, then at Seeger.

Olson turned over slowly and sat up. 'I'll kill you,' he said, 'if you're kidding.'

'While you guys are wasting your time fooling around with the infantry,' Welch said, 'I used my head. I went into Reems and used my head.'

'Rance,' Olson said automatically. He had had two years

of French in college and he felt, now that the war was over, that he had to introduce his friends to some of his culture.

'I got to talking to a captain in the Air Force,' Welch said eagerly. 'A little, fat old paddle-footed captain that never got higher off the ground than the second floor of Com Z headquarters, and he told me that what he would admire to do more than anything else is take home a nice shiny German Luger pistol with him to show to the boys back in Pacific Grove, California.'

Silence fell on the tent, and Welch and Olson looked at Seeger.

'Sixty-five bucks for a Luger, these days,' Olson said, 'is a very good figure.'

'They've been sellin' for as low as thirty-five,' said Welch hesitantly. 'I'll bet,' he said to Seeger, 'you could sell yours now and buy another one back when you got some dough, and make a clear twenty-five on the deal.'

Seeger didn't say anything. He had killed the owner of the Luger, an enormous S.S. major, in Coblenz, behind some bales of paper in a warehouse, and the major had fired at Seeger three times with it, once nicking his helmet, before Seeger hit him in the face at twenty feet. Seeger had kept the Luger, a heavy, well-balanced gun, lugging it with him, hiding it in the bottom of his bedroll, oiling it three times a week avoiding all opportunities of selling it, although he had once been offered a hundred dollars for it and several times eighty and ninety, while the war was still on, before German weapons became a glut on the market.

'Well,' said Welch, 'there's no hurry. I told the captain I'd see him tonight around eight o'clock in front of the Lion d'Or Hotel. You got five hours to make up your mind. Plenty of time.'

'Me,' said Olson, after a pause, 'I won't say anything.'

Seeger looked reflectively at his feet, and the two other men avoided looking at him.

Welch dug in his pocket. 'I forgot,' he said. 'I picked up a letter for you.' He handed it to Seeger.

'Thanks,' Seeger said. He opened it absently, thinking about the Luger.

'Me,' said Olson, 'I won't say a bloody word. I'm just going to lie here and think about that nice, fat Air Force captain.'

Seeger grinned a little at him and went to the tent opening to read the letter in the light. The letter was from his father, and even from one glance at the handwriting, scrawly and hurried and spotted, so different from his father's usual steady, handsome, professional script, he knew that something was wrong.

'Dear Norman,' it read, 'sometime in the future, you must forgive me for writing this letter. But I have been holding this in so long, and there is no one here I can talk to, and because of your brother's condition I must pretend to be cheerful and optimistic all the time at home, both with him and your mother, who has never been the same since Leonard was killed. You're the oldest now, and although I know we've never talked very seriously about anything before, you have been through a great deal by now, and I imagine you must have matured considerably, and you've seen so many different places and people. Norman, I need help. While the war was on and you were fighting, I kept this to myself. It wouldn't have been fair to burden you with this. But now the war is over, and I no longer feel I can stand up under this alone. And you will have to face it sometime when you get home, if you haven't faced it already, and perhaps we can help each other by facing it together.'

'I'm redeployable. It's so enjoyable,' Olson was singing softly, on his cot. He fell silent after his burst of song.

Seeger blinked his eyes in the gray, wintry, rainy light, and went on reading his father's letter, on the stiff white stationery with the university letterhead in polite engraving at the top of each page.

'I've been feeling this coming on for a long time,' the letter continued, 'but it wasn't until last Sunday morning that something happened to make me feel it in its full force. I don't know how much you've guessed about the reason for Jacob's discharge from the Army. It's true he was pretty badly wounded in the leg at Metz, but I've asked around, and I know that men with worse wounds were returned to duty after hospitalization. Jacob got a medical discharge, but I don't think it was for the shrapnel wound in his thigh. He is suffering now from what I suppose you call combat fatigue, and he is subject to fits of depression and hallucinations. Your mother and I thought that as time went by and the war and the Army receded, he would grow better. Instead, he is growing worse. Last Sunday morning when I came down into the living room from upstairs he was crouched in his old uniform, next to the window, peering out.'

'What the hell,' Olson was saying. 'If we don't get the sixty-five bucks we can always go to the Louvre. I understand the Mona Lisa is back.'

'I asked Jacob what he was doing,' the letter went on. 'He didn't turn around. "I'm observing," he said, "V-1s and V-2s. Buzz bombs and rockets. They're coming in by the hundred." I tried to reason with him and he told me to crouch and save myself from flying glass. To humor him I got down on the floor beside him and tried to tell him the war was over, that we were in Ohio, 4,000 miles away from the nearest spot where bombs had fallen, that America had never been touched. He wouldn't listen. "There's the new rocket bombs," he said, "for the Jews." '

'Did you ever hear of the Panthéon?' Olson asked loudly.

'No,' said Welch.

'It's free.'

'I'll go,' said Welch.

Seeger shook his head a little and blinked his eyes before he went back to the letter.

'After that,' his father went on, 'Jacob seemed to forget about the bombs from time to time, but he kept saying that the mobs were coming up the street armed with bazookas and Browning automatic rifles. He mumbled incoherently a good deal of the time and kept walking back and forth saying, "What's the situation? Do you know what the situation is?" And once he told me he wasn't worried about himself, he was a soldier and he expected to be killed, but he was worried about Mother and myself and Leonard and you. He seemed to forget that Leonard was dead. I tried to calm him and get him back to bed before your mother came down, but he refused and wanted to set out immediately to rejoin his division. It was all terribly disjointed, and at one time he took the ribbon he got for winning the Bronze Star and threw it in the fireplace, then he got down on his hands and knees and picked it out of the ashes and made me pin it on him again, and he kept repeating, "This is when they are coming for the Jews." '

'The next war I'm in,' said Olson, 'they don't get me under the rank of colonel.'

It had stopped raining by now, and Seeger folded the unfinished letter and went outside. He walked slowly down to the end of the company street, and, facing out across the empty, soaked French fields, scarred and neglected by various armies, he stopped and opened the letter again.

'I don't know what Jacob went through in the Army,' his father wrote, 'that has done this to him. He never talks to me about the war and he refuses to go to a psychoanalyst, and from time to time he is his own bouncing, cheerful self, playing handball in the afternoons and going around with a large group of girls. But he has devoured all the concentration-camp reports, and I found him weeping when the newspapers reported that a hundred Jews were killed in Tripoli some time ago.

'The terrible thing is, Norman, that I find myself coming to believe that it is not neurotic for a Jew to behave like this today. Perhaps Jacob is the normal one, and I, going about my business, teaching economics in a quiet classroom, pretending to understand that the world is comprehensible and orderly, am really the mad one. I ask you once more to forgive me for writing you a letter like this, so different from any letter or any conversation I've ever had with you. But it is crowding me, too. I do not see rockets and bombs, but I see other things.

'Wherever you go these days — restaurants, hotels, clubs,

trains — you seem to hear talk about the Jews, mean, hateful, murderous talk. Whatever page you turn to in the newspapers, you seem to find an article about Jews being killed somewhere on the face of the globe. And there are large, influential newspapers and well-known columnists who each day are growing more and more outspoken and more popular. The day that Roosevelt died I heard a drunken man yelling outside a bar, "Finally they got the Jew out of the White House." And some of the people who heard him merely laughed, and nobody stopped him. And on V-J Day, in celebration, hoodlums in Los Angeles savagely beat a Jewish writer. It's difficult to know what to do, whom to fight, where to look for allies.

'Three months ago, for example, I stopped my Thursday-night poker game, after playing with the same men for over ten years. John Reilly happened to say that the Jews got rich out of the war, and when I demanded an apology, he refused, and when I looked around at the faces of the men who had been my friends for so long, I could see they were not with me. And when I left the house, no one said good night to me. I know the poison was spreading from Germany before the war and during it, but I had not realized it had come so close.

'And in my economics class, I find myself idiotically hedging in my lectures. I discover that I am loath to praise any liberal writer or any liberal act, and find myself somehow annoyed and frightened to see an article of criticism of existing abuses signed by a Jewish name. And I hate to see Jewish names on important committees, and hate to read of Jews fighting for the poor, the oppressed, the cheated and hungry. Somehow, even in a country where my family has lived a hundred years, the enemy has won this subtle victory over me — he has made me disfranchise myself from honest causes by calling them foreign, Communist, using Jewish names connected with them as ammunition against them.

'Most hateful of all, I found myself looking for Jewish names in the casualty lists and secretly being glad when I saw them there, to prove that there, at least, among the dead and wounded, we belonged. Three times, thanks to you and your brothers, I found our name there, and, may God forgive me, at the expense of your blood and your brother's life, through my tears, I felt that same twitch of satisfaction.

'When I read the newspapers and see another story that Jews are still being killed in Poland, or Jews are requesting that they be given back their homes in France or that they be allowed to enter some country where they will not be murdered, I am annoyed with them. I feel that they are boring the rest of the world with their problems, that they are making demands upon the rest of the world by being killed, that they are disturbing everyone by being hungry and asking for the return of their property. If we could all fall in through the crust of the earth and vanish in one hour, with our heroes and poets and prophets and martyrs, perhaps we would be doing the memory of the Jewish race a service.

'This is how I feel today, son. I need some help. You've been to the war, you've fought and killed men, you've seen the people of other countries. Maybe you understand things that I don't understand. Maybe you see some hope somewhere. Help me. Your loving Father.'

Seeger folded the letter slowly, not seeing what he was doing, because the tears were burning his eyes. He walked slowly and aimlessly across the dead, sodden grass of the empty field, away from the camp. He tried to wipe away his tears, because, with his eyes full and dark, he kept seeing his father and brother crouched in the old-fashioned living room in Ohio, and hearing his brother, dressed in the old, discarded uniform, saying, 'These're the new rocket bombs. For the Jews.'

He sighed, looking out over the bleak, wasted land. Now, he thought, now I have to think about it. He felt a slight, unreasonable twinge of anger at his father for presenting him with the necessity of thinking about it. The Army was good about serious problems. While you were fighting, you were too busy and frightened and weary to think about anything, and at other times you were relaxing, putting your brain on a shelf, postponing everything to that impossible time of clarity and beauty after the war. Well, now, here was the impossible, clear, beautiful time, and here was his father, demanding that he think. There are all sorts of Jews, he thought: there are the sort whose every waking moment is ridden by the knowledge of Jewishness; who see signs against the Jew in every smile on a streetcar, every whisper; who see pogroms in every newspaper article, threats in every change of the weather, scorn in every handshake, death behind each closed door. He had not been like that. He was young, he was big and healthy and easygoing, and people of all kinds had liked him all his life, in the Army and out. In America, especially, what was going on in Europe had been remote, unreal, unrelated to him. The chanting, bearded old men burning in the Nazi furnaces, and the dark-eyed women screaming prayers in Polish and Russian and German as they were pushed naked into the gas chambers, had seemed as shadowy and almost as unrelated to him, as he trotted out onto the stadium field for a football game, as they must have been to the men named O'Dwyer and Wickersham and Poole who played in the line beside him.

These tortured people had seemed more related to him in Europe. Again and again, in the towns that had been taken back from the Germans, gaunt, gray-faced men had stopped him humbly, looking searchingly at him, and had asked, peering at his long, lined, grimy face under the anonymous helmet, 'Are you a Jew?' Sometimes they asked it in English, sometimes French, sometimes Yiddish. He didn't know French or Yiddish, but he learned to recognize that question. He had never understood exactly why they asked the question, since they never demanded anything of him, rarely even could speak to him. Then, one day in Strasbourg, a little, bent old man and a small, shapeless woman had stopped him and asked, in English, if he was Jewish. 'Yes,' he'd said, smiling at them. The two old people had smiled widely, like children. 'Look,' the old man had said to his wife. 'A young American soldier. A Jew. And so large and strong.' He had touched Seeger's arm reverently with the tips of his fingers, then had touched the Garand Seeger was carrying. 'And such a beautiful rifle.'

And there, for a moment, although he was not particularly sensitive, Seeger had got an inkling of why he had been stopped and questioned by so many before. Here, to these bent, exhausted old people, ravaged of their families, familiar with flight and death for so many years, was a symbol of continuing life. A large young man in the uniform of the liberator, blood, as they thought, of their blood, but not in hiding, not quivering in fear and helplessness, but striding secure and victorious down the street, armed and capable of inflicting terrible destruction on his enemies.

Seeger had kissed the old lady on the cheek and she had wept, and the old man had scolded her for it while shaking Seeger's hand fervently and thankfully before saying goodbye.

Thinking back on it, he knew that it was silly to pretend that, even before his father's letter, he had been like any other American soldier going through the war. When he had stood over the huge, dead S.S. major with his face blown in by his bullets in the warehouse in Coblenz, and taken the pistol from the dead hand, he had tasted a strange little extra flavor of triumph. How many Jews, he'd thought, has this man killed? How fitting it is that I've killed him. Neither Olson nor Welch, who were like his brothers, would have felt that in picking up the Luger, its barrel still hot from the last shots its owner had fired before dying. And he had resolved that he was going to make sure to take this gun back with him to America, and plug it and keep it on his desk at home, as a kind of vague, half-understood sign to himself that justice had once been done and he had been its instrument.

Maybe, he thought, maybe I'd better take it back with me, but not as a memento. Not plugged, but loaded. America by now was a strange country for him. He had been away a long time and he wasn't sure what was waiting for him when he got home. If the mobs were coming down the street toward his house, he was not going to die singing and praying.

When he had been taking basic training, he'd heard a scrawny, clerkish soldier from Boston talking at the other end of the PX bar, over the watered beer. 'The boys at the office,' the scratchy voice was saying, 'gave me a party before I left. And they told me one thing. "Charlie," they said, "hold onto your bayonet. We're going to be able to use it when you get back. On the Yids." '

He hadn't said anything then, because he'd felt it was neither possible nor desirable to fight against every random overheard voice raised against the Jews from one end of the world to the other. But again and again, at odd moments, lying on a barracks cot, or stretched out trying to sleep on the floor of a ruined French farmhouse, he had heard that voice, harsh, satisfied, heavy with hate and ignorance, saying above the beery grumble of apprentice soldiers at the bar, 'Hold onto your bayonet.'

And the other stories. Jews collected stories of hatred and injustice and inklings of doom like a special, lunatic kind of miser. The story of the Navy officer, commander of a small vessel off the Aleutians, who in the officers' wardroom had complained that he hated the Jews because it was the Jews who had demanded that the Germans be beaten first, and the forces in the Pacific had been starved in consequence. And when one of his junior officers, who had just come aboard, had objected and told the commander that he was a Jew, the commander had risen from the table and said, 'Mister, the Constitution of the United States says I have to serve in the same Navy with Jews, but it doesn't say I have to eat at the same table with them.' In the fogs and the cold, swelling Arctic seas off the Aleutians, in a small boat, subject to sudden, mortal attack at any moment. . . . And the million other stories. Jews, even the most normal and best adjusted, became living treasuries of them, scraps of malice and blood-thirstiness, clever and confusing and cunningly twisted so that every act by every Jew became suspect and blameworthy and hateful. Seeger had heard the stories and had made an almost conscious effort to forget them. Now, holding his father's letter in his hand, he remembered them all.

He stared unseeingly out in front of him. Maybe, he thought, maybe it would've been better to have been killed in the war, like Leonard. Simpler. Leonard would never have to face a crowd coming for his mother and father. Leonard would not have to listen and collect these hideous, fascinating little stories that made of every Jew a stranger in any town, on any field, on the face of the earth. He had come so close to being killed so many times; it would have been so easy, so neat and final. Seeger shook his head. It was ridiculous to feel like that, and he was ashamed of himself for the weak moment. At the age of twenty-one, death was not an answer.

'Seeger!' It was Olson's voice. He and Welch had sloshed silently up behind Seeger, standing in the open field. 'Seeger, *mon vieux*, what're you doing — grazing?'

Seeger turned slowly to them. 'I wanted to read my letter,' he said.

Olson looked closely at him. They had been together so long, through so many things, that flickers and hints of expression on each other's faces were recognized and acted upon. 'Anything wrong?' Olson asked.

'No,' said Seeger. 'Nothing much.'

'Norman,' Welch said, his voice young and solemn. 'Norman, we've been talking, Olson and me. We decided — you're pretty attached to that Luger, and maybe, if you — well —'

'What he's trying to say,' said Olson, 'is we withdraw the request. If you want to sell it, O.K. If you don't, don't do it for our sake. Honest.'

Seeger looked at them standing there, disreputable and tough and familiar. 'I haven't made up my mind yet,' he said.

'Anything you decide,' Welch said oratorically, 'is perfectly all right with us. Perfectly.'

The three of them walked aimlessly and silently across the field, away from camp. As they walked, their shoes making a wet, sliding sound in the damp, dead grass, Seeger thought

of the time Olson had covered him in the little town outside Cherbourg, when Seeger had been caught, going down
the side of a street, by four Germans with a machine gun in
the second story of a house on the corner and Olson had had
to stand out in the middle of the street with no cover at all
for more than a minute, firing continuously, so that Seeger
could get away alive. And he thought of the time outside
St.-Lô when he had been wounded and had lain in a minefield for three hours and Welch and Captain Taney had
come looking for him in the darkness and had found him
and picked him up and run for it, all of them expecting to
get blown up any second. And he thought of all the drinks
they'd had together, and the long marches and the cold
winter together, and all the girls they'd gone out with together, and he thought of his father and brother crouching
behind the window in Ohio waiting for the rockets and the
crowds armed with Browning automatic rifles.

'Say.' He stopped and stood facing them. 'Say, what do
you guys think of the Jews?'

Welch and Olson looked at each other, and Olson glanced
down at the letter in Seeger's hand.

'Jews?' Olson said finally. 'What're they? Welch, you ever
hear of the Jews?'

Welch looked thoughtfully at the gray sky. 'No,' he said.
'But remember, I'm an uneducated fellow.'

'Sorry, bud,' Olson said, turning to Seeger. 'We can't help
you. Ask us another question. Maybe we'll do better.'

Seeger peered at the faces of his friends. He would have to
rely upon them, later on, out of uniform, on their native
streets, more than he had ever relied on them on the bullet-
swept street and in the dark minefield in France. Welch and
Olson stared back at him, troubled, their faces candid and
tough and dependable.

'What time,' Seeger asked, 'did you tell that captain you'd
meet him?'

'Eight o'clock,' Welch said. 'But we don't have to go. If
you have any feeling about that gun — '

'We'll meet him,' Seeger said. 'We can use that sixty-five bucks.'

'Listen,' Olson said, 'I know how much you like that gun, and I'll feel like a heel if you sell it.'

'Forget it,' Seeger said, starting to walk again. 'What could I use it for in America?'

*(From Harper's Magazine)*

# THE RED DRESS

## BY SYLVIA SHIRLEY

*Y*OU will see how everything happens for the best, the moment I have explained it. My sisters and I had already established ourselves in America, our married brother having sent for us seventeen years ago. Papa was to have come, too, but while we waited in Constantinople for our papers he fell in love with an Armenian-Turk, or perhaps the other way around. There are strange people in Constantinople. He married her, leaving us to go on alone. That is a father for you. I ask you, would a mother do like that? Still, men will be men; the less said the better.

Ariana was the eldest, an old maid even then, that is to say: she was too clever, too critical, and she had our Papa's nose. Then there was I, who am Luba, and if I have to say so myself, very attractive. I kept house while Ariana worked and Sophie went to school. Sophie, of course, was the youngest, but not too sensible, if a little prettier than I.

When Papa died, and then his wife, their daughter Manya (already sixteen years old) wrote that she had been left quite independent and would never leave Constantinople, because it was the most beautiful place in the world. That wasn't how we remembered it, but maybe it's different now. Of course, the men were very handsome and appreciative. You cannot say less than that. Even the water vendor with his lousy beard used to kiss his fingers to us and say, which I translate for you to mean, 'Ach, beautiful Russian girls! Like sweet cream,' and smack his lips.

401

Manya wrote that she scrubbed floors by day and walked in the bazaar in the evening and that she was quite happy and would we please send her a red dress, not that she needed anything, but after all we were related by blood.

We saw red, as it is said here. But if Papa's flesh could not be denied, neither could we deny his blood and she was after all a sister to us, even if her mother was a foreigner.

Of course, we did not believe all of the letter. The part about scrubbing floors seemed a little far-fetched, nor were we much mistaken, as it soon became clear. However, we pooled our resources, that is to say: Ariana and Sophie did, because they were working and I was little mother, so to speak. But it was not enough. So we went to our married brother and enlisted his assistance, if a little grudging, and sent for Manya, which may have been what she intended we should do.

She hobbled off the boat to us in a long black gown and high-heeled slippers, a tired-looking woman-of-the-world creature. Her eyes were long and heavy-lidded. She looked at each of us fully, just once, and said, 'What ugly place. Take me at once to hotel.'

Our brother began to mutter, but Ariana said, 'Silence! You are a father yourself.' And Sophie, who is not too smart, said we better take taxi home. Cabs were a little extravagant for us, but this was an occasion, if a little bewildering. Also, people were staring, so my brother said all right he would pay. But you could see he wished Papa had had sons instead of maiden daughters.

We were not growing younger, after all, and probably our brother was afraid that now he would become involved with us more than ever. Though we all adored him, he had an American wife and it was a strain. So we did not go often to his house. We are vivacious with much laughter and some-times tears, and she serves tea with milk. She came once to us and I am marvelous cook, though I do not like to say so often, and she fished out the small pieces of onion in her plate, one course after another.

Well, Manya was left to my charge. I scalded her

thoroughly because she looked as if she did not care too much for bathing, and I was surprised to find that her eyelashes were not false or mascara. Her hands were not work-worn, her appetite was good, even too much; which is always gratifying to the one who cooks as is indication of good health.

She never spoke of what had been in Constantinople and we were much mystified and disappointed. Once I took courage and asked her questions; gently, you understand, not prying, just curious; but without satisfaction. Manya lowered the lids of her long sleepy eyes and said nothing, only a brief sigh, so that I felt quite uneasy.

It soon became apparent that our little sister was not scholarly. She was out of her element in the public school, and we despaired of finding a place to suit her temperament. But Sophie came up with a startling contribution. 'Send her to private school.' This we decided, and though we had not much money, we did not approach our brother this time.

After many inquiries, we finally registered our little sister with a very refined lady who reminded us a little of our brother's wife, that is to say: her smile was too thin. We left Manya in her care with some misgivings and much relief.

I spoke with earnestness to her that night and cautioned her to be good. Our income came to us from Ariana, who knelt all day at the feet of rich ladies to pick up hems, let out seams, or take in darts to conceal the defects in their figures; and from Sophie, whose quick fingers made the alterations indicated by the pins.

Each gown sold for more than twice their joint salaries, but we were not bitter. I was the housekeeper and thrifty, to make the most of their efforts. They appreciated me, and I tried to indicate to Manya her duty to her good sisters.

Manya was silent, but I was used to that and hoped that somehow she had been impressed. She was not really bad-hearted, only a little self-absorbed and somewhat lazy, with a good deal of prodding necessary.

For a while things moved like wheels on greased axles. Then one day there was a letter from the school principal:

would I please come and have a little talk. I was flattered
and felt almost what it must be to be a real mother.

So I dressed in my wine-colored silk, which was brought
me from the shop, and which by good fortune had been
scorched by the presser, but cleverly concealed by my sisters;
because, as you see, I have such a small waist and it is easily
taken in.

Sophie loaned me her hat with the Paris label snipped
from one of the chapeaux in the shop and I felt in fine
feather. No one can see what is inside your hat, but it does
make a difference in how you hold your head.

What is my despair when Miss Pringle, who has so cheer-
less a face it strikes a chill, said to me, 'You must do something about your sister. She has a very disrupting influence
on the others.'

In vain I explained that it is due to her heavy-lidded eyes
that Manya looks as though she has just wakened or is about
to drop off. I would not admit, aloud, that no matter how
neatly we clothed her, she had always that look of untidiness.
Then there was the matter of talking — only with her hands.

'But,' I explained, gesticulating, so that this stiff-boned
woman should understand, 'we *are* like that. It is more ex-
pressive when you make so with your hands. The meaning
of the words is better.'

No. Miss Pringle objected. So, all right, it is not refine-
ment. I will remind Manya, I promised. Alas, there were
other things, and with much hesitation Miss Pringle explained. When I finally emerged from her office, in spite of
the borrowed hat and its borrowed label, I felt much older
than it was my custom to look.

'Manya,' I said that night, 'today I have talked with Miss
Pringle. Darling, you must not whistle and make with your
hands when you want more bread with your lunch.'

Manya shrugged. 'She does not like when I stretch for it.'

'You can ask for it, no?'

'Then one would be all the time talking instead of eating.
Everything is put out of reach.'

'Miss Pringle says now all the girls whistle when they want
something. You must not be a bad influence.'

'Okay. I bring bread from home, is better?'

'Manytchka, do not joke.'

'Who jokes? One is hungry, one eats.'

'True. But do not wave your arms about.'

'Aha! Again is not right. Whatever Manya does is bad. Please God, the Devil take me soon, and you will grieve.'

'Manya! Shocking talk.' We were getting nowhere. 'You must not ask the other girls if they are virgins.'

'Why not?'

'It is assumed that unmarried girls are always virgins, besides, it is an intimate question.' I hesitated and said as an experiment, 'You would not like it if one were to ask you such a question.'

She looked at me, her eyes sliding to the corners like slippery fish, and then she closed them, so that the back of my neck was like an ant hill.

'People judge you by your behavior. You must learn to have good manners,' I said firmly, though at the moment it would have given me pleasure to cut her head from her shoulders.

'Why?' asked Manya, scratching her head.

'Because when you are courteous it pleases other people.'

'Ha! That is weakness, to want always to please others. You please yourself first, then you are happy. You are happy; you give pleasure.'

I had never heard so much talk from her before; nor could I feel altogether displeased, because there was merit in what she said. But I had promised Miss Pringle to speak to Manya, and if I could do nothing more, neither would I do less.

Soon we had a letter regretting that the enrollment for the following year was already filled. We understood what was meant. Maybe it would have been wiser to have sent the red dress to Constantinople in the first place.

'Well, we cannot take her to work with us,' my sisters said and looked at me. All right, she would stay at home.

This suited Manya very well. She slept late and trailed around in her kimono, sampling all the foods before they were fully cooked. If I gave her anything to do, invariably she did it so badly or so slowly that I took it away. It was no use to be irate with Manya, because you could not arouse her to anger or shame, neither was she ever really unpleasant or sullen. Under the circumstances, however, one could be excused for wishing that she had not been born.

Wherever Manya went, people, that is to say men, leered. Sometimes they followed her home. We could not let her go about alone. You understand, there was no real harm in her. She just had that look.

'There's only one thing left,' said Sophie, when I poured out my grief. 'We must get her a good husband.' Ariana and I looked at her, without reminding her that she had not been too successful on her own account.

'That's easier said than done,' said our eldest sister, sighing.

'It can be arranged. Sometimes it is even advertised. People are marrying all the time.'

I was horrified but interested. 'You mean to put it in the papers that we are seeking for our eighteen-year-old sister a husband?'

'If you put it that way,' said Ariana, 'we will have to offer a dowry.'

'Maybe we'd be better off letting her try by herself,' Sophie said thoughtfully. I shuddered.

'How would you like a sweetheart?' Ariana asked Manya. 'Someone to quarrel with and to kiss.'

'Someone to pay your way to the movies and hold your hand,' I added, falling in with them.

'Someone to buy you sweets,' said Sophie, insinuatingly.

Manya smiled and smiled, her prune-eyes narrowing all the while. 'Is all right,' she said, and wiped her nose mercilessly.

About this time, Ariana had pains of such cruelty in her legs that I prevailed upon her to see the doctor. It was Ariana's opinion that so many years of working on her knees had warped her bones. But the doctor said go pull teeth. Now that is a strangeness we have here, and probably why there is a need for so many dentists. As soon as one's arm aches, or one's legs, right away is the remedy, go pull teeth. But Ariana has so little patience with illness or stupidity, whether it be her own or somebody else's, that we went to seek a dentist.

Mrs. Bilbadian, who is our neighbor, recommended her relation, the dentist on our corner. And it was decided that since so many teeth would have to be repaired it would be less expensive to remove all and be fitted for new ones.

Ariana and I were impressed with the dentist, who, we subsequently discovered, lived with an old mother who was anxious to see him married before she died. He was a tremendous man, tall and rounded, with a vocabulary limited to 'Open please, wider please, spit out,' and 'Rinse please.'

I agreed with Ariana that maybe Dr. Ratzhaus would be a good thing for Manya. We wished to marry off our little sister with the least compunctions. Fat men should not be too hard to please, I reasoned, providing you can cook. Perhaps I could teach Manya something of housewifery, or I might sneak over a roast and pastry from time to time.

With much cajoling, it was finally arranged that Mrs. Bilbadian give a party, though I did not trust her too much; that is to say: she substituted water where my recipes called for sour cream.

You cannot be too sure of a woman who falsifies to her own stomach, and so I provided the refreshments. The dentist and his mother were invited.

Except when he ate, Dr. Ratzhaus did not open his mouth. Several times he got up to make his mother comfortable, while she kept up an interminable chatter about what a good wife should be.

There was no way to stretch such a frame around Manya. If she was not selfless nor persevering, neither would she martyr herself. We had to hope, therefore, that the dentist would be blinded by Manya's physical charm as others, less worthy of acceptance, had been before him.

Finally, the old lady said to her son, 'Ask her to go for a walk. She is a little too forward, to be sure, but not objectionable.'

Manya jumped up at once. 'Is beautiful tonight. The moon is shining.' But the dentist sat mute, shaking his enormous head.

'What is it?' asked his mother. The dentist stiffened himself as if for a tussle with an enemy. He lifted one huge hand and straightened a heavy finger. He pointed.

'I want that one,' and then his courage collapsed, for he bent his head into his chest. We stared.

Then Manya burst out laughing, and when she laughs, it is something to hear. 'See how red she is,' she howled, pointing to Sophie. And she was right.

Sophie had misgivings, but Ariana talked her out of them; that is to say: one cannot get a respectable proposal from a dentist every day, mothers-in-law do not live forever, and so on. That is how Sophie got married. Ariana said it was a pity it could not have been arranged sooner, because of the outrageous sum we had to pay for her new teeth. I thought Sophie might intercede and get a reduction on her sister's behalf, but it is a mistake to expect much from relatives.

Well, there was still Manya. In the excitement of Sophie's marriage we overlooked her a little, forgetting to keep a careful watch over her arrivals and departures. It soon became apparent that every time she came into the house, she brought another of God's creatures, some of them not altogether human in appearance. She was willing to like anyone, regardless of size, age, hair or lack of same, being rather amiable, but a complete simpleton about men. Manya had that look, you see, only it meant nothing.

One autumn we went to a charity picnic-bazaar, that is to say: one paid for a ticket in the first place and then, if one wanted to eat, one bought from the food vendors at the laden tables. Also there were books, and shawls, and trinkets — all trash — to buy. There was a man who tooted on a horn and another set the pace on an accordion. Also there was a woman to sing, who might just as well have been male, too, with her flat chest and deep voice. It was a beautiful day, crisp and smelling of sun-browned leaves.

'What charming odors,' said Manya, sniffing with a terrifying loudness. At hand a woman was ladling stew into a brown bowl. 'Look, goulash, what I love,' Manya pointed.

'Not now,' said Ariana, tightening her hold on her purse.

'Permit me,' said a hesitant voice behind us; and there was a little man, whose upper teeth overlapped a little. He had a startled look, as though he were surprised at his own daring, and I liked him right away.

He looked at us, one-two-three, and then again, and before we spoke he ordered four bowls, handing them to us in turn. We thanked him. When he saw how Ariana stared, he tried to close his mouth over his teeth. His chin puckered from the strain, and he blushed.

He led us to a table, put his bowl down, brushed some ants away, and ran off for some hot rolls.

When he came back, he sat down quickly, straightening his sleeves, and smiled at us. Manya dipped her bread into the gravy and filled her mouth. She was blissful.

'Please be my guests,' he said. 'I don't know anybody here. I live in New Jersey and read in the Hungarian paper about the picnic. One gets hungry for the sound of the mother-tongue.'

'We are not Hungarians,' said Ariana, with hauteur.

'Yoy,' said the little man and he looked at us, one-two-three. There are those who are always surprised to find that there are human beings in other nationalities.

'They don't like Hungarians,' said Manya, sucking the drippings off her fingers. 'Is nothing personal, is only themselves they admire.' Her voice was earnest and good-humored, and we did not think to take offense. 'What else is to eat?' she asked looking around.

'I'll show you,' said the little man, jumping up.

'Wait,' said Ariana. 'We are not acquainted.'

'She means, do you need a wife and is there money in bank,' Manya said kindly, as if to translate us to him.

'Well, I'm not married,' he answered carefully, 'and I have good business. I am cabinet maker, specialist in ice-chests. My father was coffin-maker in old country. My grandfather. . . .'

'What is your name?' interrupted Ariana, and I guessed she was sufficiently impressed.

His name was Milo Niemcy and we let Manya walk with him. We followed, but discreetly. They bought meat and green peppers roasted on skewers, and there was something new in the look on Manya's face as she watched at the open fire. It was my opinion that the scene called up something of her life in Constantinople, of which she had never spoken. But Ariana raised her eyebrows at me and pulled her lips in. I must learn not to tell everything I think to Ariana. It is disheartening to be always pooh-poohed.

Later, we saw Mr. Niemcy offering Manya his handkerchief. And suddenly I wanted to cry. I was just beginning to realize that from now on life would be different, that is to say: if Manya married, I would have to live alone with Ariana, who was daily more cranky. Do not misunderstand. I love her very dearly, but she is a little wearing.

When it was time to leave the picnic grounds, Mr. Niemcy brought our Manya to us.

'I hope you have not been too extravagant,' I said. 'Mr. Niemcy will think you are a spendthrift.' But he laughed and so did Manya.

'It's all in the echo-nomics of it,' he explained. 'She spends so much only because it is not her own.' He turned to her, as though they had settled it between them, 'When it will be yours, you'll take better care, no?'

Ariana and I exchanged looks. But Manya said, 'Will it be mine? When will it? I like something of my own, once.' She was almost wistful and I was heartily ashamed of her. He could think we had starved her, or sent her naked abroad.

He brought us all home in his little car, an unlooked-for treat. After that, he came every Sunday for three months. I tried hard to see Manya through his eyes. He was such a nice man I wondered if it was quite fair to him to let him have Manya. But to him she seemed as rich as the dark and fruitful earth of Hungary, and at the same time, exotic and simple, glamorous and naïve.

Everything went well and they were married at Christmas. Before they were to leave, however, Manya had hysterics. She cried and cried. She would not leave us, how could she go away to live with this strange man who was nothing to her, not even a relative. We coaxed and petted, and finally threatened, till she wiped her eyes and nose on the chintz skirt of the dressing table, kissed us all several times, and left.

A year and a half went by and we did not see her again. Ariana said leave well enough alone, and I did not like to ask her for the fare. You may not believe this, but I missed Manya sorely. When she wrote once or twice, the paper was so messy with ink and grease stains, it was impossible to decipher. Ariana was ill a great deal of the time and worried what would become of us if she would lose her job. Nothing I did or said pleased her. With us it was like with the dog who kept biting the end of his own tail.

Then, one summer, the establishment for which Ariana worked closed for alterations. Because she was the oldest employee, she was granted a month's pay and vacation expenses. For two vacations there was not enough money. Although Ariana offered to go to a cheap hotel, so that we could be together, I denied myself this pleasure. It was decided at last that I would travel up with her and spend the first weekend there and come back for her the last weekend.

I took the local train home and sat back to enjoy myself. For me it was an adventure. My thoughts turned to Manya, as they often did, because I could not help but speculate on how it was with her. One thought leading to another, I recalled the day at the picnic and how Manya had cried out, 'When will it be my time to have something of my own?' And I wondered pleasantly if that time ever came to anyone, and if it were ever to come to me, what was it I would like. And it seemed that this was it — just to sit quietly and watch the farm-land and the towns drift by. Perhaps I dozed. Suddenly, I heard the conductor call 'Stockwoode, next.' Stockwoode! That was where Manya and Milo lived. We had not stopped on the way up because it had been express. I would go see them. I grasped my reticule tightly and reached for my little bag; and there I was, standing on the platform.

Without too much inquiry, I found their house, stopping first at a confectioner's. It was neat and ugly like all the rest, painted tan with brown trimmings. When I opened the gate my heart began to drum so loudly and so quickly that I had to stand still, breathing deeply for some minutes. My heart does that often lately and I must remember to ask about it some time.

It was Manya who answered my knock, and she stared at me for a long time. 'Manytchka,' I said, 'you are just like always.' But it was not so. She was much thinner and seemed taller. Her heavy hair was brushed back into a roll, and her red dress was clean and pressed — only the top button was missing at the throat, and another was hanging by a thread.

'Lubitchka,' she said. Nobody had said my name like that since I was little. 'So it is you at last! Come your way in. You look so tired.' Her voice seemed charming to me as she took my hand and led me inside. 'Have you come all by yourself?'

'Yes,' and then we laughed together.

'I have brought sweets,' I said, as she took me into her living-room. It was clean and comfortable, and disappointing. There was a piano. The curtains were plain, with many pictures on the walls; but no rugs, only linoleums.

'Where is your husband?' I asked, as she undid my parcel and laid the cakes on a plate.

'Sunday is his day of reckoning,' she answered.

I was startled. 'How do you mean?'

'He sits in his shop at the end of the garden and reckons his receipts and bills for the week. Then he gives me the little papers. Is a great deal of money.'

'That is good. Money is excellent to have,' I said. She put the kettle on and broke a cake in two, giving me the larger piece. Manya is different.

'True. Always he talks about how much there is, and how much more there would be if we do not have to pay taxes.'

'What do you do with it all?'

'Spend only for what is necessary, pay taxes, and keep the rest in bank. Some is in my name.' She smiled at me in the old way, just as she used to when I set food before her.

'You are happy?' I asked her.

'Sure, look. Whole house is mine.' She led me through the tidy, barren rooms, one after another, and then into the basement to show off her washing-machine. Outside, behind the lumber shack, there was a chicken yard, and on the other side, the garden.

When we came back into the house, Milo was already there, and I could see he wondered what brought me.

Supper was a casserole of macaroni and vegetables with bits of meat. Also good warm cabbage soup. I asked if I might have a single boiled egg, my digestion is not what it used to be, and Manya brought in a half-dozen. 'From our own chickens. For you I give the heaviest.'

When I took sugar for tea, they watched me so closely, my hand trembled so that I took less than intended. Then Manya said, 'Is good to see you in my house, no Milo?' And I was glad to be there, only strange.

Afterwards, Milo showed me his shop. It was very neat with a good raw smell of wood. Over his desk hung a picture of a half-draped female. I was petrified. What kind of a portrait was this for a man's workshop?

'I have more,' he said proudly, following my gaze, and before I could stop him, he had hauled out a bunch of picture cards.

'This is too much. What for do you need these when you have our Manya?' I asked.

He bent over the pictures and with great care began to erase some thumbmarks. 'Yoy,' he sighed. 'You don't know Manya. She is a good wife and has learned the value of a dollar. But she, how shall I say? I tell you because you are her sister: Manya is not what she seems. She is sparing of everything.' He sighed again and put away his pictures.

I stared at him. What was this? 'You must be patient,' I said. 'She is very young.'

'Perhaps,' he said. But he did not seem convinced.

They did not press me to stay and although I felt that they had been pleased to see me, they seemed just as pleased to see me go. When I got on the train, bound for home the second time in one day, Manya gave me her shawl. I had no need of it, but I was strongly moved by this gesture, because I had never known her to give of herself before, in any shape or manner. Of course, the fortunes of Manya and Milo would not suffer by this gift since it was so faded and, as to be expected, badly mended. Quickly, I folded it out of sight, feeling tired and lonely and a little like the day I walked out of Miss Pringle's Day School for Girls, years ago. But I was glad that we had been unstinting in our efforts for Manya. She looked happy. But then she always had that look. As for Milo, what can you expect from a man?

It was not in me to begrudge Manya the fruits of our labor, but something was unequal here. Often there arises a predicament, even a catastrophe, and there is an axiom to prove its value. But here was strangeness, a proverb in reverse: the ten-o'clock scholar catches the worm. While we had persevered, Manya had strained neither brain nor back. Yet she had maneuvered to please herself, above all, in spite of our efforts to teach her to think of others first. Now she had a whole house to play with, money, and even a husband to manage!

I resolved not to speak of this to anyone, but the old habit of talking things over was strong. So next day, I went to visit with Sophie, the dentist's wife. While watching her bathe the fat little twins, I told her what I had learned about Manya and asked her what she thought, for I was a little confused and not at ease.

But Sophie, perhaps because she was not listening too carefully, and perhaps because she never was too sensible, handed me one slippery baby to wrap in a towel and said, 'Poor Milo, how was he to know that all that Manya ever wanted was a red dress?'

I did not understand what she was talking about at first,

but later, a little. And I would hesitate to say this to Ariana, nor do I like to set myself up as a philosopher; but the longer I live, the less certain I am that I understand men; and some women are peculiar, too. And you can see for yourself, how everything has a proper purpose and similar result, only one must shape it a little, as Manya had, without seeming to.

*(From Partisan Review)*

# THE INTERIOR CASTLE

## BY JEAN STAFFORD

*P*ANSY VANNEMAN, injured in an automobile accident, often woke up before dawn when the night noises of the hospital still came, in hushed hurry, through her half-open door. By day, when the nurses talked audibly with the internes, laughed without inhibition, and took no pains to soften their footsteps on the resounding composition floors, the routine of the hospital seemed as bland and commonplace as that of a bank or a factory. But in the dark hours, the whispering and the quickly stilled clatter of glasses and basins, the moans of patients whose morphine was wearing off, the soft squeak of a stretcher as it rolled past in its way from the emergency ward — these suggested agony and death. Thus, on the first morning, Pansy had faltered to consciousness long before daylight and had found herself in a ward from every bed of which, it seemed to her, came the bewildered protest of someone about to die. A caged light burned on the floor beside the bed next to hers. Her neighbor was dying and a priest was administering Extreme Unction. He was stout and elderly and he suffered from asthma so that the struggle of his breathing, so close to her, was the basic pattern and all the other sounds were superimposed upon it. Two middle-aged men in overcoats knelt on the floor beside the high bed. In a foreign tongue, the half-gone woman babbled against the hissing and sighing of the Latin prayers. She played with her rosary as if it were a toy: she tried, and failed, to put it into her mouth.

Pansy felt horror, but she felt no pity. An hour or so later, when the white ceiling lights were turned on and everything — faces, counterpanes, and the hands that groped upon them — was transformed into a uniform gray sordor, the woman was wheeled away in her bed to die somewhere else, in privacy. Pansy did not quite take this in, although she stared for a long time at the new, empty bed that had replaced the other.

The next morning, when she again woke up before the light, this time in a private room, she recalled the woman with such sorrow that she might have been a friend. Simultaneously, she mourned the driver of the taxicab in which she had been injured, for he had died at about noon the day before. She had been told this as she lay on a stretcher in the corridor, waiting to be taken to the x-ray room; an interne, passing by, had paused and smiled down at her and had said, 'Your cab-driver is dead. You were lucky.'

Six weeks after the accident, she woke one morning just as daylight was showing on the windows as a murky smear. It was a minute or two before she realized why she was so reluctant to be awake, why her uneasiness amounted almost to alarm. Then she remembered that her nose was to be operated on today. She lay straight and motionless under the seersucker counterpane. Her blood-red eyes in her darned face stared through the window and saw a frozen river and leafless elm trees and a grizzled esplanade where dogs danced on the ends of leashes, their bundled-up owners stumbling after them, half blind with sleepiness and cold. Warm as the hospital room was, it did not prevent Pansy from knowing, as keenly as though she were one of the walkers, how very cold it was outside. Each twig of a nearby tree was stark. Cold red brick buildings nudged the low-lying sky which was pale and inert like a punctured sac.

In six weeks, the scene had varied little: there was promise in the skies neither of sun nor of snow; no red sunsets marked these days. The trees could neither die nor leaf out again. Pansy could not remember another season in her life so constant, when the very minutes themselves were suffused with the winter pallor as they dropped from the moon-faced clock in the corridor. Likewise, her room accomplished no alterations from day to day. On the glass-topped bureau stood two potted plants telegraphed by faraway well-wishers. They did not fade, and if a leaf turned brown and fell, it soon was replaced; so did the blossoms renew themselves. The roots, like the skies and like the bare trees, seemed zealously determined to maintain a status quo. The bedside table, covered every day with a clean white towel, though the one removed was always immaculate, was furnished sparsely with a water glass, a bent drinking tube, a sweating pitcher, and a stack of paper handkerchiefs. There were a few letters in the drawer, a hairbrush, a pencil, and some postal cards on which, from time to time, she wrote brief messages to relatives and friends: 'Dr. Nash says that my reflexes are shipshape *(sic)* and Dr. Rivers says the frontal fracture has all but healed and that the occipital is coming along nicely. Dr. Nicholas, the nose doctor, promises to operate as soon as Dr. Rivers gives him the go-ahead sign *(sic)*.'

The bed itself was never rumpled. Once fretful and now convalescent, Miss Vanneman might have been expected to toss or to turn the pillows or to unmoor the counterpane; but hour after hour and day after day she lay at full length and would not even suffer the nurses to raise the head-piece of the adjustable bed. So perfect and stubborn was her body's immobility that it was as if the room and the landscape, mortified by the ice, were extensions of herself. Her resolute quiescence and her disinclination to talk, the one seeming somehow to proceed from the other, resembled, so the nurses said, a final coma. And they observed, in pitying indignation, that she might as *well* be dead for all the interest she took in life. Amongst themselves they scolded her for what they thought a moral weakness: an automobile accident, no matter how serious, was not reason enough for anyone to give up the will to live or to be happy. She had not — to come down bluntly to the facts — had the decency to be grateful that it was the driver of the cab and not she who had died. (And how dreadfully the man had died!) She was twenty-five years

old and she came from a distant city. These were really the
only facts known about her. Evidently she had not been
here long, for she had no visitors, a lack which was at first
sadly moving to the nurses but which became to them a
source of unreasonable annoyance: had anyone the right to
live so one-dimensionally? It was impossible to laugh at her,
for she said nothing absurd; her demands could not be complained of because they did not exist; she could not be hated
for a sharp tongue nor for a supercilious one; she could not
be admired for bravery or for wit or for interest in her fellow
creatures. She was believed to be a frightful snob.

Pansy, for her part, took a secret and mischievous pleasure
in the bewilderment of her attendants and the more they
courted her with offers of magazines, cross-word puzzles, and
a radio which she could rent from the hospital, the farther
she retired from them into herself and into the world which
she had created in her long hours here and which no one
could ever penetrate nor imagine. Sometimes she did not
even answer the nurses' questions; as they rubbed her back
with alcohol and steadily discoursed, she was as remote from
them as if she were miles away. She did not think that she
lived on a higher plane than that of the nurses and the
doctors but that she lived on a different one and that at this
particular time — this time of exploration and habituation —
she had no extra strength to spend on making herself known
to them. All she had been before and all the memories she
might have brought out to disturb the monotony of, say, the
morning bath, and all that the past meant to the future when
she would leave the hospital, were of no present consequence
to her. Not even in her thoughts did she employ more than
a minimum of memory. And when she did remember, it
was in flat pictures, rigorously independent of one another:
she saw her thin, poetic mother who grew thinner and more
poetic in her canvas deck-chair at Saranac reading *Lalla
Rookh*. She saw herself in an inappropriate pink hat drinking iced tea in a garden so oppressive with the smell of phlox
that the tea itself tasted of it. She recalled an afternoon in
autumn in Vermont when she had heard three dogs' voices

in the north woods and she could tell, by the characteristic minor key struck three times at intervals, like bells from several churches, that they had treed something: the eastern sky was pink and the trees on the horizon looked like some eccentric vascular system meticulously drawn on colored paper.

What Pansy thought of all the time was her own brain. Not only the brain as the seat of consciousness, but the physical organ itself which she envisaged, romantically, now as a jewel, now as a flower, now as a light in a glass, now as an envelope of rosy vellum containing other envelopes, one within the other, diminishing infinitely. It was always pink and always fragile, always deeply interior and invaluable. She believed that she had reached the innermost chamber of knowledge and that perhaps her knowledge was the same as the saint's achievement of pure love. It was only convention, she thought, that made one say 'sacred heart' and not 'sacred brain.'

Often, but never articulately, the color pink troubled her and the picture of herself in the wrong hat hung steadfastly before her mind's eye. None of the other girls had worn hats and since autumn had come early that year, they were dressed in green and rusty brown and dark yellow. Poor Pansy wore a white eyelet frock with a lacing of black ribbon around the square neck. When she came through the arch, overhung with bittersweet, and saw that they had not yet heard her, she almost turned back, but Mr. Oliver was there and she was in love with him. She was in love with him though he was ten years older than she and had never shown any interest in her beyond asking her once, quite fatuously but in an intimate voice, if the yodeling of the little boy who peddled clams did not make her wish to visit Switzerland. Actually, there was more to this question than met the eye, for some days later Pansy learned that Mr. Oliver, who was immensely rich, kept an apartment in Geneva. In the garden that day, he spoke to her only once. He said, 'My dear, you look exactly like something out of Katherine Mansfield,' and immediately turned and within her hearing asked Beatrice

Sherburne to dine with him that night at the Country Club. Afterward, Pansy went down to the sea and threw the beautiful hat onto the full tide and saw it vanish in the wake of a trawler. Thereafter, when she heard the clam boy coming down the road, she locked the door and when the knocking had stopped and her mother called down from her chaise longue, 'Who was it, dearie?' she replied, 'A salesman.'

It was only the fact that the hat had been pink that worried her. The rest of the memory was trivial, for she knew that she could never again love anything as ecstatically as she loved the spirit of Pansy Vanneman, enclosed within her head.

But her study was not without distraction, and she fought two adversaries: pain and Dr. Nicholas. Against Dr. Nicholas, she defended herself valorously and in fear; but pain, the pain, that is, that was independent of his instruments, she sometimes forced upon herself adventurously like a child scaring himself in a graveyard.

Dr. Nicholas greatly admired her crushed and splintered nose which he daily probed and peered at, exclaiming that he had never seen anything like it. His shapely hands ached for their knives; he was impatient with the skull-fracture man's cautious delay. He spoke of 'our' nose and said 'we' would be a new person when we could breathe again. His own nose, the trademark of his profession, was magnificent. Not even his own brilliant surgery could have improved upon it nor could a first-rate sculptor have duplicated its direct downward line which permitted only the least curvature inward toward the end; nor the delicately rounded lateral declivities; nor the thin-walled, perfectly matched nostrils. Miss Vanneman did not doubt his humaneness nor his talent — he was a celebrated man — but she questioned whether he had imagination. Immediately beyond the prongs of his speculum lay her treasure whose price he, no more than the nurses, could estimate. She believed he could not destroy it, but she feared that he might maim it: might leave a scratch on one of the brilliant facets of the jewel, bruise a petal of the flower, smudge the glass where the light burned, blot the envelopes, and that then she would die or would go mad. While she did not question that in either eventuality her brain would after a time redeem its original impeccability, she did not quite yet wish to enter upon either kind of eternity, for she was not certain that she could carry with her her knowledge as well as its receptacle.

Blunderer that he was, Dr. Nicholas was an honorable enemy, not like the demon, pain, which skulked in a thousand guises within her head, and which often she recklessly willed to attack her and then drove back in terror. After the rout, sweat streamed from her face and soaked the neck of the coarse hospital shirt. To be sure, it came usually of its own accord, running like a wild fire through all the convolutions to fill with flame the small sockets and ravines and then, at last, to withdraw, leaving behind a throbbing and an echo. On these occasions, she was as helpless as a tree in a wind. But at the other times when, by closing her eyes and rolling up the eyeballs in such a way that she fancied she looked directly on the place where her brain was, the pain woke sluggishly and came toward her at a snail's pace. Then, bit by bit, it gained speed. Sometimes it faltered back, subsided altogether, and then it rushed like a tidal wave driven by a hurricane, lashing and roaring until she lifted her hands from the counterpane, crushed her broken teeth into her swollen lip, stared in panic at the soothing walls with her ruby eyes, stretched out her legs until she felt their bones must snap. Each cove, each narrow inlet, every living bay was flooded and the frail brain, a little hat-shaped boat, was washed from its mooring and set adrift. The skull was as vast as the world and the brain was as small as a seashell.

Then came calm weather and the safe journey home. She kept vigil for a while, though, and did not close her eyes, but gazing pacifically at the trees, conceived of the pain as the guardian of her treasure who would not let her see it; that was why she was handled so savagely whenever she turned her eyes inward. Once this watch was interrupted: by chance she looked into the corridor and saw a shaggy mop slink past the door, followed by a senile porter. A pair of ancient eyes, as rheumy as an old dog's, stared uncritically in at her and the toothless mouth formed a brutish word. She was so surprised that she immediately closed her eyes to shut out the shape of the word and the pain dug up the unmapped regions of her head with mattocks, ludicrously huge. It was the familiar pain, but this time, even as she endured it, she observed with detachment that its effect upon her was less than that of its contents, the by-products, for example, of temporal confusion and the bizarre misapplication of the style of one sensation to another. At the moment, for example, although her brain reiterated to her that *it* was being assailed, she was stroking her right wrist with her left hand as though to assuage the ache, long since dispelled, of the sprain in the joint. Some minutes after she had opened her eyes and left off soothing her wrist, she lay rigid experiencing the sequel to the pain, an ideal terror. For, as before on several occasions, she was overwhelmed with the knowledge that the pain had been consummated in the vessel of her mind and for the moment the vessel was unbeautiful: she thought, quailing, of those plastic folds as palpable as the fingers of locked hands containing in their very cells, their fissures, their repulsive hemispheres, the mind, the soul, the inscrutable intelligence.

The porter, then, like the pink hat and like her mother and the hounds' voices, loitered with her.

Dr. Nicholas came at nine o'clock to prepare her for the operation. With him came an entourage of white-frocked acolytes, and one of them wheeled in a wagon on which lay knives and scissors and pincers, cans of swabs and gauze. In the midst of these was a bowl of liquid whose rich purple color made it seem strange like the brew of an alchemist.

'All set?' he asked her, smiling. 'A little nervous, what? I don't blame you. I've often said I'd rather lose an arm than have a submucuous resection.' Pansy thought for a moment he was going to touch his nose. His approach to her was roundabout. He moved through the yellow light shed by the globe in the ceiling which gave his forehead a liquid gloss; he paused by the bureau and touched a blossom of the cyclamen; he looked out the window and said, to no one and to all, 'I couldn't start my car this morning. Came in a cab.' Then he came forward. As he came, he removed a speculum from the pocket of his short-sleeved coat and like a cat, inquiring of the nature of a surface with its paws, he put out his hand toward her and drew it back, gently murmuring, 'You must not be afraid, my dear. There is no danger, you know. Do you think for a minute I would operate if there were?'

Dr. Nicholas, young, brilliant, and handsome, was an aristocrat, a husband, a father, a clubman, a Christian, a kind counselor, and a trustee of his school alumni association. Like many of the medical profession, even those whose speciality was centered on the organ of the basest sense, he interested himself in the psychology of his patients: in several instances, for example, he had found that severe attacks of sinusitis were coincident with emotional crises. Miss Vanneman more than ordinarily captured his fancy since her skull had been fractured and her behavior throughout had been so extraordinary that he felt he was observing at first hand some of the results of shock, that incommensurable element, which frequently were too subtle to see. There was, for example, the matter of her complete passivity during a lumbar puncture, reports of which were written down in her history and were enlarged upon for him by Dr. Rivers' interne who had been in charge. Except for a tremor in her throat and a deepening of pallor, there were no signs at all that she was aware of what was happening to her. She made no sound, did not close her eyes nor clench her fists. She had had several punctures; her only reaction had been to the very first one, the morning after she had been brought in. When the interne explained to her that he was going to drain off cerebrospinal fluid which was pressing against her brain, she exclaimed, 'My God!' but it was not an exclamation of fear. The young man had been unable to name what it was he had heard in her voice; he could only say that it had not been fear as he had observed it in other patients.

He wondered about her. There was no way of guessing whether she had always had a nature of so tolerant and undemanding a complexion. It gave him a melancholy pleasure to think that before her accident she had been high-spirited and loquacious; he was moved to think that perhaps she had been a beauty and that when she had first seen her face in the looking glass she had lost all joy in herself. It was very difficult to tell what the face had been, for it was so bruised and swollen, so hacked-up and lopsided. The black stitches the length of the nose, across the saddle, across the cheekbone, showed that there would be unsightly scars. He had ventured once to give her the name of a plastic surgeon but she had only replied with a vague, refusing smile. He had hoisted a manly shoulder and said, 'You're the doctor.'

Much as he pondered, coming to no conclusions, about what went on inside that pitiable skull, he was, of course, far more interested in the nose, deranged so badly that it would require his topmost skill to restore its functions to it. He would be obliged not only to make a submucuous resection, a simple run-of-the-mill operation, but to remove the vomer, always a delicate task but further complicated in this case by the proximity of the bone to the frontal fracture line which conceivably was not entirely closed. If it were not and he operated too soon and if a cold germ then found its way into the opening, his patient would be carried off by meningitis in the twinkling of an eye. He wondered if she knew in what potential danger she lay; he desired to assure her that he had brought his craft to its nearest perfection and that she had nothing to fear of him, but feeling that she was perhaps both ignorant and unimaginative and that such consolation would create a fear rather than dispel one, he held his tongue and came nearer to the bed.

Watching him, Pansy could already feel the prongs of his pliers opening her nostrils for the insertion of his fine probers. The pain he caused her with his instruments was of a different kind from that she felt unaided: it was a naked, clean, and vivid pain which made her faint and ill and made her wish to die. Once she had fainted as he ruthlessly explored and after she was brought around, he continued until he had finished his investigation. The memory of this outrage had afterwards several times made her cry.

This morning she looked at him and listened to him with hatred. Fixing her eyes upon the middle of his high, protuberant brow, she imagined the clutter behind it and she despised its obtuse imperfection, the reason's oblique comprehension of itself. In his bland unawareness, this nobody, this nose-bigot, was about to play with fire and she wished him ill.

He said, 'I can't blame you. No, I expect you're not looking forward to our little party. But I expect you'll be glad to be able to breathe again.'

He stationed his lieutenants. The interne stood opposite him on the left side of the bed. The surgical nurse wheeled the wagon within easy reach of his hands and stood beside it. Another nurse stood at the foot of the bed. A third drew the shades at the windows and attached the blinding light which shone down on the patient hotly, and then she left the room, softly closing the door. Pansy stared at the silver ribbon tied in a great bow round the green crepe paper of one of the flower pots. It made her realize for the first time that one of the days she had lain here had been Christmas, but she had no time to consider this strange and thrilling fact, for Dr. Nicholas was genially explaining his anaesthetic. He would soak packs of gauze in the purple fluid, a cocaine solution, and he would place them then in her nostrils, leaving them there for an hour. He warned her that the packing would be disagreeable (he did not say 'painful') but that it would be well worth a few minutes of discomfort not to be in the least sick after the operation. He asked her if she were ready and when she nodded her head, he adjusted the mirror on his forehead and began.

At the first touch of his speculum, Pansy's fingers mechanically bent to the palms of her hands and she stiffened. He said, 'A pack, Miss Kennedy,' and Pansy closed her eyes. There was a rush of plunging pain as he drove the sodden gobbet of gauze high up into her nose and something bitter burned in her throat so that she retched. The doctor paused a moment and the surgical nurse wiped her mouth. He returned to her with another pack, pushing it with his bodkin doggedly until it lodged against the first. Stop! Stop! cried all her nerves, wailing along the surface of her skin. The coats that covered them were torn off and they shuddered like naked people screaming, Stop! Stop! But Dr. Nicholas did not hear. Time and again he came back with a fresh pack and did not pause at all until one nostril was finished. She opened her eyes and saw him wipe the sweat off his forehead and saw the dark interne bending over her, fascinated. Miss Kennedy bathed her temples in ice water and Dr. Nicholas said, 'There. It won't be much longer. I'll tell them to send you some coffee, though I'm afraid you won't be able to taste it. Ever drink coffee with chicory in it? I have no use for it.'

She snatched at his irrelevancy and, though she had never tasted chicory, she said severely, 'I love it.'

Dr. Nicholas chuckled. 'De gustibus. Ready? A pack, Miss Kennedy.'

The second nostril was harder to pack since the other side was now distended and the passage was anyhow much narrower, as narrow, he had once remarked, as that in the nose of an infant. In such pain as passed all language and even the farthest fetched analogies, she turned her eyes inward thinking that under the obscuring cloak of the surgeon's pain, she could see her brain without the knowledge of its keeper. But Dr. Nicholas and his aides would give her no peace. They surrounded her with their murmuring and their foot-shuffling and the rustling of their starched uniforms, and her eyelids continually flew back in embarrassment and mistrust. She was claimed entirely by this present, meaningless pain and suddenly and sharply, she forgot what she had meant to do. She was aware of nothing but her ascent to the summit of something; what it was she did not know, whether it was a tower or a peak or Jacob's ladder. Now she was an abstract word, now she was a theorem of geometry, now she was a kite flying, a top spinning, a prism flashing, a kaleidoscope turning.

But none of the others in the room could see inside and when the surgeon was finished, the nurse at the foot of the bed said, 'Now you must take a look in the mirror. It's simply too comical.' And they all laughed intimately like old, fast friends. She smiled politely and looked at her reflection: over the gruesomely fattened snout, her scarlet eyes stared in fixed reproach upon the upturned lips, gray with bruises. But even in its smile of betrayal, the mouth itself was puzzled: it reminded her that something had been left behind, but she could not recall what it was. She was hollowed out and was as dry as a white bone.

They strapped her ankles to the operating table and put leather nooses round her wrists. Over her head was a mirror with a thousand facets in which she saw a thousand travesties of her face. At her right side was the table, shrouded in white, where lay the glittering blades of the many knives, thrusting out fitful rays of light. All the cloth was frosty; everything was white or silver and as cold as snow. Dr. Nicholas, a tall snowman with silver eyes and silver fingernails, came into the room soundlessly for he walked on layers and layers of snow which deadened his footsteps; behind him came the interne, a smaller snowman, less impressively proportioned. At the foot of the table, a snow figure put her frozen hands upon Pansy's helpless feet. The doctor plucked the packs from the cold, numb nose. His laugh was like a cry on a bitter, still night: 'I will show you now,' he called across the expanse of snow, 'that you can feel nothing.' The pincers bit at nothing, snapped at the air and cracked a nerveless icicle. Pansy called back and heard her own voice echo: 'I feel nothing.'

Here the walls were gray, not tan. Suddenly the face of the nurse at the foot of the table broke apart and Pansy first thought it was in grief. But it was a smile and she said, 'Did you enjoy your coffee?' Down the gray corridors of the maze, the words rippled, ran like mice, birds, broken beads: Did you enjoy your coffee? your coffee? your coffee? Similarly once in another room that also had gray walls, the same voice had said, 'Shall I give her some whiskey?' She was overcome with gratitude that this young woman (how pretty she was with her white hair and her white face and her china-blue eyes!) had been with her that first night and was with her now.

In the great stillness of the winter, the operation began. The knives carved snow. Pansy was happy. She had been given a hypodermic just before they came to fetch her and she would have gone to sleep had she not enjoyed so much this trickery of Dr. Nicholas' whom now she tenderly loved.

There was a clock in the operating room and from time to time she looked at it. An hour passed. The snowman's face was melting; drops of water hung from his fine nose, but his silver eyes were as bright as ever. Her love was returned, she knew: he loved her nose exactly as she loved his knives. She looked at her face in the domed mirror and saw how the blood had streaked her lily-white cheeks and had stained her shroud. She returned to the private song: Did you enjoy your coffee? your coffee?

At the half-hour, a murmur, anguine and slumbrous, came to her and only when she had repeated the words twice did they engrave their meaning upon her. Dr. Nicholas said, 'Stand back now, nurse. I'm at this girl's brain and I don't want my elbow jogged.' Instantly Pansy was alive. Her strapped ankles arched angrily; her wrists strained against their bracelets. She jerked her head and she felt the pain flare; she had made the knife slip.

'Be still!' cried the surgeon. 'Be quiet, please!'

He had made her remember what it was she had lost when he had rammed his gauze into her nose: she bustled like a housewife to shut the door. She thought, I must hurry before the robbers come. It would be like the time Mother left the cellar door open and the robber came and took, of all things, the terrarium.

Dr. Nicholas was whispering to her. He said, in the voice of a lover, 'If you can stand it five minutes more, I can perform the second operation now and you won't have to go through this again. What do you say?'

She did not reply. It took her several seconds to remember why it was her mother had set such store by the terrarium and then it came to her that the bishop's widow had brought her an erb from Palestine to put in it.

The interne said, 'You don't want to have your nose packed again, do you?'

The surgical nurse said, 'She's a good patient, isn't she, sir?'

'Never had a better,' replied Dr. Nicholas. 'But don't call me "sir." You must be a Canadian to call me "sir." '

The nurse at the foot of the bed said, 'I'll order some more coffee for you.'

'How about it, Miss Vanneman?' said the doctor. 'Shall I go ahead?'

She debated. Once she had finally fled the hospital and fled Dr. Nicholas, nothing could compel her to come back. Still, she knew that the time would come when she could no longer live in seclusion, she must go into the world again and must be equipped to live in it; she banally acknowledged that she must be able to breathe. And finally, though the world to which she would return remained unreal, she gave the surgeon her permission.

He had now to penetrate regions that were not anaesthetized and this he told her frankly, but he said that there was no danger at all. He apologized for the slip of the tongue he had made: in point of fact, he had not been near her brain, it was only a figure of speech. He began. The knives ground and carved and curried and scoured the wounds they made; the scissors clipped hard gristle and the scalpels chipped off bone. It was as if a tangle of tiny nerves were being cut dexterously, one by one; the pain writhed spirally and came to her who was a pink bird and sat on the top of a cone. The pain was a pyramid made of a diamond; it was an intense light; it was the hottest fire, the coldest chill, the highest peak, the fastest force, the furthest reach, the newest time. It possessed nothing of her but its one infinitesimal scene: beyond the screen as thin as gossamer, the brain trembled for its life, hearing the knives hunting like wolves outside, sniffing and snapping. Mercy! Mercy! cried the scalped nerves.

At last, miraculously, she turned her eyes inward tranquilly. Dr. Nicholas had said, 'The worst is over. I am going to work on the floor of your nose,' and at his signal she closed her eyes and this time and this time alone, she saw her brain lying in a shell-pink satin case. It was a pink pearl, no bigger than a needle's eye, but it was so beautiful and so pure that its smallness made no difference. Anyhow, as she watched, it grew. It grew larger and larger until it was an enormous bubble that contained the surgeon and the whole room within its rosy luster. In a long ago summer, she had often been absorbed by the spectacle of flocks of yellow birds that visited a cedar tree and she remembered that everything that summer had been some shade of yellow. One year of childhood, her mother had frequently taken her to have tea with an aged schoolmistress upon whose mantelpiece there was a herd of ivory elephants; that had been the white year. There was a green spring when early in April she had seen a grass snake on a boulder, but the very summer that followed was violet, for vetch took her mother's garden. She saw a swatch of blue tulle lying in a raffia basket on the front porch of Uncle Marion's brown house. Never before had the world been pink, whatever else it had been. Or had it been, one other time? She could not be sure and she did not care. Of one thing she was certain: never had the world enclosed her before and never had the quiet been so smooth.

For only a moment the busybodies left her to her ecstasy and then, impatient and gossiping, they forced their way inside, slashed at her resisting trance with questions and congratulations, with statements of fact and jokes. 'Later,' she said to them dumbly. 'Later on, perhaps. I am busy now.' But their voices would not go away. They touched her, too, washing her face with cloths so cold they stung, stroking her wrists with firm, antiseptic fingers. The surgeon, squeezing her arm with avuncular pride, said, 'Good girl,' as if she were a bright dog that had retrieved a bone. Her silent mind abused him: 'You are a thief,' it said, 'you are a heartless vagabond and you should be put to death.' But he was leaving, adjusting his coat with an air of vainglory, and the interne, abject with admiration, followed him from the operating room smiling like a silly boy.

Shortly after they took her back to her room, the weather changed, not for the better. Momentarily the sun emerged from its concealing murk, but in a few minutes the snow came with a wind that promised a blizzard. There was great pain, but since it could not serve her, she rejected it and she lay as if in a hammock in a pause of bitterness. She closed her eyes, shutting herself up within her treasureless head.

*(From Commentary)*

# SHOCK TREATMENT

## BY IRWIN STARK

*E*MMA RICHTER had liked him from the beginning of the night-school term. Michels, submitting to the inevitable, blamed it on his deceptively youthful manner as well as on his blond hair.

She would approach his desk after the period and inform him in a fluttery whisper, 'You said it right this time, Mr. Michels.' He would smile and continue to gather his notes, expecting more. But she would blink and scurry off.

After the third week she began to leave different specimens of literature on his desk. Michels found them there at the start of the period, and as he looked around the room he would catch her eye and she would blink back at him, smile faintly, and suddenly become very busy turning the pages of her notebook. The literature was innocuous enough, throwaways about sending food to Europe, a mimeographed paper published by someone with a revolutionary theory on God, an appeal for the humane use of atomic energy, and a bulletin on cancer or tuberculosis. He would stuff them into his pocket and forget them till he changed his suit on Saturdays.

She was middle-aged, timid, and graying, and unless Michels addressed her directly she would sit all period with her thin, bloodless lips pressed tight together. When he did put a question to her she would brush an imaginary hair from her eyes, glance nervously about the room, and mumble the answer in a hoarse whisper through which her foreign

433

accent was only vaguely perceptible. Most of the time Michels ignored her.

Eventually he would have accepted her along with the others if Mr. Goldberg, the night-school principal, had not called him into the office and asked about her. 'Miss Richter is a pupil of yours, isn't she? Noticed anything peculiar?'

'Not especially,' he said. 'She's a pretty quiet bird. Leaves some literature on my desk occasionally, but nothing unusual.'

'Nothing anti-Semitic?'

Michels frowned. 'From Emma Richter? Not in my class. Why?'

Goldberg shrugged. 'Some fellow in her Spanish class came down last night and told me she'd been making nasty remarks about the Jews.'

'I can't understand it,' Michels said. 'After all I'm a Jew, and she likes me.'

'Maybe you'd better send her to me anyhow,' Goldberg said. 'I'd like to talk to her.'

Leaving the office, Michels felt sure it was all a mistake. Emma Richter had probably tried to say something involved and muffed it. But as he thought about it, he realized suddenly that she could not know he was a Jew, because nothing he had ever said in class had advertised the fact. Whenever his classes engaged in controversial discussion he had always felt he had to be objective. Should Palestine be opened to unlimited Jewish immigration? Should the United States take practical steps to enforce the recommendations of the Anglo-American Committee? How can racial tensions be eliminated? He could hardly preserve his role as arbiter if he revealed his nationality.

Of course, it went deeper than that. He had always made it a principle to think of himself as a human being first; the Jew was incidental and irrelevant, a historical accident with little bearing on his thinking, his emotions, or his life. Not that he had ever denied his background. But there was no point in stressing it. Except when he happened to be chal-

lenged directly; then, as he once explained it, it was proper
to be belligerently Jewish — but only for 'purposes of persecution.' He rather fancied the phrase.

At the beginning of the last period that evening he sent
Miss Richter to the office and went on with the lesson. She
returned in about fifteen minutes looking blanched and haggard, slipped quietly into her seat, and remained with her
eyes lowered till the bell sounded. Then she came up to the
desk.

'Mr. Michels,' she asked, her voice trembling, 'Did I ever
make in class a remark about the Jews?'

'Of course not,' he said. 'I'm sure you never did, Miss
Richter.'

She brushed her hair back nervously. 'I am German,' she
said. 'I suffered a lot because of it. But I have not in class
made any bad remark. And Mr. Goldberg says such a remark I made some place about the Jew.'

'Someone probably misunderstood you,' Michels said, feeling genuinely sorry for her distress. 'I'd forget all about it.'

'Thank you so much,' she said. 'I wish all the teachers was
like you, Mr. Michels. It would not then be so bad.'

'Don't think about it any more,' he said abruptly and
turned to pick up his briefcase. When he turned back she
was gone.

One evening several weeks later the class was discussing
the control and use of atomic energy, and he noticed how
intently Miss Richter seemed to be listening. Her eyes
blinked constantly, and she would turn in her seat to stare
at each speaker, smiling or frowning at every new point. But
she offered no contribution of her own during the entire
discussion, and after class, though she lingered for a few
moments as if making up her mind about something, she
left without making any personal comment to him.

The next night she dropped a letter on his desk just after
the last bell and then fled. The envelope said: 'Mr. R.
Michels, Confidential and Strictly Personal.' He waited until
he was on the train before opening it.

Dear Mr. Michels:

You will remember how about three weeks ago I was called down to Mr. Goldberg about some foolish complain done by a young Jewish man from my Spanish Class? Well I only said to that young man that I don't like the Jews, not knowing he is a Jew himself. For this little incident Mr. Goldberg threatened me with expelling from the school. I attended this School for fifteen years — different Classes. In the beginning had only trade Classes, but having more love for academic Courses I decided to put myself wholly into Literature. So I was a little insulted by Mr. Goldberg's speech — and now I would like you to help me make a complain about Professor Albert Einstein at his Princeton University. If you do Mr. Goldberg's eyes will be opened why I don't like the Jews and will never like them again no matter how they should flatter me.

You know how everyone was hated by the Jews in this war who only speaks German. So what was done to me by the Jews you can guess — and what Mr. Einstein and his Jewish Scientists did and still do to me through the air is the greatest crime of immorality that ever was committed in the whole History. Unbelievable, true, but you know Science, and so I can talk to you about it without being accused I have halluzinations only. The Police seem to know it, but is afraid of Jewish trouble so sh sh everything.

However I cannot suffer insults and humiliation forever and when this Mr. Goldberg talked to expell me because for such a trifle, I think Einstein should be expelled from the University for immorality. A Professor who should look after the moral of youth, to do such things with his Science through the air, is at least in my mind a simple degenerate. Investigate to know the truth and trust no flattery. When you will find out the truth what was done to me by the degenerated Jews you will pity me greatly.

EMMA RICHTER

Monday evening he had not yet decided what to do about the letter. It would have been simple to turn it over to Mr. Goldberg and let him throw her out. Miss Richter was obviously cracked on the subject. But was she any more cracked than other anti-Semites, or less dangerous? And if not, then what purpose could be served by expelling her? While she remained in school there was at least some hope of influencing her.

But how? He was under no illusion that reason could alter her attitude. As well try to reason away the hallucinations of a lunatic. The thought suggested another idea, brutal perhaps but effective. . . . Certain types of lunacy had been cured by shock. He had heard of the insulin injection — how it completely upset the patient's cerebro-nervous system prepared it for a new and more normal pattern.

Was there a shock treatment for Emma Richter?

When she came to his desk that night he smiled to her and whispered confidentially, 'I read your letter. It was very interesting.'

'Thank you, thank you,' she murmured.

Here, he decided, was the answer. She trusted him, had faith in him, was so to speak 'in love' with him, and did not know he was a Jew. Very well, he would carry her along. He would accept her whispered compliments, and then suddenly before the term ended he would tell her. He would reveal that he too was a Jew. He would shock her with the truth, and perhaps the shock would prove so severe that her emotional pattern would be changed. It would at least be the start of a change.

As the weeks passed he continued to accept her little flatteries, even went out of his way to praise whatever harmless remarks she made in class. He prayed she would not spoil it all by saying aloud something for which he would have to reprimand her before the rest of the group. But she did not disappoint him, and the fear that suppressed her statements in public carried over to the moments after class when she spoke alone to him. She had assumed that whatever she might say would be understood by him, and there was a teasing sense of mystery in what she seemed to look upon as a private language common to the two of them.

One evening in June after the final examinations he decided the time had come. She approached his desk as usual following the bell, but this time when she started to speak he quickly interrupted.

'Won't you please sit down for a minute, Miss Richter? I want to say something important to you.'

She fluttered nervously into the first seat in front of the desk and looked at him half-smiling, wondering, not at all suspicious of him.

'I think you like me a great deal, Miss Richter?' he asked.

She turned and searched the empty room, lowered her eyes, and then looked up. 'O very much, Mr. Michels. You are best among all the teachers.'

'You think I'm an honest teacher, don't you? I have never lied to you? I have always told you the truth?'

'O yes, yes, Mr. Michels. Always you have said the truth.'

'Good,' he said. He waited for a moment and tried to fix her shifting, always agitated eyes. 'I want to tell you another truth tonight,' he went on. 'A big truth. I want to tell you that the Jews are a good people.' She opened and shut her mouth like a fish sucking air. She blinked her eyes frantically. 'The Jews are a good people. There are bad Jews and good Jews, just as there are bad Catholics and good Catholics, bad Protestants and good Protestants. Understand this, Miss Richter. You must understand what I am telling you now. There are good and bad among all people, among all races, among all religions. A man's religion has nothing to do with what he is. The Jew is good, Miss Richter, but he is good not because he is or is not a Jew. He is good because he is good as a human being. A good human being.'

He waited again, watching her closely, trying to discover what effect his words were having. Her eyes kept blinking spasmodically and she was making a futile attempt to look at him steadily. But her mouth had set tight and as he finished she started to shake her head slowly back and forth.

'And I will tell you one more thing, Miss Richter. I am telling you this because you say you like me and respect me. I want to tell you now that I too am a Jew. I am a Jew, Miss Richter.'

At first the words meant nothing to her. She went right on blinking and shaking her head. Then suddenly she became rigid. Her eyes opened wide and stared. Her lips parted and she looked for a moment like the death mask of an idiot.

'No, Mr. Michels,' she said. 'You can't be a Jew, Mr. Michels.'

He smiled. 'But I am a Jew. My mother and father were Jews. My ancestors were Jews. And I too, I am a Jew.'

She stared at him in silence for a few seconds. Then she began to laugh. It was a low, guttural laugh at first, but then it leaped an octave and became shrill and hysterical. Every wrinkle on her face was contorted.

'O Mr. Michels,' she cried, 'O Mr. Michels! I will never believe that! Never, never in a hundred years will I believe it! Never! Never!' And her voice shot off key again, and she wiped her eyes with a little lace handkerchief.

'But I am a Jew,' Michels repeated. Her laughter drowned out the statement. He pounded on the desk and her laughter stopped instantly. 'I'm a Jew!' he shouted at her. 'A Jew! Remember that I'm a Jew! A Jew!'

She arose slowly and smiled. Her laughter had vanished. She was blinking once more and pushing away the strands of imaginary hair, and a strange cloudiness seemed to haze her eyes.

'You fool a little with me, eh, Mr. Michels? I think you fool a little. We know, you and I, we know, Mr. Michels.' Then she winked at him and was gone.

He looked at the blank doorway and waited for his emotions to subside, waited for the fantasy to merge into the reality once more, for the shock to wear off.

'But I am a Jew,' he insisted almost aloud to the rows of empty and silent seats. 'But I am a Jew. . . .'

(From Harper's Magazine)

# THE WOMEN ON THE WALL

## BY WALLACE STEGNER

*T*HE CORNER window of the study overlooked a lawn,
and beyond that a sunken lane between high pines,
and beyond the lane a point of land with the old beach
club buildings at one end and a stone wall around its tip.
Beyond the point, through the cypresses and eucalyptuses,
Mr. Palmer could see the Pacific, misty blue, belted between
shore and horizon with a band of brown kelp.

Writing every morning in his study, making over his old
notebooks into a coherent account of his years on the Gala-
pagos, Mr. Palmer could glance up from his careful longhand and catch occasional glimpses, as a traveler might glance
out of the window of a moving train. And in spite of the
rather special atmosphere of the point, caused by the fact
that until the past year it had been a club, there was something homey and neighborly and pleasant about the place
that Mr. Palmer liked. There were children, for one thing,
and dogs drifting up and down, and the occasional skirr of
an automobile starting in the quiet, the diminishing sound
of tires on asphalt, the distant racket of a boy being a
machine-gun with his mouth.

Mr. Palmer had been away from the States a long time;
he found the noises on the point familiar and nostalgic and
reassuring in this time of war, and felt as if he had come
home. Though California differed considerably from his
old home in Ohio, he fell naturally and gratefully into its
procession of morning and afternoon, its neighborhood

440

routines, the pleasant breathing of its tides. When anything outside broke in upon his writing, it was generally a commonplace and familiar thing; Mr. Palmer looked up and took pleasure in the interruption.

One thing he could be sure of seeing, every morning but Sunday. The section was outside the city limits, and mail was delivered to a battery of mailboxes where the sunken lane joined the street. The mail arrived at about eleven; about ten-thirty the women from the beach club apartments began to gather on the stone wall. Below the wall was the beach, where the tides leaned in all the way from Iwo and Okinawa. Above it was the row of boxes where as regularly as the tide the mail carrier came in a gray car and deposited postmarked flotsam from half a world away.

Sometimes Mr. Palmer used to pause in his writing and speculate on what these women thought of when they looked out across the gumdrop blue water and the brown kelp and remembered that across this uninterrupted ocean their husbands fought and perhaps bled and possibly died, that in those far islands it was already tomorrow, that the green water breaking against the white foot of the beach might hold in suspension minute quantities of the blood shed into it thousands of miles away, that the Japan current, swinging in a great circle up under the Aleutians and back down the American coast, might as easily bear the mingled blood or the floating relics of a loved one lost as it could bear the glass balls of Japanese netfloats that it sometimes washed ashore.

Watching the women, with their dogs and children, waiting patiently on the stone wall for that most urgent of all the gods, that Mercury in the gray uniform, Mr. Palmer thought a good deal about Penelope on the rocky isle of Ithaca above the wine-dark sea. He got a little sentimental about these women. Sometimes he was almost frightened by the air of patient, withdrawn seriousness they wore as they waited, and the unsmiling alacrity with which they rose and crowded around the mailman when he came. And when the mail was late, and one or two of them sat out on the wall until eleven-thirty, twelve, sometimes twelve-thirty, Mr. Palmer could hardly bear it at all.

Waiting, **Mr.** Palmer reflected, must cause a person to remove to a separate and private world. Like sleep or insanity, waiting must have the faculty of making the real unreal and remote. It seemed to Mr. Palmer pathetic and somehow thrilling that these women should have followed their men to the very brink of the west, and should remain here now with their eyes still westward, patiently and faithfully suspending their own normal lives until the return of their husbands. Without knowing any of the women, Mr. Palmer respected and admired them. They did not invite his pity. Penelope was as competent for her waiting as Ulysses was for his wars and wiles.

Mr. Palmer had been working in his new house hardly a week before he found himself putting on his jacket about eleven and going out to join the women.

He knew them all by sight, just from looking out the window. The red-haired woman with the little boy was sitting on the wall nearest him. Next was the thin girl who always wore a bathing suit and went barefooted. Next was the dark-haired one, five or six months pregnant. And next to her was the florid, quick, wren-like woman with the little girl of about five. Their faces all turned as Mr. Palmer came up.

'Good morning,' he said.

The red-haired woman's plain, serious, freckled face acknowledged him, and she murmured good morning. The girl in the bathing suit had turned to look off over the ocean, and Mr. Palmer felt that she had not made any reply. The pregnant girl and the woman with the little girl both nodded.

The old man put his hands on his knees, rounded his mouth and eyes, and bent to look at the little boy hanging to the red-haired woman's hand. 'Well!' he said. 'Hi, young fella!'

The child stared at him, crowding against his mother's legs. The mother said nothing, and rather than push first acquaintance too far, Mr. Palmer walked on along the wall.

As he glanced at the thin girl, he met her eyes, so full of cold hostility that for a moment he was shocked. He had intended to sit down in the middle of the wall, but her look sent him on further, to sit between the pregnant girl and the wren-like woman.

'These beautiful mornings!' Mr. Palmer said, sitting down with a sigh.

The wren-like woman nodded, the pregnant one regarded him with quiet ox-eyes.

'This is quite a ritual, waiting for the mail,' Mr. Palmer said. He pointed to the gable of his house across the lane. 'I see you from my window over there, congregating on the wall here every morning.'

The wren-like woman looked at him rather oddly, then leaped to prevent her daughter from putting out the eyes of the long-suffering setter she was mauling. The pregnant girl smiled a slow, soft smile. Over her shoulder Mr. Palmer saw the thin girl hitch herself up and sit on her hands. The expression on her face said that she knew very well why Mr. Palmer had come down and butted in, and why he watched from his window.

'The sun's so warm out here,' the pregnant girl said. 'It's a way of killing part of the morning, sitting out here.'

'A very good way,' Mr. Palmer said. He smoothed the creases in his trousers, finding speech a little difficult. From the shelter of his mother's legs the two-year-old boy down the wall stared at him solemnly. Then the wren-like woman hopped off the wall and dusted her skirt.

'Here he is!' she said.

They all started across the mouth of the lane, and for some reason, as they waited for the mailman to sort and deliver, Mr. Palmer felt that his first introduction hadn't taken him very far. In a way, as he thought it over, he respected the women for that, too. They were living without their husbands, and had to be careful. After all, Penelope had many suitors. But he could not quite get over wanting to spank the thin girl on her almost-exposed backside, and he couldn't quite shake the sensation of having wandered by mistake into the ladies' rest room.

After that, without feeling that he knew them at all, he respected them and respected their right to privacy. Waiting, after all, put you in an exclusive club. No outsider had any more right on that wall than he had in the company of a bomber crew. But Mr. Palmer felt that he could at least watch from his window, and at the mailboxes he could, almost by osmosis, pick up a little more information.

The red-haired woman's name was Kendall. Her husband was an army captain, a doctor. The thin girl, Mrs. Fisher, got regular letters bearing a Marine Corps return. The husband of Mrs. Corson, the wren-like woman, commanded a flotilla of minesweepers in the western Pacific. Of the pregnant girl, Mrs. Vaughn, Mr. Palmer learned little. She got few letters, and none with any postmarks that told anything.

From his study window Mr. Palmer went on observing them benignly and making additions to his notes on the profession of waiting. Though the women differed sharply one from another, they seemed to Mr. Palmer to have one thing in common: they were all quiet, peaceful, faithful to the times and seasons of their vigil, almost like convalescents in a hospital. They made no protests or outcries; they merely lived at a reduced tempo, as if pulse rate and respiration rate and metabolic rate and blood pressure were all tuned down. Mr. Palmer had a notion how it might be. Sometimes when he awoke very quietly in the night he could feel how quietly and slowly and regularly his heart was pumping, how slow and regular his breathing was, how he lay there mute and cool and inert with everything turned down to idling speed, his old body taking care of itself. And when he woke that way he had a curious feeling that he was waiting for something.

Every morning at ten-thirty, as regular as sun and tide, Mrs. Kendall came out of the beach club apartments and walked across the point, leading her little boy by the hand. She had the child tuned down, too, apparently. He never, to Mr. Palmer's knowledge, ran or yelled or cried or made a fuss, but walked quietly beside his mother, and sat with her on the big stump until five minutes to eleven, and then walked with her across to the end of the stone wall. About that time the other women began to gather, until all four of them were there in a quiet, uncommunicative row.

Through the whole spring the tides leaned inward with the same slow inevitability, the gray car came around and stopped by the battery of mailboxes, the women gathered on the wall as crows gather to a rookery at dusk.

Only once in all that drowsy spring was there any breaking of the pattern. That was one Monday after Mr. Palmer had been away for the weekend. When he strolled out at mailtime he found the women not sitting on the wall, but standing in a nervous conversational group. They opened to let him in, for once accepting him silently among them, and he found that the thin girl had moved out suddenly the day before: the Saturday mail had brought word that her husband had gone down in flames over the Marianas.

The news depressed Mr. Palmer in curious ways. It depressed him to see the women shaken from their phlegmatic routine, because the moment they were so shaken they revealed the raw fear under their quiet. And it depressed him that the thin girl's husband had been killed. That tragedy should come to a woman he personally felt to be a snob, a fool, a vain and inconsequent chit, seemed to him sad and incongruous and even exasperating. As long as she was one of the company of Penelopes, Mr. Palmer had refused to dislike her. The moment she made demands upon his pity he disliked her very much.

After that sudden blow, as if a hawk had struck among the quiet birds on the wall, Mr. Palmer found it less pleasant to watch the slow, heavy-bodied walking of Mrs. Kendall, her child always tight by the hand, from apartment to stump to wall. Unless spoken to, she never spoke. She wore gingham dresses that were utterly out of place in the white sun above the white beach. She was plain, unattractive, patient, the most remote, the most tuned-down, the quietest and saddest and most patient and most exasperating of the Penelopes. She too began to make wry demands on Mr. Palmer's pity, and he found himself almost disliking her. He was guilty of a little prayer that Mrs. Kendall's husband would be spared, so that his pity would not have to go any farther than it did.

Then one morning Mr. Palmer became aware of another kind of interruption on the point. Somebody there had apparently bought a new dog. Whoever had acquired it must have fed it, though Mr. Palmer never saw anyone do so, and must have exercised it, though he never saw that either. All he saw was that the dog, a half-grown cocker, was tied to the end of a rose trellis in the clubhouse yard. And all he heard, for two solid days, was the uproar the dog made.

It did not like being tied up. It barked, and after a while its voice would break into a kind of hysterical howling mixed with shuddering diminuendo groans. Nobody ever came and told it to be still, or took care of it, or let it loose. It stayed there and yanked on the rope and chewed at the trellis post and barked and howled and groaned until Mr. Palmer's teeth were on edge and he was tempted to call the Humane Society.

Actually he didn't, because on the third morning the noise had stopped, and as he came into his study to begin working he saw that the dog was gone. Mrs. Corson was sitting in a lawn chair under one of the cypresses, and her daughter was digging in the sandpile. There was no sign either of Mrs. Kendall or Mrs. Vaughn. The owner of the house was raking leaves on the lawn above the seawall.

Mr. Palmer looked at his watch. It was nine-thirty. On an impulse he slipped on a jacket and went down and out across the lawn and down across the lane and up the other side past the trellis. Where the dog had lain the ground was strewn with chewed green splinters.

Mrs. Corson looked up from her chair. Her cheeks were painted with a hatchwork of tiny ruddy veins, and her eyes looked as if she hadn't slept. They had a stary blankness like blind eyes, and Mr. Palmer noticed that the pupils were dilated, even in the bright light. She took a towel and a pack of cigarettes and a bar of coco-butter off the chair next to her.

'Good morning,' she said in her husky voice. 'Sit down.'

'Thank you,' Mr. Palmer said. He let himself down into the steeply-slanting wooden chair and adjusted the knees of his slacks. 'It *is* a good morning,' he said slyly. 'So quiet.'

Mrs. Corson's thin neck jerked upward and backward in a curious gesture. Her throaty laughter was loud and unrestrained, and the eyes she turned on Mr. Palmer were red with mirth.

'That damned dog,' she said. 'Wasn't that something?'

'I thought I'd go crazy,' Mr. Palmer said. 'Whose dog was it, anyway?'

Mrs. Corson's rather withered, red-nailed hand, with a big diamond and a wedding ring on the fourth finger, reached down and picked up the cigarettes. The hand trembled as it held the pack out.

'No thank you,' he said.

Mrs. Corson took one. 'It was Mrs. Kendall's dog,' she said. 'She took it back.'

'Thank God!' said Mr. Palmer.

Her hands nervous with the match box in her lap, Mrs. Corson sat and smoked. Mr. Palmer saw that her lips, under the lipstick, were chapped, and that there was a dried, almost leathery look to her tanned and freckled skin.

He slid deeper into the chair and looked out over the water, calm as a lake, the long light swells breaking below him with a quiet, lulling swish. Up the coast heavier surf was breaking farther out. Its noise came like a pulsating tremble on the air, hardly a sound at all. Everything tuned down, Mr. Palmer was thinking. Even the lowest frequency of waves on the beach. Even the ocean waited.

'I should think you'd bless your stars, having a place like this to wait in,' he said.

One of Mrs. Corson's eyebrows bent. She shot him a sideward look.

'Think of the women who are waiting in boarding-house rooms,' Mr. Palmer said, a little irritated at her manner.

'Think of the ones who are working and leaving their children in nurseries.'

'Oh, sure,' Mrs. Corson said. 'It's fine for Anne, with the beach and yard.'

Mr. Palmer leaned on the arm of the chair and looked at her quizzically. He wished any of these women would ever put away their reticence and talk about their waiting, because that was where their life lay, that was where they had authority. 'How long has your husband been gone?' he asked.

'Little over two years.'

'That's a long time,' Mr. Palmer said, thinking of Penelope and her wait. Ten years while the war went on at Troy, ten more years while Ulysses wandered through every peril in the Mediterranean, past Scylla and Charybdis and Circe and the Cyclops and the iron terrors of Hades and the soft temptations of Nausicaa. But that was poetry. Twenty years was too much. Two, in all conscience, was enough.

'I shouldn't kick,' the woman said. 'Mrs. Kendall's husband has been gone for over three.'

'I've noticed her,' Mr. Palmer said. 'She seems rather sad and repressed.'

For a moment Mrs. Corson's eyes, slightly bloodshot, the pupils dilated darkly, were fixed questioningly on Mr. Palmer's. Then the woman shook herself almost as a dog does. 'I guess,' she said. She rose with a nervous snap and glanced at her watch. From the sandpile the little girl called, 'Is it time, Mommy?'

'I guess so,' Mrs. Corson said. She laid the back of her hand across her eyes and made a face.

'I'll be getting along,' Mr. Palmer said.

'I was just taking Anne down for her pony ride. Why don't you ride down with us?'

'Well . . .'

'Come on,' Mrs. Corson said. 'We'll be back in less than an hour.'

The child ran ahead of them and opened the car doors, down in the widened part of the lane. As Mr. Palmer helped

Mrs. Corson in she turned her face a little, and he smelled the stale alcohol on her breath. Obviously Mrs. Corson had been drinking the night before, and obviously she was a little hung over.

But my Lord, why not? he said to himself. Two years of waiting, nothing to do but sit and watch and do nothing and be patient. He didn't like Mrs. Corson any less for occasional drinking. She was higher-strung than either Mrs. Vaughn or Mrs. Kendall. You could almost lift up the cover board and pluck her nerves like the strings of a piano. Even so, she played the game well. He liked her.

At the pony track Anne raced down the fenced runway at a pink fluttering gallop, and Mr. Palmer and Mrs. Corson, following more slowly, found her debating between a black and a pinto pony.

'Okay,' the man in charge said. 'Which'll it be today, young lady?'

'I don't know,' the girl said. Her forehead wrinkled. 'Mommy, which do you think?'

'I don't care, hon,' her mother said. 'Either one is nice.'

Pretty, her blonde braids hanging in front and framing her odd pre-Raphaelite face, Anne stood indecisive. She turned her eyes up to Mr. Palmer speculatively. 'The black one's nice,' she said, 'but so's the . . .'

'Oh, Anne,' her mother said. 'For heaven's sake make up your mind.'

'Well . . . the black one, then,' Anne said. She reached out a hand and touched the pony's nose, pulling her fingers back sharply and looking up at her mother with a smile that Mr. Palmer found himself almost yearning over. She was a pretty, dainty little child, no mistake.

'You're a nitwit,' her mother said. 'Hop on, so we can get back for the mailman.'

The attendant swung her up, but with one leg over the saddle Anne kicked and screamed to get down. 'I've changed my mind,' she said. 'Not this one, the pinto one.'

The attendant put her up on the pinto and Mrs. Corson,

her chapped lips trembling, said, 'Another outburst like that and you won't get on any, you little . . . !'

The pony started, led by the attendant who rocked on one thick-soled shoe. For a moment Mrs. Corson and Mr. Palmer stood in the sun under the sign that said 'Pony Rides, 10 Cents, 12 for $1.00.' They were, Mr. Palmer noticed, in the Mexican part of town. Small houses, some of them almost shacks, with geraniums climbing all over them, strung out along the street. Down on the corner beyond the car was a tavern with a dusty tin sign. Mrs. Corson unsnapped her purse and fished out a wadded bill and held it vaguely in her hand, looking off up the street past the track and the pinto pony and the pink little huddle on its back and the attendant rocking along ahead on his one thick shoe.

'I wonder,' she said. 'Would you do me a favor?'

'Anything.'

'Would you stay here five minutes while I go to the store? Just keep an eye on her?'

'Of course,' he said. 'I'd be glad to go to the store for you, if you'd like.'

'No,' she said. 'No, I'd better get it.' She put the crumpled bill into his hand. 'Let her have all the rides she wants. I'll be back in a few minutes.'

Mr. Palmer settled himself on a chair against the stable wall and waited. When Anne and the attendant got back he waved the bill at them. 'Want another ride?'

'Yes!' Anne said. Her hands were clenched tightly in the pony's mane, and her eyes danced and her mouth was a little open. The attendant turned and started down the track again. 'Run!' Anne cried to him. 'Make him run!'

The crippled hostler broke into a clumsy hop-skip-and-jump for a few yards, pulling the pony into a trot. The girl screamed with delight. Mr. Palmer yawned, tapped his mouth, smiled a little as he smelled the powder-and-perfume smell on the dollar bill, yawned again. Say what you would, it was decent of the woman to come out with a hangover and take her child to the pony track. She must feel pretty rocky, if her eyes were any criterion.

He waited for some time. Anne finished a second ride, took a third, finished that and had a fourth. The attendant was sweating a little. From the fence along the sidewalk two Negro children and a handful of little Mexicans watched. 'How about it?' Mr. Palmer said. 'Want another?'

She nodded, shaken with giggles and sudden shyness when she looked around and found her mother gone.

'Sure you're not getting sore?' Mr. Palmer patted his haunch suggestively.

She shook her head.

'Okay,' the hostler said. 'Here we go again, then.'

At the end of the fifth ride Anne let herself be lifted off. The hostler went inside and sat down, the pony joined its companion at the rail, cocked its hip and tipped its right hoof and closed its eyes. Anne climbed up into Mr. Palmer's lap.

'Where's Mommy?'

'She went to buy something.'

'Darn her,' Anne said. 'She does that all the time. She better hurry up, it's getting mail time.'

'Don't you like to miss the mail?'

'Sometimes there's packages and things from Daddy,' Anne said. 'I got a grass skirt once.'

Mr. Palmer rounded his mouth and eyes. 'You must like your daddy.'

'I do. Mommy doesn't, though.'

'What?'

'Mommy gets mad,' Anne said. 'She thinks Daddy could have had shore duty a long time ago, he's had so much combat, but she says he likes the Navy better than home. He's a commander.'

'Yes, I know,' Mr. Palmer said. He looked up the street, beginning to be fretful. The fact that the woman spent her whole life waiting shouldn't make her quite so callous to how long she kept other people waiting. 'We *are* going to miss the mailman if your Mommy doesn't hurry,' he said.

Anne jumped off his lap and puckered her lips like her mother. 'And today's a package!'

Mr. Palmer raised his eyebrows. 'How do you know?'

'The fortune teller told Mommy.'

'I see,' the old man said. 'Does your mother go to fortune tellers often?'

'Every Saturday,' Anne said. 'I went with her once. You know what she said? And it came true, too.'

Mr. Palmer saw the girl's mother coming down the sidewalk, and stood up. 'Here comes Mommy,' he said. 'We'd better meet her at the car.'

'She said we'd get good news, and right away Daddy was promoted,' Anne said. 'And she said we'd get a package, and that week we got *three!*'

Mrs. Corson was out of breath. In the bright sun her eyes burned with a curious sightless brilliance. The smell of alcohol on her was fresher and stronger.

'I'm sorry,' she said as she got in. 'I met a friend, and it was so hot we stopped for a beer.'

On the open highway, going back home, she stepped down hard on the throttle, and her fingers kept clasping and unclasping the wheel. Her body seemed possessed of electric energy. She radiated something, she gave off sparks. Her eyes, with the immense dark pupils and suffused whites, were almost scary.

When they pulled up and parked in front of Mr. Palmer's gate, opposite the mail boxes, the little red flags on some of the boxes were still up. On the stone wall sat Mrs. Kendall, her son Tommy, and the pregnant girl, Mrs. Vaughn. 'Late again,' Mrs. Corson said. 'Damn that man.'

'Can I play, Mommy?' Anne said.

'Okay.' As the child climbed out, the mother said, 'Don't get into any fixes with Tommy. Remember what I told you.'

'I will,' Anne said. Her setter came up and she stooped to pull its ears.

Her mother's face went pinched and mean. 'And stop abusing that dog!' she said.

Mr. Palmer hesitated. He was beginning to feel uncomfortable, and he thought of the pages he might have filled that morning, and the hour that still remained before noon.

But Mrs. Corson was leaning back with the back of her hand across her eyes. Through the windshield Mr. Palmer could see the two women and the child on the wall, like a multiple Patience on a monument. When he looked back at Mrs. Corson he saw that she too was watching them between her fingers. Quite suddenly she began to laugh.

She laughed for a good minute, not loudly but with curious violence, her whole body shaking. She dabbed her eyes and caught her breath and shook her head and tried to speak. Mr. Palmer attended uneasily, wanting to be gone.

'Lord,' Mrs. Corson said finally. 'Look at 'em. Vultures on a limb. Me too. Three mama vultures and one baby vulture.'

'You're a little hard on yourself,' Mr. Palmer said, smiling. 'And Anne, I'd hardly call her a vulture.'

'I didn't include her,' Mrs. Corson said. She turned her hot red eyes on him. 'She's got sense enough to run and play, and I hope I've got sense enough to let her.'

'Well, but little Tommy . . .'

'Hasn't had his hand out of mama's since they came here,' Mrs. Corson said. 'Did you ever see him play with anybody?'

Mr. Palmer confessed that he hadn't, now that he thought of it.

'Because if you ever do,' Mrs. Corson said, 'call out all the preachers. It'll be Christ come the second time. Honest to God, sometimes that woman . . .'

Bending forward, Mr. Palmer could see Mrs. Kendall smoothing the blue sweater around her son's waist. 'I've wondered about her,' he said, and stopped. Mrs. Corson had started to laugh again.

When she had finished her spasm of tight, violent mirth, she said, 'It isn't her child, you know.'

'No?' he said, surprised. 'She takes such care of it.'

'You're not kidding,' Mrs. Corson said. 'She won't let him play with Anne. Anne's too dirty. She digs in the ground and stuff. Seven months we've lived in the same house, and those kids haven't played together once. Can you imagine that?'

'No,' Mr. Palmer confessed. 'I can't.'

'She adopted it when it was six months old,' Mrs. Corson said. 'She tells us all it's a love-child.' Her laugh began again, a continuous, hiccoughy chuckle. 'Never lets go its hand,' she said. 'Won't let him play with anybody. Wipes him off like an heirloom. And brags around he's a love-child. My God!'

With her thin, freckled arm along the door and her lips puckered, she fell silent. 'Love-child!' she said at last. 'Did you ever look at her flat face? It's the last place love would ever settle on.'

'Perhaps that explains,' Mr. Palmer said uncomfortably. 'She's childless, she's unattractive. She pours all that frustrated affection out on this child.'

Mrs. Corson twisted to look almost incredulously into his face. 'Of course,' she said. Her alcoholic breath puffed at him. 'Of course. But why toot it up as a love-child?' she said harshly. 'What does she think my child is, for God's sake? How does she think babies are made?'

'Well, but there's that old superstition,' Mr. Palmer said. He moved his hand sideward. 'Children born of passion, you know — they're supposed to be more beautiful . . .'

'And doesn't that tell you anything about her?' Mrs. Corson said. 'Doesn't that show you that she never thought of passion in the same world with her husband? She has to go outside herself for any passion, there's none in her.'

'Yes,' Mr. Palmer said. 'Well, of course one can speculate, but one hardly knows . . .'

'And that damned dog,' Mrs. Corson said. 'Tommy can't play with other kids. They're too dirty. So she gets a dog. Dogs are cleaner than Anne, see? So she buys her child this nice germless dog, and then ties him up and won't let him loose. So the dog howls his head off, and we all go nuts. Finally we told her we couldn't stand it, why didn't she let it loose and let it run. But she said it might run away, and Tommy loved it so she didn't want to take a chance on losing the pup. So I finally called the Society for the Prevention of Cruelty to Animals, and they told her either to give it regu-

lar running and exercise or take it back. She took it back
last night, and now she hates me.'

As she talked, saliva had gathered in the corner of her
mouth. She sucked it in and turned her head away, looking
out on the street. 'Lord God,' she said. 'So it goes, so it goes.'

Through the windshield Mr. Palmer watched the quiet
women on the wall, the quiet, well-behaved child. Anne was
romping with the setter around the big stump, twenty feet
beyond, and the little boy was watching her. It was a peaceful, windless morning steeped in sun. The mingled smell
of pines and low tide drifted across the street, and was replaced by the pervading faint fragrance of Ceanothus, blooming in shades of blue and white along Mr. Palmer's walk.

'I'm amazed,' he said. 'She seems so quiet and relaxed and
plain.'

'That's another thing,' Mrs. Corson said. 'She's a cover-
yourself-up girl, too. Remember Margy Fisher, whose husband was killed a few weeks ago? You know why she never
wore anything but a bathing suit? Because this old biddy
was always after her about showing herself.'

'Well, it's certainly a revelation,' Mr. Palmer said. 'I see
you all from my window, you know, and it seems like a kind
of symphony of waiting, all quiet and harmonious. The
pregnant girl, too — going on with the slow inevitable business of life while her husband's gone, the rhythm of the
generations unchanged. I've enjoyed the whole thing, like
a pageant, you know.'

'Your window isn't a very good peekhole,' Mrs. Corson
said drily.

'Mm?'

'Hope's husband was killed at Dieppe,' said Mrs. Corson.

For a moment Mr. Palmer did not catch on. At first he
felt only a flash of pity as he remembered the girl's big
steady brown eyes, her still, rather sad face, her air of pliant
gentleness. Then the words Mrs. Corson had spoken began
to take effect. Dieppe — almost three years ago. And the
girl six months pregnant.

He wished Mrs. Corson would quit drumming her red

nails on the car door. She was really in a state this morning, nervous as a cat. But that poor girl, sitting over there with all that bottled up inside of her, the fear and uncertainty growing as fast as the child in her womb grew . . .

'Some naval lieutenant,' Mrs. Corson said. 'He's right in the middle of the fighting, gunnery officer on a destroyer. You ought to hear Hope when she gets scared he'll never come back and make a decent woman of her.'

'I'd not like to,' Mr. Palmer said, and shook his head. Across the lane the placid scene had not changed, except that Mrs. Kendall had let Tommy toddle fifteen feet out from the wall, where he was picking up clusters of dry pine needles and throwing them into the air.

The figures were very clean, sharp-edged in the clear air against the blue backdrop of sea. An Attic grace informed all of them: the girl stooping above the long-eared red setter, the child with his hands in the air, tossing brown needles in a shower, the curving seated forms of the women on the wall. To Mr. Palmer's momentarily-tranced eyes they seemed to freeze in attitudes of flowing motion like figures on a vase, cameo-clear in the clear air under the noble trees, with the quiet ocean of their watchfulness stretching blue to the misty edge. Like figures on a Grecian urn they curved in high relief against the white moulding of the wall, and a drift of indescribable melancholy washed across the point and pricked goosepimples on Mr. Palmer's arms. 'It's sad,' he said, opening the door and stepping down. 'The whole thing is very sad.'

With the intention of leaving he put his hand on the door and pushed it shut, thinking that he did not want to stay longer and hear Mrs. Corson's bitter tongue and watch the women on the wall. Their waiting now, with the momentary trance broken and the momentary lovely frozen group dispersed in motion, seemed to him a monstrous aberration, their patience a deathly apathy, their hope an obscene self-delusion.

He was filled with a sense of the loveliness of the white

paper and the cleanly sharpened pencils, the notebooks and the quiet and the sense of purpose that waited in his study. Most of all the sense of purpose, the thing to be done that would have an ending and a result.

'It's been very pleasant,' he said automatically. At that moment there came a yowl from the point.

He turned. Apparently Anne, romping with the dog, had bumped Tommy and knocked him down. He sat among the pine needles in his blue play-suit and squalled, and Mrs. Kendall came swiftly out from the wall and took Anne by the arm, shaking her.

'You careless child!' she said. 'Watch what you're doing!'

Instantly Mrs. Corson was out of the car. Mr. Palmer saw her start for the point, her lips puckered, and was reminded of some mechanical toy tightly wound and tearing erratically around a room giving off sparks of ratchety noise. When she was twenty feet from Mrs. Kendall she shouted hoarsely, 'Let go of that child!'

Mrs. Kendall's heavy gingham body turned. Her plain face, the mouth stiff with anger, confronted Mrs. Corson. Her hand still held Anne's arm. 'It's possible to train children . . .' she said.

'Yes, and it's possible to mistreat them,' Mrs. Corson said. 'Let go of her.'

For a moment neither moved. Then Mrs. Corson's hands darted down, caught Mrs. Kendall's wrist, and tore her hold from Anne's arm. Even across the lane, fifty feet away, Mr. Palmer could see the white fury in their faces as they confronted each other.

'If I had the bringing up of that child . . . !' Mrs. Kendall said. 'I'd . . .'

'You'd tie her to your apron strings like you've tied your own,' Mrs. Corson said. 'Like you tie up a dog and expect it to get used to three feet of space. My God, a child's a little animal. He's got to run!'

'And knock other children down, I suppose.'

'Oh my God!' Mrs. Corson said, and turned her thin face skyward as if to ask God to witness. She was shaking all over:

Mr. Palmer could see the trembling of her dress. 'Listen!'
she said, 'I don't know what's the matter with you, and why
you can't stand nakedness, and why you think a bastard child
is something holier than a legitimate one, and why you hang
onto that child as if he was worth his weight in diamonds.
But you keep your claws off mine, and if your little bastard
can't get out of the way, you can just . . .'

Mrs. Kendall's face was convulsed. She raised both hands
above her head, stuttering for words. From the side the
pregnant girl slipped in quietly, and Mr. Palmer, rooted
uneasily across the lane, heard her quiet voice. 'You're beginning to draw a crowd,' she said. 'For the love of mike,
turn it down.'

Mrs. Corson swung on her. Her trembling had become
an ecstasy. When she spoke she chewed loudly on her words,
mangling them almost beyond recognition. 'You keep out
of this, you pregnant bitch,' she said. 'Any time I want advice on how to raise love children, I'll come to you too,
but right now I haven't got any love children, and I'm raising what I've got my own way.'

A window had gone up in the house next to Mr. Palmer's,
and three boys were drifting curiously down the street, their
pants sagging with the weight of armament they carried.
Without hesitating more than a moment, Mr. Palmer crossed
the street and cut them off. 'I think you'd better beat it,' he
said, and pushed his hands in the air as if shooing chickens.
The boys stopped and eyed him suspiciously, then began
edging around the side. It was clear that in any contest of
speed, agility, endurance, or anything else Mr. Palmer was
no match for them. He put his hand in his pocket and pulled
out some change. The boys stopped. Behind him Mr.
Palmer heard the saw-edged voice of Mrs. Corson. 'I'm not
the kind of person that'll stand it, by God! If you want to . . .'

'Here,' Mr. Palmer said. 'Here's a quarter apiece if you
light out and forget anything you saw.'

'Okay!' they said, and stepped up one by one and got their
quarters and retreated, their heads together and their armed
hips clanking together and their faces turning once, together,

to stare back at the arguing women on the point. Up the street Mr. Palmer saw a woman and three small children standing in the road craning. Mrs. Corson's voice carried for half a mile.

In the hope that his own presence would bring her to reason, Mr. Palmer walked across the lane. Mrs. Corson's puckered, furious face was thrust into Mrs. Kendall's, and she was saying, 'Just tell me to my face I don't raise my child right! Go on, tell me so. Tell me what you told Margy, that Anne's too dirty for your bastard to play with. Tell me, I dare you, and I'll tear your tongue out!'

Mr. Palmer found himself standing next to Mrs. Vaughn. He glanced at her once and shook his head and cleared his throat. Mrs. Corson continued to glare into the pale flat face before her. When Mrs. Kendall turned heavily and walked toward the wall, the wren-like woman skipped nimbly around her and confronted her from the other side. 'You've got a lot of things to criticize in me!' she said. Her voice, suddenly, was so hoarse it was hardly more than a whisper. 'Let's hear you say them to my face. I've heard them behind my back too long. Let's hear you say them!'

'Couldn't we get her into the house?' Mr. Palmer said to the pregnant girl. 'She'll raise the whole neighborhood.'

'Let her disgrace herself,' Mrs. Vaughn said, and shrugged.

'But you don't understand,' Mr. Palmer said. 'She had a beer or so downtown, and I think that, that and the heat . . .'

The girl looked at him with wide brown eyes in which doubt and contempt and something like mirth moved like shadows on water. 'I guess *you* don't understand,' she said. 'She isn't drunk. She's hopped.'

'Hopped?'

'I thought you went downtown with her.'

'I did.'

'Did she leave you at the pony track?'

'Yes, for a few minutes.'

'She goes to a joint down there,' Mrs. Vaughn said. 'Fortune telling in the front, goofballs and reefers in the rear. She's a sucker for all three.'

'Goofballs?' Mr. Palmer said. 'Reefers?'

'Phenobarb,' Mrs. Vaughn said. 'Marijuana. Anything. She doesn't care, long as she gets high. She's high as a kite now. Didn't you notice her eyes?'

Mrs. Kendall had got her boy by the hand. She was heavily ignoring Mrs. Corson. Now she lifted the child in her arms and turned sideways, like a cow ducking to the side to slip around a herder, and headed for the stone wall. Mrs. Corson whipped around her flanks, first on one side, then on the other, her hoarse whisper a continuing horror in Mr. Palmer's ears.

'What I ought to do,' Mrs. Corson said, 'is forbid Anne to even speak to that bastard of yours.'

Mrs. Kendall bent and put the child on the ground and stood up. 'Don't you call him that!' she shouted. 'Oh, you vulgar, vicious, drunken, depraved woman! Leave me alone! Leave me alone, can't you?'

She burst into passionate tears. For a moment Mr. Palmer was terrified that they would come to blows and have to be pulled apart. He started forward, intending to take Mrs. Corson by the arm and lead her, forcefully if necessary, to the house. This disgraceful exhibition had gone on long enough. But the pregnant girl was ahead of him.

She walked past the glaring women and said over her shoulder, carelessly, 'Mail's here.'

Mr. Palmer caught his cue. He put out his hand to Anne, and walked her down across the mouth of the lane. He did not look back, but his ears were sharp for a renewal of the cat-fight. None came. By the time the man in gray had distributed the papers and magazines to all the battery of boxes, and was unstrapping the pack of letters, Mr. Palmer was aware without turning that both Mrs. Corson and Mrs. Kendall were in the background by the gray car, waiting quietly.

*(From Harper's Magazine)*

# THE SIEGE

# BY NICCOLÓ TUCCI

*F*OR three full years, from 1915 to 1918, at nine o'clock every morning, we had waited for the postman, right before breakfast; or, if he was late, during breakfast. At times, my sister Sonia, my brother Vieri, and I went all the way to the gate to look for him on the big road, but then, if he was not in sight, we preferred to wait in the garden for him to 'ripen' from around the corner of the gardener's house. This idea of his ripening was our invention; we had coined the word and it described the situation very well. He brought news of the war, or rather of our brother Kostia, who was in it.

When the newspaper he delivered was spread open, we glanced rapidly, all of us, and in secret, and sideways, at the casualty list. There was no reason why Kostia's name should have appeared there before the next of kin had been informed, but that casualty list was like a precipice into which all our hopes might fall in one, two, three or God knows how many days. We hoped that his life would continue after that precipice was closed, that there would be peace and him again with us after that peace. But nine o'clock was an hour from another life: in fact, one could be seen idling around the house at that hour, which in itself was a crime, and even doing such terrible things as scratching one's head or putting one's finger in his nose, and rarely a word of reproach would be spoken. If then there was a letter from Kostia we had another half-hour of joy and vacation before going up to the

461

library, but if nothing arrived, then all the irregular things one had done right before nine were remembered and loudly criticized, often with sanctions, too.

One day in November 1918, almost together with the news of the armistice, came a short letter which said: 'Any day from Tuesday week you may begin to wait for me. Should my plans change, I shall get in touch with you again.' Just dry and short like that. No mention of the great event, the hard-won victory, none of the vivid tales of what had happened to him; it was almost a letter from a stranger. But of course this meant that the written word was abandoned for good as a means of conveyance. Words were now free again to go where they were needed: we had no use for them; we would soon see him, touch him, know that he was there. The postman too was no longer the sovereign of the day. This letter was his abdication.

And that was how we graduated from the calendar to the clock. Two weeks, just waiting for the right to wait. The big clock in the dark corner of the dining room, hidden by the heavy curtains between the two windows, would have a lot of work to do now, mincing away slices of time until two weeks were filled. But what is it for a strong clock to do a little extra work when it has remained idle for three years, marking fictitious hours that no one filled?

Our father was the first one to break up the joyful meeting. He had nodded to his good luck, smiled, touched his little white beard with two nervous fingers, and that seemed enough to him. 'No sense in waiting now,' he said. 'This is just another day of work. Go to the library and do your lessons, all of you.' He put on his shapeless old hat and we saw him walking angrily as usual down the main path of the park, to go and find out how much damage had been done him by the peasants, the administrator, and the wind.

When his staggering form, his hat, and his white hair had disappeared behind the last tree, mother smiled at us, we smiled at her, we did not leave, she did not tell us to leave, and we knew it was all right. She wanted to talk to someone, and for that reason we were made grown-ups by her royal decree, just as a chair is 'made' an airplane by a child. And we knew that we would hear the secret story of what had happened to us these three years.

'You know,' she said, 'the only thing one must be careful to avoid is dreams. There are little devils, microbes of dreams, around us all the time. They know our hopes and feed on them. They always come and offer us the things we want, and we are always fooled by them. We say, for instance, this is a dream, but *he* is not, because I *see* him. Kostia is here. So then we start leaving the dream with him, and then ... (she smiled) I have a word for it. I call it landing on the deserted shores of the morning.' She was crying now. Adrian, our younger brother, who was six, wanted to tell his own ideas about dreams, sensing that this was a moment for great revelations, but he was stopped by Clorinda, the white-haired maid who had exercised spanking powers on our father when he was a child, and now retained, nominally at least, the same privileges on us. She was carrying the *scaldino,* a clay fire-basket which mother held in her hands all day.

'All of you: out of here,' she said. 'And you,' she said to mother, 'don't sit there and cry like that. Do something instead. You are a fine lady who knows so many things: read, keep busy, fill this time with something else but your impatience.'

'I promise,' said mother, who in normal times would not have allowed Clorinda to address her that way.

We went upstairs, and of course did not do our lessons at all, and we could hear that mother was not doing anything either. We knew it from the noise of her rings on the clay handle of the fire-basket.

Lunch was unpleasant that day. Father sat with his head bent over his dish as if he were reading. His bald head, surrounded by white hair, looked like a wooden model for a face as it protruded against us. And when Vieri began to talk about dreams again, he said, 'Don't you have anything more intelligent to talk about? Dreams are dreams and reality is reality. It has always been that way.' This seemed very stupid to us, but his voice had the right of way, no matter what he said. He had taken his option in the conversation and now he did not know what to do with it. So, without lifting his head, he fixed his small blue eyes on us through the white curtain of his eyelashes and coughed his ill-humor into the napkin until he became red as a lobster. Then he ate his soup until he saw the blue pattern of the arms in the middle of the dish, cleaned it carefully with bread and gave the dish to the maid, saying: 'Away. The bread is for the cat. Don't forget.'

The slow, heavy afternoon was again working its way up the naked hills of Spazzavento, and dragging the old house with the peasant houses around it toward another night. At Spazzavento the sun went down at two-thirty in November, but even in June it never stayed on the horizon later than four, because the villa was built on the north slope of the stony Calvana, facing the Bisenzio valley and the north-wester that always came down that way. Only from the big window on top of the stairs one had a glimpse of the distant hills around Florence and of the railroad some three miles away and the wide, dusty new road that had been built quite recently, only forty-five years before, to link the station with the village.

Mother had not yet inaugurated her watch but she gave orders that very day to have a chair placed near the window on top of the stairs. For the next few days the maids were forever stumbling into that chair when they came down from their quarters at five o'clock in the morning, but they did not seem to mind. That chair had a meaning, like the wooden platforms they used to build in the village square a week before the procession of the patron saint. And the maids knew that the chair would stay there until after Kostia had had a chance to see it and to understand how much his mother loved him.

The house was always silent in the afternoon, or rather, the family quarters were silent. Nobody raised his voice in the corridors, in the bedrooms, in the library, or anywhere else. If father was at home, he either snored for an hour in some dark corner, under a portrait of someone who had snored there before him (I still see his white beard defiantly facing the opposite wall); or he was in the small office near the oil-mill down in the basement, where his administrator used to receive the peasants and tell them day in day out that they were thieves.

The silence of the big house, which we called the Main Silence or the Master Silence, was cut out of the eternal silence of death to which it belonged, and lifted on a pedestal made up of the various sounds that came from the kitchen, the pantry, or the fields. The sad linear song of a maid surged from the cellar and went all around that silence; out in the fields, the scissors of the peasants binding and cutting the vines for the winter broke the air like distant gunshots, and often this noise too was underlined by stripes of shapeless chanting. But when the wind moaned through the valley (indeed the name 'Windswept' was appropriate for the place), then the Main Silence became so high, so monumental, that it scared everyone in the house.

Today the wind had suddenly awakened from the air and was in one of its moods. We all felt depressed. Little Adrian, who took orders from everybody and passed them on to his toys or to chairs or imaginary people, had finished his daily battle against the Germans in the living room, and probably had found nobody in the kitchen to talk to (dreary place that kitchen, with the huge smoky pot hanging from a black chain in the fireplace and simmering all day). So he must have decided to go and see whether his beloved hero and brother, Kostia, was coming home, as he had heard in the morning, because he climbed all the stairs, stood in front of the rattling window and looked and looked. And as he saw a carriage, without thinking what he was doing, he shouted joyfully: 'Kostia is coming . . .'

Doors were flung open, the maids appeared from nowhere, we came from the library, and mother advanced on the stairs, pale, and with wide open eyes. He saw us all come toward him and began to cry: 'It wasn't Kostia, no, no, it wasn't.'

'To scare me like that,' shouted mother trembling.

'You have no business standing here,' shouted Clorinda, shaking him with anger. 'Go downstairs and do some work, you idle child, you.'

We all gave him our part of the general indignation, and mother ordered that no one should start waiting like that until two full weeks had passed. But another wall had been broken down: the fact that someone had begun to look at the street had a strange effect on her. She went downstairs, 'to prepare everything.' Then twice she climbed a few steps and compelled herself to go back to the dining room. But the third time she had another reason. She wanted to see whether the servants quarters were in good order; a thing she had not done for years because she knew that Clorinda would have resented this lack of confidence in her. As she reached the window, accompanied by Sonia, she said that after all it was unnecessary because Clorinda knew better than anyone else, and besides, three flights of stairs were already too much for her; she was no longer young. 'Let me test this chair,' she said. 'What does one see from here?' She sat down and she looked. Just for one second. And the siege of the road began.

Sonia tried to protest, but she said, 'What difference does it make, whether I wait here or downstairs? Bring me my needlework and the green book from the mantelpiece in my room.'

When Clorinda called to her not to be unwise, she answered that she was not used to carrying on a conversation from one floor to the next. It was sheer good luck that she was able to restrain herself and not add 'especially with a maid.' She would have been sorry, because Clorinda came right upstairs and took her kindly by the arm like a child, saying, 'Now you come with me.' Mother answered that she was used to doing as she pleased in her own house, but could not help laughing because she felt weak in front of this determined old woman. Finally she broke into tears and said she would go downstairs in a little while.

But the next day she was again seated up there, this time

with all her ancient pride burning in her eyes, and Clorinda must have understood from the rhythm of her rings on the handle of the *scaldino* that this was not the day to speak a word. Sonia began to pay her long visits up there, but she did not want us boys near her because we startled her with tactless questions, such as: 'Do you see that man coming down from there? Who could it be?' Or we said: 'There, a carriage slows down on the curve. It will certainly stop here.' 'Barbarians,' she used to tell us in an angry voice, just as she did when she was playing the piano and someone dared talk aloud in the room. But Sonia knew how to behave; she let mother do the waiting, the guessing, everything. She saw, of course, trains and carriages and people on foot, but she went on with what she was saying, and after they had passed and nobody had accepted to bring him or to be him, she found something interesting to say, so that mother would not have to feel ashamed of the 'defeat.' Then also Clorinda began to accept the siege. At times she stopped near mother for a second and threw a glance into the street as one throws a glance at a canvas, trying not to disturb the painter at his work.

We spent our mornings in the library as usual, then, every other day, we went to the nearby town of Prato with the carriage for our Latin and arithmetic lessons, and every time we crossed the hall we walked on tiptoes and tried to hear whether any carriages were rolling on the road. That dark figure against the glaring light of the window up there made us feel better. It was the only sign that a new era would begin. It was an assertion of our right to hope, a right that everything in that old house seemed to deny. Also the absurd idea that the road was being walked upon, that people were in the habit of coming along that road, seemed a hopeful sign: they were all part of *his* return; they kept the stream running.

Thus at the end of the two weeks, when the real expectation began, we were already a little too impatient, all of us. The first disappointment was that he did not appear in the first hour of light the first morning, a Tuesday it was, I remember so well. And then the second hour and then the third, and fourth, and then a whole morning full of hours, and then lunch-time too. The conversation stopped, as if by common understanding, every time the noise of a wheel was heard. It no longer passed on the road, it passed through the dining room, through the table, through all of us, and we resumed our talk in a state of weakness, as if we had been tramped upon by a real carriage.

How the entire third week managed to pass that way I can hardly recall. The fixity of our anguish, geared to such a high note, was the only true thing; the house, the people in it, our own actions and bodies, were all way behind. The only thing that took place in *our* world was mother walking up the stairs, determinedly, stepping on each step as if *that* obstacle had been subdued, and then sitting majestically on her throne, fixing both eyes on the top of the horizon from where the road flowed down to her like a dry stream. The road was hers, she was besieging it; it must produce her son.

Nothing could happen in that empty space that did not fall into her eyes. When people crossed the road, it bothered her, and if they stood on it for any length of time, she made impatient gestures with her hand. Because *he* was to appear from there like a small point and ripen slowly into the dear figure we knew. And once he had adopted every form we had guarded so jealously in our hearts, as a last thing he would receive his voice, and we would all be free. No more stopping to ask ourselves: What is he really like? How does he act? Have we forgotten him? Oh, to be able to say: 'These lines, this voice you take back now, for they are yours, and see whether we kept them well.' We knew we must have kept them much too well, for time brings change, and time was dead in us. Our time flew all around that point: his face, as we remembered it; that was our watch. For us it was just then and always then, and it continued to be then all day. On the night he had left, three years before, mother had put a photograph of him into the wooden frame of her small desk-watch. Now that the clock downstairs had done its work, this was the new impediment: nothing had really happened since that image had been put there. But he would come and set us free, we knew.

Oh, but too few of those small points came down the road in the afternoon. They always seemed to accept the gifts at first: Kostia's stature and way of walking; then, half-way or so, they would begin to shake them off and show that they had nothing about them even to start pretending they were Kostia: such people as old men, even women, all sorts of trespassers. Every single time we felt like shouting at them, 'We are going to extract him from the unknown, even without your help!'

After eight more days of this mother began to feel that we were all abandoning her. She was alone now on the rampart. All the doors were closed, all the hearts were closed, too: the old Nothing (another of our familiar images to describe the atmosphere of the house) was taking hold of us again like a bad winter. Now it was as if *she* were trying to conjure a dream in the midst of reality and plant it there. She had unfurled the canvas of her lively imagination with a new world painted on it, which was to cover everything — the stony countryside, the trees, the people. If there could only be a conspiracy of hope, if people helped, if they began to hold the canvas down with their feet, it would perhaps stick to the ground. If they could only fasten it under the houses, she could finish her work. If only the postman would bring that decree, empowering her with the exercise of rights she had already taken days ago, she might manage to win, but this way, all alone, it was too difficult.

We continued to work as usual in the library, and although we were too oppressed by the silence to open our hearts to any hope again, we felt defended by her faith. God, or Whoever or Whatever there was, that stood behind the curtains of the world, would find his, its, their match in the aspect of this mother who had the dignity of a queen and could want things like a queen. However, we did not communicate with

one another during those days. It was all right to be crushed
inside, but the air should not vibrate with dangerous words
of doubt, or really the happiness it was so hard to evoke
would feel offended and not come at all. Saying anything
sad was like opening the doors to the old Nothing. So we all
waited in *her* shadow and somewhat also in the shadow of
the house door. Every time the big hand-bell rang, there was
such a sinking of hearts, and the familiar faces that appeared
were so disliked! We felt like saying: 'Did you *have* to come?
Only one person has the right to come these days and you are
not that one.'

Then an incident occurred which, although we understood that it meant nothing, made it even harder for us to
interrupt our anguish. One day I saw my father come home
with a face that was not only angrier than usual, but which
said clearly: stay away, everybody. I was so afraid that I ran
to the library and waited there to be called downstairs for
tea. I heard him go through all the rooms. He was obviously looking for something and I knew what: something
wrong, something on which to hook his anger. He found it.
A chair had been displaced. He called Clorinda three times
in a voice that was almost desperate with anger, and in the
silence that followed, Sonia asked me stupidly: 'Is there any
news?' (Why oblige people to answer 'No,' when they would
give anything in the world to answer 'Yes'? There is a code
of mutual respect in such situations.) 'You fool,' I said, 'if
there were any news, do you think I would wait to tell it
until you asked me?'

Again father called Clorinda, and again his steps were
heard, and they changed from the heavy hammering of stairs
being mounted to the lighter scuffling on the same surface.
He must be in the hall now. Why didn't he say 'Good
evening' to mother up there? And then, to call Clorinda
that way, Clorinda, who had brought him up, spanked him,
used strong words with him until he was fifteen! The fourth
time he called, one note pierced the volume of his voice,
and came out in a falsetto tone. Finally she arrived; and it

was as if she had been guilty of everything that had ever happened in the world, when he asked: 'Have *you* pushed this big chair against the frame of that picture again? Can't you see that it has left a mark? . . . I . . . this precious painting . . . my orders disobeyed . . .'

It was so awful that Clorinda cried, and they both went downstairs together and way to the end of the corridor, and then a door was banged and their voices died down like thunder in the hills.

And mother continued to sit there at the window, away from all this, indifferent to the loudest expressions of reality, as if these were the threatening waters in which she did not want to drown.

Then, for three days, father was ill, and Clorinda was ill, too, and mother hardly asked about Clorinda or why she was staying at the house of her brother, the gardener, instead of in her own room upstairs. And we hardly asked about our father's health, and everybody was alone in his anguish, like a dog. Then father recovered, that is, he got up and looked so old, so terribly old, that Sonia cried one day for hours on her books, while my brother and I insulted her by way of consolation.

Then another incident, meaningless of course, utterly meaningless, but there are moments in which everything creates an atmosphere of tragedy, even though there is no reason for it. Father went up to mother's ramparts, and at first it seemed as if he, too, were interested in the road. He dragged a newspaper behind him as a child would drag a piece of cloth or a toy; and he said:

'I see here in the paper that there is going to be a League of Nations to keep the world at peace. The President of the United States of America is coming to Europe.' Strange of him, with his cynicism, to make such a remark. Mother nodded without looking at him, then he said (his voice was very quivery after his illness): 'Peace. Yes, peace for a great many years to come. At least our sacrifices will be rewarded, all of them.'

And this must have seemed strange to mother, because she screamed: 'What do you mean?' And then she was out of breath and screamed again: 'What sacrifices? *We* are beyond that and we have forgotten. *Our* sacrifices *are* being rewarded.'

He was pale and trembling and said nothing.

'But what is it?' she said. 'Why do you look so disturbed?' He did not answer, and mother rose from her chair, and asked in a terrible tone: 'Tell me, tell me right away! Why do you tremble so?'

And he said: 'Why . . . I only thought I saw someone there, on the road.'

And she sank back in the chair, crying: 'Oh, I know. I know that. It happens to me all the time.'

That evening I spoke to Sonia at length. Especially now that Clorinda was ill and no one dared scold our parents, it was necessary that we do something, because it was no longer human. Waiting had become a malady, a family epidemic, a strange fever. And we talked and talked and reached no conclusion, and the next morning she told me that she had had a dream: the wind had been so strong against the house all night that in her dream she had seen the house sailing toward non-existent shores; and it was mother's fault, because her eyes had melted down the mountains and the road, and everything had been made into a sea, and we were drifting away on it. She was trembling as she told me that dream. She said: 'You see? Even I am all upset by these silly ideas now. Kostia will laugh at this when he comes.'

'I think that he will not have the time to laugh,' I said, 'because in this state of affairs they will start quarreling with him because he did not get here on time.'

'You are right,' she said. 'And it's so silly. Let's do something. This spell must be broken.'

And I said, 'Yes, it must be broken.'

The trouble was, however, that the house held our anguish so well, just as it held the silence, and then (it was about three o'clock in the afternoon), while I was having another conversation with Sonia about it, one of the maids came and said, gasping: 'The Signora is talking.'

We couldn't help smiling at such a silly statement. 'What do you mean?' we asked.

'She is talking,' she said at last, 'alone, by herself.'

Sonia began to tremble; she was afraid for mother's health, and I felt my heart bang against my bones so that I almost resounded from it; but Sonia, who was always courageous, said: 'That's nothing,' and began to go upstairs. She found Adrian who was climbing step by step, slowly, in the hope that nobody would notice him, and she had a quarrel with him. He called mother to his defense: 'Mamma, may I come upstairs?'

And mother shouted with a voice full of hate: 'Quiet there. Go away.'

We all left. Doors were closed again, one in the face of the other, all along the hall, and there was silence, a high silence, the highest silence that ever was in Spazzavento: silence mounted on a monument of roars, moans, and cries that the wind brought from somewhere with it. Then, suddenly, we heard the voice of mother and we slowly opened the door to the library, and she was saying, as if she had a fever:

'Go away, go away. It is not true.' And then she said: 'If you are true, then I must be your dream. You reflect my desire. . . .' And then she said: 'Thank you. You are offering it back to me, for it must ache up in the air alone, detached and naked; it must suffer up there as it does here.'

And we walked to the middle of the hall and I had to lean against the wall so as not to faint. Then we began to walk downstairs, away from her, and stepped along the stairs and saw in the middle of the hall father with his red bald head, standing, as one stands at Mass during Elevation. And then mother again spoke: 'Who makes this wind of light?' (This was one of her expressions to describe the beginning of dreams.) 'Who detaches the paper from the faces, the mountains, and the houses?'

'O, my God,' murmured Sonia, 'she is ill.'

'Who puts that cup there, on a hill?' said mother again. 'Go away!' she shouted. 'Go away. I know you, devils of dream. *These* things don't happen here. . . . I know I am waiting. You don't have to tell me.' Then, in a tired tone: 'I know I have waited much too long.' And she cried quietly, like a sick child.

Sonia walked up the stairs, knelt beside her, and said: 'You are right, mother.' She said it so gently, so well, sneaking into the unreality of the situation, feigning herself unreal too; and mother looked at her and said:

'The dreams were coming again. But don't be afraid. Let me alone.'

Sonia came downstairs, and this time it was as if all of a sudden mother had lost her battle, because she greeted him with so much strength in her voice:

'Oh, here you are,' she said. 'And tell me now: how are you?' Then she whispered: 'Did you come from downstairs? Tell me,' she repeated, 'did you? Through the garden? . . . Did you batter the ground with your own feet? You are expected to do that, you know. . . . And did you see the maid? She must have let you in.' After a silence, she said, a little louder: 'No, go downstairs first and ring the bell before we sit and talk.'

Then she seemed scared by something and asked with great anguish: 'Oh, but you have forgotten! How could you just be here, without a trip behind you? Kostia,' she said, 'my darling! How did you manage to avoid that? The trainman must have seen you! You must have waited, sitting in the train, to get here slowly, with permission from them all.'

Here she laughed, and then spoke again, in a weak voice: 'That's right; you are coming to see your mother. But we mothers are the last ones to see you. First must your soldiers see you leave for home, then many other people . . . oh, so many, so many, you can never count them all.'

At this point, luckily, the dream seemed to be over, for she coughed a little, then spoke cheerfully although still in a dreamy voice: 'Because you see, my dear,' she said, 'between you and us there is this road. Yes, this road. Then that mountain. O yes, a high mountain. Your mountain. Then . . . other mountains.' She stopped to listen, as we were all crying aloud. But she went on. 'Then,' she said, 'then . . . the plain of Bologna. Then, Venice. . . . And then . . . mountains again. That's right. Mountains again. And then . . . and then . . . ?' (We could hear her breathe with difficulty.)

And then she screamed, oh, how she screamed: 'I know! I know! . . . ' and ran downstairs ranting so terribly that we all fled as if a wild, wounded beast were after us.

*(From Harper's Magazine)*

# BREAD AND GAMES

## BY JOHN D. WEAVER

*A*S *ALVIN* swung down the beaten grass path to the trailer, the phonograph music behind the crisp plaid curtains seemed to be laughing at him, reminding him of something that had happened a long time ago, but did not matter now. He tugged irritably at the brim of his straw hat, fretting it still further down over his eyes. Time for Mama's eleven o'clock medicine, and Laird's wife just sat in there playing dance music.

'Laird.'

He rapped on the back door, calling his brother instead of that flibbertigibbet. He noticed she had strung her clothesline in front of the trailer again, her pink silky things in plain view of the road, although she knew Maud didn't like it, not, as Laird had said, because Maud wore cotton underthings. Maud just didn't think it was decent, especially with young children in the house.

'It's 'leven o'clock,' Alvin said, when Laird came to the door. Eleven o'clock and Laird still hadn't put his shirt on.

'Lolly's already gone up to the house,' Laird said.

'Oh.' Alvin stepped back. He could see inside the trailer now, and he was surprised to find the bed made, the breakfast dishes put away. Laird was working over a strip of broken film coiled like a king snake in a flat silver can.

'She took a book,' Laird said. 'She's gonna read to Mama.'

Alvin stiffened. He was sensitive about Maud's not being able to read.

476

'I gotta go up to the store,' Alvin said, turning away.

'I'll drive you up,' Laird said.

'I'd just as lief walk it.'

Laird grabbed up the jacket of an army fatigue uniform, slipped it on, and trotted down the portable back steps of the trailer. Alvin shrugged. He climbed into the car beside Laird, staring straight ahead, his hands cupped over his knees.

Alvin had been eighteen and Laird ten the summer their father died. That fall Alvin would have started his last year of high school, and he had wanted to finish, he had wanted that graduation paper more than he had ever wanted anything before or since. He had walked twelve miles a day to get his schooling, six miles into town and six miles back, in rain and snow and a northern Virginia cold so sharp-toothed it chewed through his clothes. And even worse than the walking had been the town kids who used to sneak up to him at recess and pull imaginary straw out of his hair, ask him if he'd sold his eggs yet, make fun of his made-over clothes and the way Mama cut his hair. One more year and he would have got that paper, but Papa had died, and Alvin had stayed home to run the farm.

Everything had been different for Laird. By the time he got to high school the county had a big yellow bus that came right to the door, took him to town and brought him home. And nobody picked on him, because there were plenty of hill boys to stand up against the town kids and keep them in their place. Laird, without having to walk or fight, could have got the graduation paper Alvin had wanted, but Laird would skip school to go fishing, sell his books to buy cigarettes, and one day, when he was just over fifteen, he had thrown a pop bottle at the principal and run off with a circus.

'I ain't surprised,' Mama had said when Alvin brought her the news, and she had looked up at Alvin and Maud, as though seeing them for the first time after a long separation. Alvin had just begun to take on weight, his face rounding out, and Maud was six months along with her second child,

her body swollen again before it had receded back to its
old lines after the first child. Then Mama had said something that Alvin and Maud had never spoken of to each
other, but that neither of them had ever forgotten, although
it was not a thing they tried especially to remember.

'All my life,' Mamma had said, 'I've been tied down here
in this valley, them hills risin' up all around me like a high
fence, and I've never stopped wonderin' what's on the other
side of 'em. I was a growed woman with a lap baby before I
ever seen a movin' picture show, and to this day I ain't been
on a railroad train. I'm glad Laird's gone. I'm glad he got
free.'

They hadn't heard from Laird for nearly four years then,
might never have heard, except the war happened, and when
the Army yanked Laird out of the circus, he wrote home
from a camp in Missouri and told them about Lolly.

'Hmpf,' Alvin had snorted. 'A show girl.' Maud, hearing
his pronouncement, had glanced up from her ironing, her cow
eyes infinitely patient and resigned. She had nodded, then
wet the tip of her finger, touched it gingerly to the iron, and
gone back to her work.

'Laird,' Mama had said, watching Maud, 'would pick a
girl with spirit.'

Mama must have been sick even then, but she never let on.
She managed to hold out until the summer the war ended,
and then she couldn't hide it any longer. The doctor used a
word Alvin had never heard before, malignancy, but Alvin
knew what he meant. And morphine, Alvin learned what
that meant, too. Mama kept asking for Laird, and Alvin told
her he was in the Army, and Mama would say, 'But the war's
over now. Why can't he come home?' 'He'll have to wait
his turn,' Alvin would say, 'like anybody else.' But Alvin
should have known that Laird would never have to wait like
other people. Laird went to the Red Cross, they sent a
woman out to see Mama, and two weeks later Laird and
Lolly came sailing home, a green trailer bouncing along behind their 1939 coupe.

'Alvin,' Mama had said one day after Laird and Lolly had been home about a month, 'Laird's army money is running out. It's time you got 'im a job.'

Alvin hadn't said anything, but he had thought how like Mama it was to tell him to get Laird a job instead of telling Laird to go out and get it himself. Alvin had gone to see Senator Crouch, and the Senator had spoken to the manager of the new rayon plant, because Alvin was on the county school board and had always supported the Organization. The manager had offered Laird a job at twice the highest wages anybody had ever paid Alvin. But Laird couldn't work in a factory. He was a show man.

'Somepun'll turn up,' Laird had said, and two days later he had got a letter from a man in New York who had been in the circus with him and was in the motion picture business now. He had made Laird a proposition, and Laird had driven to town and talked to the man long distance.

'Folks,' Laird had announced when he came home that night, 'we're in business.'

Every night Laird and Lolly would drive to a hill town which had no movie house, and put on an outdoor show. The man in New York furnished the film and projector in exchange for a percentage of the profits. They charged fifteen cents admission, and before each show, while Lolly sold candy, Laird did a few tricks and told a few jokes, then handed out prizes which he bought at wholesale from a place in Chicago. They charged fifteen cents for the candy, which cost them three cents a box. In Laurelton, though, they never charged for the Wednesday night shows. That, Laird insisted, was home, and he couldn't charge home folks. Of course he would always sell the candy to pay expenses.

Alvin spat against the dry wind whirring past the open window of the car, as Laird rolled across the new Laurelton bridge and parked in front of Lovell Jenkins' store. Some children, mostly girls, were playing in the dusty driveway between the store and the Jenkins' big yellow frame house. The minute they spotted Laird, they stopped playing and ran over to him.

'The *show* man!'

'Trick! Do us a trick!'

Alvin shuffled into the store, the children clearing an aisle for him, then closing ranks again, swarming around Laird. He pulled two red bandanas out of his pocket, and did his disappearing knot trick. The children, who had seen him do it every show night for six weeks, pressed against him, begging him to do some more tricks, but he told them to wait till tonight. He had some special new tricks for the show tonight.

'Lov,' Laird said, shaking off the children like burrs and striding into the store, 'you're a sportin' man. Now I tell you what I'm gonna do. I'm gonna drink a cold bottle of lemon sour, and I'm gonna smoke the best cigar you got in the house, and then I'm gonna flip a coin. If you call it right, I'm gonna pay you double, and if you don't call it, I'm gonna shake you by the hand and walk on outta here with my money in my pocket.'

Alvin was reading from a list, Mrs. Jenkins hobbling about the store, getting the things down from the shelves and putting them together on the counter. 'Salt. Sugar. Coffee . . .'

'Tails,' Lov said.

'Lovell, my friend,' Laird said, bowing, 'I thank you.'

'Just a minute,' Lov said. 'I didn't git to see that coin.'

'It come up heads,' Laird said.

'But I didn't see it.'

'That's all right, Lov, *I* seen it.'

Lov slapped the side of his leg, chuckling. That Laird, he could joke his way to hell'n back.

Alvin, bent forward under the weight of his box of groceries, started toward the car. Out of the corner of his eye he had seen Lovell slip a stick of chocolate ice cream into a sack and give it to Laird. Alvin had spent four dollars and thirty-six cents, and Mrs. Jenkins hadn't given him so much as a piece of penny candy for the kids, but Laird not only got his pop and his cigar for nothing, Lovell even threw in a little treat for Lolly.

'It'd make your stomach turn,' Alvin told Maud when he

got home with the groceries, 'the way the kids all follow him around and everybody falls all over themselves givin' him treats and . . .'

He stopped abruptly, his glance lighting on four huge red tomatoes, freshly washed and laid aside. Maud followed the line of his look, her face coloring, her eyes dropping.

'Laird's so fond of 'em,' Maud said.

'If Laird's so fond of 'em, why can't Lolly help you tend 'em?'

'She's got 'er own work to do.'

Alvin picked up the four tomatoes, which were so big his hands could hardly hold them. 'I'll take 'em down for you,' he said, and Maud started to protest, then shrugged and went on with her kitchen work.

As he came near the trailer, he could hear Lolly, and then Laird, followed by a childish chorus of amazement and delight. It sounded like the trailer was filled with kids. He could make out little Alvie's voice, and he guessed that Maudie and Mattie May were there, too. Alvie hadn't swept the porch yet or brought in the wood chips, and the two girls should be helping their mother wash the tomatoes and put them away. Alvin lengthened his stride. One thing he wouldn't stand for, Laird and Lolly weren't going to spoil his children.

Lolly was standing in the trailer door, her back to him. She had on a red sunsuit, a strip of red across her back with a small red bow, and her long brown legs bare beneath the short skirt. She turned when she heard him, her yellow hair whipping lightly around her throat. He handed her the tomatoes, not looking at the sunsuit, mumbling, 'Maud sent 'em down.' Then he called to Alvie and the two girls. 'You all git on up to the house. You got your work to do.'

'Uncle Laird's gonna do his snake trick,' Alvie said.

'You finish your work,' Alvin said. 'Then we'll see about tricks.'

The trailer swarmed with children, five on the daybed, at least half a dozen scattered over the floor. Alvie started to whine, and Laird, stepping over the heads of the others, soothed him. 'Tonight,' Laird said, easing Alvie toward the door, 'you'll get to see all the tricks and a nice show besides. A Mickey Mouse.'

Lolly held up the tomatoes for Laird to see. 'Aren't they terrific?' she said, and she told Alvin again to thank Maud for them. 'Laird loves fried tomatoes for his breakfast.'

A little girl in a striped blue dress got up from the floor. Alvin wasn't sure, but when he got to thinking about it afterwards he figured she was one of the Clagett girls. She had the Clagett mouth.

'Our'n was bigger,' the little girl said.

Lolly flushed. 'Yours were nice, too.'

'Bigger,' the little girl insisted. 'Twicet as big.'

As Lolly moved to shush the child, Alvin could see the small white sink at the other end of the trailer. It was piled with tomatoes, and there were fresh peas, beets, roasting ears, even a quart pail of blackberries.

'Well,' Alvin said, 'I didn't know you were already supplied. Another time Maud'n me won't bother.'

'Laird never gets enough fresh tomatoes,' Lolly said.

'And ain't it nice,' Alvin said, 'he don't have to work for 'em.'

He grabbed Alvie by the arm and yanked him toward the house, the two girls cowering behind him. 'No show for you all tonight,' Alvin said, and the children set up such a howl that Maud came bobbing out of the house, breathless. She held court on the steps, and the children got to go to the show, but they had to promise not to go down to Uncle Laird's trailer any more. Alvin insisted on that.

'I catch you all down there again,' Alvin said, 'you don't ever git to go to the show again. You hear me?'

'But . . .'

'Now, Alvie, you heard your father,' Maud said, and that ended the argument because they had long ago learned that Daddy was always right, and even when he wasn't, they must never let on to Mama they knew he wasn't.

After supper Lolly came up to the house with an armful of magazines. She told Maud to hurry and get dressed for the show, she was going to stay with Mama tonight. Maud protested, but Lolly just smiled and shut her out of Mama's room. Maud, curious to see what kind of a show Laird put on, slipped into her next-to-best dress, a holly print, and rode up to Laurelton in Laird's car, sitting between Laird and Alvin, the children in the rumble seat. She was surprised to find how excited she was, like the children.

'If it was prayer meetin',' Alvin said after Laird had parked the car and taken the projector into Lov Jenkins' store, 'I wonder how many of 'em would be hurryin' so fast to git here?'

Maud shook her head. She could see the cars, packed with children, tumbling down the hill roads, bouncing over ruts hidden by the thickening dust. Parking in the schoolyard or along the blacktop road, wherever there was room, the families filed across the new cement bridge and down the narrow dirt driveway to the sprawling, unkempt yard behind the Jenkins' store. The children ran ahead, eager to get close to the open truck where the show man did his tricks. The older people kept to the back of the yard, talking primaries and hay-making, poking envious fun at the men who had thought to bring pillows or camp stools.

Laird set up his projector in the back of the store, training it on the portable screen already put up in the yard, then Lov Jenkins helped him run a light through the back door out to the truck, which was parked on the creek side of the yard. It was a large open flatbed truck, with sapling poles sticking up on each side. Some of the prizes, the scarves and dish towels and pan holders, were hanging on the poles, while others were scattered over the shelf of overturned crates. The bright red, green, and yellow of the prizes shone against the weathered earth color of the truck and the dark wall of trees along the creek.

Alvin edged off from the crowd, leaving Maud laughing and gossiping with a flock of women. He saw Laird stride out of the back door, glance quickly at the screen, the crowd, the truck. Laird's face was drawn tight with worry, and for a moment Alvin felt that maybe Laird was taking Mama's sickness harder than he let on.

'All right, folks.' Laird had climbed up on the truck, and, beaming, he began to wave his arms, quieting the crowd. He singled out a talkative man in a blue shirt with red armbands. 'Ab,' he said, 'if you want to entertain the folks, why don't you come up here?' The crowd tittered, the man reddened and slunk out of sight.

'Well, well,' Laird said, 'I see we got sportin' men in the crowd tonight, and I tell you what I'm gonna do. Somepun a li'l bit different. I know everybody likes somepun different once'n a while, so tonight I'm gonna pass among you with some boxes, and I'm gonna tell you beforehand there ain't a thing in them boxes, no sir, they're just as empty as my head, and you know thas plenty empty. I'm gonna hand out these empty boxes, and you're gonna pay me fifteen cents, and then you're gonna tear off the bottom of the box and write your name on it. I'm gonna put the names in a hat, not *my* hat, mind you, I got a brand new hat, but I'll take old Charley Mauck's hat here, and I'm gonna put all the names in it, and here's some of the prizes you winners are gonna draw tonight.'

He reached behind him and got a white dish towel with a red border. He held it up to his waist, frowning, as though not sure what it was supposed to be used for. A woman began to laugh, and Laird turned to her.

'Thas right, Mrs. Sowers. This here's a dish towel. *I* knowed what it was. I just wanted to see if *you* knowed. Then we got this pretty glass frame. You can put your pitcher in it, or if you never had your pitcher took, you can put your army discharge papers in it, or if you never was in the Army, you can put your marriage license in it, or if you never was married, you can put your birth certificate in it, or if you never was born, you can. . . . Well, next we got these red bandanas. Used to sell 'em for ten cents for men's handkerchiefs, but then the ladies got to tyin' 'em around their heads for show, so now they call 'em bandanas and they ask fifty-nine cents for 'em. Just goes to show you what happens when the ladies make a show of somepun. Now the grand prize tonight is somepun special, mighty special . . .'

Mrs. Sowers, who had known Laird since he was a crawling baby, began to laugh again. Every week Laird said the grand prize was something special, and of course it was always another factory-made Indian blanket. Laird stopped, stared straight at Mrs. Sowers, pretending great annoyance. The crowd got ready to laugh. Old Laird was going to let her have it.

'I reckon you think you know what the grand prize is,' Laird said, and Mrs. Sowers said sure, it was one of them old Indian blankets. 'Now thas just where you're wrong,' Laird said, and he turned back to the crowd. 'You see, folks, thas what comes of bein' too smart for your own good. Our friend here thinks she knows what the grand prize is, so she ain't holdin' her breath, waitin' like the rest of you. Oh no, she's too smart. Well, this is where she gits the surprise of her life, 'cause the grand prize tonight — now I told you it was somepun special — the grand prize is a genuine imported lap robe for your car.'

Laird held up the Indian blanket, and the crowd roared its delight. Old Laird had done it again.

'Now remember, folks,' Laird said, waving a box of candy over his head, 'these here're just empty boxes I'm sellin' tonight.'

The children eyed the familiar box, pricked by a little stab of worry. Maybe the boxes really were empty. But, no, it was just the show man fooling again.

'Who's gonna be the first sport to step up and give me fifteen cents for an empty box?'

Soley Sowers nudged Burr Rivercomb, and Burr held up his hand. 'Well, Laird said, handing a box to Burr, 'we got *one* sport anyway.' Then the others began to crowd around the truck, mostly children, the grown-ups giving them the money, figuring they ought to buy the candy because Laird didn't charge anything for the show. They knew exactly

what was in the boxes, two gumdrops, a hoarhound drop, a
licorice whip, and some little prize, a whistle, a package of
preserving jar labels, a balloon, or a couple of marbles. The
children tore open the boxes, dug for their surprise, then
gobbled the candy and traded prizes. The older children
wrote the names on the label and put them in the hat. Most
of the grown-ups couldn't read or write.

'Now, folks,' Laird said when the candy sales began to
taper off, 'tonight I got a li'l surprise for you. You all been
comin' here to the shows, and you seen me do my tricks.
Well, tonight I'm gonna show you one of the tricks of the
trade, gonna show you how to do that knot trick. It's fun to
be fooled, friends, but it's more fun to know, and once you
git the hang of it, you can fool your friends.'

Laird motioned the little Slater boy to climb up on the
truck. The child's obvious fright appealed to the crowd.
They began to clap reassuringly. Laird rumpled the boy's
red hair. 'Gonna make a show man outta this boy,' Laird
said, then he held up two red bandanas, one in each hand.
'All right now, folks, here's the way you do it. You tie the
bandanas together in a square knot, the tighter the better.'
Laird tugged at the knot, drawing it tight, then holding it
up for the crowd to see. 'Once you git your knot good'n
tight, you cover it up like this. Fold this end up'n over, and
then this end, so now you can't see the knot, but you know
it's there under them two folded ends. How about it, son?
Is the knot still there?'

The Slater boy reached up and took hold of the knot. He
nodded shyly. 'Still there, huh?' Laird said, then he motioned the boy to take hold of the knotted bandanas. 'Now
here's the part you watch close,' Laird said. He placed his
flattened hands about six inches above the bandanas which
the Slater boy was holding, then he closed his eyes and began
to spout a quick, solemn gibberish. 'Abacadabra, rootenscootenhooten, sisboombah. You hear that, everybody? Abacadabra, rootenscootenhooten, sisboombah. All right now,
let's see if the knot's still there.'

Laird reached down and took the two bandanas from the

boy's hand. They were untied. He held them up, one in each hand.

'Thas all there is to it, folks. Just say the right words. Now you can all go home and fool your friends.'

The crowd, taken in by the fast patter, caught on to the joke. They chuckled, shook their heads. That Laird.

'Lolly said he was havin' a cartoon pitcher tonight,' Maud said. Alvin glanced at her curiously. She was sitting on the running board of Laird's car, bent forward, staring at the white screen, a strange shine of excitement in her eyes. 'And a singin' cowboy,' Maud said.

Laird had the Slater boy shuffle all the names in the hat, then draw the prizewinners. Mrs. Compson won a jar with a fancy glass stopper, and the crowd howled when Laird slyly told her she could keep her elderberry wine in it. Everybody knew how Serena Compson felt about wine. Maud was the last winner. Giggling, she went up to the truck and Laird gave her two red bandanas. 'Now you can do the knot trick,' Laird said. 'Just remember the magic words.' Maud, pleased and embarrassed, went back to the running board and sat down. She gave the bandanas to Alvin. He hurriedly stuffed them in his pocket, upset by all the attention the prize had drawn to Maud and himself.

'Now, folks,' Laird said, killing the light on the truck, 'just settle back in your big easy chairs and enjoy the show.'

Darkness had settled slowly over the hills which rimmed the town like the sides of a broken blue saucer, the creek marking the break. Gnats swarmed across the lighted window, and the children, talking in whispers, kept their eyes on the screen, not wanting to miss the start of the picture. A cool breeze stirred the leaves of the sycamores along the creek, and the men leaning against the mottled trunks stared across the vast width of darkness which ended at Hogback Mountain. Above them the stars were like a great scattering of salt crystals on a blue cloth. Suddenly the children began to squeal happily, to whistle and clap their hands, then as suddenly they hushed. The picture show had started.

Afterwards, lying beside Alvin in the brass bed, Maud closed her eyes, and she could see the whole show again, the cartoon picture, the singing cowboy, even the crazy white flashes when Laird was changing the film. The picture mouse kept getting caught in the wire coil, and the big stupid dog backed into an open fire, then jumped and hit his head against the door, and the cowboy sang so loud they must have heard him down at the lime kiln, but it was pretty to listen to, and they made a nice couple, him and the girl. Maud drowsed off, and the singing played in her mind like Laird's phonograph music. When she woke up, she didn't know how many minutes or hours later, she was startled, she sensed at once that Alvin wasn't in the bed.

'Alvin?' She saw him standing by the window in his cotton nightshirt. 'You sick?'

'No.' His body jerked, like a colt shying.

'I git you anything?'

He stood with his back toward her, his hands hidden. 'No. I'm all right.' He was edgy, a sting in his voice. She lay back in the bed, and when he spoke again, after what seemed a long while, he was uncertain, he fumbled, and he still didn't look at her. 'I've tried. I've always tried to do what was right. Ain't I, Maud?'

'Why, Alvin, of course you have.'

'I've done a lot for people 'round here. They'd still be usin' coal oil lamps if I hadn't gone to the Senator and got the 'lectric lights put in out here, and the same with the phones and the government trees.'

'Sure, everybody knows that, and they 'preciate it.'

'Nobody's ever said so. They've never even said thank you. But Laird, Laird comes back and tells 'em a joke and shows 'em a picture, and they just can't do enough for 'im. Even my own kids, they hang 'round that trailer like it was a candy counter.'

'It's the tricks and the music, and Lolly makes pretty things for the girls.'

'Even Mama,' he said, speaking into the pale square of window light. 'We've made 'er a home, we work the place and pay the bills, but when she's bad off, does she ever ask for us? No, it's Laird'n Lolly. It's always Laird'n Lolly.'

She fluffed up his pillow and smoothed the rumpled sheets on his side of the bed. 'You come on back to the bed. You're tired.'

'Everything I've ever wanted or worked for,' he said, 'I've never quite got it, but always it's come to Laird, just handed to 'im, and he's turned his back on it. Why, Maud? *Why?*'

The room was quiet, with no sound except the idiot screech of the treefrogs.

'I ain't sure of things any more,' he said. 'I used to be, but not now. I just ain't sure of anything.'

As he turned toward her, his face was haggard and tormented, she saw for the first time that he was holding the two bandanas she had won at the show, and she knew what had awakened her, the sound of his clumsy tugging at the knot trick Laird did so easily.

*(From Cosmopolitan)*

# THE HIDDEN ROOM

## BY LAWRENCE WILLIAMS

*A*T THE AGE of fifty-four years it was Mr. Jolie's impression that he lived his life inside a cage. As this cage was the mining city of Grantsburgh, Pennsylvania, it was necessarily inhabited by others, but as the others, in Mr. Jolie's view, were not aware that it was a cage, they didn't mind living in it. Only Mr. Jolie by virtue of his superior sensitivity, was aware of it.

Consequently, he felt sure that only he deserved release from the cage, and that time was trying to trick him by delaying his release.

It would be difficult to say what intricate combination of circumstances had bred these notions in Mr. Jolie's mind, but it was their presence which very nearly cost him his last slim measure of security.

Mr. Jolie's first class at nine o'clock on Monday morning was English I, a class which he despised neither more nor less than any other of his classes. He sat down behind his desk, straining his eyes so that they would focus on his students waiting listlessly before him. His eyes burned and pricked in their sockets with the effort of straining, causing a splitting pain to run back to the base of Mr. Jolie's skull and to remain there the precise amount of time required for another pain to run back and replace it. The insides of his cheeks tasted acrid and sour. Very suddenly he snatched his hand off the surface of his desk because a girl in the front row had been staring stupidly at its trembling.

490

Mr. Jolie glared at the girl for a moment, then he opened the battered text book in front of him and lowered his eyes to it. He made no effort to read as there was no need. 'Page thirty-six, Act three, Scene two. Mark Antony speaks. Sophie Poliarski, read.'

The girl in the front row who had stared at Mr. Jolie's hand rose and stood in the aisle beside her desk. She peered nearsightedly into her book and began to read in a halting, monotonous voice. ' "But yesterday the word of Caesar might have stood against the world . . . " '

'Well?' said Mr. Jolie. The word was uttered irritably and was addressed not to the reading girl, but to a boy farther back in the classroom who had raised his hand.

The boy stood up. His shoulders were painfully thin, and the ribbing on his corduroy trousers had been worn to the smoothness of sacking across his knees. But he held his body very straight, and his light, intelligent eyes, set deeply into his skull, were clear and unwavering. They were curious eyes, contradictory eyes which seemed at once to be dreamily preoccupied and to see more than most eyes. These eyes looked at Mr. Jolie now, and there was some consternation in them. 'Excuse me, sir,' he said, 'we got past that Friday. We was up to "If you have tears, prepare to shed them now." '

It was this thing, this fear of forgetting which had harassed Mr. Jolie in recent months. He had tried marking the place in the book where a day's reading had stopped, but the pages had become so scribbled with pencil marks that they had little meaning. Also he occasionally forgot to make any mark at all. Once, during the previous month, he had gone back an entire chapter in the grammar book. Sometimes he could remember these things, but over week ends it was especially trying.

Mr. Jolie was not pleased to be reminded of this irritation. He raised his eyebrows, concentrating his attention upon the boy who had spoken. As he did so, a series of deep furrows appeared in the dry, yellow skin of his forehead, extending up to the scalp where the skin was of a different texture, but where there was no hair. He spoke with exaggeratedly elaborate courtesy. 'Amaric,' he said, 'I don't doubt that your long and studious association with the poet in question entitles you to conduct this class far better than I, but as others have seen fit to entrust that responsibility to me, I beg you to allow me to conduct it in my own way.'

The boy, Paul Amaric, instantly recognized the sarcasm in Mr. Jolie's tone as though from long familiarity. While his interest in the text was genuine enough, he did not place that interest in importance above a set-to with Mr. Jolie. He watched the schoolmaster's face closely, trying to determine whether he had gone too far. Then he made his decision. 'Maybe I made a mistake, sir,' he said, and started to sit down.

But Mr. Jolie stopped him with a movement of his hand. 'That is barely possible,' he said in the same tone. 'But I feel that your consuming interest in great literature should not go unrecognized. In addition to your regular homework for tomorrow, you may copy the speech ten times beginning with the lines you quoted.' He turned back to the girl, 'Continue with the reading.'

Paul Amaric returned silently to his seat. He made no effort to remonstrate against the injustice of the punishment, but only continued to stare at Mr. Jolie with his clear, defiant eyes, as though he were totting up a mental balance sheet of the score between the schoolmaster and himself.

Mr. Jolie pretended to follow the reading in the book. Actually he was trying hard not to listen. The monotony of the voices sickened him. He made no attempt to correct the frequent mispronunciations, only raising his head from time to time to call a name, when a new reader would begin where another had stopped.

Mr. Jolie enunciated these names in a way which suggested that they were not names at all, but obscenities. The names were nearly all of Middle-European sound, and Mr. Jolie always made it a point to mispronounce them. They were distasteful to him not only because he preferred his own French and English ancestry, but because he associated such names with the filth and ugliness which made up his life and all life in this city. Foreigners (as he called them all indiscriminately), fathers of these children, his charges, worked in the tortuous warp of tunnels beneath the ground to bring up each day carloads of grime to add to the ugliness of Mr. Jolie's existence.

The schoolmaster himself had been born in another, cleaner city and had been transplanted at a tender age to this one by his father who had been a mine foreman, distinctions which had not been obscured in Mr. Jolie's consciousness by all the forty-odd years of his present residence. A Bachelor-of-Arts degree at the local university had qualified him for his post as English teacher in the high-school grades, and he had held it ever since. There had been a time, a few years earlier, when he had been considered for the vacated position of principal of the school, as he was the only man remaining on the faculty. But the decision of the school board finally had gone against him. Although no reason was ever given officially, it was said privately that Mr. Jolie had been seen to enter certain buildings on Saturday nights in certain unfashionable sections of the city; it was also said that he drank.

When these rumors reached Mr. Jolie, as they inevitably did, his disdain for the citizenry perceptibly increased, if such a thing were possible. Within him there grew up a hungry longing to inform the school board that he would not have taken their contemptible job had it been offered him — that a step upward on a ladder which is totally submerged in sewage was not regarded by him as a step toward the sun.

Of course he did not say any of these things to the school board as the small income his position afforded him was all the income he possessed. Instead, he locked himself inside his house for three days, sending word to the school by messenger that he was unwell; he emerged at the end of that time with bloodshot eyes and trembling fingers.

It was on his first day back at his classes after this incident that Mr. Jolie struck one of his students, a boy of Hungarian descent, called Fekete, for some infraction of discipline. As a result of this offense he was summoned to interview the newly appointed principal, a woman, younger than himself. The subsequent interview was a humiliating experience for Mr. Jolie and an embarrassing one for the principal, but Mr. Jolie had managed to explain his behavior by attributing it to a transient nervous condition induced by his recent indisposition. He had been severely warned against any repetition of the incident, and the affair had been dropped.

Each evening for many years Mr. Jolie had experienced a recurrent waking dream — rather he had consciously practiced it. He sat alone in his small, ugly house, reaching out his hand from time to time to freshen the contents of his glass and practiced his dream of a place which he had never seen.

This place was a small university town in which all the buildings, including the buildings of the university itself, were of colonial architecture and were painted gleaming white. The students who attended this university all had been born and christened with Anglo-Saxon names, and all were very rich. The faculty members, on the other hand, were all very poor, with the single exception of Mr. Jolie who was in possession of an indeterminate private income and who invariably donated the greater portion of his salary, as holder of the chair of English literature, to a deserving charitable organization. In addition to being abjectly poor, the rest of the faculty was composed of men of markedly inferior intellect, and of men whose origin was not above the suspicion of those who comprehended the importance of such things. Because of this situation the students were quick to perceive Mr. Jolie's superior erudition and breeding, often in talks among themselves, derisively referring to the university president himself as 'Old Jolie's assistant' — a charge which Mr. Jolie was sometimes called upon modestly to deny.

His own house in this town of his practiced dream was a place of infinite charm. It was furnished with priceless museum pieces, inherited as heirlooms from pre-Revolutionary ancestors whose mode of living had been no less gracious than his own. 'I feel that they should be *used*,' Mr. Jolie would smilingly explain when visitors first exclaimed on seeing these treasures. 'After all, that's why some old boy made them. (In Nottingham, I believe. I'd have to look at the papers to be sure.) Plenty of time for them to be in a museum after I'm gone.'

Actually, only one room of this house was wholly decorated in Mr. Jolie's dream, but that was sufficient. It was the room in which his rich and sometimes troubled students came to him in quest of the understanding, satisfactory advice for which he had become so properly celebrated; and the room in which he gave faculty teas, those necessary functions which were such tedious affairs at the homes of his colleagues but which were regarded as the social high lights of the semester when conducted in Mr. Jolie's handsome room. The room in Mr. Jolie's dream was more familiar to him than any room he had physically entered in the whole of his life.

All day every day the living in this gleaming white town was scholarly and genteel, even rather elegant — a place in which one was either born to live or one was not.

Such was Mr. Jolie's waking dream, and for more than thirty years he had dreamed it, sitting alone in his small, ugly house and watching the black silt of the city sift through the crack under his front door. This was true of every evening in the week with the exception of Saturday evening, at which time he went elsewhere . . .

A bell jangled suddenly in the school corridor, and Mr. Jolie's body jerked in the chair behind his desk. Although the bell indicated that the class was over, the children made no move to leave the classroom. It was evident that they had learned the inadvisability of not waiting for Mr. Jolie's formal dismissal, and they watched his face closely. They had learned also that Mr. Jolie sometimes forgot to give them a homework assignment, a circumstance which was not as pleasurable as might be supposed for, on discovering his neglect, Mr. Jolie simply doubled the assignment for the next day.

Now he rose leisurely, surveying his class, taking evident pleasure in exercising his authority to detain them after the bell had rung. 'For tomorrow,' he said, and the children placed their pencils on their writing pads, 'a theme of not less than two hundred words on the topic: "A trip Around My Room." ' This was a standard assignment with Mr. Jolie, one which he had found years ago in a text book together with 'My Vacation,' 'My Dog (and/or Cat, Bird, etc.),' 'My Ambition,' 'Why I Am a Democrat (Republican)' and many others. Then he dismissed the class, and with the dismissal came a sudden bedlam of slamming books, stamping feet and talk.

When the last child had left the room Mr. Jolie rose, crossed quickly to the door and closed it. Then he went back to his desk and withdrew a pint bottle from the bottom drawer. While still in a stooping position he slipped the bottle under his coat and walked with it to a post behind the door where he could not be taken by surprise. He took two long swallows, then let his head roll back against the blackboard, gasping a little and drawing his lips back from his teeth. He held the bottle up to the light, studying its contents as a chemist might study the contents of his alembic, gauging what remained against the number of hours he must make it last. Finally he took another, shorter swallow and returned the bottle to the desk.

The pain at the base of Mr. Jolie's skull grew dimmer at once, and he sat down again at his desk. A stack of uncorrected examination papers lay before him which he had planned to correct in this, his free period in the morning, but he did not look at them immediately. He permitted his head to drop onto his folded arms, his eyes closed, his thin lips smiling.

As was the case with his not being able to remember everything distinctly, it was only comparatively recently that Mr. Jolie had begun to practice his dream while he was in the schoolroom. For years he had consciously avoided thinking while at work of the white university town, his house in it and his beautiful room, because it had seemed almost to defile that gracious place to think of it in the soot and shabbiness of the schoolroom. But of late when the dream had forced its way into the reality, he had let it come not because it was any less consecrated in his mind, but because he was no longer able to hold it back.

When the bell in the hall sounded the end of the period its clatter rasped against Mr. Jolie's consciousness like a physical blow on the side of his head. It seemed impossible that forty minutes could have elapsed since he had dropped his head on his arms for a moment's thinking. Blinking his eyes to clear them, he quickly jerked open the bottom drawer of his desk. He had no other free period until the middle of the afternoon, and he was angry at himself for having allowed so much time to slip by. As he reached his hand into the drawer, however, the classroom door opened and the first group of his English II students entered. For a moment Mr. Jolie remained leaning over the drawer in indecision, his fingers touching the cool, smooth surface of the glass. Then he did a thing he had never done before.

He withdrew the bottle cautiously and slipped it under his coat as he had done earlier, then walked to the back of the room and opened the door of the coat closet. Inside the closet was a strong odor of damp wool and rubber; a nearly exhausted light bulb overhead brought a faint yellow glow to the cubicle. Mr. Jolie braced his foot against the door and drank. Presently he corked the bottle and placed it carefully inside the pocket of his overcoat which hung in the corner of the closet, and went out.

This series of actions brought to Mr. Jolie a great sense of freedom, and he could not imagine why he hadn't thought to execute them before. They were so simple and at the same time so safe. The students had scarcely glanced at him. In the future, he concluded with satisfaction, he no longer need bother to apportion the minutes between his classes.

The English II class passed in much the same monotony as

did the English I class. The two sets of pupils in Mr. Jolie's view, with the exception of a year's difference in age, were interchangeable. These were equally shabby, their names equally Middle-European. Some of the names, in fact, were the same as those in English I, a coincidence which irritated Mr. Jolie as it added to the difficulty of remembering them. It was trouble enough to have to remember an outlandish name like Amaric, for example, without having to remember that there was in English I that pushy upstart, whose grades were impertinently good, Paul Amaric, and in English II, Louis Amaric, Paul's older hulk of a brother.

The conclusion of this period again caught Mr. Jolie without having issued a homework assignment. He had not been to the coat closet for forty minutes and he wanted badly to go there. He spoke the first words that came into his head. 'A theme of not less than two hundred words,' he said, 'on the topic: "A Trip Around My Room." Class dismissed.'

It was not until Mr. Jolie had emerged from the coat closet some minutes later that he realized he had given the same assignment to two classes. He was not particularly distressed by this discovery, for it was difficult to see then how it could possibly make any difference to anyone.

The themes from both classes, when he corrected them, were precisely what Mr. Jolie had expected them to be. He read through them hurriedly during his free period on the next afternoon, skimming along the lines with a red pencil, underlining misspellings, inserting commas, but scarcely following the sense of the words, so repugnant was their content to him. The themes were strikingly similar as were the lives of those who composed them, and the change of an occasional phrase could have rendered many of them identical.

Mr. Jolie had commenced his reading with the work done by English II for the reason that it was at the top of his pile. The last of these themes had been composed by Louis Amaric, and read:

## A Trip Around My Room

At the left of the door of my room when you come in is a bed. This bed is made out of some kind of iron and is where I sleep with Paul my brother. On the other side of this bed is another bed that is smaller where my brother Dominic who works sleeps. On the wall over that bed is where the window is. The glass in this window has broken but we pasted a paper over it. The paper has a picture of the president on it and it is out of the Sunday paper and it keeps out a lot of the coal dirt. Next to this window when you go around my room is a box where Paul me and Dominic keep our clothes. Over this box is a round hole in the wall where there used to be a stove pipe set in before we lived here. Now we got this hole stuffed full of paper but we get heat in my room out of the door that goes to our other room where my mother and father and my baby sister sleep where there is a stove. On the wall next to this hole is a mirror because my brother Dominic shaves sometimes. Next to the mirror is the door again where I started.

Mr. Jolie scribbled C plus at the top of this composition and placed it in the stack on the right side of his desk. Then he rose and made a brief excursion to the coat closet. On his return he breathed deeply and took up the first of the themes from English I. Attached to it by a straight pin was a thick sheaf of pages whose presence Mr. Jolie could not at once understand. He read the sentence at the top of the first page: 'If you have tears, prepare to shed them now.'

The remainder of the passage took up the whole page and was repeated ten times on ten different pages. Then Mr. Jolie recollected the penalty he had imposed on Paul Amaric the day before. He tossed the pages on the stack at his right hand and commenced reading the younger Amaric's theme:

## A Trip Around My Room

When you come into my room the first thing you notice is how white everything is. The walls are painted white and so is my bed. When the sun comes in through the big window sometimes it's so bright you have to squint to keep out the white. Next to my bed is a table where I put my portible typewriter and sometimes a box of chocolate candy, and there is a lamp on it with a long neck you can twist any way you want. Over my bed on the wall are two pointed college flags. One is red and the other is green and underneath them are two crossed tenis rackets. On the other side of my bed in my room is a sort of desk where I have my microscope. It is very interesting to look through this microscope and see all the millions of germs there are in one drop of water. Also a tiny speck of coal dirt looks like a big rock through this microscope it's so strong. Studying with a microscope like mine is how a lot of doctors found new germs.

In the drawer of my desk is where I keep my stamp collection and my coin collection and my rock specimens. I'm saving up for the museum. Next to my desk is a big victrola and a lot of victrola records so I can hear all the music I want any time and it doesn't cost me a cent. Next to that is my chemistry set where I can do all kinds of experiments. I have a lot of tubes and little heaters and all different chemicals. This is a pretty big room. There is a big fireplace here where I burn wood logs and I can keep it going all night if I want. Also I have a big closet where I keep all my clean clothes and my shoes. This is such a good room you couldn't want a better room.

It was not until after he had read several sentences of this composition that Mr. Jolie began to observe the discrepancy between this composition and the one written by Louis Amaric. A flush of blood colored his yellow skin and methodically he went back and read the theme over again from the beginning, forcing his full attention upon it.

When he had finished his second reading he rose from his desk, forgetting all the other papers from English I, and a great, unreasoning anger swelled up inside Mr. Jolie. He walked swiftly to the coat closet and rashly consumed a full two thirds of what remained in his bottle, although another forty-minute period stretched ahead of him. In the musty darkness of the closet he did not attempt to examine his anger to discover its cause. He felt that he had no wish to do so. Inside him was only a deep sense of outrage, as though he had been cheated, as though he had been robbed by design of a possession he held more dear than any other. An artery pulsed violently in his throat. 'The filthy little liar,' he said into the dark.

Outside in the corridor Mr. Jolie stopped the first child who passed and sent word by him to Paul Amaric. 'Tell him immediately after school,' he said, speaking in such a way that his lips scarcely moved, 'in my room. No excuse.'

To the recitations of his final class of the day Mr. Jolie paid no attention whatever, and he dismissed them without a homework assignment. In the coat closet he finished the contents of his bottle in two gasping swallows and walked back to his desk, his spine unnaturally stiff.

The schoolhouse had grown suddenly still with the stillness possible only in a place which sound and many people regularly inhabit. At the end of the corridor a janitor dropped his metal dust pan; the crash echoed like a gun burst in a culvert.

Presently the classroom door opened and Paul Amaric stood with his shoes straddling the wooden sill, neither in the room nor out of it. In one hand he held his books, tightly bound with a length of clothes line, the other he rubbed nervously on the leg of his shoddy corduroys. He stood stiffly, his eyes studying the schoolmaster's face, suspecting the nature of the coming interview.

'Close the door,' Mr. Jolie said, and he watched the movements of the boy with great care. 'Stand over here. No, no, over here — in front of my desk.'

Paul Amaric did as he was bidden.

Mr. Jolie raised his eyebrows so that the deep furrows creased his forehead to where his hairline had once been. 'How does it feel to be a liar?' he said.

The boy's light, intelligent eyes seemed to grow larger as wonder filled them. 'What?' he said, ' . . . sir?'

'This lie, Amaric,' Mr. Jolie said, balancing the paper very delicately on his hand. It trembled slightly. 'This one.'

Paul Amaric's eyes did not waver. 'That's not a lie, sir,' he said.

The schoolmaster's face twitched involuntarily and all color was washed from it. 'You will stay in this room, Amaric, and copy your brother's truthful composition until you admit your lie,' said Mr. Jolie quietly. The artery in his neck recommenced its furious pulsing.

The boy transferred his weight from one foot to the other. His familiarity with Mr. Jolie's punishments made him hesitate, but only for a moment. He was plainly afraid of the schoolmaster's menacing tone, but he continued to look steadily into the other's eyes. 'It wasn't a lie, sir. Not like you mean, it wasn't. It's a room I'm going to have sometime.'

Then something snapped inside Mr. Jolie. An inexplicable, uncontrollable rage surged up within him, starting in his stomach and flooding out over his body. He jerked himself up out of his chair and stood before the boy, the theme paper trembling in his hand. He ripped the page across once violently, then ripped it again and again. When it was no bigger than a postage stamp its thickness prevented him from ripping it still again, and he hurled the pieces at his wastebasket. He was breathless from his sudden exertion, but words began to pour out of him, jumbled, disconnected words which he himself scarcely heard. 'You think you can just invent a room, a different kind of life, and it will suddenly be yours for the taking, do you, Amaric? You have the impertinence to think that! You think you'll get out of this filthy place someday. Well, you won't! You'll never get out!'

Mr. Jolie smashed his fist down on the surface of his desk. It slipped on the sharp corner of the wood, rolling the skin off his knuckles in white rolls. The pain increased his fury, and he advanced a step toward the boy. 'Admit that what you wrote was a seeking, presumptuous lie!' he shouted. 'Admit that writing it was an insolent wrong! Admit it!'

Standing before the ranting schoolmaster a curious change took place in young Paul Amaric. His fear seemed to pour out of him like water from an overturned cup. His eyes grew calm, and to his mouth came a secret, understanding smile, a smile of quiet superiority. There was wonder in it, too, as though at some new and unexpected revelation.

Now when he spoke there was no trace of reluctance in his voice. His words to the frightened man before him were gentle, almost reassuring. 'Yes, sir, what I wrote was a lie,' he said. 'My real room at home is just like Louis said. It's dirty and little, and the three of us all sleep there at once. I just made up the room I wrote about. It's not a real place.' Then he slipped his hand into his pocket, and his crossed fingers made a little bulge in the shabby corduroy of his trousers. 'I guess I shouldn't have thought I would ever really live in a room like that myself,' he finished.

Mr. Jolie studied the boy narrowly for a time, then a flood of relief swept across his contorted features and the muscles of his body relaxed. He returned to his desk and sat down. There was in his posture a kind of triumph, a kind of secure invincibility. He looked across the boy's head as though he had already lost all interest in him. 'Get out,' he said absently.

Young Paul Amaric watched the schoolmaster a moment longer before he turned to go. Then he walked to the door, head erect, confidence and purpose in his dark eyes. When he reached the corridor he took his hand out of his pocket and deliberately uncrossed his fingers, flexing them as a fighter does. Then he walked out of the building, looking neither to the right nor the left, only straight ahead of him. And his mouth smiled a little.

When Mr. Jolie saw that he was alone he rose and shook himself, as a cat does to shake off water it finds repellent, and moved at a dignified pace to the door.

He had not gone two blocks of his long walk home when he discovered that without realizing it he had begun to practice his dream, again. It came to him with no effort at all, even the smallest details. Quite suddenly he knew that he was strolling down the elm-shaded avenue in the gleaming white university town after delivering an especially brilliant lecture. He could see everything very distinctly. As he walked he paused to nod to a pair of undergraduates who passed him, graciously accepting their awkward compliments on his lecture. Then he passed on, stooping once to pick one of the perfect yellow daisies which grew in profusion beside the road.

Unconsciously Mr. Jolie quickened his pace so that he might sooner reach his house at the end of the road and the beautiful white room within.

# BIOGRAPHICAL NOTICES

BRODERICK, FRANCIS L. Born in 1922, in New York, he has lived there almost all his life. He graduated from Princeton in 1943, then spent two years as a B-24 navigator in the central Pacific. In 1945, he returned to Princeton as an instructor in history and a Kemp Post-War Fellow. He is now at Harvard University, completing graduate work in American Civilization. 'Return By Faith' is his first published story, and also the first he has written.

CANFIELD, DOROTHY. This writer, equally well-known as Dorothy Canfield Fisher, was born in Lawrence, Kansas, in 1879; her father was an educator and president of several state universities. She graduated from Ohio State University and received her Ph.D. degree in Romance Languages from Columbia University after studying both there and in France. In 1907, she married John R. Fisher, and had a son and a daughter. Mrs. Fisher's writing began with academic books; in 1912, she published her first novel, *The Squirrel Cage*. Since then, she has written about twenty-five books — including novels, juveniles, non-fiction, translations of foreign works, collections of her short stories, and one play. Among her best known novels are *The Bent Twig, The Brimming Cup, Raw Material, Her Son's Wife, The Deepening Stream,* and *Seasoned Timber.* Her short stories have appeared in numerous magazines and anthologies. Holding eight degrees from American universities, she has written and lectured widely on education. Her books have had great popularity in England, and have been translated into several foreign languages. Mrs. Fisher has traveled widely in Europe, though since her marriage her permanent home has always been on a farm near Arlington, Vermont. She has been one of the judges on the Book-of-the-Month Club since its inception, and is associated with several leading educational organizations.

CAPOTE, TRUMAN. He was born in New Orleans twenty-three years ago. Since then he has lived in Alabama, Louisiana, Mississippi, Cuba, Connecticut, and presently, in New York City after a recent period at Yaddo. He attended many schools; writing steadily since his early youth, he published his first story at seventeen. His stories have since appeared in *Harper's Bazaar, Story, Mademoiselle, The Atlantic Monthly,* and some of the smaller reviews. His short story 'Miriam' was in the O. Henry Memorial Award *Prize Stories of 1946.* He is at present working on his first novel, *Other Voices, Other Rooms,* to be published this coming winter by Random House.

FONTAINE, ROBERT. Born in Marlboro, Massachusetts, thirty-five years ago, he was educated in the public schools of Ottawa, Canada, and the Ottawa Collegiate Institute. He has been a window-dresser, accountant, comptometer operator, soda jerk, radio writer, and newspaper reporter. In the last five years, he has published a couple of hundred short stories in practically every magazine in the United States and England. His novel, *The Happy Time,* was published in 1945 by Simon & Schuster and has since appeared in England and Spain. A dramatization is being made of it for a Broadway production. At present he is working on a new novel, *Blessed Are The Debonair,* and collaborating with his father, Louis A. Fontaine, in composing music and writing the lyrics and book for a musical play entitled *Spring Dream.* He is married to Stella Roscoe, also a writer, and they have two small daughters. His additional hobbies are painting, photography, and attempting to play the piano. 'Day of Gold and Darkness,' although not published until 1946, was among the very first stories he ever wrote.

GERSTLEY, ADELAIDE. She was born in Chicago in 1901 and has lived there almost continuously. In 1922, she graduated from Wellesley and was married soon after to Dr. Jesse R. Gerstley, a Chicago pediatrician. Since then, in addition to being a housewife and the mother of a son, she has been active in civic affairs and club work. Until recently, Mrs. Gerstley had done no writing other than several lengthy books when still a child, which were, she says, unblushingly reminiscent of 'The Little Colonel' stories. 'The Man In The Mirror' is her first published short story, though she has since had another accepted for publication by *The Ladies' Home Journal.*

GOODWIN, JOHN B. L. Mr. Goodwin is thirty-five years old, and was born in the United States but has lived in many parts of the world. By profession, he is both an artist and a writer. At the age of eighteen he went to London and there worked for A. R. Orage on the *New English Quarterly*, writing poetry and drama reviews. He spent the following years of the nineteen-thirties in Ireland, Spain, Austria, Italy, Corfu, Peru, and Chile. On his return to this country, he came to New York and designed jewelry for a short period. Just before the war, he moved to California, and now makes his home there on an eighty-acre ranch called 'Armageddon.' As an artist, he has had several one-man shows in Hollywood and New York, and has exhibited in New York with the surrealist group. Recently, he has been on a trip to Haiti in the West Indies.

GOSS, JOHN MAYO. His birthplace was Peoria, Illinois. He graduated from Yale in 1915, and served in the Infantry in World War I, spending over a year in France. For several years, he wrote advertising copy in Chicago, but went back to France in 1926 where he stayed for eight years working for a small advertising agency in Paris. He returned to the United States in 1933 with a French wife and lived on an Illinois farm until her death in 1941. He then spent three years in Chicago selling books at Marshall Field & Company. Since 1944, Mr. Goss has been in Tuscaloosa, Alabama, where, at the instigation of Hudson Strode of the University of Alabama, he has been writing fiction. 'Bird Song' is his first and only published story; it received first prize in the O. Henry Memorial Awards for 1946. At present he is completing a novel to be published soon by Rinehart & Company.

GRIFFITH, PAUL. He was born in western Pennsylvania and brought up in Philadelphia. In 1943 he was graduated from Yale, and since then has taught school in California, worked for two years on a magazine in New York, reviewed books, and published short stories in *Tomorrow* and *Mademoiselle*. He is now living in New York City, finishing a novel to be published by Henry Holt.

GUÉRARD, ALBERT J. He was born in Houston, Texas, in 1914, the son of the critic and historian Albert Léon Guérard and of Wilhelmina Guérard, who has published stories under the name of Graham Munro. He received B.A. and Ph.D. degrees from Stanford, and an M.A. from Harvard. During the war, he was a very itinerant sergeant in Psychological Warfare Intelligence, and was later with the Cultural Relations Section of the O.W.I. in Paris. He then spent a year in California on a Rockefeller Fellowship completing a book on the development of the modern novel. His published books include three novels (*The Past Must Alter, The Hunted,* and *Maquisard*), critical works on Robert Bridges and on Joseph Conrad, and (in France) a study and anthology of the American short story. He is married, and is at present Assistant Professor of English at Harvard. He is also at work on a new novel.

HARDWICK, ELIZABETH. Though at present living in New York City, she was born in Lexington, Kentucky, and has spent most of her life there. She was educated at the University of Kentucky and Columbia University. Her short stories and reviews have been printed in *Partisan Review, Harper's Bazaar, Sewanee Review,*

*The Yale Review,* and other periodicals; in addition, her stories have appeared in *The Best American Short Stories* previously. In 1945, Harcourt, Brace published her first novel, *The Ghostly Lover,* and her second, *A Fortunate Young Man,* is scheduled to appear this Fall.

HARRIS, RUTH McCOY. Mrs. Harris was born and raised in a small Mississippi town. She graduated from the Mississippi State College for Women, where she worked on the college paper and the town daily, and edited a short-lived humor magazine with the help of Eudora Welty, among others. She came to New York to attend the Columbia University School of Journalism, but left after a few months to marry Russell L. Harris, now an advertising executive. Mrs. Harris then worked in the editorial departments of Appleton-Century and later for Charles E. Merrill; after the birth of a daughter, she did some free-lance editing for McGraw-Hill. 'Up the Road a Piece' is her second published story; in addition, she has done occasional magazine articles, two dealing with Negroes. Her main interests are sociology and psychology, principally relative to children, and writing. During the week, she writes almost daily on the novel she is now completing; weekends, however, she and family spend in sail-boat racing, regardless of the seasons.

HEGGEN, THOMAS. He was born in 1919 in Fort Dodge, Iowa. When he was of high-school age, his family moved to Oklahoma, and he attended both school and college there. Later, he transferred to the University of Minnesota, where before graduation in 1941, he vied with Max Shulman in writing a daily humor column. In December, 1941, he enlisted in the Navy and was subsequently commissioned. He served aboard a variety of ships, and while on an assault transport he participated in the campaigns of Guam, Peleliu, Iwo Jima, and Okinawa. 'Night Watch' was first published in *The Atlantic Monthly* and won an M-G-M short story award. It is a section from his best-selling book *Mister Roberts,* published by Houghton Mifflin Company in 1946. Since his discharge from the Navy, Mr. Heggen has been working for the *Reader's Digest* in New York, collaborating with Max Shulman on the play version of *Mister Roberts* to be produced on Broadway, and writing occasional short stories.

HETH, EDWARD HARRIS. Born in Milwaukee, Wisconsin, he attended public schools there and later the University of Wisconsin. Before the war, he spent summers in Paris, Berchtesgaden, and Maine; for the last four years he has been living in New York City, where he has done some radio writing and for a period wrote the radio serial 'Mary Marlin.' He has written four novels: *Some We Loved, Told With a Drum, Light Over Ruby Street,* and most recently, *Any Number Can Play.* This last novel, published by Harper and Brothers, was sold to Twentieth-Century Fox, enabling Mr. Heth to spend his summers at a newly-built ranch house in Kettle Moraine country at Genesee Depot, Wisconsin. He has had numerous short stories in many magazines, and was represented in Edward J. O'Brien's *The Best Short Stories, 1937.* His new novel, *We Are The Robbers,* has recently been completed and will be published shortly.

HUMPHREYS, JOHN RICHARD. Born in Mancelona, Michigan, in 1918, he graduated from the University of Michigan in 1940, and then worked as a Public Opinion poll writer on the Detroit *Free Press* for several months prior to his induction into the Army in 1941. During the war, he was a Signal Corps Officer; until 1944, he was at Fort Monmouth as visual-aid editor. He served overseas in the E.T.O. on a Special Services assignment for a year. Since his discharge, Mr. Humphreys has been an instructor in short-story writing at Columbia University. His novel, *Vandameer's Road* was published by Charles Scribner's Sons in 1946. He recently received a Guggenheim Fellowship Award. He is married, has a small daughter, and at present lives in New York City.

LINCOLN, VICTORIA. Miss Lincoln was born in Fall River, Massachusetts, in 1904. She was educated at Radcliffe College, spent some time abroad for short periods, and has lived in various parts of the United States. She is the wife of Victor Lowe, professor of philosophy at Ohio State University, and the mother of three children. She has been writing for quite a few years, and is the author of the very successful novel, *February Hill*, published in 1934 and dramatized later as *The Primrose Path*. Her short stories, poems, and sketches have appeared in *The New Yorker, Harper's Magazine, Good Housekeeping, Collier's*, and other magazines. In 1944, *Grandmother and the Comet*, a collection of her pieces from *The New Yorker*, was published by Farrar & Rinehart; her latest book, *The Wind At My Back*, appeared in 1946. She is at present living in a suburb of Columbus, Ohio, running her household and working on a new novel.

LOWRY, ROBERT. In 1919, Robert Lowry was born in Cincinnati, Ohio. He attended the University of Cincinnati for six months, leaving to hitchhike around the country. At eighteen, he returned to his hometown to publish the *Little Man* books and pamphlets. He was drafted in 1942, spending twenty-three of his thirty-nine Army months in Africa and Italy with the Air Force. Since his discharge in 1945, he has lived in New York, where for a year he designed books and jackets for New Directions. His stories have appeared in *New Directions 9, Cross Section 1947*, and in several periodicals including *Story, Mademoiselle, The Western Review, Pacific*, and others. His novel, *Casualty*, was published in the fall of 1945 by New Directions.

MARTENET, MAY DAVIES. Born in Newport News, Virginia, she was educated at private schools and at the Sorbonne in Paris. Her past residences include North Carolina, Virginia, Massachusetts, the Hawaiian Islands, and a good deal of time spent in Europe, chiefly in the British Isles. With her husband and their daughter, she now lives in New York City and publishes occasional stories and articles in various magazines. She has also been a reader for Alfred Knopf.

MAYHALL, JANE. Born in Louisville, Kentucky, she lived there until her eighteenth year. She then attended Black Mountain College in North Carolina for three years, majoring in music. Between high school and college, she sang in Louisville on the radio and in a night-club; she has also played piano for tap-dancing classes and at one time had a jazz vocal trio. At present, she is a free-lance writer living in New York City. Her short stories, essays, and poetry have appeared in *Partisan Review, Sewanee Review, Antioch Review, Quarterly Review of Literature*, and others. Her writing has also been included in the 1945 and 1946 volumes of *Cross Section*. She has recently completed a long poem on esthetics, and is now working on a novel.

POWERS, J. F. This writer is thirty, has lived in various parts of the country, and for several years worked for book companies in Chicago. His stories have appeared in *Accent, The Commonweal, Rocky Mountain Review, The New Mexico Quarterly Review, The Catholic Worker*, and *Opportunity*; he has also been represented in a number of anthologies, among them *The Best American Short Stories, 1944*, the O. Henry Memorial Award *Prize Stories* of 1944 and 1945, and Bucklin Moon's *Primer For White Folks*. A collection of his short stories, entitled *Prince of Darkness and Other Stories*, was published earlier this year by Doubleday & Company. Mr. Powers was recently married; he now lives in Avon, Minnesota, where he is working on a novel.

RAPHAELSON, SAMSON. Born in New York City in 1896, he was educated in Chicago, and graduated from the University of Illinois in 1917. He worked briefly as a reporter, advertising copy-writer, and college English instructor, but soon turned to writing as a full-time career. Until recently, playwriting has been his main interest; he is the author of such Broadway successes as *The Jazz Singer, Accent on Youth,* and *Skylark* (which he also wrote as a novel). Mr. Raphaelson has been an equally well-known screen-writer since 1929, and has authored the motion-picture scripts for *Suspicion, The Shop Around the Corner, Trouble in Paradise,* and numerous others. He has been a consistent short-story contributor to various magazines, and is now devoting most of his time to fiction. With his wife and two children (a son at Harvard and a daughter at Radcliffe) he lives on a farm in Bucks County, Pennsylvania, where he is presently finishing a new novel.

SCHORER, MARK. Born in 1908 in Sauk City, Wisconsin, Mark Schorer was educated at the University of Wisconsin, where he later received his Ph.D., and at Harvard; he has been a teacher of English at both these institutions, as well as at Dartmouth College and the University of California at Berkeley, where he is now associate professor. In 1940, and again in 1941, he was granted a Guggenheim Fellowship for the writing of a long critical study on the poetry of William Blake. This work, begun on a sheep ranch in Mexico, was published by Henry Holt last year under the title *William Blake: The Politics of Vision.* Mr. Schorer has also published two novels, *A House Too Old* and *The Hermit Place.* His short stories and critical articles have appeared in *The New Yorker, Harper's Bazaar, The Atlantic Monthly, Story, Harper's Magazine,* and many others, including the leading literary quarterlies. Thirty-two of his short stories, including 'What We Don't Know Hurts Us,' were collected and published early this year by Houghton Mifflin Company in a volume entitled *The State of Mind.* Mr. Schorer is married and has two children; he is at present working on a novel with an art gallery background.

SEAGER, ALLAN. Although born in Adrian, Michigan, in 1906, he moved to Memphis, Tennessee, when he was eleven and lived there until he went to college. He was graduated from the University of Michigan and went to England as a Rhodes Scholar at Oxford University. He returned to become an editor of *Vanity Fair* in New York for a year and a half. Since then, he has been teaching English at the University of Michigan, with a year's leave of absence in 1944 to be on the faculty at Bennington College. Mr. Seager's short stories have appeared in numerous leading magazines and anthologies, including previous volumes of *The Best American Short Stories,* and his novel, *Equinox,* was published by Simon & Schuster in 1943. He is married and has one child, a daughter.

SHAW, IRWIN. Mr. Shaw is a native New Yorker, having been born in Brooklyn. His writing career began in high school; at Brooklyn College he was involved simultaneously in playwriting and football. Upon graduation, he began to write serial dramatizations of comic strips for radio, the success of which gave him the necessary leisure to write two plays. One of them was the memorable *Bury The Dead,* produced on Broadway in 1936 when the author was only twenty-three. Since then, in addition to writing occasional motion pictures for Hollywood, he has written several more plays, among them *Salute, Siege, The Gentle People, Sons and Soldiers,* and *The Assassin.* His short stories have appeared in many magazines, but most frequently in *The New Yorker.* He has been represented in previous volumes of *The Best American Short Stories* and in a number of other anthologies, and has been the recipient of two O. Henry Memorial Award prizes. Three collections of his stories have been published by Random House — *Sailor Off The Bremen, Welcome To The City,* and most recently, *Act Of Faith.* During the war, Mr. Shaw served with the United States Army in the European Theatre on the staff of *Stars and Stripes.* At present, he is living in California and working on a novel.

SHIRLEY, SYLVIA. Born in New York City, Miss Shirley has lived there all twenty-eight years of her life. She began writing in school via high-school publications. The depression interrupted her plans for studying journalism, and instead she worked at various jobs in factories and offices. Two years ago, she began writing in earnest, turning out a story every three or four weeks. 'The Red Dress' is her second published story; her first won a prize in a nationwide short-story contest. More recently, she has had stories in *Redbook* and *Collier's*. She is married to Harry Jackel, former editor-in-chief of the school publications for which she wrote; they have a seven-year-old daughter for whom they both write special stories.

STAFFORD, JEAN. Born in Covina, California, in 1915, she was educated at the University of Colorado and at Heidelberg, Germany. She has since taught school for a year in Missouri, has worked for *The Southern Review* in Louisiana, and has lived for various periods of time in Massachusetts, New York, Tennessee, Connecticut, and Maine. She is the author of two novels, *Boston Adventure* and *The Mountain Lion*, the latter published earlier this year by Harcourt Brace. Her short stories have appeared in *Partisan Review, Kenyon Review, Sewanee Review, Harper's Magazine, Mademoiselle,* and *Harper's Bazaar.* She has had a Guggenheim Fellowship, an Academy of Arts and Letters Award, has won a prize in a *Dial-Partisan Review* short-story contest, and was represented in *The Best American Short Stories, 1945.* She is married to Robert Lowell, the Pulitzer Prize poet.

STARK, IRWIN. Mr. Stark was born in Passaic, New Jersey, in 1912, but has lived in New York City since 1918. He received B.A. and M.S. degrees from the College of the City of New York, and is currently teaching English in a New York high school. His poetry has appeared in a number of little magazines and in two anthologies, Edwin Seaver's *Cross Section* and Joy Davidman's *War Poems of the United Nations*; his short stories have been printed in *The Antioch Review, Opportunity, Common Ground, Commentary, Woman's Home Companion,* and he has had articles in *Coronet* and *Esquire*. Mr. Stark's story, 'The Bridge,' was reprinted in *The Best American Short Stories, 1946.*

STEGNER, WALLACE. Although born in Lake Mills, Iowa, in 1909, Wallace Stegner received his high-school and college education in Salt Lake City, Utah, and did graduate work at the University of California and later at the University of Iowa where he received his Ph.D. degree in 1935. He has lived in various parts of the United States and also in Saskatchewan. At present, he and his wife live in California, where Mr. Stegner is professor of English at Stanford and in charge of the creative writing program there. In the past, he has taught at the universities of Utah, Iowa, Augustana College in Illinois, Wisconsin, and Harvard. He began writing in college; his Master's thesis at Iowa was a group of short stories, one of the first of the 'guinea pig' creative theses which, incidentally, he is now organizing at Stanford, too. His first novel, *Remembering Laughter,* won the Little, Brown novelette contest in 1937. Since then he has written seven books, including *The Potter's Wheel, On A Darkling Plain, Mormon Country, Fire and Ice, The Big Rock Candy Mountain,* and *One Nation,* a Life In America prize book which won an Anisfield-Wolf Award in 1946. His most recent book is *Second Growth,* a novel published this summer by Houghton Mifflin Company. Mr. Stegner has had stories and articles in many magazines; one of his stories won an O. Henry Memorial Award prize, and several of his stories have been included in previous volumes of *The Best American Short Stories.*

TUCCI, NICCOLÓ. Born in 1908 in Lugano, Switzerland, of an Italian father and a Russian mother, he was brought up and educated in Tuscany, Germany, and the United States. He had a brief bureaucratic career in Rome and in the United States as an Italian government official, and came to this country as an immigrant in 1938 to make his permanent home here. During the war he worked in Washington in the field of Inter-American Affairs until he decided that bureaucracy was about the same no matter what the country. He has since devoted his time to writing, and his stories have appeared in several publications, among them *Harper's Magazine* and *Twice A Year*. At present he lives in New York City with his wife and two children, and is working on a novel to be published by Doubleday & Company.

WEAVER, JOHN D. Born in Washington, D.C., in 1912, he attended public schools there, and spent his summers in the Shenandoah Valley of Virginia where most of his family still live. In 1932, he graduated from William and Mary College, and the following year received an M.A. degree from George Washington University. After working for several government agencies, he went to Kansas City in 1935 where he spent five years doing newspaper work. He then moved to Los Angeles to write a novel, *Wind Before Rain,* published by Macmillan in 1942. During the war, he spent three years in the Army Signal Corps. Mr. Weaver's short stories and articles have appeared in *Esquire, The American Mercury, Saturday Evening Post, Liberty,* *The Atlantic Monthly, Harper's Magazine,* and the first volume of *Cross Section.* In 1941, he was co-winner of an *Atlantic Monthly* short-story contest. He is married to Harriett Sherwood, also a writer, and they alternate between New York and Los Angeles. A play, *Virginia Reel,* which they wrote together, has been recently produced by the Experimental Theatre, New York City. Mr. Weaver is also at work on a new novel.

WILLIAMS, LAWRENCE. Born in 1915 in Tenafly, New Jersey, he was educated in France, Italy, Switzerland, New Hampshire, Colorado, and New Jersey. After an interval of various occupations — ice-cream salesman, song plugger, artist's model, truck driver, radio announcer — he became an actor, playing in stock companies around New York and New England and in eight shows on Broadway. In 1938, he went to Hollywood, and, as Larry Williams, made over thirty pictures for Warner Brothers before the war. During the war, he worked for the O.W.I. in Los Angeles as Southern California editor of the O.W.I. News and Feature Bureau. He left because of an illness which kept him bedridden for a year and a half. He began to write at that time, and has considered it his profession ever since. His stories have appeared in many magazines, both in the literary and mass-circulation category. He plans to write a novel sometime in the future. He is married to Nell O'Day, an actress; they live mostly in their house in Greenwich Village in New York City, but migrate to the California desert during the winters.

# THE YEARBOOK OF THE AMERICAN SHORT STORY

JANUARY 1 TO DECEMBER 31, 1946

# ROLL OF HONOR

## 1946

### I. *American Authors*

ANGELL, ROGER
Some Pigs in Sailor Suits. New Yorker.
ANGOFF, CHARLES
Disillusionment. Tomorow.

BENSON, SALLY
Schoolboy. New Yorker.
BERNSTEIN, WALTER
A Gathering of Friends. New Yorker.
BLONCHE, NATALIE J.
Ollie. New Masses.
BRADBURY, RAY
Homecoming. Mademoiselle.
BRODERICK, FRANCIS L.
Return by Faith. Atlantic Monthly.
BURDICK, EUGENE
Rest Camp on Maui. Harper's Magazine.
BUSH, GEORGE SIDNEY
The Way Things Have to Be. University of Kansas City Review.

CALLAGHAN, MORLEY
Lilacs for Catherine. Seventeen.
CANFIELD, DOROTHY
Sex Education. Yale Review.
CAPOTE, TRUMAN
The Headless Hawk. Harper's Bazaar.
CHEEVER, JOHN
The Sutton Place Story. New Yorker.
COATES, ROBERT M.
One of These Days. New Yorker.
Then It Happened. Harper's Bazaar.

DEASY, MARY
The Linden Tree. Atlantic Monthly.

ELDER, WALTER
You Can Wreck It. Kenyon Review.
ELLSON, HAL
The Frozen Heart. Prairie Schooner.
EMMONS, BETSY
The Secret of the Porcelain Unicorn. Today's Woman.

FIELD, BEN
Smelts Are Running. Accent.

FONTAINE, ROBERT
Day of Gold and Darkness. Yale Review.

GERSTLEY, ADELAIDE
The Man in the Mirror. Story.
GIBBS, WOLCOTT
Season in the Sun. New Yorker.
GOODWIN, JOHN B. L.
Cocoon. Story.
GOSS, JOHN MAYO
Bird Song. Atlantic Monthly.
GRIFFITH, PAUL
The Horse Like September. Tomorow.
GUÉRARD, ALBERT J.
Turista. Story.

HARDWICK, ELIZABETH
The Golden Stallion. Sewanee Review.
The Temptations of Dr. Hoffman. Partisan Review.
HARRIS, RUTH McCOY
Up the Road a Piece. Antioch Review.
HAUSER, MARIANNE
Lesson in Music. Harper's Bazaar.
Dark Dominion. Harper's Bazaar.
HEGGEN, THOMAS
Night Watch. Atlantic Monthly.
The Captain's Palms. Atlantic Monthly.
So Long, Mr. Roberts. Atlantic Monthly.
HETH, EDWARD HARRIS
Under the Ginkgo Trees. Town and Country.
HINES, DOROTHY PALMER
Mrs. Mason's Dream of General Eisenhower. Harper's Bazaar.
HUMPHREYS, JOHN RICHARD
Michael Finney and the Little Men. Cosmopolitan.
HUTCHINS, MAUDE PHELPS
From Morning Till Night. Foreground.
Innocents. Kenyon Review.

JACKSON, SHIRLEY
Seven Types of Ambiguity. Story.

KLEIN, ALEXANDER
Disavowal. Prairie Schooner.

LE SUEUR, MERIDEL
We'll Make Your Bed. New Masses.

LINCOLN, VICTORIA
Down in the Reeds by the River.
New Yorker.
Comfort. New Yorker.
Now and Forever. Cosmopolitan.

LOWRY, ROBERT
Little Baseball World. Mademoiselle.

LULL, RODERICK
The Cat. Virginia Quarterly Review.

MARCUS, ALAN R.
The Girl Without a Name. Atlantic
Monthly.

MARTENET, MAY DAVIES
Father Delacroix. Quarterly Review of
Literature.

MAXWELL, JAMES A.
Police Duty. New Yorker.

MAY, JAMES BOYER
The Ruesabords. Interim.

MAYHALL, JANE
The Darkness. Quarterly Review of
Literature.

MEYER, CORD, JR.
Waves of Darkness. Atlantic Monthly.

MODELL, MERRIAM
Ritual. Harper's Bazaar.

MORIARTY, WILLIAM
Kimmy. Harper's Magazine.

PARSONS, ELIZABETH
Behold the Hebrides. New Yorker.
The Nightingales Sing. New Yorker.

PATTON, FRANCES GRAY
Grade 5B and the Well-Fed Rat.
Harper's Magazine.

PEN, JOHN
'I Beg to Report . . .' Tomorrow.

PETERS, ASTRID
Party at the Williamsons. New Yorker.

PORTUGAL, RUTH
At the Tientsin Club. Harper's Bazaar.

POWERS, J. F.
Prince of Darkness. Accent.

RAPHAELSON, SAMSON
The Greatest Idea in the World. Good
Housekeeping.

REDFORD, GRANT H.
The Trial. Interim.

REUTERMAN, JEAN
The Death of Mr. Strum. Tomorrow.

ROBINSON, LEONARD WALLACE
Love, Let Us Be True to One Another.
Harper's Magazine.

ROSENFELD, ISAAC
Bazaar of the Senses. Commentary.
The New Egypt. Kenyon Review.

SCHMITT, GLADYS
David the Little Lad. Harper's Bazaar.

SCHORER, MARK
What We Don't Know Hurts Us.
Harper's Bazaar.

SCHWARTZ, DELMORE
A Bitter Farce. Kenyon Review.

SEAGER, ALLAN
Game Chickens. Foreground.

SHAW, IRWIN
Act of Faith. New Yorker.
Age of Reason. New Yorker.

SHEDD, MARGARET
The Innocent Bystander. Harper's
Magazine.

SHIRLEY, SYLVIA
The Red Dress. Harper's Magazine.

SMITH, JOHN CASWELL, JR.
Fighter. Atlantic Monthly.

STAFFORD, JEAN
The Interior Castle. Partisan Review.

STARK, IRWIN
Shock Treatment. Commentary.

STEGNER, WALLACE
The Women on the Wall. Harper's
Magazine.

STILL, JAMES
School Butter. Virginia Quarterly Review.

SULLIVAN, RICHARD
Saturday Nocturne. Yale Review.

SYLVESTER, HARRY
Journey South. Rocky Mountain Review.

TAYLOR, PETER
The Long Fourth. Sewanee Review.

THIELEN, BENEDICT
The Empty Sky. Yale Review.
Old Boy — New Boy. Town and
Country.

TUCCI, NICCOLÓ
The Siege. Harper's Magazine.

TYLER, DOROTHY
Fraulein Farewell. University of
Kansas City Review.

ULLMAN, VICTOR
Sometimes You Break Even. Atlantic
Monthly.

WEAVER, JOHN D.
  Bread and Games. Harper's Magazine.
WEIDMAN, JEROME
  Gallantry in Action. Salute.
WEST, JESSAMYN
  Grandpa Was Her Mirror. Harper's
    Magazine.

WILCOX, WENDELL
  A Thoroughly Immoral Story. Decade.
WILLIAMS, LAWRENCE
  The Hidden Room. Cosmopolitan.

ZUGSMITH, LEANE
  The Royal Sign. Tomorow.

## II. *Foreign Authors*

BAKER, DENYS VAL
  Passenger to Liverpool. Esquire.
BERRIDGE, ELIZABETH
  To Tea With the Colonel. Harper's
    Bazaar.

COWAN, PETER
  Temporary Job. Mademoiselle.

GODDEN, RUMER
  Snow Red, Rose White and Barbara
    Yorke. Harper's Bazaar.
  Mercy, Pity, Peace and Love. To-
    morrow.
GREENE, GRAHAM
  The Innocent. Tomorrow.

O'CONNOR, FRANK
  The Rivals. New Yorker.
  Lady in the Dark. Today's Woman.
O'FAOLAIN, SEAN

Unholy Living and Half Dying. To-
    morrow.

PASTERNACK, BORIS
  Translated by Payne, Robert.
  Aerial Ways. Kenyon Review.
PUDNEY, JOHN
  Edna's Fruit Hat. Mademoiselle.

SANSOM, WILLIAM
  The Vertical Ladder. Good House-
    keeping.

WARD, MARY JANE
  A Ring She Happened to Have. To-
    day's Woman.
WARNER, SYLVIA TOWNSEND
  The House with the Lilacs. New
    Yorker.
  A Pigeon. New Yorker.

# DISTINCTIVE VOLUMES OF SHORT STORIES

## Published in the United States

## 1946

Bemelmans, Ludwig. Hotel Bemelmans. Viking Press.

Blicher, Steen, Steensen. Twelve Stories from the Danish. American-Scandinavian Foundation.

Bowen, Elizabeth. Ivy Gripped the Steps and Other Stories. Knopf.

Brickell, Herschel, and Fuller, Muriel, Editors. O. Henry Memorial Award Prize Stories of 1946. Doubleday and Company.

Connolly, Cyril, Editor. Horizon Stories. Vanguard Press.

Dahl, Roald. Over to You: Ten Stories of Flyers and Flying. Reynal & Hitchcock.

De Jong, David Cornel. Snow-on-the-Mountain and Other Stories. Reynal & Hitchcock.

Derleth, August W., Editor. Who Knocks? Twenty Masterpieces of the Spectral for the Connoisseur. Rinehart.

Enright, Elizabeth. Borrowed Summer and Other Stories. Rinehart.

Fabricant, Noah Daniel and Werner Heinz, Editors. A Treasury of Doctor Stories. Frederick Fell.

Farrell, James T. More Stories: To Whom It May Concern. Sun Dial Press.

Foley, Martha, Editor. The Best American Short Stories of 1946. Houghton Mifflin Co.

Harte, Bret. Selected Stories. Caxton House.

Helm, Mackinlay. A Matter of Love and Other Baroque Tales of the Provinces. Harper and Bros.

Hitrec, Joseph G. Rulers' Morning and Other Stories. Harper and Bros.

Lewisohn, Ludwig. Jewish Short Stories. Berhman House.

Mansfield, Katherine. Stories: A Selection Made by J. Middleton Murry. World Pub. Co.

Parsons, Elizabeth. An Afternoon. Viking Press.

Seaver, Edwin, Editor. Cross Section. Simon & Schuster.

Shaw, Irwin. Act of Faith and Other Stories. Random House.

Steele, Wilbur Daniel. The Best Stories of Wilbur Daniel Steele. Doubleday and Company.

Stuart, Jesse. Tales from the Plum Grove Hills. Dutton.

# DISTINCTIVE SHORT STORIES IN
# AMERICAN MAGAZINES

## 1946

ABBE, GEORGE
The Bell. Rocky Mt. Review, Winter.

ALEXANDER, SIDNEY
The Return of Arthur Clementis.
Charm, July.

ALLAN, DONALD A.
Triumph of a Realist. Esquire, Oct.

ALPERT, HOLLIS
The Austrian Woman. Harper's Magazine, May.

ANDERSON, SHERWOOD
Not Sixteen. Tomorrow, March.

ANDREA, MARIANNE B.
Home. Tomorrow, Dec.

ANGELL, ROGER
Some Pigs in Sailor Suits. New Yorker,
Apr. 13.
Thursday Afternoon. New Yorker,
Dec. 28.

ANGOFF, CHARLES
Disillusionment. Tomorrow, Jan.
Mr. Harmon. University of Kansas
City Review, Spring.
Laura. Tomorrow, Dec.
Sidney. Prairie Schooner, Winter.

ANNIXTER, PAUL
Ordered Up to Nineveh. Southwest
Review, Autumn.

ASCH, NATHAN
Young Man on His Way. New Yorker,
June 22.
The Lake. Virginia Quarterly, Summer.

AUSTIN, MARY
Tomaso of the Tremblors. Southwest
Review, Summer.

AYLEN, ELISE
The Stranger from Arcady. Queen's
Quarterly, Spring.

BAKER, DENYS VAL
Passenger to Liverpool. Esquire, Jan.

BAKER, ERNESTINE MAGAGNA
The Young and the Wise. Story, Sept.-
Oct.

BARNARD, MARY
Boundaries: The Shadow. Harper's
Bazaar, Dec.

BARTLETT, PAUL A. and WINTERS, ELIZA-
BETH
Tale from an Old Port. Arizona Quarterly, Summer.
Stranger in the House. Decade, Vol.
III, No. 3.

BATES, H. E.
The Bridge. Good Housekeeping, Dec.

BATES, JOHN MCKINNEY
The Dulcimer and the Flute. Story,
Jan.-Feb.

BECK, WARREN
On the Way. Virginia Quarterly,
Winter.

BELTZ, VERNIE
Prairie Funeral. New Mexico Quarterly, Spring.

BENSON, SALLY
Schoolboy. New Yorker, Dec. 21.

BERG, LOUIS
Nasty Kupperman and the Ku Klux
Klan. Commentary, Feb.

BERNSTEIN, WALTER
A Gathering of Friends. New Yorker,
Oct. 5.

BERRIDGE, ELIZABETH
To Tea with the Colonel. Harper's
Bazaar, Nov.

BIGGS, GLORIA NEUSTADT
The Cat. Story, Jan.-Feb.

BLONCHE, NATALIE J.
Ollie. New Masses, May 28.

BOWLES, JANE
Plain Pleasures. Harper's Bazaar, Feb.

BRADBURY, RAY
The Miracles of Jamie. Charm, Apr.
Homecoming. Mademoiselle, Oct.

BRODERICK, FRANCIS L.
Return by Faith. Atlantic, Sept.

BROWN, J. A.
Meet Uncle John. Tomorrow, Dec.

BROWN, T. K. III
Poker Game. Story, May-June.
Ambush. Tomorrow, June.

BRUCE, MIRIAM
Becky and the Beautiful Afternoon.
Story, Mar.-Apr.

EASTMAN, ELIZABETH
I Must Be On My Way. Harper's Bazaar, March.

ELDER, WALTER
You Can Wreck It. Kenyon Review, Autumn.

ELLSON, HAL
The Monster of Red Hook Flats. Story, Mar.-Apr.
The Frozen Heart. Prairie Schooner, Spring.

EMMONS, BETSY
The Secret of the Porcelain Unicorn. Today's Woman, July.

EUSTIS, HELEN
Occupational, Gentlemen. Tomorrow, July.

FARRELL, JAMES T.
A Night in August, 1928. Quarterly Review of Literature, Vol. II, No. 4.

FAY, SARAH BRYANT
Devil in the Wind. Mademoiselle, Aug.

FAYE, PAUL-LOUIS
A Woman Called Pita. Arizona Quarterly, Autumn.

FEARN, JOHN
Someday After Sunday. Story, May-June.

FIELD, BEN
Smelts Are Running. Accent, Spring.

FIFIELD, WILLIAM
The Life of the Hunted. Story, Jan.-Feb.

FLYNN, PEGGY MAULDIN
Fishboat Green. Southwest Review, Spring.

FONTAINE, ROBERT
Day of Gold and Darkness. Yale Review, Spring.
A Trip Through Sex with Gun and Camera. Quarterly Review of Literature, Vol. II, No. 4.

FOREMAN, L. L.
Man Overboard. Southwest Review, Summer.

FOSTER, O'KANE
Document or Fantasy. Arizona Quarterly, Spring.
Stevedores. New Mexico Quarterly, Summer.

FREEDMAN, MORRIS
Nothing to Be Afraid Of. Commentary, Jan.

FREITAG, GEORGE
The Thief. Charm, Mar.
The Exposure. Hairenik, Sept. 26.

GABRIAL, JAN
Not With a Bang. Story, Sept.-Oct.
Voyage to the Shores of Cuautla. New Mexico Quarterly, Winter.

GASPAR, SAMUEL
Letter from Kazan. Tomorrow, Jan.

GERSTLEY, ADELAIDE
The Man in the Mirror. Story, Nov.-Dec.

GHISELIN, OLIVE
The Rain. Rocky Mt. Review, Spring.

GIBBS, WOLCOTT
Dark Cloud in the Sky. New Yorker, June 22.
Season in the Sun. New Yorker, July 6.
Love, Love, Love. New Yorker, July 20.
The Foreign Population. New Yorker, Aug. 17.
Crusoe's Footprint. New Yorker, Sept. 14.

GILES, BARBARA
The Gentle Bush. New Masses, Jan. 1.

GIRDNER, AUDREY
Fugitive. Charm, Feb.

GLEMSER, BERNARD
The Two Soldiers. Tomorrow, Jan.
The Ravine. Tomorrow, Apr.

GLENN, EUNICE
Post-Mortem for Papa. Prairie Schooner, Summer.

GODDEN, RUMER
Mercy, Pity, Peace and Love. Tomorrow, Sept.
Snow Red, Rose White and Barbara Yorke. Harper's Bazaar, Oct.

GOLDKNOPF, DAVID
Christmas Apples. Harper's Magazine, Dec.

GOODWIN, JOHN B. L.
The Cocoon. Story, Sept.-Oct.

GORDON, ETHEL EDISON
The High Places. Harper's Bazaar, Nov.

GOSS, JOHN MAYO
Bird Song. Atlantic, Feb.

GRACE, NANCY BREWSTER
Friend for the Night. Story, Mar.-Apr.

GRAHAM, RUTH
My Daughter Is With Child. New Masses, Aug. 13.

GREENE, GRAHAM
The Innocent. Tomorrow, Nov.

# ADDRESSES OF AMERICAN AND CANADIAN MAGAZINES PUBLISHING SHORT STORIES

Accent, P. O. Box 102, University Station, Urbana, Ill.
Adventure, 205 East 42nd Street, New York City
American Hebrew, 48 West 48th Street, New York City
American Magazine, 250 Park Avenue, New York City
American Mercury, 570 Lexington Avenue, New York City
Antioch Review, 212 Xenia Avenue, Yellow Springs, Ohio
Argosy, 205 East 42nd Street, New York City
Arizona Quarterly, University of Arizona, Tucson, Arizona
Atlantic Monthly, 8 Arlington Street, Boston, Mass.
Bard Review, Annandale-on-Hudson, New York
Blue Book, 230 Park Avenue, New York City
Briarcliff Quarterly, Briarcliff College, Briarcliff Manor, N.Y.
Canadian Forum, 16 Huntley Street, Toronto, Ontario, Canada
Canadian Home Journal, Richmond & Sheppard Streets, Toronto, Ontario, Canada
Catholic World, 411 West 59th Street, New York City
Charm, 122 East 42nd Street, New York City
Chatelaine, 143 University Avenue, Toronto, Ontario, Canada
Chimera, 265 West 11th Street, New York City
Circle, 2252 Telegraph Avenue, Berkeley, California
Collier's, 250 Park Avenue, New York City
Commentary, 425 Fourth Avenue, New York City
Common Ground, 20 West 40th Street, New York City
Commonweal, 386 Fourth Avenue, New York City
Contemporary, 3100 Eaton Tower, Detroit, Michigan
Coronet, 919 North Michigan Avenue, Chicago, Ill.
Cosmopolitan, 57th Street and Eighth Avenue, New York City
Country Gentleman, Independence Square, Philadelphia, Pa.
Crescendo, Box 75, B. U. Station, Waco, Texas
Crisis, 69 Fifth Avenue, New York City
Decade of Short Stories, 3642 North Pacific Avenue, Chicago, Ill.
Elks Magazine, 50 East 42nd Street, New York City
Esquire, 919 North Michigan Avenue, Chicago, Ill.
Everywoman's, 1790 Broadway, New York City
Foreground, Warren House, Quincy Street, Cambridge, Mass.
Free World, 144 Bleecker Street, New York City
Glamour, 420 Lexington Avenue, New York City
Good Housekeeping, 57th Street and Eighth Avenue, New York City
Hairenik Weekly, 212 Stuart Street, Boston, Mass.
Harper's Bazaar, 572 Madison Avenue, New York City
Harper's Magazine, 49 East 33rd Street, New York City
Harvard Wake, P. O. Box 41, Cambridge, Mass.
Household Magazine, Topeka, Kansas
Husk, Cornell College, Mount Vernon, Iowa
Interim, 1536 Shenandoah Drive, Seattle, Washington
Islander, 82 Merchant Street, Honolulu, Hawaii
Jewish Life, 305 Broadway, New York City
Kansas Magazine, Box 237, Kansas State College, Manhattan, Kansas
Kenyon Review, Kenyon College, Gambier, Ohio
Ladies' Home Journal, Independence Square, Philadelphia, Pa.
Liberty, 37 West 57th Street, New York City

MacLean's Magazine, 481 University Avenue, Toronto, Ontario, Canada
Mademoiselle, 122 East 42nd Street, New York City
Matrix, 1500 West Nedro Avenue, Philadelphia, Pa.
Mayfair, 22 West 48th Street, New York City
McCall's Magazine, 230 Park Avenue, New York City
Medusa, Amherst College, Amherst, Mass.
Menorah Journal, 63 Fifth Avenue, New York City
Negro Story, 4019 Vincennes Avenue, Chicago, Ill.
New Masses, 104 East 9th Street, New York City
New Mexico Quarterly Review, University of New Mexico, Albuquerque, N.M.
New Republic, 40 East 49th Street, New York City
New Yorker, 25 West 43rd Street, New York City
Northern Review, 635 St. Paul Street West, Montreal, Quebec, Canada
Opportunity, 1133 Broadway, New York City
Pacific, Box 467, Mills College, Oakland, California
Partisan Review, 45 Astor Place, New York City
Pharos, Box 215, Murray, Utah
Prairie Prose, Aberdeen, South Dakota
Prairie Schooner, 12th and R Streets, Lincoln, Nebraska
Profile, 106 Student Union Bldg., University of Cincinnati, Cincinnati, Ohio
Quarterly Review of Literature, 1928 Yale Station, New Haven, Conn.
Queen's Quarterly, Kingston, Ontario, Canada
Reader's Scope, 114 East 32nd Street, New York City
Reading, 67 Charles Street West, Toronto, Ontario, Canada
Redbook, 230 Park Avenue, New York City
Salute, 19 Park Place, New York City
Saturday Evening Post, Independence Square, Philadelphia, Pa.
Scholastic, 220 East 42nd Street, New York City
Script, 9480 Dayton Way, Beverly Hills, California
Seventeen, 11 West 42nd Street, New York City
Sewanee Review, University of the South, Sewanee, Tenn.
She, 521 Fifth Avenue, New York City
Southwest Review, Southern Methodist University, Dallas, Texas
Story, 432 Fourth Avenue, New York City
Tanager, Grinnell College, Grinnell, Iowa
The Woman, 420 Lexington Avenue, New York City
This Week, 420 Lexington Avenue, New York City
Today's Woman, 1501 Broadway, New York City
Tomorrow, 11 East 44th Street, New York City
Town and Country, 572 Lexington Avenue, New York City
Trend, University of Chicago, Chicago, Ill.
12th Street, New School for Social Research, 66 West 12th Street, New York City
Twice A Year, 509 Madison Avenue, New York City
University of Kansas City Review, Kansas City, Missouri
View, 1 East 53rd Street, New York City
Virginia Quarterly Review, One West Range, Charlottesville, Va.
Viva, 404 West 115th Street, New York City
Western Review, Rm. 211, Fraser Hall, University of Kansas, Lawrence, Kansas
Westminster Magazine, 683 Peachtree Street, N.E., Atlanta, Ga.
Woman's Day, 19 West 44th Street, New York City
Woman's Home Companion, 250 Park Avenue, New York City
Write, 10624-2 Elizabeth Avenue, Southgate, California
Yale Review, P. O. Box 1729, New Haven, Conn.
Yankee, Dublin, New Hampshire